Domino

'A spine of Enlightenment philosophy, wrestling with the nature of reality and existence, sits in a narrative that embraces opera, violence, plague, the South Sea Bubble, wig-making and castration. It is a convincing picture . . . more of a mystery than a thriller, with absorbingly unattractive characters'
Literary Review

'A brightly coloured, richly allusive tapestry [which] never fails to entertain . . . The debut of a novelist of such gifts is cause for celebration. *Domino* is a magnificent achievement'
Toronto Star

'As unnerving as a magician's cupboard'
The Times

'Ross King is a master craftsman of extravagant melodrama . . . and has begotten a heroine of multifarious sexuality, a lady who is no lady, perhaps a villain in drag, who may, in turn, be a woman pretending to be a man, who, in fact, may really . . . The reader's mind reels as the onion skins of false identity are peeled off'
Irish Times

'It has the pace of a thriller and black humour slivered with superb menace . . . be sure to read [it]'
The Spectator

'A fascinating and resplendent debut'
Daily Telegraph

Domino

Ross King was born in Canada in 1962
and completed a Ph.D. at York University.
Domino, his first novel, was first
published in 1995 to critical acclaim.
He and his wife currently live in Oxford.

Ross King

DOMINO

Minerva

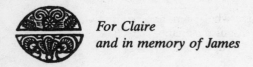

For Claire
and in memory of James

A Minerva Paperback
DOMINO

First published in Great Britain 1995
by Sinclair-Stevenson
This Minerva edition published 1996
by Mandarin Paperbacks
an imprint of Reed International Books Ltd
Michelin House, 81 Fulham Road, London SW3 6RB
and Auckland, Melbourne, Singapore and Toronto

Copyright © 1995 by Ross King
The author has asserted his moral rights

The illustrations in this book are by John Lawrence

A CIP catalogue record for this title
is available from the British Library
ISBN 0 7493 9668 7

Printed and bound in Great Britain
by Cox & Wyman Ltd, Reading, Berkshire

Conceal me what I am, and be my aid
For such disguise as haply shall become
The form of my intent.

Shakespeare, *Twelfth Night*

Do'mino *n.* (*pl.* ~**es**). Loose cloak with mask for upper part of face, worn to conceal identity esp. at masquerade; hence ~ed. [French, prob. from Latin *dominus* lord, but unexplained]

Concise Oxford Dictionary of Current English

Prologue: London, 1812

 When was the last time, I wonder, that I had a pretty young fellow such as this for an audience?

The boy—for he is hardly more than this—sits on cushions at my feet, looking rather like a student, which perhaps he is: a lissome youth, no more than eighteen years, I shouldn't think. He wears white robes—his conception of the *toga virilis*, I suppose—and leather sandals, a laurel of vine leaves (Lord knows where he found that) behind his ears. He is emulating a Greek or Roman theme, as are so many other guests at tonight's masquerade: satyrs, minotaurs and the occasional Caesar or Neptune dash to and fro, up and down Lord W—'s lengthy corridors. Occasionally a reveller pokes a masked face through the lintelled door before apologetically retreating, leaving the two of us alone in our small chamber.

Why in the midst of this happy assembly the boy should be sharing my company may appear something of a mystery, for it must be admitted that I, George Cautley, am nothing at all to look at.

True, I am tall enough, but my withered neck projects my head forward as if in perpetual deference to an invisible set of timber beams, and my elongated limbs are barely the circumference of the oaken walking-stick I must use to support myself. I have been informed by unkind urchins that my nose bears a strong resemblance to a powder-horn (though no powder-horn of my acquaintance has ever been covered so with warts and carbuncles) and, in complexion, to a grape. A powdered tie-wig conceals the sharp outcrops of my bald crown, but not, alas, the better part of two thick, overgrown ears, from which sprout great tufts of grey hair. My pate beneath the wig has sallowed where it is not dotted with great black freckles, some of which appear with only slightly less profusion on the puckered surfaces of my forehead and cheeks. My eyes are dim and grey, quenched in rheum, which occasionally drips like candle-wax down the wattles of my face, and my mouth is perpetually contracted

1

into a grimace on account of the loss many years ago of the majority of my teeth. Those few that survive discover themselves only upon those rare occasions when I twist my unpleasant countenance into a smile or, more frequently, a snarl.

No: I am nothing at all to look at, even for someone in the sixtieth year of his life. Fortunately, however, most of my infelicities of appearance can be disguised this evening—hidden behind a mask or concealed beneath the folds of my long black cloak. A person might not detect on first scrutiny whether I am young or old, handsome or ugly, nor even, indeed, whether a gentleman or a lady. This is the whole point, of course: I am at a masquerade. And what are masquerades for but to hide our true selves from one another, or even from ourselves?

But I am under no illusions about my young companion. This pretty fellow is not the least bit interested in me, whatever he may think hides behind my vizard. He is not even looking at me (blast him!), for his attention is engaged by a much prettier face, which I have put into his hands. This portrait brought us together a few moments before, amidst the whirling dancers in the salon: a porcelain miniature, the product of my own craftsmanship. I had dropped it on the floor—quite by accident, I assure you—and when it met with the toe of a dancer's buckled shoe this keen youth was gallant enough to retrieve it from its ultimate resting-place beneath our host's mahogany chess table. As he presented it to me his shy glance fell for a fatal second upon the face: and this face never fails to produce the same effect in shy young men. Believe me—for I was once a shy young man, exactly like him.

'Who is she, pray tell?' He now looks from the miniature to me, then back to the beautiful lure cupped in his palm. Such a combination of heedless alacrity and appealing *mauvaise honte*! 'Is the likeness a correct one? Why, she's the most beautiful lady in the world! Pray, sir, does she still live?'

I raise my hand to prohibit this rush of inquiry, and his pretty face suffuses with red. I pour out cups of gooseberry wine and pass one to him, relieving him at the same time of the effigy, which I return, despite his objections, to the folds of my Venetian cloak. Outside the door laughter from the other masks trills in the gallery and in the octagonal salon, where a string quartet entertains an assembly of goddesses, wood-nymphs and other dissembling selves.

Perhaps it is an effect of this partiality for the Ancients, but sitting at my feet, his vizard removed, the youth looks like Correggio's painting of Ganymede: a tender half-grown boy, all pink flesh, fat curls, and wide eyes the colour of acorns. Ganymede ... Yes: for want of his true name I shall call him Ganymede, since this is the very name given me many years before—in this very room, as it happens, and when I was of his tender years—by the woman whose portrait he has been admiring.

'So you are more interested in her,' I say, 'more interested in the miniature than you are in me, the artist.'

Once again he prepares to object, but I do not afford him the opportunity.

'Very well,' I tell him. 'I understand. You are slain by her face. Well then. Yes: the likeness is accurate, if I do not overrate my talent. I have captured her face perfectly, if I may say so myself. I was in love with her at the time, which may explain the particular animations of colour and line.'

'So beautiful,' Ganymede repeats, rather superfluously, and I wonder briefly if I am envious or pleased that my little trinket has become an object of such desire.

'In answer to your second question,' I continue, 'no, she is not living. She has been dead for more than forty years. You are in love with the face of a dead woman,' I pronounce a little violently, for I wish to shock him, to see his pretty face again turn the colour of the gooseberry wine. 'Yes! That pretty neck you have been admiring so fondly was snapped at Tyburn in front of a vulgar multitude.'

'She was a criminal? Impossible!'

'Even a beautiful lady may be a criminal,' I reply, striving to sound cynical and worldly.

'But ... who was she?' Curiosity has overcome his trepidations, or whatever an old man like myself, ugly and unknown, is capable of inspiring. 'Please—what was her name?'

'Her name you will not recognise,' I tell him as I light my pipe with a taper. 'I knew her as Lady Beauclair. Yet she also had another name, one by which the pamphlets, broadsheets and ballads proclaimed her "monstrous crime" on the corner of every street.'

3

'Monstrous crime . . .? You must tell me her history,' he commands.

I offer him my pouch of tobacco, but he demurs. I puff for a moment in silence.

'Please, sir, tell me her history,' he repeats.

'Her history is my history,' I finally tell him. 'You cannot hear about her without first hearing about me. I must declare my own interest in the matter. I cannot tell you about her without first telling you about myself.'

'Then tell me,' says Ganymede, preserving his attitude on the cushions, anxious to be swept into the tumultuous clouds and perilous draughts of an unknown world.

When was the last time, I wonder once more, that my audience was a youth such as this one, so handsome and eager?

'I first met her here,' I begin slowly, 'in this house, on a night such as this. There was a company and music. The dress was even more extravagant in those days. I had sustained a small injury, and she brought me into this same chamber . . .'

But now through the doorway I suddenly glimpse our host, Lord W—, crossing along the gallery. An insupportable young monster with the manners of a French privateer, dressed for the occasion as a general. Perhaps he presumes, a little traitorously, to represent Bonaparte. Catching my eye, he frowns from behind his mask, his eyes crossing, his tongue protruding itself in a most vulgar manner.

'I cannot continue here,' I tell my new friend. 'But if you should call upon me at my lodgings tomorrow evening . . .'

'Tomorrow evening I may not wish to know,' he promptly replies. 'I may have forgotten her face by then. Perhaps I shall walk out of this room now and see another face which will make me forget hers for ever.'

So my Ganymede is a coquette.

'That is true,' I agree. 'But should you come to my rooms tomorrow I warrant you will never forget her.'

'That is a very great thing to promise, especially to a young man. Perhaps,' he adds, 'it is *too* great a thing to promise.'

Finishing his cup, he bounds to his feet and, with a rustle of his white gown, disappears through the lintelled portal into a thronging pantheon of costumed deities.

I remain in the chamber long enough to drain the goose-

4

berry wine and tap the ashes of my pipe into the cold fireplace. Then, extinguishing the lone candle on the sideboard and adjusting my domino, I too pass into the salon.

After a moment I spy Ganymede dancing with a tall shepherdess, the daughter of an old peer who has retired to the luxury of his Jamaican estates. Insolent young man! But then, suddenly melancholy, I envy the two of them their youth, their vanity, and whatever they may feel for one another, no matter how false it is, or how brief.

Yet my sentiments become more charitable and optimistic an hour later when Ganymede unexpectedly brushes up against me as I prepare to depart. Raising his vizard and tugging on the sleeve of my domino, he whispers: 'Tomorrow, then. Nine o'clock . . .'

One

 I shall begin at the beginning. I was born in the village of Upper Buckling, in the county of Shropshire, in the year 1753. Before my birth a gypsy fortune-teller predicted to my mother that I should become a prosperous merchant or a noble statesman. My mother, fortunately, set little store by such pagan superstition, being the wife of a clergyman; and this indeed was the profession she was content to reserve for me despite these intimations of future grandeur. My reverend father likewise refused to believe that the clues to our characters resided in tea-leaves or in the palms of our hands—as the gypsy had confidently asserted—but, rather, held they were to be discovered in our faces: in the conformation of the head, the situation therein of the eyes, the length of the nose, the width of the lips, the shape of the eyebrows, the angle of the jaw. He expended a good many years and a great amount of stationery establishing the irrefutability of this hypothesis, the final fruit of which was a learned treatise entitled *The Compleat Physiognomist*. What of my own lot in life he may have glimpsed in the blots, blemishes and truculent expressions of my youthful visage he did not reveal, but in any event he was agreed with my mother on the choice of my future occupation. This prospect I did not contemplate with enthusiasm, but as a second son I relented to their wishes, however unprepossessing they were to my imagination, which instead prompted dreams of literary fame or of the popular applause I would achieve with my paintbrush in the salons and exhibition halls of the Continent.

My prospects for the clergy changed, however, with the death of my elder brother William. At eighteen years William had been purchased a commission in the army, but this career was soon terminated in battle beneath the falls of the Mississippi by the musket-ball of an Indian chieftain. Then, altering my course still further, in the following spring William was followed to the grave by my father, claimed by

6

a fever, *The Compleat Physiognomist* sadly incomplete. Since my father had entertained a philosophical carelessness to financial affairs, believing that the positive reception of his treatise would obviate the need for all worries in this area, my mother was left without a groat. Under these altered circumstances it was resolved that upon attainment of my seventeenth year I should depart for London, there to foster an alliance with my kinsman Sir Henry Pollixfen. Besides being my mother's cousin, Sir Henry was also a man of wealth and civil rank; the very sort of gentleman, in short, whose public stature the gypsy's prophecy had implausibly reserved for me.

Before setting out in the world I was made to comprehend that preparatory to any future establishment through my kinsman I should require the offices of the most cautious diplomacy, as civil contact between the families had lapsed at the time when my mother first received the addresses of my father, and then had ceased altogether upon their marriage. The causes of this breach, now entering its third decade, I understood to be a patch of arable land adjoining the estates of my maternal grandfather, as well as an eligible young man who had been legally attached to it. To my grandfather's dismay, this young gallant had not, however, been attached to the fancy of my mother, who remained devoted to my father, deaf to every advice or threat.

So it was that on the morning following my seventeenth birthday I set out for London, bearing with me on the pack-saddle twelve guineas, one suit of clothes, three ruffled shirts, two pairs of worsted stockings, my paintbox, the stained and furling manuscript of *The Compleat Physiognomist*, and a three-cornered hat which in a former service had protected the more heavily lined brow of this treatise's author. That is to say, I carried with me everything I owned in the world, and on the strength of these slender qualifications, and of my mother's letter of introduction to my honoured kinsman, I precipitated myself into the unfathomed depths of that mighty city.

My only other resource in London was my friend Topsham, or Lord Chudleigh as I now could call him. Toppie's acquaintance and subsequent avowals of friendship had followed from my father's performance of various sacred duties for the previous Lord Chudleigh, the last of which, two summers before, involved burying him. Toppie then succeeded to large estates not only in Shropshire but also in County Cork, as the legacy of a forebear's devotion to Cromwell. Determined to live among the highest company, he arrived in London some weeks after me, though his route from Shropshire had been more prolonged and adventuresome than my own, encompassing regions from Paris to Constantinople. Then, too, before repairing to London he had lingered for two months on the Portuguese coast, for after a year of dissipating studies in the less salubrious climates of the Continent he had found it necessary to recruit his health with the assistance of a painful course of mercury.

Upon his first arrival in the capital Toppie faithfully sought out my humble rooms in the Haymarket, above the wigmaker's shop; or, rather, his footman sought me out, dropping his new master's engraved card through the shop door. Many times thereafter Toppie promised to introduce me to Persons of Quality (as he called them), who, he said, would be most anxious to provide me with material assistance once they appreciated the quality of my landscapes and portraitures. The generosity of this kind offer was not lost on me, as my kinsman had so far remained impervious to my several advances. A good face may be, as *The Compleat Physiognomist* stated, 'a letter of recommendation to its bearer', but Sir Henry, alas, declined to peruse this particular document however desperately it was offered, preferring to conduct our correspondence through the person of a tall and saturnine porter, who upon my last visit to the handsome residence in Queen's Square had threatened to cudgel me should these entreaties persist. The continuing sad issue of this affair therefore predisposed me to accept Toppie's invitation to accompany him to a drum held at the residence of Lord W—, a peer well known for his convivial social habits, though somewhat infamous in the *beau monde* on account of his family history.

It was at this ball, two months into my sojourn in London, that I first made the acquaintance of Lady Petronella Beauclair and her ambiguous companion Tristano. These names are not so well known today as they once were; indeed Tristano, once so notorious, the subject of scandal and gossip, of pamphlets and broadsheets, was an old man, all but forgotten by the time I met him; and each has now been dead for more than four decades. I alone remain to tell the story of their lives, which for a few short months swept like comets within the orbit of my own, changing that orbit for ever.

Without compromising the remainder of my memoirs I shall inform you (if it not be already too apparent) that I did not become a prosperous merchant or a noble statesman, nor even a poet or an eminent painter. And neither was I to find any material assistance at the hands of my kinsman Sir Henry Pollixfen. It seems that I have spent the entirety of my life belying the gypsy's prophecy. I am, I shall confess at the outset, a murderer; and even those possessing no knowledge of my crime—for which I have been punished by my conscience alone—would say I have become a debauched creature, a monster of moral abomination reviled by all who pretend to virtue or goodness. Yet I merely ask you to restrain judgement and to hear my history, or Lady Beauclair's history, or Tristano's—whatever the case may be.

Two

 Under other circumstances I might have pursued my way on foot, for Lord W—'s house stood in St James's Square, a short distance from my lodgings above Mr Sharp's shop. Yet the invitation having come from him, Toppie saw fit to bear the expense of hiring transport—he had not yet purchased the ostentatious equipage for which he later became known—and so at nine o'clock the two of us clattered through the Haymarket in two glass-chairs borne by burly and sweating chair-men.

I should admit straight away that after two months in London the assembly was my first excursion into polite society. This may perhaps explain, if not exactly excuse, some of what follows. True, I had been several times to Ranelagh Gardens in Chelsea, where I paid half a crown for the privilege of walking round the Rotunda or watching fireworks in the presence of Persons of Quality; and the previous week I drank to the King's health with Toppie and several of his new friends after a concert at Vauxhall Gardens. But more often than not I kept only the more humble and sober company of Mr Sharp and his family, which made up for in quantity what it may have lacked in quality. This attachment was one Toppie sought to discourage: for, as he frequently reminded me, no wigmaker with seven mouths to feed could have any particular wish to commission a portrait or a landscape.

As we approached the house, situated in a moonlit square lined with chariots, phaetons, sedan-chairs, and polished coach-and-fours spattered with the mud of the country, Toppie became liberal in his assurances about the female acquaintance I might make at tonight's drum. I listened with much eagerness to his descriptions of Miss This and Lady That, for I was not always so ugly as I am now, and deep within my breast I harboured shy hopes of matrimony. He also provided encouragements regarding the quality of the company I could expect to meet and intimated that, if I created a favourable impression, there would be many faces willing to avail themselves of my pencil and paints. He spoke, furthermore, of the famous painter of portraits and founding member of the Royal Academy, Sir Endymion Starker, who, he surmised, would be in attendance tonight. He declared that there was not a famous visage in London, and scarcely one in all of Europe, that had not been reproduced by Sir Endymion's deft brush: Lord North, the Duke of Grafton, Edmund Burke, Lord Rockingham, the Marquês de Pombal, Madame de Pompadour, even King George himself—each, and many more besides, had apparently sat to this distinguished gentleman at one time or another.

'I have met Sir Endymion once or twice,' Toppie said, 'and should I see him, George, I shall introduce you, be sure of that.'

As we disembarked into the cooling air—it was early September—these words, like those of the gypsy fortune-teller, swelled into a promise that, for the moment, it seemed impossible to betray.

When Toppie announced himself at the door we were admitted into the house by a liveried footman who relieved us of our hats. This old sentinel courteously submitted a low bow, though it seemed as if he may have regarded my father's weathered tricorne and several of my other accoutrements with less esteem than he pretended. For the occasion Toppie had furnished me with one of his coats and a pair of gold-buckled shoes, to which Thomas, his footman, had with great vigour applied a rag and polish. Still, my waistcoat and breeches did not perhaps suit the occasion, and, moreover, had seen regular duty on Sunday mornings for a year or two already, a service betrayed more conspicuously than I would have preferred.

Upstairs we discovered the company assembled in a splendid salon with a corniced ceiling and walls festooned with scrolling acanthus leaves, golden sheaves and wreaths of honeysuckle. Toppie introduced me to several ladies of degree, who dropped deep curtsies and politely favoured my addresses with lowered eyes. I was on the point of engaging myself with one of them for a future minuet, when Toppie excused us and drew me into an octagonal room with red velvet walls and antique marble busts on brackets. Here a singer acclaimed for the quality of her mezzo-soprano voice had just completed an aria, and her audience now picked up their cards to resume the game of ombre.

'She's not come,' Toppie muttered into his lace cravat, in some despair.

He had been induced to attend the drum by Lady Sacharissa Lascelles, or, rather, by the prospect of seeing her again. He had made her acquaintance the previous evening as we played Dutch-pins at the Adam and Eve Tea Gardens in Tottenham Court Road. I immediately suspected that Lady Sacharissa, the daughter of a newly created peer, had made a vivid impression in his breast, for in her presence his play had been elated and uncharacteristically competitive.

I pursued him back into the crowded salon, where we partook in a glass of punch. As we drank, Toppie indicated the names and ranks of various dignitaries in attendance; but these intelligences abruptly ceased when his attention came to rest at last on the visage of Lady Sacharissa, who was in animated intercourse across the room with a small party of gamblers. Excusing himself, he crossed beneath the chandelier, and soon after the two of them were curtsying and bowing to each other.

I turned my attention to the other guests. 'Persons of the *highest* quality', Toppie had called them, in a reverential undertone, as we ascended the processional staircase, a marble cascade flowing between pairs of fluted columns.

These were the richest, most noble, most dazzling figures of the *beau monde*, all of them perfumed and powdered, equipped with gold-laced hats and silver-hilted swords, attired from top to toe in their finest ruffled and brocaded court dress. Here or there a necklace of diamonds, the glittering spoil of India or Araby, could be seen sparkling on a white bosom, while on another's alp of elaborately dressed hair rubies caught the candle-light as she laughed with a fine young gentleman who displayed a beauty-patch on a rouged cheek. Some of the ladies, I noted in amazement, had submitted themselves to a most ostentatious fashion, for bouquets of fresh flowers, bunches of grapes, young vegetables and tiny models of coaches and horses sprouted from, hung upon, or else cantered across, their *décolleté* bodices and beautiful fountains of hair. What, I wondered, might the good and sober matrons of Upper Buckling think of these practices?

More incredibly, some of the gentlemen also flaunted monstrous eccentricities of dress that surpassed all wonted bounds of fashion. Their exceedingly tight waistcoats and breeches bore the bold stripes of African zebras or the bright colours of peacocks and canary-birds, and from their pockets emerged gold or silver fob-chains of prodigious length, upon which loops oscillated one—and sometimes two—pocket-watches of seemingly inconvenient measure. In one hand these creatures clasped tiny spyglasses, through which they peered rather critically at the company; in the other, canes of fantastic length, decorated with yellow tassels. The spyglasses or canes were intermittently set aside, so that these fellows might smooth the silk neckties fastened with great bows under their chins or adjust the bearing of the tiny cocked hats perched upon the periwigs that rose to such portentous heights above their brows. Then, having settled the composition of these accoutrements, and having spotted some person of their fancy through the spyglasses, they set off across the salon in odd, tiptoeing gaits, as if their snug breeches and tiny diamond-buckled shoes caused them the most dreadful pinches and pains.

But—elsewhere—such fine dress! Such noble physiognomies! I recognised a man who held an eminent rank in the Commons conversing with a famous stage-actor who had recently acted the part of Othello in Drury Lane; beside them an old duchess, a friend to the King, exchanged gossip with an admiral and an ambassador, both in full periwigs of grey hair; and immediately to my left a peer famed for adventurous amatory practices was executing a deep bow before a tall woman whose face was obscured behind a black mask.

The only guest who appeared bereft of any wealth, bearing or distinction—apart from myself, that is—was an elderly gentleman whose attention was fully engrossed by his shoe-buckles. Though dressed in a powdered wig and elegant habiliments that comported with the occasion, his shrunken limbs and withered face subtracted greatly from their effect, the latter being the colour and texture of the shrivelled skin on a dish of one of my mother's less successful custards. So wrinkled was he, indeed, and so sickly was his hue, that he looked like an embalmed Egyptian. He occupied a rush-bottomed chair by a window, to which, when his admiration of his buckles momentarily subsided, he took occasional recurrences, as if anticipating uneasily the arrival of a particular guest.

Yet so unprepossessing was this personage that soon I forgot about him and turned my attention to the other, happier, guests. After the dancing commenced, and after a second cup of punch, I took it upon myself to join the couples disporting themselves on the dance-floor. However, much of the company had recently been transported from the Long Room at Hampstead, which accounted for a lack of inclination for minuets among the ladies. For when I begged the favour of a dance with several of the young beauties, each graciously pleaded the rigours of this previous assembly. Still, I could not avoid noticing how each found herself sufficiently revived several minutes later when prevailed upon by the young peer.

Resigning my pretensions, I presently found myself in the company of three men who, having witnessed my ill luck with the ladies, demonstrated their sympathy by courteously inviting me to their card-table to take a hand at whist. When I confessed my ignorance of the game—for, remember, I was of the household of a clergyman—one of the gentlemen patiently explained its concepts and rules while another disembarrassed me of my cup, which he kindly replenished. We played for a time at threepence a game, and, being swift of apprehension, I acquitted myself with some expertise and soon found myself wealthier by half a crown. I received the

13

handsome congratulations of my new friends, who commended me as a clever youth. They pleaded to be allowed to retrieve their losses, and I speedily agreed, for I was enjoying their company, and the goddess Fortune had thus far gazed upon me with favour. We doubled the stakes and resumed play. I had every expectation of improving my winnings, but after one auspicious game the goddess displayed some fickle behaviour and then finally forsook me altogether in favour of Mr Larkins, one of my antagonists, a gentleman bearing a spyglass and tasselled cane. In due course I was relieved not only of my half-crown but of the remainder of my capital as well. My companions would have permitted me to recover my losses, but I was forced to explain the unhappy condition of my purse.

'For you must understand that I am a poor artist,' I said, 'who has as yet to make his impression in the world. But I am reckoned to possess a fine skill in portraiture,' I felt it wise to append to my confession, 'and so have great hopes for the future.'

This speech my companions did not regard with indifference.

'I have seen evidence that you are a clever youth,' responded the partner of Mr Larkins, a gentleman in a claret-coloured waistcoat with a silver brocade. He roused himself to my rescue upon the mention of my occupation, which he seemed to endorse with a sympathetic smile. Beneath its heavy application of powder and its mouse-skin beauty-patch his face bore all the symptoms of a good and kindly disposition. 'I do not doubt you will improve your state,' he continued, 'both in the game and in your profession; therefore I will advance you a guinea, or, if you wish, two guineas, and we may recommence our play.'

He smiled ever more kindly as he opened a weasel-skin purse, drew out some coins and pushed them across the table. I reflected upon how unmannerly I would seem should I refuse this generous offer, and indeed I had been enjoying myself tremendously; accordingly, I did not scruple to accept the coins. Once again we doubled the stakes, this time at my own request, and cheerfully continued our play, each of us fortified by a tobacco-pipe and another cup of punch. However, the goddess was not so benevolent towards me as my opponent had been, for she demonstrated further capricious behaviour and presently did with the gentleman's two guineas what she had with my half-crown. Thus once again I was obliged to empty my purse and acknowledge my losses.

My opponents sympathised mightily. Mr Larkins and his partner both conjectured that this singular desertion by Fortune could only be of a temporary nature, and both now graciously offered the assistance of their purses. Prevailed upon in so generous a manner I accepted three more guineas from the same weasel-skin purse, promising as I did so to repay the earlier loan as well. Despite my best efforts, however, I suffered further calamities and discovered myself unable to discharge either obligation. The gentleman in the claret waistcoat nevertheless accepted his loss of five guineas with great equanimity, naming a house in St Alban's Street at which, if I found the arrangement convenient, I could present myself for repayment in two days' time.

'But I don't have five guineas in the world,' I should have confessed to the kind gentleman. Yet I feared this admission of a lack of security would appear a breach of his good faith and kindness. So I assured him I found his proposal suitable, whereupon he exchanged smiles with Mr Larkins, who was dropping his winnings into his purse, and Mr Storch, a more taciturn gentleman, who had been my partner and who had been inflicted with similar losses.

'Now we must take leave of your company,' said the gentleman from St Alban's Street as the three of them stood in unison and knocked the ashes from their pipes, 'but I shall look forward to your call next week, Cautley, and not only, I may say, for the sake of my five errant guineas. You should ask for Sir Endymion Starker,' he finished, before the three of them disappeared into the press of hoop-skirts, bustles and tasselled canes.

The discovery that I had lost five guineas to Sir Endymion Starker, a gentleman who had painted the faces of so many Persons of Quality, including that of the King himself, had, as you may well imagine, a most profound effect upon me. For the next few minutes I am sure that my face was a study in contrasts: a mixture of eager anticipation and acute dismay. Yet when I considered how I now had an engagement with so great a Person of Quality as Sir Endymion Starker, a paragon of my aspiring profession, it seemed that perhaps Fortune had not dealt me such a miserable hand of cards after all.

Removing myself from the card-table I assumed one of the beech chairs by a window, from where, partially obscured by a heavy damask curtain, I pondered how I might redeem and even ingratiate myself at this conference. In the midst of my contemplations I realised I had commanded a chair next to the old gentleman whom I had earlier remarked. No longer preoccupied with either his shoe-buckles or the window, this forlorn soul seemed to have fallen asleep, providing me with the opportunity to study him more closely. His stature appeared to be a little below the middle size, but despite the exiguous limbs, which tapered into tiny hands and feet, his belly was prominent beneath a gosling-green waistcoat. The custard-skin face was of small dimensions, but for a fleshless nose that bore a strong likeness to the bill of a sparrow-hawk. This crooked beak passed at its lowest point within a fraction of the strutting protuberance of a hairless chin, and in doing so all but concealed a mouth of the minutest calibre. Every so often this pinched orifice struggled open, expelled a brief draught that bedewed the cravat, then snapped shut, tortoise-like. As this singular creature slept his feet were thrust out before him, liveried in silk stockings whose colour repeated that of the waistcoat, and his head had rolled forward to such a degree that the continued adhesion of his periwig was in some doubt.

As I studied this creature, something about his appearance made me uneasy, as if in the midst of this gaiety he represented a ghostly ambassador from an unhappy province far away. It seemed to me that one or two of the guests now and again favoured him with an anxious gaze, almost as if they, too, suspected that something tragic and unknown had advanced a pace or two towards them across the sparkling salon; but then their faces returned to their partners so quickly that I could not be at all certain.

My interest was presently diverted from this creature by a nearby conversation between two ladies whose countenances were concealed behind Japanese folding fans. They were discussing our host, whom I had not yet seen.

'Has his lordship lived for very long in St James's Square?' the first was inquiring as she adjusted the position of several oranges and bananas inhabiting the regions above her brow.

'Yes, my dear,' replied her companion, whose own head was adorned with the replica of a windmill, the mobile vanes of which winked with jewels. Her languid voice seemed accustomed to conveying such minor intelligences. 'For all his life. The lease was purchased by his father.' A pause. 'Surely you recall him?'

'Yes, a Turkey merchant, was he not? I am told he lost a fortune in the South Sea Company.'

'He lost more than that, upon my word.'

'Oh?'

'Why, have you not heard the story? About his wife, Lady W—?' Another pause; then, hissingly: 'Such a scandal!'

What the rumoured scandal of my host's mother might have been I was not to learn—at least, not tonight—for no sooner had the conversation continued beyond the range of my hearing than the creature to my right, who had stirred perceptibly at the mention of Lady W—, suddenly sat upright. Then, giving the two ladies a startled glance, he flew from his seat and, nimbly taking resort to his feet, fled the salon with a facility that belied his years and the earlier imbecility of motion.

I looked round the room for confirmation of this strange event: the ladies who evidently prompted it appeared to have witnessed nothing; nor did anyone else register the phenomenon. It was as if from my chair at the window I had beheld the departure of a ghost or walking spirit visible to no one but myself.

The conversation between the ladies continued apace, once again within range of my hearing; but the subject had changed, and now its freedom of comment regarding some of our fellow guests offended my delicacy. I was then, may I remind you, a very virtuous youth. Presently I experienced more than a mild discomfiture, as though, trapped in my window-seat, I was witness to scenes and privy to conversations and unpleasant discoveries that should have been concealed from my eyes and ears. Mention of the previous Lord W—'s losses in the South Sea Company had reminded me once more of my own, newly incurred obligation, and once again I became slightly apprehensive in the midst of the riotous gaiety.

Shortly afterwards another glass of punch partly disordered my senses, and the pungent spices of perfume, so light and refreshing at first, made the corniced ceiling and its chandelier, a bejewelled crystal octopus, wobble unsteadily above my head. Wishing to take some air, I rose from my

17

chair and took leave of the crowded salon. In the process I bumped my shoulder into the singer, who reproached me with a mezzo-soprano voice that was no longer as sweet and gentle as when it had produced the aria. I stuttered an apology and stumbled through a set of doors and down a stair.

I was half-way down, clutching the banister for assistance, before I realised these tapering steps were not the processional ones—the marble cascade—from which I had access to the salon an hour or two before. They opened at the foot on to a tribune whose ceiling was upheld by four fluted pillars, between each pair of which were inscribed armorial bearings. The alcoved walls served as repositories for more urns and canvases, as well as for casts of classical statuary. The canvases in particular engaged my attention for a time. All portrayed either Italian landscapes in the manner of Claude Lorrain, or, more numerously, broad-countenanced gentlemen clad in military dress. Several of these heroes were painted with a rare art and appeared to be productions of the great Sir Godfrey Kneller. The proud martial faces that frowned in their gilt frames displayed all the tokens of eminence that in my fond reveries I imagined marked the visage of my distinguished kinsman, which as yet, alas, remained unknown to me.

The only face dissenting from this illustrious masculine line, which quite reasonably I took to be Lord W—'s forebears, was that of a young lady in Turkish costume, who posed with her hands on one hip and regarded her portraitist with disdainful feminine coquetry. Though she was not, perhaps, perfectly beautiful—her nose was rather too extended, her eyes too narrowly set, and her limbs not quite so delicate as my youthful standard of beauty prescribed—her features nevertheless kindled my fascination and even a few flickers of awe. The sharp, hooded eyes that fixed me in my spot conveyed an infinitely more intense version of the haughtiness aspired to by the military gentlemen in their swords and epaulettes. The habit, moreover, was arrayed carelessly about her shoulders, exposing to profile a bosom to whose perfections had been added a large jewel, mulberry in colour, sculpted into the shape of a tear-drop. I could not help wondering who she had been; a stage player perhaps? A wealthy courtesan well known in the court of Charles II? Or perhaps, I wondered, recalling the rumoured occupation

18

of Lord W—'s father—perhaps she had been a Turkish slave-girl transported back from a riotous caravanserai on the blossom-scented shores of the Levant?

In another time, and in better illumination, I should have tarried longer to inspect the masterful execution of fine detail in these mighty physiognomies. But as my eyes were weary, and as I still required the benefit of air, I presently crossed through the tribune and passed into a corridor, on either side of which stood a closed door, leading, I supposed, into sculleries, larders, wine-vaults, bedchambers for butlers and house-maids. Reluctant to chance these portals, I continued forward and a moment later attained the terminus of the gallery, which now executed a sharp turn into a cramped closet.

At this point I heard a series of sounds advancing behind me: a pair of shuffling feet assisted by a walking-stick, the base of which was, every two or three paces, struck down heavily on the tiled floor. As this pedestrian slowly approached, something in the sound of his progress, especially in the arhythmical tapping of his walking-stick, assumed ominous inflections.

Conscious, suddenly, of my status as an interloper, I crept into the closet, a tiny dressing-chamber furnished only with a mahogany chair, and held my breath as the tapping grew nigh. My curiosity was sufficiently excited, however, that I positioned myself behind the door, left open to permit a view of the advancing passenger. My desire was gratified a moment later when who should pass through the gallery but the ancient porter, assisted by a twisted walking-stick and bearing a velvet cape. Remembering the uncharitable glances this old retainer had bestowed upon my father's tricorne, I had no wish to reveal myself and shrank back into the closet. A second later I detected the rasp of a latch, then the voice of the porter as he heaved open a door.

'*Signora!*' he commanded, in what sounded like the prelude to an expostulation, and in a voice that ill concealed his disdain. '*Signora!* You will not presume again—'

A female voice returned from beyond the door, seemingly equally disdainful, though garbled and unintelligible, as if its owner had not yet mastered articulate speech.

The footman resumed in his contemptuous tone. 'You are not to show yourself above the stairs, especially not tonight.'

19

To this reproach the strangely garbled voice responded with a mewl registering an even higher pitch.

'You were warned,' intoned the footman.

Another unintelligible garble—the angered bark of a timid wolf bitch.

'You may stay in the garden all night if you wish!'

The door clunked shut, then the footman tapped his way back into my view, this time disburdened of the cape. Only when the tapping and shuffling grew inaudible did I creep from my hiding-place. My first instinct was to return immediately to the tribune; but once again my fear was overborne by my curiosity, and so I cautiously inspected the gallery for the secret entrance to the garden. In the poor light I discovered no door, but high on the wall was a small casement, which I was able to reach with the assistance of the mahogany chair purloined from the closet. So supported, I stood on tiptoe and looked outside, holding my breath. At first I saw nothing. Then, seconds later, a movement below attracted my eye. I peered into the unlit garden, to see the peculiar old gentleman who had fled the salon staring up at me with close-set, hooded eyes, his thin shoulders encircled by the velvet cape. I vented my breath in a short cry that echoed the garbled voice—though this yap of alarm was sounded not only on account of the strange figure in the garden but because, in that same second, I detected the soft whisper of a footfall behind me.

When I spun round to confront my unexpected companion the force of this motion played havoc with the bearing of the mahogany chair, and with my position on it; and so instead of discerning the tall lady with the black mask— for she it was who had now arrived—I found myself gazing up at a coved ceiling painted with beribboned Cupids and the allegorical figures of Time and Love. Only when I raised my head a few seconds later did I glimpse the face that, as its vizard was removed, tallied in every point with my youthful standard of beauty.

20

Three

 'Please.' Blackness. 'Please, sir.' Light.

The terracotta tiles had delivered my brow such a nasty bump that not until a full minute had passed were my eyes able to fix themselves once more upon this *beau idéal*, this emblem of feminine beauty. I blinked—twice, thrice, four times—at this particular physiognomy, which I now noticed was etched with an expression of the most tender concern. I also noticed that, high above, populating the vast territories of her hair, there appeared a large green caterpillar and several other insects, all encased in blown glass. Whether by accident or design, entire regions of the impressive mane descended here and there in black cataracts, swirling in a soft spume about the ears and neck. This last was long, arched, impossibly slender, and circumscribed by a set of jewels whose reflections, even in this poor light, were much too vivid for my aching eyeballs. Their owner was dressed in an open-fronted gown, the extremities of which remained somewhere far behind her in the corridor, and whose ornamented frontispiece threatened to engulf me in its ample waves.

'A tiny sip will recruit your strength in a trice,' said a gentle voice as my lips were plied with a small flask produced from the multitudinous folds of the tremendous gown. 'I prithee—drink.'

I submitted myself to the flask, though under the influence of its contents I felt even less inclined to find my feet. I had been expecting the lady's animadversions, but now her hand, heretofore gently supportive of my head, even more gently caressed the back of my neck. She unfolded her fan, bringing the buffets of a soft breeze across my brow.

'Surely I dream,' I said aloud. 'Where am I?'

This rescuing angel stroked my cheek with a gesture that seemed to savour as much of passion as of tender concern for my health, and the folds of her dress drew even closer

21

round. I watched, dumb, as Cupid, Time and Love executed a fairy dance in the coves far, far overhead ...

In retrospect—that is, when I thought of this face in the days that followed—a passage from *The Compleat Physiognomist* never failed to revolve through my head: 'The great *Plato*', my father had written in his introductory chapter, 'regards all physical Beauty as a Sign of the Beauty of the *Soul*: outward Appearance—notably the *Physiognomy*—he believes, is shaped by the *inward Disposition*. Likewise doth his worthy Pupil, *Aristotle*, postulate a close Relation between the *Body* and the *Soul*; moral Dispositions such as Gentleness or Kindness or Stupidity (as he says in the *Physiognomonica*) being most capably surmis'd from physical Appearances manifest in the *Countenance*. Thus may we say, following *Aristotle*, that the Countenance is the *Mask of the Soul*; yet with this Difference: it is a Mask which does not *disguise* its Wearer, but instead *reveals* him to our Eyes.'

Yet now as I saw the stranger's graceful countenance hovering before me, its lovely brow furrowed with concern, I asked myself why a lady as beautiful as this should require a mask. And this is the question about Lady Petronella Beauclair—for this she presently told me was her name—I was to ask myself many times in the weeks that followed.

Several minutes later, after I had submitted to the ministrations of her cambric handkerchief and many sympathetic cluckings of her tongue, Lady Beauclair exalted me to my feet and offered to conduct me up the stairs. Only when we passed through the tribune did I spy the strange caped figure—the '*Signora*'—standing in the corridor behind us, evidently a witness to the scene. For a second I was fixed in my place by its dark gaze. Through the allusions in my father's treatise I was reminded—again in retrospect—of those physiognomies painted a century before by Charles Le Brun in his *Traité de l'Expression*: human faces with eyes or noses of eagle or camel or sheep, though in the case of this caped creature in the corridor I was reminded of the watchful eyes of a badger or a stoat.

I wished to demand an explanation for this mysterious presence, but either the bump on my head or the contents of the flask—or perhaps a combination of the two—had robbed me of my powers of speech, so that my first attempts at the question were barely more articulate than the sounds of the *Signora*. I had also been robbed of my equilibrium, for which reason I was required to lean for support upon Lady Beauclair's shoulder, an act to which it seemed she submitted with unusual alacrity.

Her interrogation as we ascended was very brief, concerned only with the particulars of my name and street, which, discovering my powers of speech, I saw no reason to withhold. When I informed her I wished to reunite myself with my friend Toppie, or 'Lord Chudleigh' as I said, she responded that his lordship had departed not five minutes ago. Her voice as she imparted this information was incomparably sweet, a rival, surely, to that of the esteemed mezzo-soprano. Still, I could not help wondering whether this sweet voice spoke the truth, for at that instant I was certain I spied Toppie's periwig bobbing towards me across the salon.

Be that as it may, Lady Beauclair pre-empted a reunion by escorting me into a vacant chamber. Here she seated me on a low sofa and, with the assistance of a young serving-girl, proceeded with the manufacture of some variety of poultice for my brow, a remedy I now insisted was unnecessary, though to no avail. In the midst of these ministrations, likewise accompanied by Lady Beauclair's gentle words and the cluckings of her tongue, I presently found the nerve to make my inquiry.

'Who, pray, was the—person,' I asked, 'that I saw below the stairs just now?'

At some point during our ascent Lady Beauclair had replaced the vizard, so her lovely white face was now hidden from me, a mysterious blank.

'So you are still curious,' she replied teasingly as she superintended the serving-girl's efforts with the poultice. 'The bump on the head evidently has not taught you the lesson about curiosity! Perhaps,' she continued in the same playful voice, 'perhaps, then, you are more interested in the gentleman downstairs than you are in me? Can you be so ungrateful, Mr Cautley?'

As she asked this question she leaned closer than perhaps her services truly required. Her delicate fingers touched my cheeks, whose colour, I suspect, grew even brighter; while under the influence of this lingering contact, to which was added the tickles of her lace sleeve, an ungovernable force in my breeches now slowly asserted itself into, I feared, shamingly conspicuous proportions.

23

'Of course not,' I stammered, even more distressed now by the fact that the eyes in the mask appeared to take account of the altered disposition of my breeches.

'Perhaps, my Ganymede, your curiosity does not extend to Amy either,' she continued, indicating the serving-girl, whose colour and diffidence now repeated my own. 'And Amy is such a lovely girl,' she reflected in an admiring tone. 'Such a beauty!'

As if to convince herself of the veracity of these claims she now stepped back to appraise Amy, the eyes in the mask taking a particularly loving account of the discomfited girl's bosom. The hand that had caressed my face now reached out and did the same with Amy's, before descending gradually to the throat, then to the bodice, which Amy's hands fluttered quickly to protect.

'Amy, like you, is newly arrived in town. Are you not, Amy?'

Amy made no reply other than to achieve an even deeper degree of scarlet.

'So fresh and clean . . .' Lady Beauclair's hand deftly breached the girl's blockade. 'Touch her,' she suddenly commanded of me, reaching for my hand. Her sweet and gentle voice had, like her face, been replaced by a more inscrutable alternative.

'Please, ma'am,' responded Amy, whose delicate countenance had now gone startlingly pale.

'Kiss her,' Lady Beauclair commanded, more insistent now as her own fingers insinuated themselves into the bodice, which had begun to heave in some alarm. She ignored my silent refusal and, following her own injunction, kissed the trembling Amy on the hollow of the neck, then began working the buttons of the girl's blouse.

'Please, ma'am!'

With some effort Amy managed to twist herself free of Lady Beauclair's attentions and rush to the door. Lady Beauclair's response to this tearful evacuation was a shower of careless laughter, whose effect on me was, I must admit, a desire to follow hastily in Amy's footsteps.

'I would fain speak to my friend Toppie,' I blurted.

Lady Beauclair precluded my departure by seating herself beside me on the sofa and grasping my cold hands in her warm ones. Her exertions with poor Amy caused her to fetch her breath in long sighs, whose fragrant plumes now

24

caressed my cheek. Several slender strands of pomatum-slick hair had freed themselves from their bondage among the pullulating insects to dangle in curls about the eye-holes of her satin mask, and once more the folds of her dress threatened engulfment.

'Very well,' she said after a moment. 'I shall tell you about the gentleman, since you are so insistent.'

I now denied any inclination to learn the gentleman's identity; in truth, I had quite forgotten him. But Lady Beauclair's sweet voice had returned, and her aspect was now more modest; so for the moment I relinquished my hopes of an escape and submitted to the closeness of the masked face and the delicate perfume of its breath.

'That gentleman,' she said in a conspiratorial voice, though no one else was about, 'that gentleman is a kinsman, of sorts, of Lord W—, who is also a relation of mine. I cannot tell you of him here, but should you call upon me tomorrow morning, when I shall be receiving calls . . .'

I reminded her that, as tomorrow was Sunday, I would be attending holy service in the forenoon. Such was my unfailing custom—one from which I was unwilling to deviate even for the sake of a woman as beautiful as Lady Beauclair. She hastily acknowledged her forgetfulness.

'I meant to say, of course, that if you would call upon me on *Monday* . . .'

'That, I regret, will not be possible,' I protested, remembering my assignation with Sir Endymion. I told her of this appointment, omitting, however, its immediate occasion. Yet Lady Beauclair, curiously, appeared to know my circumstances in regard to my new acquaintance and intimated that, should I call upon her, she might find herself capable of rendering material assistance.

'I shall be dining at four o'clock,' she said, naming the more fashionable hour rather than the three o'clock ceremony maintained by Mrs Sharp. 'You will be welcome at my table then, at which point, if you still wish, I shall tell you the history of Tristano.'

'Perhaps I might paint your portrait,' I was bold enough to venture. 'For I am reckoned to have a great skill in portraiture . . .'

'I should like that very much,' she replied. 'I will be your patron. Or is it your *patroness*?' Into my hand she now dropped two golden guineas. 'Well then—may I command you?'

So for the sake of curiosity, for the promise of gold, and for the encouragement of something else that as yet I was not near to comprehending: for the sake of all of these things, I agreed that she could.

Four

 Two wigmakers owned shops in the Haymarket in the year 1770. A signboard above the more venerable establishment proclaimed in gilt letters the trade of 'Jules Regnault, Perruquier', beneath which the finest specimens of M. Regnault's craft were represented in a rank in the polished bow-windows, perched atop leather wig blocks like elegantly coiffed marble portrait busts. Starch-white wigs with bags of red silk in the shape of roses or with long queues tied in satin bows; wigs with fat sausage curls or three tiers of tight *boucles*; full-bottom wigs for judges, barristers, and aldermen; riding wigs, campaign wigs, fantail wigs, full dress bob-wigs; wigs decorated with the feathers of mallards or sprinkled with gold dust or tinted green or yellow and smelling sweetly of orris-root and pomatum. These creations, of which a new style was invented each fortnight or sent by the Paris post, perched upon, or dangled from behind, the finest and most noble heads in London.

The other shop, three doors away and on the opposite side of the street, served an altogether more modest clientele. In place of a coat of arms—for, unlike M. Regnault, he had none—its proprietor had posted a signboard on which was represented Delilah clipping the golden locks of a languorous Samson. Beneath, a couplet:

> O *SAMSON*, thou unlucky PRIG,
> Why didst not wear a *PERIWIG*?

Then below this inscription, though in larger script:

26

BOBS, BOB-MAJORS, SCRATCHES,
CAULIFLOWERS, & other *WIGS* made here,
also POWDER for the ITCH; also TEETH
EXTRACTED, SHAVES, and BLEEDS.

And below this, in yet larger script:

Mʳ S. *SHARP*, Prop.

The grizzled inventory, woven from, or stuffed with, the hair of horses, goats and cadavers, was displayed in a window of indifferent transparency. Items left the shop clapped on to the heads of coachmen, market porters, apothecaries, clergymen, grocers, shopkeepers, pamphleteers, poets, chandlers, tavern-keepers—in short, upon the crown of anyone who could not afford the more fashionable and expensive productions of M. Regnault. These humble gentlemen became the subjects of my first portraits in London, for as Mr Sharp measured their heads, shaved their chops, or powdered their wigs with great sneezy clouds from his dredger, I sat on an elbow-chair in a corner of the shop and rendered their knobby crowns with my pencil or, after mixing cakes of paint in mussel shells, represented their peeled-potato or boiled-beetroot complexions in watercolour. Occasionally one of these fellows objected to a portrait of his naked skull, and so in order to appease him I was exiled into the street by the normally benignant Mr Sharp. At such times I lingered alongside M. Regnault's door, through which, each time it was opened, there wafted into the street a great nimbus smelling of orris-root and the extracts of orange and jasmine blossoms.

And here, as my thoughts were borne upwards upon these scent-drenched clouds of powder, I clutched my sketchbook to my breast and dreamed of painting the refined heads that tilted and nodded and bowed inside. For in those days to me the world had divided into two separate spheres: one filled with those humble souls who purchased their wigs from Mr Sharp, the other with the much more elevated ones—the Persons of Quality—who swept through the chiming doors of 'Jules Regnault, Perruquier'. I lived in one sphere—rather, two storeys above it—but I wished one day to pass through the singing portals of the other.

On the morning following Lord W—'s drum I awoke in

this humbler sphere, my little chamber above Mr Sharp's shop. My dreams had been filled with the dressed heads and noble faces of Lord W—'s company—and two heads and two faces in particular—so that, upon being awakened by the creaking hinges of Samson and Delilah, I was unpleasantly surprised to discover myself lying on my thin pallet beside a dead fire.

But despite this small shock, and despite my copious consumption of punch and the profound knock on my brow, I was in splendid fettle. I leapt out of bed, and out of my nightcap and slippers, before a single Sharp was stirring below stairs. I performed my matutinal devotions; lit a small fire; consumed a breakfast of two halfpenny rolls, a hasty pudding and a dish of tea; dressed; and then enjoyed a brisk perambulation through the mist in St James's Park.

By the time I returned, the majority of the Sharps had roused themselves, and at length we proceeded together along Piccadilly to take communion at St James's Church. The family was a pious one, though its younger members were somewhat clamorous in their devotions. My attendance in church was a popular attraction for these latter, who competed among themselves for the spaces beside me on our pew. Ordinarily I was happy enough to indulge these attentions, but this morning for the first time I was more than a little troubled to be seen in the midst of the manifold and vociferous members of this clan, having already recognised among the parishioners the white periwigs, silk coats and bone-tipped canes of some of the guests from last night's assembly. For despite Mrs Sharp's best efforts, the younger members of the family preserved the remains of their breakfast of tea and buttered rolls on their hands and faces and, in the notable instance of little Miss Henrietta, in a stain that encompassed the preponderance of her tiny lace frock. Surely no Person of Quality would wish to grant a commission to a portraitist who kept such untidy companions?

The vicar of St James's possessed a fine voice, whose sepulchral timbre had on previous Sundays inclined my thoughts to sober reflections. Yet despite the solemn performance, and despite the occasional poke or pinch from a young Sharp, this morning my eyes presently roved across the heads of my fellow parishioners, occasionally settling on the visage of a fair young votary as she bent over her prayer-book. Then my thoughts began to rove as well, and in the midst of a sermon recounting 'By What Means We Shall Learn to Tread the Path of Righteousness' I became wholly insensible to the vicar's sage words.

Though I was to meet with Toppie this afternoon, you may be certain that this was not the engagement now occupying my thoughts, which turned, first, to my forthcoming interview with Sir Endymion, then to the one with Lady Beauclair. In either case, but especially in that of the latter, my thoughts spun to and fro like a frantic weathercock, tilting first in one direction, then in another. For the moments could not pass nimbly enough whenever I thought of my lady's amiable glances, the agreeable touch of her hands, her tender exclamations of concern; yet at the same time each moment was filled with squirming agitation, perhaps even dread, if I reflected upon the expressions of her more mysterious passions. Before parting from me the previous night, she had provided me with a *carte-de-visite*, between whose black borders an address in the parish of St Giles was inscribed in a gilt script. A dozen times during the course of the sermon I extracted this token from the pocket of my coat for inspection, as if to convince myself that what had transpired had been more than, as it now seemed, an antic dream.

After the conclusion of the service I stood in the sunlight and watched as our fellow parishioners were handed into their carriages by liveried servants and then transported to what I imagined were their great homes in Piccadilly, Pall Mall or Mayfair. As I smelled the perfume of their wigs and white lace I suddenly felt faint with yearning and sick at my own unworthiness, like a Tantalus thirsting for those receding waters.

You have heard of Tantalus, the son of Zeus? How his punishment in Hades was to stand neck-deep in waters that retreated whenever he, perishing of thirst, attempted to drink of them? At this time of which I speak, in the autumn of 1770, I, like Tantalus, suddenly seemed within reach of everything I had thirsted for, dreamed of; yet I feared that if I leaned too far forward, or raised my hand too quickly, all might fade at a stroke and vanish as swiftly as it had appeared.

Some hours after the service I was sitting with Toppie in

the Piazza Coffee-house in Covent Garden, having spent some of the intervening time engrossed in my father's treatise, the rest waiting upon Toppie. I had it in my mind that through *The Compleat Physiognomist* I might develop a talent for physiognomical readings and thereby look into men's—and women's—souls, which I then would commit to canvas. Surely a Person of Quality would pay dearly for a portrait of his soul? Moreover, this study would, I anticipated, doubtless repay itself in other ways, for the talent of reading countenances would surely be an invaluable resource in London, where the perfidy of men—and of women—was legendary.

Now, reading my gazette, I chanced upon a remarkable account of the perfidies of these latter. Lately it had become my custom to spend a good part of the forenoon here, drinking dishes of coffee and exclaiming with Toppie upon the iniquities of the world. This day these iniquities—if my gazette could be credited—involved the ladies, for I was reading how an Act of Parliament had been passed by our political representatives in order to preserve the interests and reputations of gentlemen tricked into marriage by the more dissembling members of this fairer sex. 'All Women, of whatever Age, Rank, Profession or Degree,' this law stated, 'that shall betray into Matrimony any of his Majesty's Subjects, by the Scents, Paints, cosmetic Washes, artificial Teeth, false Hair, Hoops, high-heeled Shoes and bolstered Hips, shall incur the Penalty of the Law in Force against Witchcraft, and the Marriage shall stand null and void.'

How I chuckled into my dish of coffee! ''Tis a silly fellow,' I remarked to Toppie, showing him the piece, 'a silly fellow indeed, who weds the outward shape of beauty!'

Yet Toppie was less inclined to inveigh against such practices, which he asserted were as prevalent among the gentlemen as the ladies. 'Consider, George,' he said, 'how by a few trifling bits of cloth and ribbon we make our judgements of a man's wealth and character.' He had tipped his head back like that of a sword-swallower, or as if addressing the beams above our heads; a posture invariably adopted during his pontifications. 'Each of us is greatly indebted to his tailor—for his public self. Walking through this city, George, are many folk who have no existence other than that which a tailor bestows upon them. Stripped of their fine garments, these shape-shifters are quite a different species, having no

30

more relation to their dressed selves than they have to the King of Prussia. Thus the habits the tailor fashions disguise us every bit as much as those of the costumier. Where, I would know, lies the difference?'

As it happens, we had, a short time before, visited a costumier's—Mr Johnson's Habit-Warehouse, round the corner in Tavistock Street—to which we had proceeded after meeting at Toppie's new mansion in Grosvenor Square. I had been anxious to see him, for I wished to tell him of my new acquaintances and to seek his advice about how I should best conduct myself. I reasoned that Toppie, as a Person of Quality himself, understood such things.

Yet on this count our meeting today had so far proved something of a disappointment, as I had not yet managed to solicit his advice. Two hours earlier I had been greeted outside his residence by Wheelwright, an old campaigner lately plucked from the Chelsea Hospital. Toppie had dressed him in the regalia of a Swiss Guard and installed him beneath the pediment to call out the hours of the clock and safeguard his riches against the designs of house-breakers. These riches were many and varied, for Toppie was determined to have one of the finest homes in London, no matter the cost or effort. Soon after his arrival he had purchased the lease of a house and assorted moveables for £4,000 and then, with much vigour and idiosyncrasy, set about his endless and seemingly ineffectual renovations and decorations. Each day, it seemed, some new furnishing arrived on a wagon drawn by two exhausted grey-spotted mares employed at the shops of Gumley & Moore, and each day a little more progress was made by the Italian craftsmen on the rococo carvings and gilt mouldings above the fire-places and doorways. These craftsmen had an uncertain livelihood, being hired, dismissed to Italy, recalled, then dismissed again. In consequence, chambers and corridors often remained in an impaired state for weeks on end, while at other times activity was so intense one had to be wary upon arrival of fragments of timber sailing out of third-floor windows or chunks of plaster dropping unexpectedly from the ceilings.

This morning, however, all had been still, and the draper-ies—huge blue folds with gold tassels—were tightly drawn. I employed the brass knocker, on whose second repetition Thomas, the footman, appeared. Toppie was 'indisposed',

Thomas informed me, and had not yet rung the bell or made an appearance. I was perfectly welcome to await his stirring in the Green Velvet Room.

The Green Velvet Room had evidently gained its name during the house's earlier incarnation, for not one inch of its walls, floor or knotted carpet was now either velvet or even remotely a shade of green. It was employed primarily for the storage of items of furniture whose final places had yet to be determined, or else older pieces exiled from their former stations. For twenty-five minutes I had sat among these armchairs and cabinets, patiently awaiting, much like them, Toppie's favour.

After Wheelwright had bellowed out the arrival of the noon hour, Thomas appeared with a pot of black tea. He was a cheerful young fellow of quite handsome appearance, though his cheeks bore the scars of the smallpox, a defect which he was endeavouring to conceal with the assistance of a pair of side-whiskers. These, proving unequal to the task, sprouted from the stippled surfaces at irregular intervals and in filaments of unequal length, like the tufted roots of a small turnip.

After seating himself on one of the superfluous items of furniture he made brief references to the weather, then unexpectedly confessed an amorous alliance with one of the kitchen-maids. He explained with a leer that, when the master was asleep, the two of them would steal into the wine cellar and celebrate their new fellowship, to the chiming accompaniment of Toppie's bottles of claret. None of this frivolous banter—to which I knew not how to respond—could quite manage to conceal rites of a similar nature being celebrated above the stairs: a number of rapid, almost frolicksome footfalls; the cries of spirited laughter; the unmistakable sound of a lute, whose sweet melody drifted intermittently down the banisterless, plaster-dusted staircase.

As Wheelwright proclaimed the quarter-hour I finished the tea and rose to my feet. The lute was clearer and more insistent now, solacing the 'indisposed' Toppie with a sweet rendition of 'O Mistress Mine'. I frowned and told myself that, really, I had been better treated on my visits to the Pollixfen residence in Queen's Square. As I passed through the front door a triangle of plaster fell to the floor, missing my head by a bare six inches.

32

But Toppie, his unwigged head protruding from an open window in one of the upper storeys, hailed me a moment later as I trudged towards Brook Street; I therefore spent the next while—until Wheelwright observed the arrival of one o'clock—back in the Green Velvet Room, waiting for him to dress, or, rather, to be dressed by Thomas. Then we proceeded in a hackney-coach to Tavistock Street, there to purchase costumes for the masquerade to be held in a fortnight's time at Vauxhall Gardens.

The habit-maker's shop occupied a tall, narrow building that was a kind of emblem of the proprietor, who was himself tall and narrow, his wrists extending well beyond the reach of his lace cuffs and his stockings terminating several inches shy of the hem of his breeches. His face seemed to have been composed principally of nose cartilage, which occasioned many a new customer (no doubt hard of seeing) to mistake it for a Punch mask like those on pegs behind his head. By entering his shop we had roused him from a slumber behind the counter, and he hastily assembled himself, extracting his periwig from his pocket and plopping it on to a bald crown, which was bordered on three sides by a thin furze of grey hair. He offered us peeps inside his catalogues—which boasted a 'Very Large Assortment of Character and other *Masquerade Dresses*'—then bid us ramble through his remarkable inventory, recently complemented with costumes seen this past season at the Carnival in Venice.

I was soon agog, for the shop held a collection of the most fantastic appearances, all suspended on pegs in ranks along the walls. A promiscuous congregation of millers, haymakers, milk-maids, country swains and other rustics swarmed with chimney-sweeps, pirates, witches, ward beadles, watchmen, pilgrims, ghosts, Falstaffs, comical-looking Devils, ruffled Pierrots, colourful Harlequins, black-hatted Quakers, Tahitians with grass skirts, Mohawks in bearskins, Turks with feathered turbans and studded brilliants, furred and frogged hussars, and a hundred other fanciful habits, including the silk hoods, lace capes and huge pleated cloaks of Venetian dominoes of every size and colour. Above these costumes, lining the wall in similar profusion, were row upon row of velvet and satin masks, their empty eyes our sightless audience.

Under the pressure of these uncanny gazes I presently

33

decided upon one of the dominoes—a black one—but, when I presented it, Mr Johnson arched a black-quilled eyebrow and ran his long finger down the side of his similarly protracted nose.

'Ah,' he said, offering me a meaningful wink. 'Who, pray, is the lady?' Upon seeing that my face remained as blank as the masks above our heads, he continued: 'Confess, young sir—you have in mind some mischief, some intrigue!' I hastily assured him I had in mind nothing of the sort, but his insinuations did not abate. 'No one, young sir, shall be a domino unless he or she—it being so confounded difficult to know the difference sometimes—truly holds some box of secrets kept slyly hidden from the other guests.' He laughed, quite inexplicably, through his long nose. 'Before the close of the evening we shall all discover who is Punch or Pierrot, but not even I shall be entirely the wiser which gentleman or lady, or which cock-bawd or molly, has been the black domino, that mysterious cipher creeping around the dark paths of Vauxhall.'

So alarmed was I by his insinuation that I returned the garb to its peg and for some minutes regarded all of the costumes with an equal revulsion. But then, after many deliberations, and upon Toppie's somewhat impatient command, I settled upon the costume of a lady, that of an old midwife named 'Mrs Midnight', whose habit comprised a lace bonnet, a checked apron and tattered grey petticoats. I was somewhat reluctant where the petticoats were concerned, being loath to transgress even in play those boundaries that distinguish the sexes one from another; but in the end economy won the day: for, although the apparel would cost me £5 (which in truth I did not yet possess for payment), this expense was by far the lowest to be found and I balked at assuming a greater debt.

Toppie's selection, on the other hand, was contracted to lighten his purse by almost £50. Being a complete stranger to economy where such things were concerned, he staked his claim with Mr Johnson for a 'macaroni' costume such as the one worn at the drum by Mr Larkins and some of his friends. This most ostentatious of disguises would include a voluminous periwig, whose uncommon height was complemented by a queue descending almost to the heels of his diamond-buckled shoes. At the peak of the astonishing structure was to roost a tiny cocked hat, which it seemed he would require the services of his sword to doff. A bouquet of flowers and vegetables—endives and tomatoes—would grow upwards to his ear from his left shoulder, which, like the right, was possessed of an epaulette through whose overlarge brocaded loop the fleeing Israelites might have passed; and his waistcoat and breeches would be spotted like the hide of a leopard and so reduced in size that I conceived how they would surely constrict his respiration and exhibit in general outline the conformation of his manhood.

So excited was Toppie by this costume that now, as we sat in the coffee-house, he could scarcely talk about anything else, thus granting me little opportunity to raise the subject of my altered fortunes. The topic of the macaroni habit was then revived with much enthusiasm upon the arrival of some of his friends—young gentlemen whose fortunes set them above the necessity of any employment other than cards, drink, gossip and ladies. Eventually these fellows guided the conversation from masquerade habits to other topics— the unreliability of footmen, the expenses of enclosure, the antiquities of Rome, the personal fortunes of certain heiresses set against their physical attractiveness—which excluded me altogether.

I had the impression, moreover, that Toppie was not especially anxious for me to remain at our table. It must be admitted that I was maladroit and nervous among strangers: I dribbled coffee on to my shirt-ruffles as I laughed at one of my own witticisms that, alas, raised a titter of mirth in no one else; and then a minute later as I reached for the ale I overturned a small herring pie, which on its descent to the floor avoided my neighbour's lap by a scant two inches. My neighbour, introduced earlier as Sir James Clutterbuck, accepted my apologies, but in the meantime I caught his friends sniggering into their scent-sprinkled handkerchiefs and dishes of coffee. Toppie, for his part, merely frowned painfully. No doubt he regarded me as I had the Sharps, an unwanted makeweight that slowed his flight along a rushing path of fresh new breezes.

After an hour I departed unnoticed, without having wished Toppie a good night, and without having found an opportunity to relate to him the names of my new acquaintances or to press him for more reliable advice. As I walked home without a lanthorn or linkboy, fearful that every shadow was, or concealed, a robber, I wondered if I wished to rise in the world after all, and if perhaps I truly belonged only in Upper Buckling, where a herring pie or a splotch of coffee had no powers to ruin a man's reputation.

Yet I need not explain that I did not return to Upper Buckling, and it was at this point—as I walked almost tearfully homeward—that another actor in the theatre my life was now to become suddenly appeared for the first time upon the stage, dressed in the guise of a villain. For I had passed through Leicester Fields and crossed the dark and narrow length of a court leading into Coventry Street, when I discerned the tapping sounds of a pedestrian approaching from my left, in Oxendon Street. I quickened my pace lest my fellow-traveller should prove himself a thief or ruffian. Despite this precaution our paths soon intersected and then became contiguous, for the fellow—it was, I perceived, a man—was headed in the direction of the Haymarket. My heart commenced beating swiftly, and I tightened my iron grip upon my purse, looking about somewhat hopefully for the Night Watch.

Yet soon after sneaking a glance at my new companion as we passed below a lighted lamp I recognised how little I had to fear, for he was dressed like one of the fancy fellows from Lord W—'s drum, his periwig and cane both being of an uncommon height, and his breeches striped in black like the hide of a zebra. His periwig was surmounted by a handsome tricorne whose borders were marked in gold *point d'Espagne*, and his hands as he strode by my side flashed in white parabolas, being elegantly gloved in kid leather. Why, I had more cause to fear a tailor's dummy!

'A fine evening,' he said in a cordial voice, whose timbre did nothing to belie his foppish appearance.

I agreed that it was, noticing the bold contribution made by his eau-de-Cologne to the softness of the evening air, and the pleasant sounds—the tick-tock of a long-case clock—made upon the flagstones by the heels of his diamond-buckled shoes and the tip of his elongated stick.

'Whither do you travel at this hour?'

'My lodgings are yonder in the Haymarket,' I replied, 'above the shop of the perruquier.'

'Ah—so you are acquainted with Monsieur Regnault!' the fellow responded with some enthusiasm, pronouncing this

Gallic name with the most expert accentuations. 'Indeed! I know the gentleman well.'

I found myself loath to contradict this fellow of fashion and confess that my lodgings were not with M. Regnault but, rather, with plain Mr Sharp, so I pretended to cough, permitting him to interpret my loud strangulation as he may.

'Perhaps I shall accompany you as far as your lodgings,' he said in a kindly voice, 'for on a night such as this the footpad plagues the streets, and I have no wish to encounter such a rogue solitary.'

'Yes,' I told myself, sneaking another glance at his finery, 'surely the footpad would make a juicy meal upon this fine fellow!' None the less, I assented to this proposition immediately, for I was now laughing at my former fear of the stranger and considering how a creature of fashion accoutred thus, a veritable macaroni, had more cause to flee my presence than I his. And since the fellow was disposed to be friendly, I could make no objection.

'My name is Robert...' he began in a pleasant voice, extending his white-gloved hand. Yet having arrived in the greater light of the meeting-point of Piccadilly and the Haymarket, where he took a sly account of my countenance and then supplemented this snatched glimpse with a more searching gaze, my new friend did not see fit to complete his introduction and all at once seemed anxious to rescind his companionable offer. He dropped my hand quite abruptly and then, appearing distracted and uncertain of what to do next, drew hastily back and quickened his step as if eager to part from my company.

'Possibly he thinks I shall snitch his periwig!' I thought, much amused at the fellow's vanity and presumption. 'Perhaps he considers that I am a robber who has taken a harmful fancy to his silk-tasselled cane!'

Now two or three steps in advance of me, this unpredictable stranger halted in some further confusion at the great intersection and then, after shooting me a backward glance, betook himself hastily into the pitch-dark corridor of Shug Lane.

'Well!' I was now affronted more than amused by this unmannerly behaviour, which I interpreted as being occasioned by a sight of my comparatively humble dress. Suddenly Toppie's sniggering companions rose up in my mind, and my blood began to boil. 'Perhaps this fellow, like them, fancies himself too fine a gentleman to be acquainted with the likes of me. Is that the affair, then? Well, I shall teach him some graces!'

I rapidly took to my heels, recoiling from the path of a hackney-coach bound for Piccadilly and then leaping into the narrow lane, at the end of which I perceived the bobbing periwig. His diamond-buckled shoes and elongated cane must have incommoded his flight, for soon I caught him up in Marybone Street, laying hold of his silk collar and preparing to shake him by it until his teeth rattled in his head. Yet those accoutrements that had slowed his escape now did my combatant much better service: with a short cry he brought the tasselled cane down forcibly upon my crown, spilling my hat into the dirt and knocking my wig over my eyes, thus blinding me and making me wellnigh insensible in one go; and though its contribution was no longer truly necessary, one of his dainty shoes twice buried itself in the softest part of my belly. I keeled over, and only when my wig fell into the gutter did I see the white gloves for a last time, flashing in Glasshouse Street like two fading meteors.

I rolled on to my back and lay still until the only pain I felt was not that in my belly or head but, instead, a deeper one; a weak, wincing feeling nudging at my bosom, nibbling at my heart. Oh, that fine frippery should disguise such an ill-mannered rascal! I lay motionless longer still, staring at the starless sky above me—a great, empty canvas—and wondering about the perfidious and unknown ways of my new world.

Then I picked myself up and limped into the Haymarket, the few coins I had left to my name jingling and chiming in my purse, sounding to my ears very much like the bell of an approaching leper.

Five

A fine night's sleep restored my spirits to me. Upon rising I quickly put a taper to a letter to my mother (written after my return from the coffee-house), in which I confessed my diplomatic failure in the Pollixfen mission, the loneliness of my impecunious existence, and my urgent desire to return to Upper Buckling. For upon returning from Marybone Street I had looked about my dark chamber and despairingly asked myself if my place in the world was truly meant to be these small lodgings. A bed, a wainscot table, two old chairs with cane seats, a looking-glass in a deal frame, a tattered window-curtain that imperfectly blocked the draughts, an iron stove, a poker and shovel, a pair of tongs, an iron candlestick, a tin pint-pot—these wretched little items represented the sole furniture of my world, and, alas, I did not own even them.

Yet this morning I was cheered not only by a recollection of my engagements today, but also by the sight of a letter from my old friend Pinthorpe, delivered by the morning post. Pinthorpe, a childhood neighbour, had studied at Oxford for two years before entering into holy orders last spring; treading, in other words, the path along which, at one time, I had myself been expected to follow. He now had the charge of a tiny parish in Somerset, where, having failed among the farmers and stonemasons of his congregation to make a single proselyte to an idiosyncratic philosophy imbibed at the university, he occupied his evenings by writing long letters, or, rather, treatises, which I found more and more perplexing. These were meant to persuade me of the virtues of this particular species of philosophical inquiry he had derived from Bishop Berkeley (whoever this gentleman might have been). I could make no sense of Pinthorpe's theories of 'immaterialism', but his letters explained how this fellow had with a single stroke done away with material substance and proved the entire world—its colours and lights and sounds—to be merely an illusion.

Visual qualities such as light and colour, he claimed, upon the bishop's authority, had no existence in matter but were only 'ideas in the mind'.

'I am convinced that the Reality of sensible Things', his letter now read, 'consists solely in their *being perceived* by sensible Beings; that is to say, you or I. The material World of Trees and Houses and Streets and Rivers has no Existence, I am content, in and of itself; nor do Qualities like Colour, Sound, or Taste; nor even do *other People*, who, like all else, exist only as they are perceived. For all Things of this World are, truly speaking, Appearances in the Mind. As Bishop Berkeley writes, "*Esse est percipi*"—that is to say, "to be is to be perceived". Consider the Words of the eminent *Treatise concerning the Principles of Human Knowledge*, wherein this great Philosopher vouches that "all the Choir of Heaven and Furniture of the Earth, in a word all those Bodies which compose the mighty Frame of the World, have not any Subsistence without a Mind—that their *Being* is *to be perceived or known*".

'Consider the Situation', continued Pinthorpe, 'in which you light a Candle in your Chamber at Dusk and observe the Colour of the Paper upon the Walls. Now if you extinguish the Candle and once again observe the Colour of the Wall-paper, I believe you will discover that this same Object, viz. the Wall-paper, presents quite a different Colour to the observing Eye. What may we conclude from this Phenomenon but that, because Colour admits of alteration, it cannot therefore be considered a *Real Property* of an Object, one possessing an existence in Matter. From this evidence the learned Berkeley suggests that all Qualities of Objects, that is, Colours, Shapes, and whether an Object is in Motion or at Rest, do not exist independently of the Perceiver, but are contingent upon his Mind and exist only in their being perceived by him.

'From this we may conclude, I think, that all such Appearances, such outward Signs inscribed in the World, are therefore most *deceiving*. Thus, George, you will consider that all the Colours which illuminate our World, like all of its other Sights and Sounds, are but *Tricks of the Light*.'

Pinthorpe switched topics in his final paragraph in order to relate news of the progress of his physick garden and the encroachments upon it by the village cats—this rivalry had been deepening all summer—but in truth I paid little heed to his strategies and complaints, for I was still considering Berkeley's dictum. I was much confounded by—and had a strong mind to refute—this strange creed, which (if Pinthorpe's interpretation could be trusted) seemed to allege that the objects in the world, including perhaps the people about us, were the products of our deceived and dreaming brains. Doubtless my reverenced father could have scuttled the argument with aplomb, for *The Compleat Physiognomist* maintained upon the precedent of Plato that external forms arise from internal ones, of which they are the signs. But now this nonsense. Did Pinthorpe mean to imply that, because I could not at this moment see my fob-watch, which this morning I had somehow mislaid, *ergo*, my fob-watch did not exist? By the same token, if I could not see Pinthorpe, did this mean that Pinthorpe did not exist? And if he did not exist—such foolishness!—why should I pay any heed to his letters?

My deliberations upon this most vexatious subject were shortly terminated when Mrs Sharp summoned me to her breakfast-table. Then, an hour later, with my periwig freshly powdered by Mr Sharp's dredger, I stepped into the street, where the heads in the display window of 'Jules Regnault, Perruquier' seemed to nod in encouragement and urge me on my way.

First, Sir Endymion Starker's residence in St Alban's Street. As I walked I attempted to compose the speech with which I would address the worthy gentleman, but as my journey proved to be such a very short one—round the corner at Norris Street, down Market Lane, right into Charles Street, then right again—I arrived without having proceeded beyond plans to offer a grovelling apology for not yet being capable of discharging my obligation and a fumbling reiteration of my aspirations for the future.

Yet so surprised was I upon arriving in St Alban's Street that I very quickly forgot my speech. I thought at first I must have misunderstood Sir Endymion's instructions, for the house that presented itself to me was of mean appearance and not in especially good repair: certainly not, I was sure, lodgings that might befit a gentleman of Sir Endymion's appearance and bearing. A handcart depleted of its store of coal lay beside the door, overturned, and a dead rat of barely credible dimensions reposed alongside on a heap of soot-blackened straw, its body, bloated by the sun, host to a noisy congregation of bluebottles.

My suspicions were increased when a series of applications with the door knocker went unremarked. When the knocker broke in my hand on its third entreaty I tiptoed to a window; but its panes, grimily opaque, refused to provide any distinct impression of the interior. What I discerned, however—a vacant and disused parlour, one which seemed in more brutal disrepair than Toppie's gutted chambers even in the midst of their most frenzied renovations—led me to conclude that my debt, as well as my newly kindled hopes for the future, had been forfeited.

As I prepared to return to the street, giving the deceased rat another generous berth, I heard the sound of a casement creaking open far above my head. I looked up to see a head—a female head, its superabundance of bright ochre hair obscuring the visage—protruding into the pale sunshine from a window on the third storey.

'Yes, who calls?'

'George Cautley,' I replied, executing a low bow. 'I am seeking Sir Endymion Starker.'

The head vanished inside the window, then reappeared a moment later, shaking its ochre tresses, which it seemed descended almost to the sash of the window below. These tresses by their volume and strategic disposition concealed from me a full view of their owner's milk-white appurtenances, for I could not help but take note that, in her haste to communicate with me, this fair lady had arrived at the window in a state of some impudicity: to wit, she had neglected to cover herself with any clothing whatsoever.

'Sir Endymion is not here,' this pretty creature now announced, seeming somewhat out of humour, either at my presence or Sir Endymion's lack of it.

'But I am to see him today. Pray, mistress, is this the residence of Sir Endymion Starker?'

'Sir Endymion Starker is not here,' the lady reiterated. With a small hand she pushed the plentiful tresses from her brow, and for an instant I glimpsed a greater portion of her visage, which was a dead white: not the magnolia-blossom complexion of Lady Beauclair, powdered and painted with lead, but the ghastly and unsalubrious colour— or, rather, the non-colour—of one rarely suffered to experience the sun.

'But . . . I have an engagement,' I said, quite flummoxed, and pressing my case more assiduously than was perhaps truly wise.

'Here, then!' The tresses swirled back inside the window, reappearing a few seconds later. 'Bear this to your *engagement*!'

With this injunction, the last word of which was fairly spat out, she tossed down a bright object. It missed my head with less room to spare than Toppie's triangle of plaster had and bounced off the handcart.

'I bid you good-day, sir,' she said, and the casement closed with a sharp bang.

I stooped to retrieve the object, inspection of which revealed a silver pendant suspended on a slim chain; inside the pendant, the water-colour miniature of a lady's face: the face, it now appeared upon further scrutiny, of the lady who had just slammed the window.

I weighed this object in my hand, looked to the window, then studied the portrait once more. Though of rather modest workmanship and not, to my unpractised eye, a product of especial value or talent, it seemed to create a further obligation in me to locate Sir Endymion. So for twenty minutes I stood outside the door, looking, I fancied, rather like a meaner version of Wheelwright keeping guard beneath Toppie's magnificent portico.

As the minutes passed I sadly pondered this latest failure and wondered whether Pinthorpe would argue that, because I did not see Sir Endymion, then he assuredly could be said not to exist; or even that, because I was so miserably alone, so bereft of the world's attentions, I myself—like 'all the Choir of Heaven and Furniture of the Earth'—had no existence either.

Then the stench of the street overcame me, and I trod back to my lodgings, feeling unwanted and inconsequential once again, much as I had at Toppie's residence the day before, and much as I had after my several previous visits to my kinsman's residence. I wondered how many more doors in London would remain closed to me; how many more of its citizens would ignore or avoid me; and how, if this behaviour recurred, I should ever find my place in the world.

Would Lady Beauclair's door also remain closed to me,

43

then? Would she, too, despite her importunity of two nights before, suddenly have forgotten my existence or else not wish to recognise it?

I believe I may be forgiven for entertaining such apprehensions as, some hours later, I set out for the parish of St Giles, my paintbox tucked under my arm, my gallipots in a small satchel. In honour of the occasion I had spent much of the intervening time contemplating the clothing with which I might attire myself. Over the past few weeks Toppie had charitably supplemented my small wardrobe, mainly for the purposes of our excursions to Vauxhall and Ranelagh Gardens. These frocks, knee-breeches and the occasional pair of silk stockings had so far proved the most material benefit of our friendship. I inherited them as he swiftly shed them, like a moulting bird of paradise, after his thrice-weekly trips to his tailor in New Bond Street. I had come to enjoy these visits to the shop, with its row of journeymen sitting cross-legged upon a board, carefully sewing, the empty arms and legs of their limp garments spread across their knees and over their shoulders, turning each into a kind of *pietà*.

Having taken to heart Toppie's lecture about appearance, I too was now determined to show myself in style, to fashion an identity for myself. Upon first arriving in London I had fretted greatly over the possible rusticity of my gait and speech, fearful of walking or speaking like a Shropshire ploughboy. Yet after many exercises in deportment before my small looking-glass I considered myself—splotches of coffee and herring pies aside—as polished and polite as any fancy fellow, especially when attired, as now, in Toppie's fashionable apparel. For this evening I had selected a parrot-green frock, a blue waistcoat trimmed in gold, black knee-breeches with thin white stripes, a black coat with a blue-and-gold brocade, and white silk stockings with flowering vines embroidered in colours up the sides like pairs of snakes twisting up to bite my knees. Several of my toes protruded through a large hole in one of the stockings, the breeches had seen duty the night before and needed a brush, and I wished I owned a silver-hilted sword like the one that Toppie bespoke at a sword-cutter's shop in the Strand the previous week. Yet as I confirmed the constitutions of my ruffled collar and heavily powdered bobbed periwig in a cheesemonger's window as I made my way up Greek Street,

I told myself that, on the whole, I would pass even the inspection of Lord W—'s uncompromising footman.

So impressed was I with my new appearance that for some moments I paused to admire the reflection created in this window, all the while performing foolish conceits, such as tapping my buckled shoe on the flagstones, oscillating my walking-stick like a pendulum, and offering an invisible companion a pinch from my snuff-box. This little charade led me to ponder, as I continued my journey, how I appeared to the world at this time in my life; for as I have said, I was not always so ugly as I am today. Though my nose (inherited from the Pollixfens) extended itself somewhat more than the fashion prescribed, it had not yet attained either its bulbous shape or its profusion of warts and carbuncles; I fancied that it made a quite respectable appearance, one which *The Compleat Physiognomist* might have interpreted as being, by dint of its conformation and length, the symbol of a sanguine temperament compounded with a versatile intelligence. Likewise, though my ears and chin were more prominent than I would have wished, neither represented too lamentable a subtraction from the general appeal of my countenance; indeed, they apparently—so my father would have held—betokened a good listener and a firm resolve respectively. My shoulders, it is true, were thin—poor William had acquired the broader set—but my posture was correct; and my legs, though rather slender in Toppie's stockings (which, alas, failed to merge with my breeches), were none the less shapely enough from their exertions in pursuit of the game-birds and hares that dwelt among the hills of the Welsh Marches. This last imperfection could be remedied, Toppie once pointed out to me at Ranelagh Gardens, by padded stockings; and several defects in my complexion, he further noted, might benefit from a touch of *maquillage* and the application of one or two heart-shaped beauty-patches.

'A lady will forgive you such little secrets,' he had assured me when I objected to such imposture, 'for if you are lucky she herself will never present a face to the world that has not first been patched, painted and plucked, according to its need. We live in an age of deception,' he had continued, his head adopting its sword-swallower's pose. 'This is an age of disguise, George, of tricksters and shape-shifters and chameleons who change their colours at every hour. Each

45

one of us hides *something*—under a wig or patch, beneath a padding, behind a mask or fan or a thick coat of ceruse. For the face is "the chief seat of beauty", especially in the case of the ladies, and it must therefore be treated, truly, as a work of the highest art. Yes, George—the lady is as artful with *her* brush and palette of paints as you are with yours. I warrant you, the most beautiful lady is always an artist of the most scrupulous talent and genius—a true Canaletto or Reynolds. Why, look upon *her*!'

He had pointed with the tip of his cane at a well-known lady of fashion, the youngest daughter of an ancient duke. She was perched in one of the handsome painted boxes above our heads, accepting refreshment from a beau who was known to be worth £5,000 per annum. She was indeed a beauty; a fairer creature I did not see that evening.

'Such a way she has with light and colour,' Toppie said with a smirk, 'with paints and pastes, daubs and creams! Such a fair masterpiece she produces! Shall I describe her secret arts? A wash of mercury water and the thickest appliqués of white lead and pearl-powder conceal the scabs of a pox upon her cheeks and neck. A cork plumper gives volume to her cheeks, hollowed by a cruel distemper of Venus. Her brow has been plucked naked of its native growth, for which she substitutes the hide cultivated from a mouse, whose sacrifice also shows in the beauty-patch glued upon the blemish of her chin. Red lead mixed with carmine and vermilion produces those healthful spots of colour upon her fevered countenance and emphasises her failing eyes, lending their milkiness a most fetchingly amorous fury. She is bald as Caesar, but what of that? Vast loads of false hair conceal the shining peak, raised to their great altitude and stiffened into position with a thick paste of mutton suet, hog's grease, and tallow, then powdered with ground meal and drenched, like the rest of her, in eau-de-Cologne. If unrolled, the ribbon affixed to its peak would stretch from her home in Hanover Square to her milliner's door in New Bond Street.

'Look well upon her,' he had concluded with a superior wink, turning his back on the lady in her box, 'for like all good paintings this one will soon crack and fade; and therefore, George, you must gaze upon it and enjoy it whilst you may.'

I had refused to endorse such practices, explaining that I

hoped the ladies would dispense with the fine art of painting, if such forgeries were the be-all and end-all of their efforts. Moreover, I had declined to tamper with Nature myself, being on the whole a lad of pleasing appearance, padded stockings and beauty-patches or not. And so as I posed before the cheesemonger's window it did not seem to snap credibility to tell myself, as I did now, that a creature as beautiful as Lady Beauclair might perhaps take an interest in me.

Lady Beauclair's card (which by this time I had inspected upon at least one hundred delicious occasions) conducted me to an address close by St Giles-in-the-Fields. As I entered St Giles High Street I began to doubt the wisdom of displaying my finery, such as it was, in so conspicuous a manner, since the neighbourhood was far from genteel. Upon turning the corner, I was presented with the perfect likeness of Mr Hogarth's *Gin Lane*. On the left side of the street stood an establishment dispensing vendibles of no particularly benign nature, if the behaviour of its patrons was anything by which to judge. As I passed before it, two fellows emerged noisily from the narrow door, one of them attempting to break the crown of the other with an empty gin bottle. The bloodied victim promptly returned the obligation with a bottle of his own, but then, apparently reluctant to prosecute the dispute any farther, fled down the street, bumping into me as he passed. His antagonist slumped to the stones and, extracting another bottle from his pocket, celebrated his victory with a solitary libation.

The right side of the street hardly presented a more favourable aspect. To avoid the discord of the gin-shop, which had begun to fill the street with a few more combatants, I swiftly crossed to the other side, hopping over the straw- and dung-clogged kennel in the middle. This action, however, succeeded in rousing the aspirations of three young ladies in scarlet petticoats, who lounged at the windows of the rather mean-looking edifice before which my flight had taken me. One of them inquired in a sweet voice whither I was going and, when I announced my engagement with a lady, offered me the softest smile and ventured her opinion that the lady whom I sought dwelt within those very doors.

'I am sure it is not so,' I replied, for once again I had withdrawn the *carte-de-visite* for inspection, and its evidence, as well as the opinion I had formed of this decrepit edifice, greatly conflicted with her testimony. I was therefore surprised when this position was endorsed by her companion in the next window, who bid me enter, 'so that you may see her for yourself'. In the course of this invitation she casually unfastened two of the uppermost buttons of her scarlet petticoats and fixed me with an impudent stare as the tip of her tongue performed a languorous circuit of her carmined lips.

I declined this lady's proposal and politely assured her that she and her companions were mistaken; but having done so, I became the subject of their stern reproaches, and as I walked was forced to cover my ears so I did not hear the worst of the vile language with which they abused me.

'How strange it is,' I thought to myself (for I had never before heard such words upon the lips of ladies), 'how very strange that creatures of such fair shape and demeanour should be capable of uttering such terrible blasphemies!'

When I finally attained it, Lady Beauclair's residence was not at all the sort of establishment the gilt script on the card had suggested to me. Indeed, had I not received this card from Lady Beauclair herself I should scarcely have believed she lodged here, the building before which I stood being mean and decrepit, even by comparison with the meagre lodgings in St Alban's Street, and scarcely in better repair or more distinguished in appearance than the abode of the ladies in scarlet petticoats. Certainly it was not the residence of a lady, especially one who claimed kinship with Lord W—. From its tiny windows hung great heaps of damp linen, some items of which were suspended on a cord that traversed the narrow space to bear in like fashion the bed-clothes and table-cloths of a neighbour across the street. A rough wind or some other force of Nature had toppled most of the chimney, and the black smoke, thwarted in its path, now vented itself in great, irregular clouds above the ruins.

Outside the door reposed two malodorous figures, whom I was required to step over in order to make my application. Fortunately the response to my request was swift, and I was led inside by a woman whom at first I mistook for the maid, but later learned was in fact the proprietress: a lady of no comely appearance, and of perhaps fifty years, who wore an apron and a bonnet that she might have had on loan from one of the supine inhabitants of her porch. Yet she inspected my plumage with a kindly smile, and her greeting was of a gentler and more welcome variety than I had grown accustomed to hearing in this great city.

Despite her considerable breadth and a wheeze in her chest, this good lady nimbly conducted me up two sets of dark stairs and into a chamber with barely any greater illumination. And here, perched in a reading chair, her glory somehow undiminished by the squalor of the street below, sat Lady Beauclair.

'Mr Cautley,' she said in a bright voice. 'I am so very happy to see you.'

Six

 If you are to understand my story—to understand, that is, what has become of me—you must first of all understand my feelings towards Lady Beauclair. At this time of which I speak, all my hopes resided in her person, for she—along, perhaps, with Sir Endymion Starker—was a lone star in the otherwise dark and desolate firmament. My hopes in her—in this *beau idéal*—were strangely combined, however, with something else: with fear, though I knew not what I feared.

Yet, when I saw her now, this capricious weathercock rotated swiftly from fear to hope. For the past two days I had derived a greater pleasure from anticipating the execution of my portrait than from the prospect of hearing the promised history of the forlorn creature in the garden. Never before did I possess so fair a subject, not even when, one fine afternoon the previous summer, Jenny Barton, the handsome daughter of the tallow-chandler, had after many requests submitted herself to an uncomfortable posture for two hours while I daubed happily at my canvas and attempted to duplicate the auburn tints of her hair and the behaviour of the sunlight upon her brow. Then, apart from Mr Sharp's reluctant customers, for a long time after my arrival in London my only sitter was 'Mr Knatchbull', a wooden figure, eight inches in height, whose joints could be manipulated to mimic human attitudes, and whose rather skeletal form put me in mind of Mr Knatchbull, my ancient watch-making neighbour in Upper Buckling. More recently my subjects had been found among the more acquiescent Sharp children, who, once posed, invariably became the prey of fidgets, sneezes, hunger, cramps, fatigue, yawns, sore necks or spines, antagonistic siblings, fits of choler, importunate bladders and a dozen other complaints, all of which precluded me from ever completing their portraits.

Of course, I was not paid a penny for these efforts either. I had great hopes, on the other hand, of gaining recompense from Lady Beauclair—or, at least, I had entertained such hopes until the shabby conditions of her lodgings were exposed.

Yet, strangely, Lady Beauclair's lodgings, which consisted of three rather commodious chambers, each with its own fire, belied in size and furnishings their forbidding exterior. Perhaps Lord W— treated her with more favour than that which my own wealthy kinsman bestowed on me.

As the proprietress now disembarrassed me of my hat, Lady Beauclair politely invited me to seat myself on an armchair.

'I must confess, Mr Cautley,' she said as she observed the departure of the woman, 'I am almost surprised at your arrival. I thought that you would perhaps not keep our engagement.'

Reflecting on recent experience I assured her that I never failed to keep appointments, for, whatever the custom of others, I remained true to my word.

'I hope it will always be so,' she responded as she freshened a bouquet of jonquils that brightened the parlour. 'Yet I feared, Mr Cautley, that perhaps you may have found something improper in our engagement.'

I confessed I could find nothing at all that could be interpreted as improper, as we were merely to have dinner, and I was to paint her portrait.

'And I,' she added, 'am to tell you the history of Tristano.'

'Of course,' I agreed. In truth, I had for the moment quite forgotten this clause in our contract.

'Very good,' she exclaimed, 'for you must understand that I do not invite everyone into my home. There are so many rascals abroad, especially at routs and drums. Yet you impressed me immediately as a most virtuous youth.'

I confirmed the accuracy of her impression and expressed a wish that I should never counteract it.

'This world is a difficult and dangerous place for a lady,' she remarked with a triste sigh.

'I believe that it is,' I said.

'A lady must be very circumspect where virtue is concerned,' she continued her observation. 'It is truly a commodity which, once traded away, cannot be purchased back, even with the wealth of both the Indies.'

I considered these to be words of wisdom, and told her as much. Still, I could not help thinking that such wise sentiments conflicted with her erstwhile conduct towards the unfortunate Amy, whose virtue, it seemed, Lady Beauclair had been prepared to trade at a bargain price.

'Well,' she said brightly, her mission among the flowers complete, 'shall we sit to dinner?'

Any lingering impression of Lady Beauclair's seeming indigence was dispelled with the arrival of our dinner; for she, or, rather, her landlady, assisted by a small child not much the senior of Miss Hetty, produced a very plentiful repast: Westphalian ham sprinkled with peppercorns, partridges in onion sauce, pickled oysters, pease, rhubarb tarts, China oranges, figs and a melon imported from Lisbon. Toppie himself could hardly have furnished our table better.

I pronounced a grace before we began, but then we spoke very little as we ate from the fine china plates, upon which our silverware chimed and rang. I interpreted the silence as an unhappy failure on my part. I was nervous, fearing a repetition of the kind of incident that had shattered my social pretensions the night before when my herring pie toppled to the floor. I answered her questions about my engagement with Sir Endymion by relating a few details of the most strange incident in St Alban's Street. Yet I made no mention of the peculiar lady, nor did I emphasise the dereliction of the premises, lest my observations should reflect adversely upon her own accommodation: this would have been a greater *faux pas*, I knew, than dropping an oyster into my lap, which, alas, I now managed to do in the course of my narration. Lady Beauclair affected not to notice this mishap and merely reached across the fig- and orange-laden epergne to replenish my cup of wine. Certainly she did not titter into her handkerchief, as my previous acquaintances had done, and for this I was most grateful and felt my heart warm. Instead she now asked if I had seen some of Sir Endymion's paintings.

'In them you will see some very famous faces,' she told me after I confessed that this pleasure had not been mine. 'Yes—Dr Johnson, Parson Sterne, Abel and Bach, even poor old blind Handel the year before he died. Voltaire—another old man. The astonishing infant Master Mozart. Who else? Horace Walpole, Dr Burney, the great actor Mr Garrick. Many others—French counts, Prussian princesses, Habsburgs, Marlboroughs ... on and on; one can hardly keep count. Oh,' she finished, taking a sip of wine, as if exhausted by this catalogue, 'he is indeed a great man, your friend Sir Endymion.'

Each of these names as it was pronounced became one more stick tossed upon the hungry fires of my ambition, which now burned most scorchingly inside me. Suddenly I was more determined than ever to find Sir Endymion—even if I had to take myself to the Royal Academy itself. Still, I was somewhat perplexed by Lady Beauclair's account of this great gentleman, for his lodgings in St Alban's Street, with the dead rat and the abusive and pale-visaged young lady, did not seem entirely consistent with his eminent public character.

But my puzzled ruminations upon this discrepancy were presently interrupted by Lady Beauclair.

'I wonder, Mr Cautley, how will you paint me? I am most anxious, for my portrait has been painted only once before.'

She gestured with her eyes at the canvas with which she had generously supplied me. It had been professionally sized with oil, gypsum and white lead, so that it now appeared a virginal white, prepared to receive its new impression; yet she had explained to me that beneath this smoothly primed surface there was painted a previous, now obliterated, portrait executed a year or two before.

'It was an unsuccessful attempt,' she said. 'Since I was not at all contented by the likeness, I commanded a colourman to paint it over. I am sure, Mr Cautley, that yours will be the better.'

I bowed my head in modesty, looking for a moment at the white surface of the canvas—as marble-white as my lady's face—and wondering if I saw, beneath, an indistinct shadow of colour, a roundish contour, perhaps of a face? No: nothing. Only a trick of the light.

'I am told,' she said at length, 'that one may hide nothing from a good portraitist, and that the most superior artist— Sir Endymion Starker, for instance—may paint on to a canvas the very soul of his sitter. I wonder, Mr Cautley, can this be so?'

I assured her that this indeed was the power aspired to by all painters of portraits, for 'the individual expressions of our countenances', I explained, 'are nothing so much as masks behind whose peculiarities we may glimpse traces of the universal. It is the object of the portraitist to remove the mask and display to the world the naked visage of his sitter.'

Lady Beauclair appeared to colour slightly at my exposition of this philosophy, and I could not help observing how her fan rose an inch or two higher, until it removed from view three-quarters of the particular visage—the *beau idéal*—I had been contracted to display to the appreciation of the world.

'If what you say is so,' she ventured after a moment, 'then portraiture, it seems to me, must be an unkind business.'

'Can it be unkind for one to show Truth in all her glory?'

My lady's only reply to this inquiry was to agitate her fan to an even greater degree, and to conceal with it further territories of her beautiful visage.

In the midst of these obstructions I began to consider in what attitude I should pose my lady and what complementary objects I might place in the background. For Jenny Barton's portrait I had incorporated her dog, an ancient spaniel named Dick, who it must be said was a much more co-operative subject than his young owner. Mr Knatchbull I often placed in the company of the Arch of Constantine or the ruins of Palmyra. But what object or landscape was competent to the task of complementing the beauty and grace of Lady Beauclair? Perhaps a background of Elysian fields—tall cypresses, orange groves, a company of nymphs and reapers disporting themselves on a green hillside? Or possibly an allegorical painting in which Lady Beauclair, in the garb of the Angel of Truth, battered down the twin demons of Envy and Falsehood?

My reflections now led me to study my subject more closely and frankly. Her appearance was somehow different from that of two nights before; more modest and feminine, perhaps. The worries which had overtaken me on St Giles High Street, namely that I had dressed too much the cox-comb, had been dispersed upon my first sight of her, since she had greatly exceeded my own sartorial efforts. Her clothes were hardly so voluminous as on that first occasion, yet they were of elaborate design, consisting now of an embroidered green stomacher and a blue gown whose fron-tiers were patterned with a series of gold fleurs-de-lys. Her hair, too, was of more modest dimensions and—somewhat to my relief—minus its complement of encased insects. Nevertheless, when she stood, its summit reached almost to the timbers of her low ceiling, and it was powdered a pinkish hue, as if lit by an August sunset. I knew that such a head could only be a product of 'Jules Regnault, Perruquier', certainly not of my homely landlord.

However, it was her face, which of course was unmasked, that had changed most of all. The duties of the vizard had been assumed by heavy applications of paint and powder, and by a beauty-patch of the variety that Toppie had recom-mended for my own use. I remembered what he had said about this being an age of deception and disguise—and also what our members of Parliament had said about dissembling ladies being witches—and through my mind trickled the unwelcome thought that Lady Beauclair was deceiving me. Certainly her face ran the gamut of artful tricks that Toppie had alleged to be the recourse of all ladies of fashion, and which our political representatives had so roundly con-demned. Her lips were painted the colour of apricots, as were her cheeks, which were swelled out (I suspected) by a cork plumper that lent her a most engaging lisp, and which were emblazoned with two bright orbs that looked like twin suns sinking into the dusky horizon of her jawline. The charge once given to the mask had also now been assumed, as I have said, by a folding fan, with tortoiseshell sticks that maintained its perpetual position before her chin even as she ate. Unfolded, this fan displayed in triptych the struggle between Zeus and the young Ganymede.

The reason for Lady Beauclair's subterfuge—for her fan and her beauty-patch—I had surmised before our dinner was served. For upon satisfying herself with the composition of her flowers she had passed near to a wall-sconce, and the candle in that second showed a face that was not perhaps as youthful as its proprietress would have wished, nor indeed as I had truly expected. Having guessed her secret—she was, I estimated, a lady of perhaps some thirty or thirty-two years—I smiled inwardly at my discovery. For it was pleasing to think of her applying powder and paint, splattering herself with eau-de-Cologne, and fastening her shift and corset and selecting a gown—all for my sake. Once again I felt my heart gently warm. Heretofore I had regarded the affectations of the female sex as mere guile and a gaudy symbol of ladies' natural weakness; yet as I observed Lady Beauclair play with her fan and cock her head this way and that as she delicately supped, I was forced to revise my opinion.

After due consideration, and after our dinner-service was cleared, I chose to place Lady Beauclair in one of her armchairs, her hands folded demurely in her lap and her face slightly upturned and smiling chastely. I told her that, as Mr Hogarth writes in his *Analysis of Beauty*, the dispositions of the body and limbs appear most graceful when seen at rest, and this therefore is the attitude most conducive to the representation of beauty, sensibility and intelligence. The flowers I would place alongside, for, as I explained, I possessed an uncommon skill as a botanical artist. By such positioning, I further explained, I hoped to achieve an effect of quiet and passive spirituality, and to capture with my oils the eternal and immutable that lies behind our individual expressions.

'For it is the true function and first principle of art,' I told her, resuming my earlier theme, 'to represent not outward accidents but the inward form of things. It is the task of the artist to portray not the external surface but the permanent, insubstantial Truth that resides in all human form.'

Lady Beauclair, however, dissented from my choice, the studious philosophy of which appeared either uncongenial to, or entirely lost upon, her. Instead she expressed a wish to stand erect, with her hands placed on her left hip; meanwhile her face, exposed to profile, would adopt a somewhat wanton stare from over the top of her left shoulder. Strangely, I remembered this posture from somewhere, though exactly where I could not then say. It smacked rather too much of feminine coquetry for me, and as such I was sentimentally opposed to it; yet, as I have just noted, my opinion on this topic had lately begun to soften, and so I relented without argument.

'And what, pray, shall I wear?' she next inquired.

I studied the green stomacher, the gown and the fleur-de-lys pattern, humming and hawing for a minute before pronouncing them excellent for our purposes since I possessed in my paintbox adequate quantities of verdigris and royal blue, which were both very noble colours found in Nature's own great canvas. Once again, however, she chose to ignore my advice.

'Would you care to examine my wardrobe, Mr Cautley?' she offered. 'Perhaps there we may find something even more excellent for our purposes.'

And so, notwithstanding my faint objections, I was thrust into that most private of places, a lady's wardrobe. I was forced to consider the virtues and detractions of a series of costumes whose splendour and quantity, like the other furnishings, betrayed the damning evidence of the street. Unfortunately, I was too flummoxed by the number and variety of these costumes, and by the closeness of Lady Beauclair herself, to offer any opinion.

At length she selected one of the more antic residents of the wardrobe: some kind of Mahometan dress of ultramarine damask, embroidered with pearl and gold, its train a full six feet long. To this costume she proposed to add a turban of the Turkish mode, from which was suspended a loose fold of white sarsenet fastened at the pinnacle by a small jewel. I meekly assented, thinking how greatly my powers of verisimilitude would be taxed, and how difficult it would now be to achieve an appearance of quiet and passive spirituality or to delineate insubstantial Truth.

We agreed that she should tell me the history of Tristano as I painted her portrait. Lady Beauclair intimated that the fulfilment of our contract—the completion of both the story and the portrait—would take more than a single evening; a forecast with which I silently agreed, since by now I anticipated that she would be an even more demanding and censorious subject than Jenny Barton. And thus I was faced with the not unpleasant prospect of sharing another of her bounteous dinners. But next time, I resolved, I would take greater pains to avoid the social tragedies of my tongue-tied silences and spilt oysters.

In recompense for my efforts Lady Beauclair now offered me, besides the history of Tristano, a more material reward: five guineas—the sum of my debt—to be paid upon completion of the portrait. I agreed to these terms and suspected that further commissions certainly awaited me, for she was, as she said, a kinswoman of Lord W—. Therefore, as I lay out my palette, brushes and pigments, and set my canvas upon my knees, I was able to forget my former humiliations and contemplate instead how high I might rise in the world with the benefit of her patronage. I imagined being borne up in the voluminous swirls of her gown, on the billows of ruffles and lace, swept as high as the summit of her great pink-powdered alp of hair, from which I could look down, triumphant, over all adversity and persecution.

Lady Beauclair disappeared into her bedchamber to dress herself with the assistance of the landlady, who was summoned from the scullery by the jingle of a bell. I stood alone in the parlour, listening anxiously to the rasp of fastenings, the rustle of silk, the slight gasp as a whalebone corset was drawn tight.

When she finally emerged from the bedchamber it was my turn to gasp, for the strange Mahometan costume adhered to her figure in a manner which without a doubt proved the truth of Mr Hogarth's observation that 'the form of a woman's body surpasses in beauty that of a man'. The ultramarine damask did not descend quite low enough to conceal in their entirety two well-turned ankles; nor was it altogether adhesive enough to contain or conceal the ample swells of her bosom. Moreover, through either the negligence of the landlady or the design of Lady Beauclair, the habit exposed to view the whole of her left shoulder, upon which dangled a fat serpentine curl.

'How do I look, Mr Cautley?'

As she adopted her chosen position, experimenting with several haughty glances, I realised all at once where I had seen this particular posture and, moreover, where I had seen this particular costume: for Lady Beauclair, as she stood before me, was the exact image of the portrait of the lady I had seen among Lord W—'s collection, a small mezzotint engraving of which I now saw propped on her sideboard; and this print, I further detected, with an even greater start, was inscribed with the signature 'E. Starker'.

'Well,' said Lady Beauclair, 'shall we commence?'

Seven

'His name, to begin at the beginning, was Tristano Venanzio Pieretti. Quite a mouthful, is it not? Well, of course no one knew him by this long name; for our rude tongues it was always abbreviated to Tristano. Simply Tristano. You recollect now? No? Ah—so I must tell you everything, then . . .'

For the sake of her story Lady Beauclair's defiant posture forfeited some of its rigidity, as did her ultramarine costume. In its brief tenure this habit had already contrived to slip several fractions of an inch lower and expose ever greater territories of her left shoulder. It seemed that the garment had originally been designed to adorn a person of dissimilar proportions. Thus for the sake of modesty she was required, every few seconds, to rescue the situation by hiking her sleeve to a more seemly altitude—a small drama which, I fear, at times greatly distracted me not only from her story but from my painting as well.

'When he was born I do not pretend to know,' she continued as her dress began one of these little descents, 'nor, I believe, does he know, not precisely. I gather that his parents were very poor and that he was born somewhere in the Kingdom of Naples—in a village far in the south, along the arch of that peninsular boot. A humble origin indeed. Can you conceive it? Imagine a poor, rocky place, too cold in winter, too hot in summer; the natives rude and ignorant, their manners unpolished, their condition miserable. Can you see his village? Mountains, olive groves, skinny goats, stone walls, a clutch of straw huts in a dry valley. Imagine a single inn, seldom if ever required to admit a paying customer into its squalid precincts. Imagine a fly-specked church whose campanile is a rusty bell attached to a rotting post, and whose priest is an indolent and a drunkard.

'Can you see the villagers? Hired labourers, most of them; dirty *garzoni* working in a prince's olive groves. Can you

58

see the ragged troop of men marching into the trees at first
light, pruning-knives in their belts, then returning home at
dusk, their faces red and their necks black? Imagine their
wives—bell-shaped women threshing flax on the dirt floors
of their kitchen, drying it in stone ovens, groaning before
casks and oil-presses in the cellar, ceasing in these exertions
only to give birth each year to a sickly child; a replacement
for the one who died the year before, itself a replacement for
another sickly predecessor.

'Now, if you can,' she went on, 'imagine Tristano. Can
you see him as he was at the age of eight years? Imagine a
child who is ignorant, illiterate, uncultivated; the son of
a man named Tommaso, who is also ignorant, illiterate,
uncultivated. There is a dead brother on either side of the
boy, two small mounds of clay behind the church; but having
cheated the swellings and fevers and poxes that claimed his
siblings, he is now a robust and lively child, the favourite of
the priest. Imagine him singing in the church's choir; ringing
its bell each morning with a keen though unpopular enthusiasm; squashing spiders and scorpions on its floor in the hot
weather; catching green lizards that wriggle under its pews
after the rains; hanging damask and streamers on its pillars
and pulpit and silk on its windows, windows begrimed and
clouded with fly-tracks. Can you see him yet, Mr Cautley?'

The privilege of hanging damask and streamers the boy
enjoyed several times each year, whenever the groups of
strangers arrived in the village after having braved the heat,
the banditti, and the steep Via Romana. Most of these were
diseased, blind, crippled—a sorry lot indeed. They travelled
on bandaged feet, leaning on sticks, or arrived on the backs
of bony donkeys turned white with dust, some of which
drew the most decrepit in small wooden carts. The purpose
of these rigours was the privilege of whispering a few words
over a stone chest housing the finger-bone of St Vitus and
the skulls of two of the virgins who attended St Ursula;
or, on more rare occasions, of witnessing the miraculous
liquefaction of the blood of St Januarius.

It was upon one of these occasions, a notable one when
the liquefaction failed, that the boy performed a miracle of
his own and afterwards escaped the misery of his former
condition.

He was perhaps nine years of age when one of these feast
59

days drew an unusually large group of pilgrims into the village. The priest at this time was Father Antonio Molinari. An act of penance had brought him to the village six years before, after he committed a series of vague indiscretions in a seminary where he once taught. The bishop had promptly exiled him to this tiny parish, where, quite rightly, he now owned the reputation of a rake and a sot. All but his most fractious parishioners had relinquished any hope that the bishop would shift him elsewhere during their lifetime, and so were resigned to any behaviour short of the most egregious folly. Father Antonio was resigned to his fate as well. Because he believed that no penance could possibly be more humiliating than the charge of this miserable little parish, he did little to mitigate the habits which brought him into it, and which with each recurrence ensured that he would never escape. It was one such casual imprudence, however, that revealed to the village the nature of the child's particular genius.

Normally indifferent about his duties, Father Antonio nevertheless relished feast days, albeit with an enthusiasm not always entirely benign, for on these occasions his vices, ordinarily indulged in solitude, were often exhibited in public. So it was on the evening of the feast. The pilgrims were expecting evening Mass, yet an hour after the hoarse and dissonant tolling of the rusty bell there was no sign of the priest. Someone dispatched a search party of older boys from the choir, but they returned empty-handed an hour later, and the Mass only proceeded when Father Antonio finally emerged, quite unexpectedly, from the darkness of the vestry, blinking and smiling and muttering vague apologies for his state of dishabille (for he was stripped to his waist, thus exposing his pale, prodigious belly, which he wisely endeavoured to conceal with his surplice).

After urging the pilgrims into their pews and mumbling a Mass in the same disorderly fashion, Father Antonio withdrew from the reliquary the saint's phial of blood, still a brown crust. This, of course, was the moment everyone had been waiting for, the reason why they had risked their necks and purses on the Via Romana in the growing heat of early May.

—Dear brethren! Father Antonio proclaimed from the pulpit in a loud voice, shaking the phial at his audience like

60

a mountebank recommending a new nostrum. My dearly beloved brethren!

As the pilgrims looked on, there followed a few more of these jovial hailings, then a series of less comprehensible addresses and invocations, the force of whose delivery caused the priest to lose his balance once or twice and seize the pulpit for support. At the conclusion of these exertions he triumphantly flourished the phial, whose contents, however, looked very much the same as they had a moment before. Father Antonio was, alas, the last to remark upon the failure of his miracle.

—Yea, my dear brethren! The blood of St Januarius! Behold!

By now several of the pilgrims had perceived an unsteadiness in the priest's posture and a slightly dislocated expression in his eyes.

—Yea, behold, Father Antonio dimly repeated, his voice now reflecting his diminished convictions and his eyes attempting to focus on the phial wavering before his nose.

—Yes, behold! someone shouted from the rear of the congregation. Behold the priest! A drunkard!

Those nearest the pulpit were able to confirm this charge since Father Antonio's pungent exhalations had now begun to reach them. He was sweating heavily and very nearly dropped the phial on to the floor.

—Yes, yes! Father Molinari is a drunkard!

—A disgrace!

—Drunk in the Lord's church!

—A scandal!

—A profanation!

Father Antonio's whole face blinked, then he lapsed into troubled silence, oblivious to the execrations being hurled at him, his eyes crossing and uncrossing as he inspected the recalcitrant substance at the bottom of his phial.

—Fellow brethren, he murmured, dribbling down the front of his surplice.

Several of the more able-bodied pilgrims had leapt to their feet and appeared set to rush the pulpit. They may well have done so had Father Antonio not righted himself and then, with a faltering bow in the direction of the choir— whose members sat frozen in their chairs—gently commanded:

—Please, ah, Tristano, if you will . . .

What followed next was perhaps more miraculous than the liquefaction of the saint's blood (which, incidentally, the priest finally managed to effect to the satisfaction of his audience a few moments later, discreetly warming the phial in his sweated hand). The child obeyed this cryptic command from the priest, stood, and slowly began to sing:

'*Ammo Christum, qui renovat juventem meam,*
Ammo Christum, qui gemmis cingit collum meum . . .'

After the first few bars of the hymn, old men who had been preparing themselves for the bloody strangulation of a priest quietly resumed their places, sinking placidly into the pews, gentle smiles suffusing their sun-peeled faces; and old black-frocked crones who had filled the church with their denunciations immediately fell silent, scarcely daring to breathe.

Yes—such a voice! The tongue of an angel! No one—none of the pilgrims—could remember hearing anything so blessed—and from one so young! And so when the hymn was completed and the bright red blood of St Januarius swirled round and round before their eyes, it was the opinion among the majority—a superstitious lot to begin with—that this child's voice and nothing else had produced the liquefaction.

A miracle? Yes—perhaps. But not all miracles have happy endings. You see, in Italy it is a sorry thing for a child to possess a beautiful voice and to be the son of a poor man. A sweet voice may become a fine currency, more valuable than the casks of oil or the squirming pigs carried away, bouncing, in the back of one of the prince's wagons. A voice—no prince, surely, can take that away? Well, yes, he can, but he must pay more than for a pig or a chicken. Much, much more.

So it was that one week after this miracle, and on the eve of another holy day, the boy was rehearsing with the choir when an enormous man in a brimmed hat appeared in the doorway of the church, completely blocking the slanting rectangle of afternoon light and the better part of Tommaso, the boy's father, who hovered behind him. A prince? One may well have thought as much, so enormously fat was he; but no, this was instead Signor Piozzi, the great maestro, proprietor of a *scuola di canto* in Naples.

62

After singing for the maestro, who sat on one of the pews with his fingers interleaved on his large belly, the boy was conducted into the vestry. He sat alone for a few minutes while the three men spoke outside the door. Their intonations were echoic, barely audible. Tommaso and Father Antonio stood alongside Signor Piozzi, two small moons girdling a mighty planet. Then the jingle of coins as twenty-four ducats changed hands; twenty-four ducats knelling his fate.

The child departed from the village a fortnight later, on the morning after yet another feast day brought to the church yet another collection of mule-drawn cripples. He saw his village for the last time from the swaying back of a pack-mule, a spirited old beast that had permitted him to clamber aboard only after a great show of reluctance. He was to travel in the company of the pilgrims, all mounted now on more accommodating animals. Father Antonio, dressed in a cap and a white surplice, pronounced a prayer and cast cool showers of holy water on to the procession, beast and human alike. The weeping child gave his mother a last kiss, then the muleteer slapped the fly-bitten haunches of the lead animal, and they were away.

Within an hour the road changed, the dirty old Via Romana, down which the boy had trudged a thousand times—all mule droppings and gorse in summer, mule droppings and mud in winter, ruts and bumps always—becoming a place of the most remarkable wonders. Indeed, the whole world changed once he surpassed his previous limits, marked by a whitewashed chapel a league beyond the village wall. As they descended from the steep hills at the end of the first day the procession crossed the edge of a forest of junipers filled with deer owned by a duke. At dusk a passage-boat bore them and their mules across a broad river, sweeping them downstream to disembark into painted meadows, fields of bergamot, groves of mulberry hung with the white cocoons of a million silkworms. In the morning they tramped past white villas with marble terraces growing out of hills whose sides were thick with ilex and orchards of lemon. Here and there snatches of a silver lake winked through gaps in the black cypress, and many leagues later another dusk showed the broken-tooth yawn of an overgrown amphitheatre. Then at dawn six long humps of an aqueduct marched through the valley like the coils of a petrified sea monster, its tail a crumble of red rock stretching into the hilly distance.

In the middle of the third day the procession met with disaster. One of the pilgrims, an old man named Giuntoli, had pointed out the cavern refuge of a reputedly beautiful bandit queen; it lay at the bottom of a deep ravine overgrown with wild asparagus, copsewood and thickets of young chestnut. But the pilgrims met not the bandit queen: rather, a few less legendary, though equally fierce, members of her profession. They had passed the hottest part of the day in the shade of a grove of walnuts and elms, nibbling cheese and dried figs. In the midst of their refreshments three banditti appeared on the narrow trail that the Via Romana had now become. One of the trio discharged his pistol at the sky. An ancient widow in a veil fainted dead away into a bush of wild roses, from there rolling down the steep bank and into the river. The other pilgrims were extorted at the point of the weapon, forced to open their panniers and calfskin purses and deliver their small treasures: a few ducats and Roman coins, a tarnished chatelaine, a dented goblet, a handful of old *bijouterie*, a watch with a broken fob-chain, three silver spoons, a few sorry-looking relics. These were poor people.

Having less of anything to relinquish than his companions, the boy attempted to appease the urgent demands barked out by these three fellows by proffering a pewter figurine of St Orontius, which had been conveyed to him at the last minute by Father Antonio. This trinket was tossed into the river and its owner afforded a knock on his crown.

When he awoke, all—banditti, loot, pilgrims, mules, even the ancient veiled widow—had vanished, and the slender shadows of the elms now stretched across to the far bank of the stream.

He discovered the mules first, all but his own: they stood at the side of the trail, beyond its first bend, munching thistle and broom, patiently awaiting commands. They must wait an eternity, for every pilgrim, save the widow, who must have been swept away and drowned, lay still at their hoofs, limbs askew, neat holes in their foreheads. Giuntoli's eyes were prominent in his white face, his mouth agape, his tongue protruding stiffly as if preparing to receive the Communion wafer.

How long or how far he ran the boy could not say. At

some point he must have ceased running and, overcome, flopped down into the scratches and stabs of broom and gorse. When he opened his eyes in the cold dawn, what did he see? Shining alabaster domes and bright pavilions, a carmine-and-rust tartan of tiled rooftops, a score of sharp spires spiking the hard blue sky, a thousand windows collecting and shattering the early sunlight. Beyond, a blue bay, a shoal of dolphins, men casting hoop-nets into the waves . . .

Eight

'A place of safety and refuge,' I said, hopefully.

'You will discover soon enough,' replied Lady Beauclair. She stretched her limbs and appeared to take account of me for the first time in quite some minutes. 'Yet now, Mr Cautley, I am wondering how my portrait progresses . . .'

'Very well,' I replied, though the truth was that, because of the distractions, my progress had been very slow.

Thus far I had laid a ground of blue-black, grey and white. These ground-up pigments I had diluted with turpentine from my gallipot and then spread thinly and evenly across the top half of the canvas, which soaked them up and quickly dried. Then, more precisely, I had blocked in a head, using a thicker mixture of paint—carmine and more white, each mixed with wax dissolved in turpentine. Next, drying oil, then yellow lake, more carmine, more white, all mixed with wax; then linseed oil spread across the ghostly cloud of my lady's oval visage, which, in truth, at this point may have been reasonably mistaken for the visage of almost anyone.

'Why do you not continue, Mr Cautley?'

'I must await the drying of the paint,' I replied as I blew on my canvas, growing somewhat dizzy in the process.

'What, may I ask, is that most unpleasant smell?'

'Turpentine,' I replied, whisking my brush in the gallipot

that contained this offending substance, which only a painter can love. 'Turpentine and wax and balsam and resin.'

'Your concoctions do reek abominably. I believe the art of portraiture is a messy and malodorous business, is it not?'

Alas, it was just as I suspected: my lady was proving a rather difficult sitter. Much of the problem, you will guess, resulted from her Turkish dress. Because of its precarious adhesion, this costume in the moments of its lowest suspension not only captivated my attention more than her story, it also disabled my paintbrush, which would quiver above the canvas as if registering the tremors of a distant earthquake. I had heard stories of how, at his excellent Academy in St Martin's Lane, the late Mr Hogarth instructed his students in a 'life school', by which was meant a gentleman or lady was paid a guinea for the favour of removing his or her garments and perching on a table in the attitude of an Achilles or a Venus. So negligent did she become in the midst of her story that once or twice I truly thought Lady Beauclair might expose me to the benefits of just such a 'life school'—though her sleeve and *décolletage* were always adjusted at the last possible moment.

Yet this dress created, or would create, other difficulties as well. I expected to encounter some trouble of a financial nature in duplicating these folds of ultramarine, for Mr Middleton, the colourman whom I visited in St Martin's Lane, demanded five guineas for an ounce of that particular pigment; even an ounce of ultramarine ashes, an inferior grade, would subtract 25 shillings from my purse; and I had already discovered that this gentleman's cheapest alternative, 'blue verditer', made from copper, turned bright green after only a month. (Several of my landscapes had unfortunately suffered from this kind of economy, though as a result they greatly delighted the Sharp children, for whom Upper Buckling had become a magical place of absinthe rivers and richly verdant skies.) So I began to regret that I had not promoted more assiduously the case of the fleur-de-lys mantua, which, in comparison, would have been a great bargain.

Still, the matter of the background had not presented as great a difficulty as I feared, for I had hit upon the idea of placing my lady against a backdrop of darkness (and a darkness had indeed descended behind her, as the landlady, Madam Chapuy, had, at Lady Beauclair's instigation, extinguished several candles upon her departure with the oysters, melons and epergne). I had determined that I would illuminate her, as Mr Joseph Wright of Derby might have done, solely with the light of a single candle, which now was bowing and dancing and wiggling uncertainly on the sideboard, its existence at the mercy of the draughts that entered through my lady's leaded window-panes. In a moment of inspiration a few minutes before, I had also decided to call my painting *A Lady by Candle-light, Holding a Fan, Dressed in the Turkish Manner*. Or, if the moon ever saw fit to emerge from behind its misty shroud, and from behind the baroque steeple of St Giles-in-the-Fields, I should call it *A Lady by Moonlight*, etc. When I informed Lady Beauclair of this plan, she suggested instead *A Lady at Midnight*, but I balked at this contribution, which seemed to raise connotations not especially consistent with the august moral purposes motivating my brushes and pencils; and in any case that particular hour had not yet come upon us.

Greater difficulties arose, however, from Lady Beauclair's many gesticulations during the course of her narration, and the temporary abandonments of her magisterial posture (to the further detriment of her dress's adhesion) as she imitated the inebriated priest, the execrating pilgrims, the trilling Tristano, or the murdered Giuntoli. She acted these parts as well, truly, as any player in Drury Lane. She seemed to possess a great talent for mimicry, to be capable of assuming, with expert ease, any role she wished. Thus it almost seemed that at the most acute moments of her story the execution of the portrait slipped her mind entirely, and she resumed her posture (and straightened her garment) only upon my repeated encouragements.

'My lady,' I had frequently been obliged to say, putting my hands on my hips and turning my head to its side in a rather limp imitation of her lapsed posture. 'Have you forgotten . . .?'

'Forgive me, forgive me. Yes, yes—now where was I? Ah, yes . . .'

Every few moments, moreover, my lady had demanded to see her portrait and only slightly less often complained, like the Sharp children, of a sore neck or aching back, the results of her uncomfortable posture. Even more inconvenient, the tortoiseshell folding fan had resumed its prior duties and now and then obscured her face entirely, interceding between her nose and the precariously flickering candle and thus casting her entire face into shadow. How could I be expected to create the likeness of her countenance if all I could see was a black shadow and *The Rape of Ganymede*? Already I was aware that, despite further applications of carmine and then a few dark highlights of asphaltum and additions of yellow gamboge for the candle's light, I had begun to strain the likeness. The image on the canvas before me, though incomplete, looked hardly at all like the lady who stood before me; or, rather, sat before me; or, rather, now stood again, flapping her arms in the air, her costume slipping downwards in the process. What if, through such distractions, I should paint a portrait like those of Monsieur Le Brun in the *Traité*, turning my lady's exquisite physiognomy into that of an eagle, an owl, or a tigress?

'Please, my lady . . .'

'Yes, of course, forgive me. I quite forgot myself. Now— where was I?'

It almost seemed that my task would be much easier if I turned my attention several degrees to the left and concentrated it not on my rambunctious story-teller but on the engraved print that sat quite prominently—and quite obediently—on the sideboard. For as I have pointed out already, both Lady Beauclair's posture and her costume were perfect counterparts to those of the sitter in the print. And so it was that after several more admonitions about the fan and the lapses in posture went unheeded, or, rather, were heeded for only a few short seconds, I did turn my attention to the print, wondering, as I had done in the house in St James's Square, who this remarkable sitter was. From what little detail I could discern, there seemed to be a facial resemblance between her and Lady Beauclair, though of course this may have been the result only of the affinity in posture and costume. Now, too, there existed the other questions: that is, how Sir Endymion had come to engrave the portrait, whether or not he had executed the original, and what relation existed between him, her and Lady Beauclair. Puzzled as I was by these fraying threads of my inquiry, I was pleased by what this token on the sideboard seemed to confirm—to wit, that my lady truly was Lord W—'s kinswoman, part of that great and noble family tree: an exotic flower blossoming, I imagined, on one of its higher, more

68

slender branches. The portrait of such a relation would undoubtedly find favour with Lord W—, and perhaps one day might even hang in his gallery, alongside the broad-countenanced gentlemen with their cutlasses and dignified frowns.

I was on the point of inquiring about Sir Endymion's mezzotint and its mysterious subject, when my deliberations were interrupted by a sudden draught of wind. The gust breached the borders of my lady's window-panes with a particularly violent rattle, then extinguished the lone candle, leaving us in a darkness more profound than the one requested of Madam Chapuy or required by my painting. One might have tested Pinthorpe's hypothesis about candle-light and wallpaper had not the embossed scarlet paper on Lady Beauclair's walls now been rendered wholly invisible. Indeed, so unmitigated was this blackness that for a moment I could not descry my own hand before my face, let alone the form of my subject, who was now continuing her narration as if nothing in particular had happened.

'Three years,' she was saying; 'that is how long Tristano spent in the *conservatorio* before Signor Piozzi—'

'If you please, my lady,' I said as she made no apparent effort to relieve the darkness, 'I must have light if I am to accomplish your portrait. Have you a flint?'

'I beg your pardon? Oh! Well . . . I believe there is a taper here—somewhere beside me,' came her voice out of the darkness. 'If you would be so good as to fetch a flame from Madam Chapuy in the scullery . . .'

'I cannot seem to locate it,' I said after a moment's search for the taper, during which reconnoitre I barked my left shin upon the leg of the table and stumbled over an invisible chair. I yelped in pain, but picking myself from the floor I attempted to preserve a good humour.

'This table,' I proclaimed as I rubbed my shin, 'aptly disproves the theory of Bishop Berkeley that *esse est percipi*, that "to be is to be perceived". I see no table before me, yet from the bump on my leg I know that it exists.'

'More to the point,' said my lady, whose playful voice did not seem to take very seriously the bishop's (and his disciple Pinthorpe's) idiosyncratic philosophy of material substance, 'the wax taper. Does *that* exist? Yes, I know it is here somewhere . . .'

Resuming my search I soon knocked to the floor some

other invisible object, one somewhat less sturdy than a chair or table, and it broke with an explosion of glass.

'Dear me,' I said aloud, thinking in despair how much worse was this destruction than the near convergence of my herring pie with the buckled shoes of Sir James Clutterbuck. 'Oh, dear me! My lady, forgive me—so very sorry . . .'

Yet Lady Beauclair did not seem troubled by the dilapidation of this object—whatever it may have been—and instead announced in a triumphant voice that she had located the taper.

'Yes,' she said, 'it is precisely as I thought: the taper exists. Now, Mr Cautley, if you cross the room you will soon learn if *I* exist.'

Mindful of invisible chairs or other impediments, I advanced through the darkness, my heels grinding into the floor the splinters and shards of the article my elbow had displaced from the sideboard. I reached the spot by the window where Lady Beauclair had been posing—I could have sworn this was it—only to discover that she no longer stood there.

'Please, my lady,' I said, 'the taper . . .'

'Closer,' came her voice—from the opposite side of the chamber, it seemed. 'Come closer, Mr Cautley.'

I turned round and doggedly pursued the direction of the voice, my heels again scraping and crunching across the broken shards, my shin again encountering the leg of the table, across whose invisible surface I was sent sprawling and yelping—again.

'I am waiting, Mr Cautley,' came the voice, this time from nearer the door. 'Come, Mr Cautley. What is it? Can you not find me? Can it be that your bishop was right after all, and that we exist only as we are seen? That we have no being apart from our appearance in the eyes of others? That we, like all the world, are only the dreams and fantasies of one another?'

You may imagine that my mood for philosophising had passed, especially since my hand had just come into contact with my canvas, whose highlights of asphaltum were far from dry.

'Where are you, my lady?' I demanded as I wiped my hand with a handkerchief and caressed my smarting shin-bone. 'I beg of you—enough of these games.'

These words had barely passed my lips, when I sensed

her at my side—that is, above the stink of turpentine I caught the gentler scent of the eau-de-Cologne with which she had sprinkled herself. A second later I felt the sarsenet trickle across my forearm, its whiteness passing before my eyes like a soft cloud on a windy night. And then I felt something else, too, for her invisible hand touched my belly and her breath blew softly at my ear. An instant later her lips and then—oh!—her tongue grazed the line of my jaw, at which moment the moon slipped out from behind the segmented steeple of St Giles-in-the-Fields. Now I could see her eyes, only inches from my own, and her left shoulder: a denuded white promontory that had achieved its fullest exposure thus far.

'Do not fear. Here I am, Mr Cautley. Do not fear—I exist.'

'The taper,' I said as the pair of eyes drew closer, larger, the fragrant cologne flowed about me like clouds from an unholy censer, and deep within my belly an ancient serpent raised itself from its lair of moist and heavy coils. 'Hurry, my lady—I must light the candle. Quickly—before my pigments dry . . .'

'Three years,' Lady Beauclair was saying a few minutes later, after I had hobbled back up the stairs with a flame and applied it to the extinct candle. Nothing in her face suggested the moment that had passed, for once again she had entered a kind of trance. 'Three years—that is how long Tristano spent in the *conservatorio* before Signor Piozzi deemed him worthy of demonstrating his soprano in the Royal Chapel and then at the Teatro delle Dame in Rome. After this he was conducted to a small town—but forgive me; I run too far ahead of myself.'

Nine

For three long years, Tristano roused himself each morning at the mellifluous demands of the angelus bell and, surplice pulled over his flannel petticoats, pattered down the cold stone steps to invoke the saints in the elbow-prodding company of the other young *figlioli*—that is, the other students. Three years of music—of ear-training, counterpoint, composing with chalk and learning letters and notation on a chipped *cartella*. Three years of violins, dulcimers, harpsichords, oboes, lutes, bassoons. Three years of duos and ensembles, of Vespers on Saturday, of the Passion in Holy Week, of alms walks on feast days; of studying Graziani, Cazzati, Pitoni, Vivaldi . . .

Most of all, though, three years of singing; of learning to play that most difficult and beautiful of instruments, the human voice. For the human voice, as Signor Piozzi informed his pupils, was the greatest, most divine, of all musical instruments, the one to whose perfection all others aspired. It was the workmanship not of man, who at best humbly tuned it or trifled imperfectly upon it, but of God, who had offered it as a gift to His greatest creation and by so doing separated him from the beasts.

—When you sing, the maestro told the *figlioli*, I wish you to think of your voices returning in gratitude to Him. I wish you to think of them flying through the air to Him as if on the wing-tips of angels.

Signor Piozzi more particularly expected the voices of his very best pupils to fly on wing-tips through the air to their Creator from, for instance, the Royal Chapel or the stage of the Teatro San Bartolomeo, or at least from the palatial halls of dukes or princes—thereby showing gratitude not only to God but also, more materially, to Signor Piozzi himself, the humble tuner who under the terms of an agreement with these institutions received a sum of ten ducats and two carlini for each performance. For this was no charity-school, after all; the maestro had thirty-odd mouths to feed, violins and cornets to repair or replace, stipends and taxes to pay, candles and coal to purchase, two nags to keep in oats and straw. Frugality had lately become necessary, for it seemed that Naples hosted almost as many *conservatori*—Sant' Onofrio, Santa Maria di Loreto, Poveri di Gesù Cristo, the list went on—as there were theatres, chapels, or nobles willing to part with ten ducats and two carlini per performance. And that was without counting the many private singing-masters and their ever-ripening crops of little prodigies. So to defray some of his expenses the maestro had begun to cultivate a herb garden and, less profitably but more ambitiously, to compose operas—eleven so far. He hoped to have these staged at the Teatro San Bartolomeo, but until the city's doltish impresarios recognised the true genius of these masterpieces the voices of his students and the fennel and oregano from his garden would, alas, remain his only source of income.

Singing, then. Three years of Signor Piozzi's meticulous tuning—of his screaming asperity and flying batons, his fits and rebukes, his face (which each year assumed more and more the dimensions of a pig's fat hind end) turning scarlet as he disputed a weeping orphan's music capabilities or threatened another's eviction. Three years of learning trills, roulades, portamento, arpeggios, runs, *gorgheggi, passaggi*, the full *messa di voce. Gorgheggi*? That is, shakes—the sound of a fairy beating the throbbing tonsils with a silver mallet. *Passaggi*? Changes of register, the voice smoothly climbing into the falsetto range, those delirious, gossamer-shrouded peaks that so few will ever scale. The *messa di voce*—pianissimo to fortissimo and back again on one gulp of air. Three years, also, of learning how to make the voice echo—no, resonate—in the face, in the cavities of the head: as the French say, *dans le masque*. Of exercising his palate, tongue, cheeks, lips, lungs; of holding his breath for sixty, seventy, eighty ticks at a stretch; of singing ariettas before a full-length looking-glass, a mouthful of pebbles weighing down his tongue and bulging out his cheeks . . .

Hard work? Yes, yes—but there was much more work, too, of a completely different variety: scrubbing, polishing, sweeping, peeling, chopping, weeding . . . before retiring to a tiny chamber (shared with four other boys) at the final angelus, the oil lamp still burning. For Signor Piozzi was determined to have his ducats' worth out of his little charges, whether in the *conservatorio* or on the stage. They may have possessed the holy voices of angels but, for all that, they still required sustenance and lodging, they still grubbed up lutes and balustrades with their dirty little fingers, or tramped mud and rainwater into the corridors and music-rooms.

So there were always plenty of tasks to be done: drawing slopping buckets of water from the well in the piazza, for example, or bearing basket-loads of coal up a ladder from the pitch-black cellars. Or sweeping the courtyard and *porte-cochère*, and dodging the blows of their resident beggars. Bottling jellies in the low-beamed kitchen, or chopping parsley, purslane, zucchini, anchovies; or halving pears, slicing lemons, shucking oysters. Twisting the heads of chickens, decapitating and scaling skate, whiting, sole, trout. Weeding the herb garden or scooping manure into the dung-cart. And afterwards there were always rugs to be beaten and frocks and bed-linen to be laundered; bows to be resined; sideboards, looking-glasses and *cassoni* to be polished with a cheesecloth, as well as chalices, straining spoons, and the sleek surfaces of violoncellos, mandolins, gold cornets, a harpsichord, and trombones whose coils and bells reflected shifting, gold-burnished anamorphic images of the music-room. And then much heavier scrubbing and shining when that was finished: floors, steps, window-panes, chamber-pots, a flagstoned entryway, iron grilles on the gate, table-clocks, silverware, china cups and dishes, goblets and wooden spoons, brass fittings in the chapel, flagons and copper pots hanging on hooks in the steaming scullery alongside wreaths of garlic and dried figs.

What else did he remember of those years? His fellow inmates, of course: their pranks, chatter, smell, lice, their shrill pursuits of pleasure, their pustulated little faces and arses, and most of all their constant, ceaseless, inescapable, all-enveloping *presence*. Sleeping, waking, eating, praying, singing, laughing, weeping, bathing, even pissing and shitting in their midst: bastards and orphans, most of them, from all over the Kingdom, some from even farther away, from other, unknown kingdoms and dukedoms and tiny principalities whose roads and farms and villages were as forsaken and now as distant and as impossible to imagine as his own. Girolamo, Marco, Pietro, Daniele, Gioacchino, Giuseppe Maria, little Farinello, the scamp . . . What had happened to all of them? Despite the enforced intimacy of these com-

74

panions he forgot about most of them, their names and faces as well as their plans and ambitions, soon after he left the *conservatorio*.

Well—all but one: the great Scipio. The school held many disagreeable shocks—its unsparing regimen, its draughty windows, its thin blankets on cold nights, its endless tasks with the broom, pitchfork, or wash-bucket—but most loathsome of all was surely Scipio, or 'Il Piozzino', as he was popularly known out of respect for his maestro.

Worst of all, then: three years of Il Piozzino.

Perhaps you have heard of Il Piozzino, who once sang upon the English stage? No? Well, then, a few words are in order. Tristano had heard much about this young soprano from the other students before he actually laid eyes upon him or heard the celebrated voice. Scipio was entitled to better lodgings than most of his young peers—a warmer chamber, which enjoyed a private stair, the attentions of a maid, a view of a flagged piazza. He had also gained a dispensation that preserved him from the more menial duties in the kitchen or scullery. Another rule exempted him most mornings from devotions, and well after the final ringing of the angelus the old gatekeeper who locked up at sundown was frequently the recipient of angry summonses and curses, ordered from his cheerless little room to admit the young virtuoso upon his return from an evening of secretive amusements.

These privileges in themselves created no resentments among the other pupils. True enough, Scipio was resented very deeply—several of the children would have murdered him had they possessed either the courage or the means— but they did not take umbrage merely at this immunity each morning from emptying chamber-pots or kneeling down to invoke the saints. No: their resentment grew out of fear— no, out of terror. For Scipio's amusements were not confined to the world beyond the gates of the school: just as often he pursued them within its walls. Indeed, it appeared to be his privilege, among these others, to submit his fellow pupils to any number of cruel torments. These ran the gamut from relatively innocuous forms of verbal abuse—exaggerated mimicries of speech defects or dialects, invented stories that robbed their subject of his good reputation—to other tortures which routinely concluded not merely with mental, but also with physical, trauma. Spiders with noxious mandibles were slipped into the beds or surplices of unwary victims, others of a less hazardous species into the squirming mouth of anyone who could be held down long enough, his nose tightly pinched. Other victims were locked overnight in a cellar—the favoured site of his diversions—where they were assailed by its more compliant captives, a dozen or so large rats. The younger children were sometimes persuaded by the promise of a few scudi (never actually forthcoming, of course) to kiss the snout of a rat or lizard, often receiving a bite in return; or to bloody each other's noses and claw each other's faces in gladiatorial battle below the stairs.

When the full extent of his eccentric appetites could not be gratified by the blood and tears of his little fellows, Scipio occasionally amused himself with the lower forms of life he cultivated in alarming abundance in the darker, wetter recesses of the school. His commodious chamber regularly became a blood-splotched theatre of anatomy, to which curious pupils were admitted—at a modest price—for evenings of entertainment. Here the legs of frogs and lizards were excised one by one and fed to a fat black viper who inhabited a small airing cupboard; then, when their contortions became tiresome, the amputees themselves were disposed of in similar fashion. Sometimes he turned his thoughts to jurisprudence, and the chamber became a court of law. At least once a fortnight one of the rats was summoned from its dark nest in the cellar to respond to some fanciful charge; invariably it was found guilty and then in accordance with Scipio's enthusiastic sense of justice was starved to death in a stoppered bottle—this often took the best part of a month—or else was hanged, or fed to the insatiable viper, or forced to ingest a few drops of an evil-smelling fluid which Scipio asserted had been concocted according to the recipe for the Poison of the Inquisitors. True or not, the rat lurched, kicked and twitched its way out of this world as painfully as any heretic.

Against these measures it was no good for a victim or frightened witness to appeal to the authority of Signor Piozzi; whatever pleasure the maestro took from wrathful execrations against his students stopped well short of any chastisement of Scipio. Indeed he would hear nothing at all said against the boy. In the absence of offspring, he regarded Scipio as his son and as a plentiful source of the income that would endow his retirement. In his rare moments of volubility he was fond of predicting that in the space of a few years Il Piozzino would earn in excess of 3,000 ducats per year—and, of course, then he would not forget his old teacher. Yes—and *then*, by heaven, those eleven operas would be staged!

But Signor Piozzi did not know Scipio like the other pupils did. This little scaramouch frequently explained how he would have parted company with the fat monster years ago but for a contract he had signed, very unwisely, upon first entering the school: but when this accursed contract expired he would be gone!

—Which will be the last I see of you foul little turds, he invariably finished; a proposition that was not especially unattractive to his audience.

Tristano encountered this malevolent little creature two or three days after his arrival; at precisely the time when a student was most vulnerable to Scipio's pitiless whimsies.

—Peasant! was his judgement upon first encountering Tristano after matins. He was standing on the stone staircase. The famous soprano voice that had so lately bewitched a congregation of the devoted at the Madonna di Loreto in Rome assumed an ugly screech:

—Lout, clodpole! Don't track your pig-shit on to my stair!

He might well have continued for some time on this theme (which soon expanded to include Tristano's alleged preference for sexual congress with goats and his mother's availability to the more perverse passions of Turkish soldiers in Apulian bagnios) had there not suddenly come a commotion from the bottom of the stairs. One of the *figlioli*, a boy named Concetto, was being borne swiftly up the steps by the organist, a moon-faced man almost as fat as Signor Piozzi. Concetto was moaning and whey-faced, a patch of blood having spread across most of his lower abdomen and upper right thigh.

—Idiots! Signor Piozzi was screaming from somewhere below. Why send him back so soon? The last time! Idiots! The last time, I say!

Scipio stepped back to allow the duo to pass, a look of amusement briefly crossing his face.

—Concetto, he called after the boy, a lacertian grin stretching across his face, you shall recover soon enough! Am I right, Giulia?

The maid had appeared beside him on the steps. She was

77

a girl of perhaps fifteen years, who, like many of the *figlioli*, remained devoted to Scipio despite frequent maltreatment. In truth she remained the most loyal of all, for she was a regular visitor to his chamber, and it was not unusual to witness Scipio skipping down the narrow stone stairs that led to her lodgings in the tiny garret.

Giulia tittered her affirmation, then the two of them disappeared up the steps, Scipio swatting her wiggling buttocks. Their titters and shuffling feet remained audible until a door somewhere high above banged heavily.

The stricken boy had been carried into the chamber Tristano shared with four other boys, and here he was laid on a sixth pallet, breathing in soft hitches and moans. He remained there for the next two days and nights, occasionally slurping weakly at cold broths that Giulia, leering, conducted from the kitchen and submitting his wrist to a thin physician whose grim composure intimated a certain familiarity with the affliction. During one of these conferences Tristano overheard this man whispering gravely to Signor Piozzi, whose presence in the chamber had blacked out the light of the candle before Tristano was scooted into the corridor to listen at the half-open door: Most delicate . . . the doctor at Bologna . . . a complete loss . . . the ecclesiastical laws . . . maiming . . . the most scandalous . . . surely appreciate . . . severe compromise . . .

On the third day Concetto rose from his pallet at the sound of the angelus and, leaning on Tristano's shoulder, limped down the steps to murmur his devotions. His sudden appearance in the chapel occasioned a good many nudges and sidelong glances, as well as a few smirks, though upon his entrance two or three kneeling boys seemed to gather themselves tensely, as if the sad little fellow's affliction somehow threatened them as well.

A fair boy with whitish curls and the pink eyes of a rabbit, Concetto stood squinting painfully in the sunlight. He was so palely complected that Tristano decided that either his affliction had drained him of every drop of blood in his body or else the sun had never once showed itself in his place of birth, some far-off dukedom whose ruler was reputedly the boy's patron. Today, and then each day thereafter, he dressed in a black frock, which marked him out from the ordinary society of the boys who were largely indistinguishable in white frocks, red belts and Turkish berets. Scipio,

78

too, wore black, but only, of course, when it suited his fancy, which was not often: more frequently he obliged his tastes with blue velvet coats brocaded with gold thread, or with poppy-coloured frocks and corresponding knee-breeches, all supposedly the gifts of his admirers beyond the school walls.

A small contingent of other boys wore black as well, perhaps seven of them all told. Like Scipio, they inhabited more capacious lodgings above the stairs and enjoyed both a greater quantity of linen on their beds and a better quality of fare at the dinner-table. And they, too, had won reprieves from any scrubbing, chopping or polishing. Yet this was a Pyrrhic victory, for despite their more mature years—they were on average perhaps a year or two older than the other boys—and their mysterious brotherhood with him, they represented some of Scipio's most favoured victims. And indeed whenever Signor Piozzi's back was turned the other boys took much delight in ragging them, usually with pranks plagiarised from Scipio's repertoire: and so once or twice a fortnight, having been missed at matins, one or other of these poor fellows would be liberated from the cellar, shivering, rat-bitten, sucking back sobs, smearing tears and snot over his cheeks. Very occasionally one of them disappeared altogether. Tristano suspected one of Scipio's more lusty diversions, but beside their names in the gold-embossed roll book Signor Piozzi always entered the same words: *'se n'è fuggito'*—'he ran away'.

If Tristano was hoping to learn the secrets of this tragical fraternity by sharing his chamber with one of its members, he was soon disappointed. On the fourth day Concetto and his portmanteau were swept up the stairs to enjoy the domestic benefits of his new position. Tristano then might have forgotten Concetto altogether but for events that occurred almost two years later; events which for a few days disturbed the routine so rigorously prescribed at the school.

'But these events are, perhaps, better left for another time,' said my lady. 'For the hour has grown late, and I fear you grow weary. No? Dear Mr Cautley, I do enjoy your company. But now I am curious to see the progress of your work, and I see that Madam Chapuy has delivered us a dish of strawberries.' (For the good lady had arrived a moment before and now was peering over my left shoulder, breathing heavily and casting a shadow across my canvas.) 'May I propose that we meet again in three nights' time, when I shall continue the history of Tristano?'

As I walked down the narrow stair twenty minutes later, lighted by Madam Chapuy's young daughter, who escorted me most graciously with a candle held high, my passage was momentarily blocked by a small party—two gentlemen and a lady—squatted upon the landing. Though dressed well enough in velvet coats and clean white cravats, the two gentlemen wore rather ill-looking countenances, out of which eyes red-rimmed from an excess of drink—which perhaps accounted for their slumping postures—regarded us with a brief suspicion. As I passed, pressed flat against the wall, the lady—an unwholesome-looking jade with a great volume of greasy ringlets tumbling down her back—drew one of the gentlemen unsteadily to his feet and then, making good use of her superior weight, dragged him through a curtained doorway, saying: 'What have you brought me tonight, Mr McQuarters? Hmm? What have you brought your Betty tonight?'

The fellow who remained on the steps squinted at me again and then demanded in an imperious tone of unwonted familiarity: 'Is there a jakes upon these premises, then?'

'Through the door, Mr Lockhart,' replied my young companion, Esmeralda, pointing. 'You know where 'tis found,' she added, encouragingly.

Once in the street, whose aspect was not improved by darkness, I pitied Lady Beauclair these unmannerly neighbours. But I reasoned that perhaps she did not know them, for in a great city such as this the faces and names of everyone, even those of our nearest neighbours, can remain a mystery, a blank.

Ten

The morrow was a most irksomely miserable day. Showers of cold rain were driven slantwise through the streets by a north wind that threatened to unhinge Samson and Delilah, who creaked and swung wildly at the force of the attempt. Failing in this assault, the hyperborean blast swirled about in the chimney until at last it succeeded in extinguishing the fire I had kindled for my breakfast, suffusing my chamber with a black billow of soot. The rain drummed upon the roof-tiles like the fingertips of an impatient giant contemplating what he might do with me today.

The miseries of my cold pudding, and of my lodgings, which, fireless, had become as frigid as the regions of Nova Zembla (for the wind had infiltrated my windows and, a little later, the rain my ceiling), were presently surpassed by the woes of having to precipitate myself into the streets. This morning the Haymarket and its neighbours were awash in muck, resembling a muddy Ganges and its streaming tributaries: thick waves lapped and sucked at shop doors and the boots of anyone either desperate or foolish enough to venture into the elements. Even the establishment of 'Jules Regnault, Perruquier' was not spared these encroachments, for in spite of the efforts of two apprentices equipped with straw brooms the river gulped and gurgled at its door, and at the buckled shoes of bicorned footmen who gingerly picked their way into the shop, their masters' bag-wigs tucked under their arms in rain-drummed pasteboard boxes, their muddy-legged horses splashing and steaming at the kerb.

As I navigated these murky streams I was accompanied by my own would-be footman, Jeremiah Sharp (ten years of age the previous month), who held under his arm not a boxed bag-wig but a French morocco satchel, in which I had placed a collection of sketches: pastel crayon portraits of Mr Knatchbull in the posture of the dying General Wolfe, in Cossack garb, and as a naked gladiator preparing for

81

battle; as well as one or two prospects of the hills above Upper Buckling, painted in water-colours (and therefore with more orthodox skies of blue); the charcoal likenesses of some of Mr Sharp's more compliant patrons; and even last night's *A Lady by Candle-light*, which was woefully incomplete and as yet unrecognisable as my lady, but not, I thought, without a certain suggestion of talent. Works, in other words, with which I hoped to impress Sir Endymion Starker.

At his own behest Jeremiah had been granted an exemption from his morning duties—sweeping the floor and threshold of his father's shop—in order to accompany me on my errands; for though each one of the seven Sharp children was tenacious in his or her dedication, competing for the seats beside me on the pew or at the supper-table, and sometimes coming to blows with one another over the honour of bearing my paintbox or sketch-book, young Jeremiah remained most touchingly assiduous. Indeed, after appraising my talents more kindly and anticipating my prospects more optimistically than the rest of society had thus far deemed appropriate, he could envision no occupation more rewarding than that of entering my service and travelling with me through the capitals of the Continent. Often while sweeping the powder from his father's floor, plucking errant hairs from his hackle, or emptying buckets of bleach into the gutter, he would solace himself with reveries of a more idyllic life in which he shaved me each morning and brushed my clothes, prepared my paint and brushes, set up my easel, read poetry to me in my moments of recreation, answered my correspondence, managed my accounts, admitted or debarred my visitors, interceded in my disputes with jealous husbands or cast-off mistresses and tenderly ministered to me during my periods of illness or melancholy. If on previous occasions his modest ambitions had struck me as sweetly amusing, and everyone else as, alas, ludicrously misplaced, this morning as he marched down the street before me, picking a passage through the sludge and endeavouring to shield me with his small frame from the depredations of wind and rain, his own brow defended from these assaults by a straw bonnet, it assumed a special poignancy: for last night, before I had been awakened by Mr Sharp's creaking sign, I had been dreaming of performing a set of very similar tasks for Sir Endymion Starker.

Stressing his qualifications a fortnight before, Jeremiah had pledged himself to follow me wherever my genius might see fit to take me, 'from Frobisher Bay to Timbuktu'; yet this blustery forenoon, when his heroic fidelity was given its first test, I planned that he should be required to attend me only as far as St Alban's Street, that is, to the lodgings of Sir Endymion, to whom, once again, I was hoping to pay my address. However, on this most miserable of mornings I took my new servant much farther afield; as far afield, in fact, as Chiswick; and I knocked, in the end, on three different doors. In his hopeful catalogue of duties Jeremiah had made no mention of knocking on doors; yet this, I felt, was the task most demanded of anyone in my service, since here in London it seemed my life was being measured out in the intervals between door knockers, between a series of unheeded applications and hapless attempts to gain admittance into privileged spaces that for some reason were forbidden me.

First, then, the door on St Alban's Street. Jeremiah picked his way to the house on tiptoe, then made a gallant motion for me to follow in his steps, but to avoid a starburst of vomit on the flags and an ochre splatter where a cart-horse had lately evacuated itself in the gutter.

'Nobody at home, Mr Cautley,' he opined, pressing his nose to the bottle glass of the side-window as I had done a day before. 'Shall we go to Pall Mall, then? He must be in Pall Mall, Mr Cautley.'

'Tarry a moment,' I said, wondering if in a moment of volubility earlier that morning I had been wise to make the lad privy to my plans. 'Tarry just a moment, Jeremiah.'

I looked round the front of the house, which in this weather, as its eaves dripped, its tiles flapped, and its chimney howled, seemed a more abject dwelling than ever. However, the rodent whose corpse had defiled the doorway a day earlier had vanished, no doubt swept away by the torrent. The handcart had also vanished, less plausibly a casualty of the rains, and I took this alteration to be a sign of possession by the master.

I looked up, sheltering my face against the deluge. The window from which the pale-visaged lady had scowled down upon me was shut, dark, its curtains drawn.

'The knocker, Jeremiah.'

'No knocker, Mr Cautley,' he replied, gesturing to the

implement that had snapped in my hand the day earlier and now lay in the stinking muck. ''Tis broken, sir.'

'Strike the door, then.'

Jeremiah thumped the wood with his small fist; the sound, being barely audible to me, two feet behind him, hardly risked rousing anyone two sets of stairs above us: it was indeed a small, lost sound, I reflected, in the midst of such a great and noisy world.

'Harder, Jeremiah,' I commanded when this petition went unremarked.

'I hear someone, Mr Cautley.'

Yes—voices; coming, it seemed, from one of the upper windows: screams, rather; two people arguing, a gentleman and a lady; or, rather, a gentleman shouting and a lady sobbing.

'Can you hear, Jeremiah? What do they say?'

My footman shook his straw bonnet and again thumped the door. No response, and after another minute, and after Jeremiah's third appeal, the voices fell silent, or at least grew inaudible. Yet before this extinction I thought I detected the gentleman angrily denounce his weeping antagonist as a 'jade' and a 'whore', though as the wind had chosen that particular moment to wail in the chimney and dislodge a tile I could in no wise be certain of my ears. And whether this execrating fellow was Sir Endymion, and whether the sobbing lady was the pretty mistress who a day earlier had pitched the miniature at my crown, of these things I was still less convinced.

Jeremiah was persuaded to apply his knuckles to the door for a fourth time, but when this by now somewhat reluctant entreaty met with no better reception than the earlier ones I turned on my heel in the mud of the cracked flags and led the way into the street.

'Come, Jeremiah,' I said, in what I tried to make sound like a brave and cheery voice. 'To Pall Mall, then.'

'Yes, Mr Cautley.'

By now my young footman was soaking wet; his thin shoulders were shivering, his teeth were chattering and clicking, and his knuckles, poor fellow, no doubt were smarting. Making matters worse, several times in the course of our expedition the wind had succeeded in lifting the straw hat from his crown and dropping it in a puddle of mire, from which it was unhappily retrieved, wrung out, and clamped down more forcefully upon his brow, only to blow away a minute later. There was something amusing but also admirable in his perseverence—as indeed there was, I suppose you will say, in my own persistent habit of petitioning locked doors.

'Yes, Mr Cautley,' Jeremiah repeated as we commenced our walk south towards the Carv'd Balcony Tavern and the entrance to Pall Mall, where, even though it was the middle of the morning, the lamps were still glowing in their crystal bulbs. Once again Jeremiah shielded me from the wind as he picked our way round the most treacherous of puddles and the steaming leavings of cart-horses. Now, I suppose, the prospect of entering Pall Mall, and indeed of entering my service, was a somewhat less alluring one to him than it had been twenty minutes before.

Second, a larger door. We forded Pall Mall at its shallowest point, crossing to the south side near Market Lane. The building to which we directed our steps was modest in size and of a disappointingly humble aspect, having in its previous existence been a print warehouse. In the bulbous knob of a brass knocker I was able to appraise the composition of my wig, which now was sopping wet and, I feared, beginning to smell like the beast from whose tail it had been cultivated. Despite Jeremiah's best efforts, furthermore, my breeches were soaked, my stockings splattered, and my shoes rendered wholly invisible beneath several tenacious strata of mud and dung that my vigorous essays with an iron mud-scraper failed to depose. I doffed my hat in the shelter of the portico and, as Jeremiah wrung it out, mopped my face with a handkerchief, which, extracted from my pocket, proved at least as sodden as my other accoutrements, and, worse still, was stained by last night's asphaltum, which I succeeded in smearing across my nose. What *A Lady by Candle-light* and my sketches of Mr Knatchbull might have looked like by now I was loath to imagine.

'Bless you,' Jeremiah whispered absently as I sneezed into my dripping handkerchief. He was contriving to put a more attractive knot in the red ribbon that I had affixed to my wig, but in spite of this endeavour I was, I fear, a most unsightly attraction. One glimpse of my frizzled head and asphaltum-smudged nose in the brass knocker and I was prepared to beat a hasty retreat to my lodgings. No doubt

I would have, too, had it not been for Jeremiah, who, sensing the crumbling of my resolve, seized the knocker and struck it viciously four times upon the plate. The response to this action was one that neither of us could have predicted.

'Lessons have commenced,' said a gentleman who swung the door ajar and then hastily enlarged the aperture to admit the two of us, but not the wind or rain. 'Hurry now—inside—come now, come now . . .'

Jeremiah and I exchanged looks, and I was on the point of broaching my business, but the gentleman, who was equipped with an ear-trumpet, beckoned us inside, then pointed down the corridor with his trumpet.

'Please, sir,' I said as he slammed the door with a bang that seemed to dislodge the words from my throat, 'I am seeking Sir Endymion Starker, if you please—'

'Hasten, hasten,' he said in a loud voice, taking no account of my statement. As the trumpet was once again pointing down the corridor, thereby forsaking its more orthodox employment at his ear, he was, I surmised, quite unable to hear a single syllable. I therefore addressed him in a louder voice, but he merely placed a hand in the middle of my back and, doing likewise with Jeremiah, moved us forcibly along the corridor.

'On with you,' he said; 'already you are late by an hour.' Then, giving us each a final push, he slipped away into one of the chambers whose oak doors lined the corridor.

Jeremiah and I exchanged looks once again, though just as he was venturing in a small voice that we should depart, 'for surely this gentleman has mistaken us for somebody else', my eyes drifted from the visage of my young footman to that of a Diana, who, high on the wall of the large chamber we now were passing, was disarming Cupid, while next to her, in another gold frame, Juno was preparing to receive the cestus from Venus.

'The Exhibition Room,' I said, my attention engaged now by a stern-looking Regulus in the process of departing from Rome, as well as other likenesses of Venus that were either hung on the walls or propped against the base-boards: Venuses directing Aeneas, lamenting the death of Adonis, subduing Mars, suckling the infant Cupid, or posing half-naked in the sea, the fortuitous disposition of her plentiful locks barely managing to conceal her breasts. Then, too, there was an Achilles, distraught, bearing the bluish-pale body of Patroclus; several full-length portraits of the King and Queen; the bicorned heads and brocaded and besashed breasts of martial Persons of Quality; scenes of the Roman *campagna* and the ruins of the Colosseum—all suspended in gilt frames, and covering, so it seemed, every available inch of the blue velvet walls.

I would have stopped and gawped for ever, but, high on the wall, I noticed one particular Venus—a thinner, fairer rendition of the goddess—whose pleading white visage and cataracts of ochre tresses recalled those of the miniature which that morning I had carefully placed in my fob-pocket and had been fingering for the better part of the expedition.

'Mr Cautley . . .' said Jeremiah, who was not awed, as was I, by the many wonders of the Exhibition Room. 'I think, sir, that we should depart. Please, Mr Cautley, surely someone will see us.'

But someone had seen us already, for in the midst of the Exhibition Room was ranged a group of boys, some no older than Jeremiah (who was now actually tugging at my sleeve), each draped in a smock, equipped with a sketchbook or an easel, and busily producing a copy of Venus or Achilles. One or two of the less industrious among them had turned their gazes towards us, leaving their brushes or pencils suspended in the air over their half-finished sketches.

'I am seeking Sir Endymion Starker,' I said in the important voice I had learned from my father, who had employed it when addressing his congregation or purchasing fish at the Shrewsbury market. 'Can you tell me, sirs, if he is about today?'

One of the older students (for so I took these fellows to be) raised his paintbrush—its bristles were gummy with a generous dollop of Mr Middleton's finest ultramarine (which was the colour of the gown adorning the particular Venus he was reproducing)—and pointed, or, rather, dabbed, in the direction of another door.

'Try the Cast Room,' he said, then returned his ultramarined brush to the bright folds of the goddess's robe.

The Cast Room I found to be under an occupation similar to that of the Exhibition Room. (Jeremiah, who had pledged to follow me to Timbuktu, had quailed at the sight of the suggested door and now, I presumed, stood outside in the rain.) The floor of this new room was filled with more sketching boys, for a similar exercise was underway, though this time the students were inscribing on to their papers and canvases the effigies of a dozen or so marbles that stood around them: figures throwing discuses, playing flutes while leaping over logs, brandishing swords and shields, placing feet or shin-guards on the necks of writhing foes, or engaging themselves in more amorous recreations with naked young maidens. Here, too, stood more Venuses—one shyly shielding her bosom with her hands and hair, another, in a less decorous posture, carelessly exposing a breast to view while she placed a sea shell to her ear and a bearded figure with a triton crept up behind her.

These silently sketching students were superintended by a drawing-master, who now crept up behind me, much like the figure with the triton behind the unsuspecting Venus. If his colleague at the door had been deficient in the sense of hearing, this fellow, it seemed, was strangely wanting in another faculty, one generally considered indispensable in his profession: for after squinting ambiguously into my face, he addressed me familiarly, though with much irritation, as 'Spencer'.

'You're late as usual, Spencer,' he said in a croaking voice. 'The lesson commenced an hour before. Take your seat, boy—hurry now.'

'Yes, sir.'

Assuming the convenient disguise of this perpetually tardy fellow, I took a seat on the floor and, removing a sodden portrait of Mr Knatchbull from the satchel, began adding muscles to his limbs and a discus to his outstretched hand.

'If you cannot arrive in Pall Mall at the prescribed hour,' continued the master, unwilling to drop the matter, 'however do you expect to arrive in Chiswick on time? Sir Endymion is not so tolerant as I am, and you shall learn soon enough that he does not stand for such things. You had best set out early tomorrow if you expect to arrive in time. Remember—ten o'clock. You will be painting draperies.'

'What, sir, is the address, if you please?' I begged. 'You know how forgetful I am . . .'

Perhaps I felt guilty at having brought poor Spencer's tattered reputation into further disrepute; but after I received the address, and after the lesson ended and I had slipped out into the rain, I was thinking not of Spencer—whoever he was—and not even of Jeremiah, who was faithfully awaiting me, shivering feverishly beneath the portico and hopping about like a Quaker, but, rather, of Sir Endymion; that is, I suppose, I was thinking only of myself.

Eleven

 Behind the third door, then, many hours later, I discovered Sir Endymion Starker; or, rather, behind the third door I discovered Lady Manresa and then finally, behind her, Sir Endymion.

Chiswick was not Timbuktu or Frobisher Bay, it was a matter of perhaps only two leagues; yet we had a long and eventful journey none the less, even if the rain *had* finally stopped by the time we reached the turnpike at Hyde Park Corner and turned on to the gravelled carriageway leading to Knightsbridge. By this time we were part of a company, for at the bottom of Tyburn Lane we had encountered two gentlemen, likewise on foot, who expressed a wish to travel with us, as they were on the road to Kensington.

'On such a journey there is a greater security in numbers,' explained one of these fellows, who had introduced himself as Mr Brownrigg. He was a cordial, well-appointed fellow with a silver-brocaded coat, a silk waistcoat with lace trimmings, and a bone-tipped cane. A swift physiognomical reading of his eyes and brow proclaimed him as a sturdy, honest fellow given to friendly association and beneficent gestures. The accuracy of my reading was soon confirmed, for as we proceeded he explained that, as this road was so notorious for its highwaymen, a bell was sounded at regular intervals, on most days, at the bottom of Tyburn Lane, mustering into a group those who wished to travel to Kensington; but 'as no bell has sounded this morning, Mr O'Leary and I have taken upon ourselves the task of assembling fellow travellers for our mutual preservation'.

'It is a fine day indeed for the highwayman,' Mr O'Leary observed, indicating the quagmire of the carriageway before us and a mud-splattered coach that was now lurching arduously towards the paving-stones of Piccadilly. 'The Knightsbridge Turnpike is plagued by the worst mud in the kingdom, as thick as a hasty pudding—a condition much beloved by the rogue.'

'No one, alack, is spared his perils,' Mr Brownrigg continued in a cheerful voice of a pleasantly musical modulation, 'for it is not so long ago that our late King George was himself robbed of his watch and purse on this same stretch of the highway.'

'Yonder lie the Five Fields,' Mr O'Leary further elaborated. He was an Irishman of comparably fine dress and deportment, now pointing with a clouded cane to the empty meadows that opened on our left. In the distance a brick kiln was smoking thinly, behind which smirching screen rose the mist-draped hulk of the Lock Hospital. 'No day passes, I do believe, but an unwary traveller has his hat or his wig snitched within their precincts, or his sword or purse stolen.' Suddenly he lowered his voice, as if fearful of being overheard by passers-by (of whom, in truth, there were none). 'Only last spring,' he said in this hushed tone, 'a merchant returning by coach from Chiswick was murdered as he crossed the Ranelagh Stream, which flows not so far from this very road.'

'The poor gentleman was shot through the heart,' said Mr Brownrigg, who was ruefully shaking his head at his recollection of this event, 'just as his coach traversed the "Bloody Bridge".'

'Most aptly named, Mr Brownrigg,' exclaimed the Irishman. 'Alack, most aptly named.'

'Oh, a man is never truly secure in his possessions,' lamented Mr Brownrigg, 'once he passes beyond the gates of Piccadilly.'

You may well imagine that Jeremiah and I were grateful to enjoy the companionship of these two sturdy fellows as protection against the perils to which we had so unknowingly exposed ourselves. Jeremiah (whose eyes had grown very wide as he learned the fate that befell the unlucky merchant from Chiswick) was particularly gratified, and as we walked he maintained a position very close to Mr Brownrigg, who was the larger of the two gentlemen.

As we progressed past the hamlet of Knightsbridge, the mud squelching and sucking at our shoes, Mr O'Leary

90

pointed out Knightsbridge Green, which, he said, had served as a burial pit during the time of plague.

''Tis maintained,' he continued, 'that on days such as this, when it rains so very heavily, the skulls of some of these poor souls are exposed to view, though I have not myself witnessed the phenomenon.'

At this macabre piece of news, Jeremiah drew even closer to Mr Brownrigg and, averting his gaze from the green, exclaimed that he should not feel safe until we arrived in Chiswick. Mr Brownrigg, upon learning our destination, then announced an alternative to the Kensington Road; this, he conjectured, might shorten our journey by as much as a quarter of an hour or more. When Jeremiah and I expressed interest in this new itinerary, the good gentleman, however, proposed a *caveat*.

'For 'tis true that this path, which descends to the river, owns a more notorious reputation than the Kensington Road, on account of the footpads who find its isolation most expedient to their perfidious purposes.'

'I believe it to be the very passage favoured by the poor merchant,' offered the Irishman.

'That it was, Mr O'Leary, alack for him,' replied Mr Brownrigg in a sympathetic tone. He now drew up short on the road and addressed Jeremiah and me with an aspect of kind though anxious concern. 'On this account,' he said, making a particular study of Jeremiah's satchel of French morocco, 'if you are determined to embark upon this pathway I am bound to ask if you possess any valuables—perchance some coin or jewellery—which might excite the avarice of a footpad or highwayman. Now you must understand,' he continued before either of us could respond, 'that as 'tis some time before Mr O'Leary and I are required in Kensington we should be most honoured to accompany you along the stretches of the route from whence it derives this infamous reputation.'

After a brief conference, Jeremiah and I found that whatever fears we entertained of footpads and highwaymen were overborne by a desire to reach Chiswick before we caught pneumonia, and by the guarantee of our kind companions, who seemed satisfied with our decision, however dismayed they might have been (as their sympathetic smiles implied) by our confessions of poverty.

'For you must understand that I am a poor artist,' I told

these gentlemen, 'who has as yet to make his impression in the world. Yet I have expectations,' I saw fit to append, 'for I have been engaged to paint the portrait of the kinswoman of Lord W—.'

Our companions were duly impressed by this intelligence, and only a show of modesty on my part prevented Jeremiah from extracting the finer examples of my craft from the satchel for their inspection.

'Come—I believe the path is this way,' said Mr Brownrigg a moment later as he led us into a field populated here and there by spotted hogs, which were rooting about noisily in two foul-smelling heaps of refuse. The field (in which no path immediately presented itself) was also occupied by several small contingents of bewhiskered fellows, dressed in rags, who were cooking their midday repast—likewise retrieved, it appeared, from the foul heaps of refuse—upon the hellish-looking flames of two brick kilns. Under other circumstances Jeremiah and I surely would have provided these fellows with a broad berth, but today we were emboldened by the presence of our new friends. Even so, I noticed how Jeremiah never ventured more than two feet beyond the elbow of Mr Brownrigg.

'Lo,' said Mr O'Leary quite suddenly, after we had tramped for a quarter of an hour across fields and through thick stands of elm and chestnut. 'Behold—the "Bloody Bridge".'

I heard Jeremiah catch his breath at the sight of this infamous piece of engineering, a wooden construction barely broad enough to permit two horses to pass abreast. Beneath it bubbled the Ranelagh Stream, which was swollen by the rain and hastening at an immoderate pace to its appointment with the Thames.

'I believe 'twas upon this very spot, Mr Brownrigg, that the merchant from Chiswick encountered his unfortunate end,' said Mr O'Leary, who had assumed a position upon the near side of the structure and was pointing with his cane to the bank of clay above the stream.

'Yes, upon that spot precisely,' agreed Mr Brownrigg. 'God rest his soul.'

'How the rogue pleaded,' said Mr O'Leary.

'Yes,' agreed Mr Brownrigg, 'and how he screamed.'

'But alas, there was no one to hear him,' said Mr O'Leary.

'And if no one hears a scream,' suggested Mr Brownrigg, 'then truly 'tis as if no one had screamed at all.'

Neither I nor poor Jeremiah gave any special credit to this hypothesis (which in retrospect sounded rather like the philosophy of my friend Pinthorpe, though you may be quite sure this did not cross my mind at the moment): for no sooner did Mr O'Leary produce a pistol from his handsome waistcoat and express a desire to inspect the contents of the morocco satchel than the two of us began shrieking at the top of our lungs, appealing both for the assistance of our fellow men and the mercy of our treacherous companions. When this action produced neither result, we took other measures: to wit, we began to run. Yet this attempt produced no better effect, for poor Jeremiah was apprehended by Mr O'Leary after only five steps, at which point he recommenced his screams.

'Into the river, Jeremiah!'

When my own pursuer began to close the gap that separated us, I had myself involuntarily taken recourse to this same channel of escape, for I slipped on the clay bank and tumbled head over heels into the stream. For the sake of his fine clothing, perhaps, Mr Brownrigg seemed most loath to follow—a quite understandable reservation. Instead, he stood cursing me from the bank and flourishing his bone-tipped cane like a sword.

'Into the river!' I repeated while the current swept me under the 'Bloody Bridge', nearly knocking me into one of its wooden arches.

'Yes, Mr Cautley!'

With a violent twist my young footman leapt free from the grasp of Mr O'Leary and, throwing the satchel before him, jumped into the rushing water with a faint splash. The current treated him as harshly as it had me, thrusting him into one of the bridge's splintered supports and promptly dunking him below the surface; but then it bore both of us beyond the reach of the figures on the bank, who shouted, pursued, flaunted their walking-sticks, discharged their pistols, then diminished and, finally, disappeared.

'This way, Jeremiah!' I called as the force of the current swept us downstream like two small chicks in a stormy kennel.

'Coming, Mr Cautley! I'm coming, sir!'

A few minutes later the stream discharged us into the Thames at Chelsea, near Ranelagh Gardens, the arches and encircling colonnades of whose great wooden Rotunda were visible as we were washed on to the bank, coughing, spluttering, and soaking wet. As I stumbled ashore with Jeremiah, my stockings squishing noisily in my gold-buckled shoes, I realised that only two weeks before I had stood near this very spot in the company of Toppie. We had been smoking tobacco-pipes and watching as masked and costumed Persons of Quality promenaded, two by two, past the scented and candle-lit fountain and into the enchanted palace. Today, of course, the Persons of Quality were absent and the fountain was still. The colonnade and the Venetian windows were dark and gloomy, and the shrubs in the garden looked very small and miserable, like little green animals huddled together against the cold and wet; much, I suppose, as Jeremiah and I must have appeared if anyone had been watching.

As it transpired, someone *was* watching. We had begun wringing out our clothes, and I my wig, which had relinquished its dredger-load of powder into the stream, and I had sadly inspected the damaged contents of the satchel, when a voice suddenly hailed us from a short distance along the river bank.

'How lucky you are, my good gentlemen, that the tide is low, or else surely you would not have washed up before Greenwich!'

Our misfortune was evidently a source of amusement to the speaker—an ancient fellow in an eel boat, who was gathering in his nets beside a small dock—for he completed his observation with a loud chortle that must have carried across to the Battersea Fields on the other side of the Chelsea Reach. He was an ill-favoured old codger with only a single eye, which had itself been reduced to a squint; yet as he appeared set to put himself into the river I discerned an opportunity to find our way home: for quite soon after our introduction to the Ranelagh Stream we had abandoned the idea of Chiswick.

'Pray, sir,' I called to him, 'in which direction do you travel?'

'Chiswick,' he replied.

Jeremiah had quite reasonably been reluctant to entrust the pair of us to the custody of yet another stranger. However, as this fellow offered each of us a piece of his cheese, supplied us with flannel blankets with which to dry and then bundle ourselves, and even bid us sip from a goatskin flask, from which he treated himself with many noisy gulps (Jeremiah prudently declined this last hospitality that soon made my head reel one way, my stomach the other), the eel boat, and even the long ride to Chiswick, did not present an altogether unfavourable prospect. The disadvantage of this new form of transportation, we discovered, was that a good part of the old fellow's cargo reposed upon the tarry and seaweed-strewn boards at our feet. These creatures slithered, squirmed, worked their tiny gills and jaws, then expired and, finally, began to stink up our small craft. The journey did not end one minute too soon for Jeremiah, who scrambled off the boat one hour later, before it had quite arrived alongside the draw dock in Chiswick. I believe he never again partook of Mrs Sharp's eel pies with the same relish.

Our little boat had docked alongside that of a group of osier-cutters who had been labouring on a nearby eyot. They persuaded our companion to share with them in a pot of beer at the Burlington Arms, whereupon we bid him adieu and set out in search of Sir Endymion's house. The dock where we disembarked was, however, nearby the St Nicholas church, where, I happened to know, the dust of the great Mr Hogarth had been interred some five years earlier. Thus over Jeremiah's objections—his spirits had not recovered since I fished him out of the Thames—the two of us made the short pilgrimage to his grave, and as we shivered on the edge of the burial ground I read aloud Mr Garrick's inscription upon the stone monument. As I did so I detected a tremble in my voice—and it was not only from the cold: I was filled with sorrow at the knowledge that I should never encounter this great man in the flesh, for he meant to me every bit as much as Bishop Berkeley (apparently also deceased) meant to my friend Pinthorpe. Though it may sound impious, I confess that in those days the *Analysis of Beauty* was my bible.

Yet soon I was cheered by the prospect of encountering a living artist, one who was perhaps as esteemed as the gentleman interred at my feet.

'Come, Jeremiah,' I said. 'Let us find the house of Sir Endymion Starker.'

The house was not hard to find, being one of the largest of those overlooking the river: a handsome brick structure, three storeys in height, and with an ox-eye window and a green door shaded by a mulberry tree; the very sort of residence, I was relieved to see, to suit a gentleman of genius as celebrated as Sir Endymion Starker.

The door swung open with a sharp creak almost as soon as Jeremiah struck it with the oaken branch he had found in the churchyard and now employed both to sustain himself for the remainder of our journey and to defend us against highwaymen, should that unfortunate situation again arise. Yet his effort, forceful though it was, in truth was extrinsic to the result it apparently produced, for the door lurched open so immediately that poor Jeremiah very nearly applied his staff to the stern brow of a tall and formidable lady of middle years, who, in turn, very nearly knocked him over as she swept busily outside.

'Have you brought my carriage round?' she demanded of him.

'Lady Manresa,' came a voice from inside the dark hall, 'surely you do not intend to abscond just yet?'

'I intend to do the very same thing, for I have an engagement tonight,' she retorted, naming a fashionable peer at whose residence in Richmond she had been invited to dine. In the meantime she stretched a pair of silk gloves over her large hands and affixed to her head a straw bonnet embellished with two Prussian-blue ostrich plumes.

'Four sittings already!' she complained. 'Truly, Sir Endymion' (for indeed it was that gentleman—my erstwhile companion at whist—who now appeared in the doorway) 'I fear if you are any more dilatory in the accomplishment you will have to *add* wrinkles and *subtract* my teeth!'

'Lady Manresa,' responded Sir Endymion in a placating voice. It seemed that he noticed neither Jeremiah nor me. He was wearing a Spencer wig, and a lace cravat and ruffled holland shirt were visible beneath his grey smock, which was freckled with dried paint—vermilion and yellow lake, it appeared, and perhaps a few traces of asphaltum. He took one of the lady's gloved hands in his own.

'Lady Manresa,' he repeated, 'have no fear of that, whatever my progress, for I warrant this lovely cheek' (the paint-splotched back of his hand traced a tender circle upon this detail of her countenance, which at the touch turned the exact hue of the vermilion staining the knuckles) 'this lovely cheek will bloom and glow for many a year to come . . .'

'Oh, Sir Endymion!' exclaimed the lady, who for a few seconds seemed in considerably less haste to locate her carriage; but remembering the lord and her engagement with him in Richmond, she presently spun round and once again addressed Jeremiah in the same forthright tone.

'My carriage, I say!'

'One more hour, Lady Manresa,' said Sir Endymion in a voice that seemed to combine both the command and the supplication. 'That is all I ask, my lady. Thirty minutes.'

But the lady had spotted her carriage and, hoisting her skirts above the mud, and with the ostrich feathers flapping and quivering above her rich mound of hair like two fluttering standards raised atop a windswept promontory, she negotiated the series of ruts the street had become, then was ceremoniously handed inside by a servant dressed in red livery with epaulettes of gold brocade.

'Until next week,' she called through a window, from which, for the sake of the carriage's low ceiling, her feathers were required to project themselves.

'A most trying lady!' exclaimed Sir Endymion to himself in the doorway, punctuating his observation with what sounded like a sigh.

'George Cautley, sir, at your service,' I took the opportunity of saying when this indomitable creature had been towed away. I had removed my tricorne (still quite soggy) and now performed a low bow. 'I have come, sir, to discharge my debt,' I persevered, deepening my bow by several inches when its initial performance created no discernible effect.

Sir Endymion blinked at me, then at Jeremiah, as if seeing us for the first time.

'Of course,' he said. Now his handsome visage was perfectly expressionless, and not even our muddy clothes and my frizzled, powderless wig seemed to daunt him. 'Mr Cautley. Of course. The painter. Yes, yes. Good, good. I have been expecting your visit.' He returned my bow and opened the door to its fullest limit. 'Gentlemen! Do please come in.'

Twelve

'Now—yes, good—pull this over your head,' Sir Endymion was commanding a few moments later. 'Jeremiah will assist you with the stockings—yes, that's it. Excellent. Good lad. And the wig; yes, yes. Now . . . wherever is my lady's fan?'

As Sir Endymion searched the chamber for this accessory—we were in his studio, two floors above the river—Jeremiah unrolled a pair of white silk stockings over my calves, then proceeded to fasten them above the knee with a black garter. This accomplished, he released my hoop petticoat, which had been supported by his forearms; it bounced and swivelled as my mantua, likewise disengaged, tumbled about the dainty pair of white shoes into which my feet had quite mercilessly been squeezed. Then a lady's fashion wig, complete with feathers and ribbons, was placed upon my head, my own wig being removed and placed by the fire in an adjoining chamber to dry with my clothes.

'Perfect,' said Sir Endymion, who, having located the fan and handed it to Jeremiah, now returned to his easel. 'A perfect fit. I do declare—Lady Manresa herself.'

In the space of a few short hours, in less than a single day, I reflected, I had switched roles: I had moved from one side of the canvas to the other—that is, from portraitist to subject. Moreover, at Sir Endymion's behest, and to my chagrin, I had moved across that more inveterate divide and now breached the boundary which separates the sexes one from another. You may well suppose that it took not a few entreaties before I was persuaded to assume this unnatural guise, but Sir Endymion was at pains to explain that he had attained a vital point in the composition, the entirety of which Lady Manresa's abrupt departure for Richmond now had placed in jeopardy. Having told him that I, a fellow artist, could appreciate this pickle, there was nothing for me to do but to become the lady's substitute, to pose stiffly in her side-hooped petticoats and quilted sack, my head half-turned to the opened casement, my hands occupied by the fan, a string of pearls and a parasol.

Sir Endymion meanwhile hummed and daubed at his canvas, his precise gaze taking frequent account of me, or rather of my sack and feathered *tête*. His small, paddle-shaped palette was smeared with red lake, yellow ochre and ultramarine blue, which he deftly transferred with a brush to the canvas. I suppose I should have seized this golden chance to inspect the intimate secrets of a master at work; yet the truth was that my feet were causing me grave trouble, as was my stomach, constricted by a corset, and as was, most gravely troubled of all, my manly vanity and pride.

'Jeremiah!' I was moved to hiss at regular intervals. 'Perhaps you find something amusing in my situation?'

'No, Mr Cautley,' my servant would reply, his small shoulders quaking with mirth. Evidently his spirits had returned.

To cap it all, the sitting was constantly interrupted by the comings and goings of three or four boys—young gentlemen, rather, of perhaps my own years—who were employed by Sir Endymion and occupied themselves (besides sniggering at my petticoats) by cleaning his brushes, grinding his pigments, priming his canvases, painting the draperies of his half-finished portraits and in general performing whichever tasks their master saw fit to assign them.

Except for Sir Endymion, in whose eyes my task was no different from these others, the only person present who did not seem disposed to enjoy this great joke at my expense, either frankly or furtively, was Lady Starker, who made one or two brief appearances in the studio with cups of tea and a morose pug. How shall I describe Lady Starker? She put me in mind of those portraits by Giuseppe Arcimboldo, the Milanese painter whose subjects' physiognomies, upon closer inspection, prove to be vegetables or fruit. I hasten to say that none of this lady's features put me in mind of a carrot or a plum: for in her case it almost seemed that she had been painted by a divine artist whose living portrait, if one looked at it closely enough, was truly a willow tree in the early spring, gently and gracefully draping itself upon a riverside bank of flowers. Oh, exquisite being!

Yet Sir Endymion's studio was, excepting my hermaphrodite appearance, a gentleman's place, and after her introduction, and after she had dispensed the cups of tea, Lady Starker floated out of the chamber and down the stairs, not, alas, to be seen again on that afternoon.

As I posed I presently grew bold enough to raise the issue of my debt, which Sir Endymion had thus far not deigned to mention, and I was pleased to discover that he was not at all adamant in this respect. He replied that it could quite easily be discharged—to the benefit of each party.

'Perhaps I can find more tasks for you here,' he said as he painted my gown, 'and you would doubtless work off those few guineas in a short enough space of time. Better work, I promise you, than your present duties,' he added with a gentle smile. 'For not even the depredations of the rain and the river' (we had told him our story) 'have succeeded in effacing your talents, which I judge propitious.' He gestured with his palette in the direction of the next chamber, where the satchel and its wares were submitting themselves to the warmth of the fire. 'Think of your duties here,' he concluded, 'if you wish, as an apprenticeship.'

Nothing, I believe, could have been more welcome to my ears. To become an apprentice to Sir Endymion Starker! The catastrophes of the morning—the rain, the perfidy of Messrs Brownrigg and O'Leary, the perils of the stream, the stink of the eel boat—all melted away as if they had been nothing, mists burned away by a bright morning sun. This joyful news was not even spoiled a minute later when, from the corner of my eye, I caught one of the young fellows who was grinding pigments nudge his friend, stick out his tongue at me, then dissolve into giggles.

Finally, after what seemed like hours, Sir Endymion put aside his half-finished portrait of Lady Manresa, and I was at last permitted to attire myself in my breeches, which a maidservant had brushed and now presented to me. Though they were still a little damp, I had never felt so glad to don them.

After clothing myself in my more customary apparel, I lay aside the fashion wig, the parasol, the pearls, and last of all the fan, which, as I placed it on a small table, dropped on to the floor with a loud clatter. Silently cursing my clumsiness I plucked it up, only to discover that its clasp had come loose and, as it had unfolded, I was now staring at *The Rape of Ganymede.*

'Do not trouble yourself over the fan, Mr Cautley,' said Sir Endymion, who must have witnessed my shocked expression. He had removed his smock and replaced it with a handsome coat of snuff-coloured velvet. 'It does not belong to Lady Manresa, and if it is broken, well, 'tis no great matter.'

'It is an uncommonly striking fan,' I said, placing it more carefully upon the table with a hand whose tremble I fear was ill-concealed. 'Did you paint it yourself, sir?'

'Many years ago,' he said, shying his paint-flecked hand through the air and removing his smock. 'Any fan will do for the painting, any at all. I tell you, 'tis no great matter.'

'Oh—I very nearly forgot,' I said a few minutes later as Jeremiah and I prepared to quit the green door and begin our homeward journey. I drew from my fob-pocket the portrait that the young lady had tossed at my head. Though blotched, it had survived its dip in the river, and the face was still quite recognisable. Now, suddenly, it was Sir Endymion's turn to blanch.

'Where, pray, did you discover this?'

I explained I had paid a visit, as requested, to St Alban's Street, and that the fair creature represented in the water-colour had appeared in the window and instructed me to bring it with me to our engagement.

'She is a most trying lady,' he said in a low voice, drawing me towards the green door and quickly slipping the minia-ture into his pocket. 'Most trying indeed. I am sorry you had to meet her—so very sorry. Now, Mr Cautley,' he said in the same wellnigh inaudible tone, 'if you will come to my studio in St Alban's Street in three days' time, I shall present you with a proposition. This time, I promise, I shall be more punctual, and the proposition, I hope, will be well worth listening to.'

As we began our journey home we passed the Burlington Arms, outside which two osier-cutters were sharpening their blades upon a large whetstone. Inside the tavern two rush-lights burned brightly, and through the window I could see the head of our eel boat captain, which, like those of his table-mates, now sagged under the weight of the day's labours and the strength of a gaily shared potation. A few yards away the boat with its complement of eels still rocked gently at the draw dock, and the reaped osiers stood on the bank in pale shocks, like silently consulting ghosts.

Farther along the road we passed Mawson's Row, and I pointed out to Jeremiah the house which, many years ago, had been home to Mr Alexander Pope. Jeremiah had not heard of Mr Pope, much less 'Eloisa to Abelard', which (as I informed him) had been composed behind those handsome brick walls. And so in order to pass the time as we took ourselves home, and to steer Jeremiah's thoughts away from fears of highwaymen, I told him the story of those two famous and tragic lovers, Abélard and Héloïse: that is, how after secretly marrying Héloïse and giving her a son named Astrolabe, the great philosopher and teacher Abélard had been maimed in his generative parts by her angry father, Canon Fulbert of Notre Dame Cathedral in Paris.

'Yet the cruel subtraction of Abélard's manhood did not diminish the passion of the two lovers,' I explained, 'nor did the retirement of Héloïse to a convent, nor even did the death of poor Abélard on the road to Rome, where he had hoped to appeal to the pontiff against a charge of heresy made by Bernard of Clairvaux.'

I quoted for my young companion's benefit several of the more tender passages of Mr Pope's poem, including,

> *Even here, where frozen chastity retires,*
> *Love finds an altar for forbidden fires,*

and

> *I view my crime, but kindle at the view,*
> *Repent old pleasures, and solicit new,*

and finally,

> *O curst, dear horrors of all-conscious night!*
> *How glowing guilt exalts the keen delight!*
> *Provoking Daemons all restraint remove,*
> *And stir within me every source of love.*

Jeremiah was, I believe, much affected by these passages (though mention of the 'horrors' of the night once again put him on the alert for every shadow). When I had finished the story—we were now following the Great West Road in

102

Hammersmith, approaching the turnpike in North End Road—he inquired: 'I believe, Mr Cautley, that this Héloïse is a most noble lady. Pray, does she still live, sir?'

I laughed and told him that the events I had described occurred more than six hundred years ago. 'For you must understand, Jeremiah,' I explained, 'such terrible things do not happen now, in our age and time.'

Thirteen

 Besides being the custom of Signor Piozzi's students to serve the Masses in city churches, it was also their practice to appear together in the choirs of the city's theatres. The pyramid of candles at the high altar, the martyred saints peering down from frescoed ceilings, the angels poised gracefully on the reredos above a quiet and humble congregation—these holy precincts gave way on such occasions to cavernous rooms with crimson arabesques, taffeta curtains, festoons of gilt flowers, sweeping marble balustrades, dozens of wax torches flickering on golden sconces high on the wall. And the tranquil congregation became a noisome mob, flapping and squawking in great terraced galleries and tiers of plush-velvet boxes: a flock of raucous crows tricked out in frost-white wigs, loops of silver, huge bustles, waistcoats of lemon or mother-of-pearl silk, which suggested the origins of some of the more conspicuous items in Il Piozzino's *armoire*.

Il Piozzino himself was, of course, the primary attraction on these occasions, the recipient after each performance of applause, flowers, *billets-doux*. He was the recipient as well of the competitive attentions of the ladies who admitted themselves to quarters behind the stage—countesses, duchesses, ladies with equine faces, ladies whose significance was proclaimed by their arrival in open chaises shaped like dolphins or scallop shells, their side-panels inscribed with the insignia of ancient families. They presented him with embraces and kisses; or sometimes, more materially, with gold coins, gilt pouncet-boxes, bottles of scent with cut-glass stoppers; and sometimes even, more unusually, with peacocks, foxes, caged doves, once even a small leopard on a gold chain. Lord knows what became of these creatures; perhaps they were scornfully returned—or perhaps they were claimed by Scipio's passion for natural philosophy and ended their lives beneath his scalpel or between the jaws of the monster in the airing cupboard.

These ladies, of course, witnessed nothing of Il Piozzino's darker side. His quarters behind the stage were a merry place, free from the sinister tastes indulged hugger-mugger within the walls of the *conservatorio*. Here cool waters made with fruit and wine were served until late into the night or, rather, until early in the morning, or sometimes indeed until late into the morning, for Scipio's performances on the stage generally commenced, as was the custom, at eleven o'clock, not concluding until three or four hours later. Here games of *trente-et-quarante* were hosted at velvet-topped card-tables, and here the devil's bones rattled and tumbled in the hands of his pretty little accomplices: ladies in mantuas sprinkled with eau-de-Cologne; ladies in masks, low *décollet-age*, ballooning skirts; ladies who resembled great ruffled bells, their silk legs the dainty clappers. They were borne to the Teatro San Bartolomeo from white palaces high in the hills, or else, so it was rumoured, made the considerably shorter journey from some of the neighbouring bordellos. Here the finest ladies in Naples jostled with the most degenerate harlots, each hoping to be the one most favoured with Il Piozzino's conversation and, later, in another nearby chamber, smaller and wainscoted and featuring a four-post bed, his quieter and more intimate regards.

One day, however, a singularly vigorous engrossment in these pleasures demanded Scipio's confinement in his dark-ened chamber. On this bleak morning even Giulia was excluded, ordered neither to scrub and clean nor to perform her more stealthy offices, which had, of late, been much less in demand in any case. Hence, at Signor Piozzi's command, Concetto abruptly exchanged his position among the choir in the gallery for a jewelled crown, a purple cloak trimmed with ermine, and prominent place on stage before a paste-board sea. Which opera was this? At last: one of Signor Piozzi's long-neglected eleven! With the smallest amount of plagiarism and historical inaccuracy this work, *Oeneus*, told the story of a beautiful Lydian princess and her lover, Oeneus, King of Calydon.

The role of the princess was, alas, a most inauspicious début for poor Concetto. As he minced on stage the audience rustled its brilliant plumage at the unaccustomed sight of the new soprano, then most of the boxes were shuttered with loud claps as their inhabitants reverted to draughtboards, cups of wine, leonine yawns. Yet by the middle of the first scene, as Concetto fluttered his cloak and pined sadly for Oeneus, who was lost beyond the pasteboard sea, these crows tucked away their draughtsmen, swung open their shutters, roused themselves from their indifference: for it was obvious from the start that Concetto's singing was all wrong, completely unworthy of Il Piozzino. The corset he was compelled to wear compressed his round little stomach (on his better diet and exemption from menial tasks he had become a plump boy and could not easily pass for a lady, let alone the dainty princess called for by the libretto), and so the expended notes died with a hoarse whisper before serving their proper time in his throat or on his carmined lips. His shoes, too, incommoded his performance; he wobbled on the heels and jerked like a puppet whenever obliged to take a step, thus raising the comical possibility that the princess had resorted to tippling in the absence of her lover.

All of this soon became too much for the audience to resist. On the malicious inspiration of two or three patrons—those among Il Piozzino's most competitive admirers—the desultory attentions of the flock turned to hisses and outbursts of laughter. This commotion spread swiftly from the galleries to the boxes, then to the masked ladies in the front rows, at which point several silk-bound librettos flapped on to the stage like dying sea-gulls.

—*Dentro, dentro!*

More whistles, more laughter; a moulting flock of librettos, some fluttering all the way from the gallery.

—Off the stage! Off the stage!

By now Concetto had reached the middle of a particularly difficult coloratura aria it was Il Piozzino's distinction to execute with flawless ease. He had also reached the middle of a precarious wooden construction intended to represent the deck of a ship progressing across the seas in search of the Calydonian king (who was at the moment, in fact, peering out from the safety of the coulisses, nervous and alarmed).

This tempest aria was Signor Piozzi's intended masterpiece, to be sung with great passion while the ship (its rope-lines tugged by stage-hands concealed in the wings) rocked from side to side, narrowly avoiding the rocks off the rough coast of Lydia, painted on to a backcloth:

> *Un' aura soave crudel gli diventa,*
> *e in porto paventa di franger la nave . . .*

The gentle breeze, that is, *turns into a gale and threatens to destroy the vessel*. Or something like that.

Concetto's voice faltered first, then his heels. The tempest had become too violent, as if Concetto's incompetence had somehow spread to the stage-hands tugging their rope-lines, and now the ship began to bucket and toss uncontrollably on its sea of painted waves. Concetto lurched across the *faux* deck—three stuttering steps—then toppled overboard. His purple robe flapped over his head just in time to protect it from the blow of a libretto cast down from one of the boxes beneath the proscenium arch, but the impact succeeded in removing his crown, which rolled into the orchestra pit.

The audience roared. The orchestra fell silent. Trumpets froze before still-puckered lips; violin bows poised motionless over hunched shoulders. One of the violinists finally broke rank, timidly retrieving the crown and tossing it back on to the stage as if it were an unexploded petard. The theatre's manager leapt to his feet in the front row and madly windmilled his arms.

—Stop this! Play on, play on! Stop this, I say!

Concetto's patron, the duke, a thin scarecrow of a man with the beard of a goat, made similar appeals from his box, shaking a malacca cane in one hand and a silver-hilted sword in the other. But such supporters were in the minority, and no one paid them any mind, though Concetto, at the joint urging of the impresario and the *primo uomo* (still fretting in the wings), gamely hoisted himself from his knees. Alas, it was a most ungraceful attempt: a cow, heavy with calf, responding to the nudge of a milkmaid's toe.

The gallops of laughter were renewed at the spectacle of so ungraceful a princess. In the torchlight Concetto's pink eyes had grown as wide and frightened as those of the dead Giuntoli, and beneath a thick crust of paint his face was

dazed and grinning sickly, as if his mouth as well as the ship
was being manipulated by the antic jerks of the incompetent
stage-hands. He hastily retrieved his crown, clapped it on
to his wigged head—the wig by now sat lopsidedly over his
brow—then gathered his cloak about himself with an air of
downtrodden authority.

—Please, he commanded in a ridiculously polite tone, but
his persecutors declined to relent.

—*Dentro, dentro!*

The patrons in the first rows had now begun stamping
their feet and making horns at him with their candles. The
orchestra haltingly struck up, ceased, struck up again even
more haltingly; the violins mewling, the horns groaning like
sick calves. After a second, Concetto's mouth struggled
open—a trout gulping at an invisible hook, the vanished
aria that had been flicked effortlessly beyond his reach.
When no sound emerged from these contortions he fell back
into the pasteboard waves, his crown tumbling again into
the dissonantly braying pit.

—A catastrophe! screamed the manager. A catastrophe!
For God's sake, get him off the stage! Off, off, *off*!

A day later Il Piozzino resumed the stage and plans were
hatched for the disgraced Concetto to be removed to Bologna; an apprentice still, he would ply his trade in churches
and theatres, in competition with other singers whose
careers had reached similar passes. But he never arrived in
Bologna, this place of failure and exile, for on the evening
before his departure he leapt to his death from the organ
gallery in one of the *conservatorio* music-rooms. He was
buried three days later in the preserve of beggars and
unchristened bastards, a broom-overgrown patch of unequal
ground in the lumpy hills a league from the Appian road.
The duke, who did not attend the funeral, none the less
paid ten soldi for Masses to be sung and then, with another
contribution, for repetitions on the seventh and thirtieth
days thereafter.

A day after this latter occasion, Il Piozzino again fell ill.
By this time Signor Piozzi had begun instructing Tristano in
the difficult acrobatics of the tempest aria, and in the art
of the Lydian princess's role more generally. For, as he had
recognised some time ago, Tristano's soprano and vocal
technique, his larynx and his lungs, were superior to any
other pupil's—excepting (of course) those of Il Piozzino. So

it was that Tristano now found himself exempted from keeping the dishes and the courtyard clean, and at liberty to practise in the inner sanctum of the Black Frocks. And when Il Piozzino fell ill—an innocent ague, that was all, but one that kept him indisposed for the better part of a week—Tristano was hastily stitched into the quilted petticoats and purple robe.

Yet if Il Piozzino hoped that this latest understudy would repeat Concetto's performance he was sorely disappointed. Tristano stepped on to the rocking wooden ship and presented a Lydian princess whose golden throat caused a stir of a very different sort. To be sure, he was an ugly little fellow—not even the powder and paint could quite disguise that. But, oh, his voice! Or *her* voice? For it was so difficult to tell ... but no, no: surely no lady's voice could be as beautiful as this one—this stream of golden silk that unravelled and then soared, up, up, to the galleries, borne aloft like an eagle floating upon thermals rising above plunging cliffs ...

And so Signor Piozzi's new Lydian princess soon caused the world—by which I mean the royal courts in Dresden, Vienna and Moscow, the churches in Florence and Rome, and the theatres in Naples, Venice and, of course, in London—to forget all others.

Fourteen

 Lady Beauclair was standing in the same posture, and in the same gown, as three nights previously. Now, however, rather than ignoring me, as she had done before, she fixed me with a concerned gaze as she spoke.

'If you will forgive my saying so, Mr Cautley,' she said, interrupting her story, 'tonight it seems to me your face is very pale, as if perhaps you are suffering from some malady. Are you certain that—'

'Yes, my lady, of course I am quite well.' Now it was my turn to show my impatience, for she had inquired after my health twice already: first upon my arrival, and then as we sat to our meal—partridges in prune sauce, hog's pudding, oyster loaves, green-pea soup, turnips, strawberry fritters, and pickled mangoes from India—which, I must confess, I hardly touched. 'Thank you kindly for asking,' I added, a little more graciously.

If the truth be known, however, I *was* feeling quite poorly, and my first sight of the roasted partridges, and then the behaviour of their prune sauce inside my belly, had very nearly set me dashing to my lady's fireplace, heaving and retching; only two or three sips of elderflower wine had managed to revive me at the last second. This lamentable condition was not occasioned by my expedition to Chiswick two days before, as one might have expected; it was the result of a visit I had paid with Toppie to Pancras Wells on the previous evening. This establishment, one of those places that Nature created as a resource from distemper and disquiet, had, far from serving its salubrious purposes, succeeded instead in making a perfect wreck of my constitution.

Yesterday morning I had awakened—feeling much refreshed after the toilsome journey—to discover that Thomas had left a card requesting my presence upon these fashionable premises that evening at eight o'clock; Toppie, as usual, would bear the expense of coach-hire, but I could expect to assume the admission charge of one guinea. My high spirits at the prospect of an evening's entertainment were soon brought low, however, since as I lit a fire for my breakfast it was reported to me by Miss Hetty that Jeremiah had taken ill in the night and now was faring poorly. This account of my footman I confirmed a moment later when I paid him a visit in the chamber he shared with three brothers. I found him to be in a very miserable condition indeed—sneezing, shaking, coughing, shivering, his face the colour of a parsnip, his eyes glossy and spherical, his teeth chattering and clicking with even more violence than the day before. Mr Langley, the apothecary, had been to call already, and the lad had since been induced to swallow various potions and apply foul-smelling poultices to his neck, chest and brow. Earlier he had been flopping and thrashing in his bed, but now, perhaps as a result of these nostrums, he lay peaceful and still.

'The poor child was in the most frightful state,' said Mrs

Sharp, who was sitting beside his bed, 'raving about mur-
therers and giant eels.'

'Doubtless 'tis the fever,' I surmised, creasing my brow.
For we had neglected to tell Mr and Mrs Sharp many details
of our expedition.

I made haste to my chamber and returned with a flask of
mineral water, with whose beneficial properties I hoped to
complement, or perhaps counteract, Mr Langley's malodorous poultices and potions. This water had been pumped
from the Well at Hampstead, and I had purchased two
bottles at the Piazza Coffee-house three nights before.
According to its label, as well as the testimony of the gentleman who sold it to me at a price of threepence a pint, it
possessed the most effective curative powers, being 'highly
successful', as the label stated, 'in curing the most Obstinate
Scurvy, Leprosy, and all other breakings out & defilements
of the Skin, including Running Sores, Eating Ulcers, & the
Piles; also Scrofula, Dropsy, the King's Evil, Surfeits, Gout,
any Corruption of the Blood & Juices, the Rheumatism &
all Inflammatory Distempers, most Disorders of the Eyes,
Pains in the Stomach & Bowels, Indigestion, Diarrhoea, loss
of Appetite & Sinking of the Spirits & Vapours, the most
violent Colds, Worms of all Kinds, the Stone & Gravel, the
Stranguary, or total suppression of Urine; in Young or Old,
and in either Sex'.

Mrs Sharp had been sceptical about this remedy, being
prey to vulgar prejudices and lamentably old-fashioned and
unenlightened where the science of physick was concerned;
but when I dribbled this general and sovereign aid to Nature
down Jeremiah's throat it seemed to take its effect soon
enough, and his complexion rapidly lost something of its
parsnip hue, which was displaced by a rosier blush that did
much to cheer his anxious mother. Still, throughout the day
his condition caused me considerable worry, and I offered
up several fervent prayers on his behalf; I also resolved to
purchase more flasks of this panacea, especially since I knew
that an elixir with similar properties would be available that
night at the Pancras Wells.

Thus my thoughts were still very much upon poor Jeremiah when, at eight o'clock in the evening, Toppie and I
bounced and shook and creaked up the coach road towards
Hampstead and turned on to the narrow coachway leading
to the Wells. Situated close to the St Pancras Church, which

110

was joined to them by a diagonal footway, these wells were a short coach-ride from London, occupying several pleasant acres in the open countryside. We disembarked from our hackney-coach before a collection of three buildings of undistinguished appearance cobbled together at various angles to each other and surrounded by plantations of trees, parterres of flowers, and shaded footpaths. From the central building, the House of Entertainment, I could detect the babble of voices and, below them, the mournful lowing of a bass viol.

'Ah! Lady Sacharissa! My dear!'

I had been in the midst of relating to Toppie my strange experiences of the day before and their auspicious conclusion at the house of Sir Endymion Starker, but as I did so I sensed that my friend's attention was engaged elsewhere—to wit, upon Lady Sacharissa, whom he had arranged to meet, and whom he now approached, executing a low bow and doffing his hat, my story utterly forgotten.

'Allow me to say I am delighted to see you looking so fine tonight, my lady.'

'You are very kind, Lord Chudleigh.'

Lady Sacharissa was in the company of not only Mrs Redwine, a guardian of the most saturnine countenance, but also a young lady who was introduced as Miss Arabella Longpré, a cousin visiting Lady Sacharissa from a place vaguely denominated as 'the country'.

As the evening was mild and the lugubrious groans of the bass viol prevailed, we decided to take a turn through the gardens, which already hosted a dozen or more strolling couples. Since Toppie had drawn Lady Sacharissa aside at the first opportunity and now steered her off in the direction of a new plantation of lime trees, I found myself under the obligation of entertaining Miss Longpré and her gloomy guardian, who hovered close upon our heels. Miss Longpré I soon discovered to be a charming companion, who, unlike Toppie, listened most attentively as I described my affiliation with the renowned Sir Endymion Starker. Into my conversation I casually dropped references as well to 'my footman' and to Lady Beauclair, 'who perhaps you know is the kinswoman of Lord W—?'

'I have not heard of him, sir,' replied Miss Longpré in her sweet voice. 'You must forgive me, for I am from the country and know very little of society.'

'In any case,' I continued, made bold enough by this confession to grasp her elbow as we walked, 'I am in the process of executing her portrait, for which I am being paid a pretty sum. I believe it will hang in Lord W—'s gallery—that is, in his house in St James's Square. Perhaps, Miss Longpré, you have visited this house?'

'Regrettably, no.'

'A most beautiful house,' I continued, describing the drum that had been held there, as well as the various guests in attendance, the names of many of whom moved my companion to small cries of wonder.

These 'oohs' and 'ahs', some of which had been reserved for my own alliances and accomplishments, soon induced in me such confidence that, as the five of us entered the Pump Room to partake of refreshments, I began to perform some of the silly coquetries I had practised in the window of the cheesemonger's shop. That is, I displayed my snuff-box to Miss Longpré's frequent view; twirled my walking-stick in my fingers and pointed it unnecessarily at objects or persons of interest or contempt; affected dainty sneezes that I might extract my perfumed handkerchief and flutter it in the air; and carelessly pendulated my watch on its fob (for this object I had found, *pace* Pinthorpe, beneath my wainscot table)—all the while preening and posing and lisping like the most incorrigible pretty fellow ever seen on display. If Miss Longpré seemed suitably impressed by this repertoire, Mrs Redwine clearly was not, interposing herself between the two of us when my grasp on her charge's elbow intensified and my hand then elevated to the middle of her back or descended to her dainty waist. I made several other such essays in between ferrying my companion cups of tea, punch, and hot water from the pump, but Mrs Redwine was, alas, most officious in her duties and nipped all attempts in the bud.

'Perhaps later we shall dance a minuet,' I whispered to Miss Longpré after Mrs Redwine had parted the two of us with a strength and vigour that belied her considerable years.

'I fear I have never danced before,' lamented Miss Longpré, 'excepting the morris dance.'

This confession pained me very much, and I was most grateful it had not been overheard by any of the other young ladies or gentlemen loitering about us, all of whom I

112

believed had been somewhat jealously admiring my fashionable deportment and cocking their heads whenever (in a voice somewhat louder than was truly required) I uttered the names of Sir Endymion Starker and Lord W—. The morris dance indeed! A sudden image of Miss Longpré hopping about upon a village green, attired in ribbons and bells, greatly distressed me. Why this rustication should have troubled me so deeply I did not know, for not so very long ago I had been dreaming fondly of Jenny Barton, the tallow-chandler's daughter who each year frolicked round the maypole erected upon Buckling Common; but it did none the less, and now I began to see my companion in a new and less favourable light. I realised, upon more critical inspection, that, though fair of brow, Miss Longpré perhaps lacked the elegance and sophistication of many of her contemporaries on parade tonight. No beauty-patches and only a minimum of paint adorned her face, which, though of a pleasing enough shape, suffered with a slightly defective complexion that surely would have been improved by such measures. I noticed as well that, to her further discredit, her eyebrows were not only rather more abundant in themselves than I would have preferred but they also very nearly encountered one another in the delta above her nose. Furthermore, her hair, while of an admirable chestnut hue, was timorously confined beneath a lace cape rather than displayed to its best advantage, to wit, stuffed with wool, stacked upon pads, slicked with pomatum and twisted into the serpentine curls that dangled so appealingly upon the shoulders of, for example, Lady Sacharissa or Lady Beauclair.

I recalled now what Toppie had said about this 'Age of Disguise', about how one day I would thank my lady for her patches and paint. All at once I was disappointed and then, more forcefully, irritated that Miss Longpré had not made more of an effort to flatter my vanity. Perhaps in her opinion I was not worthy of the effort? With much gravity I tucked away my watch and snuff-box, and my cane ceased its oscillations.

'Mr Cautley, I wonder if I could trouble you for another cup of tea?' Miss Longpré now inquired, after providing a description, which I scarcely heeded, of how she had sewed her morris costume with her own needle.

I stalked to the tea-booth, pondering how I might extricate myself from Miss Longpré's company and instead impress some of these other, more refined, young ladies. I soon caught the eye of a young beauty (who had applied one heart-shaped patch to her chin, another to her neck) and contrived to flaunt my snuff-box and dangle my cane for her pleasure. However, this peacockery was abruptly interrupted when I bumped into Sir James Clutterbuck—quite literally, that is—and caused him to spill punch down the scalloped ruffles of his shirt.

'You clown!' this gentleman snarled, reaching for his handkerchief. 'Oh—it's you.' His expression softened somewhat, though the pronoun, which he had peculiarly emphasised, suggested sniffy recognition more than congenial familiarity. 'Ah, Mr . . . Mr George, was it? An acquaintance of Lord Chudleigh's, I recall.'

The young beauty who had been the intended beneficiary of my conceits had turned away, and now I saw Toppie and Lady Sacharissa watching my exchange with Sir James from beneath a fir tree planted in a tub. Lady Sacharissa was attempting, unsuccessfully, to stifle a titter—oh, how that cut me!—while Toppie's face remained perfectly and unnaturally expressionless.

'No harm done, no harm done,' said Sir James as I stuttered my apologies and fumbled at his breast with my own handkerchief. 'Do not concern yourself. That your lady over there? Very comely, Mr George. You must introduce us.'

I returned to Miss Longpré with her cup of tea, thinking how the accident had been her fault, really, and how I had no wish at all to introduce her, a morris dancer from the country—one who sewed her own costumes—to a haughty fellow such as Sir James Clutterbuck. I made no further assaults either upon her back or her waist, and I pretended not to hear when she requested the privilege of inspecting the pretty lapis-lazuli panels of my snuff-box.

'That clumsy fellow,' she said uncertainly several moments later, trying to break my malicious silence, 'he should have seen you coming . . .'

Sullenly, I made no reply.

Presently we were in the company again of Toppie and Lady Sacharissa, who now expressed a wish to enter the House of Entertainment for some minuets. They had been joined, I was dismayed to see, by Sir James, who I noticed had successfully removed the splotches of punch from his ruffles. I consented to their plan, but as they entered the

114

hall I lingered behind, beside a mass of auriculas growing in terracotta pots, then quite intentionally lost myself in the crowd. When my companions had been swallowed up by this many-headed monster, I slipped back inside the Pump Room and crossed to a refreshment booth. I purchased a cup of wine, then rather gloomily surveyed the hall, hoping to espy the young beauty whose attention had been drawn to the flourishes of my snuff-box and cane, which I now prepared for further service. Alas, I soon saw that she was maintaining a whispered conversation with two hard-favoured fellows whose choice in drink inclined them towards the less wholesome offerings of the stalls. This conference was punctuated liberally with titters, and occasional glances in my direction led me to wonder if I had somehow excited whispers, and if a rumour was now circulating to my prejudice. Perhaps, I thought (quite appalled by the possibility)—perhaps my reputation was suffering from my earlier alliance with that bumpkin, Miss Longpré, whose rustication everyone must surely have remarked upon?

I soon lost sight of this trio when the eddies of the crowd forced me against a wall, from which post I continued my sullen watch. Yet I could not help noticing that, to Miss Longpré's small advantage, some revellers among the company, especially certain of the ladies, could hardly be mistaken for persons of the best sort, if their clothing and manners were to be allowed as evidence against them. I recalled Toppie's complaint, made during our coach-ride, that in such places 'the more genteel people are too often swallowed up by a mob of impudent plebeians from the purlieus of Butcher Row, Blackfriars, and Botolph Lane'. It did indeed appear that in the press of the crowd a promiscuous mingling was underway, and the guests mixed in this monstrous jumble without regard to either rank or fortune. Individuals whose robust visages suggested that they lived by the labour of some toilsome trade jostled elbows with the most notable Persons of Quality—sons and daughters of dukes and marquesses and wealthy knights and baronets— whom it had been my great pleasure, a few minutes before, to point out for the benefit of Miss Longpré. To my left a well-dressed gentleman in a silk bag-wig was conversing with a young lady whose insolent expression and forward manner recalled the ladies in the scarlet petticoats and suggested that she, like them, had long since been lost to shame.

Behind her a fellow attired hardly any more formally or immaculately than a chimney-sweep appeared to have gained the favour of a fair creature whose apparel advertised all the best that the world of New Bond Street had to offer. The details of their conversation—conducted with a few furtively swift caresses—taxed my imagination most severely.

A more homogeneous group had gathered at the gaming-tables, each of which was occupied by rapt players, who were snapping their cards and clicking ivory draughtsmen upon the boards. This scenario cheered me, since suddenly I remembered how, under similar circumstances, Sir Endymion and his companions had sympathised with me after my previous disappointment with the capricious sex. Reflecting that the loss of those five guineas had perhaps been the best fortune that had ever befallen me, I decided to celebrate this cheerful thought with another cup of wine. Beyond the wine-booth, however, I noticed a fellow selling flasks of spa water, and this reminded me of my obligation to poor Jeremiah.

I made directly for the stall, but on the way encountered a small group of young gentlemen gathered round another booth, from which spirits of a somewhat less salubrious quality were being dispensed. From their expressions I guessed that these fellows had seen my coquetries and overheard my references to Sir Endymion and so fancied me a very toplofty fellow, 'too good to drink with the likes of us', as I distinctly heard one of them say. I hesitated for a moment as I stood in their midst, then purchased a mug of Ringwood beer and proposed a drink to the King's health.

This strategy won them to my side, at which point a good many more bumpers were drunk: I believe we celebrated the health of most members of the Royal Family at least once. It was only after these displays of patriotism began repeating themselves for a third time, and only after quite a succession of mugs of Ringwood had been drained and replenished, that I recalled my mission at the water-stall. However, these fellows convinced me to tarry longer by their booth and sample two other varieties of table-beer, Dorchester and Marlborough, in order to settle a dispute that had grown up among them as to which of the three was truly the most refreshing. I officiated in this dispute as best I could, eventually naming Ringwood as my champion, though in truth my palate was quite numb by this point, to the detriment of my speech as well as my taste. Soon another contender, Calvert's, presented itself, but after a methodical sampling, during which not a few drops of this new competitor were splashed down the front of my waistcoat, I staunchly reaffirmed my claims for the butt of Ringwood. My new friends were satisfied by my decision and kindly repaid my services by purchasing me a parting cup. After I finished it, I shook their hands and, I fear, stumbled most ungracefully in the direction of the water-stall, only to discover the vendor had closed up shop.

'There will be pump-water for sale in the House of Entertainment,' said one of my new friends, noticing my plight. 'Come, George, one more drink—here, my good fellow, try some of this excellent porter—and we shall all of us step inside.'

I must have made my appearance in the House of Entertainment at some point, for I still have a very vivid impression in my head of Sir James Clutterbuck kissing Miss Longpré upon the cheek in the middle of the dance-floor while she offered me a reproachful smile. If in that second Miss Longpré was not the most beautiful creature I had ever seen, then I was blind as Mr Knatchbull. Yet I recall nothing else of the House of Entertainment, and certainly I found no water. Perhaps the spectacle on the dance-floor sent me in search of a stronger concoction than spa water, for I awakened some hours later upon the footway that traversed the fields behind the gardens and led the way into Gray's Inn Lane.

By now the House of Entertainment was dark and silent, the gardens and coachway empty. The assembly had obviously dispersed hours ago, and as they took themselves home, I realised in horror, many of the revellers—half of London society—must have stepped over my prostrate body as I lay snorting and drooling in the dust. Oh, how they must have chuckled and pointed if they recognised me as the pretty fellow with the snuff-box and fob-watch! I scarcely dared imagine what a terrible blow I had struck against my reputation. Perhaps Toppie and Sir James had been witnesses? Perhaps Lady Sacharissa had sniggered behind her delicate white hand while Miss Longpré fixed me with another reproachful smile . . .

With a few groans I attained my feet, upon which I swayed

117

unsteadily for a few minutes before essaying a few experimental steps. Then I started up the path to the coachway, still wavering as if perched in the middle of an eel boat rocking gently in a high tide. A tide of Ringwood and Calvert's, I thought grimly. Oh, what a fool I was to drink so much! The most modest calculation, performed the following morning, put eleven pints of beer under my belt, not to mention untold cups of wine. 'Through thy lips, George,' I could hear my abstemious father intoning from beyond his grave, 'thou hast provided entry for an enemy who has snatched away thy brain!'

By now the contents of my belly had begun to seethe and mill like the goat's milk in my mother's churn, and I promptly disburdened myself into a small hedge of hawthorn. This resort made me feel slightly better, but then when I stood erect again the sight of the moon—white and fat, hanging low over Highgate—hurt my eyes something rotten. Once awakened, this sharp pain radiated outwards in a series of dull pulses until it encompassed both hemispheres of my poor skull. Only when I clutched my brow in mournful sympathy with this ache did I realise that my wig was gone, and only after bemoaning this loss—for truly it was gone, not to be found, as I briefly allowed myself to hope, lying behind me in the dirt—did I realise that my coat had also disappeared, as had my purse, my fob-watch, my snuff-box, my cane and even my gold-buckled shoes.

I had been robbed, I realised, sinking back down in the dirt. Robbed! The realisation was appalling. I had frustrated the malicious designs of Brownrigg and O'Leary a day before only to be waylaid at Pancras Wells, in the midst of some of the nation's most esteemed citizens and finest Persons of Quality. Surely, I thought—surely some notorious fellows are indeed afoot at these places!

For several minutes I wept noisily into my fists, then once again emptied my churning belly into the hedge with a few more gags and plashes. Finally, after drying my effeminate tears with a few last juddering sobs and relieving myself into the branches of a young juniper, I trudged to the coachway, still somewhat unsteady on my feet (one of whose stockings, I now noticed with further dismay, had been breached in several places by my toe-nail). For reasons of safety I had decided to return to my lodgings along the coach road rather than the footway, but now as I set out,

118

the stones hurting my feet, I realised I possessed nothing of value, and so a highwayman could truly hold no fears. This was, you may imagine, a most ambiguous comfort.

I had crossed through Battle Bridge and entered Constitution Row, from which I could see, on my left, the brickfields with their ash house and enormous dust heaps, and before me the distant pyramidal rooftop of the Foundling Hospital, when I was overtaken by a phaeton drawn by two white horses. This vehicle, which had been travelling at an unrestrained pace, slowed when it drew even with me, then jolted to a stop at the command of one of its passengers. A face now peered at me through the window.

'It appears, young sir,' said the gentleman, whose countenance looked familiar as he appraised my sorry condition, 'it appears that you have suffered some misfortune.'

'I have been set upon and robbed,' I explained in a voice that made no effort to conceal my distress. I deemed it wise to abstain from the full truth, though no doubt this fellow could smell the stale fumes of Ringwood upon me, and I fear my waistcoat, though mercifully spared the predacity of the thieves, now bore evidence of my late regurgitations. 'My wig has been snitched,' I continued, 'as have my watch, my purse, my cane . . .' In the midst of this catalogue I very nearly began to blub again.

The gentleman shook his head in sympathy, at which point another face appeared alongside: another gentleman who also looked strangely familiar. Yet this second gentleman, upon seeing me, swiftly retracted his head and commanded the driver to resume his pace.

'Robert,' protested the first fellow, 'we must take pity upon the young gentleman. Pity, as Monsieur Rousseau tells us, is the first human passion, that blessed quality upon which all human civilisation reposes. The mirror by which, in the face of another, we recognise our own.'

This treatise appeared to fall upon deaf ears, for Robert repeated his command to the driver, this time pronouncing it with considerably more urgency and insinuating that I was a wastrel or a footpad. 'Robert', I remembered with a start, was the very name of the impudent scoundrel who had cudgelled me in Marybone Street. I was in the midst of trying to confirm that this was indeed the same fellow when I realised that the other gentleman was Mr Larkins, one of my companions at the card-table. He now contradicted

119

Robert's injunction to the driver, who respected this greater authority.

'Please,' Mr Larkins said to me with a kindly smile, 'will you accept a ride from two strangers? I believe your sorry condition would excite sympathy in any human breast. You must forgive Robert' (who displayed no signs of any such arousal in his own bosom as I squeezed inside; rather, he shrank against the far door and averted his face) 'for we have been at Hampstead Wells and he is most anxious to repair to his lodgings.'

'You, sir, are no stranger to me,' I said as I settled myself on to a cushion beside Mr Larkins and the crowded phaeton resumed its hasty pace, 'for we have been companions at whist, Mr Larkins.'

Mr Larkins expressed his pleasure at having encountered me once again, 'even if it is under such lamentable circumstances', and then the two of us chatted quite pleasantly—I told him how I had entered the employment of Sir Endymion—until our vehicle arrived at the bottom of the Haymarket.

'We shall leave you at this point,' said Mr Larkins, 'for we have some distance yet to travel.'

When I expressed my gratitude, the good gentleman merely shied his gloved hand through the window in a brief white arc.

'No man, I believe, could have done otherwise,' he replied. 'Sympathy—'tis what separates us from the beasts of the field.'

Robert had, however, remained curiously unmoved throughout this journey. He said not a word as we progressed first down Gray's Inn Lane and then High Holborn and St Martin's Lane, though I had the impression that he and Mr Larkins occasionally communicated with each other through a series of sharp prods and nudges that bespoke some degree of mysterious conflict. Robert, moreover, kept his face, which was partially shielded either by his tricorne (rather foppishly trimmed with gold *point d'Espagne*) or his hand (gloved in a kid leather so white it fairly glowed), turned to his window. It was almost as if he hoped to frustrate my attempts—ultimately, as a result, unsuccessful—to place him. I was offended by this lack of *politesse*, which duplicated his previous conduct and which I found equally provoking; but on account of Mr Larkins's

120

hospitality I said nothing about it. Only when I limped down the Haymarket, whose flags had been scattered with straw and were therefore somewhat softer on my feet, did I begin to contemplate who he was. Perhaps it had been Mr Brownrigg, I considered, or Mr O'Leary—for after tonight I was quite prepared to believe that a rogue might well dress himself in silk and travel to Hampstead Wells in the company of a true gentleman.

'I am perfectly recovered,' I was now informing Lady Beauclair, 'but my footman, I regret to say, has contracted a most violent cold, on account of which, you see, I have been most concerned.'

'I am very sorry to hear of it.'

So interested was Lady Beauclair in the details of my health, and so solicitous was she about my new wig (which had been purchased on credit that morning from Mr Sharp and fitted my aching skull very poorly), that I almost began to wonder if somehow she had learned of my disgraceful performance at Pancras Wells. Surely there was now some tattle buzzing about the town at my expense? Perhaps she had been apprised by one of her acquaintances or, worse still, had been—God forbid!—in attendance herself. I felt my face turn red at the thought, though this blush, mistaken for a bloom of health, apparently convinced my lady that my condition was not perilous; and so, resuming her posture, she recommenced her story.

'Where was I? Ah, yes. After Tristano's first performance, and after those at the Royal Chapel and the Teatro delle Dame, there was no question of it being done: of his credentials being confirmed . . .'

Fifteen

 Still, Signor Piozzi had waited until the last moment—almost until it was too late—for he was determined that there should be no more Concettos. But now—well, there was simply no question.

Yes: Tristano's entry into the Black Frocks, the *musici*, that most mysterious brotherhood.

So it was that on a wet morning at the end of Holy Week the boy was transported to a small town in the Papal States, on the border of the Marches. Instead of riding in Signor Piozzi's monogrammed carriage, which recently had begun ferrying him to the Teatro San Bartolomeo or the Royal Chapel, or to wherever he might express a wish to go, he travelled by post, in a calèche, staying at out-of-the-way inns and post houses, whose lice and filth were mitigated only by the linen and cutlery with which he had been wisely instructed to equip himself. This sudden parsimony on the part of the maestro he found most puzzling, as he did the instructions to dress himself in neither the bright frocks and breeches nor the feather-trimmed tricornes or fobbed time-pieces that lately had come into his possession through the generosity of the fine ladies in the theatre's upper boxes. He may have attributed this prescription to the danger of banditti had it not been accompanied by another, even stranger, directive: namely that he should powder and paint his face and don the petticoats, mantua and lace cape of a young lady.

For it was decreed that he was to pass as the bride of Gaetano, his only companion on the journey, a young poet whose duties as librettist for Signor Piozzi's latest operas had been combined with employment of his less plausible talents as the *conservatorio*'s cook and now his even more dubious versatility as an amorous young bridegroom. Gaetano was a timid fellow with anxious brown eyes, sparse side-whiskers, and a rapid stutter that created much amusement and distraction among the *figlioli*. He maintained many long silences on the rutted roads between the posts, as if unwilling to tempt Tristano, or as if, and perhaps more likely, he was abashed by the presence of a wife, even if she was a sham one.

Like all men, though, he soon taught his young bride her place. In the evening he refused Tristano permission to take his supper in the table d'hôte, confining him instead to their mutual chamber, away from the prying eyes of ostlers, muleteers, postilions, chambermaids and road-weary diligence passengers. And all details of the journey were left to him. Inside his cloak he retained their passports and a leather purse, constantly displaying the one and depleting the contents of the other—soldi, scudi, lire, carlini, crowns, ducats—as they ran a costly gauntlet of doganas, bridges, passage-boats and toll-gates, each of which demanded a fee in return for the privilege of entering a new state or traversing a river that they had crossed at similar expense two hours before. This proved an even costlier business than advertised. Most of the men in the doganas explained how it was inconsistent with their consciences to leave any coach unsearched for less than, say, five soldi. The moral sentiments of the fellow who guarded entry into the Papal States were especially sensitive in this regard; he boldly suggested an even larger sum for their relief—ten soldi plus a Roman crown for good measure. In order to salve their consciences Gaetano never failed to untie his purse and slip into their outstretched hands the requested amount, no matter how outrageous. Tristano found this complaisance most peculiar, since the coach really held nothing of value besides the bed-linen and the few pieces of plate.

—It is y-you, and not the plate, that I d-do not wish them to d-d-d-discover, Gaetano finally explained when questioned by Tristano, though this reply really left him none the wiser, and the morose poet declined to elaborate.

After twenty posts, two nights in filthy inns, and untold riches extorted at the doganas, the calèche at last arrived at its destination, a small town scattered among hills covered with the suture-like marks of vineyards. Arriving at the house of a doctor named Monticelli, Tristano was instructed to unpack his small, uninspected portmanteau in a musty chamber, where he was presently served his dinner by Monticelli himself. This cheerless and unrepaying meal—dry bread, a thin soup, a few strips of salted pork—he then

123

enjoyed alone in the chamber, which was hardly more hospitable than those in the filthy inns, comprised sparsely as it was of a straw mattress, a three-legged stool, and a plaster cross hanging crookedly on its nail. Monticelli himself was equally spare of composition, an ancient and impecunious stork who dressed in black from top to toe and wore a pair of spectacles askew on his distended, constantly sniffling proboscis. A silent stork he was, too, for upon questioning he proved every bit as unforthcoming as Gaetano, who by now had vanished, his sham marriage for the moment abandoned.

Next morning Tristano was roused by the bells of a nearby church ringing the angelus. After prayers he was fed again: more bread, even drier now, and more soup, an even thinner broth. To his surprise, however, Monticelli made recompense for this exiguous fare by pouring a generous cup of red wine. Tristano tried to explain that apart from the wine drunk at Communion . . .

—Drink, ordered Monticelli.

When Tristano complied, the doctor swiftly replenished the cup.

—Drink.

By the time the second cup had been dispatched, the doctor presented another unexpected luxury, a claw-foot enamel tub into which a maid was pouring urn after urn of steaming water. Monticelli filled another cup of wine and gestured with a long finger at the tub when the girl's efforts raised the water's level to within an inch or two of its brim.

—In, he commanded, adding a perfume from a stoppered bottle to the hot water, which had begun to fog his spectacles as well as a bull's-eye window behind his head.

Tristano hastily undressed and complied, accepting as well a third cup of wine, which Monticelli had darkened with the addition of several drops of a brown syrup from another stoppered bottle.

—Drink, he said.

The water was hot, but he dared not protest, and so, gritting his teeth, he submerged himself to his neck, in the process sipping experimentally at the latest cup of wine, which was considerably more bitter to the tongue than its two predecessors.

—Relax, Monticelli now commanded in a softer voice, his back turned as he busied himself at a small table.

124

Tristano found himself strangely able to comply with this request as well, for presently the water did not seem so hot, nor the wine so bitter. He closed his eyes, remembering how the sulphurous waters of the hot baths outside his village had slurped, just so, at his chin when he took the waters with his father. Yes, yes, it seemed so long ago now, like something from a dream . . .

The wine had made him dizzy. He was only vaguely conscious now of Monticelli bent over him, only distantly aware of the pressure of the doctor's thin hand on the side of his neck, just below his ear . . . and then at some point he must have fallen asleep in the soothing waters.

Light. Voices.

When Tristano awoke—it may have been days later—he saw the pinched, bespectacled frown of Monticelli, whom he did not recognise for a long moment or two.

—Is he aw-wake? a voice—Gaetano's—finally inquired.

—Yes, yes, replied Monticelli, cross. Now leave me to him, if you please. Go back to your whores. I shan't have you fainting like a girl again this time if I can help it.

He turned to Tristano, placing another cup of darkened wine before the boy's lips.

—Drink.

Then darkness, silence.

Soon, though, more light, more voices. And pain. Oh, yes. Pain. Pain. *Pain.*

—Quiet, muttered Monticelli, banging the shutters and filling another glass of wine. It won't hurt for ever. Drink.

No, no: it didn't hurt for ever. But it did hurt for ten days. Which can sometimes feel like for ever.

Eleven days after arriving at the house the nervous bridegroom handed his young bride into the calèche, which bumped away through narrow alleys, then back again through a gauntlet of doganas, toll-gates, ferries, bridges. It bled coins at every stop, halted each sunset at the most obscure inns, different ones this time, though equally filthy and inhospitable, filled with lice and spiders and smelling of sheep's dung and horses' piss. Needless to say they ate from their own crockery and cutlery, slept in their own linen. But now Tristano's linen was stained with blood; despite several industrious attempts, Monticelli's chambermaid had been unable to launder them clean. Tristano's blood, of course.

—The b-bridal sheets, snickered Gaetano. But then he became more serious: We shall b-burn them when we reach N-naples, he added with a frown.

It seemed to Tristano that it was an uneasiness over these sheets that prompted Gaetano to pay the leering gentlemen even more than they admitted their consciences truly required. For now he knew—it had been explained to him by the doctor on the evening before his departure—that anyone concerned with the 'operation', as Monticelli called it, was subject to excommunication. That, at least, was the punishment in the Papal States, which also imposed several unpleasant civil penalties, though none of them quite so drastic as that prescribed in the Kingdom of Naples: there, Monticelli explained, a practitioner such as himself would promptly be put to death.

—The warrant would be signed, he informed Tristano with a sliver of a smile, by the same men who the night before had been enjoying the fruits of my labours in the Royal Chapel. But do you know why I make no bones about this hypocrisy? Because you see I am a hypocrite myself. That is to say, I despise music. Yes, my boy, he said with a cawing laugh, it's all cats-coupling-on-the-rooftop as far as I'm concerned!

Yet if he despised music, during the ten-day visit Monticelli had allowed himself to grow fond of Tristano—even though the boy spent at least half of that time in a stupor, occasioned by the endless cocktails of opium-steeped wine. Towards the end of the convalescence, however, the cups of wine had resumed their regular hue, and Monticelli frequently treated himself to them as well, becoming more kindly and voluble as a consequence. Often the three of them—that is, if on the occasion Gaetano could be persuaded to forsake the town's flesh-pots—played spinado, slobberhannes, piquet, or other games Monticelli had acquired during an apparently idyllic apprenticeship in Padua. But then on Tristano's final day in the house a calèche drew up, and a little fellow in a ribboned hat hopped on to the cobbles. One of the angels from the famous Pietà dei Turchini in Naples. A new playmate for the doctor.

—I despise the music, Monticelli muttered under his

breath, adjusting his spectacles as he prepared to greet the newest arrival, but I love the money.

Yes, the money. Who could believe that there was so much of it available? Not at first, no, but after a few years ... Once, he had earned 2,000 ducats in a six-month period; he was aged only seventeen or eighteen years then—unprecedented.

Where did it all come from? The opera houses, mostly; first those in Naples and then, later, in Florence and Venice. Yes, Venice ... But I must not get ahead of myself. First there were the churches in Rome and the Papal States, holy places no female voices were permitted to contaminate. Yet these paid only four crowns for a performance, and so the theatre, the Aliberte, for instance, was much more lucrative—and ladies' voices were not suffered to be heard there, either. So there was no end of roles: Tancredi in *Gerusalemme liberata*, Termancia in *Onoria in Roma*, Claudio in *Messalina*, Anastasio in *Giustino* ...

What is that? Perhaps you find it amusing that the great kings and villains of history and mythology—Tamburlaine, the Caesars, Aeneas, Orlando, Tancred—should be reduced to this, the voice of a boy—or, indeed, one might say to that of a girl? Yes, of late the taste has changed, such heroic roles going to tenors ... but then, fifty years ago, the most heroic roles called for the most beautiful virtuoso voices; nothing less, nothing else, would do.

So there were lucrative, private performances at the *palazzi* of cardinals and nobles: the Palazzo Matthei, the Villa Pamphilia, and the Villa Borghese, where Cardinal Gualtieri paid him 1,000 scudi for four performances. Or the silk-draped theatre in the Palazzo della Cancelleria, where Cardinal Ottoboni watched from his private apartment, tears trickling down his cheeks during an *aria grazioso*—or so it was reported. Another 1,000 scudi. Then, from outside Rome, those who had witnessed these performances battled for his services—the Prince of Modena, the Countess Grimaldi in Genoa, the Saxon Court in Dresden, the Grand Duke of Tuscany; even, on several occasions, Cardinal Grimani, the Viceroy of Naples.

All of this, I have said, occurred in good time, after several more years of developing, several more years of humbler, less well-paying engagements. His very first patron, a somewhat homelier sort than a viceroy or a duke, had been awaiting him upon his return from Monticelli's house. A *nobiluomo* none the less. Tristano had been acclimatising himself to his new chamber—Concetto's—and its view of the piazza and the castle, Il Torrione del Carmine, in the distance. A black frock lay on the pallet. Then Signor Piozzi entered with a young man whom he introduced as the Count Annibali.

—I bid you a welcome return to Naples, the Count said, jerkily removing his brocaded tricorne and affecting a low bow. I trust the waters of the spa have improved your health?

—Yes, thank you. Signor Piozzi leapt in when Tristano failed to respond. (Spa?) The spa—yes, sir. Tristano? Yes, sir, excellent for the health. He is quite as good as new. It was—an ague, that is all.

—I am most glad to hear it, replied the Count, and in that case I wish to put forth a proposition.

Annibali, Tristano's first count, was a rather disappointing member of the species—short, goggle-eyed, and so bandy-legged that it seemed he must have sat all day on the backs of mules before learning his first steps. Yet, remarkably, this jasmine-scented and silk-draped little frog was a notorious one for the ladies, who, if the rumours could be given credit, cheerily reciprocated his affections. All but one, that is: Caterina-Speranza, a great beauty, whom, perhaps for the sole reason of her resistance, he wished to wed.

A fortnight later Tristano was engaged by the Count to attend a *ridotto* at his villa and at the end of the evening to sing for this stubborn creature, besides the now-famous tempest aria from *Oeneus*, a sentimental song of his, Annibali's, own composition. It was a wretched piece, such rubbish that not even Signor Piozzi and his eleven operas needed to fret about competition. Tristano, however, earned 30 scudi for his troubles. In return Annibali expected to earn the love of Caterina-Speranza. Yet still she was unyielding—to the Count at least, though not to Tristano. No, she was quite charmed by this ugly child with the beautiful voice, inviting him to her father's villa in Ischia, making him gifts of tortoiseshell snuff-boxes, gold flacons of eau-de-Cologne, a peacock from Japan . . .

An omen of what was to come. He was dismissed from the Count's services, but quickly found more patrons. There was no shortage of other ladies and gentlemen willing to part with small fortunes in return for the pleasure of hearing his voice drift to them across the darkened theatres or balconied halls. Of course, in those early years much of the wealth went back into the *conservatorio*. As a result, Signor Piozzi was able to cease tending his herb garden and even hatched plans to expand his *conservatorio* and transplant it to more commodious lodgings in the shadow of the Castel dell' Ovo; but alas, he died while these were in preparation: one morning he was discovered on the floor of the chapel, head inverted, arms thrusting, eyes prominent; a rigid, staring, bluish-white statue of the maestro pushed from its pedestal. But by this time Tristano had fulfilled his obligation to the maestro and was living in Venice.

Yet Signor Piozzi—perhaps you know him as Gasparo Piozzi? no?—lived on, immortal, through his works: that is, through his operas—seventeen of them by the time the chambermaid discovered him lying belly-up on the cold stone floor. *Penelope, Fulvia vendicata, Dido e Aeneas, Il trionfo di Lucina, Ifigenia abbandonata, La forza d'amor*—perhaps you have heard of these? No? Not quite so immortal, then. But surely *Philomela*, considered by many to be his *magnum opus*? No? Ah, well. Perhaps on their own they are nothing very special—mere handbooks for virtuosity, their artistic integrity too eagerly sacrificed upon the altar of popular demand. Their melodic invention may be banal, their style occasionally monotonous and arid, their librettos execrable; true enough. Yet it was with many of these works, with their arias, their bravura style, that Tristano first made his mark.

But if the—granted, inferior—operas of Gasparo Piozzi brought Tristano such renown, what then might he do with those of the true masters—Scarlatti, Bononcini, Handel? All wrote for him—yes, they were just as clamorous for his attentions as everyone else. In their hands Tristano may have been—no, *should* have been—the greatest soprano in the history of the opera. Next to him, Farinelli and Senesino were squawking gulls. Nicolini and Porporino? A pair of squealing pigs! Faustina, Cuzzoni—those two, squabbling, squawling geese?

And Il Piozzino?

Ah. It was Il Piozzino in part, together with the Count

129

Provenzale in Venice and then, later, with Lord W— in London—

'But once again I am getting ahead of myself,' said Lady Beauclair, 'and if you will pardon my saying, Mr Cautley, truly you do not look at all well.'

I am certain that indeed I did not, yet the cause of my stricken complexion was not now the prune sauce, nor even my immoderately consumed cups of Calvert's or Marlborough and the endless bumpers to our King. Rather, my sudden affliction was the result of something I had glimpsed a moment before, immediately preceding this intermission in her story. Why I had not glimpsed it—or, rather, *them*—at an earlier interval in the evening I do not know, for they were exposed quite plainly to my view, sitting atop the sideboard where the engraved portrait had formerly stood: a three-cornered hat trimmed at its edges with gold *point d'Espagne* and a pair of kid leather gloves, gleaming in the candle-lit chamber like polished bones.

Sixteen

 'Come, Cautley, come—my smock, my pigments. Hop to it, my good man, hop to it! Hurry—there is much work to be done!'

How many times over the next fortnight did I hear this command, or one of a thousand others like it? How many times did I abandon the duty to which I had hopped a moment before in order to hop instead to this newer, more urgent one? For I was now an apprentice in the studio of Sir Endymion Starker; I was, as the historians of the subject would say, of the 'school of Starker'.

This school, as it transpired, was a most uncompromising one. Sir Endymion insisted upon a strenuous and varied regime for his apprentices, of whom there were five, myself included. Most of our days were spent mixing his concoctions of paint and then applying them, under his supervision, to the draperies sketched into his half-finished portraits. Of these it seemed there were hundreds, enough to keep a hundred hands painting draperies for a hundred years: gouache miniatures, silhouette miniatures, head-and-shoulder bust portraits, kit-cats, head-size fancy pictures, bishop's half-lengths, whole-lengths, and even some larger-than-life representations of entire families, which for the future pleasures of projected generations were destined to be suspended in the cavernous libraries of distant country seats. There was no shortage of such work, for Sir Endymion's sitter book, a fat ledger into which it was the task of one of the apprentices to inscribe an endlessly expanding list of names, was 'completely full up', as Sir Endymion once explained over a cup of porter, which had succeeded in establishing an air of informality in the studio—'full up for the next three years at least. Unless, as is likely, a few of the old birds I'm sworn to paint pay their debt to Nature before I can discharge my own obligation to them.'

Such moments of conviviality were extremely rare in the capacious studio two stairs above the river in Chiswick. While at work, Sir Endymion was not prone to fits of either humour or relaxation, and he expected this somewhat severe disposition to influence those of his apprentices, among whom he tacitly discouraged most of the recreations to which young men of their years were acutely susceptible. The reason for this formality was that the studio was host to a constant succession of sitters, often as many as six or seven each day. And though to my knowledge no one of the stature of King George or Lord North passed through the studio's doors, a good many Persons of Quality did indeed arrive in all the pomp of their equipage and sit to Sir Endymion: Portmans, Cavendishes, Grosvenors, Chesterfields, Cadogans, as well as admirals, bishops, squires, philosophers and wits, actors from Drury Lane, sopranos from the King's Theatre in the Haymarket, distillers of rum from Jamaica, the editors of magazines, a Cherokee chieftain, the King's jelly-man, furniture- and china-makers, potters, perfumers, architects, magistrates, Whigs, Tories, together with the wives or mistresses of the above, sometimes their heirs, and only somewhat less frequently their parlour poodles, cats, macaws, or canary-birds. Sometimes three or four parties arrived at the green door at once, a phenomenon never failing to occasion much dispute and even the kind of violent exchange that once resulted in a

131

magistrate's periwig landing in a puddle and a dowager duchess's spaniel slipping its leash and absconding to Brentford.

These important persons sat before Sir Endymion's canvas for two-hour sessions on consecutive days, most somewhat more patiently than Lady Manresa. Since it was Sir Endymion's opinion that the subjects of his portraits, no matter how handsome, could never be properly dignified nor have their 'universal essences' exposed in modern dress, they were persuaded to attire themselves with the general air of the antique or the pastoral.

'I abhor such fashionable frippery,' he would expostulate whenever one of the sitters appeared at his house in a Turkish or Persian costume. 'Is this a masquerade? No, it is not. I am concerned with *Truth*, not with disguise. I am concerned with *universal essence*, not with mere show. Not with the latest milliner's fashion or the new rage at Vauxhall. Not with the most fanciful whims of the Court or the newest costume arriving by the post from Paris. No, no, *no*. How the devil, I ask you, may one reveal the *inward spirit* if the *outward shape* comes draped and feathered like a half-naked harem-girl?'

Thus those sitters who had the folly to appear at the green door in these prohibited costumes were sent away and ordered to return in classical costume—white robes with chaplets of flowers upon the shoulder and sashes round the waist—so that posing together in the studio or standing outside their coach-and-fours they constituted small pantheons of somewhat morose-looking deities. Or else they were made to concede to the 'elegant simplicity' (as the master called it) of black dresses and raised collars, thus creating the startling impression that they had stepped out of one of the portraits executed in the previous century by the great Messrs Vandyke, Velázquez or Rubens.

'Much better,' Sir Endymion would exult as he circled his sitter, squinting with a critical eye at the new costume. 'Ah, *much* better. Yes, yes. Now one may see not the troublesome particularities but the outline of the *universal* and the *ideal*. Yes—perfect!'

Sir Endymion's philosophy was, as well you may imagine, a most congenial one for me, and I was greatly pleased to discover myself in such close agreement with so fine a mind. Still, I wondered with some apprehension what he might

132

make of the 'Turkish frippery' of *A Lady by Candle-light* when it was completed. Or perhaps I should have said *if* it was completed, for my association with Lady Beauclair had been threatened by what I had seen in her lodgings and, perhaps even more, by my inadvisably impudent behaviour towards her.

'You have had a visitor,' I had managed to say that evening, in a voice which I fear had grown both hoarse and accusing.

'A visitor, Mr Cautley?' she had replied, blinking her eyes as if in puzzlement. 'No—no, I do not believe so . . .'

How it pained me to hear such a sweet voice pronounce this lie!

'The hat,' I said, in a voice barely more than a whisper, pointing. 'The gloves . . .'

'Ah,' she said smoothly. 'Yes. A friend, Mr Cautley, that is all. A gentleman friend called upon me several evenings ago. Yes, yes—I had quite forgotten. Yes—his hat. He left behind his hat, the silly fellow.'

So Robert had been within that very chamber! No wonder, then, that the rogue had treated me so shabbily in the cramped phaeton. Lady Beauclair no doubt spoke well of me, and perhaps he perceived me as a rival.

'He is no one you might know,' she had continued. 'An acquaintance, that is all. A gentleman of no importance—a cousin, visiting from the country. Why, Mr Cautley,' she said after a short pause, 'I *do* believe you are envious!'

Envious? Was I? *Ought* I to be?

As I shut her door and walked along St Giles High Street I knew only that my dislike of Robert—whoever he was, cousin or not—had darkened a shade or two. And my regard for Lady Beauclair? As I walked I could hear inside my head the endless repetition of her lie. Or *was* it a lie? Had she truly forgotten, or had she wished to deceive me?

Over the following days I sought relief from these questions by immersing myself in my duties in the studio. These duties were both numerous and various, yet always of a rather humble nature. After Sir Endymion had completed the face and dress, I daubed carmine into the folds of the drapery that bordered them or spread *terra verte* on to the immodest expanses of grass and oak that comprised the prospect behind. The sitters then paid Sir Endymion 50 guineas for the finished product if it was a kit-cat and as much as 200 if a whole-length. I must confess how my mouth watered at these transactions, which were accomplished without either party so much as blinking an eye. My contribution to this profitable enterprise earned me only a single guinea at the end of each week, at which rate I was expected to discharge my gaming debt in a little over a month.

Yet the full value of this experience could not, of course, be measured simply in guineas or by any other cash denomination, for I was learning my chosen craft at the feet, so to speak, of a master—or at least from Mr Lewis, the master's 'head assistant'. I learned much from the grudging Mr Lewis about Sir Endymion's technique, which rested upon a series of strange concoctions with which he constantly muddled and experimented. Indeed, he possessed as many potions and nostrums as any sorcerer or apothecary, or (if Toppie was to be credited) as any lady of fashion; and his cupboards, which were filled with flasks, phials, jiggers, trowels, mortars and calabashes, which in turn were filled with waxes, oils, resins, balsams, gums, and pigments of every hue, boasted more provisions than Mr Langley's armamentarium with its many foul-smelling powders and steaming poultices. It was to the creation of these potions, these great omnium gatherums, that I devoted most of my time—that is, when I wasn't cleaning gummy brushes, rinsing out gallipots and demijohns, or scrubbing the stair. Under the instruction of Mr Lewis I boiled combinations of linseed and nut oil over red lead in order to create drying oils, which I then mixed, at precise ratios, into the pigments I had fetched from Mr Middleton's shop in St Martin's Lane. Or I blended these oils with a special resin, mastic, which I had dissolved in spirits of turpentine, thus creating a buttery medium much favoured by Sir Endymion for painting the flesh. I made varnishes for him with egg-whites or, more laboriously, by dissolving another resin, copal, in drying oil and then crumbling the pigments into the result. Occasionally a certain pigment could not be obtained from Mr Middleton, or else Sir Endymion would receive the recipe for a rare and experimental one from an associate, and so I was set to work with earthenware pans, a measuring-scale, and a hotchpotch of resins and minerals—aniline, celadon, tragacanth, white lead, ammonia, aluminium, and who knew what else. After emulsifying the noxious compound I set these pans to bubbling and spluttering and spitting over a fire for seven or eight hours at a stretch, the membranes of my eyes and nose becoming inflamed, and watering from the smoke. Once the pans had boiled dry I would scrape the crusty residue into a gallipot and then grind it with oil or turpentine mingled with wax. The creation of great works of art was, I could see, a messy and laborious business.

What else? I assisted with copperplate printing. I inked Sir Endymion's incised plates with a pigment—'frankfort black'—ground in linseed oil before rubbing it off with a stiff tarlatan and then the chalked palm of my hand. I soaked the paper and placed it into the rolling-press, whose spoked wheel I rotated with much sweating and grunting until I pulled the print—the black-and-white mirror-image—from the plate. I assisted the master with the execution of a species of portrait recently invented in France by M. de Silhouette, placing the ladies in a special chair, a 'silhouette machine' (as my master called it), to whose side a piece of paper had been affixed and then made translucent through the placement of a candle opposite. I watched over his shoulder as Sir Endymion sketched the shadow that fell upon the paper, creating a perfect profile of his subject, one he claimed most effectively transcribed the universal and the ideal.

'For in these silhouette drawings,' he explained, 'all particularities are abandoned, and one may perceive the strengths and weaknesses of their characters—their virtues and their vices—in the line of their brows or the angles of their jaws, which here are denuded of the paints and powders of disguise.'

What more did I do? Mr Lewis set me to work on the canvases. I primed them by, first of all, soaking the cloths in boiling-hot drying oil, then spreading their surfaces with more hot oil and red ochre, and finally, when the surfaces had dried before the fire, applying more hot oil and a final coat of white. Once sized, the canvases were stretched over their frames, and it only remained for me to watch the master apply his gobbets of the thick, waxy, stinking conglomerations I had spent the previous day concocting. Indeed, they were often applied so thickly, and were themselves so messy and oily, that occasionally whole planes of colour—entire faces—slid down the canvas and spattered on to the floor at his feet. Then I incurred my mentor's

135

gentle reproach, along with the not so kindly rebuke of Mr Lewis.

It seemed, alas, that I was forever incurring the displeasure of either Sir Endymion or, more often, his head assistant; for although I was swift of apprehension, being, as Sir Endymion himself had noted during our game of whist, a 'clever youth', I made several alarming blunders in the course of my duties, one or two of which, I was made to understand, had risked the lives of the house's residents. I believed, however, that these errors were not altogether my fault, for my wheel was constantly being scotched, so to speak, by the perfidious Mr Lewis, whom I had recognised immediately, much to my chagrin, as the young fellow from whom my appearance in Lady Manresa's sack and petticoats on that first afternoon had elicited the most maliciously persistent titters and even his impudent pink tongue.

My first disaster occurred when, cleaning out a gallipot with turpentine, I tossed the contents, upon Mr Lewis's advice, into the fireplace; whereupon a great flame shot up into the chimney, necessitating the arrival of two firemen, whose services cost Sir Endymion £5, as well as (he sighed) something of his good reputation among his neighbours. I was heartily sorry for this dangerous misadventure and made profuse apologies, duly accepted by my master. Yet he chastised me further for pleading in my defence that Mr Lewis had invited me to cast the turpentine into the fireplace, for 'Mr Lewis has been in my house for these past two years, and never in this time has he succeeded in lighting fire to it in such a manner as this'.

The disastrous situation was nearly repeated a day later when, after being instructed by Mr Lewis to place an unfinished portrait of a famed countess to dry before the fire, I returned from my tea-break to discover the good lady smouldering and blistering, the most flammable hues of her countenance burned away and dropping in smoking blobs on to the floor, which they succeeded in scorching.

'Great heavens above,' cried Sir Endymion, after the two of us had succeeded in extinguishing the flames with our boots, thereby damaging the countess's visage even more severely, 'never again shall you put one of my canvases so near to the fire! What the devil were you thinking of, Cautley? The painting I can replace,' he said in a grave tone; 'my home and family, however, I *cannot*.'

136

Once again I was forced to render my apologies in the greatest abundance; but I could not help thinking that, in truth, I had *not* placed the countess quite so close to the flames, and that as I partook in my dish of tea she had somehow managed to migrate several inches towards the grate. The mystery of this short but fatal voyage was cleared up somewhat a moment later when I turned from the scene of the mishap to discover the tongue of Mr Lewis standing out in great prominence from his smirking face. I said nothing at all to Sir Endymion of my suspicions, but I determined to remain on my guard, Argus-eyed, against the further treacheries of the head assistant.

Yet this vigilance unfortunately was not rewarded, for another disaster soon befell me, easily the most disquieting so far, and one which I fear greatly, and perhaps permanently, lowered my esteem in the eyes of Lady Starker. Paint, and not flame, was at the root of this débâcle; specifically, 'yellow orpiment'. This was one of Sir Endymion's favourite pigments, by reason of its suitability for highlighting the hair; it was therefore a colour that complimented the heads of many fine ladies of fashion who came to sit in the studio. On the fourth day of my apprenticeship Sir Endymion discovered me admiring his application of this appealing colour to the hair of one particularly handsome lady.

'It is indeed a pretty hue,' he agreed when I commented upon its peculiar glow, 'but one must be most cautious in the application. For mark my words, George, that yellow orpiment is a very poisonous compound.'

'Poisonous!' I exclaimed, recoiling with a start from the handsome yellow head.

'Indeed it is,' he replied, 'for yellow orpiment is composed of sulphide of arsenic, which is a most harmful substance. Therefore, George, I bid you always take the greatest caution when grinding this pigment, which you must never leave lying about the studio, but instead lock away securely in the cupboard.'

You may be certain that I heeded Sir Endymion's words to their last syllable. From that moment I never touched yellow orpiment without experiencing a few palpitations in my breast and a slight shaking in my fingers, which trembled like tuning-forks, as if they were handling not a cake of paint but an unexploded rifle-ball or dozing serpent. Thus

137

it was that at the close of the second day, after Sir Endymion had finished applying daubs of this pretty poison to the head of a fair lady of fashion, I scrupulously locked the pigment in its cupboard, scarcely drawing a breath until I had done so.

'How strange it is,' I thought to myself in the midst of my tremulous performance of this momentous duty, 'how very strange that a colour so beauteous as this one should hold such frightful perils!'

Sir Endymion, having removed his smock, now accepted a dish of coffee from his wife. 'Is the yellow orpiment safely stowed?' he inquired of me in a casual voice. I assured him that it was indeed and then accepted from this gracious creature a dish of my own.

I was aghast, then, when a few minutes later a cake of this most dangerous pigment was discovered by Mr Lewis in the chubby fists of young Alciphron Starker, who one week before had celebrated the commencement of his third year, and who, had his activities been discovered a few seconds later, would surely not have observed another. As a result of this troublous and puzzling event I was greatly discredited and once again was sternly reproached by my master.

Yet in spite of these many reproaches I could not in these days have held my new master in any higher regard. Back in my lodgings each evening I sought to imitate not only his techniques of painting but also the flawless manners and noble bearing so casually demonstrated in his rare moments of ease. For perhaps I believed that by duplicating his postures or polished habits I might imbibe something of his genius for painting. Thus I stood leaning my elbow against the chimney-piece as I read a small volume of poetry, or, when sitting down with the book, I crossed my legs and dangled one foot in the air while slowly flexing my ankle, as if working it free from a noose. Lifting my chipped teacup from its cracked saucer I would balance it in the fingers of both hands as if making an offering to some gracious deity: just as, I suppose, I was raising and offering myself in humble supplication to a grand and gracious idol.

That this idol may have possessed feet of clay or been raised upon shifting sands was intimated one evening by Stubbs, the youngest and by far the most amiable and loquacious apprentice. Welcome as his fraternal advances had been, I could not, however, approve of their source or what had increasingly become their import. For this fellow, a freckled youth with carrot-coloured hair standing erect in quiffs above his small skull, possessed a great talent for mischief as well as for painting; and despite his modest years—he was not much the senior of Jeremiah—he had already been afflicted with a number of unwholesome vices. Most of his evenings, as well as most of his wages, were, I gathered, frittered away in those twin occupations, gaming and drinking, which so often lead to a third, brawling. In consequence of this business he frequently appealed to me for the loan of a few shillings, which I always forced myself to deny him with much sternness and gravity.

Whether the other apprentices, to whom he made similar petitions, responded with greater generosity I do not know; but in any event his sparse funds none the less allowed him to persevere in his activities such that he appeared one morning in the studio with his upper lip double its normal proportions, and with his countenance covered in purplish blotches more malign in appearance than the spattering of freckles. That evening, as the two of us returned together to London on the mail-coach from Bristol—whose motions, he lamented, pained his tender ribs most grievously—I saw fit to warn him (after refusing him a shilling for the second time that day) that his activities were certain to prejudice his position in the studio. To my surprise, however, he laughed at this counsel and gave me to understand that Sir Endymion was himself a great one for the vices against which I inveighed. I must have looked surprised—and indeed I was—for he laughed again and asked:

'Have you not heard the stories about him, Cautley?'

'I have heard that he is one of our nation's finest painters,' I replied somewhat defensively, 'who hangs in our finest homes.'

'Aye—hangs indeed!' He produced another of these inexplicable titters, this one abbreviated, however, by a sudden sideways jerk of the coach. 'Aye, hangs indeed,' he repeated after having clutched at his ribs and cursed the driver with much foul language. 'Have you not heard of how Sir Endymion was once condemned to the gallows?'

'Condemned! The gallows!' I exclaimed, before falling speechless.

'Aye, 'twas for murther,' Stubbs continued somewhat gleefully after wetting his inflated lip with the tip of his tongue. 'Some five years ago he was convicted at the Old Bailey of "wilful murther" and sentenced to hang. Aye—cut the throat of one of his drinking companions, so 'twas said, in a house of ill fame near Charing Cross.' His bruised face leered at me through the gathering darkness. 'An argument over a strumpet, so 'twas reported. He and the other fellow were gambling for her favours. Both in drink, of course. Sir Endymion lost the hand of cards but, after claiming his friend had cheated, tussled with him, and then—*pssht*!' He drew his index finger across his throat and twisted his distorted lips into a repulsive and painful-looking half-smile.

Sir Endymion, he proceeded to explain, possessed a good many friends in high places, and after the conviction a royal pardon was sought by some of them—lords and ladies, other painters; that sort. Grub Street hacks wrote poems and pamphlets in his defence, while the Quality petitioned the King for mercy. In the end he was released from Newgate Prison after spending only three weeks fettered in a condemned cell.

''Twas said'—Stubbs was leaning closer, his voice lowered to a scratchy whisper—''twas said, though, that this pardon was granted not because of the pamphlets and painters; rather, it was because of Sir Endymion's close relations with a countess'—another leer—'who in turn was close to the King.'

I was frowning deeply, trying to absorb this—surely scurrilous?—information. After we had reached the turnpike at North End Road and paid our fare, I said: 'If all you say is true, then this must have been before he married Lady Starker ...' For I was thinking how the softer passions of the ladies were proverbially successful in taming the ruder ones of men.

'Not at all, Cautley!' Another delighted cackle, followed by a moment or two of fond reflection. 'Lady Starker—aye, there is another story, Cautley, another scandal. Surely you have heard of the duel he fought for her sake a year or so before this conviction for murther ...?'

How I was wishing I was deaf as Stubbs chattered about the violent passions that had caused our master, first, to kidnap Lady Starker—or Miss Bridges, as she was then known—from her father's home in Wiltshire after old Squire Bridges had declined to permit his daughter to wed a

140

painter; then, when discovered, mortally to wound the brother seeking to redeem her honour; and, finally, to keep her as a virtual prisoner in Chiswick, granting her none of his own extensive liberties.

'How strange it is,' I exclaimed, 'that a hand that so delicately and so skilfully holds a paintbrush, that creates such wondrous works of art, should be capable of such acts of terrible violence!'

But Stubbs did not hear my sorry reflection, for upon our coach arriving in Piccadilly he had hopped on to the paving-stones. Now his carrot-coloured head was bobbing away in the direction of a tavern, out of which an unwholesome firelight was spilling, along with three or four raucously exclaiming patrons. As I sprang to the stones myself a few minutes later at the top of the Haymarket, I reflected sadly that, if all he said was true—which indeed I very much doubted—then it was perhaps Stubbs, not I, who made the more faithful model of our master.

True or not, Stubbs's story made me think of the strange creature I had seen in St Alban's Street and now, after a few days in the studio, almost forgotten. But then after three days of work in Chiswick I was invited to this mean edifice by Sir Endymion, whose actions I interpreted as a sign of his favour. More, I interpreted my admittance to these latter premises—which were a great secret, being unknown to the apprentices in Chiswick, including Mr Lewis and even Stubbs, and, for aught I knew, to Lady Starker as well—as being something of a privilege. Indeed, it was the singular honour of this intimacy that made the best recompense for the miseries so inexplicably visited upon me by the perfidious head assistant. Thus as I ground pigments for the master or stared into my sputtering earthenware pans, coughing and sneezing, watched all the while by the disapproving eye of Mr Lewis, or sometimes by the sadly reproving one of Lady Starker, I thought about my secret privilege and was cheered.

So my third visit to St Alban's Street was, at last, a successful one. Jeremiah expressed a wish to accompany me, but as his nose was still a leaky nozzle and his complexion not entirely rid of a disquieting tint of parsnip (even if it had been improved each day by my prescription of further pints of spa water, as well as by two efficacious new remedies, 'Dr James's Fever Powder' and 'Dr Hill's Essence of

Waterdock'), he was persuaded to preserve himself in his sick-bed while I made the short journey alone.

As promised, Sir Endymion greeted me at the door of these lodgings, which still languished in the same state of dereliction and were as different as seemed possible from the charming edifice in Chiswick, as if the buildings were the absolute opposites to each other.

'Mind your head,' he warned, pointing to a perilously low timber-beam, which none the less managed to dent my brow as I entered. Then, advising me about a series of similar hazards, including uneven and even missing steps, he conducted me up a narrow back stair and into a small chamber. During our ascent I had been expecting that, when they presented themselves, these lodgings would be of the same obscured grandeur as Lady Beauclair's—for the quality of a book, I had learned, cannot be judged by the condition of its binding.

How surprised was I, then, when the chamber to which he conducted me was, if anything, more miserable even than the most disadvantageous glimpse of the exterior of the decaying edifice would have suggested. Indeed, in comparison to this chamber—no more than a garret—my own modest lodgings were a veritable palace. I discovered it to be unadorned by any furnishings other than a small pallet, a looking-glass, a chair, an easel, and a demijohn that was employed to capture the drops of water which fell at regular intervals from the ceiling. The ceiling, besides admitting the rain, also gave ready passage to a cool breeze, and furthermore appeared to have subsided to an angle alarmingly at odds with those of the walls, which in providing their uncertain support had buckled and cracked in numerous places; expanding stains now stood upon them like continents on a great, sullied map. The bare floor lay at as incongruous an angle as the ceiling, for which reason a person with no knowledge of this caprice upon entering the chamber felt himself being propelled by the force of gravity to its far side: to which, indeed, I now leaned and stumbled, as if down a short hillside. All at once my feelings of honour at gaining entry to this *sanctum sanctorum* were somewhat diminished.

'Eleanora,' called Sir Endymion, who had anchored himself in the doorway. 'Eleanora!'

Before this garreteer appeared—she was, as I had been

142

expecting, the lady from the casement—I noticed her effigy upon the canvas situated on the easel in the middle of the chamber: a fair creature, whose abundant hair was the colour of the honeysuckle that blossomed each spring beside my mother's door; a hue which on his easel Sir Endymion was reproducing with a pigment that I recognised as yellow orpiment. Her face he had executed through the application of much carmine and white flake, which had been glazed and scumbled and varnished and waxed until it fairly glowed. Yet when the subject of these efforts appeared before me, I could not help but notice that, perhaps through charity or indulgence, Sir Endymion's Art had departed some distance from Nature; for the complexion of his sitter, though fair, was truly somewhat unwholesome, being so pale as indeed to be almost translucent, thereby putting me in mind of the tiny blind fishes that live in the dark waters of the deepest subterranean grottoes. Her eyes, moreover, which in the portrait appeared as soft orbs of copper-blue, in their original were, by marked contrast, unwelcoming squints whose pink and puffy margins suggested some late expression of sorrow. And the testimony of the portrait was contradicted, finally, by this creature's hands, which instead of gently bearing a nosegay, as the painter had interpreted them, now clutched and then released an iron salamander, which directed itself with a lethal force at the crown of my host. Sir Endymion swiftly ducked his head, however, and the implement missed him by a few scant inches, crashing noisily into one of the continents upon the wall.

'You jade!' he cried in a voice that I had not heretofore heard him employ. 'By heaven, I shall reward you for that impertinence!'

But then, remembering me, he appeared to reconsider whether or not he ought grant this reward (whatever it may have been) in my presence; and he proceeded instead to perform graceful introductions, Eleanora's assault seemingly forgotten. She reminded him quickly enough, though, for no sooner had he said, 'And this, Eleanora, is my apprentice, Mr Cautley,' than she launched herself at him, endeavouring to embed her finger-nails in his face and her teeth in his arm. A fierce struggle then ensued; however, despite several successes scored by his antagonist's incisors Sir Endymion swiftly established himself as the victor, and the lady allowed herself to be thrust into the lone chair, where she sat, rocking and weeping.

During the course of this short battle I had retreated uphill, towards the door, preparing to flee should this mad lady (for so she certainly seemed) succeed in her violent assault against my master and then perhaps set her ambitions upon me.

'I do apologise, Cautley,' Sir Endymion said, restoring the salamander to its place by the empty fireplace and then mopping at his brow and dabbing at one of the small inflictions upon his forearm with a lace handkerchief, which came away blotted in red. 'I am truly sorry—youch!—that you had to witness this.'

Upon seeing the wounds of which she had been the authoress, the lady ceased her rocking and rose from her chair. I prepared to take rapidly to my heels, but in the course of the past few seconds this mad creature's opinion of my master had evidently sailed across the tumultuous oceans to its stark antipodes. For rather than visiting upon him the wrath of her teeth and nails, she now imprinted his face with a series of kisses, muttering all the while, 'My love, my love!' and 'My dearest master!' and tenderly sleeking with her palm those territories which, barely two seconds before, she had been endeavouring to maim. 'The human heart,' I thought to myself, 'is indeed a wonder. How swift is the shift of the passions from one extreme to the other!'

Sir Endymion resisted these new attentions almost as vehemently as their contraries, grasping her by the wrists and setting her once again upon the chair.

'Your costume,' he said. 'Where is it? No, no—never mind. *I* shall find it.'

He disappeared into another chamber, one even smaller and more wretched than the first, furnished (I could see through the rhomboid portal that had not been dignified by a door) only by a close-stool, an oak-framed rolling-press, and a few of the lady's toiletries and garments, which in the absence of an *armoire* or dressing-table had been heaped in some discord upon a portmanteau. He proceeded to toss aside these garments—stays, shifts, and stockings in diverse states of repair—before extracting one or two items from the portmanteau. The lady remained as indifferent to this enterprise as she was to my presence. As we waited she did not even lift her gaze to acknowledge me, but instead wrapped her arms about her rib-cage and shivered. Sir Endymion then emerged with the costume he had selected, a linen shawl and a chemise of white muslin; the very sort of Grecian apparel, that is, which he so favoured for his sitters in Chiswick.

'Here,' he said, 'attire yourself in this, Eleanora. This day you shall be the Goddess of Liberty. Quickly now!' he commanded when she failed to move. 'Cautley,' he said turning to me: 'my smock, my pigments. Yes—hop to it, hop to it! Come, there is much work to be done! Hop to it!'

'Yes, sir—straight away, sir!' I said, opening my master's box of pigments, helping his head through the small hole in the hessian smock, and sounding to my own ears exactly like Jeremiah.

Seventeen

 Hours later, I was seated by my fire, pondering a letter. A cup—port wine—sat at my elbow, and I had just finished observing the ruddy sun reflect itself in the shop windows across the street until a forest of shadows planted along the gutter grew steadily upwards, swallowing in its cubical foliage suns and casements alike. I was dressed in a ruffled holland shirt and a waistcoat of watered silk, and beside me, on the floor, a white starburst showed where Samuel Sharp the Younger had recently applied powder to my periwig. Nearby was my paintbox, *A Lady by Candlelight*, and a pair of buckled shoes borrowed from Toppie and diligently blacked by Samuel. For this evening I was appointed to pay another visit to Lady Beauclair.

Or, rather, this evening I had been *aiming* to visit Lady Beauclair; but now this letter, inscribed in a looping hand upon a cream-coloured paper, creased twice and then sealed with a wafer, informed me that she would be unable to keep our appointment. This intelligence startled me, and the pleasure I had been deriving by imagining her lips moistening the disc of wafer quickly evaporated. Perhaps my behaviour the other evening, my suspicions, had offended her? Perhaps she no longer wished to see me? Possibly this letter—a very short one—was intended to terminate our acquaintance?

'Samuel,' I said, addressing the young Mercury who a few seconds earlier had fetched me this correspondence, which I now waved in some consternation beneath his nose, 'who, pray tell, delivered this letter?'

'A gentleman brought it to the door,' replied Samuel, who in the event of Jeremiah's illness had assumed some of his brother's duties. Not quite a year Jeremiah's senior, he aspired not to be my servant, but, rather, more grandly, a painter. He was a bashful, blushing little fellow, possessed of a great enthusiasm for all things concerned with painting and drawing. He marvelled no end at my pencil-sketches and, even more, at the image of Lady Beauclair magically appearing upon my canvas. I suspected him of having made several private attempts to develop his own abilities, for often upon returning to my chamber I discovered my pencil to be an inch shorter than it had been at my departure, and I could not help but observe how the pages of my sketch-book were being depleted at an unaccountable pace.

'A gentleman? Are you certain?'

'A gentleman, Mr Cautley,' he repeated.

'The penny post?'

'No, sir. A gentleman. A handsome fellow, very finely dressed. He dropped it through the door.'

I leapt to my feet and started to the window, the chair legs scraping sharply on the floor, the chair then overturning. In my haste I very nearly dropped the letter into the fire.

'Is the fellow yet below?' I asked, catching the paper in the last second before its incineration.

'Sir?'

I swung open the casement and thrust my head outside. The wind billowed in my face and snatched at my wig. Outside, barely visible through the forest of shadows, a slim figure receded north along the Haymarket, his floating hat trimmed at its corners in gold *point d'Espagne*, his gloved hands flashing at his sides in white arcs. Robert!

'That's him, sir,' said Samuel, who had joined me at the window. 'That's the fellow yonder. Mr Cautley!' he said as I rushed from the window to the door. 'Whither do you go? Mr Cautley, please wait!'

146

I did not wait. A minute later I was in the street, my heels clopping on the flagged surface as I pursued the gentleman into Great Windmill Street, past the School of Anatomy, and then—for I was certain I had seen him turn into it—Knaves Acre. Truly a most fitting name! Yes—the knave would make an account of himself here or, by heaven, I would cudgel him!

Yet when I crossed through the narrow passage of Milk Alley and into Soho, out of breath now, my clopping heels not quite so rapid or assertive, and the street lamps neither so numerous nor so closely spaced, I could detect no sign of him. I proceeded more slowly up Dean Street, my passage impeded at every step by butcher's carts, empty butts, gaping cellar doors, projecting doorsteps and bow-windows, heaped lay-stalls, slumbering mongrels, and a clutch of hunger-bitten wretches grinding street organs or selling brick dust in the shelter of shop doors.

'Out of my way,' I commanded the animate and inanimate alike. 'Stop that fellow! Pray allow me passage!'

Half-way down this busy thoroughfare I believed I spied the gold-trimmed hat turn the corner into Queen Street and from thence—I was running once more, leaping and dodging the obstacles—into Greek Street. Yes, there he was! I hailed him by name and called upon him to halt, but he either failed to hear my appeal or else his wish to avoid me was as resolute as it had been inside Mr Larkins's phaeton. After crossing Compton Street he passed into Moor Street, his white hands scything through the darkness and his head turning never so much as an inch to either left or right.

'Stop-*op*,' I bellowed, my voice echoing against the overhanging edifices. 'Please-*ease!*'

Having lost sight of him soon after this second petition met with an identical response as the first, I made two abortive ventures into Holborn, first up Monmouth Street, then down West Street, until in my confusion at the doubtful maze spreading about me I wandered a few minutes later into the Seven Dials.

I was panting for breath by now, and my scalp itched and was sweating copiously under my wig. I looked about me, wondering whither to turn. I was spoiled for choice, for no less than seven streets now led outwards from the spot on which I stood, each one a dark and unpromising corridor. At the centre of this great rendezvous a tall pillar rose up, surmounted by a clock and six faces, each of which gazed down a different avenue. I followed their example, peering down each passageway as I performed a weary revolution round the centre of this great asterisk. Each street was scarcely to be distinguished from its neighbours. Linen was suspended below the windows, swelling in the breeze like jibs. The windows themselves were many of them broken, imperfectly repaired with papers and snatches of cloth. Below these, the shop signs of pawnbrokers and bootmakers creaked on their hinges, flapped, straightened, flapped again. Invisible dray-horses snorted and stamped in their stables, and here and there passengers appeared along the narrow precincts, though none of these skulking peripatetics was to be mistaken for Robert, either by his gait or his dress. At the sound of my heels some of these fellows left off their mysterious and solitary occupations, and there seemed to be a sudden and general movement in their ranks. For the first time I became sensible of the possible dangers into which I had rashly delivered myself, since from its appearance I concluded that this spot was a general rendezvous not only for streets but perhaps for footpads and robbers as well.

'Ho,' called a gruff voice, 'who goes there?'

I spun round as a tall figure suddenly emerged from behind me in Great White Lion Street, one of the emptier avenues, at whose terminus, a short distance hence, I could discern the more familiar, more well-lit, length of Monmouth Street. In one hand the figure bore a lamp, whose aureole succeeded in illuminating everything about his person save his feet and his head; the latter, it seemed, was suspended in the darkness a good twenty hands above the former. The long staff, in his other hand, he employed to punctuate every second of his steps, thereby attracting not only my notice but that of the figures skulking in the other streets as well, and they swiftly dissolved into the shadows.

'Ho,' the gruff voice repeated itself. 'I said, Who goes there?'

'George Cautley, sir,' I replied, bowing and making to doff my hat—which, in the midst of this execution, I now realised I had left behind in my lodgings.

'What, pray, is your business, young scamp?' he inquired, his gruffness wholly unmodified by my abortive expression of *politesse*.

I explained that I had become separated from my companion, 'whom perhaps, sir, you have witnessed in the course of your travels?' Unwilling to attend to my description of Robert, however, the tall fellow—whom by now I had recognised as a watchman—elevated his staff and threatened to smite me with it should I fail to 'clear off home'. When I unwisely protested that, as an Englishman, I enjoyed the liberty of walking the streets of the capital as much as any man, he attempted to make good upon his warrant, and I was required to preserve myself from the persecutions of this brutal ruffian by fleeing into Great St Andrew's Street. His shouts and the echoes of his staff pursued me until I rounded the corner.

By now, not knowing whither to direct my steps, and having relinquished my hopes of laying hold of Robert and forcing him to make an account of himself, I wandered the streets and narrow laneways for several minutes, quite lost among the dark terraces with their blackened, unwelcoming countenances. Soon, however, I discovered myself to be back in Greek Street, passing before the shop of the cheesemonger whose window had formerly granted that much-savoured illustration of my fine deportment and borrowed luxury. I was now a sorry sight by comparison, for at each step my right stocking progressed another inch towards my shoe, which was chafing my toes, and my ill-fitting wig migrated back and forth across my pate, once or twice descending over my brow like a visor and thereby temporarily rendering me blind. I hastened onwards without stopping to attend to these awkwardnesses, but then I realised, suddenly, how very near my pursuit had conducted me to my lady's residence.

'Perhaps I will call upon her,' I said to myself, considering how an explanation for her unexpected behaviour had been mysteriously absent from her letter, if indeed she was its authoress. Briefly my mind's eye cast itself upon an exceedingly unpleasant tableau of Robert seated at an escritoire, nodding and sniggering beneath his gold-trimmed hat as he penned the missive. Yet then my deliberations affixed themselves upon a different, though equally disagreeable, image.

'Perhaps my lady is ill,' I considered, imagining that, like Jeremiah, she was now lying abed, her fair complexion translated by a fever to some equally insalubrious colour. 'Or perhaps'—the scenario grew worse still—'perhaps this Robert has harmed her in some manner, for certainly he seems a disagreeable fellow! Yes, yes—surely I must go to her at once!'

My step quickened as I arrived in Hog Lane, from which I could see in the distance the lobster's-tail steeple of St Giles-in-the-Fields raising itself above the jumble of tiled rooftops and tumbledown chimney-stacks of its surrounding hovels. By the time I reached Denmark Street I was running swiftly once again. My feet clattered upon the unevenly flagged surface, and lanthorns and lighted windows wavered towards me, then floated past my head.

But what was this? I halted in my tracks as soon as I entered St Giles High Street—for what did I see at some short remove beyond the gin-shop, and an even shorter remove beyond my lady's door, but a dark figure, attired in a gold-trimmed hat, stepping inside a waiting hackney-coach. Before I could take a step or speak a word, its small door slammed with the brief comet-flash of a white-gloved hand and the coach clattered away in the direction of High Holborn, a long whip curling and looping like a ribbon in the lamplight above the head of the coachman. But—where was my lady? I perceived that her door, which had been opened at an angle of a few short degrees, also banged shut, though not before I had glimpsed a head, wearing a bonnet, peering through its small aperture. My lady? I rushed forward and pounded the door with my fists. A second later it creaked open, and Madam Chapuy stood before me in a narrow fan of light.

'Stars above,' she said, 'such a racket! What the devil have you forgot now? Already you are—oh!' Her expression changed as she now peered more discriminatingly into my face. 'Mr Cautley—I do apologise. I thought . . .'

Addressing me with much courtesy—more, it appeared, than she had accorded the departing Robert—she explained that at this moment Lady Beauclair was not at home. It was just as I suspected. This intelligence had already been communicated to me a few seconds previously by the sight of my lady's unlit casement. I hoped to put further inquiries to this good lady, not the least of which concerned the identity of Robert; but I was interrupted as soon as I opened my mouth again by a long and anguished lamentation, which

150

issued from somewhere within the house's darkened interior.

'Esmeralda, my daughter, is ill,' Madam Chapuy explained in response to this expression of grief; then, making a hasty apology, she bid me to call again. The fan of light snapped shut and the anguished wail was muted.

I plodded back slowly, dragging my feet, in the direction of Denmark Street. I was cold, shivering uncontrollably inside my waistcoat. Outside the gin-shop two men were engaged in a violent dispute, while a third unsuccessfully adjudicated, a fourth copiously disgorged himself on to the stones, and a fifth slumbered noisily alongside, sweetly oblivious to the commotions. I limped across the street, ignoring the scarlet flashes of petticoats in the windows and the sweet voices of the pretty sirens who beckoned me inside.

'Why hurry so?' said one of them. 'Do come inside, sir. Please, Mr Cautley—tarry a moment in our company . . .'

I was in Greek Street, passing the window of the cheese-monger's shop, before I thought to wonder how these lost creatures had learned my name.

What I may have dreamed about that night, if I dreamed anything at all, I do not remember, but I opened my eyes the next morning to discover Mr Knatchbull standing in a puddle of light on the wainscot table. His limbs were disposed into a most peculiar posture, his hands resting upon his hips and his head turned to the side, as if as I slept his sightless sockets had been regarding me with a haughty gaze from over his wooden shoulder. Directly behind him, echoing this posture, was *A Lady by Candle-light*. My lady's face, scumbled and glazed the day before, was also watching me, yet this morning it appeared tallow and insubstantial in the sunlight, as if about to fade from the canvas and disappear.

I sat up and looked more closely at the canvas. From this angle, and with the sunlight so disposed, I could see for the first time the very faint outline, the ghostly contour, of the image that lay beneath; the hillocks of the shoulders, the peak of the head. The sharply angled planes of the . . . what? The hat? The paint had been applied thickly and almost seemed to be bleeding to the surface, blending into my own efforts. Perhaps Sir Endymion . . .? But surely my lady

151

would not pay a colourman to paint over a portrait accomplished by Sir Endymion Starker. Who, then? Who had been my mysterious competitor? And what—I was running my finger over the gentle ridge, the faintest shadow of colour—what had this extinguished portrait looked like? Why had my lady been dissatisfied?

I rose and lit my fire, and soon enough my thoughts were occupied and exercised not by Lady Beauclair, nor even by Robert or the other, unknown, portraitist, but instead by Sir Endymion, for whose studio in St Alban's Street I was already late.

Eighteen

 It was in this tiny studio—if indeed those two most unfavourable chambers could be honoured with this title—that Sir Endymion claimed to execute his finest works, those for which he would be remembered, he told me, 'with the highest approbation in one hundred years' time, like Rubens or Rembrandt'. The studio in Chiswick, where he painted his many portraits and collected his bags of guineas, he dismissed with a wave of his paint-specked hand.

'Can you appreciate, Cautley, how very difficult it is to extract the universal essence from the visage of His Majesty's jelly-man, or from that insupportable she-devil, Lady Manresa? From the evil-humoured Countess Kinsky— or whatever her name is—and that even more disagreeable poodle bitch she drags about on its gold chain? No,' he said with a violent shake of his head, which very nearly dislodged his periwig, '*no*—for it is history-painting in the grand style, and not portraiture, that is the topmost branch of Art. History-painting, Cautley, is a liberal profession; portraiture merely a mechanical trade, like making a pair of boots. And it is from this most lofty of branches, and from no other, that we may pluck the fairest flower of universal essence.'

Sir Endymion's paint-dappled hand gestured grandly at the canvas over which he had hunched for the past two

152

hours, spattering upon it great waxy gobs of carmine, asphaltum and yellow orpiment. The painting, an allegorical one, was to be called *The Goddess of Liberty Receiving the Garland from Harmodius and Aristogiton*. It was a fine work indeed. Eleanora, the model for the goddess, had maintained a low curtsy for much of the forenoon, while I had perched above her, first in the posture of Harmodius, then as Aristogiton, wearing a chemise of white linen cinched at its waist by a red sash, my calves bare and my head unwigged. I felt as ridiculous as I had when I represented Lady Manresa.

'These fellows were the two founders of Athenian democracy,' Sir Endymion had explained as he mixed paints on his pallet, 'who, you will remember, murdered the tyrant Hipparchus. How the acts of a few men may alter the course of history and civilisation! For it was from this act of tyrannicide that there then followed in a short space of time the Athenian democracy, the statesmanship of the great general Pericles and the unsurpassed marbles of Phidias.'

I fear this explanation, learned as it was, had made me feel only slightly less foolish. I clinched the sash tighter, for it was constantly slipping and thereby exposing part of my belly to the bowing Goddess of Liberty.

Nearby, propped against one of the walls, stood *The Rape of Lucretia by Sextus Tarquinius*, also unfinished and also destined to hang above the supper-boxes at Vauxhall Gardens. A day before I had played the role, so to speak, of the treacherous Sextus, standing for most of the afternoon with my hands pawing and tearing at Eleanora's muslin robe and my features contorted into a lecherous frown. That duty completed, I had removed my garb—the same inadequately adhering one that I had worn to impersonate Harmodius and Aristogiton—and spent the last hour painting plinths and draperies in the background.

'The fair Lucretia committed suicide,' Sir Endymion had reminded me as he painted, 'but her death was avenged by Junius Brutus, who drove out the Tarquins and became the first consul of Rome. Consider again the effects that flow from the actions of men. From this one act of terrible barbarism performed by Sextus there arose the greatest civilisation—the greatest government and the greatest art—that our world has ever known. It is ever such, is it not? There is no document of civilisation that does not have roots

153

which reach down into the dark and wretched soil of such barbarisms that in our own enlightened age we may only recall with a cringe.'

'Can such acts of barbarism,' I inquired, 'be justified or redeemed because of the works of art that issue from them?'

'I speak not of justification, which is a moral concept; rather, I refer to causal effects. Seeds of political and artistic renewal sprout through the fissures opened by acts of the vilest desecration. Pass me the sable-haired brush, if you will . . .'

'But, sir'—I was pensively chewing the tip of this brush— 'can such art then truly be properly hung upon a wall, or be loved and appreciated, when we know its cost in blood or violence? When we know what horrors it disguises?'

'Yes—for, to adopt your moral terms, it is innocent of those forces that create it and will indeed point the way to nobler aspirations.'

'Must all art, then, base itself in such suffering and destruction?'

'Only the very best art will do so—that which probes the mystery of what it is to be human. For as your Mr Hogarth writes . . .'

And so on, and so forth. When I now think of those days it seems as if we shared not the dank garret but a green hillside in some distant Arcadia; as if we sat not on the treacherously sloping floor but in the tapering shade of a group of teardrop-shaped cypresses. On such occasions I was all ears as he described, for example, Plato's cave. Do you know this particular subterranean grotto, this prison of the senses in which reflections and illusions are cast and created by other reflections and illusions?

'In the *Republic*,' he would tell me, 'Plato describes a race of men fettered in such a way that they may not turn their heads from a stone surface before them. Behind them burns a bright fire, and before this fire stands a low wall not unlike that seen in puppet-shows. Behind this wall, which stands, in turn, behind these prisoners, another group of men carry images—cut-outs made from wood and stone, like shadow-puppets—representing men and animals, and so forth. The shadows of these cut-outs—do you follow me, Cautley?— the shadows are cast by the firelight upon the stone surface before the prisoners, being mistaken by them for real objects.

'Now, Cautley, what if one of these prisoners should one day be released from his fetters and for the first time glimpse the wooden shapes moving above the wall, casting those flickering shadows? Will he be disabused, do you think, of his old illusions? No, no: he will think the shadows are truer forms than the wooden shapes; he will mistake the shadows for the originals, which are in turn, of course, shadows and images of something else. For it is not just any man who is able to avert his eyes from the shadows and recognise these other forms . . .'

And so on, and so forth. Such was my life in Sir Endymion's studio. There was so much to learn from him, and I could not have done better, I do not believe, had I been one of his students at the Royal Academy. In the many hours we spent together in the garret he spoke to me of many things—of his Grand Tour, for instance: of encountering the Young Pretender at a masquerade in Rome and sharing with him in a cup of punch; of watching the eruption of Vesuvius from the isle of Ischia; of touching the frozen corpses of porous stone at Herculaneum; of seeing a tarantella dance in Lecce; of reading one of Virgil's manuscripts—'fourteen hundred years old, Cautley!'—in the Vatican Library, as well as the love-letters Henry VIII composed for Anne Boleyn. Above all, though, he spoke of his passion for art—of making copies of the works of Titian and Correggio and Poussin and Claude; viewing the paintings and marbles in the collection of the Duke of Bracciano; discussing optics and atmospheric perspective while playing faro with Canaletto in Florian's café beneath the arcades of the Procuratie Nuove in Venice; painting the portrait of the bejewelled Dauphine Marie-Josèphe of Saxony and a dozen other noble beauties; producing a prospect of Rome from the heights of Mount Testaceus and sketching the antiquities of Mount Esquilinus and Mount Celius; setting up his easel in the Piazza del Popolo in Rome or before the Basilica di San Marco . . .

And in those first few days I hung upon every word he said. I wished to read every book that *he*, my wise master, had read, to cast my eyes upon every marvel of painting, sculpture and architecture that *he* had seen—for perhaps then I would be as great an artist and as much of a gentleman as he was.

'One day, Cautley, I shall show you these paintings,' he told me once, 'and if you wish you may copy them.'

It was now a little more than one week since I first entered the studio, and my relations with Sir Endymion, as you will guess, had come to occupy a favourable pass, my former catastrophes with the countess and the yellow orpiment notwithstanding. This was my most cherished time of day. We had just sat down to our supper—hog's cheek, neat's tongue, a wedge of Suffolk cheese, and some choice eel pies, which had been heated in the oven at the Carv'd Balcony Tavern and now sprouted long florets of steam that rose to the crooked ceiling and fogged the lone window of the garret as we cut into their crusts. Sir Endymion added to our victuals the further cheer of a pot of porter, which disposed him to a degree of loquacity altogether unknown in Chiswick. On this day he had also attempted to create in the garret—or rather the 'studio'—a more congenial environment, for he had spread herbs—bay and lavender— upon the damp floor and placed a scented candle by the fogged window. At times such as this, as we ate our supper and drank our cups of porter, he often spoke eloquently and at length, not only about the highlights of his Tour but also about some of the more philosophical matters that the cups of porter prompted him to entertain.

Yet if I was an eager student of these learned discussions, Eleanora on the other hand regarded Sir Endymion's lectures—if I may call them this—with a great apathy; which indeed was her response, it seemed, to most conversations and occurrences. Today none of his efforts—not the sprinkled herbs, the pot of porter, the eel pies, nor even his happy volubility upon the subject of Athenian democracy or history-painting in the grand style—had quite succeeded in raising her spirits. She now sat at some remove from us, apparently in dejection, picking distastefully at her pie and not so much as nibbling her cheese. Not even when Sir Endymion spoke fondly of her as his 'Muse' had she responded with the briefest smile.

Eleanora was indeed a puzzle. Perhaps struck by the incongruity of her situation—viz., that his Goddess of Liberty in fact enjoyed very little liberty herself, being, as far as I knew, cooped up in the garret both day and night— earlier in the evening Sir Endymion had permitted her the benefit of a constitutional, with the two of us as her companions, one on either side. Yet when we stepped out into the air she appeared wholly indifferent to her new privilege, for her eyes remained glued to the straw-strewn paving-stones as we ventured the length of Pall Mall. Two fellows with a footstool and a long taper were lighting the street lamps, and as the faint smell of sizzling fish blubber wafted to us on the chill breeze the sallow flames, which leapt and sputtered inside their crystal globes, had cast their light upon her pale face and yellow-orange hair, revealing an unbecoming scowl.

Seeking with an ever greater determination to raise her spirits, Sir Endymion had presently stepped into a hatter's and made her the purchase of a bonnet with a lilac ribbon. Then he purchased a flacon of lavender and bergamot cologne, 'Parisian Delights', from the shop of the royal per-fumer, and finally a flask each of apricot wine and nectarine gin from the wine-merchant under the colonnade of the King's Theatre. Eleanora received these gifts as disin-terestedly as she had her brief spell of liberty, and when we returned to the garret an hour later she ungratefully cast them out the window and then subjected her benefactor to one of her daily assaults with the salamander. Catching him by surprise this time, she succeeded in knocking his periwig on to the floor and opening an inch-long gash upon his cheek. As he mopped at this wound his eyes had said to me, 'Alas, do you see how it is, Cautley? At first you believed me cruel, yet do you see how the lady refuses all my charity? I am a kind man, Cautley—and such is my reward!' My eyes looking back at him told him how per-fectly I understood.

After consuming my pie I returned to one of the canvases, for my pigments had not yet dried upon the palette. Often I worked until nine o'clock in the evening, sometimes later, for I enjoyed my duties in this studio more than those I performed in its counterpart in Chiswick, where (perhaps as a result of my terrible débâcles) they were now in less demand. I believe I should have stayed at my easel all through the night had it not been for Eleanora, of whom you may imagine I was exceedingly wary, having no wish at all to find myself alone in the chamber with such an unpredictable creature, whose persecutions I believed could surpass even those of Mr Lewis.

Now I recommenced work upon my favourite of Sir Endy-

157

mion's canvases, *The Miseries of Life*, which bore the subtitle *The Fair Garreteer at her Casement, Holding a Nosegay*. This painting, commissioned to hang upon the wall of the General Court Room in the Foundling Hospital, was that which I had seen propped upon the easel when I first entered the studio almost a week before. Now I had been assigned the task of painting the darkened wall and draperies that composed its background and applying a glaze to the melancholy visage of the subject, a young tatterdemalion. It was a most remarkable work, and I took as much pride in my efforts upon it as I did with *A Lady by Candle-light*. Eleanora, dressed in rags, her countenance smudged with dirt or soot, her hair loosened and spilling in some disarray upon a naked shoulder (itself lightly smudged), gazed mournfully at the spectator, or rather, it seemed, over his left shoulder, as if she were contemplating some distant object. She appeared to be fetching a triste sigh, as though resigned to the tragic loss or inaccessibility of that object, whatever it was.

'Perhaps it is the churchwarden,' I conjectured to myself as I took up my brush, 'who is taking one of her tiny babes into parish-keeping. Or perhaps a cherished heirloom that her flint-hearted landlady removes to sell for rent, or which she herself has decided to pawn for money to appease the baker or the butcher. Or perhaps the poor creature takes account of a depleting pile of coal that she knows full well will not suffice to see her through the winter...' As always when I looked at this fair creature, I felt a sympathetic stirring in my breast.

'I have never seen a painting so like life,' I now told Sir Endymion as I blew upon my fingers, warming them for the task ahead. The lady had been rendered so exactly that, as I began to paint the papered wall behind her, I almost expected her to move her lips to speak, or that she would reach out one of her hands from the canvas and tweak my nose.

'All art must provide an enchantment,' Sir Endymion replied as he poured himself another cup of porter. 'The sole function and beauty of art lies in its illusion. Through such pleasing deceit the cloth and colours show living figures that trick the eye into a belief in solid flesh, when, truly, nothing exists but light and shadow. As the Earl of Shaftesbury tells us in the *Characteristicks*, the purpose of this pleasing deceit is to persuade us, the spectators, to emulate acts of public virtue. Thus'—he gestured a hand at *The Miseries of Life*—'thus are the terrible miseries of the poor brought home to the spectator, exciting his affections and disposing him to sympathy, the amiable passion that is the finest principle in human nature and the basis for the social virtues.'

Inscribed beneath, he added, would be a quotation from Proverbs serving to remind spectators how 'he that gives to the Poor, lends to the Lord'.

I was duly impressed by the nobility of this intention, yet I was none the less somewhat puzzled by the painting, which seemed to deceive (to use Sir Endymion's own word) in quite another manner. For although it was, as I have said, very like life, yet, as I have also said, it departed in no small way from Nature, looking in truth very little like its original subject, the scumbled and varnished visage of carmine and lake bearing little resemblance to the scowling physiognomy that I had seen lighted by the lamps a short while before in Pall Mall. Indeed the handsomely downcast figure with the bright nosegay and blooming cheeks was scarcely recognisable as the creature who was now making sulky attempts upon her eel pie. For the countenance of the 'fair garreteer', while melancholy and smudged across the bridge of its nose with soot, yet possessed in its resignation a certain peaceful beauty; and I could not help but notice how its suggestion of poverty and privation was mitigated to some degree by the roseate sun that spilled through the casement and suffused it with a pinkish radiance. Needless to say, I had never seen the thin and pale Eleanora disposed to quite this advantage. This creature upon the canvas also held a posy of fresh flowers whose colours reflected to their best advantage the tones of their owner's skin, eyes and dress. This last, though torn, was of no mean quality and was, moreover, disposed in a fashion whose suggestions did not seem entirely chaste, thereby stirring in my breast certain aspirations more dangerous and much less lofty than charitable assistance.

But as Sir Endymion had himself explained upon a previous occasion, when I commented upon this remarkable distance between Art and Nature, this figure was 'not truly the Eleanora whom each day we see in the studio. True painting does not, in servile fashion, imitate external Nature.

159

I have painted instead the image that we might see of Eleanora were we to extract her from her local habitation, from her history, and from the accidents and idiosyncrasies of her personal appearance. The genius of all art,' he had continued, expanding upon what was one of his favourite themes, 'lies, above all, in its *generalisation*. For you must understand, Cautley, that the business of the true painter is to examine not the *individual* but the *species*. The former is of interest only insofar as it displays the latter. The beauty and grandeur of art consists in being able to rise above singular forms, particularities, accidents and petty details, all of which are deviations from the universal rule and merely pollute the canvas with deformities.'

I was much satisfied by this explanation, for of course it was just such an image that I had myself been attempting to capture—alas, less successfully—in my portrait of Lady Beauclair. Still, mention of Eleanora's history had roused my curiosity and set me to wondering how she had reached her sorry pass in the garret; but I did not think it wise to ask my master, much less Eleanora herself, so I daubed at *The Miseries of Life* in silence.

'Cautley,' Sir Endymion commanded a few minutes later as I was putting the final touches of 'turchino', a deep blue, on to the walls behind the yellow head of the garreteer. He had put aside his porter and now resumed work on *The Goddess of Liberty*. Eleanora was once again bowed before him, barefoot, wearing her muslin chemise. 'Cautley,' he said, 'will you please see to the door?'

I trudged down the stairs, limping slightly on account of a small wound inflicted several days previously by the Countess Kinsky's monstrous poodle. Tripping as usual over the fourteenth step, which was of a height unequal to its fellows, and the twentieth, which was absent, I asked myself who could be calling upon us. The application—three heavy knocks—I felt was most unusual, for no one thus far had visited us in all the time that I had been employed in the studio. While a steady tide lapped at the green door in faraway Chiswick, bearing upon its crests the flotsam and jetsam of London society, here in St Alban's Street—in the heart of fashionable London—we had never once been disturbed.

An old gentleman removed his hat and bowed slightly when I creaked the door on its hinges and peered outside

160

into the rain. In lieu of the knocker, which still lay in the mud, he had made his petition with an oaken walking-stick, now raised as if ready to strike again.

'I have come to call upon Sir Endymion Starker,' he said, lowering his stock, replacing his hat and fixing me with a rather imperious gaze, such as one would bestow upon a servant. He looked familiar, though as I opened the door to admit him and then led him up the stair I could not think where I might have seen him. His pockets chinked and jingled and he struck his twisted stick upon the steps as we climbed the stairs. He was quite out of breath by the time we reached the top.

'Sir Endymion,' he puffed.

'Ah. Mr Fox.'

'I trust they are prepared?'

'Quite so.' Sir Endymion lay down his brush and slowly wiped his hands, one of which he extended to the old gentleman. 'This way, if you please.'

The ancient visitor was conducted into the smaller of the two chambers, where a short conversation took place, followed by the musical chinking of coins. The two of them emerged a moment later, the old fellow burdened by a canvas sack at whose corners the contents, whatever they were—they almost looked like the copper plates from which I pulled prints on the press in Chiswick—made sharp impressions. Sir Endymion's pockets now provided the music as he escorted the gentleman to the door.

'Good, good,' Mr Fox was saying, still puffing, 'he shall be most pleased, most pleased.'

So saying, he paused long enough to cast his eyes in the direction of Eleanora, who had taken advantage of this unexpected intermission to hug at her rib-cage and, alternately, massage her toes, which in the course of the forenoon had gone from red to white to the faintest purple. At the sight of Eleanora in her muslin chemise an unpleasant expression passed over the gentleman's countenance, one not at all unlike that which contorted the frozen features of Sextus Tarquinius, who was leering at us from the fire, where the *The Rape of Lucretia* had been placed to dry. Then, as he shifted the canvas sack under his arm and bid Sir Endymion adieu, this fellow's eyes briefly met mine, and I realised where I had seen him: for as it took account of my speckled smock and ill-fitting wig his gaze was the same disapproving one that not so very long ago had appeared to object to the weathered condition of my late father's second-best tricorne.

'Cautley,' said Sir Endymion after this old gentleman had departed with his sack, 'I will not stand to have you gawping like this. To work with you, to work!'

Later that evening, after his humour had been improved, and his tongue loosened, by a pot of porter, as well as by several drops of a preparation I had procured earlier in the day from an apothecary on Oxford Street, Sir Endymion confirmed that the gentleman had indeed been the footman of Lord W—. Lord W—, he explained, was a most discriminating connoisseur. It was he, for instance, who had christened Sir Endymion 'the English Titian'.

'Lord W— appreciates the superior beauty of the most sensual masterpieces, such as those painted by Titian, Correggio or Raphael. Have you seen these works, Cautley? No? Titian's *Danaë*, or his *Venus and the Organ Player*. His *Diana and Actaeon*? No? Ah—a great pity! The richness and extreme subtlety of the palette is surpassed in these paintings only by the sensual delight one finds in the subject matter, which the great Titian draws from the most dramatic episodes in myth and history. I have done many such works for Lord W—,' he said reflectively, lowering his voice, 'many, many such works—many Venuses, for example . . .'

We were seated in the Carv'd Balcony Tavern, smoking our pipes and playing bezique, a game in which he had been tutoring me. This tuition had proved quite dear, rapidly making me poorer by half a crown. I hoped to gain a form of recompense, however, for in the course of our game I had made inquiries not only regarding the footman but about Robert as well. I reasonably assumed that, if the fellow was known to Mr Larkins, then surely he was known to my master as well. I had already broached this topic a day or two earlier, but at my mention of Mr Larkins's name Eleanora's head shot up (she had been in the pose of the Goddess of Liberty, and I in that of Harmodius) and her extreme discomposure became evident. Sensible of this alteration, Sir Endymion appeared reluctant to discuss the nature of his acquaintance with this gentleman, and so I now chose my opportunity more cautiously. Yet despite the porter (the landlord has just delivered us another pot) and the mysterious tincture from the apothecary, whose potion had succeeded in contributing an unnatural brightness to my master's eyes, as well as an equally startling bloom to his countenance—despite these potent stimulants to conversation, Sir Endymion still remained somewhat resistant, as though I had unwittingly put a check upon his affability.

'Mr Larkins? Yes, I know him well. An impresario. Works in Covent Garden. I have done set designs for him. A fine gentleman. Careful, Cautley!' He pointed at one of my turned-up playing-cards from the piquet pack. 'Do you forget the rules of our game so soon? The ten ranks *above* the knave, not below as in whist. Ha!' He drew a card from the top of the stock on the table between us. 'An ace! The trick is mine!'

After he earned several subsequent tricks with similar outbursts of pleasure—for I fear I was not concentrating upon our game—he scratched his chin and asked, 'Robert?' and I won my only trick of the evening. 'I may know many Roberts,' he continued, oblivious to his loss, 'if I stopped to ponder the matter . . .'

I could not help but suspect that this casual attitude was feigned, since at my mention of Robert's name, as well as my account of this mysterious varlet's distinguishing hat and gloves, Sir Endymion's countenance had momentarily sacrificed some of its rubicund virility to the same pale hue that had overtaken it when I placed the water-colour miniature in his hands.

'He is, I believe, the cousin of Lady Beauclair.'

'What?' He snapped out of some private reverie. 'A cousin of Lady Beauclair? Oh, yes, yes—I believe I know the fellow. Yes, yes. I do believe I have met him. I once painted his portrait, if I am not mistaken.' Over his fan of cards his eyes suddenly shot me a somewhat mysterious, perhaps suspicious, look. 'How are you acquainted with this fellow?'

Without bringing the opportunity for too many recriminations upon my head I explained how after my outing to Pancras Wells he had been unwilling to assist me in a moment of need, and how now he had interceded in my affair with Lady Beauclair, apparently to my disadvantage.

'He seems a most unpleasant, discourteous and disagreeable fellow,' I finished, somewhat heated.

Sir Endymion was silent for a moment. I did not know if he was pondering the peculiarities of Robert, his cards, or me.

'You are yet very young, Cautley,' he said at last. 'You do not yet know how, nor do you possess the right, to cast judgements upon the world. You see only the appearances, not the substance that lies beneath.' He paused for a second. 'You are like the dwellers in Plato's cave, who, upon seeing the shadows created by the flickering reflections of the fire behind them, foolishly mistake these for reality.'

Towards the end of this last sentence his consonants had become somewhat tangled, his vowels nasal. He paused long enough to inhale deeply from his tobacco-pipe and wet his apparently encumbered tongue with more porter, which did nothing to disburden it.

'There will be many things, many people,' he continued, 'that you do not understand. Your judgement in these cases must not be made in haste. If you live long enough you will find that these things, these people, are not perhaps what at first they seem. Robert,' he said, concluding this most peculiar lecture, 'your Robert, I believe, is one such person.'

I must have looked alarmed or puzzled—for indeed I was both—since he now burst out laughing.

'Sir?'

He lay a knave upon the table before me, then a queen. 'Double bezique, Cautley!' His laugh disgorged smoke from the bottom of his lungs and rattled off the timber-beams. 'Five hundred points!' He accepted my money, another half-crown. 'Be guided by my counsel,' he said after a moment, 'and I warrant you shall not go wrong.'

What he was speaking about, whether of Robert or the game of bezique, I could not be certain. However, he would say no more upon the former topic. He was much more inclined, it seemed, to discuss his work for Lord W—, to which topic he now steered our conversation. After the landlord delivered to us still another pot of porter and we rekindled our pipes from the fire that crackled at our side, he explained that in the *Characteristicks* Lord Shaftesbury had prohibited Venus as a proper subject of painting. 'Unless,' he said, giving the qualification to this famous earl's interdiction, 'unless, that is, the artist intended to exhibit the dangers of falling prey to her sexual temptations.' He puffed smoke at the timbered ceiling for a few seconds before exclaiming, 'Utter rubbish!'

As he explained how he himself had long ago abandoned the dicta of this particular philosophy and had painted an

164

entire series of this 'most dangerous goddess' (as he called her), I remembered the many Venuses I had seen on display in the Exhibition Room at the Royal Academy. I was on the point of asking about them, but with the arrival of a third pot of porter the topic had changed, and Sir Endymion had resumed an earlier and much favoured theme, describing how the universal essence could best be appreciated if the sitter was bereft of 'local and temporary particularities like jewellery, fashion wigs and—yes, my dear fellow—dress. Especially, perhaps, dress,' he whispered, leaning confidentially close, so that I could now smell the mixture of tobacco and porter on his breath. 'The Truth I seek is an *unapparelled* one; for all apparel, Cautley, is a disguise, a mask, the essence of *deception*.'

I was reminded of Toppie's remarks on this topic, and also of Sir Endymion's physiognomical remarks about the silhouette as the image that most perfectly discovers the sitter's character. I was on the point of broaching this latter subject, by way of making a comparison, when it occurred to me, not for the first time, that Sir Endymion was scarcely the most disciplined practitioner of his own teachings, especially where apparel was concerned.

Perhaps I have recounted the figure made by my master? No—I believe not. What shall I say of him? If a finer specimen of that creature Man had been struck from the mould, I had yet to set eyes upon it. The initial impression gained across the card-table at Lord W—'s drum—viz., that in his handsome features one might trace the symptoms of kindly disposition—had been many times confirmed: the forehead elevated perpendicularly above the well-shaped eyebrows; the nose partaking slightly of the Roman character; the compressed mouth; the expressive eyes—these features marked him as a gentleman of resolution, kindness, charm, warmth, intelligence, munificence. Yet it must be admitted that these fine features were too often obscured, even in his moments of casual recreations—as, for instance, now—by a heavy *maquillage* that might have done justice to some of the most prodigally patched and painted harridans who visited him in Chiswick. Moreover, he showed a personal relish for the fine clothes—the frippery—he so condemned in these sitters. In short, he was not given to Grecian simplicity in his own case, and while it was not precisely that of a macaroni—the sort of garb worn by, say, Mr Larkins or Robert—his *armoire* surely rivalled Toppie's in its exhaustive repertoire.

Now as he inveighed against the deceptions of dress he did so in the conspicuous splendour of a black silk bag-wig tinged with green powder and fixed with a ruby bow; a claret-red silk frock-coat with analogous waistcoat, both embroidered and gold-buttoned; olive knee-breeches with emerald fastenings; and a pair of ox-tongue shoes with blood-red heels, highly polished. A strong scent, recognisable from our journey to the royal perfumer's shop as 'Foolish Pleasures', insinuated from his person with such importunity, and in so wide a compass, that gentlemen along the most distant wall of the tavern occasionally ceased their smoking and drinking to sniff the air, their faces quizzical.

'The Greeks believed,' he now continued, 'that the body divested of its raiments—to wit, the naked body—most effectively reconciled contrary states, bringing sensuous shape together with the rational mathematical order it betokens, and making this order a perfect delight to the senses. Do our clothes possess a mathematic order?' he inquired of me, blinking at his own waistcoat and breeches. 'No—I believe not at all, especially when in the hands of that clothes-mangler known as the English tailor. But the human body! Ah—surely the height of perfection! The handwriting of the Almighty! The *beau idéal*! The human face, the *belle tournure* of the finest specimens! Long ago the Roman architect Vitruvius believed the ideal proportions of the human figure to be possessed of a perfect geometry whose curves and dimensions are described in the heavens. Likewise, Plato in the *Timaeus* argues that all components of the material world—the body included—are models of those higher forms existing'—his consonants were again entangling themselves, his vowels exiting through his nose—'existing in the spiritual world . . .'

I suspected that this philosophy may have found an ally in the author of *The Compleat Physiognomist*, who in his second chapter—through which I had lately struggled—ventured the hypothesis that each of the body's moles, birthmarks, pockmarks, warts and freckles was possessed of the most meaningful cosmic significance. Before I had time to reflect any further, however, Sir Endymion had extracted a small object from the pocket of his waistcoat and fumblingly passed it into my hands. In the process, his pupils dilated and his eyebrows rose so high into his admirably perpendicular brow that they very nearly disappeared beneath his greenish bag-wig.

'The Greeks and Romans—the great Phidias, for example—favoured the male body in their representations,' he was saying, 'but, as your Mr Hogarth says, "the form of a woman's body surpasses in beauty that of a man". Open it.'

'Sir?'

One of his paint-splotched fingers indicated the object in my hand, which I now looked at for the first time: a pewter pendant of the sort that upon our first encounter Eleanora had thrown at my head.

'I beg of you—open it.'

Back at my lodgings a short time later—my head reeling both from drink and the sight of the miniature—I discovered two letters awaiting me. The first, from Pinthorpe, related more preposterous but disturbing news hardly designed to calm my agitated mind. For now my friend was championing a view that not only were the people round about us the mere inventions of our imaginations, but so also, if I understood him right, was the perceiving self unstable in its own identity. These absurd propositions, he claimed, had been clearly established by several eminent British philosophers.

'*David Hume*', the letter began, 'tells us in his *Treatise of Human Nature* (Bk. I, pt. iv, sect. 6) that the Mind is a *Theatre* before which our Perceptions of the World slip and glide like so many Flats and Backcloths sliding to and fro and rising up and down as the Waxlights flicker and change before an Audience: to wit, before our perceiving Selves. Mr Hume observes how we most illogically grant an *Identity* and *Sameness* to these Objects of Perception—in short, to these People, or, we might say, these *Actors*—who pop into the Stage's ever-changing Lights to strut the Boards and then pass away into the Wings, to reappear again and again, seemingly the same. This is to say that, when we encounter our Friends Peter and John in the Street today, we naturally assume that these are those same Friends, Peter and John, with whom yesterday we engag'd to meet at this same Hour of the Forenoon. *Yet*, Mr Hume would ask, wherefore do we say they are *the same* Peter and John? On what Basis, and for what Reason, do we grant our Friends these self-same Identities? " 'Tis certain", writes this Philosopher in his *Treatise* (Bk. I, pt. iv, sect. 7), "there is no Question in Philosophy more abstruse than that concerning Identity." 'Tis for no good Reason, he observes, that we say they are the same Persons, as we can have no Proof; and our Assumption regarding their Identities derives, rather, only from our *Imagination*, from what he names a "Fiction of continued Existence" with which we must comfort Ourselves in the Face of the Flux.

'But the Problem of Identity, George, does not end here,' this boggling missive continued, 'for we may consider the flapping and gaping Hole breach'd by Mr Hume's philosophical Predecessor, *John Locke*. In his Principle of Identity (*Essay*, Bk. II, chap. xxvii), Mr Locke explains that one Thing cannot have two Beginnings, nor two Things one Beginning. Yet he observes that because human Identity depends upon Consciousness of the Self, the same Person may through Accident or some other Misfortune become so alter'd—because, for example, of Madness, of Drunkenness, of an Injury to the Brain occasioning Memory Loss, or even of Sleep or the Passage of Time—as to seem *another Person entirely*. (Consider the perplexing case of Saul on the road to Damascus.) If Personality is constituted, as Mr Locke says, not by Substance but by Consciousness, which is ever changing, then Personality, too, must be ever changing. And if no Man possesses the same Consciousness Today that he had Yesterday, then how can he know *Himself*, let alone Peter or John? Thus does the Deist *Anthony Collins* assert that for Mr Locke human Identity is impermanent and transitory, "that it lives and dies," Mr Collins argues, "begins and ends continually: that no one can remain one and the same Person two Moments together". Locke, we may say, gives us no Lock upon Identity, for Personality is in his Account ever *metamorphosing*, not the same from one Day—or one Hour, or one Minute—to the next.'

That one man might be two different people! Half-way through this treatise I commenced alternately snorting and chuckling, and then finally contemplating how possibly the identity of this Pinthorpe in the tiny parish in Somerset had metamorphosed from the identity of the Pinthorpe I had known in Shropshire—which is to say, the former had gone quite mad and so, as Mr Locke presumably would have argued, was altogether unlike his former self. I also contemplated the identities of these strange philosophers—how they must have lived supperless and hollow-eyed in leaky garrets, their clothing patched and their stockings atwist; how they must have stumbled about in the streets, bumping into and being abused by those in whose existence they stubbornly refused to believe, let alone recognise.

Then I creased this letter and quickly tossed it aside—along with my memories of the Carv'd Balcony Tavern—when my eyes lit upon the second, more welcome, letter inscribed in a familiar looping hand. Upon the page—scented with a sweet perfume—Lady Beauclair presented her compliments and made 'the sincerest Apologies for failing to maintain our Appointment'. She claimed to be 'heartily sorry, for nothing could be less desirable to me than to disappoint you'. She begged my forgiveness and asked me to understand that 'only an Event of the most urgent Nature prevented me from making good our Engagement'. Finally, she assured me that she was in health, thanked me most gratefully for my concern, and wondered if we might meet tomorrow evening at nine o'clock.

'Jeremiah!'

As I stumbled into his chamber, Jeremiah's face rose from its pillow.

'Jeremiah,' I said, flapping the cream-coloured paper under my chin like a lady's fan, 'who, pray tell me, delivered this letter?'

'A gentleman, sir,' he replied.

'The same gentleman as before,' added Samuel, whose white face, too, had just arisen from its pillow. 'I should surely recognise him anywhere! Exceedingly handsome fellow,' he said, 'exceedingly well-dressed.'

Early on the morrow I was sent by Sir Endymion to Mr Middleton's shop in St Martin's Lane. I had progressed up the Haymarket as far as the Theatre Royal, when I saw that, it being a market day, the avenue was blocked by a dozen hay-carts and, worse still, at least fourscore people, all of them milling back and forth, as thick as the revellers at Pancras Wells. Preparing to take a detour along Panton Street, I suddenly realised that I had neglected to collect money for the pigments, which would cost several guineas at least.

Cursing my bad luck, for it was a cool day and the first

drops of a chill rain had spattered my brow a moment before, I turned on my heel and trudged back to St Alban's Street. I returned with some reluctance, for on this day Sir Endymion had been somewhat abrupt with me, perhaps as a consequence of his rather immoderate consumption of refreshments the evening before. Or perhaps it had been how I had impugned Robert? Possibly they were friends— dear companions. 'Unpleasant', 'discourteous'; doubtless I had gone too far there. '*Disagreeable*'—what the devil had possessed me? Little wonder my master had been so anxious to scoot me out the door this morning!

Or perhaps—I was now reconsidering as I passed Market Lane, even more crowded with carters—perhaps instead it had been my Shaftesburian response to the pendant? I closed my eyes and once more saw its image as clearly as if it had been painted upon the inside of my eyelids. I had to shake my head to rid myself of it. I wondered, had I dreamed it? Had the innumerable cups of porter somehow placed this alarming image in my brain? It did not seem possible, what I had seen. That Sir Endymion, who had painted the visage of our King—that *he*, a man of such genius, my master, should have painted such a thing!

So inconsistent was the miniature with *The Fair Garreteer* or *The Goddess of Liberty* that I could almost believe, with Pinthorpe and Mr Hume, that a person did indeed alter his identity day by day; that the Sir Endymion I knew had somehow slipped and shifted and twisted like a posture-master and then appeared in the strange and novel shape presented to me last night.

'You do not yet know how,' I heard his voice again, 'nor do you possess the right, to cast judgements upon the world. You see only the appearances, not the substance that lies beneath...'

As Sir Endymion had provided me with a key of my own, I now opened the door and started up the narrow staircase. What would have happened, I wondered later, if I had bumped my head upon the beam and cried out in pain, as I usually did? Or if I had placed my foot down unawares upon that non-existent twentieth step and fallen headlong with a loud clatter to the foot of the stairs? Then, surely, I would have provided Sir Endymion with sufficient warning; and then, surely, as I reached the top I would not have seen

170

what I did: the more terrible image which was to supplant from my dizzy brain that of the pendant.

But I neither stumbled nor cried out, and it was I, not Sir Endymion, who heard the sounds—cries, they sounded like, then a bump; or perhaps, I thought, the sound of something being cast upon the floor, followed by further cries.

I climbed swiftly, two steps at a time, and by the time I had attained the final dog-legged turn, I realised that the cries were those of a man—of Sir Endymion.

'It is happening,' I said to myself, '—she is murthering my master! The she-devil is murthering my master!'

I reached for the small coal-shovel that lay by the door, then bounded through into the studio, stumbling as usual down the steep floor. The chamber was empty, *The Goddess of Liberty* propped on the easel, smelling of turpentine and yellow orpiment, over which scent I could identify the powerful and distinctive bouquet of 'Foolish Pleasures'. More cries, more plenteous and insistent now. The two of them had joined battle, it appeared, in the smaller chamber. I rushed inside, the shovel aloft.

So great was the racket that for a second or two neither participant in the raging contest detected my entry, and I had almost managed to retreat, lowering the shovel, before the linen that covered the thrashing twosome fell away under the force of some great gesture. It revealed to my startled eyes a shocking and immodest tableau—the image on the pendant come to life, framed in the rhomboid doorway. For with this inopportune unveiling I now was witness to the sight of my master crouched upon the pallet, very much in the posture of Sextus Tarquinius, though minus the linen chemise and red sash; and in fact minus any garments whatsoever, including his wig, in whose absence his head proved completely bald. His Lucretia—I could not avert my eyes from this spectacle—cringed beneath, likewise divested of all concealments, her white limbs and even whiter trunk fully exposed, including that particular theatre of my master's most urgent pleasures, which, as they tumbled together, willingly received its patron.

Such a sight was she to behold! Not the plump Venus of the miniature with its full belly, undulant hips, and bulb-like breasts—rather, a spare figure whose bosom had been most stingily composed, whose corrugations of rib clutched at her narrow trunk like the splaying finger-bones of a witch or

171

sorceress, and whose shoulders wore the whitish strands of scars inflicted, it appeared, by some long-ago lash. Truly Life was unlike Art! Yet—remarkably—for all of her fragility Eleanora shifted and wriggled as forcefully as her partner, summoning those energies ordinarily reserved for furious endeavours with the salamander, and directing them to a new and different purpose. As she did so, her yellow hair spread like a fan across the pallet, and her head moved from side to side as if she were observing through her closed eyes a tennis match played at a frantic pace. Her swivelling face was upside-down to me, and her mouth emitted startling sounds such as I had never heard from the throat of a woman.

'Ah, good sir,' she was crying, 'spare me not—spare me not, sir—oh! oh! oh! *oh*!'

'Oh, you jade,' my master's reply came on top of it, 'oh, you whore, you shall have it now, by heaven!'

I stepped backwards, my eyes still fixed on this most appalling—yet most magnetic—of sights; but opening her eyes at the creak of my shoes, Eleanora gave a shriek whose timbre—modulated differently from its more joyful predecessors—served to alert Sir Endymion. His cries and agitations ceased as his naked head—the top of which was speckled like the back of a pigeon—rose up before me, his expression indignant, shamed and surprised, all at once.

Yet this expression could not have been more indignant, shamed and surprised than my own, for my master made for an even more alarming sight than his lady. As I gawped in horror at this spectacle, I could only think: Alas, Vitruvius—alas, Phidias—*how wrong you were*! For there was naught of perfection about the denuded body of my master now flopping and floundering before me, from the pigeon-spots on top of his bald skull to his posteriors—red as any baboon's and withered like an old man's chaps.

'My wig!' this unrecognisable figure shouted as it strained for the handsome, green-tinged bag-wig reposing on the top of the close-stool. 'My wig, man—for mercy sake, *pass me my wig*!'

I walked slowly to St Martin's Lane and purchased the pigments from Mr Middleton on credit. Then, even more slowly, I walked back.

'You do not yet know how,' I heard Sir Endymion's voice

172

saying inside my head all the while, 'nor do you possess the right, to cast judgements upon the world . . .'

Did I not? No. Yes. *No.* I did not know. I only knew that the veil which had slipped two hours before had revealed something more to me than two thrashing bodies; something of the great perplexities of this world. My head now whirled in confusion, as if I were on the tip of a windmill's flashing vane, spinning so quickly I couldn't see or feel or think.

'You see only the appearances, not the substance that lies beneath . . .'

Nineteen

By the great clock on the arcaded bell-tower of San Giacometto the hour was past six in the evening when, one warm evening in the early spring of 1720, a gentleman entered a small shop on the Rialto Bridge. The proprietor, Domenico Belloni, had been preparing to lock his doors and shutter his display windows, and had already dismissed his assistant, Cametti. At this late hour the appearance of the gentleman—indeed, of any customer—was something of a peculiarity, for trade had been quite scant all day long. Belloni had been expecting no further customers for the remainder of the week—in fact, for the remainder of the season, since with Lent now only a few days hence his business never failed to suffer a decline that would continue unabated until Ascension Day, when the Carnival finally resumed. This slump in Signor Belloni's commerce was easily explained, for his trade was in masks and masquerade habits—that is, in disguises. And even in Venice the appetite for disguise has its rare moments of recession.

As it was now past six o'clock, Belloni was hoping this fellow would depart from his shop as abruptly as he had entered. He wished at this moment to lock his doors, cross the bridge and drink a dish of coffee and smoke a pipe of Spanish tobacco under the shade of an awning with old

Grossi, the wigmaker, whose custom suffered equivalent gains and losses according to the season, thereby making him an unreproaching companion with whom to celebrate or commiserate. After ten minutes of chit-chat—they would be complaining, today, about their lack of trade—he would knock the ashes from his pipe into the canal, bid Grossi farewell, and begin the journey to his lodgings near the Campo San Polo. He knew the precise route he would follow, since he had pursued it with few variations for the past thirty-three years. Leaving Grossi on the bridge, he would walk along the Riva del Vin, where the stink of the canal mixed with the fragrant pallets of grapes in the *fondachi* and the barrels of wine unloaded from moored gondolas. Then he would cross the mostly empty Campo San Silvestro and five minutes later attain the Fondamenta della Tette, which would not be quite so empty. For here several ladies would lean across their balconies and brashly bare those objects from which the Fondamenta derived its name.

—Signor Belloni, one might say as she exposed these articles of her trade, will you come to bed with me tonight?

—Signor Belloni, another might inquire in a piteous tone, why do you leave me to sleep alone?

—We are so lonely, Signor Belloni . . .

Modestly ducking his head, the little costumier would hasten towards the Campo San Polo, where he no longer heard their laughter croaking behind him. Yet however abashed he may have been by these bold exhibitions, as a merchant, and as a purveyor of illusion, Belloni perfectly understood the candid guarantee implied by these open blouses. For who comprehended the prevalence of imposture and disguise better than someone who advised gentlemen in the purchase of stays, underpetticoats and crimson mantuas with tassels and tiers of French lace, or adorned beautiful ladies with silk waistcoats, velvet breeches, jackboots, and burgundy frocks with braided epaulettes and gold froggings?

At this hour the Campo San Polo would still be crowded, and Belloni would be obliged to skirt its edges, hugging the pilasters and bay-windows fronting the great hulks of the *palazzi*. And, as always, he would sneer at what he saw and heard. Such a racket! Such foolishness! Pantalooned tumblers and jugglers, posture-masters, a mountebank

174

perched on a wine barrel, a gentleman eating stones, cages displaying tigers or dwarfs, two fellows tottering across the grass on pairs of stilts, two others in bright red hose baiting a bull snorting at the end of its short tether. Then, too, the usual groups of maskers: husbands spying on their wives, wives on their husbands, or each trying to avoid the attentions of the other. Belloni had no time for such frivolity: anyone foolish enough to stand and gawp at this lunacy deserved to open his purse a quarter of an hour later and discover how its contents had been cunningly emptied by the fellows who were now pushing themselves into the midst of the unwary maskers. Not that Belloni himself did not occasionally pause at the edge of the *campo*, but naturally his interest was strictly professional, the admiration of a particular costume that had come into his view: the Turkish janissary crossing in front of the church, for instance, or the Siberian Kamchatka standing on the lip of the Canàl Sant' Antonio. If the habit had been purchased from his own shop, he might smile secretly at the handiwork and attempt to divine its effect on passers-by. If, on the other hand, it had been procured from a rival costumier, he would study it with either envy or lofty disdain, depending on the quality.

Such moments when he allowed himself to stand at the corner of the swarming *campo* he was afforded another secret pleasure, one which in many ways provided a costumier with his greatest satisfaction. For Belloni knew on these occasions that, of everyone thronging the *campo*, he alone could guess the identity of, say, the masked lady whose white domino was lined with pink taffeta, or the gentleman displaying the armour of a conquistador—for, of course, he had sold these same habits only a few days before. He alone knew that the richly dressed Moor who paraded before the Palazzo Maffetti-Tiépolo on the arm of the bearded corsair was in fact the blue-eyed wife of a wealthy perfumer, and that beneath the black beard her companion, the corsair, was truly her unmarried sister, one of Venice's most notorious courtesans. He alone could guess that it was none other than the Marquess of V—, disguised as a mikado, who was handing the Countess of B—, the veiled odalisque, into the waiting gondola at the same moment that the Count himself, in the hat and garb of a cossack, slipped into the shadows behind the Palazzo Cornèr-Mocenigo, a young *carabiniere* in tow—an English duchess, if Belloni's memory served him properly.

Who knew what other intrigues and imbroglios Belloni may have divined had he the least inclination to show himself more conspicuously in Venetian society, not merely lurk unobtrusively in a corner of the Campo San Polo? Cametti, the young fool, aspired to these circles, but the truth was that Belloni lacked the moral toleration for such things. He knew better than anyone how a few frills and furbelows, along with a simple silk mask, could remove the checks and restraints of modesty; how they encouraged a liberty the guilt at which their owners' blushes would betray were they but bare-faced, as God had made them. He saw such evidence each day, or, rather, each evening, as he returned home through the torchlit *campo*: it was as if his costumes granted a strange power to the people who donned them— or else perhaps they caused a *loss* of sovereign control in their wearers. They were like the vestments one read of in the tales written for children in superstitious times: cloaks or hats having the power to consume and trick the right mind not only of those who witnessed whosoever should put them on but of the person so arrayed himself. So it was that a young lady who in the forenoon had timidly asked to inspect the sabre and leopard-skin robe of an Amazon queen would, upon donning the habit that same evening, transmogrify herself into a haughty sovereign prepared to assume her place at the belligerent phalanx of half-naked warriors. The chaste daughter of a senator or councillor might sweep through his door and a quarter of an hour later emerge with a boxed habit—a Venus or an Iphigenia, perhaps—whose low *décolletage* and diaphanous clouds of lace were quite enough, a few hours later, to communicate delicious quivers into the deepest pilings and sturdiest balks of female virtue and male restraint.

No, no—this little Prometheus had no wish to regard the full extent of his transformative powers: these glimpses from the shadows were quite enough.

So after only a few minutes of such observation Belloni would scurry across the bridge spanning the Rio di San Polo and soon, after several twists and turns down the capillaries of dark *calli*, find himself safely seated at his dinner-table across from Signora Belloni. And, since it was Friday, Signora Belloni would have instructed the cook to fry a sole caught that morning in the Lagoon. There would be blue cabbage and beetroot purchased from the Erberia, a bottle of wine and, to finish the meal, the sweetmeats with which he treated himself after a good day's work . . .

Yes, yes, in his mind's eye Belloni could see it all now, and would be tasting it soon enough, too, if only this dilatory young fellow would make up his mind. Through his display window he could see old Grossi seated beneath the awning, waving to him, sucking happily on his carob-wood pipe . . .

—May I be of assistance? Belloni presently inquired of the gentleman, hoping to speed the process on its way towards a conclusion.

—I am seeking a certain costume, he replied slowly, but alas, sir, I cannot seem to find it.

—Pray, good *signore* (for Signor Belloni was unfailingly polite, no matter how impatient), which costume might this be?

When customers entered his shop, Belloni was, after thirty-three years of trade, able to venture reliable conjectures as to what sort of habit each might select for the evening's banquet or *bal masqué*. That is, he knew before they did that the finest citizens—the wealthy merchants, for example, but especially those patricians whose names were inscribed in the Golden Book—would invariably choose to clothe themselves as scullery maids, orange girls, flower sellers, market porters, mob-capped washerwomen. On the other hand, the poorer folk—that is, the *real* scullery maids, orange girls, flower sellers, market porters and washerwomen—naturally wished to turn themselves out resplendently in the regal garb of caliphs, maharajahs, sultanas, pharaohs, czarinas and admirals, or even, sometimes, with the *corno* and ermine-trimmed robes of the Doge himself. Then of course the bold-faced strumpets, ladies of spotted fame, and those cavaliers given over to the most flamboyant vices, would without fail request the smocks and scapulars of nuns and monks, the calottes and pleated surplices of priests or muftis, the long robes and maniples of cardinals— while the nuns and friars unabashedly demanded the costumes of bawds, courtesans, procuresses, concubines or satyrs, and sometimes, indeed, even the red and black robes and pitchfork of the Devil himself. Illiterate peasants would favour the black tabards and miniver-trimmed hoods of academicians, just as learned professors could be counted

177

upon to adopt the straw hats and baggy hose of ignorant rustics. The young? They selected the long beards and oaken sticks of age, while their grey-bearded elders preferred the bibs, rattles and bonnets of infancy. The judges? The collars and chains of prisoners and galley-slaves. Physicians? The hooded robes of stumbling lazars. And this fellow . . .?

—The costume of a Hungarian hussar, he replied at length, examining the ranks of eyeless satin faces suspended upon the wall, a spectacle that never failed to give pause to the first-time visitor.

Yes, thought Belloni, who in fact had guessed it would be something of this variety. For the young gentleman, now that Belloni saw him more closely, moved about the shop with a modest and unsteady diffidence, and his face was smooth, scarcely capable of producing a single whisker. His limbs, though well-shaped, were delicate; his voice, in its rare moments of employment, was not of the most virile calibre; and he was scarcely an inch or two taller than Belloni, who, because of a tuberculosis of the spine, was self-consciously low of stature. Yes, thought Belloni: the costume of a vigorous and warlike hussar was certainly in constant demand among young fellows like this one, those who needed to steal from their dress some of the manliness they so obviously lacked in their person.

—A Hungarian hussar, Belloni now repeated. His pride as Venice's finest costumier was roused by this quest, and now he was only too anxious to assist. Perhaps you wish to inspect my catalogue? he said. He had perhaps a half-dozen hussar habits at his disposal, all with various choices in accessories, swords and pistols and the like. Surely this fellow would require a sword?

The gentleman displayed no inclination to examine the proffered catalogue, but instead continued to search through the costumes displayed on mannequins or else dangling on the racks below the rows of velvet and satin faces. Such a haphazard search might easily consume the remainder of the night and a good deal of the following morning, for Belloni's inventory was a substantial one: toreadors, Circassian maids, shepherdesses, Polish princesses, pirates, gypsies, Muscovites, harlequins, Pierrots in calico and huge ruff collars . . .

—Ah, remarked the fellow after a moment's careful scru-

178

tiny of one particular item, yes, here it is! Yes, yes! I must have it!

Such a fuss for an ordinary fur-trimmed hussar costume and a gold satin *moretà*! Mind you, thought Belloni, it *was* expensive—150 florins, a price that swelled by a quarter when the gentleman was persuaded to complement the habit with a sword. Belloni packed the mask and costume into a box, accepted the fellow's money and then (at last!) hastily steered him through the door.

—Thank you, *signore*, thank you. Good evening . . .

As the gentleman stepped on to the crowded bridge, Belloni realised that the fellow had not offered his name. Well, no matter; no doubt he was no one very important— and now, ah, there sat old Grossi, waving to him . . .

Prescient as his trade had made him, Signor Belloni had been incorrect to assume that this gentleman was no one of any consequence. The little costumier's reluctance to precipitate himself into Venetian society was no doubt responsible for his error. Had he attended either an opera at, for example, the nearby Teatro San Giovanni Grisostomo or a *bal masqué* hosted by Count Provenzale, or had young Cametti, who attended to such things, been present in the shop, then Belloni may have been honoured with the knowledge that he had sold a habit to one of Venice's most famous singers. As it was now, however, he would not even have recognised the name had it been pronounced in his face; yet soon enough, a few months hence, knowledge of it would bring about his death.

But as if casually indifferent to what fate had in store, Belloni did not so much as cast an eye in his direction as the young gentleman crossed down the slope of the bridge to the San Marco side, then turned left on to the thoroughfare leading into Cannaregio. After stopping a few minutes later at the Teatro San Giovanni Grisostomo, where tomorrow night he would sing the part of Rinaldo in a revival of Handel's opera of that name, the gentleman reached his lodgings in the upper floors of a skinny *palazetto* behind the scaffolded campanile of the Church of Santi Apóstoli at the same moment that the little costumier was planting a kiss upon the plump cheek of Signora Belloni. After an hour, and after a few ablutions of rose-water, a change of knee-breeches and the application of perfumed starch to a periwig—a handsome *perruque à marteaux* purchased a day before from Signor Grossi—he donned the fur-trimmed hat and cape, placed the *moretà* over his face and fastened the small sword to his belt.

A black gondola with a purple canopy awaited him at the *stazio* on the Rio dei Santi Apóstoli. The gondola's canopy was decorated with paper lanterns and the gondolier was clad in red velvet and silver lace, the livery of Count Provenzale. After being assisted aboard, the singer was borne into the Canàl Grande, back beneath the broad stone arch of the Rialto Bridge, which was now filled with revellers much less retiringly modest than Signors Belloni and Grossi in imbibing their delights. Perhaps moved by the spectacle of this riotous assembly, the gondolier began to sing an aria from one of Gasparo Piozzi's eleven operas, though the piece was rendered so execrably that the maestro would no doubt have been reluctant to claim it as his own.

—Please, requested the lounging hussar, whose hand was trailing in the cold waters of the canal, I believe the Count employs you to row, not to sing.

The fellow ceased his racket, applied his oar more responsibly to the waves, and a few moments later manoeuvred them, bumping and rocking, into the emblazoned mooring-posts below the Palazzo Provenzale. The *palazzo*, one of the newer ones at this bend in the canal, was an ornately crenellated bulk standing across from the Ca' Foscari, near the Campo San Samuele, on to whose stone flags light was now spilling from the ranks of bay windows. Also welling over into the *campo* was the music of violins and, above this oratorio, almost drowning it out, the babble of what sounded like a thousand voices. There may well have been that number, too, for tonight was the last—and greatest—masquerade of the season, Count Provenzale's annual *festa*: a banquet, an orchestra, fancy dress, fireworks over the Canàl Grande. The last chance for an amusing diversion before Lent. And such a diversion! Of the many pageants, processions, operas, masked balls, and *fêtes galantes* that were the Carnival, the Count's masquerade had long owned the distinction of being the most spectacular, and often the most notorious, episode of the season.

—There, said the gondolier with a wink, *I* rowed for the Count. Now I believe *you* will sing for him.

180

—I beg your pardon? replied the hussar, startled at having been recognised. Do you presume to know me?

—You must not forget your sword, *signore*. Once again the fellow was all meekness and solicitude. Now, allow me to hand you ashore.

The *stazio* was crowded with a dozen other gleaming boats whose lacquered sides reflected long canal-scapes. The gondolier helped the singer—very unsteadily—on to the short *fondamenta*, where they were approached by a porter who had been waiting between a pair of Corinthian pilasters flanking the door. Or at least the fellow performed the offices of a porter, though he wore the habit of a Tartar soldier. Unlike the gondolier, he displayed no sign of recognition.

—Please, *signore*, this way if you will . . .

Most of the masks were above the stairs in the great *portego* that ran the width of the building and occupied almost the entire second floor. It was from this enormous chamber that the lights—a score of wax torches in gold sconces—and the sounds of the oratorio and voices had issued. And it was here that the Tartar soldier now conducted the hussar, leading him past assorted nabobs, huntsmen and Chinese mandarins traversing corridors or descending the semicircular staircase, some sliding downwards, side-saddle, on the scrolled balustrade and landing with squeals of laughter in brightly costumed heaps at the bottom.

At last they reached the door of the *portego*, whose overmantel was surmounted by two gilded cherubs and whose apple-green ceiling was coved, its cornice a white border of gilt plasterwork with emblems of tritons bearing overflowing urns and tridented goddesses astride sea-horses. A little below the urns and sea-horses' tails a balustraded gallery projected itself in two tiers, each now filled with musicians from San Giovanni Grisostomo, twenty-two of them in all, dressed as aigretted Moors, their playing desultory and almost inaudible. Below them, a long mezzanine, over which some of the company hung, silent and incurious, like bored housewives peering at their children in the street below from laundry-festooned second-floor casements. Below this, finally, an antic and promiscuous crowd, the Count's more enthusiastic guests.

So many maskers! Oh, how busily employed must Signor

Belloni have been! Here by the broad doorway a Persian shah conversed with a Negro page-boy in a plumed turban, while beneath the bank of windows overlooking the canal a Turkish bravo with a smouldering hookah courteously presented a cup of punch to a liveried footman wearing a gold-edged bicorne. In chairs nearby a parlourmaid and a shawled fishwife were enjoying the attentions of a Don Quixote and a gypsy woman clad in a silver girdle and bright red kerchief. And everywhere amid the throng, rustling silk cloaks and black lace mantellinas, their heads hooded in black, moved white-masked dominoes, the multiplying images in a shattered looking-glass. A hundred of them, two hundred, stalked the room. Who were these people? Tonight even Signor Belloni's powers of divination would have been severely taxed. For the little costumier knew that of the many habits and disguises that altered the moral deportment of his clients this plain garment was perhaps the most powerful of them all, the habit for those who truly wished to stay incognito, who for their own mysterious—often nefarious—purposes wished to pass incognito among their more ostentatious brethren.

The hussar entered the hall without attracting anyone's notice, not even that of the musicians in the gallery, who for the past fortnight had seen him each evening at the opera. But by the time he had crossed the floor and reached one of the punch-bowls, his progress had been marked by a Roman centurion wearing a silver breastplate and visored helmet; yet when the hussar turned his head towards him, almost as if in recognition, the centurion quickly looked away, then retired into the throng.

A cup of punch, a dance with the gypsy; another cup, another dance, this time with a shepherdess. The shepherdess was drunk, leaning very close, her breath noxious.

—My flock, she giggled into the hussar's ear as her crook clattered to the floor behind her, narrowly missing a scarlet domino, I fear, good sir, that I have lost my flock . . .

After a moment's struggle the hussar was extricated from this embrace by a tall figure in a black domino.

—Accept my apologies, the domino said very formally. It took me some moments to see you.

—At least there are no other Hungarian hussars.

—That would have been inconvenient.

—Most embarrassing.

182

The white *gnaga*—the grotesque mask—leaned closer. Were you recognised?

—The gondolier...

The domino shied a white-gloved hand through the air and shook the silk hood. The fellow doesn't know as much as he thinks.

—No.

—Apart from him?

—No. And you?

—Who can know? I do not care, the domino said with some emotion, the lace veil over the mouth billowing lightly. The white-gloved hand appeared again from inside the black cloak and touched the hussar's fur-trimmed belly, then progressed cautiously upwards, where it met with no resistance. Now?

—Yes.

—Go, then. You know where? I shall be along—five minutes, yes? Ah! The voice, hollow and muffled behind the mask and veil, was already addressing someone else before the hussar had turned away, fur cloak flapping. I surely can guess who *you* are, my lady! Not even the shawl of a fishwife can hide *your* most charming beauty!

The hussar ascended one set of stairs, then another, narrower one, its steps tapered and uneven. By the time he reached the top he was breathing heavily—from exertion and excitement both—and the floor seemed to shift slightly beneath his boots, the deck of a boat shifting in deep swells. He was sweating inside the hussar costume, and his breathing inside the mask was loud, a raucous whisper. He stopped for a moment to steady himself, one hand upon the wall. Here the sounds of the *portego* had been muted, the lighting was poor, and fragrant aromas of cooking—onions, garlic, purslane, some variety of fish—filtered through the narrow corridor from a kitchen somewhere above, from which there also issued the distant clang of pots, the hiss of steam. He paused longer, hearing footfalls now, the swift shush-and-pat of bare feet receding down the corridor, round one of its bends. Then, silence. Drawing a slow breath he proceeded round a corner, down past two doors, his own feet clopping on the beeswaxed tiles, then turned left into a chamber, whose door he shut solidly behind him. Instinctively his hand moved to the latch before he stopped himself.

The room, a bedchamber, was modestly furnished by comparison with the baroque excesses that characterised the rest of the *palazzo*: a canopied bed with a japanned headboard, a small *armoire*, a silver candelabrum and candle-snuffers sitting on a *cassone*, a gilt-framed glass on one of the walls, which were hung with embossed paper. All familiar enough . . . but what was this? The embroidered counterpane was askew and the candles, three of them, had burnt low and now filled the chamber with an uncertain light and, more confidently, their scent. And there on the floor, a blue ostrich feather—part of an aigrette. The leavings of someone's costume?

—Hello? He stooped to pluck the feather from the knotted carpet. Please—is someone there?

No reply. Shadows flickered on the *armoire* and the papered walls as the candle burned with soft sputters. The violins were audible again, dribbling into the courtyard; below them, the heavy thrumming of a *gamba*. The window, the hussar realised, was open. He moved across to it, a tall arch with a small balcony overlooking the enclosed courtyard. Removing his mask, he pressed his nose against one of the leaded panes, which was open at an angle of 30 degrees. Outside, three floors below, a gabled cistern stood in the centre of the flags, whose borders were edged with a small herb garden and a potted orange tree. Beyond the walls the darkened channel of the Salizzada San Samuele was briefly illuminated by the glow of lanterns, whose yellow light flickered and swayed in short arcs as caped figures were lighted either down to the canal or away in the direction of the Campo Santo Stéfano. The top tiers of the *campo*'s wooden stands, erected for the bull-running, were visible over the intervening tiled rooftops, and over the growing fog of the hussar's breath.

He began to swing the window wide and had placed one soft boot on the balcony, when the door behind him sighed open. The ensuing breeze, a cool rush, very nearly extinguished the candles, whose flames bowed and rose, and bowed again.

—Ah, said the hussar, turning round as the black domino closed the door with another short sigh. It's you.

—Who else? Come, my love.

—But the bed . . .

—I do apologise. The house-maids . . . The cape shrugged.

184

—Please, lock the door, said the hussar, remembering the patter of feet in the corridor.

This was accomplished with a short rasp.

—The candles, whispered the hussar, pointing.

—No, said the domino. I wish to see you.

With this, the white gloves reached upwards, folded back their owner's black hood and removed the white *gnaga*, thereby revealing to the hussar the well-known visage of Count Provenzale. It was a fearsome countenance, almost singular in its grotesqueness, bisected from one ear to the other by a pair of black eyebrows, above which rose a formidable forehead, itself bisected at various angles by a number of thick creases, and below which projected a rubicund Roman nose that overhung a pair of fat lips, the upper of which in turn overhung the lower. The jaw was square, of the same dimension and width as the scored brow, and the neck was short and equally thick, not manifestly distinguishable from the shoulders above which the quad-rangular head gave the impression of being forcefully but inadequately raised.

—Come, the Count's voice rumbled as he peeled away his gloves and then extended his hands, as dark and square as his countenance. The three-cornered black hat removed, a snow-white periwig glowed in stark contrast to the swart features. Come, my coy young fellow.

The hussar crossed the chamber, four short steps, during which passage the boots and cape were shed. Next to be cast off was the wig from Signor Grossi, which fell to the rug, splotching it with a fragrant white plume of starch; then the sword, a muffled clatter; then the stockings, trailing to the floor like ribbons.

—Ah, groaned the Count, falling back on to the embroidered counterpane as he unbuckled his leather belt with one hand and worked the buttons of the hussar's silk frock with the other. Yes, my boy—oh yes, yes, my fine little fellow . . .

—What was that?

The hussar was sitting straight, the frock half-removed to reveal a shoulder as white as the Count's periwig. The candle flames bowed sideways in a breeze, and the shadows of the figures on the bed, barely separate, shimmied and leapt across headboard and wall.

—The window . . .

—I hear nothing, whispered the Count. The shoulder disappeared beneath his black hand, which then slowly peeled away the rest of the frock.

—Someone comes, began the hussar, thinking once again of the hurried footfalls.

—No one, replied the Count. No one important.

On the papered wall his great square shadow rose up and seemed to swallow whole the smaller one of the hussar.

Twenty

 'Yet the Count was wrong,' said Lady Beauclair, 'for there *was* someone. Have you guessed? Yes—outside, on the balcony, pressed flat against the cold bricks. Have you guessed who? No? Why, it is Tristano. The hussar? *You* thought—? No, no, no. My dear Mr Cautley, I fear you must listen more closely . . .'

My lady was right: I had not, in truth, been attending as closely as I might have; I was a poor audience tonight, paying close heed neither to the story nor to my painting. Upon first setting eyes upon me earlier my lady had kindly inquired, as on our last occasion, whether I was ill; and indeed tonight I felt quite as horrible as then. Madam Chapuy's feast—a duck roasted in slices of hothouse pineapple, a salmagundi with herrings and pickles, a potato pudding, venison pasties and gingerbread—I consumed indifferently. I showed a little favour only to three cups of Rhenish wine.

The cause of my downcast spirits no doubt you will have surmised. After purchasing the pigments I had been unable to return to St Alban's Street. Instead, I walked down Whitehall and Parliament Street, then across Westminster Bridge to the south side of the river. There I sat upon the bank for many hours on end, in a kind of moral shock. In fact I sat there all through the day, until the sky had darkened and the sunset was spread like quince jelly across the jumble of rooftops; across the Abbey and the Admiralty, the walls of the Banqueting House, the mud-flats of the river. Here and there lamps were lit along Bridge and Parliament Streets. Linkboys appeared, joggling lanthorns. Rushlights glowed cheerily in the taverns and ale-houses. Torches moved to and fro in soft sweeps behind the wall of the Privy Garden. Like a drowning man gasping and gawping at the stars, I stared for a long time at these trembling sparks across the river—this *ignis fatuus* of London—and thought of the people I knew, or thought I knew, moving invisibly among them, behind them: changing every day with each glance or each bewildering flicker of light, like maskers at Vauxhall or Ranelagh Gardens, possessing no more form or substance than a glove-puppet or a tailor's dummy. For, you see, in these matters I was now almost becoming a sceptic, a confirmed Pinthorpian.

'I am first affrighted and confounded', Mr Hume had written in his *Treatise* (according to Pinthorpe's letter) after his disturbing study of personal identity, 'with that forlorn Solitude, in which I am plac'd by my Philosophy, and fancy myself some strange uncouth Monster, who, not being able to mingle and unite in Society, has been expell'd from all human Commerce, and left utterly abandon'd and disconsolate . . .'

After the philosopher's words had passed through my head a score of times I suddenly recollected—almost too late—my engagement with Lady Beauclair; the only society, it seemed, I had left. And in a panic I had rushed back to the Haymarket for my canvas.

'Perhaps your friend—your footman—' she was now saying as she poured a red ribbon of wine into my cup, 'perhaps he is yet ill?'

'No, no, he is very much improved, thank you,' I replied. The truth was, however, that these past few days I had scarcely spared poor Jeremiah a thought; he might have been sweating with the Black Death for aught I knew. Many was the time in the past week that he—and sometimes also Samuel—had hoped to accompany me either to St Alban's Street or Chiswick; but in denying their hopes and repulsing them from my door I had been as adamant and heartless as my kinsman. For then, a few days before—indeed a few *hours* before—I had been filled with a sanguine spirit, and I had regarded the young Sharps as tethers upon the gondola of a great oiled-silk, primary-coloured hot-air balloon

187

I was on the very brink of releasing into a glorious morning sky.

'I fear you are angry with me,' said my lady in a searching tone.

'No,' I replied in a dredged voice meant to conjure exactly the opposite meaning. For there was now another reason for my low spirits this evening, and therefore for my desultory progress on *A Lady by Candle-light*. After we had sat to the table I found myself made bold enough by my desperate temper to ask my lady if I might assume the privilege of escorting her to the masquerade at Vauxhall. She confessed to being flattered by this request but dithered prettily about whether or not she might comply with it. I pressed her further, and then her answer had become more precise.

'I regret, Mr Cautley,' she said, lowering her eyes, 'that I shall, alas, be incapable of requiting this kind wish of yours.'

My beautiful balloon bumped to the ground, its hundreds of yards of silk slack, its tethers limp.

'Yet I must confess,' she added after a few thoughtful seconds, 'that I shall in fact be in attendance at Vauxhall that evening—and so perhaps we shall encounter one another there *after all*.'

Far from being contented with this revelation and its hypothetical coda, my spirits were all the more perturbed. I smelled a rat, to wit, Robert—though I dared not bring myself to ask if this scent-sprinkled little villain was the pre-empting party. Upon my arrival I had, of course, searched the chamber for signs of him, even sniffing the air for the fragrant leavings of his perfume; but there had been no traces of any kind. Yet I was not tricked: doubtless she had merely been more cautious.

I gnashed my teeth for a moment in silence, showing the heat of my displeasure; then, when she must have received my unspoken message, I inquired which costume she proposed to wear.

Lady Beauclair steadfastly refused to divulge its nature. 'If I should tell you, Mr Cautley,' she said in her familiar teasing voice, which tonight I found considerably more provoking than before, 'why then I would surely spoil our sport altogether!'

Coquettish female! I wanted to tell her that I did not wish our relations to be governed by the rules of sport or separated at riotous masquerades by masks and disguises. I wanted to tell her how I wished the two of us might be more candid and artless with one another; how we might found our dealings upon a sturdy Gibraltar of faith and trust, not upon trickery and intrigue: for Life, like Art, was not to be directed by artifice and deception but ruled, rather, by truth and a strong sincerity of intent, by a fidelity to the universal, the ideal, and the inward form of things. (You see, I was not yet so much of a Pinthorpian after all.) But, sadly, my old philosophy now served to remind me of its spectacular betrayal by my master, seemingly its greatest proponent; so again I said nothing.

I felt my lady's eyes upon me as I effected a few fidgety daubs upon the canvas. No doubt she now regarded me as an impetuous young fellow unable to govern his passions, but at that moment, for the first time, I did not care so much for her opinion.

'It is no matter,' I said. Once again I was employing a tone intended to imply the contrary. 'Perhaps I shall see you at the masquerade . . . perhaps not. Now,' I said, furrowing my brow and tightening my lips, 'do, if you are not fatigued, resume the history.'

Twenty-one

Tristano had arrived at the Palazzo Provenzale more than an hour before. Like the hussar, he arrived by gondola, though from the opposite direction, leaning on his cushions and drinking a cup of wine as his own gondolier sang just as execrably. On one side, the sun shone upon the parabolic dome-line of Santa Maria della Salute, while on the other the Piazza San Marco, from which he had come, was filling with harlequins, long-nosed *Punchinelli*, musicians rattling timbrels and salt-boxes, vendors of sweetmeats, and more indeterminate figures crossing the *campi* and arched bridges in their silk hoods and black lace mantellinas.

What does Tristano look like now as he lounges on the

cushions, drinking his wine? What sort of figure does he cut at this time? Tonight he is wearing a Vandyke costume (he, too, is a patron of Signor Belloni, who sold him the habit two days before at a price of 250 florins): a dark-pink, ermine-lined cloak, a white silk hat trimmed with ostrich feathers, a lace cravat, a white velvet mask. At first he is not easy to recognise—the mask notwithstanding—for it is almost ten years since we saw him last. Not everything about him has changed, of course. Were he to lift his white mask, we should see that his dark eyes are still too closely set and his nose yet comes boldly forth in its sharp and irregular curve. But he is taller now, as we would expect, though perhaps an inch or two shy of the majority of his fellows. The deficiency in his height must be the result of an abbreviation in his trunk, since his limbs as well as his neck appear long, slim, graceful; and he has thus far avoided corpulence, something of an occupational hazard in his profession. As he traverses the *fondamenta*—for his gondola has now arrived before the *palazzo*—his gait is lengthy and slow, as if he were wading through water.

From the *fondamenta* he was conducted by the Tartar soldier into the *portego*, which was already crowded. Like the hussar, he ascended the staircase unrecognised. For someone of his eminence this anonymity possessed obvious pleasures. Ordinarily when he entered a hall such as this he was besieged in an instant by frowsty old dukes and uniformed young gentlemen with needle-thin swords and primly simpering smiles. Even more aggressively, he was set upon by their ladies, those gaunt, bored creatures whose eyes momentarily kindled to life when they caught sight of him. Then, with a frou-frou of silk and satin, they began their rush forward: a tide of gold stoles, paper fans, pink tassles, panther-skin muffs, yapping poodles. Unhappily, their husbands were quite content to relinquish them to his custody; the Italian husband is often a most indifferent lover, foisting his wife upon whomsoever he may and thereby leaving himself at liberty for other pursuits—the tobacco-pipe, the gaming-table, someone else's palmed-off wife. As a result of this honoured custom of domestic politics, Tristano had spent many of his evenings listening to chatter about obdurate daughters, neglectful servants, sequins lost at faro, larger fortunes dropped at the milliner's, wealthy parents-in-law who clung spitefully to life.

Now, free from such attentions, he stepped inside the hall, the blue plumes of the aigrette bowing and floating above his head. Or was he indeed free? He noticed one of the masks—a Roman centurion—taking stock of him from behind a visored helmet. Or was he in point of fact watching? With a swirl of red cape the helmet ducked and disappeared into the mob.

At the punch-bowl he was set upon by a lady in the costume of a shepherdess. He declined when she requested the favour of a dance, but she took advantage of the pressing crowd to push herself into him, in the process knocking his plumed hat on to the floor with her long staff.

—A drink, then, kind sir, she said when he retrieved the hat. I'm so very thirsty...

She raised an empty cup, whose irregular oscillations before her masked face suggested that the lady had attempted to quench her thirst for a good while already.

As a consequence of these oscillations, as well as of some-one's straying elbow, most of her replenished cup was, how-ever, splashed on to the floor. During their descent a few pink drops also splattered the lace hem of her costume and one of her kid-leather slippers.

—Look, she lamented, her eyes blinking almost tearfully behind her mask.

Tristano, whose elbow had truly been innocent of this fateful glance, none the less knelt at her feet and mopped at the stains with his handkerchief. During this application the spirits of the shepherdess evidently improved. One of her feet now slipped out of its shoe and elevated itself to the middle of his right thigh, then the left. Having established its bearings it progressed upwards to their intersection, the toes wriggling in a pink stocking. Tristano tried to rise, but the crook of her staff quickly encircled his neck.

—Come, she said, keeping him down with a force that belied the earlier flaccidity of her limbs. She was still balan-cing on one foot, and the eyes in the mask were hard, shining. Come—I know of a place.

Tristano may well have consented, for the unexpected touch of her wriggling toes had not been entirely unpleasant. Yet from his subservient position he had glimpsed the face behind the veil, and what he had seen—a dimpled chin upon which neither the sharpest razor nor the heaviest application of powdered lead could entirely disguise a bluish gloss—

191

made him first start and then twist free from the confinement of the staff. In the process of acquiring his liberty he fell backwards into the ruffled skirts of a lady, who then toppled on to him with a squeal. When he elevated her to her feet—the shepherdess by this time had disappeared—the lady assured him that she had sustained no injury, accepted his apologies, then handed him the plumed hat, which in the confusion had come down lopsidedly upon her own head. The hat, she pointed out in a good-humoured way, was not entirely incompatible with her costume, for she too was in Vandyke dress—a raised lace collar, ruched overskirts, slashed sleeves decorated with artificial flowers and tiny pink ribbons.

—Now, *signore*, she said with a charming laugh, if on the other hand you had been bedecked in the fur hat of a hussar . . .

They drank a cup of punch together; then the lady, who thus far had been quite charming and demure, whispered, Come—I know a place. Upstairs, *signore*. She took his hand and started to lead. Please, come.

Tug—tug—tug. She pulled him along with precise jerks, the pressure on his hand not relenting even when they reached the top of the second staircase and his resistance, mild as it was, finally diminished. This opposition had arisen not from the memory of the shepherdess but, rather, from the sight of the Roman centurion whose visored gaze unmistakably took account of their progress across the smooth terracotta tiles of the great *portego*.

—Inside, she now said, leading him round a corner and gesturing to a chamber on their left. Quickly now.

She had escaped with only seconds to spare, for hardly had she slipped through the doorway, clutching the parts of her costume that she had not been able to step into or hastily pull over her head, than another figure, that of a man, appeared. For want of other opportunities—he had considered, then abandoned, the idea of diving beneath the canopied bed—Tristano, in a similar state of dishabille, dragging the breeches and frock discarded only moments before, leapt on to the tiny balcony.

When they first heard the footfalls on the stair Tristano had been in favour of remaining in bed, such as they were; for it would hardly have been the first time, would it, that a couple was surprised in these circumstances, especially at a masquerade? Even if he entered the chamber, the interloper, whatever his business, would retreat hastily, blurting a surprised apology. Besides, though Tristano could not vouch for her face (for she had not yet removed her mask), the loosened corset into which he had just plunged a hand gave testimony that she was a fair lady indeed, not one to be callowly relinquished. And so at the first clop of the heels he merely lowered his head and kissed the lightly downed vale of the bosom, which had been elevated by a startled gasp.

—Someone comes . . .

—My lady, he murmured, half reproachfully, before restoring the intimate congress of lips and bosom. These soft swells, he noticed, were at the point of their deepest cleft distinguished by a peculiar W-shaped constellation of moles: Cassiopeia, he thought, his osculations increasingly ardurous as they progressed lower and the draw-strings of the corset were further released.

But the lady for some reason would not be compromised. In fact, it almost seemed that as he struggled with the folds and fastenings of her costume she was listening for these footfalls, which, indeed, arrived soon enough. Certainly the passion that moved her to tug him up two flights of stairs seemed to dissolve the very second they reached their destination beneath the canopy. Perhaps this was her husband, some jealous, violent fellow. The centurion, perhaps? Yes—after she fled he had been expecting to see the visored helmet arrive at the door, and so how surprised was he when in the triangle of light he glimpsed instead the fur-trimmed hat of a hussar. At this point he had then been tempted to step back inside the room and announce himself to the fellow, for there was no need for discretion now that the lady had safely absconded. Yet something in her manner—she had been in fear of something more than her reputation—persuaded him to remain on the balcony, half-naked and shivering though he was. And so he kept silent, kept to the shadows, even when in coming to the window the fellow was close enough to have his nose tweaked.

The appearance of the black domino, whom he soon recognised as the Count, made an escape even more impossible. Tristano was well known to the Count, of course. Who do you think brought him to Venice in the first place? Count Provenzale was from an old Neapolitan family whose wealth, even in Venice, was legendary. Still, even in his most ceremonious moments he looked, Tristano always thought, like a thick-shouldered beast that had reared itself on to a pair of unfamiliar hind legs, bellowing and trampling its lair. What, Tristano now wondered, was he doing with this fellow, the hussar? The Count had a great sexual appetite, to be sure, though it was not known to extend itself in this direction . . .

He dressed himself awkwardly on the balcony, hoping that the Count might draw the bed-curtains and thereby allow him to tiptoe past. He also hoped that none of the figures who had begun appearing in the courtyard below— a loose knot of drunken revellers—would raise his eyes to the window just yet. He very nearly disclosed himself, however, when one of the plumes remaining in his hat tickled his nose—it was either that or the hussar's abundantly perfumed powder—and he sneezed with a short, squelched cry.

He froze. The shadows on the wall froze. Laughter— directed at him?—rose, echoing, from the courtyard. After a few seconds the shadows inside the chamber resumed their exertions, moving to and fro like fighters in a dumb show. Articles of clothing, discarded, flopped to the floor.

But what was this?

After a moment Tristano had pressed his nose to the window-pane, anxiously checking the composition of the bed-curtains. What he saw made him forget his escape, for much to his surprise he saw that, like the shepherdess, the hussar had been an impostor: having disencumbered his partner of the frock and breeches, the Count, still in his black cape, was hunkered over what could now be recognised as the body of a young lady. By the light of the candle Tristano could see her pair of wishbone legs, at whose dark intersection the Count first introduced his great, fleshy nose, and then, after fumbling for a few seconds beneath the cape, a bow-shaped member whose prodigious dimensions attested to the justness of his envied reputation.

The lady received him with a short cry, replying to the motion of his hips with a few further cries and then a series of concurrent heaves. Alas for her, the Count's boasted equipment lacked all powers of endurance. After a short moment his motions ceased with a suppressed cry, one which

194

in truth sounded rather like Tristano's stifled sneeze. The lady sympathetically reproduced a version of this utterance, and then after the Count rolled heavily sideways they lay together on the bat-wings of his cape, panting rapidly, as if their pleasures had defied the hours and not terminated after a duration of barely two minutes. Upon the lady's instigation they next indulged in a few caresses and turtle-billing kisses, hers being by far the more artful and moti-vated, evidently provided for the purposes of rousing her lover's forces to their former state of glory. But the Count was already preparing his retreat.

—My guests, he murmured apologetically, gathering up his cloak and drawing his breeches over his copious and rather woolly posteriors, his mighty appendage in the course of this operation striking like a clapper between his legs. The Countess, he said, shrugging.

—Yes, the lady agreed, in no particular manner, looking away.

—You will be ready for the performance? He was all business now, adjusting his hat and periwig, smoothing his domino.

—Yes, yes . . .

—Farewell, then, my young fellow.

Chuckling at this private source of amusement and offer-ing his lady a final kiss upon the brow, he clapped the white mask over his broad countenance, then unlatched the door and departed without another word, his cape billowing behind him.

After the door thudded shut the lady seemed disinclined to resume her costume with any special dispatch, and indeed even to move. Instead she lay upon the cushions in a lazy posture that concealed few secrets of her person. If her inducements had failed in the case of the Count, she could have counted upon a fresh reinforcement from the window, for the truth was that, as he peeped through the pane (his nose had scarcely left it for a second), Tristano's own forces had achieved a state of the highest plight. Yet by now the expressions of this passion, the exhalations of a series of deeply fetched breaths, had succeeded in fogging the pane, and thus obscuring his stolen prospect. He was doubting whether he dared apply his handkerchief to it, and thereby perhaps inadvertently announce himself and so spoil this view in any case, when something—a small pebble—struck him sharply in the middle of the back.

Before he could turn to discover whence it came, another such missile, though a slightly larger one, whispered past his ear and struck the mortar beside his right hand with a dull crack. He peered quickly into the courtyard in time to see three upturned faces—masks, rather—and two outstretched arms, each of which had released a further brickbat. A number of shouts and insults were likewise being hurled, and so in order to preserve his reputation as well as his crown he had no further option. He pushed open the window and stepped inside.

The lady cried out, of course, and was roused very abruptly from her languorous indifference to all motion. To protect her exposed charms she first seized the tangled counterpane and then, a second later, recovered her fur-trimmed cape. This last effort, however, disturbed her balance, and she tumbled part way on to the floor.

—Sir! she cried, scrambling back on to the bed and encircling herself in the folds of counterpane and cape. Please! What—?

—Do not be alarmed, my lady, he said in his most mannerly tone, while performing a low bow to complement it. Do not be frightened. I am Tristano, the famous castrato. Perhaps you have heard of me?

This announcement was motivated, first of all, by a desire to allay her fears. Perhaps she was ignorant enough to believe, as was indeed a current enough opinion, that impotence attended his artificial condition, and that as a result he could pay a lady no disrespect. But it was also prompted by vanity—yes, he was as vain as the rest of his tribe—as well as by an aspiration to succeed to the Count's late pleasures: for his name, as we have seen, often moved even the most chaste and noble ladies to the pursuit of what the philosophers tell us are the baser comforts of our existence.

Yet he was inexplicably defeated in these last hopes. If the lady had been calmed to some degree by his courteous words and their attendant bow, her alarm increased upon the pronunciation of his identity. For now she not only sought to conceal those lovely parts that had lately granted the Count his brief though intense delights, but her countenance as well, hurriedly draping it with her cape. After

196

obscuring herself in this manner and venting a few distraught murmurs, she frantically gathered the remainder of her costume and then felt her way through the door and into the corridor. Whereupon she left her admirer to ponder his strange fortune as, for the second time that evening, he stood in the centre of this chamber and watched as a lady unaccountably fled from him in a hectic swirl of garments, like a distressed vessel travelling under a toppled mainsail.

Tristano expected neither to learn who this lady was nor to see her again, and after receiving the more steadfast attentions of a shepherdess—an authentic one this time— he had almost succeeded in forgetting her. So how surprised was he when in the *portego* two hours later this hussar, accompanied by the Count, moved to the bank of windows overlooking the canal.

—Ladies and gentlemen, announced the Count, whose mask had been removed to expose his rubicund visage. He gestured toward the hussar, whose own mask had likewise been deposed, revealing to the company the soft countenance of the young gentleman who earlier that evening had transacted his business with Signor Belloni. May I present for your pleasure this evening, he said, the gentleman who has of late been singing in my production of *Rinaldo* at San Giovanni Grisostomo—the famous castrato Il Prizziello!

Her name, he learned later, was Maddalena Broccolo, though of course no one knew her by this. At the Ospedale della Pietà—that is, at the foundling hospital, which was really a *conservatorio* for young girls, only some of whom were actual foundlings—she was known briefly as 'La Maddalena' to those who heard her sing from the gallery high above the concert chamber. Later, after she met the Count at one such assembly, and after he bore the expense of private tuition in the house of the great Roman maestro Ottaviano Prizzi, she went through a transmogrification more profound and enduring than any effected by Signor Belloni and was from that time known as 'Il Prizziello'. Four years, now, of Il Prizziello. Four years of masquerade.

—He shall kill you if you dare say anything.

—Do you threaten me?

—The Count is a most powerful man.

—It is not for the sake of the Count that I keep my peace.

—Do you blackmail me?

—Need you ask?

—Yes, she replied. These days one suspects everyone.

Tristano rolled out of the bed and padded to the window. In the distance, above the dark planes of the dovecot and a family of narrow cypresses—two tall, one short—he could see the triangulated roof-line and melon-shaped dome of the Count's villa. Beyond, to a few ragged cheers, the first fireworks blossomed in the dust-coloured sky: a school of swimming lights followed by great jellyfishes of grey smoke. The Count was always a great one for fireworks. Fireworks and gaming. And hunting and duelling and intriguing. And ladies—usually of the vilest sort. If in previous times the citizens of Venice had been known for their skill in seamanship, as explorers and merchant adventurers, or as painters and poets and musicians, now they were known as gamblers, pimps, intriguers; the brothel-keepers of Europe. A decline, Tristano thought, marked nowhere more spectacularly, more lamentably, than in the case of this newcomer, Count Provenzale.

—When shall you quit his protection?

Maddalena stirred beneath the quilt. She had shrouded herself for reasons of modesty more than anything else, for it was now early July, the summer *villeggiatura*. Venice, a dozen leagues away, was hot and empty, its lords having scattered to the countryside, to places like this. Here the Carnival continued. Last night there had been music in the Count's ballroom, this morning a banquet in a cool glade a league beyond the villa's gate. The Count, she thought, had been watching them as their chariot returned to the villa through the serpentine sweep of poplars, elm and ilex. He and Il Piozzino—yes, Scipio was here, too, a great favourite of the Count's—had followed in a chariot of their own. Yes: as he disembarked on to the footstool by the plashing, violet-scented fountain, the Count was most definitely watching, judging. What did he suspect from behind that smile? And then this evening it had been so difficult to slip away. Only the confusion of the *festa* had permitted them to steal—undetected?—through the garden with its crescent-shaped beds of oleander and acanthus. Past the marble statuary—boars, griffins, Cupids astride dolphins—that glowed a soft white in the dusk. Through a horseshoe archway, then along a low wall of mortared rubble. Finally, into one of the small, whitewashed cottages behind the dovecot and the semi-spherical rear of the Temple of Worthies.

—He will never allow it, she replied after a moment.

—Then it is he who blackmails.

But the affair, as well he knew, was more complex than this. Already—a half-dozen times—she had explained. This continuing masquerade was needful, for after all she was a woman. In the Papal States—this was where she had commenced singing opera—a lady's voice was considered a scandal to piety, prohibited not only in the churches but upon the stages as well. Elsewhere things were scarcely any better. Il Prizziello, the disguise, had been the Count's idea. He had seen her perform at one of the Pietà's public concerts. Rather, he had *heard* her perform, for the assembly was deprived of the privilege of a full view of the girls, being limited to what could be glimpsed of these remarkable creatures through an iron lattice. A host of angels, invisible to the eye. One day later he was received as a visitor, albeit on the opposite side of another grille. 'La Maddalena' wore a gold crucifix and a pleated bodice of blue moiré silk, but still he could not see her face, which the sisters had artfully veiled. Two days later, and after a modest contribution to the *Pia Congregazione*, he was delivered by one of these pious ladies to the girl's bed.

—He will have us both murdered, she said, in a voice that betrayed little. You remember poor little Calvé? He, too, professed his love.

A year before, the little Frenchman, a painter of landscapes, had pursued her with his attentions in the conviction that Il Prizziello was truly a man. In the course of his payment of these respects, which became ever more ardent for being coldly rebuffed, Calvé had imperilled her identity. Last autumn two men fishing for mullet in their *bragozzo* raised him from the Lagoon in their nets.

—Tonight, my lady, we have more important things with which to concern ourselves. He returned to the bed and kissed her brow. Come, the fireworks have almost finished. We must not arrive late at the masquerade. Where, pray, is your costume? Am I to know your identity tonight, my fine young fellow?

Maddalena's white hand reached out from beneath the quilt and touched a cream-coloured pasteboard box, flipping off its lid. Folded inside was the long caftan of ultramarine

199

damask and jewelled girdle of a Turkish costume, which two days before she had purchased at Signor Belloni's shop on the Rialto Bridge at a cost of 200 florins.

—Thank you, *signore*, the little costumier had said, with a polite bow and a wide smile. Thank you. An honour, Il Signor Prizziello. Truly an honour!

Twenty-two

 'But how was it that Signor Belloni now knew his—or rather *her*—? That is,' I resumed, 'how came he to learn the name Il Prizziello?'

Lady Beauclair had interrupted her story long enough to pour each of us another cup of Rhenish wine, and to accept dishes of strawberries from Madam Chapuy. Much of my earlier impetuosity had been dissolved by four cups of the wine, which at each swallow seemed to swirl, lazily and soothingly, in the centre of my breast. With my lady's permission I had lighted my tobacco-pipe from the candle's flame and was now blowing fat plumes of foetid smoke at her ceiling, giving her chamber the aspect of a smouldering brush-fire.

'Why, he learned it from Signor Cametti,' she responded, after coughing daintily into her hand because of this great holocaust, 'for Signor Cametti, I have said, was a great one for operas and masquerades. Indeed, he was in attendance that night at the Palazzo Provenzale.'

'Yet I have marked him as a lowly apprentice,' I said as I added a few more cirrus clouds to the conflagration. 'Surely this fellow has been mixing above his station?'

She smiled faintly at this observation. 'Have you not visited Venice in the time of the Carnival, Mr Cautley?'

I admitted that the pleasure had not been mine, feeling deflated by this forced confession of my deficiencies as gentleman of the world. At the same time, however, I was somewhat flattered that the question had been posed in the first place, as it seemed to attribute to me the worldliness that I so craved but did not exactly own. 'Not during the

Carnival,' I added hastily, counterfeiting a cough and placing my pipe rather self-consciously between my teeth and giving it a fierce champ.

'In Venice during the Carnival,' she explained as another slim red ribbon curled into my cup, 'this mixing between the stations—as you call them—is the strict order of the day. Everyone wears a mask at all times, from the doge to the lowliest kitchen-maid. Indeed, one scarcely glimpses a bare face or an ordinary suit of clothes for the whole of the Carnival, which, beginning in October, extends until Christmas, resumes upon Twelfth Night and continues once more until Lent, before recommencing for the fortnight that succeeds Ascension Day. And because of these perpetual masks and disguises—because their wearers become anonymous, mysterious, incognito (or, perhaps, incognita)—all of the citizens of the republic share equally—if unwittingly—in their joys. For you must understand, Mr Cautley, it is a time of innumerable possibilities!'

This description naturally put me in mind of the promiscuous crowd I had witnessed at Pancras Wells, then of my own mask and disguise chosen from Mr Johnson's Habit-Warehouse in Tavistock Street. What 'innumerable possibilities', I wondered, might await me at Vauxhall Gardens?

My attention was, however, presently occupied by a mask—if I may call it such—of a different variety. Half-way through my lady's description of the riotous assembly of Venice I had commenced slopping turpentine across the right-hand corner of my canvas, behind the steadily resolving waxed image of my subject's partly veiled head. I was applying a very liberal dose, *à la* Sir Endymion, and the effect produced was now as peculiar as it was unexpected. So abundant was my application, and so aggressive was my brush, that I succeeded in diluting and then stripping not only the paint lately applied (this in fact had been my design, for through my earlier fit of pique, and also perhaps because of the three cups of Rhenish, I had made a wretched mess of the drapery behind her turban) but also the paint—the priming—that lay beneath. In short, I had opened a small window upon the hidden portrait over which my own effort was superimposed.

Yet before I had occasion to scrutinise this palimpsest more closely, my lady offered an impish smile and wondered aloud whether or not she might be allowed the privilege of a puff from my tobacco-pipe. I responded that if she had so much as sucked a breath of air in the past five minutes then most assuredly she had done so already; but not being dissuaded so easily she extended her hand, and I relented, wondering, however, why a lady of such refinement should wish to partake of such a masculine pleasure.

She accepted the pipe with great alacrity, but then swiftly became more tentative, studying it for a few seconds as if uncertain of whither to suck. But soon she pushed aside the veil and placed the stem between her carmined lips, pursing them daintily upon it. At first she suckled and nursed so softly and prettily that, as I watched with a delicate and inexplicable pleasure, I feared for a moment that the flame would extinguish itself; but then, as if these tender efforts were not being requited as expected, she soon commenced the most prodigious sucking. I worried that she might gather into her lungs not merely the smoke—against whose intoxicating properties I was now giving her a concerned warning—but also its smouldering source, which with each great pull glowed as bright hell-fire in the bowl.

'Take heed, my lady,' I said in a tentative voice, remembering my first tuition in this art from Mr Sharp a month before. I had sucked eagerly at the good man's pipe as if trying to draw a camel through its slender reed, in the midst of which exertions my chaps had shrunk, my eyes had crossed, and my lips, which advanced half-way down the stem as if threatening to gobble up the entire pipe, had wagged like those of a beached trout with a hook in its mouth. My prompt reward for these endeavours had been a most painful and groaning illness. 'You must take care not to inspire the smoke,' I now warned in the gravest tone.

Yet she merely persisted with her tremendous gulps, between which she offered the opinion that she was mastering the habit. Alas, the upshot of these imprudently vigorous aspirations was in good time, as I feared, a fit of violent coughs, through whose unrelenting percussions her face attained the colour of our Rhenish wine.

'My lady,' I repeated with some concern when this fit showed little sign of subsiding and was now attended by several gags. Streams of tears advanced down her cheeks, which had maintained their bright colour even through the layers of white lead. So profuse were these tears that presently they began to act upon her countenance in the same

202

fashion as the excess of turpentine upon the corner of *A Lady by Candle-light*, partially stripping away the thick covering of paint, the rouge and powdered lead, and revealing stripes of the foundation—the flesh—that lay beneath.

You may well imagine that I did not stop to bear witness to this phenomenon. I rushed to the window, threw it open, then rushed back to her side. Placing my hands on her sides, which were contracting and contorting beneath the confinement of the corset, I steered her to this aperture and commanded her to breathe. This she did with a few stertorous rasps—before promptly recommencing her violent coughs and gags. The gushes of evening air (which, alas, smelled almost as disagreeable as my pipe) seemed powerless to counteract the intoxicating fumes, and when I persuaded her to withdraw her head from the casement a moment later she scarcely seemed any more composed. She seemed, indeed, much the worse for it, her complexion having translated itself from a brilliant crimson to a bluish white. Great droplets stood out upon her brow, and her eyes as they reflected the candle seemed prominent and burnished to an unnaturally vivid lustre.

'Please,' she rasped weakly, 'Mr Cautley—'

In the middle of this supplication she swooned into my arms, falling upon me with a force that very nearly landed both of us upon the floor. I managed to brace myself against an elbow-chair, into which, once my balance was recuperated, I gently transferred my insensible burden, shouting all the while for the assistance of Madam Chapuy. But since this good lady had evidently immersed herself in some duty far below the stairs and so did not catch my appeal for volatile salts, I was required to slap my lady's wrists and cheeks and then, when these measures failed to revive her, to liberate her from the rigid confinement of her stays and thereby permit her to breathe unencumbered.

A most delicate task! For a second I appraised the voluptuous disorder of her dress as she spread across the elbow-chair, then drew a deep breath and plunged my hands into the soft ultramarine fabric of her garment, which I sought to loosen. In any other circumstance such an action would surely have been interpreted as indecent—and despite the circumstance I was not, I fear, wholly exempt from a few indecent thoughts. For though I was a virtuous youth, and though I was frantic with fear, yet I could not help but pause for a second when my paint-smudged hands discovered how the Turkish costume and then, especially, my lady's naked skin were both of them inconceivably soft, like finely ground frankfort black when it is rubbed betwixt the fingers.

Startled from my fixation by a short moan and a few convulsive twitches in my subject, I quickly proceeded to tug and jerk at the laces of the whalebone corset into which Madam Chapuy had squeezed her some hours before. As it transpired, this soft cry was a prelude to a revival, for my patient regained her senses in the very second when I had unlaced the corset and exposed her shift. Yet my relief at my lady's swift recovery was greatly qualified by the construction that she appeared to put upon my actions.

'What—?' Coming alert and seeming greatly vexed and affrighted, she blinked in horror at her drooping costume, her exposed corset, both of which she quickly endeavoured to compose with a reserve wholly out of keeping with her previous character. 'Fie! What is this? I declare!'

'My lady—' I leaned forward and sought to assist her with the lacings, but she resisted my efforts with a violent species of fury.

'Unhand me, sir! Base man, how you surprise me! A scandalous villain! To take such callow advantage of a lady! I pray you have not dared—not—! Do not touch me! *Do not gaze upon me*!'

It appeared she knew not where to place her hands, whether across her bosom, which was partially exposed, or over her streaked countenance, whose cosmetics were rapidly waning in power.

I averted my face from this spectacle, but when my protests and attempts to come to an *éclaircissement*, and thereby pacify her, went for naught, succeeding only in raising her temper, I chose to reclaim my reputation by providing assistance in a fashion that could not, surely, be prone to any false interpretation: I removed my handkerchief and made to daub at the rivulets which had carved their way down her cheeks during the most explosive moments of the fit. I was strongly reminded of some of Sir Endymion's portraits when the master's great slathers and gobbets of paint slipped and slid down the canvas and spattered on to the floor, as if the faces of the princesses and merchants' wives were melting in a mighty heat.

My lady's response to my services at her own melting face—for such it almost seemed—was, however, equally as obstinate and violent as her previous actions; for she very nearly tipped her elbow-chair on to its back while striving to avoid my attentions. Nothing could equal my astonishment—my dismay—at her suspicions, at this inexplicable alteration in her character.

'Away from me!' she commanded, once more curtaining herself with the veil and then for good measure concealing her face from detection with her hands as well, as if made terrified by the thought of me peering into it. 'Begone!' her voice squeaked through this ten-fingered mask. 'Let me alone! *Let me alone!*'

Whereupon she blew out the candle and then, gathering her bedraggled garments about her, fled into the adjoining chamber, banging the door and bolting it, and leaving me standing in the middle of an unrelieved darkness.

Ten minutes later, however, she had composed not only her costume but also her temper. Her face, too, had been composed, artfully repainted with rouge and pearl-powder in the privacy of her boudoir. When she emerged in an oblong stretch of light she discovered me upon the point of departing, standing frozen at the door like a statue; like Harmodius or Aristogiton, though now bereft of his deity. The chamber was yet dark as pitch.

'First Sir Endymion, now my lady,' I had been thinking a minute before as I crawled across the floor in the darkness, gathering my paints and my pipe: my offending pipe, the apple for which, surely, I was to be expelled from Eden. 'Now, George, you have lost both of them. Irreparable breaches have opened. Whither now will you go? What now will you do?' My head had bumped itself painfully upon the leg of the table.

She lighted the candle, now a stub. Then she filled our cups with wine.

'Please.' Her voice was calm, though her hand quaked slightly, and one or two droplets spilled on to the table, like dots of blood. 'Be seated, good sir. Drink.'

I seated myself, warily, reluctantly. I took the cup and drank. My hand, too, was trembling, spilling one or two more dots of blood. I was still clutching my paints and the wet canvas; the fragments, the *disjecta membra* of my life,

205

assembled in darkness. She refilled my cup; the bottle was very nearly finished, a half-inch of wine remaining.

'Drink,' she repeated.

For the next five minutes she begged gently for my forgiveness. She knew my attentions had been proper, she said. She thanked me for my concern. Truly, she could not thank me enough. She apologised a thousand times, in a thousand ways. She said she had been ill, frightened—out of her senses. Gentlemen, she claimed, had taken liberties before—taken advantage of her; never mind how. Gentlemen whom she had trusted. Oh, the stories she could tell! The villains she might name! So . . . did I blame her? A lady was required to protect her virtue and gentlemen were so—deceptive. Yet (here she smiled gently, confidentially) she knew I was not so, and assuredly she did not condemn the species for a few of its vilest members! My virtue, she said, was what had recommended me to her; what attracted me to her. She knew—she was *convinced*—that I should never betray her faith or trust.

Once this monologue had been completed she daubed at the corners of her eyes, which in the course of her defence had grown moist and, it appeared, once again threatened the composition of her *maquillage*. Yet no tears fell, and she raised her head. She appeared to be awaiting my reaction.

Silently I set up my canvas and easel and opened my box of paints. 'We shall need a fresh candle,' I said at last.

'The display of fireworks ended,' she was saying a moment later as she lighted a new candle from the flame of the old one and then assumed her familiar posture. 'The last pyramids, columns, and lions' manes of light reflected in the short strip of canal and the villa's windows, then died away . . .'

As I recommenced my own work I hid from her view the exposed patch upon the canvas, the window that had unexpectedly opened—upon what? For I was wondering, would my lady have sought to draw a veil across that as well?

Twenty-three

 The guests clambered down from the rows of benches raked twenty feet high and proceeded inside the Villa Provenzale. An orchestra—thirty-four instruments—was playing in the immense carved gallery above the Great Room, but their music was soon overcome by the commotion of the arriving guests, of whom there were perhaps two hundred, all masked and costumed.

The Villa Provenzale, almost as capacious as the Palazzo Provenzale, was once no doubt a distinguished edifice, having been designed by the great Palladio for one of the Count's forebears almost two centuries before. But after the Count's endless and seemingly indiscriminate additions and 'improvements' (including, so it was rumoured, the incorporation of a number of secret staircases) the house and its outlying wings had now come to resemble a collection of hat-boxes jumbled across the green-velvet surface of a faro table. Inside, a similarly untamed order of aggrandising restoration prevailed, and as a result the Great Room, a grandiose octagonal saloon, made a spectacular and imposing sight. Its four doors were architraved, its walls panelled in mahogany, scrolled with golden vines, husk-chains and honeysuckles, and furnished, wherever these decorations permitted, with busts and urns in brackets, as well as some twenty paintings: biblical scenes and martyrs by Ricci, townscapes by Carlevaris, and portraits by Carriera, including one of the Count himself, whose vicious face glowered upon his guests from a rococo frame set in a specially reserved alcove. The saloon was ceiled by the melon-shaped dome, which had been divided into plaster coffers whose painted scenes—Sebastiano Ricci again—were classical and military in inspiration. By day it was lit from the drum of the dome by semicircular windows, and at night, as now, by scores of scented candles burning smoothly beneath the vast span.

Spectacular and imposing—yes. The Count fancied him-
207

self quite a man of taste. At one time or other he had summoned the most skilled and esteemed artists and craftsmen from Italy, France, England and Greater Germany, then sent them away with an obligation to produce wrought-iron entrance gates, marble chimney-pieces with caryatid supports, spiralling banisters carved from lime-wood, jewel-cabinets inlaid with ivory, armchairs upholstered in cut-velvet, frescos and friezes, flamboyant stuccoes, voluptuous vases, silver spoons, candelabra, doorknobs, sconces, clock-cases, or a dozen other enrichments to his house. Sculptors, cabinet-makers, plasterers, iron-workers, woodcarvers, painters of mountainscapes—the Count scattered his commissions among them like the steward of a grand estate impulsively sprinkling a bounty of corn into a pool of hungrily plashing carp.

None of the maskers paused to admire their surroundings, for most had been here many times before on previous summer evenings. Indeed, despite their laughter and apparent exuberance, despite their competitive bustle at the punch-bowls and tables of venison tarts or the enthusiasm with which they approached a game of faraone or participated in a quadrille, there was something familiar, practised, and therefore unnatural, about these festivities. They had the air of age and honoured custom, as if these same two hundred people had been assembling, mingling, dancing and drinking here for a hundred or more years; as if someone—the Count, perhaps—had manipulated a set of ingenious pulleys and levers, thereby springing them into this mechanical, almost clockwork, motion.

The curiosity of the guests—or, rather, their prurience, for these were people incapable of any seemly interests—was roused only by the arrival half-way through the evening of the unknown guest in the Turkish habit of aquamarine damask with a feathered turban and a veil of white sarsenet. It seemed the costume was as spectacular as the late fireworks display, for as the lady crossed the saloon, the embroidered borders of the dress trailing a full two yards behind her sandalled feet and the damask slipping to reveal the soft mount of her shoulder, a score of masked faces craned in unison, like flowers following the passage of the sun. Dozens of voices murmured, conferred in unison: who, whispered one and all, was *this*?

208

—Madame de V—, a man in a tiger costume confidently affirmed.

—Donna Rosalba Lombardo, offered another, dressed in a *faux* suit of armour, naming the famous courtesan.

—No, no, the Countess of B—, a paladin speculated.

—No—*I* am the Countess of B—, came the tart reply from an orange-girl standing alongside.

—Never fear, I believe we shall all learn her identity before the evening has ended. A Roman centurion was watching the lady from over his hand of cards. He was playing piquet at a table beside the punch-bowl, a tobacco-pipe protruding from beneath his visor. She shall let it slip anon, he said, you may be sure of that. The purpose of such a costume is always to reveal an identity, not to disguise one. He waved his pipe about like a baton as he spoke. All disguise, he said in a soft voice, is merely a prelude to a great revelation—one depends wholly upon the other.

But no one, not even his companion at the card-table, was paying heed to him, so he placed his pipe between his teeth and, champing down upon the stem, helped himself to another cup of punch.

—She shall be known, he said under his breath as he contemplated his cards. Sooner or later. But once again no one paid any heed, perhaps because none of them, not even his companion, had guessed who he was.

The dancing continued: in rows, in circles, in pairs, in figures-of-eight; the ladies scurrying under arches of gentlemen's arms or turning like tops, their skirts rising and swelling, smoothed down by their hands and changing shape with each rotation, like clay spinning on a potter's wheel. The mysterious Turkish masquerader had joined their numbers, and whenever she drew nigh to a partner he would bring his mask into contact with hers, peering inquiringly into it. To no avail: the veil of white sarsenet suspended from the summit of the turban prevented a glimpse even of her eyes.

After the dance was completed, drinks and venison tarts were pressed upon her. Gentlemen deserted disgruntled partners to request the pleasure of a galliard or a *pas de deux*. Their ladies, recovering, moved to her elbows and engaged her in conversation, suggesting games of backgammon, faro, bassetta. Did she play? No? Did she *wish* to play? For they would be *most* grateful to teach her.

All were pre-empted by the Count, slightly the worse for

drink, dressed in the smock and hose of a peasant, a furred codpiece (which his hand recurrently stroked and smoothed) completing his disguise. He bowed before her, his fat overlapping lips caressing her hand; a pilgrim kissing a sacred relic. His hand touched her elbow, the bared contour of her shoulder, then moved slowly up the long column of her neck; he did not seem so pious now. He had been watching her from beneath his portrait with a mixture of lip-gnawing consternation and goatish desire. At first the former bulked larger than the latter, for, though he was a man who loved to promote curiosity and intrigue among his guests, he did not so much enjoy being made curious or intrigued himself: bafflement and confusion were for lesser people than a Provenzale. *And* he did not enjoy his fireworks or his magnificent saloon or his musicians from the Teatro San Moisè being upstaged like this. No question—the lady possessed too much temerity.

Still, that *costume*: for *its* sake he could find it in his heart to forgive very much—oh yes. And now as he touched her soft nape he felt a familiar serpent stir its fat coils: lechery, that is, had swung into the ascendancy. No doubt, he thought, the lady was a beauty; he could sense such things, even through a mask. One had to be careful, of course: a masquerading lady was so often like the dish that, when covered, causes the juices of digestion to heat and flow but then, its lid lifted, turns the stomach. Yet upon the evidence of this creature's bared shoulder, her bold deportment, the pear-shaped conformations of her trussed-up bosom . . .

—*Signorina*, he said in his politest tone, leading her on to the floor, beneath a bower of arms, thinking already of the chamber upstairs prepared for just such an eventuality as this: one of the little shrines where he celebrated the rites of Venus.

—The Count dances with her, came the whispers. For everyone, of course, knew who *he* was, peasant costume or not. Once again the heads craned to watch.

The Count, it transpired, was an inept and ungainly dancer. As he bowed and stepped and turned or swung his partner he looked less graceful than one of his peasants. Why, he might truly have been the clod whom his costume represented. He was less graceful, too, than the tamed mountain bear that had danced for his guests during the previous *villeggiatura*, earning great acclaim. Half-drunk, as

210

now, he was even clumsier, more ponderous than usual: the elegant steps he translated into those of a field-hand stumping up a hill or trampling down a seeded furrow. Performing the figure-of-eight, he traipsed with all the grace of a blind ass in an olive-mill. Then he tripped; a few people sniggered. He righted himself. Taking the lady's hand, he passed her through the wreathing and unwreathing arms. Then he stood unsupported in the line, breathing heavily, swaying uncertainly, until either exertion or drink, or some debilitating compound of the two, toppled him to the floor: a soldier struck by a musket-ball collapsing in the middle of his battle formation. Cries of alarm; two dozen hands projecting themselves at him like the fronds of a great heliotrope. Assisted to his feet, he roared bearishly, brushing them away. His hose was sagging, his mask askew: he had become a Janus-faced creature now, one visage white and impassive, the other florid and vexed. Both frantically searched the saloon, each peering in an opposite direction. The beautiful masquerader, the lady in the Turkish habit—she was gone, he had lost her, she had disappeared into the throng.

—Where is she? he growled. He was beside the punch-bowl and the card-players. Then, more quietly, into his mask: *Who* is she?

The Roman centurion folded his hand of cards and knocked the ashes from his pipe.

Tristano, tonight a black domino, had also disappeared, five minutes earlier. Exhausted by the unvarying festivities almost before they commenced, he had passed through a door and along by a gaming-room, where bassetta and faraone and other games of chance were being played. Sets of dice clicked across a walnut table. He climbed a spiral stair. At the top he turned left and pushed open the door to a chamber. It was small, simply decorated: a torchère stood by a sideboard surmounted by a looking-glass, a sofa lay beneath the window. A vase of white lilies, a small console table against the wall, a citrus breeze. Beside the torchère, a closet, its door closed.

He moved to the window and, raising his mask, inhaled deeply. These festivities with their drink and tobacco smoke—they were certainly no good at all for the voice. Already Scipio's—the victim of every vice, a small golden child whipped each night by his drunken father—was

211

becoming ragged, stropping. That evening during Holy Week at the Teatro San Moisè, for example, when (together on stage for the first time) the two of them had sung Couperin's 'Troisième Leçon à Ténèbres' as the candles were extinguished one by one: as he sang the words of the prophet Jeremiah, Scipio had sounded at times like a knife-grinder sharpening implements upon granite; at others, like a raven choking on rubbish. Fit only for the *opera buffa*, if that. Did the Count not realise? Surely so: though he was stupid, he was not yet deaf. By no means a religious man, he none the less had been in his box for Tenebrae; watching, appraising. It had been a test, surely, putting the two of them together like that. And yet still it was said, even after that disgrace, that Il Piozzino, not Tristano—and not even Il Prizziello— would be the Count's *primo uomo* again when the opera season commenced with a revival of Scarlatti's *Tigrane*.

Through the open casement he could see the dark swirls of shrubbery in the knot-garden, to which it appeared two or three of the guests had repaired, their masks a luminous white. Beyond, to the left, lay the service wing; beyond that, the Count's grotto; and beyond the grotto, his folly—a small collection of thatched huts with various tethered farm animals. More 'improvements'. A whimsical fellow, the Count. The grotto possessed its own hermit, paid 100 sequins per year to live in his little cell and make occasional appearances when guests strolled about the garden. He was given a dusty tome to carry—*De Imitatione Christi*—but in fact he was illiterate, unable to read his own name, let alone Latin.

The thatched huts held curiosities of an even more peculiar order—products not of Gothic fancy but of 'scientific interest'. Yesterday the Count had displayed some of them for his most privileged guests, all the while invoking the magic of the new science and extolling the virtues of progress inherent in an 'automaton' that played the harpsichord tolerably well, a waxwork effigy of a man whose penis came erect by means of clockwork concealed behind his ears, and the shrunken remains of a two-faced infant preserved in a jar of viscous liquid.

—Are they human, then, inquired the Count, or are they not? He was making a close study of this last curiosity, squinting into the bottle, which he suddenly flourished before their startled faces.

—A monster, replied one of the ladies, Donna Francesca,

212

crossing herself and averting her eyes from the ill-formed production of Nature.

—By means of the technical skills brought to us by scientific progress and invention, he continued, placing the jar aside, the inhuman looks—and *acts*—like the human, deceiving the eye into a belief that life exists where none truly does. Who shall tell us any longer what is *real* and what is *mere illusion*?

Despite his prediction that ingenious inventions such as the harpsichord-playing automaton would one day be baking his breakfast, lacing his boots and pruning his garden, the Count next revealed how he had not yet turned his back on the world of the living, for an adjoining hut was home to a creature—rather, upon closer inspection, a man— to whom Nature had been most grudging with her charms. Introduced to the guests as 'Salvestro', his only response was to grunt and then lower and shake his head in a some- what bullish manner. He was altogether remarkable in appearance: his brow and nose were as flat as if they had been smitten by a fry-pan; his ears were tapered at their tops; and each of his tiny eyes appeared to be strangely enamoured of the other, so close together had they been set and so intently did each gaze into the other's cloudy and bewildered depths. Yet it was Salvestro's conduct that was the true source of his curiosity. The Count explained how some years before he had been discovered inhabiting a wood near Vicenza, capable of no words except a kind of 'wolf-language' (as the Count called it) composed of grunts and growls. His diet had consisted solely of berries and small rodents captured with his own hands and consumed raw; his clothing, of foul-smelling animal skins.

In previous years Salvestro had been a frequent sight at these *fêtes*, for which occasions he was outfitted by the Count's tailor in an embroidered frock-coat and breeches, and, by his wigmaker, with an immense peruke. He was daubed with perfume, a cravat was tied at his throat, his feet were sheathed in buckled shoes, and a cane was placed into his rough, berry-grubbing hands, which were squeezed into a soft pair of kid-leather gloves decorated with precious stones. A French dancing-master had been employed to provide him with a more becoming gait—in short, an upright one—and the Count took it upon himself to teach him piquet, draughts, backgammon and bagatelle. Soon learned doctors from the academies were hired for quite different lessons, endeavouring to tutor him in Hebrew, Greek and German, hoping thereby to discover the ancient secret of which of these tongues was truly the first to develop after the confusion of Babel, and whether speech in fact preceded writing or vice versa. Alas, these exciting endeavours went wholly unrequited, and the learned doctors were forced to conclude that after Babel our ancient ancestors had communicated with one another in a primitive wolf-language of grunts and growls supplemented by a limited repertoire of crude gestures. The dancing-master and the Count fared no better with their pupil. Not only had the steps of the *pas seul* and the rules governing the movements of the Count's ivory draughtsmen been woefully beyond his talents, but Salvestro remained unequal to even the simplest of tasks, sadly unable to cope with the intricacies of forks, spoons, buttons, buckles, wig-curlers, powder-puffs, doorknobs, chamber-pots and stool-pans, no matter how expert or how ruthless was his tutor. Thus, after all of these experiments had concluded in disappointment, the Count bored of him, exiling him to this cottage where he now dressed in rags and indulged private and inexplicable amusements.

—Is my Salvestro human or is he not? the Count inquired of his guests, placing a hand upon the matted head in a fond gesture of proprietorship, as one might do with a favourite wolfhound. Does he possess a rational soul like you or I? Ought he to be baptised? Was he begot upon a lady's body by a wolf or a man? Is he indeed the issue of a lady's womb?

—He is a devil, replied Donna Francesca, who crossed herself once more as she averted her eyes.

—Human or inhuman? inquired the Count, who did not seem to have heard her, so closely was he preoccupied by his subject. What, pray, are the boundaries of our species? Is it our rational soul? Is it our speech? Our clothing? Our art? Do you remember, my friends, the definition of Plato? *Animal implume bipes latis unguibus*, he answered his own question with a proud flourish. He seemed to be enjoying his role as a learned doctor. Ah, *well*—my Salvestro has no feathers and when he wishes he may walk upon his hind legs. Yet I ask you, my friends, is he therefore a man?

Salvestro chose that precise second to scratch vigorously at his crotch, thereby betraying through his leather breeches

214

the outline of a not inconsiderable manhood. The company laughed.

—More of a man than some! one of the ladies, a marquise, stage-whispered to Donna Francesca with a titter, nodding at Tristano and Il Prizziello. Donna Francesca laughed loudly, brittly.

—Shape without reason, proclaimed the Count. What are we to understand from it?

When no solution could be proposed for his philosophical conundrum he led the way outdoors, taking them behind the hut to a small wooden cage. This last wonder was an equally sorry sight: a black panther, fretting in its confinement, paced to and fro in the cage and displayed enmity by snarling sickly at the guests. A thread of silver spittle hung from its right jowl, its ribs were visible, and the skin hung on its back like uncut velvet. The yellow eyes were blinking slowly, like a drinker's.

—He is sick, explained the Count sympathetically. But a year ago, when I bought him—oh, he was such a magnificent creature then!

Now, alone in the chamber, listening to the voices swelling and falling behind him in the Great Room, Tristano could not forget the beautiful ruins of that slack-jowled face. He, Scipio, Maddalena—they were of course truly no different from the poor beast or from Salvestro: mere 'curiosities' collected for the Count's passing amusement. Even his operas themselves were curiosities, full of strange novelties and feats of the most bizarre and sometimes perilous showmanship. The props, the set designs—all outrageous mixtures of reality and 'mere illusion'; a magic show, nothing more, suitable only for the amusement of the rabble and, as such, humiliating for a singer, utterly wasteful of his talent. How many times had Tristano been required to sing an aria from the back of a triumphal chariot as it was drawn across the stage by green-scaled mechanical dragons whose nostrils spouted plumes of smoke and balls of flame? Or upon the brink of a sulphurous volcano belching cinders and great black clouds into the alarmed audience? On flower-laden barges floating down 'the Nile', a water-filled conduit that upon one memorable occasion burst its banks and very nearly drowned the orchestra? Through the air above the stage, supported by ropes and pulleys? On smouldering catafalques pushed out to the sea, a huge cistern with slopping waves? Beneath fountain-like waterfalls created by complicated arrangements of vats, tubes, pumps, jacks and weights? Before windmills whose sharp-edged vanes rotated scant inches from his head? On the swaying decks of fully rigged galleons or the prow of a scale model of the *Bucintoro*? Among huge casts of legionnaires, centurions, Amazons, harems, courts, councils, Athenian mobs, Roman slaves, suicidal Hebrews—all of them together enough to collapse the stage?

Yet, as before, Tristano would escape his confinement: for last month, while performing in Dresden, he had been offered a contract to sing in London—1,500 guineas for a single season. It was said that Italian opera was popular with the English nobility. The English king—the German—had formed an academy of music; another German—Handel, whom Tristano had once encountered in Naples—was Master of the Orchestra, and his new opera, *Radamisto*, was being performed with much success. His *Rinaldo*—Tristano knew it well—had earlier been a great success in London. So he would go. No one yet knew—not the Count, not Maddalena; but by the time the sun set tomorrow he would be gone, crossing Lombardy Plain beneath a poppy-coloured sky, approaching the French Alps through the falling darkness.

Yes; let Scipio have *Tigrane*—and the flames and smoke and waves and fireworks and whatever else, whatever new spectacle, the Count might have in mind. He, Tristano, would leave all of it behind.

—Tristano?

Including Maddalena.

He turned round to see the glowing ultramarine, the plumes of the aigretted turban that now floated towards him as the door swung shut. Yes, the dress was certainly a curiosity: little wonder, then, that the Count had been so fascinated. Tristano had seen him lovingly stroking his codpiece.

—I have created a sensation, she said, pleased. No one has guessed.

—The Count?

—Especially not. We shared a dance. He frowned in response to this, but she added quickly: Did you not see him? Why, he is so deeply in drink that I might have been the Countess herself.

216

—Heaven forbid.

—Since my time in La Pietà he has not seen me in the apparel of a lady. She was studying her reflection in the glass, the torchère highlighting her mask. That is, not more than once or twice. For sometimes when they were alone together (this she did not tell Tristano) the Count had dressed her in the habit of a nun and then defrocked her with frenzied hands. Tonight, she said, he believes I have selected a black domino—which I have, of course. For later.

—Must you remind me? Then his voice became lighter, and he gestured at his cloak. I shall be mindful, he said with a laugh. Perhaps the Count will make an error.

—I mean that later I am to *sing*.

—In that case, he laughed again, there will be little chance of such a mistake.

As she moved to the sofa she plucked the snuffers from the sideboard and extinguished the candles. The Turkish habit was loosened and had descended half-way to her sandalled feet, and the mask and turban had been removed, when suddenly the door creaked open.

—Oh! She made to conceal her face, snatching the mask from the floor.

The Roman centurion. He retreated quickly with a polite bow, closing the door precisely.

—Who—?

Tristano shook his head. One of the Count's men. One of his spies, no doubt. Your heart is beating—

—Please—not here.

—Yes. The final time, he thought. *Come.*

She had locked the door and relented, when, a few moments later, another door—the closet door—swung open. In the sheaf of light cast by a lanthorn there appeared a peasant in drooping hose. His mask was turned sideways, over the left ear. In the wobbling light his squarish face, half of it cast in shadow, was suddenly visible: the flushed visage of the Count, rendered even more florid by drink. The mythical staircase, thought Tristano as he tried to shroud Maddalena in his own cape; one of the secret passages the Count uses to keep his assignations—or to spy.

—Ha, the Count said thickly. What, what . . .?

Fortunately he was badly inebriated now, worse even, it seemed, than a few minutes before: he hung upon the door, swaying, his eyes rolling and blinking slowly at the tableau before them. His overlong tongue rolled around in his mouth, salaciously licking his lips and then sticking out like a pink eel extruding from its coral grotto. With his thick shoulders and short neck he might have been Salvestro; his brother at least. After a second his eyes widened like those of the drunk who draws himself arduously erect and wishes to appear sober; but he was, rather, attempting to align his slowly gyrating eyes and fix them upon the spectacle before him. He lurched clumsily forwards and in doing so looked ever more like Salvestro.

—Trissh-shtano, he spluttered, his lolling tongue not quite able to negotiate the syllables. A eunuch in my seraglio? Ha! Who have you there, boy? His eyes completed a wobbly revolution and fixed upon the Turkish costume, which Maddalena, who had swiftly masked herself, was clutching to her breasts, though not before he had favoured her with an unsavoury stare. So, he said, stumbling towards them. Ha, ha! My fair masquerader! My honoured guest! Now all your secrets shall be unveiled!

This predicted revelation was pre-empted by a series of screams from below, in the Great Room. The Count halted in mid-lurch, cocking his head. In doing so he again resembled a mountain bear, one stopping and scenting in a small forest clearing, raising itself to an uncertain pair of hind legs and sniffing the breeze. More screams, then a clatter from below the spiral stair. A louder cry—a lady's. The Count turned—slowly, slowly—and, unlocking the door, lumbered through the opening, butting one side of the frame and then the other before negotiating its narrow passage into the greater light.

—Salvestro! someone, a man, was screaming over his laughter, somewhere outside. No, Salvestro, *no!*

A little more than an hour later Maddalena (or, rather, Il Prizziello), a black domino, sang for the assembly. The audience was indifferent to his performance. Tired of dancing, even tired of playing faro and drinking punch, they had slumped into chairs, or on to the floor, their backs bent at various angles against the wall; or they half-listened from the front portico or the knot-garden: all of them a scattered collection of run-down clockwork. There was nothing to drink in any case: the punch-bowls were empty except for a few triangles and crescents of sodden and discoloured fruit. The last of their more fortifying contents were to be seen in a few sticky smirches on the chequered floor-tiles, like blood-stains after a battle. Masks, cups, playing-cards, also littered the tiles. A few ribbons and feathers, moulted by their wearers. And many of the candles had extinguished of their own accord and now smouldered like tree stumps after a forest conflagration. Already the serving-maids had started their task of cleaning.

The Count disappeared even before Il Prizziello commenced his singing. It seemed that the mysterious lady in the Turkish gown had been forgotten; as, perhaps less readily, had Salvestro, conducted back to his cottage, arms confined. When exactly he had entered the Great Room no one could say; though it could safely be testified that his copious attentions to the punch-bowls were now responsible for their premature depletion. When he took to the dance-floor under the stimulation of these audacious potations his presence was at first cheered by the onlookers. Emboldened by this unwise response, he seized one of the ladies—it happened to be Donna Francesca, dressed as Minerva—and led her through a grim, groping *pas de deux*. The steps, bubbling up from the deep recesses of his brain, were, as he now executed them, more the inborn actions of a reptile or extinct predator than the product of the French dancing-master's season of unsuccessful tuition. Donna Francesca immediately objected, but these protests merely encountered several fierce tokens of her partner's growing ardour: he kissed her heartily upon the lips and then foraged with his hairy hands at her bosom, hips and prodigiously ample rump. Her protests registered themselves ever more clamorously, yet once again they served only to aggravate Salvestro's immoderate desires. Now her quaking peaks and most delicate vales received his even more violent regards as they were forcefully divested of their raiments, whose loudly ripping seams accompanied her shrieks of fright. Undaunted by an audience and prey to this ungovernable and impetuous passion, her aggressor struggled for a second with his own breeches before springing from them a member whose dimensions surpassed the expectations even of those who had witnessed his scratching at the exhibition a day earlier.

By now two of the more heroically inclined guests were draped on his back, but, persevering under this restraint, Salvestro thrust himself forward at his intended partner

219

like an ox lunging and bucking in its yoke. Fortunately the intervention was sufficient to permit Donna Francesca to twist herself free and totter across the saloon into the protection of more beneficent embraces.

The Count had not been so drunk when he appeared—finally, stumbling into the saloon—that he was unable to restore a sort of order upon this scene of chaos. Donna Francesca's torn costume was hastily restored while she herself was likewise ordered, comforted by many hands and induced to consume great amounts of cordial-water. Salvestro, cringing beneath a good many kicks and blows from those whose courage and sense of justice had failed them seconds before, was led by a steward and a footman to his hut, where a more professional punishment was administered; that is, for the next day he was denied his customary ration of sweetmeats. One of the revellers who leapt to Donna Francesca's assistance, and then had his nose bloodied by Salvestro's elbow in response to this act of valour, was also borne away, conducted to an adjoining chamber into which he trailed tiny crimson starbursts.

—Drink, the Count had then commanded the remainder of his guests. Eat! Dance!

The Count himself did not, however, follow his own bellows of advice. He stumbled back up the stair and, after pissing torrentially into a chamber-pot, toppled into bed, emitting tigerish snores almost before his head touched the goose-feather mattress. Which happened to be the moment at which Maddalena commenced singing: first a sentimental aria, followed by vengeance and funeral arias. Then, after a short break, a farewell aria:

> *Partirò, ma teco resta,*
> *questo core incantenato ...*

Tancredi's farewell, this is, from *Gerusalemme liberata*.

Most of the guests had already bid their own farewells by this point, and the Great Room was almost empty. When she had finished, Maddalena searched a moment, unsuccessfully, for Tristano. Then she climbed the stair to the Count's chamber. Hearing his clamorous snorts, she told herself that he had seen—had understood—nothing. It had been dark; he had been drunk. She—and Tristano—were safe; they might continue as they were. And so, an hour later, Tristano filled her dreams as she fell asleep in her own chamber.

Which was the precise moment that the Count's own dreams were filled with the lady in the Turkish costume, who slowly danced and unveiled herself before him, though her face remained an unresolving blank.

Which was the precise moment that Tristano, a stair above, had completed filling his three portmanteaus. When Maddalena and the Count awoke from their dreams, hours later, he had departed.

Twenty-four

 If Lent brought a decline in a Venetian habit-maker's trade, during the summer *villeggiatura* Signor Belloni had even more cause, and even more time, to commiserate over his carob-wood pipe with old Grossi. Which was why, several days into July, just after the bell-tower of San Giacometto had proclaimed six o'clock and he had sent Cametti home to his mother, Belloni was surprised to see three of Count Provenzale's men—he recognised them by their red livery—enter his shop. As everyone knew, Count Provenzale was at his villa. The Count brought him a good trade during the Carnival, but now during the hot season . . .

—Gentlemen, he said, always at his most unctuous whenever the Count was involved. Gentlemen, may I please be of assistance?

—I believe you most certainly can, said one of them—the tallest, named Anzolo in a genial voice. He offered a wholly mirthless smile. Yes, I am interested in a habit. A Turkish habit. Perhaps, *signore*, you will remember it?

Early that morning—it was now the day after the *fête*—Anzolo had been roused from his bed by his master; roused, that is, from the side of Donna Francesca, to whom he had spent much of the evening offering his most private consolations. He had expected the Count to be angered, shocked—to be *something* at least—at the sight of the two

221

of them clasped in such intimacy, for it was rumoured that Donna Francesca had once shared the Count's bed. And now she slept with a servant. Even if this was the *villeggiatura*, a time when in true republican fashion no barriers of birth or station applied in a new, topsy-turvy world of wildly interchanging equals, surely Anzolo was devaluing the Count's sexual currency just a little? He had cringed beneath the linen as the great malformed burgundy visage appeared above his pillow. Yet, strangely enough, the Count scarcely honoured Donna Francesca (still asleep as a result of her many cordials) with a second glance as he pulled Anzolo from his bed and bumped him on to the floor, telling him to hurry, to get dressed, that he was travelling to Venice this day. Hurry, the Count had commanded, or by Heaven he would feel the back of his hand!

—A Turkish habit? Signor Belloni was now inquiring, wondering why one of the liveried gentlemen was locking the shop door and another shuttering the windows. Ah, yes. Gentlemen! How could I possibly forget? One of my finest.

—Yes, I am confident it has many admirers, Anzolo replied very amiably. For example, Count Provenzale.

—Yes, the Count, he responded somewhat apprehensively.

—More to the point, however, Count Provenzale has been admiring the lady who donned it.

Belloni blinked.

—The lady?

—Yes. A charming smile from Anzolo. Yet the lady ... well, she proved reluctant. The smiled had turned knowing.

—I fear my trade binds me to the greatest discretion. Belloni was attempting to duplicate Anzolo's smile with his own crooked yellow teeth, withered chops, twitching lips. Surely the Count can appreciate ...

The gentleman at the shutters drew a sword from his scabbard, Anzolo a pistol. Though he did not show it, Anzolo was puzzled. Why did the fellow not simply confess? *Discretion*—how absurd! Anyone knew there was no such thing in Venice. Yet he had also been puzzled by the Count, ordinarily so glutted on the ladies that scarcely did he ever bother to cross the street in either search or pursuit. Assuredly the lady, whoever she was, had been a fine-looking morsel: Anzolo himself had craftily bumped into her once or twice during a quadrille. But why the devil should she

222

inspire this sudden trip into Venice's dry and empty summertime husk? The coach had rocked and bucketed as the coachman—the fellow now brandishing the sword—whipped the frothing horses until their blood sprayed the tiny oval forewindow. Surely some strange intrigue was astir. Had it something to do with one of the damned castrati, Tristano, stealing away in the night like that? Ah, yes—that was the next job set by the Count: lay hold of Tristano.

—Who, inquired Anzolo, now making a great show of his patience, was the lady?

—The lady? repeated Belloni, eyes flickering from one weapon to the other as he backed away from the counter. I do not understand, my good *signore*. *What* lady? His voice was shrill, womanish. What lady is this? I know of *no lady*! It was a *gentleman*—it was the Count's young man. I know because my assistant, Signor Cametti . . .

—A gentleman? Anzolo lowered his pistol, frowning. The Count's man? What the devil do you talk about, you silly old fool?

—Can I be expected to know for whom he bought it? No. Perhaps it was for himself—yes, I thought of that. In his fear, Belloni had begun to blather. Suddenly, overpoweringly, he need to urinate. Why, those fellows are prone to such things, am I correct? So it is said, yes? I myself could hardly be expected to know, but I assure you that Signor Cametti—

—*What* gentleman?

—Il Prizziello, he blurted in his shrill old woman's voice. It was the castrato, Il Prizziello! He purchased it three days ago—I had specially tailored it for him . . . fitted him in my own—

—Impossible! From his tiny bedchamber Anzolo had listened to Il Prizziello's farewell aria as he struggled with the seemingly endless successions of clasps and hooks and buttons comprising Donna Francesca's half-shredded Minerva costume. The castrato, he had noted during the earlier arias, had worn a black domino, like Tristano's. You lie!

—No, no, no, no! In a moment of inspiration Belloni hastily produced his book of accounts. He flipped noisily through a few heavy pages that seemed as large as staysails, then spun the book round on the counter, stabbing one

223

of the entries three times with a desperately triumphant forefinger. There!

Tomà, the sword-wielding coachman and the only member of the Count's party who had learned his letters, squinted for a second at the page and then confirmed Belloni's claim. Anzolo's brow furrowed as he lowered the pistol. So the costumier was correct. There was nothing for it but to return to the villa and address a few questions to Il Prizziello; he would surely know, and could be made to reveal, the masquerader's identity. The Count must have been mistaken about what he saw last evening; little wonder after he poured an entire punch-bowl down his gullet. To give the old devil his due, though, both castrati *had* been wearing dominoes . . .

—It must have been Il Prizziello, he said, almost to himself, and not Tristano who . . .

—Il Prizziello it was, Belloni interrupted him, exulting. A perfect disguise. Perfect! Why, I should never have guessed myself!

—Guessed what? Another frown.

—That he was a man! Belloni positively beamed. A perfect travesty—*so* like a lady, *signore*. No, no, I should never have guessed. Why, the little fellow might have tricked all the world!

Anzolo's frown deepened still more, until his brow nearly eclipsed his eyes.

Belloni's smile twitched and then abruptly vanished.

—What? he stammered. *What*?

But suddenly he knew. Great purveyor of disguise, witness to all manner and variety of deceptions and concealments, he at once realised the import of what he had just said.

—Hail Mary, he whispered fumblingly as Anzolo, who had also guessed, raised his pistol. Hail Mary, full of—

Tristano had arrived in Venice well after first light. He crossed the ruffled waters from Fusina on the mainland to the Cannaregio canal in just under an hour. A light rain was falling; the tops of the campaniles and clock-towers were shrouded. He was to meet an English lord in a *palazzo* across the Canàl Grande from Santa Maria della Salute, but upon arrival was informed that the lord—evidently a dissolute fellow—had not yet returned from last night's festivities. Was it known when he might make his belated appearance? The servant winked and shook his head.

After his trunks were lugged through the water-gate, Tristano impatiently abided the lord's return in the *piano nobile*. Coffee was brought to him; then, as the hours passed, wine. He consumed a meal, sardines marinated in an inferior white wine. It was abominable, nauseating: the cook was at a villa in the country, explained the servant with a smirk; he had prepared the meal himself. Tristano paced the *portego*. Five times he requested the lord's chambers be examined for evidence of his return. Five times the servant returned with the same smirk. Was it known at least *where* the lord was indulging his fancy? The servant winked again, and only after much prompting, which included at last the irresistible incentive of five silver sequins, did this Brighella name a well-known house of recreation in San Polo. Tristano wondered if he might forward a letter to this ... establishment? No, came the reply: the other servants, like the cook, were in the country; there was no one about who might carry it.

Late in the afternoon, therefore, Tristano summoned a gondola. It bore him through San Marco, carrying him up the stinking, rain-stippled passages of the Rio San Moisè and the Rio San Luca until he disembarked in San Polo near the Palazzo Coccina. From there he travelled on foot to the Fondamenta della Tette, the flared skirts of his tight-waisted black *velada* billowing behind him. The breeze caught his parasol as the rain drummed applause across its silk top.

The Fondamenta della Tette was all but deserted. A street-sweeper pushed his empty wheelbarrow into the warren of narrow *calli* running to the sides; an old man slumped against a wall with an empty begging bowl; an inexplicable cockerel marched purposefully towards the Campo San Polo. Tristano walked briskly in the opposite direction, after a moment crossing beneath an archway whose keystone was a frowning face. He arrived in a small stone-flagged courtyard, its surface slick with rain. Here a fountain and a well-tended kitchen garden with a dripping box tree were overlooked by a tall *palazetto* with a narrow façade, an overhang, and an ancient wooden portico, newly painted. Above the portico, a small balcony with a wrought-iron rail, bay windows, and a light cornice, also painted.

225

From the balcony a young lady shielded by a silk parasol not unlike his own was lowering a basket on a rope for a delivery of grapes and pomegranates. High above her rose a chimney with a conical flue, its smudge of smoke looking heavy and woollen in the rain.

Tristano watched for a moment as the lady raised the small load. So fair and virginal was her complexion that she might have been a singer or musician at one of the city's famous *ospedali*—the Pietà, the Mendicanti, the Incurabili—rather than an inmate of one of its equally famous brothels. Of course there was, he knew, a happy commerce between the two: many young ladies graduated from the former to the latter; hence the refined quality of the courtesans one found in Venice. Most of these creatures began life—like Maddalena, for example—as foundlings on the steps of the *ospedali* or churches; but these humble origins belied the circumstances, for the foundlings were most often the offspring from the finest families, all of whom for sensible reasons of self-preservation observed a strict economy where heirs were concerned. As a result of this practice only one son, normally the youngest, ever married, his brothers being denied the chance to expand, and thereby fragment, the family and its centuries-old fortune. How many great families had destroyed themselves through the dissipative productions of their children's loins? Yet for these sons to be unmarried was one thing, to remain celibate quite another: they relieved the dolour of their domestic solitude with the attentions of mistresses, who were in much demand, and who as a matter of natural course presented them with the occasional child. These unwanted parcels, because of the observances that brought them into being in the first place, were never acknowledged; rather, they were placed in the *ospedali*. Once of sufficient years, they became either musicians or the mistresses of a new generation of enforced bachelors; and often both.

After the lady had raised her basket and disappeared inside, the door of this civil-looking establishment was opened upon Tristano's summons by a serving-girl, who quickly fetched her mistress. This handsome lady was dressed in great finery: a gold dress with low *décolletage* and ballooning skirts edged with lace. A beauty-patch had been placed above her artfully reddened cheek-bone, near one of her large, painted eyes.

—*Signora*, he began somewhat hesitantly, removing his hat and performing a bow.

The lady said something, very rapidly, to the serving-girl, who disappeared. These Venetians—he could scarcely understand a word they said: so many lisps, slurs, sucked vowels, chopped syllables; impossible to understand everything. He felt his face redden.

—*Signora*, he resumed, suddenly conscious of his own rude peasant tongue. He may have possessed one of the greatest voices ever heard in the churches and theatres of Venice, but in Florian's and the other cafés the patrons mocked his supposedly vulgar speech, his mangled pronunciations. If he sang like an angel, he spoke, to their ears, like a goatherd.

Yet the lady did not mock. She smiled gracefully and lowered her eyes.

—Do not fear, she said more slowly, her syllables now liquid and plashing like the rain and fountain-water outside the door. I know why you come, *signore*.

So: the young fellow, this Englishman, was expecting him. This he found most peculiar, though perhaps the lord used the brothel like his club in London, having his newspapers and correspondence delivered, a pipe sent from the tobacconist, a suit of clothes from the tailor. How very civilised, these English. He smiled privately as the lady drew him inside and relieved him of his dripping parasol, which she placed in a basket by the door filled with—great heavens—a half-dozen other dripping parasols. So neither the rain nor the hour nor the season had quite managed to discourage her commerce. She led him to the foot of a processional staircase, rather grand for the building. In a small chamber on the left he could see a young lady in dishabille bleaching her long hair with somewhat malodorous unguents of sulphur, lead and alum. Next door two ladies, dressed more formally, were practising violins; a third, seated beside them, read a book.

The fine lady crooked a finger at this last lady, who then put aside her book—it appeared to be a Greek translation of the Old Testament, therefore intimating its reader's piety and scholarship both—after carefully marking her page. Entering the corridor, she greeted Tristano with a swift curtsy.

—Excuse me, *signora*. But the mistress of the house had

disappeared behind a heavy curtain. Excuse me, *signorina*, he addressed himself to the learned young lady. Evidently there had been a misunderstanding. But the lady had taken hold of his hand and now pulled him—tug, tug—up the wide staircase. He stumbled to keep pace. At the top, corridors branched left and right. She conducted him left into a maze, passing red-and-gold rooms decorated with tasselled and embroidered fabrics hanging in great folds from the walls; with paintings in heavy frames, thick rugs, gold-leaf cornices, lacquered furniture, vases whose bodies were shaped like those of young maidens. Then into a smaller chamber with saffron walls, empty but for a bed decorated with chinoiserie and spread with a great counterpane.

—You do not understand, he whispered when he had determined that the lord was not inside reading his English gazettes and enjoying a tobacco-pipe. But by now the fold of curtain had toppled to behind them and she was pressing herself into his belly.

—Shall I summon a lady to assist me as I undress?

—No. Please—

—You are welcome to observe, if you wish. Or to assist.

—No, you do not . . .

Already she was peeling away her stomacher and allowing the mantua to slide from her shoulders. And already—for they had been forced upwards by the pressure of her corset—he could see the peculiar W-shaped constellation of moles, the Cassiopeia, marking her breasts.

He stared in wonder, in fear, at this bodily inscription, thinking: *Now all your secrets have been unveiled . . .*

Half-way across the Campo San Polo he realised that he was being observed, perhaps even followed.

The rain had ceased, the sun appearing in time to dip behind the buildings of Cannaregio and send hugely elongated shadows across the *campo*. And there, in the growing shadow of the Church of San Polo, a costumed figure: the centurion.

Tristano turned round and, walking back towards the Palazzo Maffetti-Tiépolo, hailed a gondolier lounging by the bridge, swatting mosquitoes.

—Please hurry, he said, naming the *palazzo* where the truant lord was expected.

After climbing in, his knees weak and tremulous beneath

the *velada*, the gondola rocking and dipping, he was carried down the Rio della Madonetta. The centurion was no longer in view. Into the wider waters of the Canàl Grande, empty but for a few lighters bearing catches of fish and casks of oil. After a minute they encountered a funeral gondola, a great catafalque draped in black and decked with unnaturally bright wreaths, its centre supporting a statuette of the Virgin. Four black-frocked gondoliers were silently dipping their oars; a veiled widow stood at the prow, motionless as the Virgin behind her. Tristano, shuddering, crossed himself like Donna Francesca at the thought of the white and silent body lying prone inside, hands folded, eyes stitched shut. He glimpsed his own face—was it truly that pallid?—reflected in the long lacquered side.

After they rocked for a moment in the wake of this funereal bark, Tristano's gondolier oared them past the uneven crescents of the canal-side *palazzi*. The rows of semicircular windows were mostly dark, their upside-down skeletons wavering in the water. At this hour it looked as if these elegant façades projecting themselves into the air were being tugged down, silently, into a subterranean darkness, into this other, darker, world of their shadows and reflections. The only sound to mark the event was the gurgle and suck of the water on the hull and oars; the noise of a fitfully sleeping beast.

After a few minutes the gondola drew abreast of the Palazzo Provenzale. A few intermittent windows above the water-entrance cast their light on to the water. Had the Count returned? Tristano craned his neck as they passed. He tried to think, to plan, but could not. The lady in San Polo, in the house: had the Count . . .? Was she . . .? He knew nothing—only that he must reach the English lord.

The gondolier grunted at his oar. The brief gold planes and the reflection of the Count's rearing edifice were soon broken by the waves into score after score of gold sequins and small glittering sickles. Tristano thought he heard a voice from inside, then its echo. This was indeed a city of reflections and mirrors and echoes, he thought; a place where the Count's 'mere illusion' prevailed, enfolding the known world, superimposing itself upon it like a painted stage-flat; the whole city one of the Count's 'curiosities', an optical trick accomplished with mirrors and hidden cogs. As if below the shining surface of the canal, below the tide and moonlight, there rippled an inverted world, half-seen, half-imagined, black and murky.

As they swept round the bend the golden bulbs and twin campaniles of Santa Maria della Salute broke into view above the curving line of *palazzi* in Dorsoduro, as well as, across the canal, the Palazzo Ducale, a great pinkish glow. In the distance stood a thick, gently swaying forest of naked main- and mizzenmasts, a few yellow sails like washing hung out to dry on the horizon.

—Turn, Tristano suddenly commanded. Left. *Now.* Quickly, quickly!

In the darkening water at the mouth of the canal, near the water-gate of the English lord's *palazzo*, he could see three gondolas floating at various angles to the *fondamenta*, their hanging lanthorns illuminating the passengers, all dressed in red livery.

—But *signore*, protested the gondolier, who was already puffing from the swift pace Tristano had been demanding.

—*Now.*

Grunting, the gondolier steered them—so slowly, it seemed—into the mouth of the Rio del Santíssimo. Then he halted his efforts altogether, allowing them to yaw lazily and rock in their own wake. He was peering back over his right shoulder.

—There is no need for all of this, *signore*, he said calmly, fraternally. He had turned forward and was steering the craft to a small mooring-point. I believe the Count simply wishes—

But before he could finish Tristano had leapt to the *fondamenta*, his toes splashing the water and his stockinged knees painfully grinding the paving-stones. The gondolier cursed, clambering ashore himself a few seconds later as his boat bumped the tarred pilings. But he was a big, thick-set fellow, soon outpaced by Tristano's clicking heels.

At the edge of the Campo San Maurízio Tristano turned right and began running eastward, in the direction of the Piazza San Marco, the top of whose campanile he could see bathed in a last dusky-orange light. As he passed a church—San Fantin—his heels not clicking quite so rapidly now, he glimpsed the three gondolas, one behind the other, plying their way up the ink-dark Rio San Moisè, opposite the theatre where he had sung during Holy Week three months before. The shouts of the gondolier approached from behind. His lungs burning, his spittle hot and thick, he turned into a series of narrow *calli* overlooked by awninged or shuttered windows. The cramped buildings were topped by crumbling chimneys and tilted weathercocks. Their windows were dark, some of them boarded.

He halted after a few minutes, lost, listening. Steam rose from his brow. The campanile had disappeared from view. One or two passengers shuffled past, peering into his face. A cat meowed plaintively, unseen. Then he detected more insistent noises—footfalls, voices hailing one another. Hugging the walls, he doubled back on his tracks, skirting behind the Teatro San Moisè and, a few minutes later, emerged on to a short, half-flooded *fondamenta*, which opened on to the great *bacino*. Behind him, towards the lord's *palazzo*, he could distinguish two running figures, now joined by the burly gondolier, who had resumed his shouting.

He turned and, splashing away in the opposite direction, had just arrived between the red and grey granite columns marking the entrance to the Piazzetta—its surface thinly flooded because of the high tide—when he saw three men approaching from the enormous square, wading smartly through the inch-deep waters. Approaching casually, unhurriedly, as if they had spent the previous hour drinking coffee in a café beneath the arcades: the Count and two of his men, long swords bouncing in scabbards at their thighs. Two steps behind strode the centurion. Or rather, since his visored helmet had now been removed, it was Scipio who followed in their wake, a smile twisted on to his face.

Tristano spun round again, ran a few steps along the puddled *fondamenta*, and then, without thinking, leapt over the bow-shaped mooring-posts and into the water. He was sucked under the chill, salty, bubbling waves. Bobbing to the surface a few seconds later, he bumped his head on the smooth hull of a gondola. Immediately a hand with a laced cuff reached down and clutched him by the collar of his *velada*. Then another pair of hands helped pull him aboard. He flopped on to the vessel's floor like the morning catch netted in the Lagoon, gasping and choking. His clothes weighed him down. When he looked up a second later he saw a face suspended above him, peering at him with the most arresting eyes he had ever seen: one of them green, the other brown.

—Signor Tristano, said an unfamiliar voice. Permit me to

introduce myself. The voice was rough and hollow, like a rusty sword being whetted on the walls of a deep cavern. I am Lord W—. He extended his ruffled hand and laughed raucously. Well done! Well done! So you are coming to England with us after all!

Twenty-five

For three weeks they travelled. Three weeks of coaches, springless calèches, crowded diligences, a *coche-d'eau* tugged up the Rhône by oxen, a storm-tossed packet-boat, post-chaises, sedan-chairs, horses, mules and, sometimes, when all else failed, their own feet. Roads, rivers, mountains, mule-trails; sleeping in *auberges* on the edge of tiny villages crouched fearfully beneath great white-capped peaks, or in the occasional château where Lord W— was known and somewhat grudgingly provided with claret and a bed.

On the first evening two coaches awaited his lordship at a *locanda* outside Fusina. On the morrow, much more punctual than the previous day, he set out with his three servants—and with Tristano—at six o'clock in the morning. As a precaution against the vengeful designs of the Count, Tristano was obliged to dress in a fashion to which he had become strangely accustomed—that is, he applied a heavy *maquillage*, donned a silk mantua and laced petticoats—and greeted the leering gentlemen in the doganas with a squeaking voice and a modest flutter of his eyelashes. Lord W—, who provided this habit, was much amused by its effect, frequently proclaiming to English fellow-travellers over table-d'hôte suppers how proud he was of his shy Catholic mistress.

Indeed, the lord, who remained an incomprehensibly jolly fellow throughout the many adversities of the journey, was in especially high spirits at its outset. After the coaches had been loaded he made a great show of inserting a brace of large horse-pistols into an outside pocket, proposing to use them in the event of banditti. Before noon three members of this occupation duly appeared, and the lord, true to his word, put a bullet through the temple of each. As their rivulets of blood trickled into the dry ruts he celebrated his victory with several swallows from a silver flask, which was never inconvenient to his hand. Observing this strange Englishman's contrasting eyes glittering with mirth and drink and from the sight of blood, Tristano wondered if he had perhaps exchanged one villain for another.

Soon enough, however, he had other worries. At the end of the second day—when at last he resumed his breeches and *velada*, thus being spared the lord's many salacious comments—the small party reached the foot of the Alps and commenced the dangerous ascent into the rude and lonely peaks of the Savoy. Three times Tristano's coach overturned, spilling him on to the steep mountain road. He snapped his cane, broke the lid of his snuff-box and chipped a tooth. On his third, most violent, fall the clasp broke on one of his portmanteaus and his clothes were scattered across a muddy reach of ditch. On that occasion one of the coach's wheels was also damaged, delaying the journey by twelve hours.

Two days later the road worsened, and when passage by coach became impossible they were obliged to mount horses. These beasts were presently replaced by mules, and these, finally, by humans: Savoyard porters who bore them in wicker hampers suspended on long poles. The air was thin and cool. Tristano was given a fur cap, which he pulled over his eyes. Mountain goats appeared, licking salt from the rocks. A grey wolf crossed their path, challenging them with its yellow eyes; it was frightened away only by the prodigious report of one of Lord W—'s horse-pistols. Higher they climbed, thinning pine woods and the grey faces of cliffs replacing the sheep-filled meadows and the few huddled villages. Rocks toppled into gorges far below. One of the Savoyard porters fell, too, bouncing and pirouetting like a dancer until his body, like his scream, was swallowed by the deep vale. For hours at a time life depended upon a single step. Twice Tristano's own porters had teetered on the brink of a steep precipice before righting themselves as he swung wildly in his basket, reciting a miserere. For the hundredth time he repented his flight. At long last, though, they began a descent.

—France, reported Lord W—, who had borne the tribulations of the journey with the aid of his apparently fathomless flask, to which Tristano had also commenced taking resort. Tristano knew nothing of France except that here castrati were banned from the stage. He was impatient for England. Onward they journeyed, day after day, crossing and recrossing first the Loire, then the Seine, then the Oise. Chambéry, Lyons, Vichy, Moulins, Châteauneuf, Malesherbes, Paris, Chantilly, Amiens, Abbeville, Calais.

Lord W— was in no particular haste. In Lyons he lost 3,000 livres at the gaming-tables in a fashionable assembly. Five days and sixty-five stages later, in Paris, 2,000 more. In Paris, also, he conducted Tristano to a monastery to view the preserved corpse of an English king exposed in a coffin alongside his daughter. Apparently mistaking this fellow for a saint—James was his name—pilgrims had snapped off parts of the coffin and clipped snippets from the brocaded cloth hanging in the room. He was not a true king, Lord W— explained, rendering a brief account of recent English history that, to Tristano, sounded very like the libretto of an opera, so much fighting and treachery was there. Surely these English were a passionate people.

The French, too, were passionate. That same day they witnessed an angry mob rush the doors of the Banque Générale, waving paper notes in the air. Two of them were bayoneted by a guard. Later a bonfire was ignited from this strange currency. Scraps and ashes floated over the grey river like volcanic ash.

—The old things no longer possess any value, Lord W— explained simply when Tristano puzzled over the reasons for this madness. Their money, he said, is as worthless to them as if a poem or a song was writ upon it.

An omen, though neither knew it, of what was to come in England.

One day later, at Versailles, they watched another king— a live one, this time a young French boy—consume his dinner, a roasted lamb, in public. Lord W—, apparently as proficient in the French tongue as in the Italian, discoursed knowledgeably on politics and philosophy with some of the courtiers, then dropped 5,000 livres on games of chance. He was consoled by a contessa whose acquaintance he had made at the *ridotto* in Venice. Like the French ladies, the contessa had smeared her face, neck and shoulders with *fard*, or white lead, then dabbed her cheeks—or, rather, the entire surface of her face from chin to eyes—with bright blotches of rouge. Tristano was reminded of a glacier in the Savoy stained with the blood of a mountain hare slain in sport by one of Lord W—'s pistols. Yet not unless the ladies applied these hideous masks, the Englishman had explained, were they suffered to appear at Court.

On the morrow they visited the shops on the Pont au Change. Lord W— dropped even vaster sums at these establishments, emptying his purse of its stock of gold louis d'or to purchase pillbox hats, feathered head-dresses, gold cuirasses, embroidered gloves, watch-cases, patch-boxes, *nécessaires*, perfumes, stockings, scarves and cobweb-thin jewellery for every digit and limb. All were for Lady W—, who, like a faithful Penelope, was patiently awaiting her traveller's return. The lord seemed rather patient himself about his return. Why he should be so Tristano found puzzling, for a miniature he had glimpsed among the lord's bright litter of possessions gave a most favourable account of the lady's countenance; and, moreover, one of the servants had confided to Tristano in a voice which mixed both envy and wonder that Lady W— was truly the most beautiful lady in England.

Three days later the travel party reached Calais. A packet-boat bound for Dover was set to sail at nine o'clock in the morning. When they arrived along the shore of the *basse ville* by stage from Amiens, the sea behind the custom-house was rough and grey, the waves topped by white scythes of foam. In a chill rain near Chantilly two days before, Tristano had contracted a violent cough, attended by a fever. His throat began to ache. At night, in the *auberges*, he would dream of the Count's gloved fingers taking hold of it, choking him. Three times a night he would wake, screaming in pain and fear. From next door would come Lord W—'s loud command that he save his howling for the king's opera house.

Now Tristano was huddled in a blanket on the windy dock on the edge of France, coughing and shivering and sweating. He hoped to return to the *auberge*, miserable and flea-infested as it was, but the captain was not one to be daunted by the elements. He impatiently ushered the passengers aboard as the master took their money—six guineas—and the porters grunted beneath their portmanteaus.

—Six guineas for a passage, said Lord W—, eyeing the waves, which looked more murderous by the minute. I declare, not a bad stake on our lives. Not bad at all! My good man, he said, flipping another two gold coins into the surprised master's palm, I shall raise you by two! Whereupon he laughed harshly and stomped up the gangway, his boots clicking and the silver flask winking in his pocket.

They took possession of a small cabin that stank of tar and sodden wood. Beyond the tiny porthole the sails rippled and snapped. A few minutes out to sea the packet pitched and tipped as much as their coach in the foothills of Piedmont. Indeed, much more. Tristano was thrown on to the creaking floorboards, breaking his fob-watch. His portmanteaus migrated from one wall to the other, crashing violently at each terminus. A second clasp broke, and soon the cabin was littered with his frocks and breeches and with Maddalena's Turkish costume, packed on the evening of the *fête*. His cough and fever worsened by the second, to which complaints he very shortly added a most excrutiating seasickness. He vomited painfully through the porthole, which in return admitted through its small aperture a great number of waves, like wash-buckets emptied from balconies. He drank a bottle of cordial-water, which in short order was spewed through the window. This time the waves snitched the wig he had purchased on the Pont au Change and bore it away to a cold and sloppy doom.

Lord W—, anchored to a bench and taking frequent recurrences to his flask, seemed immune to either fear or illness, and as a result was greatly amused by the hardships experienced by his companion.

—Never fear, he said, interrupting a song he had been singing, we shall be upon dry land soon enough, my good fellow. A short hop, that is all. Why—look you!—there lies England now.

Through the porthole, which in one second showed nothing but water and in the next nothing but sky, Tristano was able to catch the odd flashing glimpse of England: a grey-white beast rearing from the foaming sea, its head smirched by mist and rain, its patched green coat groomed by the fierce wind. But the little packet skirted this great beast, making brief sallies at its sandy feet before falling helplessly back. From the other cabins there now rose the wailing sounds of women—funereal sounds, like those of

236

black-veiled widows perched on the lips of the oblong graves behind his village church. The men on board showed little more valour. The cabin-boys and certain members of the small crew could be heard despairing of their lives, proclaiming unhappily that they were undone.

—Say your prayers, people! Undone, alack—all undone! Say your prayers, people!

Tristano had already taken this desperate refuge, kneeling on the wet boards and skittering back and forth through the puddles in concert with the scrapes and slides and splashes of his trunks. After he had chipped another incisor and showered the floor with coins from his purse—sous, livres, sols, francs, louis d'or—the violent motions at last relented. He crawled to the porthole. The beast rose mightily above them, its head now crowned with a castle, its sandy paws projecting jetties and cupping an inn, blue lighters, a dozen tiny people.

—We have arrived, Lord W— croaked in triumph. Welcome to England!

Twenty-six

 'Tristano fell back on to his knees and wept— for what, the past or the future, because of hope or fear, he did not quite know. All the while his hands squeezed the soft, and now the wet, fabric of Maddalena's costume . . .'

Lady Beauclair's posture had lapsed, her attention fully occupied now by her garment, which she appeared to study with a sadness equal to, and as inexplicable as, that of Tristano.

'Your costume,' I began. 'Is it . . .?'

'Yes,' she replied. 'The very same. It belonged to *her*.'

I was silent for a moment. My earlier disappointment over the Vauxhall masquerade had been forgotten, as had my puzzlement over the canvas and, somewhat less completely, the catastrophe with the pipe. Now I was trying to fit together the straying pieces of her story. When my lady

237

offered no further explanations, her story apparently finished for the evening—for indeed the hour was now very late—I softly cleared my throat and said: 'But—I do not understand.'

She looked up, then quietly asked: 'What is it you do not understand?'

'Many things, my lady. The lady in the bordello,' I said after once more clearing my throat, 'that is, the lady with the moles. Who, I beg of you, was this fallen creature? Some cruel traitoress, I shall warrant,' I said with some warmth. 'Doubtless she is to be blamed for Tristano's misfortunes.'

At her mention of moles I had remembered the excursus upon this subject in *The Compleat Physiognomist*. Like Ludovico Settala in his *De naevis* (1628), my father condemned the frivolous attitude of previous physiognomists who had ignored the import of moles, which he, like Ludovico, believed to possess the greatest significance in the art of divination. Ludovico and my father were positively adamant upon this matter, believing that we ignore these tokens at our peril.

'Misfortunes . . .' my lady repeated somewhat absently, as if she had not attended to the full of my sentence. 'Without these misfortunes,' she continued after a moment, still speaking as if to herself, 'he should never have arrived in England, in which case we two should not be holding this conversation.' I must have looked confounded—and indeed confusion had seized me—for she continued: 'That is to say, if Tristano had never arrived in England I should not be sitting here this evening. In short, I should not even be alive . . .'

I was puzzled by this strange confession and would fain have heard an elaboration; but apparently she had said her piece. I wondered to myself, had Tristano, that withered little creature from the drum, somehow rescued and preserved the life of this mettlesome lady who now stood before me? It seemed impossible.

'Perhaps this lady with the moles,' I said after a silence had endured for a moment or two, 'perhaps she was in the service of the Count?'

'No, no.' She shook her head, which at last seemed to clear away her reverie. 'This fallen lady, as you name her, had nothing at all to do with the Count. To his dying day— which, incidentally, I believe was yet a good many years

238

hence—I am convinced he possessed no knowledge of her existence beyond, perhaps, the rustle of costume that he may have detected in his corridor. *Who* she was is surely of little importance; she might have been anyone, for indeed, as I have described, there were so many of her *métier* in that city of earthly delights. Moreover'—her voice was somewhat arch here, though her countenance none the less pleasant— 'I believe you to be rather too harsh upon her calling, Mr Cautley, as well as upon her conduct: an innocent involved for a night in an intrigue for the sake of a few silver sequins, that is all. It was surely mere coincidence and nothing more insidious that upon his last day in Venice Tristano should have encountered her in that most civil establishment where she plied her trade.'

'But,' I protested, unwilling to acquit this lady from my charge, 'the centurion—Scipio—was loitering outside—'

'Ah,' she said as if she had tasted something delicious. 'Good! You have surmised the true villain, have you not? Well done, Mr Cautley. Yes—the centurion. For it was assuredly *he* who engaged this lady's services on that first evening at the *palazzo*; *he* who arranged that she should conduct the gentleman in Vandyke costume—doubtless she never knew Tristano's name—into the prescribed chamber. *Why* should he do so? Must you ask? It is very simple, surely? For when the opera season resumed a few months later with *Tigrane*, there remained only a single *primo uomo* in the Count's company.'

I contemplated this statistic for a few seconds. 'What, then, became of Maddalena?'

My lady engaged in silent contemplation of her own; then she sighed, her attention once again taking refuge in her costume.

'I fear Tancredi's farewell aria was her last to be heard in public. Her career upon the stage might so easily have continued. Signor Belloni was dead. Anzolo, too, might have been silenced, one way or the other, had it been required. Yet by now the Count did not give a fig for the masquerade, for his great *primo uomo*. The crime now in question was not that of transgressing the boundaries of the sexes and appearing upon the stage in the guise of a man; rather, it was one of transgressing other boundaries—those prescribed by the Count. In short, she had betrayed him, and in the most egregious fashion—with a castrato.

239

'Maddalena, to answer your question, was most easily disposed of, because of course she did not exist in the first place. Il Prizziello, naturally, was somewhat more difficult; a famous singer after all. Yet he vanished—from Venice at least. After the *villeggiatura* concluded and the nobles and merchants flocked back to their city it was reported that he had accepted a contract in Naples, at the Teatro San Bartolomeo. But imagine the surprise of a dozen or so of his closest admirers who made the pilgrimage only to learn that in fact he had never arrived in Naples, his engagement truly having been—so a new report asserted—in Florence. Meanwhile, in Florence it was understood by half the populace that the great Il Prizziello had deserted their theatres even before his arrival in order to accept a lucrative contract from the Elector Palatine, by the other half that he had departed for Moscow. This latter theory eventually gained a measure of credence over the former, in the process acquiring certain sorrowful dimensions: it was given abroad—upon an authority nobody could ever quote—that Il Prizziello had been thrown from his horse and killed only a few short leagues from his destination in Russia; or, alternatively, that he had been murdered by bandits *en route* in Bohemia, his golden throat pierced by a cheap poniard. In any event, it is with true sadness that I must relate that he—that *she*—was never more heard upon the stage.'

Once more Lady Beauclair appeared to contemplate the fate of the original owner of her costume. And now I myself looked at this habit as if for the first time. The ultramarine damask glowed, seeming to light the chamber more successfully than the candle's fluttering flame. It seemed as if a part of my lady's story had raised itself from the frozen past and fluttered towards me like a downy seed-petal on the breeze, blossoming in the chamber now before my eyes; a small piece of Art that upon these evenings had been granted a brief Life. Maddalena had vanished—through whatever villainy or mischance—but *it* remained, a still point at the centre of the inscrutably revolving world; the hub around which lives had circled and chained and intertwined and come apart like dancers on a chequered floor. I wished to inquire of my lady how it had come into her possession, and how she had come to know—and been preserved by—Tristano; but these, I knew, were the subjects of another evening. Instead I posed a different question.

'Scipio,' I said at length, when I had started from this reverie. 'What then, may I ask, was the fate of this most terrible little rogue? I presume he remained in Venice.'

Lady Beauclair looked up sharply. 'I fear you presume wrong, Mr Cautley. For soon enough Scipio, too, arrived in England.'

This time as I departed from Lady Beauclair's lodgings there was no sign of either Mr McQuarters or Mr Lockhart. Neither did I encounter Betty, though upon the narrow stair a different, equally unwholesome, lady was bidding a passionate adieu to, or perhaps hungrily greeting, a finely dressed gentleman whose waggling scabbard struck my knee as I passed. Outside in the street, the abode of the ladies in scarlet petticoats was dark and silent. For indeed the hour was very late.

As I placed my wig on its stand by my door an hour later and commenced unbuttoning my shirt and breeches, I stared fixedly at *A Lady by Candle-light*. The countenance in the foreground was, despite the veil, slowly becoming recognisable as Lady Beauclair; yet a more extensive application of turpentine revealed someone else in the portrait: someone peering over my lady's half-bared shoulder; someone whose head emerged from behind hers; a shadow, a dark contour; unrecognisable. By now I was more intrigued by this visage—this ur-painting—than I was by the half-finished portrait of my lady. I wondered, did I dare strip the remainder of the paint and sizing? Did I dare uncover this dark original?

Yet as I slipped my night-shirt over my head, donned my nightcap and blew out the candle, I was thinking once again of the Turkish costume: that traitorous cynosure by which lives were guided and wrecked on mountainous waves and hidden reefs.

And then I was imagining Lady Beauclair pushing aside its delicate sarsenet, unfastening its moulded buttons, letting it glide down her soft legs and release from its folds the exquisite fragrances of her skin . . .

I fell to my knees at the edge of my pallet and, as on every evening, whispered a prayer for the protection of my soul.

Twenty-seven

In the days that followed The Unveiling—as I had come to think of what had passed between my master and Eleanora—I saw much less of Sir Endymion in the studio in St Alban's Street. Indeed, I saw much less of him altogether, for my services were apparently no longer required in Chiswick.

This is not to say that my duties for Sir Endymion had concluded on that chill morning, though in the first hours after The Unveiling this was what I had feared—and perhaps desired? But there was still much work to be done on *The Goddess of Liberty*, *The Miseries of Life*, and *The Rape of Lucretia*, and Sir Endymion was anxious that I should finish everything on time. So I walked each morning to the studio, applied the pigments and varnishes, and departed well before nightfall, feeling quite forlorn. For the truth was that despite what had happened—whatever it had been—I missed my master. I missed the eel pies and pints of porter served at dusk; the stories of Plato's cave and the Grand Tour; the discourses upon history-painting in the grand style that spilled over into our regular board beside the fire at the Carv'd Balcony Tavern. I even missed his voice calling out, 'Hop to it, Cautley, you sluggard! Hop to it, or we shall never finish on time!'

Sir Endymion, I knew, still visited this little studio. Each morning I could not help but observe how in my absence herbs had been burned in the fire or placed in the corners of the chamber; how bottles of port-wine were reproducing themselves beside the table. Scented candles burned to short stubs and were succeeded by others, which in turn burned low. Bouquets of lilies or jonquils occasionally appeared, faded, were replaced by new ones. Each morning, too, I noticed that the hair of 'the fair garreteer' became richer and the features of Lucretia and the Goddess of Liberty more clearly defined. How such small tokens rebuked me!

242

Each morning, also, a note—usually a single line—arrived by the penny post, giving my instructions: '*The Miseries of Life* must be completed by St Michael's Day', or 'Ultramarine and canvases from Mr Middleton'. Contact with my master had dwindled to these few terse communications. One morning, however, the note, again a single line, commanded something quite different: 'Take Eleanora for constitutional'.

I blinked at this strange missive, hoping I had misread it, and then wondering—when I realised I had not—if I should toss it through the window. No task assigned by my master could possibly have been more odious to me than this request. If my relations with Eleanora had been restrained before, in the absence of Sir Endymion they were now guarded by the most extreme reserve. Though we spent hours together in the studio, we never exchanged so much as a word. As soon as I arrived she retreated to the smaller of the two chambers, where she remained until my departure, silent except for the occasional interval of sobbing. I did not know why she sobbed, nor did I care. She was to blame for what I had seen—*she* was; no one else. It was plain enough: she had seduced my master. Yes—after a day or two of deliberations I was certain of this. The Scriptures, history, mythology—all abounded with examples of the villainy of her sex: Jezebel, Medea, Judith, Delilah, Salome, Lady Macbeth, Tanaquil; the list went on. Yes—she had betrayed my master. That a gentleman so devoted to virtue would *actually* . . . well, it was simply not possible. And yet . . . such ruin! I nearly sobbed myself when I thought of young Alciphron and his adoring mother—that happy family. But I did not for a trice believe that *she*, this madwoman, this arch-jade, this second Eve, this 'most dangerous goddess', was weeping for *them*.

Now I handed her the note, or, rather, left it for her upon the chair, pointing to it with my paintbrush. She picked it up after a minute and seemed to require some moments to decipher it. Perhaps the jade did not know her letters. Or possibly she was as disbelieving—as reticent—as I had been.

'Very well.' Was that an insolent tone in her voice? 'Whenever you are prepared, sir.'

I made her wait a good while. I was her master now—or so it felt like. Her keeper, in any case. The perambulation, when I saw fit to grant it, was a short one: down Cockspur

Street to Charing Cross, then past Northumberland House and a short distance along the Strand before returning. We exchanged not a word.

On the following morning I received a note containing, alas, similar instructions. We walked as far as Covent Garden. For a time we strolled among the stalls, trestles and carts in the Great Piazza, then along Drury Lane, past the theatre and into Great Hart Street. I noticed she was weeping. This area I knew to be notorious for its venereal commerce. Perhaps Eleanora had been of the sisterhood of Covent Garden?

'Come,' I said, shivering in my coat, filled with revulsion. 'We must return.'

On the third day I allowed her a more copious liberty, even though Sir Endymion's instructions had made no mention of any such privileges for her. We ventured down Whitehall and Parliament Street, then at her behest turned into Bridge Street and Channel Row, which conducted us through a narrow court and on to the Manchester Stairs. At the top of these steps she stood for some time, gazing at the back-and-forth procession of barques, barges, oyster-boats, fishing-smacks, and the jumble of wharves and timber-yards scattered across the far side. Then she seated herself and withdrew from her pocket what looked to be a novel.

As the day was fine and dry I had carried my sketch-book under my arm and, likewise seating myself, now began a drawing of Westminster Bridge. In the absence of sitters I had upon my arrival in London begun some architectural studies: views of Buckingham House from behind Rosamond's Pond in St James's Park; Burlington House from the doorway of St James's Church in Piccadilly; St George's Hospital from beneath the shade of a lime tree in Hyde Park; as well as a half-dozen or so of Mr Wren's churches.

Now, with the sun warm upon my shoulders, I removed my coat and lay it by, then tucked my wig into my pocket and removed my shoes. I forgot about Eleanora, though she sat only five feet away, still engrossed in her novel. The river slurped and slopped an inch from my toes, its incoming tide stirring up great clouds of tea-coloured silt and sending past our station a constant parade of colliers, wherries, hoys and hay-boats. I added a few of their number to my drawing. Great argosies of clouds scudded overhead; I added a few of them as well. Beside Lambeth Palace—visible above the arches of the great bridge—a horse-ferry crossed back and forth, laden with carts and liveried watermen; they, too, were represented. I imagined myself as the still centre, the vital axle, of all of this activity; its silent registrar. Alas, I was an imperfect registrar, for after much critical inspection I decided that my bridge looked akin to a sea monster or serpent uncoiling across the river; so I erased it and attempted another—slightly better. I added a few coaches to its top, drawing swiftly now; then a few of the people— no more than ants, really—moving to and fro along the wharves, water-gates and timber-yards of Southwark. Behind them, far in the distance, I sketched the rotating vanes of a windmill.

When I looked at her—it may have been an hour later— Eleanora was weeping. What about? Her novel? After putting on my coat and wig, I assisted her to her feet. I felt none of my previous revulsion; only a little awkwardness, embarrassment. As we walked back to St Alban's Street in our customary silence, for the first time I walked beside her instead of, as I had been doing, two steps in front.

Only when we were back in the studio some twenty minutes later did I realise I had forgotten my sketch-book. I imagined it lying at the top of the Manchester Stairs, its pages flapping in the breeze like the wings of a great crippled sea-bird.

On the fourth day, another walk. No instructions had arrived from Sir Endymion and I had at present no further duties to perform. My master seemed to have abandoned me. I felt a twist of pain at the base of my heart. Yet—how pleased I was to see this—he had abandoned Eleanora as well: no bottles of port-wine, no new candles or flowers had appeared overnight. So today, moved more by charity than obligation, I indulged her with a much longer perambulation: up Ludgate Hill and past St Paul's, along Butcher Row and then the broader pavement of Cheapside, into Cornhill, which in turn led into Whitechapel Road. So long was our journey that my feet were smarting even before we returned, and in Whitechapel we stopped at a cook-shop upon my request and ate suet-pudding and potatoes swimming in pork fat. Or, rather, Eleanora ate, sitting across the board from me, her chin upon her breast as if she were praying over her unwholesome victuals. She consumed this exiguous repast almost greedily, dispatching half of my pudding when lumps of fat the size of filberts scuttled my own hunger and forced me to place the greasy potatoes as well as the pudding aside. The other patrons of this establishment were noisily enjoying shin of beef, tripe, cow-heel, jugged pigeons and other delicacies whose particular method of preparation, glimpsed through a doorway and smelled at a much further remove, fairly turned my stomach. Our reckoning amounted to twopence and a halfpenny each, which I was happy to pay for the privilege of departing.

When we stepped back outside it was raining. Grey clouds slid across the western sky like a herd of migrating beasts. People pushed past us, wearing pattens and riding-hoods, their white stockings as streaked with mud as the legs of postilions. The street was thick with newspaper-boys, shovel-hatted porters, pot-boys carrying belch. Carts rumbled past us; colliers emptied their loads into cellars, the coal-dust rising up in thick black plumes. The air stank, besides, of the chandler's cauldron, of the trout and salmon rotting in the fish-stalls, of boiled beef and mutton fat sputtering in the cook-shops.

I wished to turn back, but Eleanora was untroubled by all of this, seeming to regard our environs as, strangely, a form of paradise. Occasionally—because we now were speaking, however inconsistently and fragmentedly—she would say (albeit mostly to herself), 'Yes, yes, I remember', 'Ah, so it still stands', or some such thing as that. By the time we turned up Brick Lane I realised that she, and not I, was now—and indeed had been—our leader. We turned into Brown's Lane and then proceeded along Lamb Street, from where the pitched roof and square turret of Spitalfields Market could be glimpsed over the mossy slates of the rooftops on our left.

'Where do we go?' I finally saw fit to inquire, hopping quickly through the puddles now to keep up with her increased pace. 'Eleanora' (this being the first time I spoke her name to her) 'Eleanora, I believe it is high time . . .'

She did not seem to have heard; she would not be stopped. We entered Spital Square and then turned into a narrow court whose buildings were represented in an uneven row, some leaning forward, others backward, and their rank interrupted in the middle by a pile of rubble overgrown with ragweed and crab-grass. The immediate neighbours of this irregular pyramid had each slumped to a degree where it seemed they, too, would contribute further to the picture of ruin. Yet as if heedless of this danger, their inhabitants—children with blackened face, mothers in aprons sprinkling a scanty fare among the scuttling clouds of chickens—peered from the windows and lounged in the doorways, watching us incuriously.

Eleanora drew up short before the heap of rubble, upon which I now saw a band of ragged urchins.

'A sorry end,' I said after a minute, staring at the ruin above which the grey herd was driving northwards, as if fleeing before some approaching disaster.

'On the contrary, sir,' she replied. 'This is where all began.'

My lodgings when I returned home that evening were dark and cold. I lighted a small fire, which reflected upon the double countenances of *A Lady by Candle-light*.

A note from Johnson's Habit-Warehouse sat upon my wainscot table, as did a letter from Toppie. No doubt they had been conducted hither by Jeremiah or perhaps Samuel. With each of my rebukes and denials, their devotions appeared to grow and their attentions became more determined. Each evening I returned home to discover the linen on my bed tight and smooth. Coal sat at the ready in my grate. My pipe had been cleaned of spittle and its cud of tobacco and was filled afresh from a pouch, likewise replenished. My clothes for the morrow were brushed and spread upon the bed. My letters, as now, were sorted and placed on the wainscot table, which, like my boots, and like my window-panes, bore unmistakable evidence of a shine. I had been making inquiries to Mr Sharp about having a bolt fixed upon my door.

I broke the seal on the first letter and learned that my costume had been completed and could be collected at my convenience. Toppie enclosed in his letter a ticket for the Vauxhall masquerade. The ticket bore an engraving of a maiden perched upon the back of a plunging dolphin. In one hand she carried a harp, in the other an unfurling banner. The inscription on the banner proclaimed 'Ball at Vauxhall'. Beneath, amid the curling waves: 'No Gentleman or Lady admitted unless in Full Dress. Price 1 shilling.'

'It will be the final Vauxhall Masquerade of the Season,' Toppie wrote in the brief note. He predicted that, if the precedent held, it would therefore be a more riotous evening than one might ordinarily expect, 'more violent than an Uprising of irate Silk-weavers in Spitalfields. Truly, George, *anything* at all might *happen!*'

I tucked the ticket between the leaves of *The Compleat Physiognomist*, atop of a page in which my father had painstakingly outlined the difference between physiognomy and other forms of divining the future: necromancy, pyromancy, neomancy, pedomancy, hydromancy, geomancy, chiromancy and metoscopy—'all of which', he had written, 'were most strictly proscribed by successive Popes in the Time of the Holy Inquisition'. It transpired that the physiognomist belonged to a dangerous and much persecuted profession, for on this same page my father noted with no little regret that Queen Bess had passed a law against the tribe, stipulating that anyone professing 'knowledge of phisnognomie shall be openly whipped untill his body be bloudye'; and that even our own late King George had denounced them as 'rogues and vagabonds'.

As I climbed into my night-shirt—which had been folded in tissue paper, like a gift—I wondered which of these methods of divination might foretell what lay in wait for me, in a day, a fortnight, or a year. And as I placed my head upon my pillow—which had been lovingly fluffed and plumped—I listened to my heart beat and wondered if I was as affrighted by the future as these popes, kings and queens.

Twenty-eight

 Eleanora Clitherow had been born into a family whose fortunes had never entirely revived after her great-grand-uncle rashly committed himself to the Duke of Monmouth's forces in 1685. For his efforts this gentleman was transported as a slave to the sugar plantations of the West Indies, while the Clitherows suffered to remain upon English soil wisely avoided all subsequent turmoil and prospered under the first of our two Hanoverian mon-

archs, busily enclosing as much of the Buckinghamshire countryside as the Parliaments of the day generously permitted. Alas, an unanticipated decline in stock prices some years previously had required the removal of the family seat from a villa near Aylesbury to a set of surpassingly modest lodgings in Spitalfields. Here chambers were let on a weekly basis to itinerant strangers, and here Eleanora lived with her valetudinarian parents, devoid of any possessions but for those boasting the highest sentimental interest.

'I entertained great hopes at this time of appearing as a player upon the stage and thereby providing a measure of relief for my poor parents,' she was telling me upon the morrow, after we had taken another, shorter, ramble through Spring Garden into St James's Park. 'These hopes were first raised in me by a gentleman who now lodged above our stairs, an actor from a company appearing at the Covent Garden Theatre. This fellow was a flatterer and a most egregious coxcomb, yet he seemed kindly disposed towards me and promised to make an application on my behalf to a gentleman who was in the Cabinet Council of that same playhouse. This gentleman, I was allowed to believe, was a person of no little importance in the world of the playhouses. My coxcomb persuaded me to believe that, if this vital gentleman could be suitably impressed, then I should have an opportunity to commence my career in a comic opera or some other silly piece. Into this fellow's hands, then, I entrusted my fortunes.—Pray, sir, does this posture aptly suit your purposes?'

'Perfectly, Miss Eleanora. Now, if you would maintain it a few moments more . . .'

I was completing a sketch of her head, having placed her by the window a few minutes before, where she now stood very much in the pose of 'the fair garreteer'. The nosegay having wilted and drooped—for still there was no sign of Sir Endymion—I had provided her instead with the iron salamander, the sight of which in her hands even two days ago would surely have struck into my heart the most trembling terrors. Now, however, I had begun to regard her less fearfully, no longer worrying that she might attempt to cleave my skull with this favourite of weapons. Indeed I was quite at ease, even though it was now past dark, well beyond the hour when it had been my wont to scuttle and twist down the broken steps and return to the Haymarket. She had asked me to tarry, as if fearful of what this night should bring, or perhaps of what it should not. As we betook ourselves back from Spitalfields yesterday she had made several starts to her tale, which, however, moved her to shed some tears and promptly discontinue; only after she had been composed by her more familiar surroundings, it seemed, was she able to recommence this sorrowful history. And despite Sir Endymion's many proscriptions against misery not being given a particular name—'It possesses only a family name, Cautley, not a proper one'—I found myself curious to know what forces conspired to bring her into this deplorable state.

As she spoke, the stubs from two candles burned and spat lightly, and the window was fogged from our hot supper—eel pies. After returning from our perambulation I had fetched them—as in the old days little more than a week before, I thought with a twinge—from the Carv'd Balcony Tavern. I could not help observing that Eleanora consumed hers with more relish than she showed any of those provided by my master's purse, and for some reason I could not help but smile inwardly with pleasure at this transformation. Yet then I felt a worm of guilt burrow into my belly at the same second that my first bite arrived.

'Will Sir Endymion be drinking some cheer with us this evening?' one of the tap-boys, an amiable young fellow, had inquired of me as he pricked our pies and slipped them into the oven. He contemplated his own red-hot salamander. 'He has not been about for a few nights—not like him! No, not like Sir Endymion! He likes his pint of porter, Sir Endymion does.'

I kept silent, no longer feeling I knew anything at all of what was like or unlike my master. My own victuals I consumed only half-heartedly.

'I believed by this time that our lodger had taken a fancy to me,' Eleanora was continuing her tale as I reached for my—that is, Sir Endymion's—brushes and pigments. 'He was, as I said, something of a coxcomb, but I fear I was most susceptible to amorous impressions, being an inveterate reader of novels of romance. And, as he was a fine-looking fellow, very well-dressed, I reciprocated what I interpreted to be his honest affections. Soon it did not concern me that this gentleman's intercession with the manager was continually deferred, nor that upon more sustained

250

interrogation he proved to be not an actor at all, merely a prompter and sometimes a dresser. For the heart is not a rational creature, nor a perspicacious one. It is an accomplice to many crimes, being so willingly deceived . . .'

She reflected upon this sad wisdom for a moment before continuing.

'My dear father had by now hit upon a contrasting prescription for the relief of our misery. A debtor's writ was about to be served upon him, and surely the gaol awaited. Thus he had commenced negotiations with Squire Waghorn, one of our neighbours in the brighter days when we enjoyed a more comfortable estate than our miserable abode in Spitalfields. Soon a deal was struck between them, and I was contracted to wed the squire's second son. I was borne out of London and back into the country in the squire's coach. I was shown a small thatched cottage upon the edge of the estate, hard by a forest, where it had been decided that the two of us should pass our connubial days and nights. Another rustic cottage close by was destined for my parents. It was an even humbler dwelling, surely the lowliest hovel in the Kingdom—but didn't my poor mother wring her hands and weep for joy when she clapped her eyes upon it? *She*—who had been mistress of a thousand acres, a score of rooms, a dozen maids and servants! And my poor, gratified father? This poor Lear, dispossessed of his kingdom and now gratified by the prospect of a wind-blown shelter hunkered on the edge of the hills!

'Then—oh, only *then*—was my intended husband revealed to me.' She paused, biting her lower lip and seeming to ruminate critically upon this foreordained person. 'What shall I say of him?' She shrugged, frowned. 'The second son is always a superfluous fellow—'

'Alas,' I said to myself, 'this is most true . . .'

'—the fifth teat on the udder. But—*this* fellow?' She shuddered for a few seconds, clenching her fists upon the salamander as if preparing to break the odious fellow's skull with it. 'Oh, how swiftly the fair maidens of Buckinghamshire had fled from the attentions of this lout, this most beastly of beaux. How sincere were their cringes of horror at his gruesome propositions! A clodbrain—you cannot conceive him, sir—a veritable changeling, a beast, an *ogre*. His bloody eyes as he cast them lecherously upon me each gazed in a contrary direction, then rolled like tops in their fleshy sockets before disappearing beneath the inundation of his two eyebrows; these were the size of weasels and indeed wriggled and writhed as if struggling in the snare a farmer had set for them. Nature had been no less prodigal with the other details of his appearance, which were scarcely more comforting. His nose, narrow at the bridge and portentously wide at the terminus, hung like a clapper over his thick lips, between which protruded a tongue two sizes too large for his mouth. This contorting orifice was still most capacious, ample enough to confine the major part of two incomplete rows of teeth comparable in measure to those of a donkey. Like his tongue, his belly also rebelled against all confinement, protruding in hairy hillocks through the straining buttons of his shirt. His waistcoat was unfastened and dripped like a slabbering bib with generous morsels of his late repast, some of which also betrayed themselves in the corners of his mouth, upon the black hairs of his moustache, and even upon the bulby tip of his great nozzle. His side-whiskers, spared this anointment, stood out a full six inches from either side of his chops, thickened still more by an abundance of bristles issuing from his ears.

'In deference to the occasion he had donned a filthy tie-wig, which perched upon his overlarge skull like a small verminous creature, its knotty tail descending as far as his rump, where it was fixed with a short red ribbon; and his shoulders had been squeezed into a silk coat whose gold buttons and bright brocade presented the same ludicrous effect as they would had they been ornamenting a wild bear in its forest den, or an orang-utan in the jungle. The formalities of the occasion did not preclude him from allowing his foxhounds to share in his joy at his expected union, and they capered noisily round the drawing-room, occasionally receiving a howl of rebuke and a whack from his cane whenever their exuberance brought their paws, tails or muzzles into contact with the toe elevated to great prominence upon an elbow-chair. This swelling, yellowed protuberance with its cracked and blackened nail had been denuded of its stocking on account of the gout, a condition whose pains he was seeking to mitigate with a pint of strong ale and a series of loud oaths.'

Eleanora closed her eyes and shook her head, as if to rid herself of the terrible image of her intended. Then she fetched a breath and continued.

'To sanctify his son's goatish lust through the solemn rites of the Church the determined Squire Waghorn had recruited far and wide, in ever expanding circles in the towns and villages round their copious lands, until at last I fell within the compass of this dreadful forage. How I then begged my dear father to rescind this hateful contract! I believe I should have done anything to crack in twain this beastly betrothal. Yet my father, fearing the debtor's gaol, could see—would hear of, could brook—no other means.'

'Your career upon the stage?' I said, hopefully.

'My father disapproved mightily of all players,' she said, shaking her tresses. 'To him the gaol was an immeasurably preferable place to the stage, which he deemed the broadest entryway into hell.'

'Ah, yes—there are many of his mind.'

I was nodding vigorously in sympathy, remembering how my own dear father had regarded playhouses as the Devil's nurseries, places of the blackest arts.

'Yet now I am convinced,' Eleanora broke in upon my recollections, 'that this prejudice does not altogether pay the playhouse and its denizens an injustice, nor are those who profess to it entirely wanting in sense. How do I know this? Ah, upon that best of authorities, sir, that most wise and remorseless of teachers—folly and sad experience. Yes,' she said with a sigh, her face somewhat discomposed, 'bitter experience has been my heartless tutor. For so convinced was I of our lodger's affections that on the eve of the day of my loathed union I crept through the window of my chamber in the squire's manor-house and fled on foot into Oxford. In the morning I was bouncing into London on the post-chaise, and at the same hour as that dreaded ceremony was prescribed to commence I found myself in my home in Spitalfields, weeping in the arms of my beloved. How different he was from my prescribed husband—the very opposite! His beautiful clothes with their polished buttons; his elegant manners, fit for the Court; the soft scent of the cologne with which he had sprinkled himself; even the hat cocked at the jaunty angle upon his periwig ... "A tailor's dummy, not a man," my father had once said, sniggering. "A mincing fellow of fashion!" But if clothes proclaim the man, this gallant was spotless, noble—an ornament, a glittering star in heaven!

'He wasted not a moment, summoning a hack and delivering me upon an instant into the presence of his friend. This powerful personage dwelt in a fine residence in Mayfair. My beau—for, you see, by now I thought of him as such—applied himself to the door. He was known here. A manservant admitted us, addressing him courteously by name. There, in a parlour, the great man awaited; another fellow of fashion, brightly attired. My circumstances were explained. I was frankly appraised. Alas, my spirits were greatly agitated—I feared for what impression might be taken from such a trembling mould: I did not sit right upon my chair, I spoke rarely, and then only with a squeak, and my eyes took a continual reckoning of my hands, which reposed fitfully in my lap, twisting and untwisting a lace handkerchief. The men moved apart, into an adjoining chamber. Cups of brandy; pipes; a maidservant moving within and without through a communicating door. My beloved, I could hear, was deferential; the gentleman, hearty. Was that the chink of coins I heard, or of brandy-glasses? Then the two gentlemen emerged. My charming gallant was smiling! Yes: it was decreed—a role would be mine; so I was assured. This manager—for such, I believe, was his title—this manager made me the most solemn promises, affected the most kindly smiles, spoke about the many favourable opportunities in his company. Soon, a day later, I was ensconced in lodgings—in Great Hart Street, round the corner from the Theatre Royal. Small rooms, yes, but I had expectations, prospects! First, a small bit in *The Way of the World*, then *Every Man in His Humour* . . .'

She closed her eyes again, though this time the image that she contemplated was a considerably fonder one. The end-point of this joyous deliberation was, however, a regretful sigh.

'Upon the following day—in the evening, rather—this good gentleman sent up his *carte-de-visite*, desiring most urgently to wait upon me. I readily admitted my kind benefactor into my chambers, where he greeted me with great politeness, kissing my hand. I was compelled to receive him in my bedchamber, which, tiny though it was, constituted the least incommodious of my chambers. The gentleman, however, was not daunted in the least. "Queen Bess was wont to receive guests in her bedchamber," he said, "so surely with this as your precedent you need make no apology! See here—I bear a gift," he appended in a jolly tone,

254

holding out for inspection a large pasteboard box: a costume, fresh from Mr Johnson's Habit-Warehouse. I was to be Foible, he said. Would I attire myself in her costume? He had a great wish, he confessed as he raised the lid on the box, to witness for himself the effect this piece might produce upon the stage.

'I readily obliged his wish, donning the habit in an adjoining chamber, among a small litter of pint-pots and stiffened pudding-cloths. Outside the door he related with much enthusiasm his plans for the production. We should go on the road presently—to Bath. Did I fancy that? Yes, very much. Truly, however, I paid very little mind to his prating, pondering happily upon my altered fortunes, and particularly upon my gallant, who had been responsible for them. Though I had not seen him for two days—that is, since the successful issue of our conference in Mayfair—all this evening I had been solacing my romantic imagination with warm remembrances of him, and only slightly less so with anticipations of the fame that awaited me upon the stage and the generous subsistence which thereafter would reward the sufferings of my dear parents. So rapt was I with these reflections upon my agreeable circumstances that I did not take heed of how my costume—once it was fitted— could scarcely be conceived as any sort of decent attire for display in the public arena, and might in fact lower still further my dear father's inveterate opinion of the stage.

'Yet when I returned to my bedchamber the good gentleman confessed himself most favourably struck by the habit, albeit he insisted upon effecting one or two alterations concerning the allocation of the silken material across my bosom. His hands were rather too liberal of movement in these regions for my true comfort, but he smiled gently upon me when these lingering arrangements were completed and then said in a tender voice that I should make a pretty picture indeed upon the stage. I had scarce finished thanking him for this kindness, when his brow knit itself critically and he allowed that his professional mind was not altogether at ease with the distribution of the costume across my stomach (in truth, it fitted most tightly over the corset) nor the colour of the scarlet stockings, which were peeping in the briefest hints from below my skirts. When I admitted doubts of my own, his hands went to work again, fastening and unfastening, cinching and pinching, until at last he recommended

255

that I remove the stockings so that our impression of the habit not be marred.

' "Come, come—let us have no shyness now," he said in a jovial voice when I made a few steps in the direction of the other chamber. "Shyness is no virtue upon the stage, mind!" And so I accomplished this change in his presence, aided in the unfastening of one of my garters and the unrolling of a stocking by his own pair of hands, which by accident tickled my knee and ankle to no modest degree. "Hum!" he pronounced when this transformation was complete, "I fear even so that something is not right and proper . . ." After a further moment's careful scrutiny he advised that the corset be removed. "Tut-tut," he said with a comical smile, wagging a finger at me as once again I set off for the adjoining chamber, "shyness will never do you a service upon the stage!"

'He now described how he, like my young gallant—"for whom I have great hopes"—had begun his career as a dresser, having fitted and unfitted some of the finest ladies of the stage. Had I heard of the celebrated Mrs Charlotte Charke? Of course I had heard of her. Who—what hopeful stage-player—had not? The youngest daughter of our late poet laureate, Mr Colley Cibber; the sister of Mr Theophilus Cibber, the actor-manager at Drury Lane; as well as a famed player and dramatist in her own right. Well, as a young man (my benefactor explained) he had been Mrs Charke's dresser on those enchanting evenings when she played Captain Macheath in *The Beggar's Opera* at the King's Theatre in the Haymarket. Yes, Macheath—for she was famed for her masculine roles, her Roderigo in *Othello*, he said, being another triumph of note. Yet she dressed the part of a gentleman in her private life as well, my benefactor explained: this indeed was her greatest role. She adopted the name of "Mr Brown" and wore a gentleman's clothes in public. She learned to shoot and hunt; she was a hog merchant; a pastry-cook; a farmer. In short, she became a man. She played the *valet de chambre* to a young nobleman who could not pierce her disguise. She took heiresses as female companions. When they proposed marriage she was required to disabuse them in great haste. They were aghast—they had not suspected, even during the most intimate moments spent together.

' "Yet I was on those occasions in her dressing-chamber

256

permitted to peep behind this secret disguise which tricked all the world," my gentleman said with a wink, "and can testify to any magistrate in the land that Mrs Charke *was no gentleman!*"

'He was made so merry by his recollections of Mrs Charke that for some moments he appeared to forget that I shared the chamber with him. Presently, though, his attention fixed itself again upon the corset, and he proposed that we go to work upon it. The removal of this item necessitated many variations in the disposition of my dress, as well as a good deal of tugging and wrestling. My benefactor (still in a merry temper) considered these proceedings highly amusing and seemingly could not refrain from tickling my arms and legs at occasional intervals in the course of our struggles. I was preparing to object to this licence, when one particularly extravagant tug, of which he had been the author, dramatically freed my corset and sent the both of us toppling in a heap on to my small bed, and then from there to the floor.

' "Please, good sir," I said, highly sensitive to the indecency of our posture, which he seemed reluctant to alter, even though in the course of our thrashes his own garments had unaccountably loosened themselves, thereby duplicating my own dishabille. "Please, good sir!"

'He remained highly amused by our situation, laughing boisterously and, upon the pretence of tickling me some more, advancing his hands into the more delicate regions concealed—and, in one or two cases, not in fact quite concealed—by my habit. I made further objections, but now his countenance as it thrust itself into mine at once assumed a more grave expression, and suddenly he confessed his passion for me in the strongest terms. I drew back in horror— I could scarce believe his words! Before I could respond to this alarming declaration he punctuated it with a prolonged kiss upon my lips, which fairly smothered me and, when it had at long last run its course, left me gasping in fright.

'He took advantage of my perplexities to raise me on to the bed and then, loath to delay his felicity for another moment, swiftly unlocked the cabinet of Venus and robbed me of that most precious gift which in its more wanton and fervent transports my imagination had seen unwrapped and tenderly cherished by my gallant young beau.

'When he had finished his business he buttoned his breeches and gathered up Foible's costume, leaving me

naked and ashamed, cringing and weeping. He departed
with scarcely a word, though upon the morrow his *carte-
de-visite* was again delivered to me—and then upon the
morrow—and upon the morrow. Each time a new costume
was produced, and I was requested to exhibit it for his
critical gaze. Yet each time he spoke less and less of Foible,
and it seemed that the costumes were less and less plausibly
those of a stage-player. His alterations to them were
now swift and decisive, made with freely roving hands.
Once or twice the costume was intended for his own demonstration—silk stockings and shifts, garters, a dainty chemise,
a fur stole. Once he squeezed himself into a corset and I
was persuaded to unlace it, calling him "my lady". On that
memorable occasion he also painted his cheeks and lips and
attired himself in some kind of strange oriental habit. Or,
citing the noble precedent of Mrs Charke, he would dress
me in breeches, a gentleman's silk coat, a brocaded tricorne
and a pair of black boots. Then he would take me outside
for short perambulations through Covent Garden, where
we purchased roots and herbs. But soon, despite these antics,
he grew bored with me. Our time together contracted; our
business was transacted in minutes and was of a more con-
ventional dealing. Once or twice he did not show. Then one
forenoon I walked past the Covent Garden Theatre—and
what did I see? *The Way of the World* had been running for
three nights, was closing in a fortnight, was touring two
other playhouses next month. Oh, poor, poor Foible!'

'But what of your gallant?' I inquired. 'Surely he might
defend your honour and cudgel this roguish manager?'

'Defend my honour!' She shook her tresses in some agitation, then resumed more calmly. 'I had indeed been puzzled by his absence, not having seen him in all this time. In
the meantime I had grown quite sick with love. In search
of him I returned to Spitalfields—on foot, as yesterday—
and what should I see? That same pile of rubble that yet
distinguishes the very spot upon which my dear father's
modest lodgings stood. It had collapsed in the dead of night,
during a rain, like an old dray-horse dropping dead in the
street.'

'Ah—and your young beau was killed,' I said with a sympathetic sigh.

'No, no,' she protested. 'Oh, would that were true! He
escaped harm, more is the pity. No, no—it was my dear
258

parents, who had returned in sorrow, in disgrace, from the squire's home. Both of them . . . crushed . . . their bones yet—yet—yet beneath . . .'

Eleanora found herself unable to render a full account of the fate of these poor souls, yet I was nevertheless moved almost as passionately as she. Then after a short interval, during which she took frequent recourse to her handkerchief, she daubed at her eyes a final time and continued.

'Gallantry, they say, is comprised of every vice. Yet it is equally so that vice is comprised of every gallantry. My beau arrived a day later at my lodgings in Great Hart Street, to which I had retreated in my grief. He had been, he explained, on tour with a company—in Bath. He was chief prompter; he had been promised a speaking part, but alas, he had been duped . . . But had I not received his letters? No? Surely not! Some villain, he exclaimed, was interceding. What was that? Mr Larkins? No—surely not. *No*—a gentleman of the most unimpeachable character, Mr Larkins . . .'

You may imagine that I sat rigidly upright at the revelation of this name, my brush very nearly dropping through my fingers.

'Mr Larkins,' I interrupted. 'This fellow's name was *Larkins*?'

'Most cursed name,' she replied. 'Synonym for every vice and evil under the sun. Yes, Larkins; that is the name of this treacherous persecutor, the author of my ruin—the *co-author* at least. My gallant,' she rushed on, oblivious to how my countenance had discomposed at this information, 'was convinced soon enough of this manager's villainy and forthwith removed me from my abhorred lodgings, ensconcing me instead in the household of his aunt, a lady somewhat advanced in years and of a most kindly demeanour. Mrs Cook was her name. This modest-seeming soul kept a coffee-house opposite St Paul's, Covent Garden. Yet mark you how gallantry passes hand in glove with vice! How villainy may don the pleasing mantle of goodness. In my new lodgings—this new household—I found myself in identical circumstances as before—the same, only more so. Need I tell you these circumstances? Need I shower myself with even more shame? My dream had been granted—after a fashion. For I now performed in Covent Garden, though not in the manner I had hoped. I made my début upon a stage—of sorts: in the window of a bagnio. My name and qualifications were to be found not in a playhouse programme but in the *List of Covent Garden Ladies*. I appeared in the playhouses, true, and donned a costume—but it was a black satin vizard. I was seated in the front row, behind the orchestra. I manipulated my fan, tossed my head this way and that, awaited the applause. After the play I visited gentlemen in their boxes or met them more informally in the shadows of those arcades through which we—you and I—took our stroll these two days ago. Yes—a *fille de joie*. A strumpet, a punk. I was borne back to their lodgings in sedan-chairs and requited their every devilish pleasure. Our business over, I was turned into the street, half-clothed— into the squares of Mayfair and St James's, or the dark warrens and rotting byways of Whitechapel or St Giles. Twice or thrice I was taken up after hours by the watchman and condemned to Bridewell by a magistrate in Bow Street, who denounced me as a common strumpet. Stripped naked from the waist up I was flogged in front of the alderman, in front of the roaring audience whose privilege it is to observe this proceeding. I yet bear the scars—see? Here, and here . . .

'In the confines of Bridewell I was tutored in the art of glove-making and, unofficially, in the more gainful trade of house-breaking, cutting purses and picking pockets. Each time I was released from custody after no more than a month and, despite my expert tuition and a few successes, reverted to my old living. Bridewell is a preferable fate to Tyburn, where I watched one of my best teachers do her dance in the air after riding backwards up Holborn Hill. It was after the third time,' she said after a pause, 'that I made the acquaintance of Sir Endymion.'

'This meeting was at the playhouse?'

'No—at Mrs Cook's. In my private chamber. Returning by sedan-chair from one of Mr Garrick's performances in Drury Lane, he had spied me in the window. You must consider the figure presented by the majority of my sisters. Some had been actresses, true, or fair maidens from the country; but now most of them were the most sorry-looking creatures—one might have thought the most stinking beggar from the town's end would never have touched them. Such emblems of female ruin! As a penalty from Venus the pert noses that once they had wrinkled at their gentlemen had dissolved into thin air, on account of which they wore masks

260

or veils. Their teeth, too, had disappeared—many could boast only a single snag, now bent sideways and turned the colour of egg yolk. Some were missing an eye, one a leg—though the surviving partner was rumoured to be of a most incomparable shape. Their dugs were either withered and shrunken or vast and bouncing as if inflated by a bellows. Their tresses hung down in stiff knots beside their sunken chaps or else stood out like quills, pointing simultaneously in every direction, the hospitable abode of all manner of creepers. These *têtes* had no need of a pot of pomatum, having produced gratis a brand of their own grease, albeit of a less fragrant concoction. The charms of this perfume were combined with a more potent odour, which could be traced to the dark crescent moons that besmirched the armpits of their dirty smocks and the unsavoury gusts that billowed across their cankered gums. A few well-placed plasters attempted in vain to conceal the manifold imperfections of their visages—the sprouting pustules and seething sores, the inexplicable variegations of colour, the thick black hairs upon their chins which no tweezer might extract—'

'I can conceive these creatures—verily!' I interrupted, fearful that this catalogue should for ever spoil my appetite for the fair species of which these unfortunate creatures were surely the lowliest members.

'It was not Sir Endymion's wont,' she then continued in a more moderate tone, 'to sample such wares as these, blaze themselves across the Great Piazza as these doxies might while he was conducted past their windows. I, however, never cried out in this impudent manner favoured by my sisters, keeping my eyes lowered for shame—for even now I was far from being immune to the pricks and prods of conscience. Yet one such evening my sorrowful deliberations were interrupted by the sight of this gentleman's chair halting before my window. I proved the maxim bitterly repeated by these Covent Garden vestals throughout the days that followed, to wit, "she shall get what she wishes for, who does not wish for it". He did not stop in that evening; my prize instead was a drunken alderman, who flashed his hash on my pillow while at the height of his pleasures.

'Yet upon the morrow Sir Endymion was conducted into the privacy of the chamber where I entertained. He stepped through the heavy brocaded curtain, which swung once and fell into place behind him. An officer entering a tent on a battlefield, I thought. "Undress, if you please," he said. So he was not one for preliminaries, then, unlike Mr Larkins. I divested myself of my cream-coloured silk robe. "Lie yourself down." I stretched myself upon the bed, closing my eyes. After a few seconds—nothing. Then, scratching. I opened my eyes. My visitor was squatting at the foot of the bed ... sketching? Yes—fully clothed. "Lie yourself down," he commanded. "Maintain that posture, I beg of you." He sketched some more. "I could not resist," he added after a few minutes of this most eccentric activity. "Your posture, the way the light fell slantwise across your body ... it reminded me of a painting by Titian I once saw in the gallery of the Duke of Parma." He set his pad to the side after a critical appraisal that consumed some minutes. "Come!" he said at last. "Allow room for me."

'Afterwards he prepared to execute another of his sketches. My gown yet lay crumpled upon the floor. When I reached for it, he forbid me. He spoke about how nudity was itself a costume, or rather an "anti-costume"; how to be naked was to be oneself, to be without disguise. Yet all the while, strangely, he remained clothed; his breeches, his waistcoat, his ticklish cravat—none were removed. For his performance on the bed he had undone perhaps two or three of his buttons, no more. Why, even his shoes remained—the buckles clicking and clacking on the footboard, the heels scuffing the linen ... Well, not all philosophers follow their own teachings, do they?

'The rest you will know,' she said, 'or by now have surmised. He collected me two days later from Mrs Cook. From behind my heavy curtain I detected the chink and jingle of coins. I had been purchased, like the fruit and herbs and roots in the market outside my window. I was conducted hither. How long ago this was I do not remember. Years perhaps. How many winters have I spent shivering in this chamber? Two? Three?'

'But why do you not seek to flee this confinement?'

Her bright tresses shook like autumn leaves stirred by a brief wind as she laughed mournfully, mockingly. 'And where would I go, sir? Back to Covent Garden? Back to my beastly beau in the country, Mr Waghorn?' I made no reply; but then after a few seconds her face brightened. 'Indeed, I cannot flee—I do not *wish* to flee—for Sir Endy-

262

mion needs me. Yes—I believe he loves me, and I,' she finished somewhat triumphantly, 'I love him.'

Doubt must have ploughed deep furrows across my brow. I thought of what she had said a short while before about the heart being a willing accomplice in its betrayal. But now, upon seeing my sceptical expression, she hastily sought to provide testimony of my master's esteem.

'This past year,' she explained, 'Mr Waghorn, my intended, came storming hither to, as he phrased it, "redeem" me. How he discovered me I cannot imagine. But his situation had by this time grown altogether desperate and called, apparently, for desperate measures. He had been unsuccessful—to my little surprise—in persuading any lady to marry him. This would have been no great loss to him had not in the midst of these countless abortive courtships his elder brother, and Squire Waghorn's heir, toppled from his horse and crushed his skull against a tree stump while pursuing a fox through a wood. Old Waghorn then named his married nephew as heir presumptive, with the understanding that this claim would be superseded should his remaining son—that is, my erstwhile intended—marry and produce a son of his own. Now, as this nephew entertained a lusty and enthusiastically reciprocated hatred for him, the younger Waghorn would not be able to rely upon a groat, much less his rustic little cottage, should this enemy inherit.

'In the face of such promises and pressures, after a particularly vehement rebuttal from a prospective wife, and under the influence of a great quantity of ale, Waghorn one day grew rash and daring. After spending the better part of the forenoon in a tavern near Charing Cross—evidently his frantic search had now conducted him as far as London— he came pounding upon my door while Sir Endymion, alas for me, was absent. I foolishly allowed him entry, upon which he with no further ado seized my arms and endeavoured to force me into his waiting carriage. I managed to twist free and flee up the stair, pursued at each step, however, by this dreadful beast, whose drunken indictments I dare not repeat. He caught me at the top and no doubt would have borne me back to his lair in the country had Sir Endymion not then suddenly returned.

'Such a terrible sight he made upon the stair!' She closed her eyes for a second, a serene smile having spread across

263

her countenance. 'Waghorn at once released me,' she continued, 'his courage fleeing him more quickly than I had. He whimpered something—an apology or explanation—but Sir Endymion had already drawn his sword and advanced threateningly towards him. Waghorn's whimpering grew louder and less intelligible as he backed away in great haste. But as he moved backwards up the stair his boot in seeking the missing step discovered only air, thus causing him to plunge forward, down the steps, and into the point of Sir Endymion's blade, which pierced his breast.'

I swallowed hard when she paused. 'A mortal wound?'

'No, alas. The creature yet breaths.'

'''Twas an accident,' I said, swallowing again, and wondering why my heart had begun to beat so quickly, and my abdomen and fingertips to tingle. 'Sir Endymion surely did not intend—'

'He intended to kill him,' she replied rather fiercely, tossing her yellow hair. 'Nothing else but to kill him. He has told me as much many times.'

I fell into silent contemplation of these words. Even taking Stubbs's assertions into account I could not help thinking they cast the whole of her story into doubt, becoming the few stones that, removed from their places, brought the entire castle tumbling into a pile of rubble and dust. I wondered if perhaps her entire story was simply that—a story, an invention; a fantasy with which she entertained herself during her many lonely hours in the garret. Then something else suddenly occurred to me.

'Your gallant,' I asked as I lay my brushes and paints aside. 'What of him?'

Her countenance assumed a sorrowful expression and soon required the further services of her handkerchief.

'I did not set eyes upon him again,' she at length found herself able to reply, 'not since that black day when he so traitorously ensconced me in the lodgings—in the bawdy-house—of Mrs Cook. How my thoughts now choke upon him! Now I know him to be what he is—a flash man, a cock-bawd. Yet, foolishly, in those evenings when I sat in the window overlooking the piazza I many times watched out for him, hoping that one day it would not be merely in my imagination that I should see him crossing towards me, saying, "Eleanora, Eleanora, please forgive me; I shall never

leave you!"—and I replying: "Robert, Robert, my love . . ."
But, alas, I was never to see him more.'

No, I thought, perhaps not. But *I* had seen him; of that I
was certain: for now she was showing me a miniature—she
had retained it all these years; and not even her most vexed
tears had succeeded in extinguishing the outline of—nor
fashion altered the subject's devotion to—a foppish, gold-
trimmed tricorne and a delicate white glove, the fingers of
which were cupping, rather coquettishly, the wearer's cheek.

My great consternation at this revelation was not exactly
relieved when, upon returning to the Haymarket, I discovered yet another letter from Pinthorpe; one at least as
disconcerting as that I had received a week before. I lighted
my candle and read how, upon studying a work of Soame
Jenyns entitled *A Free Inquiry into the Nature and Origins
of Evil*, my friend had been struck with fear by the author's
disturbing thesis that we are perhaps the sport of higher
beings who 'deceive, torment, or destroy us for the Ends
only of their own Pleasure or Utility'.

'Not only, that is, do the Objects about us in Space have
no material Existence, as Mr Berkeley has suggested,' Pinthorpe elaborated for me, 'but they are perchance the cruel
Tricks of malignant Deities.' This worrisome possibility
raised by Mr Jenyns had immediately sent my friend scuttling to find comfort in the *Meditations* of Descartes, 'who
had puzzled profitably upon this troublous Proposition long
before. For in employing his philosophical Method of Doubt
this Gentleman recognised how we must so often doubt the
Evidence of our Senses, even that Evidence which appears
most obvious and indubitable, viz., that tonight I sit here
beside my Fire in a Dressing-gown, with my Paper, Pen and
Ink-well before me on a Table. For as Descartes inquired,
how do we not know that some Evil Genius has not
employed his fearsome Energies in deceiving me, not only
regarding these Objects in my Chamber, but about the Sky
and the Earth as well, and even about myself?'

The solution to this perplexity apparently involved, for
Descartes, the doubt which it raised so vertiginously in the
first place: 'For as this philosopher observes, all may be
doubted save Doubt itself. If I doubt my Existence, or that
of my Hands or my Dressing-gown, these Acts, which cannot
be denied, in themselves *prove* my Existence, and that of

my Mind; for if I had no Existence, how then might I doubt it? Faith, Belief, Truth; all of these Things, George, must therefore depend wholly upon Doubt, through whose Circuit they first must pass. For the Temple of Faith must be erected from the Stones of Doubt.'

So Truth, I mused (inventing another metaphor), was to emerge from behind the scrubbings of the India rubber of Doubt. I gazed doubtfully upon the canvas of *A Lady by Candle-light* and slowly ran a finger across the rough and wiggling contours of its surface.

But then I flopped on to my pallet, whereupon all my doubts and fears were erased by the India rubber of sleep.

Twenty-nine

 When the evening of the masquerade at last arrived—it was one day later—Toppie decreed that we should each take a sedan-chair to Vauxhall Gardens, the better to 'cut a fine dash' among the company. I assented to this extravagance, though swiftly regretted my compliance once the chair-men, who presented themselves at the door as Wheelwright was proclaiming eight o'clock, announced their price of one shilling per mile. Thus when we set out along Brook Street a few minutes later and turned south towards Berkeley Square, I was fretting for the sake of my purse with each of their steps.

I was soon fretting, too, over our creeping pace, since I feared that at the present rate we should not arrive at our destination in the parish of Lambeth—by my anxious calculation, a good two shillings distant—until the festivities were concluding. My fears were supported when we arrived in Piccadilly and encountered the most grievous difficulties turning into St James's Street, both of these thoroughfares being crowded with the densest traffic of chariots, coaches, chaises, phaetons, and sedan-chairs like our own. The entire city, it appeared, was proceeding with us to Vauxhall. The masked visages of witches, nabobs and Floridian kings peered out from the windows of the vehicles inching beside us down the street. Some of these maskers shared my impatience, and here and there noisy disputes arose among them. A party of Harlequins and Pierrots in a hackney-coach battled with a one-horse chaise bearing a Spaniard and a huntsman in white buckskin for the right of way into Little Jermyn Street; and as neither proved capable of triumphing in this contest both vehicles now sat together, stuck fast like ships run aground. A short time later we encountered a priest of Rome and a black-frocked Quaker unmasked and exchanging blows in the midst of the crowded street behind St James's Palace, their efforts cheered by groups of costumed foot-passengers not ordinarily enthusiastic about theological controversy.

Toppie, whose chair was some feet in advance of mine, was unruffled by these commotions and impediments. He explained that Persons of Quality purposely arrived late at Vauxhall, at an hour when the rabble were obliged to go home to their beds so they might open the shutters on their smithies and butcher shops—'or however these persons of inferior birth occupy themselves'—early the next morning. He was in high spirits, greatly enjoying himself, or, more specifically, his costume. Anxious to be recognised by one and all, with every few steps of his slowly advancing chairmen he raised his mask upon the pretext of fixing a tiny spyglass to his eye; then, peering with feigned consternation at the congested street before us, he would sigh, shake his head, cluck his tongue, all the while snitching crafty glances hither and thither in order to detect who might have paid homage to his finery. He was indeed a spectacle difficult to disregard. To his pleasant surprise his macaroni costume had rendered him especially conspicuous despite his confinement in the chair, for on account of the volume of his periwig he was required to project his head from one of the windows, while the great tasselled cane rose like a bishop's staff through the other, twice or thrice imperilling the crystal of a street lamp or the eyeball of an unwary horse or pedestrian.

I was somewhat less determined to be spotted. After we collected our habits from Mr Johnson earlier in the afternoon, I had been favourably struck by the appearance of an old woman—'Mother Midnight', an ancient midwife—that I presented in Toppie's looking-glass. Scarcely did I

267

recognise myself as I curtsied and scampered round the dressing-chamber in my hoops, shift and stays, to which I presently added patched grey petticoats, a frizzled grey wig that looked like a gooseberry bush, a red-and-white checked kerchief and, finally, to complete the effect, a squeaking voice, which Toppie insisted I employ in all my conversation. I was somewhat abashed by the prospect of presenting myself in this manner to public view, and so was glad of the white mask. Still, I soon warmed to my role and blushed with a secret pleasure when first Thomas and then Wheelwright failed to recognise me in my garb, and again when my chair-men mistook me for a lady as they assisted me on to the cushions.

'Pray give me notice, dear lady, should you lack any comforts in the course of our journey,' one of these fellows had murmured as his hand lingered unnecessarily upon my glove, whereupon he tipped his hat and favoured me with a lecherous wink.

'Be assured that I shall,' I squeaked in return, withdrawing from his tender clutches with a flourish. 'It is as if,' I then said to myself, smiling behind my mask as we set off, 'as if another George, myself and not myself, now travels to Vauxhall. Yes—surely anything at all might happen this evening!'

If, that is, we ever arrived. My anxieties about our progress were raised to a higher pitch when, on entering Pall Mall, we beheld scores of horses stamping and snorting in their harnesses along its crowded length, their drivers' whips hanging idly above them, as motionless as the rods of anglers. I was not to be placated in the least by Toppie's assurances about the practices of the *haut monde*. I was in haste to reach Vauxhall because I was in haste—a great haste—to reach Lady Beauclair. After learning Eleanora's history the day before, I had dispatched an urgent letter to St Giles by the penny post, warning her most urgently about the true nature of Robert's character—'I have spied the cloven foot!' I wrote—and demanding to see her at her earliest convenience. When no reply was forthcoming in the ensuing hours, I set out by foot, reaching her street an hour after darkness only to discover—first by the sight of her darkened window, then from Madam Chapuy—that my lady was engaged for the evening at another house, 'though I know not whither, good sir'. Yet when I proposed to await her arrival, this lady's story now became something altered. She recollected, all of a sudden, that my lady had in fact taken ill—'a very minor complaint, I do assure thee'—and hence had long since retired to her bed, from which the apothecary who had mixed her a potion an hour before had implied it would be unwise to rouse her.

Today two further letters of similar import, though conveying an increased alarm, had failed to raise any more positive response, or indeed any reply. The second had been hastily penned and then dispatched from Toppie's house after I witnessed a sight at Mr Johnson's Habit-Warehouse that struck a desperate chill into my heart. For as we arrived in Tavistock Street our wheels clashed with those of a hack travelling in the opposite direction, approaching the intersection with Southampton Street; and my attention at this moment was diverted from my gazette in good time for me to witness a familiar white-gloved hand tip a familiar gold-laced hat at me while the owner of these distinguishing articles, the top half of his face concealed by one of Mr Johnson's satin masks—a *baùta*—smiled contemptuously out of the window. So Robert, vile scoundrel, would be afoot tonight!

By the time we reached Charing Cross—it seemed an hour later, Pall Mall having been as thronged with wheel-traffic as Piccadilly—Toppie had a sudden mind to make his appearance by water; and so after being conducted into the Strand and paying our chair-men (whom I had not enlightened and as a consequence was forced to suffer two or three kisses upon my hand from each) a shilling per vehicle, we engaged the services of a linkboy, walked down to the Black Lyon Stairs and clambered into a slender wherry. The river, we discovered to my extreme displeasure, was scarcely any less teeming than the streets. As we progressed towards Westminster Bridge and then passed beneath one of its arches, we were jostled and splashed by a great number of other vessels with a similar destination in mind; and when we finally arrived at Vauxhall—by now I was in a terrible lather—we were forced to compete with them for landing-space on the south bank and, in doing so, very nearly capsized ourselves. Once this heated competition was finished we commenced a fresh one, pushing and thrusting and bumping our way up the Vauxhall Stairs and through the narrow entry gates to the gardens—until at

269

last we spilled into this most splendid of London's pleasure gardens.

My appreciation of Vauxhall's wonders was considerably tempered, however, by the size of the crowd. In the Grand Walk, a great gravelled promenade, the maskers were as thick and boisterous as those in Piccadilly. Indeed, so very dense were these guests—all masked and attired as Dutch skippers, lunatics, mountebanks, and the like—that immediately I despaired of discovering Lady Beauclair among their numbers. The design of the spacious gardens, moreover, rendered my task even more impossible, for at regular intervals as we walked along the promenade—or, rather, were bumped and pushed—we encountered narrower passages leading into other passages, even narrower, all of them bounded by high hedges and canopied by cedars and the loftiest elms. Everywhere a thousand distractions rose from among the trees and avenues: grottoes, temples, pavilions, obelisks, domes, arches, statues (one of Milton, another of Handel, in a morning cap, plucking at a harp), a rotunda, an orchestra, feathered minstrels, colonnaded supper-boxes hung with monumental paintings, and everywhere great numbers of lamps suspended in the branches of elms or above porticoes, all of them shaped like suns or stars and ranged in brilliant constellations, though none quite succeeding in casting its rays of illumination into some of the more isolated byways.

'Yonder lies the Lovers' Walk,' Toppie remarked, pointing with his cane at one of these avenues, down which I could discern nothing but two or three dark shapes, like those shadow-images cast by Sir Endymion's 'silhouette machine'. These skulking inhabitants I did not mistake for lovers, at least not the most common variety. 'You would be wise to keep yourself without its precincts,' Toppie warned me, 'and those of the other "dark walks", unless, George, you have some intrigue in mind! For these places are the retreats only of thieves and of the most anomalous lovers.'

Elsewhere we encountered further sights that might have been created in Sir Endymion's studio. Some of these curiosities were most cunning and perplexing, intended to deceive the unwary eye and confound it as to whether it cast itself upon Art or Life; to make the mind reflect upon whether 'all the Choir of Heaven and Furniture of the Earth' were, as Pinthorpe claimed, of no true subsistence.

270

Thus as we crossed through an avenue and emerged into the South Walk, likewise a grand parade but, unlike its neighbours, spanned by magnificent arches, we were confronted by a prospect of the Temple of Neptune, with the deity surrounded by tritons; yet after we progressed along the parade I presently discovered to my great surprise that this temple, which from a distance looked perfectly like marble and seemed to comprise four dimensions, was truly nothing more than a clever painting upon a large flat. At the terminus of a different avenue we were similarly tricked by another *trompe l'oeil* (as my master had called this cunning effect) into the conviction that the ruins of Palmyra existed not in the deserts of Syria but in the parish of Lambeth, being disabused of this notion only after approaching within ten feet of these tumbledown arches. In yet another spot an illuminated cascade—whether or not it was truly water I could not have said—appeared to flow past a miller's house and rotate the wheel of his watermill, all to the excited acclaim of the spectators. Everywhere we turned we stumbled upon a more subtle craft, pictures painted with translucent pigments upon calico or oiled paper such that the eye might peep through their scenes to witness the oblivious throng of masqueraders who strolled on the nether side. 'How this strange world of Vauxhall vibrates,' I thought, 'with a thousand false appearances and tricks of the light!'

'Is it not most confounding,' I said with some admiration as we gazed upon, or, rather, through, one of these little pieces, 'for as we peer into this transparent world how may we say what is bona fide and and what is mere illusion?'

'What is forsooth bona fide,' responded Toppie, who was swiftly becoming bored by this sport, 'is that my guts are full of emptiness.'

He therefore proposed we retire to a supper-box, there to await the arrival of his other guests. False appearances did not abate, however, as we returned along the Grand Walk. I was startled after a few minutes to glimpse my own face leering back at me from the inside of a great picture frame, as if by magic my form had been cast upon a great canvas: for upon the wall of one of the supper-boxes I now saw *The Rape of Lucretia by Sextus Tarquinius*, around which a small company was gathered. I would fain have known their conversation, which was very merry and supplemented by fingers pointing rather expressively at the figure of Sextus. Suddenly I regretted my mask—for what a triumph I should certainly have made had these fashionable people only recognised me, George Cautley, as the model for Sir Endymion's painting, and also as the clever apprentice whose delicate brushes had painted the folds in Lucretia's ripping gown, the crimson draperies behind her orange-yellow hair, the broken column rising up in the misty distance ... Yet no sooner had this pleasing prospect crossed my mind than a dark cloud scudded across in tow. As Toppie hurried us onwards, being himself required by the tight adherence of his macaroni breeches to walk as if kneading dough between his knees, I tried to recall the moral lesson my master had attached to this picture, viz., 'there is no document of civilisation that does not have roots which reach down into dark and wretched soil'—and as this dark cloud swelled and parted I remembered Eleanora for the first time this evening.

Our box, we discovered, having fought our way back to it, was situated in a serpentine sweep of colonnade that overlooked the South Walk and, beyond that, a leafy quadrangle in which the orchestra had commenced rehearsing, sounding for the moment like rattling candlesticks and dolorous livestock. We also enjoyed a view of a platform that had been raised under an awning for dances—rigadoons, louvres, galliards—though, as these had not yet begun, several young bucks had taken possession of it for a noisy game of battledore and shuttlecock. Favourable as it seemed, Toppie was none the less vexed by our location, thrice wishing aloud in a peevish tone that he had bespoke one of the boxes opposite, facing upon the Great Walk; the better, I supposed, for the company to ogle him. Accordingly he sought to compensate for the perceived disadvantage of our station with such an egregious repertoire of foppish behaviour that by comparison my conceits before the cheesemonger's window in Greek Street had displayed all the meekness of a Quaker. These complaints and posturings were nothing abated by the arrival of his friends—some eight or ten persons, among whom were Lady Sacharissa, dressed as a watercress girl, and Sir James Clutterbuck, a Highland chieftain—nor that of our victuals twenty minutes later. Indeed this latter event provoked in him a good many laments concerning both the quantity and the quality of his dish, through whose thin slices of beef he asserted he might read his gazette, a hypothesis he in fact tested before the project was curtailed by several of Lady Sacharissa's cross whispers and sharp prods.

When neither Lady Sacharissa nor Sir James had succeeded in piercing my disguise, Toppie in a fit of merriment introduced me as 'Miss Miranda', his cousin lately arrived from Shropshire; and so I was required to adopt this fictional personage for the duration of our meal, responding in the counterfeit of a young lady's voice whenever addressed. This sport I indulged and even enjoyed until the illusion was punctured after the arrival of our drinks—cups of red porter, a bottle of burgundy, another of champagne, and many quart mugs of table beer. For while courteously filling my cup with champagne, Sir James had all at once inquired:

'I say, Toppie, what the deuce became of that baffle-headed fellow who used to follow you about town like the king's fart-catcher? Now, what the devil was the name of that addle-pate?'

'Cautley,' replied Lady Sacharissa without the hesitation of so much as a second, a sour titter escaping from behind her mask. 'George Cautley.'

'The very same. A lubber born under a halfpenny planet, if ever I saw one. Why, Toppie—*I say*, what the blazes is so damnably funny?'

If blushes suffused the face of either Sir James or Lady Sacharissa when Toppie forced me to come to an *éclaircissement*, these were hidden by their masks, and in any case could not have been half so fierce as mine.

After we ordered further drinks a lady with a fine voice sang a number of sentimental ballads and sprightly ditties, among them 'I'll Assure You', 'Thro' the Woods, Laddie' and 'You Tell Me I'm Handsome', this latter being a silly piece about a coquette. By the time we had emptied these latest cups and bottles with toasts to King George, Queen Charlotte, Lord North and a series of other worthies, this lady had been replaced by a gentleman with an even more exquisite soprano. He was a tall fellow of the middle years, somewhat inclining towards stoutness and possessed of the gentle countenance of a provincial vicar. His chest as he sang swelled magnificently, his ruffled shirt and silk waistcoat billowing like a mainsail, and his mouth dilated and contracted with the most marvellous facility, all the while releasing

273

the sweetest sounds, as if it had swallowed a nightingale. Announced to the company as 'Cavalier Giovanni-Battista Orlando, a knight of St Mark's', he became the subject of much adoration among the ladies in our box, and much scoffing and sly merriment among the gentlemen.

'Here, George, we gaze upon yet another confounding sight,' Toppie whispered to me as the tall cavalier completed his second aria amid the most enthusiastic applause, 'for this strange thing from Italy looks very like a gentleman and yet sings very like a lady. Which, therefore, need we say it is?'

I made no effort to reply, still being out of countenance, grumbling in my gizzard at Sir James's remark; but one of Toppie's friends, who was dressed as a haymaker, quickly interposed: ''Tis neither the one nor the other. A third sort of creature, I warrant you.'

'I believe this to be so,' remarked Lady Sacharissa, whose eyes had been caressing the cavalier, 'for truly he bears the voice neither of man nor woman, but of a god.'

'That of a capon, I should say,' muttered the haymaker. 'Cock-a-doodle-doo!'

'You were nearer the mark,' Toppie whispered in reply, 'had you chopped away that first syllable, as the doctor has done with him.'

After these buckish witticisms had further declined into a train of sniggers involving how the cavalier should make an inferior competitor at battledore and shuttlecock on account of 'not keeping the cock up finely', the ladies proclaimed their gentlemen envious rascals. I, for my part, was paying heed neither to the singing—beauteous as it was— nor to the fiddle-faddle it occasioned; for immediately upon assuming my seat and then throughout our meal—and even more assiduously after suffering Sir James's insults—I had been peeping through my spyglass at the maskers who strolled arm in arm past our box. I was hoping to descry Lady Beauclair, whom I was certain I would recognise at once, disguise or no. Yet I met with little success and was much relieved when a stroll through the gardens was proposed.

We settled the reckoning, my share of which, I was alarmed to learn, had been estimated at five shillings sixpence, then proceeded along the Grand Cross Walk. After passing the dancing platform, where the shuttlecock players had at last been displaced by an equally roistering company of dancers, we promenaded round the quadrangle, exhibiting ourselves to the rest of the company, who in turn exhibited themselves to us, as if we were actors and audience both, all watching a drama and performing in it at the same time. Presently my party ventured farther afield, at which point we steadily lost members of our company to the temptations of the many pavilions—the Turkish Tent, the Chinese Pavilion, the Temple of Comus, the gloriously ornate Music Room alongside the Great Walk—until at last I was dismayed to discover myself quite alone.

The saddest regret pricked my heart when I considered how differently the evening would now be unfolding had Lady Beauclair only consented to accompany me. How the masked faces in the supper-boxes would have craned after us as we strolled past! How the Turkish garment would have excited a buzz of whispers, questions, all of these attentions then making Lady Sacharissa envious of her, and Sir James—and perchance even Toppie—of me. Now, however, bereft of these disagreeable companions as well as of my lady, I passed through the laughing company as if I wore not the garb of Mrs Midnight but a cloak of invisibility; as if I were no more real, no more made of flesh and blood, than the painted shadow of Sextus Tarquinius.

By this time I was strolling along one of the more distant reaches of the South Walk, near the Temple of Neptune, beyond which I could espy dark and empty fields. The company here was a good deal sparser, the majority having congregated at the opposite end to take pleasure in the dancing, music and other more public entertainments. A small group of those maskers with whom I shared the broad path I noticed to be attired in costumes—those of gypsies—highly authentic in appearance, scarcely to be distinguished from the real thing. One of their members wore the gold ear-hoops and bright kerchief of King Prig, while the others promoted their likeness to this gypsy monarch's subjects by conversing among themselves in the kind of gibberish peculiar to this nefarious order of thieves. My spirits were raised by this sight, and so pleased was I with the clever inventiveness of these masqueraders that I was keen to pay my regards to one of their number. I was prevented from doing so, however, when a terrible rumpus suddenly ensued among them, apparently motivated by King Prig's interpre-

275

tation of one of his subordinates' comments about the queen, who tarried at his heels, her tiny dog in tow.

'I shall lump your jolly nob for that one,' the king cried in a tremendous voice. 'By thunder, I shall knock out your cogs for that!'

'A flea-bite, forsooth!' taunted the offending party.

'Shut your bone-box or you will soon find how I fan you sweetly! Oh yes—I shall give you your bastings, rogue!'

'In a pig's eye,' was his antagonist's impudent response as he stood before him, arms akimbo. 'You're dicked in the nob if you think so, my good sir.'

The other members of the tribe were not slow to form alliances in the dispute, and soon the night air was full of further menaces upon similar themes—'I shall smite your costard!' and 'I shall crack your napper!' or 'give you a fine dowse upon the chops!' being much repeated phrases—though despite the heat of their delivery none of these threats, so far as I could detect, was ever truly executed. Soon the stretch of avenue was teeming with other guests, a goodly number of whom willingly precipitated themselves into the fray in a more physical fashion, so that in a few more seconds the gravelled walk was swarming in a more general mêlée, whose battle-lines had become much confused, costumed figures shrieking and running harum-scarum in every direction.

I, too, was at the ready to lend my diplomatic services but was soon startled to see the former antagonists among the gypsy tribe seemingly lay aside their previous differences and commence working in concert, some of them casting handfuls of snuff into the masks of the interceding combatants while others, including the queen, plundered these choking gentlemen of their fob-watches and pocket-books before disappearing, in the midst of this even more heightened confusion, into the 'dark walks' that opened in narrow tributaries along the sides of the South Walk.

'Accursed gypsies,' sputtered one of their victims—from his knees—as he clawed off his mask and ground his knuckles into his smarting eyes. 'Prigged by a band of dirty gypsies, by heaven!' At which point he began complaining about his coach fare to Stoke Newington and a fob-chain that had once been the property of Mr Beau Nash.

Once again I made ready to intercede, this time to assist the pillaged victims, but as I approached the citizen of Stoke

276

Newington I was startled to see standing at some remove from the fray, beyond one of the Chinese arches, a solitary lady wearing a Turkish habit and a black oval mask. Her habit was fashioned from scarlet rather than ultramarine damask, and the turban was gold in hue and not nearly so voluminous in size nor equipped with a sarsenet veil; yet after extracting my spyglass and fixing it to my eye I was in no doubt at all—I had at last discovered Lady Beauclair. Yet, perhaps seeing me, my lady now withdrew quickly, retiring in some haste into one of the narrow lanes communicating between the South Walk and the darker lengths of the Lovers' Walk.

'My lady!' I appealed, greatly dismayed by this shy response and forgetting all at once the plight of the penniless and fobless dandy kneeling before me. 'My lady—I beg of you!'

Petticoats hoisted, I rushed down the wide avenue in the direction of the Temple of Neptune, at each step dodging the howling victims of the gypsies and the snapping jaws of the queen's mongrel, which had slipped its tether during the pageant and was now celebrating its liberty by contriving to fasten its sharp little teeth into my heels. By the time I shook off these attentions and entered the narrow lane whence she had appeared and then retired, there was no sign of my lady—indeed, no sign of anyone.

After a minute's cautious tiptoeing through the rising hedges I reached the Lovers' Walk, but, recalling Toppie's earlier warning, I was loath to advance any farther. Yet I was even more profoundly affrighted by the thought of my lady wandering this treacherous avenue alone, and so I crept a few feet into it, then paused to peer in each direction. How strange it was that a few moments ago I had been at the centre of a great hurly-burly and might now have been wandering the precincts of the darkest and loneliest forest in Britain! The music and voices dimmed behind me and my path at each step grew thicker with shadows, as if splattered everywhere with asphaltum or frankfort black.

'Lady Beauclair,' I called in a tentative voice that was little better than a whisper, then cocked my ear for a reply: but now the cavalier's voice had vanished and the only sound besides that of my slippers on the gravel and my breath sucking within my mask was the twitter of invisible nightingales in their nests above my head.

But upon turning a corner I could hear the voice again—beckoning, it almost seemed. Yet this wellnigh inhuman strain proved an unreliable guide back into the Grand Walk and the illuminated environs of the pavilions. For so much did it swirl in the faltering breeze that I was conducted first up one of the dark walks, then down another, as if wandering between the tall hedges of a maze like that within the grounds of Chudleigh House, in whose leafy labyrinth I once passed the best part of a Sunday, bewildered and discouraged by every false turn as Toppie howled with mirth in the liberty of the far side of the hedge.

I glimpsed a few intermittent lights through the trees, and so departed in this new direction. I had not progressed any great distance before I discovered myself approaching a motionless silhouette beneath the branch of an elm overhanging the verge of the Lovers' Walk. Having no wish for society of the sort reputedly encountered in these dark walks, I made to hasten past the figure—a gentleman, it appeared—with my head ducked low. Yet as I was hoping to reacquaint myself with my companions, and as my curiosity, as always, surmounted my discretion, I chanced to steal a look at the fellow, whereupon I was given a great start: for though it was partly concealed by the silk hood of a black domino, and more successfully by the darkness, there was no disguising the gold-laced tricorne that now swivelled round as the mask—a white flash—spun to face me. Yet before I could speak a word or steal a closer look, the figure deftly withdrew with a whisper of silk and a crunch of stone into one of the narrower paths, the black cape swirling behind.

I paused, my heart quickening. So—had the rogue recognised me, then? Surely not. No. Impossible. The darkness, my mask: he could not have done so. Yet soon enough he would, I told myself—for, by heaven, I would now make him acknowledge me, his rival!

Thus I raised my petticoats and scampered after him, turning into the dark lane whence he had slipped, to see him disappear yet again, this time swirling into another, even narrower, lane whose hedges, when I reached them, were barely sufficient to grant passage to my billowing petticoats. Having lost sight of him in this stretch, I halted in my tracks, quite confounded. But then a second later I espied him tarrying at the overgrown entrance of still another pathway, backing into it, so it seemed, only when certain that my eye had indeed caught him. I therefore advanced into this new avenue with great wariness, clawed by branches with each step and very soon discovering that I had entered a cul-de-sac. At its terminus a short distance away the glow of the *baùta* was visible, as was that of the white-gloved hand, which now crooked a finger and beckoned me forward. I was still more confounded. What did he desire? And who, I wondered, was pursuing whom? I stopped after another step and, as I was not anxious to disclose myself just yet in this kingdom where false appearances reigned, hailed him in the high-pitched voice of 'Miss Miranda':

'Robert!'

The figure did not so much as move an inch. The hand had disappeared and the mask and hat hung in the air above the black cape as if disembodied, as if part of yet another Vauxhall curiosity: a *trompe l'oeil*, perhaps, or one of the transparent paintings suspended from branches, a masked head painted upon calico through which I might see more darkness, other heads. I had almost convinced myself that such was the case, when the *baùta* inclined itself as if stirred by a sudden breeze and then spoke: 'Who . . .?'

I shook my own mask at him and again spoke in my squeaking voice. 'One, sir, whom your designs have harmed most grievously.'

'What do you say?' The mask did not stir. 'Who—?'

'Fie, sir! And have you harmed so many,' I scolded, 'that you fail to recall the individuals?'

'Nay, madam, I understand you not. I have harmed no lady.'

So—I had deceived the rogue!

'Eleanora,' I said in an outraged tone, 'Miss Eleanora Clitherow! Well, rascally knave! Sure you dare not deny me now?'

Oh, how I should have enjoyed to witness the impudent rapscallion's visage at the mention of this name, to have seen how it smote his conscience like a coachman's lash! But now the mask merely rose up an inch or two as if stirred again by the soughing breeze, which carried upon its wings the strong scent of 'Foolish Pleasures'.

'So—it is *you*, is it, after these many years?' The voice, ruffling the black veil beneath the mask, had turned contemptuous. 'What, pray, is the cause of these strange aspersions?'

'Peer into the sink of your heart and you will know the answer,' I proclaimed in a heated tone, playing my part as expertly, I fancied, as any actor in a playhouse. 'For it is none other than your most cruel deceptions. I proclaim you an arrant blackguard with more tricks and shows in your cruel repertoire than we find on display in these wondrous gardens! Yes—for your world is false as this one! You, sir, showed me hope, promise—behind whose beautiful painted illusions there shimmered, unseen to my innocent eyes, the most treacherous villainy.'

'You know not what you say,' he snarled, as impertinent as any stage-villain. 'I never promised you aught.'

'You were as artful and subtle in your dealings with me as anything put upon the stage in Drury Lane. Shall I name the players, then? The cast of villainous characters whom you summoned to act their parts? Mr Larkins ... Mrs Cook ... Sir Endymion—'

'So I find you are a thankless wench as well as a silly one.'

'And you, sir, are a cock-bawd, a flash man. Yet let me not speak to you of my own tragedy—for such, yes, was the role you created for me in the end: a tragic one. Yet all this you, as its author, know well enough. No: let us talk of others; for *now* I learn—never mind how, you good-for-naught knave—that you have begun still another drama, formed your wicked designs upon yet another maiden, one of noble birth.'

'Then you have been wrongly informed, Miss Clitherow, as in all else.'

'Be assured I am not. Shall I name her?' I stepped forward. 'Can your ears hear her name pronounced without reproaching your black heart?'

'My heart, little miss, troubles me very little.'

'I am sorry to believe that for once you do not lie, black-hearted scoundrel that you are. Yet still I may make it squirm a little.' I advanced another step into the cul-de-sac, the scent of 'Foolish Pleasures' growing ever stronger, a beautiful bouquet disguising the vilest stench. 'Lady Beau-clair,' I said.

'What is this?' The villain truly seemed confounded. For

a second he was struck dumb. 'What do you mean to say? I know not—'

'Lady Petronella Beauclair,' I repeated in a firmer tone, through which my own voice had begun to break. 'Do you deny your actions?'

As he remained all-a-mort I advanced another step so that only a few feet of darkness stood betwixt us. His guilt was palpable in this silence. Yes—by heaven, I had the dog now!

'What promises do you make to *her*?' I was close enough to wring his neck. 'What plans have you for *her*? The same role in your drama, I'll warrant, that you awarded *me*.'

He stepped backwards, encountering the trunk of an elm. 'I know not of what you—'

'Then, by thunder, soon enough you shall!' So bellowing in my natural voice, I ripped the mask from my visage, which I had formed into a terrible stare. 'For 'tis *I*, George Cautley, who accuse you! And now, enough of your trickery and your false appearances—for I shall unmask you as well, sir, and speak to you barefaced.'

Before my hands could reach his mask, however, they were struck forcibly by his own, the right of which then reached quickly for the sword in a glinting scabbard beneath the black cloak. I had not, alas, glimpsed this instrument earlier, so now was forced to retreat before it. Yet the scoundrel did not press his advantage, instead resorting to his heels as he had that night in Coventry Street, brushing past me and achieving the liberty of one of the wider footpaths before I had time to move. And then, as before, I pursued him through many twists and turns before laying hold of his collar and spinning him round—only to be knocked once again to the ground, this time by the broad side of his weapon. By now we had attained the South Walk, and a small group of costumed figures halted in their promenades and gathered round to witness our dispute. One of their number, in the long robes and full-bottomed wig of a magistrate, seemed inclined to arbitrate, and advancing towards us asked of me while pointing at Robert, who stood above me, gasping, his sword aloft:

'Pray, sir, has this gentleman paid you some offence?'

'The payment has not been to my account, sir,' I responded in a stout voice, 'but to those of unfortunate others known unto me.' I raised myself from the gravel and

281

then persevered in an even louder voice, one which would admit of no doubts or misconstructions among my audience. 'I accuse him of the darkest villainies, namely: corrupting the morals, destroying the virtue, and blackening the good reputation of Miss Eleanora Clitherow of Buckinghamshire, and for attempting the same upon another lady—one of noble birth who is most dear to my heart.'

The wretched malfeasant again sought to take flight in the face of this public proclamation, but I seized his arm, in which his sword now began to droop; and he was further detained by the figure in the magistrate costume. This fellow appeared to enjoy the respect of the mob, as if truly partaking of the powers symbolised in his gown.

'These are the most grave charges,' this Vauxhall judge now declared. Then, turning to Robert, he addressed him in a solemn tone: 'What is your reply? *What*, sir? Have you none to make? Well, sir, I declare if you are a man of honour as your sword implies and not the scoundrel for whom this gentleman vouches, then you shall break your silence and respond to his charge with a pair of pistols at the Ring in Hyde Park tomorrow morning at dawn.'

The gathering loudly assented to this proposition, but I believe I was as taken aback by it as Robert, who appeared to shrink from the suggestion, struggling fiercely with the magistrate, who none the less confined him fast, inquiring in his importunate voice: 'Ha? What of it, then, sir?' I myself squirmed inwardly for a moment; yet so inflamed was I with anger that all too soon I consented—or, rather, I heard my voice consent, loudly declaring my intention to procure my satisfaction through this violent method.

'Well, sirrah!' The judge turned to Robert. 'The gentleman cannot be more respectful of your honour than that. So—may we command you?'

The masked head, bowed now, nodded its slow assent, the rim of gold *point d'Espagne* wavering up and down and glittering as bright beneath the swaying lamps as brush-strokes of yellow orpiment.

An hour later I was crossing Westminster Bridge. Having been unable to discover Toppie among the walks and pavilions, I found myself without a shilling for a coach, a chair, or even a linkboy, and so was forced to wend my way home on foot and in darkness. I was shivering in my shawl, and so numb were my feet inside Mrs Midnight's slippers that I felt myself to be walking upon pillows or ascending steps fitted with a plush carpet; steps leading I knew not where.

The passion that had inflamed me an hour earlier was likewise cold and shivering, perhaps because I had been even less successful in my search for Lady Beauclair. I wondered, had I encountered her this evening, quite unknowingly, and passed her by? Or had she perchance recognised me—and then declined to unmask herself? Anything seemed possible, including my having blundered into this perilous new encounter for the sake of a lady who nursed no tender feelings for me; who instead would side with the varlet whom I was engaged to fight—to kill.

Whatever the case, even before departing Vauxhall to the melancholy strains of Cavalier Orlando—ominously, a funeral aria—I regretted having committed myself to this ancient code of honour. What was happening to me, to my life? I was the passenger in a bucketing phaeton driven forward by an invisible coachman who cracked his whip in a box-seat high above me. If only I could glimpse this mysterious coachman's visage, I thought, then perchance I might take hold of the whip myself and guide the racing horses down the road twisting and untwisting ahead.

Thirty

 So it was that daybreak discovered me creeping with Jeremiah through Hyde Park Gate, then up the narrow pathway towards that infamous field of blood known as the Ring. The park appeared empty, its trees headless in the still morning fog, a succession of twisted grey columns rising from the green earth. Piccadilly, too, had been empty as we walked its length; its lamps snuffed, its rooftops and chimneys likewise shrouded, as if a lace veil had descended during the night. There were no scraps or signs to speak of the costumed revellers who had crowded along its stones only a few hours before; the wild merriment had

all been part of some insubstantial pageant, it seemed, no more real than the swirls of mist or the wondrous shows and follies of Vauxhall.

Determined to cut a fine dash for this occasion—for what was perhaps the final appointment of my mortal life—I had dressed myself in the height of fashion, as if my engagement was not with a villain flourishing duelling pistols but with some beautiful lady whose favours I sought: freshly laundered small clothes and stockings, black velvet breeches, a brocaded frock-coat recently fashioned for Toppie's figure by the scissors of his tailor and given a careful brush a short time before by Jeremiah, who was yet half-asleep. So full of patches and holes were his clothes, by contrast, that he resembled a heathen philosopher. He was, moreover, in a cursed funk, pleading with me for the entire journey not to follow through with my terrible obligation, reasoning that in the scheme of things it was infinitely preferable to live as a coward than to die as a man of honour; to live for him, my loyal footman, than to die for Lady Beauclair, of whose affections, I had admitted to him, I was gravely uncertain. By the time we reached Tyburn Lane he had very nearly convinced me to turn back; but then as we passed through the gates he at last fell silent, perhaps hoping upon the evidence of the ghostly trees that he was in fact still deep in a strange slumber and would soon awaken from this nightmare to discover himself lying upon his pillow next to Samuel.

He had been dreaming when I shook him awake some thirty or forty minutes earlier. Hardly had I fallen asleep last night, it seemed, than I was awakened by a fierce creak from Samson and Delilah and a sting from one of the fleas with whom I shared my mattress. Seeing a nimbus of light in the sky above the roofline of the buildings across the street, I crept into his bedchamber and gently prodded his shoulder. Two minutes later he was shivering beside my fire, blinking over his hasty pudding and a cup of tea, coming fully awake only when I suggested he tiptoe into his parents' bedchamber and purloin the brace of pistols I knew Mr Sharp to keep close by his pillow as he slumbered. Mrs Sharp possessed a terrible fear of house-breakers and therefore persuaded her husband to adopt this practice, which had served the family well upon more than one occasion while I shared their roof. I had purchased new powder and shot

284

for these weapons a fortnight before, since which time I knew they had not been discharged.

Jeremiah had nearly dropped his hasty pudding into my fire upon hearing my request; but finally, more relieved by my renewed attentions than cowed by their dangerous import, he acquitted his duty loyally and without questions, appearing a few minutes later with the weapons in his hands and an affrighted, uncertain smile twitching upon his sleep-creased face. My smile in return, I'll warrant, was likewise affrighted and uncertain, for I now had even less inclination to fight than the evening before. As we crept into the grey shadows reaching across the Haymarket like the long-fingered hand of a giant, I felt myself being gathered into a world I did not control or own. Once again I was not wholly and truly George Cautley—rather, someone quite other, myself and not myself: I was to play a role in a strange masquerade; not that of Mrs Midnight, but one for which I was equally unsuited. The impression did not quickly abate, for walking up the Haymarket we encountered an alderman, a small-coals man, a guardsman, an oyster girl, and two chimney-sweeps with soot bags—and for a second I was confounded as to whether these were characters in a Vauxhall masquerade or genuine fellow-citizens of London.

Now as we approached the Ring—which was to be found some short distance west of one of the reservoirs for the Chelsea Water-Works—we detected the sharp report of a pistol ring out upon the still air. Rushing through the strands of fog we soon discovered not Robert, of whom there was no sign, but a number of young fellows assembled upon this infamous spot, obeying summonses as inexplicable, perhaps, as my own. The proceedings were oddly inelegant for such a famed theatre of valour. A pair now stood square to one another, the first having discharged his piece to no visible effect upon his opponent, whose own weapon was proving a reluctant participant in the affair. This young cavalier— he was of no more than twenty years—was shaking like an autumn leaf as he excitedly rebuked his pistol for this unreliability, whereupon it unexpectedly obeyed his wishes with a mighty flash that, when the cloud eventually cleared, was revealed to have blackened his face and burned his fingers, but spared his antagonist, who stood unimpaired at his station, cocking his firing mechanism to the urgent instructions of his second. This advantage the gentleman failed to seize, for when his own pistol flashed the event proved material only to one of the headless trees, into whose trunk the shot embedded itself with a loud splintering sound. As this oak stood in no great proximity to the intended target, and rather nearer the excited seconds, one of whom confessed in some alarm that the ball had buzzed close by his hat, the contest was swiftly declared a draw, and the young fellows quitted their ground to make way for another party of aggrieved gentlemen of honour.

In all, three duels were fought that morning as Jeremiah and I stood upon the perimeter, awaiting our turn that would come with the arrival of Robert, who it seemed was in no great haste to answer my charge. The next two contests produced results scarcely more satisfactory than the first, though at last some telling shots were fired, the most spectacular by an astonished young booby from the country—a tall, gawky fellow in foul-looking linen—who put his bullet through the shoulder of an abdominous baronet; a wound that, despite the baronet's terrible howls, did not seem likely to prove mortal. The other engagement was conducted with even less dignity, both parties still being under the spell of the concoctions which had delivered them to this spot in the first place. With their abilities to aim their pistols so prejudiced, their exchanges were at first of a strictly verbal nature, though at length one inflicted a scorching wound upon the buttocks of the other, who had stooped to retrieve the weapon that had slipped from his grasp a moment or two before.

The reasons behind these heroic struggles we were never to learn, for when the business was completed the participants marched through Grosvenor Gate, or, in the case of the vanquished, were bandaged and borne away in sedanchairs to seek the comforts of a surgeon in New Bond Street. Jeremiah and I then waited in nervous silence, hopping from foot to foot, until at last, just as I was about to declare with some disguised relief that the cowardly Robert was obviously not fain to show, a figure appeared beneath the gate; a lone figure, without a second. A headless figure, too, I saw after a moment, one invisible above the shoulders on account of the swirls of fog.

Jeremiah's whole face squinted as this disguised figure slowly approached us, cutting a path through the mist. 'Sure that cannot be the fellow, Mr Cautley?'

'No,' I replied, 'it most certainly is not.' For, having come closer, the figure's bright petticoat and sack were now clear, as was, a moment later, the visage I had searched for so desperately the evening before and would have recognised anywhere. 'No, Jeremiah,' I said as she crossed the notorious field of Mars to stand before us, 'pray allow me to introduce Lady Beauclair.'

Thirty-one

 Mr Robert Hannah—such, according to Lady Beauclair, was my antagonist's name—meant her ladyship no harm, of that I could be assured. This she told me in the stoutest terms. Perhaps, she said, if I understood something about him . . .

So I listened. I had little choice. But—did I believe her? Even now—already, as we walked south towards the lodge at Hyde Park Gate—I was possessed of the uncertain impression that my lady was not always so addicted to the truth; that, as she spoke, the margin between the truth and invention shifted, becoming fluid or foggy.

Robert Hannah was the only son, she claimed, of a distinguished family from the western regions of Scotland. At the age of seventeen years he entered a dispute with his father over the choice of his bride, and when this quarrel finally proved resistant to all arbitration he was required to flee his native country in order to prevent the odious match from being prosecuted. So, bereft of the fortune of his ancestors, he contrived to make his way in the world through other means, joining a troupe of strolling players in Liverpool. With these glorious vagabonds he traversed the country for some few years, until, arriving in London at last and seeing its grander temples of Thespis, he gained loftier aspirations for his trade and was successful in procuring a livelihood at the Covent Garden Theatre.

'A livelihood? No,' Lady Beauclair was saying, 'for two years he was a "house servant", sweeping the stage, lighting candles, scrubbing the necessary houses, sticking bills upon every dead wall in the town. Two shillings he was paid for each performance. Those two years became three, those became four . . . until, at last, he was promoted. To the pit door. Then, after a season, to the lobby door, then the gallery door. Then finally, when there were no higher doors, into Wardrobe, to the office of a woman's dresser. Three shillings a performance. Four more years of drudgery; of patching and brushing costumes, smoking them in sulphur to clean out the stains and smells, or collecting them from, or returning them to, Mr Johnson's Habit-Warehouse. Darning stockings, blacking boots, purchasing ribands, wash-balls, wig-curlers, silk laces, garters, corking-pins, needles, pin-cushions. Stitching and lacing before each performance like a milliner who visits a great lady in her boudoir.

'At last, however, he achieved his wish and began to act again. At first in the smaller theatres. In the Chapel at the Lock Hospital, in the Grotto in St George's Fields, in the Black Bull Tavern in Pudding Lane. Many other taverns—I forget their names. Then Ranelagh and Mary-le-Bone Gardens in the summer season; getting soaked to the skin if it rained. The Great Room in Panton Street, at the corner of the Haymarket. Then, in time, with recognition, in our finest theatres—Covent Garden, Drury Lane, Lincoln's Inn Fields, the King's Opera House, the Little Theatre in the Haymarket. And everywhere such acclaim! He was applauded by the critics in the roles of fops, fools, young sparks of the town—'

'I have no doubt of this,' I murmured.

'—in *The Devil Upon Two Sticks* or *The Lying Valet*—'

'The fellow knew his business,' I mumbled.

'—yet he also performed others to an equal regard. The plays of Shakespeare, for example. For at length he became one of the Queen's Players, a company formed by Mr Larkins. Ah—may I assume from your expression that this great impresario is known to you? Yes? Then you must know, too, of the Queen's Players, the troupe that contrived to present the plays of Shakespeare in their purest and most original manner. Perhaps you have attended one of Mr Larkins's productions at the Globe Tavern—as it was named—in Southwark? No? Alas, it is gone now—burnt down—but until lately it staged these plays in a spirit as close as possible to the original, it being Mr Larkins's conviction that these masterpieces were ill served by our modern playhouses. Thus a small platform-stage was built inside the tavern, a curtain hung across it; black for the tragedies, motley for the comedies. The most authentic habits of the times were employed, as were cannonades, fireworks, hautboys, rebecks; the whole arsenal of Elizabethan stagecraft. Child actors, too—young boys. You know of course that ladies were not suffered to appear upon the stage during the reign of Queen Bess. So—boys. Mr Larkins was very adamant upon this issue. Yet these young fellows ultimately proved not to be the most suitable. For how might a cheeky boy of eleven years render the sweet charms of a Juliet, the wanton seductions of a majestic Cleopatra, the fragile tenderness of a poor Ophelia? And, besides which, the silly young scamps were forever forgetting their lines.

'The solution? Very simple. Presently Robert—and others among the players—assumed these troublesome roles. With great success. Robert, especially, was acclaimed. A most convincing figure! His mincing step, his voice either dainty and soft or shrewish and scolding—why, soon it seemed all of London was travelling to the tavern to see him play Rosalind in *As You Like It*, Viola in *Twelfth Night*, or Portia in *The Merchant of Venice*. Do you know these plays, Mr Cautley? Yes, I am certain that you do. And I am certain that you can recall how these heroines for various reasons— for love, for protection, for the purpose of finding their place in the world—disguise themselves as young boys; how the beautiful Rosalind, for instance, disguises herself as a boy named Ganymede, or how Viola assumes the personage of Cesario, a eunuch, until Duke Orsino falls in love with him—that is, with *her*.'

She sighed, then fell silent. At length she said in a quiet tone: 'Yet at the height of Robert's triumphs a most peculiar scandal broke, and his career, alas, was at its end. It is upon this account, I believe, that he is become a fugitive figure, unwilling, for instance, to expose his true face to the public—to you, for one. For, you see, on account of this scandal Robert must travel incognito—that is to say, in disguise. His life, in short, has become a masquerade.'

I kept my silence for a moment, waiting for her to proceed. When she did not I frowned as deeply as I could and said: 'I believe I have learned of this scandal.'

She turned her face to me, or, rather, the white satin

289

mask with which a few minutes before she had concealed her face, on account, she explained, of the wind and sun. These she asserted were most disadvantageous to the complexion—never mind that at the moment there was no wind and very little sun. The latter now shone rather weakly above the roof-tops of Mayfair and Piccadilly as the three of us walked up Constitution Hill in Green Park.

Yet I had never seen my lady by sunlight, however weak. As she spoke I had been reflecting on how this was the first time I had set eyes upon her either out-of-doors or by this more natural light of day; the first time we had come together—barring our first meeting—in a public place. Under these circumstances she looked something altered. The masses of hair, which by candle-light had been black, now proved tinged with the most attractive shade of auburn, though undoubtedly in their original had adorned the head of someone else; some fair young maiden in a country village, perhaps. In the wan sunlight her powdered cheeks— before being hidden by the mask—were so pale as to be almost blue, like skimmed milk, yet they sparkled even in this dimmish light like mother-of-pearl or the iridescent purple-and-verdigris necks of the pigeons scattering before our feet. Her nose, strangely, appeared more prominent, her lips thinner, despite their layer of carmine, and her countenance as a whole stronger and more angular, as if looked at through the flaw in a highly polished looking-glass. The same lady, yet different, as if two different people were overlapping one another, their appearances dovetailing and becoming indistinguishable; the one perceptible only from a certain angle, with the advantage of a certain light, like the shadowy figure on my canvas bleeding through into *A Lady by Candle-light*. I tried to recall Pinthorpe's curious theory about the candle and the wallpaper, the one that by some twist of logic had done away with the existence of wallpaper: something about colours admitting of alteration; about objects or persons not appearing the same in two different lights; about light—and people—tricking, disguising, deceiving, as if each person were only a painted stage-flat or *trompe l'oeil*.

Whatever the case, I would have gawped with pleasure at this new spectacle—and, even more eagerly, have painted it—had Lady Beauclair, who hitherto had successfully defeated all of my physiognomical designs, not appeared uncomfortable with my attentions. Indeed, she had averted her face whenever I rested my gaze upon her, casting it purposely in shadow, hiding it behind the pleats of her fan, nervously consulting its image in a pocket-mirror, and then finally producing the mask.

Not only was Lady Beauclair's appearance markedly different in this new light; her behaviour, too, was altered—sadly, for the worse. I was greatly confounded by her reaction to my presence in the Ring a few moments before. My affair of honour had not been quite of the nature I had anticipated, being even more ignominious in its own way than the previous contests—for I had been soundly whipped by a lady. My great surprise at her unexpected appearance was exceeded only when her gloved hand (which, upon the precedent of the chair-men, I was attempting to kiss) struck my left cheek, then the right, then the left again. Then I was pummelled upon the breastbone until I seized her fists. At which point a series of eloquent chastisements had commenced. How I had disappointed her! How she had misjudged my character! Did I think she would be impressed—flattered—by this foolhardy risk? Was she to thank me for this display of barbarism? I was accused of being 'prey to ungovernable passions', 'hell-bent upon misadventure', 'hot for the gallows', 'a rowdy young buck', 'a petulant child', 'a mischief-maker', and a score of other charges for which this plummeting avalanche of reproach admitted of neither Jeremiah's protests nor my apologies.

'It is ever the same,' she had lamented as we walked towards Hyde Park Corner through the rising veil of fog. 'The violent passions of men! You are like Tristano—yes, yes—he, too, fought upon this very spot, this same bloody field of battle! Oh, the foolish pursuit of honour, valour! The love of a woman! Mark what has become of him! And now *you* proceed down this same destructive path . . .'

This comparison was not, as I at first thought, the prelude to a story about Tristano—this, perhaps, I would learn at a later time, if I ever saw her again, which now truly seemed rather doubtful—but one concerning this 'Robert Hannah', whose unruly passions she claimed to have successfully tamed, for the moment at least. Thus by the time we crossed into Green Park and thence on to the path conducting us up Constitution Hill (where we were walking I believe none of us knew) her reproaches had been replaced by this account of Robert's life. She had asserted that the fellow would have 'shot out my lights' had he appeared, 'as, mark you, Mr Cautley, he had every intention of doing, had I not, fortunately, persuaded him otherwise. Why, I have never witnessed such an unholy rage! Should you have but seen him this morning! The vigour with which he cleaned and polished his pistols! The meticulous glee with which he ground the edge of his sword, caressed its blade, spoke of slicing your throat in twain and drinking your blood to its last drop!'

At this description of the violent character possessed by my intended antagonist the blood had drained from the face of my young second, who then commenced trembling noticeably and casting his eyes heavenward, as if paying thanks to the Almighty for her ladyship's intervention. I, however, had with a much greater equality of comportment demanded a more precise account of this fellow—'who he is and the like'—which she had duly been providing; painting this picture of him, however, that was not especially consistent with the furiously execrating rogue with whom she had terrorised Jeremiah.

'You have learned of this . . . scandal?' She now seemed perplexed, but then swiftly proceeded with more confidence. 'Yes, yes—he said you mentioned a lady. But no—I speak not of a scandal with a lady; not of the ruin of some silly girl from the country. Yes—he mentioned some fiddle-faddle concerning this person. Come, what was the name . . .? Miss Clitherow?'

So for the next five minutes—until we passed through the gates of St James's Park—it was my turn to talk, to tell a history. And though I made no mention at all of Sir Endymion—I was, you see, still faithful to my master—you may be quite certain that I did not shy from adding not a few unflattering daubs to the portrait she had begun of Robert.

When I finished, however, she responded quite differently from how I expected, seeming to ignore entirely, and to exempt from all comment, Robert's perfidy and Eleanora's tragedy. Instead, the only interest my story held for her ladyship resided—much to my disappointment and frustration—in the character of Eleanora herself. She asked a great number of questions regarding the girl's appearance and bearing and so forth. Was she pleasant to converse with? Fair to look upon? How old? What colour was her hair? Her eyes? Was she tall or short? Her complexion—dark or fair? In what manner did she dress, speak? My painting of her—was it completed? Might she perchance see it?

I was greatly exasperated by this interrogation, and though I could by no means provide Eleanora with favourable references upon all of these counts, I was surprised to find myself defending her rather ardently, exaggerating her beauty, charms, disposition. At the same time I wished to shout out that I was describing not an automaton or a tailor's dummy, not a figure in a painting or a character in the pages of a book, but instead a human being suffering in a garret. Presently, though, I discovered myself flattered, my heart warmed by the intensity and general direction of this interest: for perchance my lady suspected—or feared—a rival for my affections?

This not unpleasant impression of my lady's jealousy was strengthened if not quite confirmed soon after, for upon reaching one of the tree-lined promenades in the park—which, as it was Sunday, had begun filling quite rapidly with Persons of Quality taking the air before attending a holy service—she quite unexpectedly threaded her arm through mine. Quite unexpectedly, that is, because hitherto it seemed she was determined to be Robert's ally in both affairs; to blame me—and Eleanora—for these events. And so I had become increasingly vexed, not wishing to suffer any longer a lady whose moral sentiments were so deficient.

Yet now, as the sun emerged more strongly, this sudden display of ... what? Affection? I dared not resist, and so we strolled arm in arm together past other couples, also arm in arm. Jeremiah, still clutching the pistols, prudently fell two steps behind, then three, then after another few steps lagged even further in our wake until presently he was quite forgotten.

Our dispute over Robert had likewise been forgotten, left somewhere outside the gates of the park. I now discovered myself enjoying the pleasures denied me at Vauxhall, as it seemed we had become the subject of general observation and comment. Perhaps these good people recognised my lady despite her mask? As the last of my resentment drained away I drew myself erect and carefully altered my gait, affecting the graceful deportment I had rehearsed so often before my glass. I permitted myself to imagine what a handsome couple we must make. This flattering opinion was soon ratified when two fine young ladies in lace caps and hoop skirts turned their heads as we passed, then conferred with waiting-maids who carried lap-dogs in fur muffs. Then a milkmaid selling penny mugs of milk curtsied as deeply as if we had been King George and Queen Charlotte themselves. Handsome gentlemen on horseback doffed their hats; others on foot bowed respectfully, swords rising behind them like silver tails. Old ladies smiled kindly upon us from the windows of passing sedan-chairs, their painted faces, as they did so, framed by draperies, as if these ancient dowagers had become head-and-shoulder portraits of themselves; as if the chair-men carried not a cargo of withered flesh and brittle bone but an oil-painting—one of Sir Endymion's kit-cats—on its way for an exhibition in the Royal Academy.

After a short promenade Lady Beauclair and I also became a painting of sorts, for upon crossing the open conduit that carried water from the Tyburn brook into the duck-filled Canal we paused on a short foot-bridge to peer at the reflections—little more than shadows—shivering below our feet. I began to wish my lady might remove her mask, not only because then our fellow promenaders would see the beauty of my companion but because, as I squinted at its image in the water—a white blank, almost skull-like—I suddenly felt as if I were in yet another Vauxhall masquerade, confounded for the moment as to who or what was bona fide. Then a duck, quacking noisily, swam with much vigour across the portrait, and our images warped and bowed and wiggled as if dancing a rapid minuet, then vanished.

By the time we approached the Horse Guards the fog had lifted, like the curtain rising to reveal a magnificent stage design rushed into place by invisible scene-shifters: the Treasury and Abbey to our right, Pall Mall and the Admiralty to our left, the Parade before us, everywhere the spires and terraced squares of Westminster; a stage set, I thought, for one of those plays—something by Mr Etherege or Mr Congreve—in which Robert had played his rakish men about town.

Still arm in arm—and with Jeremiah still a discreet five or ten yards to our backs—we turned to our left hand and walked through Spring Garden into Cockspur Street. Then—as my lady was leading—we turned left again and entered the Haymarket. My silly conceits vanished, and I felt fear flutter in my breast, like a bagged partridge. Where was she leading us? To Mr Sharp's shop? To my lodgings? I was boggled. However did she learn . . .?

I had no desire for Lady Beauclair to set eyes upon my modest place of dwelling and so endeavoured to steer us into Pall Mall, for whose advantage over the Haymarket I vouched in the strongest terms. Yet as either her strength or determination—or perhaps both—proved at least the rival of mine, I discovered myself being dragged up the street like the Countess Kinsky's recalcitrant parlour-poodle struggling at the limit of its tether. Before we had progressed very far in this manner she drew to an abrupt halt and indicated with a nod the domed and colonnaded building to our left.

'Do you know it?'

'Yes,' I replied, relieved that this, and not Mr Sharp's humble shop, had been our destination. 'The King's Theatre.'

'Yes—the Italian Opera House.' She paused, gazing upon the great edifice. 'I wonder, can you conceive it?'

I was perplexed. 'Conceive . . .?'

'The masquerades, the operas. This is where it all commenced, Mr Cautley—or, perhaps I should say, where it all ended.'

Still I was perplexed. 'Do you mean to say that Robert—?'

'No, no.' She shook her head. 'I mean to say nothing at all about Robert. No, no, it is Tristano I am speaking of.'

An hour later we were seated together in one of the rooms that the White-Conduit House reserved for tea-drinking. Our window overlooked an ornamental pond filled with orange goldfish. The morning had now turned soft and fine, the sky clear. Our cups of tea were ochre with cream, and a hot loaf steamed the air between us. Our tea equipage glistened in the column of sunlight sprouting aslant from our table.

Another public place. We had come at my lady's suggestion. She summoned a hackney-coach at the foot of the Haymarket. After I handed her inside, the two of us bid Jeremiah adieu and then rattled away to Islington, half a league distant, maintaining a merry and preoccupied silence for most of the journey. The favours she had shown me in

295

St James's Park now continued. Our hands assumed a secret conversation, communicating with one another through a series of pinches, squeezes and dandling caresses. So eloquent was my lady in this language of gesture that as we clattered into St Martin's Lane I contrived to inflate its value by removing her mask and planting a kiss upon her cheek, to which deeds she coyly submitted and then replied—inflating the value even further—by pressing her lips into mine.

This joyous commerce may well have sustained itself for the duration of our voyage had not three successive events occurred, the most immediate being that our left front wheel selected this crucial second to encounter a particularly deep crevice between two flagstones, thus causing us to pitch first forwards in our seats, then backwards, and finally to the side, whereupon I very nearly crushed my lady's ribs and caused her to squeal sharply in pain. The second was that a moment later—after I made my profuse apologies and we resumed our delicious congress—we entered the narrow passage of Little St Andrew's Street and approached the Seven Dials; the vicinity, in other words, into which I had once unsuccessfully pursued the elusive Robert. In this neighbourhood and then again some moments later in Battle Bridge I could not but observe how my lady, growing unaccountably anxious, sought to avert her face from the window and then draw the curtains, as if apprehensive of what she might glimpse outside in the decrepit streets.

Or perhaps it was *being glimpsed* that she feared—for when she failed to resume these strange precautions in the Pentonville Road the third event occurred. Here we were unexpectedly hailed from the gutter by a gentleman of no favourable appearance: a hard-looking rogue whose frock-coat and linen did not look spotlessly clean, and whose surly expression appeared to originate from his having received a strong hint of his own foul odour. His lewd observation as we passed—that my lady was an incontinent bawd whose services I had engaged at no luxurious sum—so enraged me that at once I hollered for our vehicle to halt, whereupon I contrived to hop to the stones with the plan of cudgelling the impudent rascal within a bare inch of his life. I would have done so, too, had my lady not precluded this display of valour—my second of the morning for her sake—by slamming the door on my fingers while importuning the

296

driver to recommence our journey with the greatest possible haste. The scoundrel in the gutter then laughed boisterously and advanced a few more choice imputations, which, fortunately for him, the blood pounding in my ears prevented me from discerning with any great accuracy. None the less I had to be pressed forcibly into my seat by Lady Beauclair, who insisted I should pay the villain no heed. Yet by the time we halted before the White-Conduit House I was still hopping mad and laying plans for my hot revenge.

By this time I was perplexed, too, for it soon appeared that this impudence had worked a strange and unaccountable alteration in my lady's mood, seeming to have affected her views of both Robert and myself. For whilst daubing at her eyes with a perfumed handkerchief as we disembarked, she announced—quite out of the blue—that I should forget about Robert; that she had done with him; that I should forget he ever existed; that she had already proceeded to do so; that I should never see him more; that she only regretted I had encountered the villain in the first place; and finally that she wished most desperately that I had opportunity to plant my bullet into his foul heart.

You may well surmise how much I was astounded by these declarations, especially in view of her earlier warm defence of the rascal. Yet she being disinclined to elaborate, I was unable to puzzle out the reason for Robert's dramatic oscillation in her affections. Thus as we walked through a number of the house's prettily disposed walks, sat for a time in a pleasant arbour, then wandered into a shrubby maze, my mind was as confused, as subject to starts and stops and wrong turns, as our faulty and meandering steps. Alas, I was always confused thus in the company of Lady Beauclair! My thoughts on these occasions seemed to travel in all directions at once, like vines creeping and twisting through the undergrowth, blindly embracing all.

Now as we sat to tea in one of the booths I was no less confounded. Yet at least her spirits had improved by this time, and though our words again were spare we had resumed our increasingly articulate body language. Our arms were linked and our shoulders pressed as closely together as if perhaps we had been the product of one of Count Provenzale's curiosities. Our dual reflection was returned to me from the window, where it was superimposed upon the fish-pond and a distant meadow of cricket-players:

a peculiar man-woman; two heads and one body, this last being encompassed by my lady's petticoats, whose billows and frothy borders had encroached upon my breeches, fairly swallowing me up. A strange creature indeed, such a one as no traveller had ever seen.

We finished our tea and ordered another pot. By now I was laying plans other than ones for revenge; not the designs of a warrior, but the softer ones of a lover. I believe I must have been deaf to the chimes of St Mary's Church summoning the faithful to a holy service, for not once during that long day did I remember how this was the sabbath; and as the righteous citizens of Islington tramped along Penton Street to the pealing of the bells I suddenly lent words to my importunate gestures.

'I must have you, my lady,' I whispered as the goldfish splashed and the cricket bats popped outside the window, in the unreal world beyond our doubled image.

If my lady took heed of this rash confession of my passion she gave little sign. Instead, she popped a piece of bread into my mouth, poured another cup of tea and inquired: 'I wonder, Mr Cautley, do you remember the tragic tale of Philomela?'

Thirty-two

 The new opera—if Mr Handel ever managed to complete it—was to be performed in the Haymarket in November of 1720, shortly after the king dragged himself back from Hanover with his two mistresses in tow. This work, the topic of much discussion in London society during the summer months, was to open the second season of the new Royal Academy of Music. Expectations—for Mr Handel, for his new opera, for the Academy—were lofty since the Academy's first season at the King's Theatre had been the most tremendous success, closing the previous spring with the triumphant *Radamisto*.

Yes: the triumphs of the spring. Tristano had heard of

little else since arriving in London a fortnight after the curtain finally descended upon that first season at the end of June: the crush of the crowds in the Haymarket; the clerks and subordinate staff who had to be hired in order to meet the rush for tickets; the noble gentlemen offering forty shillings for seats in the footman's gallery and being turned away; the intemperately warm evening when the theatre doors were left open, causing a mob of hundreds to assemble in the Haymarket and along Cockspur Street, as peaceful as if entranced by the lute of Orpheus. And everywhere one went that summer—coffee-houses, cockpits, churches—people were humming the arias from *Radamisto*, the lovely '*Ombra cara*' especially. A beautiful enough melody, no doubt, but how much better would it be—and how superior would London's new Italian opera venture become—once the Academy presented singers of the best quality in the roles of, say, Radamisto and Zenobia; when the poorly trained and barely competent English sopranos— Mrs Anastasia Robinson or Mrs Ann Turner Robinson— were replaced by the finest singers from Italy?

At his villa in Richmond, Lord W—, for one, had contemplated this question with no mean enthusiasm. This relish extended beyond strictly musical considerations, for indeed his lordship had never so much as heard an opera in his life. Yet he happened to be one of the largest stockholders in the Academy, having oversubscribed by a factor of six and extravagantly pledged £1,200 to the enterprise as soon as it was floated. It was, he proclaimed, a favourable hazard, though even before the curtain rose on *Radamisto* in April he dispatched himself to Italy in order to safeguard this investment. He and another equally generous subscriber, that is: the Earl of Burlington, who had returned from Rome with the great composer Bononcini. Then, too, another singer—the castrato Senesino—was to arrive by the autumn, also in time for the new season. With these forces behind it, the new venture surely could not fail. As soon as Tristano and Senesino opened their mouths and sang one of Mr Handel's arias in a pitch hitherto unheard upon the English stage, 'why then,' Lord W— had been predicting in every villa that admitted him that summer, 'our opera stock shall raise itself from eighty, when they begin the ditty, to a hundred when they finish!'

Yes—stocks: this was the other great prepossession that

summer. All one heard of was operas and stocks—and, increasingly by the end of July, more of the latter than of the former. Subscription lists, joint-stock companies, projects, schemes of every description, chartered and unchartered, sound and unsound, enlisting the shrewd and the foolhardy—there was no end to them; London was mad, obsessed. Foremost among these lunatics, Lord W—. Not only had he subscribed generously to the Academy, he had also pledged similar amounts to several less illustrious schemes: a house-breaker alarm; a machine-gun with revolving chambers; a musket-proof chariot; a perpetual-motion machine; an appliance for turning salt water into fresh; another for fixing quicksilver; yet another for extracting silver from lead. He was little daunted when the mines of Terra Australis, in whose apparently favourable prospects he had invested, proved barren of all gold save the bags of guineas he had imprudently pledged to a stock-jobber at Jonathan's Coffee-house in Exchange Alley. Nor was he discouraged when a plan to resettle the poor of England's parishes along the banks of the St Lawrence River near Montreal drastically miscarried when its advocate closed up shop in the middle of the night and disappeared without a trace into those remote regions. For these were optimistic days, and his lordship responded in each case with the same cheerfulness that had served him at the gaming-tables of Paris and Lyons. Besides, scarcely had he time to contemplate his fleecing than he was happily allowing himself to be fleeced anew, drawn by another stock-jobber into a new project by which silkworms would be bred in Chelsea Park, or saltpetre refined from the night-soil collected from tavern jakes and lay-stalls.

Like the Academy, however, other projects that summer possessed more encouraging aims and extractions. During the run of *Radamisto*—when Lord W— was, alas for him, yet in Venice—the King had given royal assent to a Parliamentary bill for the grandest scheme of all: the redemption of the nation's debt through the South Sea Company. No doubt you have heard of this enterprise, of what our journalists call the great Bubble? The Company was launched a decade before with a keen eye for commerce with the Spanish colonies of South America. Its proprietors proposed to buy up the public debt—greatly swollen because of Marlborough's wars with France and Spain—in return for the privilege of holding a trade monopoly in Spanish America. These colonies were a prize much hankered after by English merchants, being much closer than India, therefore much less perilous for ships to reach, and long closed by the Spanish kings to foreign trade. These colonies would ship back to England dyestuffs, logwood, cochineal. All valuable commodities, especially cochineal, a scarlet dye made from the dried bodies of insects fed on cactus; a very popular colour for silks, damasks, cottons, for dresses and draperies; indispensable, in other words, to fashionable society, to their balls, assemblies, operas.

In return the colonies would receive ... what? Why, Negro slaves. Spain's lone trading concession was the coveted Asiento grant, the right to introduce slaves into the domains of Spanish America. Since the Pope spared the peoples of his dominions the degradation of this servitude, these colonies possessed the greatest appetite for African slaves, who enjoyed no such exemption. So as part of the Treaty of Utrecht in 1713 our nation acquired the privilege of docking ships named the *Hope* and the *Liberty* at the ports of Buenos Aires, Caracas, Cartagena, Panama, Porto Bello, Havana—wherever their services were required—and supplying the lands of the Spanish monarch with five thousand Negroes per year. Ten pounds per head was paid, one quarter of the profits going to the Queen's civil list—her court, palaces, living expenses, the salaries and offices of her ministers in Whitehall. The remainder was paid in commissions to the sea-captains, as royalties to the Spanish king, and finally, what was left, to the proprietors in the Company. One of these, incidentally, was Mr Handel, who in 1715 invested £500 and in return for his generosity received a handsome dividend.

This trade resumed for many years—indeed until not so very long since. Yet it was not altogether so gainful as hoped. Returns were poor, and entire cargoes were disposed of at a loss in our colonies in the West Indies when Spanish officials in the New World proved dilatory, hostile to this new arrangement. Further trading facilities were denied; slaves were the sole import, nothing else being allowed to breach the borders.

No, it was not until the next decade, until 1720—this period I now describe—that the Company, for a brief time at least, became a more profitable venture. The money raised by subscription and through slaving was used in other speculative adventures. After the Bubble Bill passed through Parliament—assisted, as was the custom, by generous bribes—and then received royal assent, the Company's shares immediately rose a thousand per cent. Nothing of this sort had happened before; scarcely could it be conceived, this great inflation of wealth. Tremendous fortunes were made in a single forenoon. Footmen soon purchased ancient estates along the Thames, shopkeepers new mansions in Hanover Square. Everyone—from housekeepers to clergymen to dowager duchesses—pawned anything of worth, parting with heirlooms at starvation prices in order to lay their hands on money to invest, whether in the South Sea Company or, failing that, the latest schemes taking subscriptions at the coffee-houses in Exchange Alley. Gold and silver coins—the gradual products of honest industry— were traded for paper credit, for an imaginary wealth that flew up on the Daedalian wings of paper; on these promises, shadows. Yes, shadows: like the dog in the fable, people were catching at the shadow of wealth—its illusion—and resigning the substance.

Oh, but how alluring was that illusion! Share prices in the Company were at 375 in April, 495 in May, 870 by July. It was said that at eight o'clock each morning of that summer a breeze ruffled through the city as everyone opened his newspaper to read how the stock was being quoted. Those in the Royal Academy of Music rose in sympathy, as did those in the Royal African Company, which was under contract to supply the Negro slaves to the South Sea traders. As did everything rise. The price of land, for instance. That near London attracted forty-five times its previous annual rent. A grand new square—'South Sea Square'—was planned for the south side of St James's Park. Bennet Street, Cock Yard, narrow little St John's Street, all would be knocked away to make room for the grand mansions of the new men of fortune. In the City a magnificent new 'South Sea House' would be built in Threadneedle Street, a short distance from the Company's great rival, the Bank of England. In the west—along the river in Chelsea, Chiswick, Richmond—the construction of villas commenced.

And so suddenly—this was Tristano's first impression of London—the entire city looked, and sounded, like a stone-mason's yard. Everywhere that summer were piles of wall-

302

stones, paving-stones, stacks of ashlar and slate, bags of lime. Everywhere the bark of hammers, the rasp of trowels, the cough of saws. Old buildings were knocked into rubble, new ones built over them, rising up like the feet and calves of unfinished colossuses. Blocks of marble, cairns of red bricks and heavy sacks of sand slumped like sleeping drunks alongside the rims of new excavations. Convoys of carts in the streets like a migratory herd. Overhead, drum winches, scaffolding that crawled up the sides of half-finished mansions, a thousand protrusions of wooden planks. Workmen in yokes clambering up and down ladders. More hammering in the coachmen's yards and, to the south and east, in the shipyards. More, more—more of everything was bought, built, sold, all shunted along by these flickering shadows and pernicious decoys of money, by this frivolous fever of speculation, this fury of gaming. Greed, self-interest, vanity, getting and spending, the indulging of every luxury, vice, profligacy, whim, ostentation, criminal passion: these it seemed were now the sole pursuit. People rushed from coffee-house to coffee-house, hoping to invest. Threadneedle Street and Exchange Alley became counting-houses and were blocked with desks and clerks. The river choked with new barges, the streets with new equipages, the monstrous homes with new furniture and sumptuous draperies that could not be unloaded quickly enough from the merchant ships and lighters crowding the Port of London. And everything, it seemed, choked with a white dust that floated through the air like a fog, descending everywhere in a thin, gritty film, as if overnight the fairies had sprinkled a magic powder upon the city, driving its citizens into madness.

Not so long after Tristano's arrival, though, this madness began to abate, or, rather, to trickle into a new channel. Lord W— had anticipated that his new singer would introduce himself to London society through a series of conversaziones at the finest homes: singing at the harpsichord after a hunt or a massacre of game-birds in the park, after a magnificent feast of roasting pigs and sea turtles from Jamaica, or on other such occasions. Yet on account of this omnipresent substance coating each window-ledge, cartwheel and hat brim, Tristano spent his first day in London sneezing, his second coughing, and his third struggling in some alarm for his breath. Perhaps foreseeing a decline in the worth of his stock, Lord W— promptly transported his singer by barge from the mansion in St James's Square to his villa in Richmond. Here Tristano might have recuperated quite peacefully had not that same week two workers unloading wool from a merchant ship on to the docks at Marseilles by an unhappy coincidence also sneezed and coughed, presently complained of dizziness and then, with no further ado, fallen dead in their tracks. The plague.

Within a fortnight 30,000 were reported dead of the pestilential contagion in southern France—in Marseilles, Arles, Aix. Cordons appeared along French rivers as the affliction rapidly spread northwards. In Toulon 178 people were massacred by soldiers as they fled their quarantine. In the northern ports, merchant ships from the south were forbidden to unload; some bound for Holland were burned at sea, their crews forced to wade ashore naked or suffer a similar end. In the London papers quarantine regulations and tolls of the dead in France appeared alongside the financial reports. And in the villa in Richmond, Tristano, under the anxious instructions of Lady W—, was incarcerated for five days in a chamber, 'under quarantine'. A caged songbird.

Yes; Lady W—. Oh, if only Tristano might have been quarantined against *her*, against this most beautiful—and most dangerous—of creatures! But forgive me; I run too far ahead of myself.

Tristano presently recovered, was released from his bondage, returned to London. By this time, though it was only August, a fortnight later, the city had changed quite remarkably. As he rode into London through Hyde Park Corner with Lord W— beside him in the coach-and-six, they were approached by a strange little fellow who was naked but for a pair of drawers held fast about his waist. His countenance was full of horror as it thrust itself inside the carriage.

—How doth the city sit solitary that was full of people! his hot breath shrieked into Tristano's face. How is she become a widow!

This jeremiad earned him a blow upon the ear from the back of his lordship's hand—thus occasioning another even louder lamentation as he toppled into the ruts—but as they drew into Piccadilly Tristano discovered that the miserable fellow had not been greatly mistaken in his appraisal of the city. The people of fashion had retired to their estates in the country, or to the spas—to Bath, Epsom, Tunbridge Wells—and in their absence, with their mansions shut up, the new squares appeared dark and lifeless. Here and there the hammering and sawing and chiselling continued, though it was something diminished, as if the workmen were expecting some imminent interruption of their labours. Indeed, building supplies and, especially, home furnishings—calico, silk, cambric, muslin, indigo, cochineal, tapestries, broadlooms—were running short, for the Port of London, though not empty, was silent, most ships being forbidden by law to unload; some were even held in the Downs, in the Medway, their cargoes and crews under quarantine. The plague, that is, had closed up the avenues through which the new signs of wealth had flowed into London: those paths by which had arrived the riches from Arabia and both the Indies now threatened to bring the plague to the doors of its newly wealthy citizens. In consequence, even Exchange Alley now was emptier, less frenzied.

Lord W— was undaunted. Tomorrow, he said, as their portmanteaus were unpacked at the mansion in St James's Square, he would go to South Sea House in Old Broad Street and subscribe for more stock; pay with cash for some of that being exchanged—foolishly—by nervous investors; by 'phlegmatic hypochondriacs with all the nerve of old serving-women'. He was shading his narrowed eyes as he watched the pulleys and winches that hung from his magnificent home, the ropes that dangled like tails, the stacks of bricks, the scaffolds and ladders with workmen who scampered about like so many monkeys on their perches.

—This talk of the price of stocks falling, of the plague coming, 'tis nonsense, I say, all of it! A plot by the Tories and Jacobites to distract the nation! They hope to steal our liberties and put their Pretender on the throne. *They* are the only plague I see.

A light fog—the thin dust—had drifted down from the cornices of the house, causing Tristano to sneeze.

Not until a week later, upon the eve of St Bartholomew's Day and the start of the great fair in Smithfield, did Tristano finally encounter some of the grand patrons who had conspired to bring him to London.

On this evening he was conducted by his lordship's coach-and-six—one of the grandest equipages to be seen in London, in or out of season—into a back street near Clerkenwell Green, a neighbourhood of no happy or welcoming mien. Several inhabitants appeared to express an interest in the coach and its passengers, attentions they abandoned only when Lord W— casually exposed his horse-pistols to their view. But other hazards soon presented themselves. The street into which they had turned proved an exceedingly narrow and difficult passage, barely capable of giving berth to a handcart, let alone a monstrous carriage. His lordship loudly cursed the driver when the vehicle's sides were scraped on either side as the poor fellow dodged the Scylla of a bow-window only to encounter the Charybdis of a palisade. Once out of the carriage, he vowed to repair the damaged veneer with funds extracted from the wages of the unhappy driver, who was struck thrice with his own whip and afterwards commanded to straighten his master's cravat, which had come loose in the exertions of the beating. Then his lordship conducted Tristano to a door, at which point the two of them were required to negotiate an even narrower passage, a set of steps rising above a dark stable in which heaps of something—was it coal?—had been stacked in bins.

—Yes, coal it is, replied Lord W— as he crawled four or five steps ahead, in the process showering Tristano with crumbs of dirt from his boots. Did I not promise to introduce you only to gems of the first water in London society? And so I shall: the fellow who lives here is the finest small-coals man in England!

With this he broke into a laugh, whereupon his left boot in missing a stair—which in fact no longer existed—clipped Tristano smartly on the forehead.

At the top of the steps a further hazard awaited Tristano's brow: the ceiling, on which he bumped his head, was so low that for the duration of his visit—three hours in all—he was required to hunch forward and bend his neck. In this pose he was introduced to a small company, most of whom were also bent out of a similar respect for this architectural caprice, so that together they resembled not 'gems of the first water' but freaks escaped from Count Provenzale's thatched huts. Besides being low of ceiling, the loft also proved dark, noisome with the smoke of tobacco-pipes and mercilessly without windows. Crooked stacks of books rose from the floor like stalagmites, giving the chamber the aspect of a grotto, though this grotto proved to have been furnished,

306

most incongruously, with a wing-shaped harpsichord and a small chamber organ.

It was also furnished with a most distinguished assembly. Its proprietor—the small-coals man—was named Mr Britton, an enterprising fellow who for the past decade had enhanced his humble living by presenting in his tiny loft concerts of no little renown. The best musicians, the wealthiest and most noble citizens in London, all were willing to crawl up the narrow stair for the pleasure of one of his musical entertainments. This evening the unique impresario was joined by the Earl of Burlington, known in the intimacy of this little circle as 'Dick'; a handsome, well-appointed young fellow—he could have been no older than Tristano— in a full-bottom wig. He stepped forward and addressed Tristano in Italian, politely asking after Signors Scarlatti and Vivaldi (each of whom Tristano had met but once) and expressing his sorrow at the recent demise of Maestro Gasparo Piozzi. Tristano was likewise addressed cordially in his native tongue—or in a variety thereof—by the gentleman next to Lord Burlington, a black-clad Irish clergyman with a kindly face and glittering eyes, who was introduced as the renowned philosopher George Berkeley, of Trinity College, Dublin.

Several of the other guests who now followed were somewhat less genial and distinguished in appearance. Beside the philosopher stood a tiny little fellow much too short to be required to hunch, though he seemed to do so anyway, perhaps out of sympathy with the others. He had contorted his shrunken body into what looked to be a most uncomfortable attitude, but one from which he did not extricate himself for the remainder of the evening. His bow, accomplished with a slight delay, appeared either reticent or painful. This, Lord W— announced, was the esteemed poet Mr Alexander Pope.

Next to the dwarfish Mr Pope, an even stranger sight, a man who eclipsed in spectacular fashion the saturnine poet's peculiarly deformed little body. As this fellow now stepped forward to make his bow, Tristano very nearly gasped in fright at the visage that appeared in the light of the lanthorn. A rare physiognomical study; surely the very summit of ugliness! So frightful was this countenance, indeed, that scarcely did it seem possible for beneficent Nature to have created it—rather, some cruel mask-maker working gleefully by torchlight. His brow was formed of a series of assymetrical bumps, from beneath whose rough promontories peered two fierce eyes, one significantly larger and situated at a greater elevation than the other. Voluminous chops were suspended below each, their surfaces so pockmarked that one might have played a game of cribbage in them. The black hairs, of no trifling length, that grew from these pits intimated a casual attitude towards tonsorial duties, the most conspicuous of these hairs sprouting from the tip of his nose and thereby lending the initial impression that a black spider had taken up habitation there. This scabby appendage was of a disproportionate length and seemingly strove for an encounter with an equally long chin at a point before the pair of fat lips which these two great protuberances—misshapen and purple, like the bulbs of hyacinths—very nearly eclipsed.

This grotesque Punchinello was introduced as the manager of the King's Theatre in the Haymarket, the impresario who brought both masquerades and Italian operas into London: the Swiss count Johann Jakob Heidegger. (In the coach a few minutes earlier Lord W— had been somewhat less flattering, asserting that Count Heidegger brought masks into fashion so that he might disguise himself; for otherwise the ladies were, he said, too affrighted to look upon him.)

Yet the hideous appearance of the Count belied his nature, for he smiled benevolently and—unlike Mr Pope— made a ready bow.

Finally—after a viola da gambist, an ancient duke, an organist from a City church, and another poet less distinguished than Mr Pope, both in his appearance and, apparently, his verse—another strange figure. This one was rather poorly attired, his frayed cravat and ill-fitting waistcoat both being stained with snuff, his boots in need of a blacking, and two of the seams in his breeches requiring, but apparently being stubbornly denied, the offices of a tailor. His wig, moreover, resided at an eccentric angle to his swarthy brow, which appeared to be creased in some display of discontentment. At least Count Heidegger's linen and waistcoat were, respectively, clean and of an expensive cut, and Mr Pope's wig was curled as delicately as any lady's head, his tiny frock-coat—scarcely larger than that of a tailor's beeswax doll—immaculate. A mug of ale sat by this grubby fellow's elbow, which rested on the tiny chamber organ; and between his yellow teeth he clenched a tobacco-pipe that in refusing to remain alight for a duration of more than ten seconds occasioned a constant slurping and gurgling and muttered cursing in some unfamiliar foreign tongue.

—Permit me to introduce the great composer Mr George Handel, Lord W— said to Tristano, who made a bow, though Mr Handel, far from returning the obligation, simply nodded with much rapidity, as if impatient for the entertainment to proceed.

The musical side of the entertainment did not, however, proceed with any great haste, for, upon the request of Lord Burlington, Mr Britton uncorked two bottles of wine which his lordship had lately transported from Italy. After cups were poured and the quality of the vintage exclaimed over, the Earl lamented having lost a crate of the same at Dover, where he had been required to pay a handsome bribe in the custom-house for the privilege of importing two others.

—I had such a devil of a time on account of the plague, he explained. In more healthful times such cupidity will be satisfied with a single bottle.

At this piece of news Mr Berkeley turned quite as red as the liquid in his beaker, his kindly countenance for the moment assuming the gloomiest expression.

—Is it not a fine state of affairs, this philosopher inquired, when a pestilence delivered to punish our waywardness then becomes the avenue to a greater avarice?

—Pshaw, remarked Lord W— as he lit his tobacco-pipe and poured himself a second cup of the Earl's wine. 'Tis surely a strange way for the Almighty to punish Londoners, by murthering Frenchmen.

Not appearing to have hearkened to this remark, Mr Berkeley, seconded by Mr Pope, proceeded to cast the blame upon the stock-jobbers—to blame the greed and debauchery they had exposed—for the imminent coming of the plague. Why, had it not after all been a *merchant* ship— Captain Chataud's vessel filled with its fatal cargo of wool from Syria—that had ushered the contagion to Marseilles in the first place? Anyone, they argued, could see this was no accident.

—Nay, said the philosopher, surely it is the judgement of heaven, the reckoning of the Almighty, an impending punishment for the sins of our nation, for the debaucheries and levities that have prevailed among us. For our obsession with wealth and speculation, buying and spending.

—Nonsense, Lord W— growled at the pair of them, moving on to his third cup, which exhausted the bottle. I suppose you will say that because the Great Fire of the last century began in Pudding Lane and concluded at Pye Corner it was caused by the sin of gluttony?

Mr Berkeley remained conspicuously silent on the matter.

—No, his lordship continued, downing his cup, we have behaved more abominably, more sinfully than this, and then avoided or survived any reprisals—if such they are—cast upon us by the Almighty.

—Our turn may yet arrive, the philosopher remarked in a grave tone. The corruption of manners, mark you, never faileth but to draw after it some heavy judgement, be it war, famine, or pestilence.

—Then let it be war, urged Lord W— in a hearty voice, for there is much more profit to be made by this than by these others. There is a good trade in war, forsooth.

These sentiments were received with no great enthusiasm by Mr Berkeley, nor by a number of the other guests, whose wigs wagged in some consternation.

—There is profit for some, surely, Mr Pope remarked in his cheeping little voice, who pay not one bit to its charge; yet what of the noble families of landed interest who bore the heavy burden of taxes for our late wars against the French king? Their losses were the gains of the stock-jobbers and self-interested merchants in the City.

—Where, I would know, is to be found the difference? His lordship's mighty voice seemed to reduce the little poet's to the mewling of a sick kitten. 'Tis either the one or the other, and, so long as there is wealth, I declare our nation shall prosper, no matter who holds it.

—If these riches promote an honest commerce among men, Mr Berkeley said amiably, then I would dare not disagree; for history—the example of Rome, or that of Venice—shows us that commerce most certainly begets virtue, culture and patriotism.

—What is more, added Lord Burlington, commerce is in all times and all places a necessary condition if the arts are to flourish. How, sirs, may these thrive without it? The citizens of London wish to see an opera. Very well. Yet a price must be paid for this pleasure. We have, for example,

310

Mr Handel to pay (he gestured at the composer, who was tuning the harpsichord and paying him no mind), as well as (another gesture) the salary of the great Tristano. All art presents such reckonings!

—Which, fortunately, we may settle upon the heads of a few black slave boys, Lord W— chuckled mirthlessly.

—Therefore, continued Lord Burlington (who apparently had not heard, or chose to ignore, this remark), let us hear none speak against wealth, for all of our arts depend most vitally upon it.

—Yet, said the philosopher in his gravest tone, yet, your lordship, I fear our wealth is not always used with such prudence; for we must observe that whenever riches are made an instrument to luxury and private vice—as happens now, and as has happened, increasingly, since the reign of King Charles II—they enervate and dispirit us, and these admirable ends are sadly forsaken.

—These new moneyed men with their easy wealth, Mr Pope remarked in a harsh tone as he nodded vigorously, show the disease that afflicts the body of the public, which is grown vain and effeminate.

—The pot calling the kettle black-arse, Lord W— murmured into his cravat.

Mr Pope, who had not detected this remark, continued in a tone grown even more acerbic:

—Our merchants in the East India Company, he said, are become like foolish beaux who woo a vain and silly lady, bearing her gifts that she may adorn her body in the most egregious fashions at her dressing-table. Precious stones from Africa, incense from Arabia, coffee, tea, chocolate, tobacco—

—The fruits of civilisation, declared Lord W—, interrupting him. The spoils of empire!

—No, your lordship—the products of corruption and vanity. The rewards of a race of dunces who cannot rise above trifles.

—I believe, sir, that you own some little stock—a 'trifle', no doubt you will say—in the South Sea Company?

At this revelation the little man turned red beneath his powder and a cross expression took fierce hold of his unpleasant features. Meanwhile those more agreeable ones of his ally, Mr Berkeley, had transformed themselves into an attitude of pensive concentration.

—The wisdom of our legislature, he said, must interpose itself and curb these vices, these pursuits of luxury that Mr Pope speaks of with such reason. I am referring to sumptuary laws, which may most effectively discountenance the display of gold and silver, either in clothes or equipage.

Lord W— snorted at the philosopher.

—Then, sir, he said, you will discourage trade, choke our merchants, and, by your own logic, throttle the arts.

—On the contrary, your lordship: then shall we save our bullion as well as our arts and our morals—and also, may I add, our immortal souls.

This time it was the turn of Count Heidegger to snort his disapproval.

—You are therefore suggesting, he challenged, that the Almighty will denounce a gentleman or a lady for the wearing of a certain jewel or costume? Hell would in that case be a veritable pleasure palace, filled with our finest citizens.

—Can there be any doubt, I ask you, continued Mr Berkeley, that the luxury of dress, especially a disguise, giveth a lewd and immoral behaviour to women, who are thereafter so often corrupted by sparks similarly attired in the modish way? She who dresses as a strumpet or an odalisque will, I warrant you, soon enough act the part as well.

—The truth or behaviour of a lady does not in every case tally with the cut of her dress, said the Count, whose gargoyle features appeared to have deepened into a frown, though his voice was yet modulated in its pleasing bass. The strumpets among the arcades at Covent Garden, he continued, were not made so because of their garments. You speak, doctor, as if the world were governed by *mere appearance*.

—Indeed, sir, I hope that I do; for there is no world distinct from appearances; and are we not, I ask you, governed by these appearances, by the sights that each day meet our eyes? Are not the objects of vision—as I believe I have shown—a universal language which regulates our moral actions, either for good or ill? We know only, and only act upon, that which we are able to observe; and if all we observe is corruption, folly and vice, then surely our actions will follow in kind. He paused long enough to offer the Count a kindly but triumphant smile. Is it not therefore, he concluded, most advisable to take great care of appearances, whether of dress, theatre or streets?

Count Heidegger rubbed vigorously at his hyacinth-bulb nose, which under this exertion seemed unnaturally pliant, as if capable of being squashed flat or removed. Then he said:

—You know I am a humble man, doctor, trained as a soldier in the Guards, as a man of business, and I understand none of your philosophy. Yet this I do understand. What is the consequence for a lady's immortal soul if of an evening she piles high her hair or wears a bustle, a mask or a jewel as she sits in her box at the opera? Surely the Almighty is astute enough to study the soul, not the body or its masks or vestments.

—The Almighty, yes; but as for the rest of us, I fear no. Mr Berkeley shook his head and regarded the Count with no little disappointment.

—As one of the Ancients has observed, added Mr Pope, the direct way to ruin a man is to dress him up in fine clothes.

—Then praise be, Lord W— snorted, that we have progressed beyond the Ancients!

—Surely you agree with me, Mr Berkeley addressed Count Heidegger, that virtue and good manners rise or fall in connection to the assemblies we encourage? These masquerades lately come to London, to your theatre in the Haymarket, are not merely pernicious in themselves, satisfying as they do the sinful appetites for gaming, dressing, intriguing and luxurious eating; they are an abridgement or abstract of—a symbol for—all of those senseless vanities that have ever existed under the sun.

—Dressing: a *sin*? expostulated Count Heidegger, shaking his head. Eating fine food: a *sin*?

—You say you understand no philosophy. Perhaps you will understand this, then. Mr Berkeley now turned to Mr Britton, who had been observing these exchanges somewhat anxiously. Pray, good sir, have you a Bible in your house?

Mr Britton blinked in alarm at the question, as if it were an accusation.

—Certainly, sir, he replied, scurrying away and then returning a moment later with the book, which to his credit looked well-worn. The Irishman fluttered the furling leaves for an instant before halting at a passage, which he stabbed with a manicured forefinger.

—Need I remind you, he asked, directing his attention to

313

the company in general, how the prophet Isaiah, under instructions from the Lord, denounced the luxurious dress of the ladies of his time?

The murmured—and somewhat abashed—consensus was that he must.

—Very well, then, I shall. He cleared his throat and wet his lips. *Because the daughters of Zion are haughty,* he began in a mellifluous voice, *and walk with stretched forth necks and wanton eyes, walking and mincing as they go, and making a tinkling with their feet; therefore the Lord will smite with a scab the crown of the head of the daughters of Zion, and the Lord will discover their secret parts. In that day the Lord will take away the bravery of their tinkling ornaments about their feet, and their cauls, and their round tires like the moon, the chains, and the bracelets, and the mufflers, the bonnets, and the ornaments of the legs, and the headbands, and the tablets, and the ear-rings, the rings and nose-jewels, the changeable suits of apparel, and the mantles, and the wimples, and the crisping pins, the glasses, and the fine linen, and the hoods and the veils. And it shall come to pass that instead of a sweet smell there shall be a stink; and instead of a girdle a rent; and instead of well-set hair, baldness; and instead of a stomacher, a girding of sack-cloth; and burning instead of beauty.*

When he closed the book with a triumphant slap a short silence ensued in the chamber before Mr Pope remarked:

—The scab, the stench, the burning—these, surely, we may interpret as the pestilential symptoms even now making their way across France like an avenging army. Shall we say that our folly and corruption have been so different?

—It is to be feared, said the philosopher, his lilt now turned lugubrious, that the end of our State now approaches, should we not mend our ways.

Lord W— scowled at the poet and, advancing a step or two forward, exhaled a thick plume of smoke into the little fellow's face, causing him first to cough and, secondly, to attempt to even the score by tossing a punch, which landed with no great force in his lordship's belly. Lord W— then prepared to respond in kind, but Mr Berkeley, Mr Britton, Count Heidegger, Lord Burlington, the viola da gambist, the organist, the poet of lesser distinction, all now pressed forward in a scramble of boots, either to officiate in this uncivil dispute or to prosecute it farther—it being difficult

314

in the poor light and close quarters to distinguish intentions—until in the mêlée the two bottles of wine, now emptied, broke on the floor and a tallow-candle was tipped, spilling and then igniting a pool of grease. These two accidents had the unfortunate effect of raising, and perhaps confusing, passions, and who knows what further violence may have ensued in the loft had not at that moment Mr Handel commenced playing upon Mr Britton's harpsichord.

Neither he nor Tristano had been attending the debate—nor even, now, the pushing, incipient fisticuffs, and flaming floor-boards—with any special regard. When the battle had begun to erupt the two of them had been leaning over the harpsichord, peering inside at the rows of jacks and the silver rails of string, looking as they did so like two mourners bent over a coffin, paying their final respects to a deceased relation. The composer had propped open the instrument's polished lid (whose underside was inscribed 'CONCORDIA MVSIS AMICA') with three leather-bound volumes plucked from one of the nearby stacks, and for the past few minutes he had been fiddling with keys and tuning-pins, the insistent *ting-tong-tung* as he tightened the strings and struck the keys at times almost drowning out the arguing voices. Then, having decided upon '*Cara sposa*', the famous aria from *Rinaldo*, the two of them began their performance with a continued obliviousness to the company.

—*Cara sposa*, Tristano sang over the growls and oaths, half-hidden by a cloud of greasy smoke,

> *Amante cara,*
> *Dove sei?*
> *Deh! Ritorna a' pianti miei!*
> *Del vostr' erebo sull' ara,*
> *Colla face del mio sdegno*
> *Io vi sfido, O spirti rei . . .*

The company, fortunately, was not so oblivious to the performers as they to it, and the combatants first stomped upon the flames and then quickly scraped their chairs and sat to the performance, their unruly passions likewise extinguished, tamed as if by the strains of Orpheus.

—*Where art thou gone, my love, my dear betroth'd*, Lord Burlington was translating in a whisper for the old duke.

315

Where are thy beauties now? Return alas! Thou ravish'd Heaven, return to an abandoned lover's sad complaint and save a life that dies for loss of thee—and so forth until the old duke, a veteran of the siege of Namur, was reaching for his handkerchief to wipe a tear from his mustard-coloured eye. Since the piece was normally sung—as, for example, by the castrato Nicolini in the Haymarket nine years earlier—amid fire-snorting dragons on a stage enveloped in a mysterious cloud of black smoke, into which the sorceress Armida had vanished, some might say that the sooty chamber was not an entirely inappropriate venue for Tristano's performance.

Certainly there were no critics in the audience this evening. As Lord W— sat peacefully beside Mr Pope, listening to this aria finish and then another begin—'*Augelletti, che cantate*', the famous 'bird song' from *Rinaldo*—he could not help but smile and feel cheered by the knowledge that his most prestigious investment, if no other, was safe, prospering. Indeed, as this small but distinguished company sat quietly in the loft, hearing the sweet music—and, in the far distance, not charming birds sweetly singing, as the song suggested, but the silvery clang as stakes were driven into Smithfield Market for the stalls and show-booths of the coming fair—none of them could have guessed that this brief performance was to be, alas, the only successful collaboration between the two great artistes.

Yet as the second aria was finished, one of the harpsichord's strings suddenly broke with a bright *ping*! and flew out of the wing-shaped coffin, flapping wildly about like a snake crushed by the wheel of a cart. A second later, perhaps as a consequence, the three books slid from their perch, causing the instrument's lid to clap down with a bang as loud in these close quarters as the report of a pistol. (The ancient duke came smartly to attention and, tossing aside the handkerchief, reached for his blade.) This sharp noise was followed, finally, by a more prolonged reverberation in the sound-board, which hummed in a deep timbre, and, for what seemed like an eternity, filled the small chamber with its portentous noise; seemed, indeed, to make the chamber itself hum and throb, as if, far in the distance, an unknown disaster had struck, its tragic effects reaching them now in rippling tremors.

316

Two hours later this sound still trembled in Tristano's head. Indeed, it was grown louder now; a sonorous buzz.

After leaving Aldersgate Street at the conclusion of the concert the coach-and-six had passed through Smithfield, this site of rare activity occupied by a band of workmen labouring by torchlight, tearing up the paving-stones. St Bartholomew's Fair was to begin on the morrow, Lord W— explained; the English carnival. Perhaps Tristano wished to pay a visit? No?

—Count Heidegger's masquerades will soon be resuming, too. Ho! Such liberty and licence, you shall never see the like! Why, I hope those Tory blockheads have not scuppered your desire for a little entertainment?

Tristano shook his head again; for it had been Count Provenzale, and not the philosopher or the poet, who had scuppered his desire for such things.

Yet his lordship had insisted upon the visit, and so a fortnight later—a warm, sunny day early in September— the coach-and-six returned to Smithfield so that Tristano might enjoy the privilege of clapping his eyes on spectacles whose foolishness was equal to anything seen in the Campo San Polo. For him the privilege was, however, truly one of escaping from the disagreeable presence of Lady W—, who a week earlier had arrived from Richmond for the commencement of the London season, accompanied by her three serving-maids, six spaniels and twelve portmanteaus packed with clothing of every fashion and baubles of every description; the 'fruits of civilisation', no doubt, which her husband had transported back from the Levant.

If during the past month Tristano had grown accustomed to, if not exactly fond of, the habits of Lord W—, he was considerably less successful in his dealings with Lady W—. Since his involuntary sequestration for the 'plague', and even after his recovery and liberation, Tristano and her ladyship had not suffered one another at all well. That is, for some reason that despite his lordship's inquiries had remained quite inexplicable, she could not abide to remain in the same house as Tristano, even if that house was as capacious as the villa in Richmond or the mansion in St James's Square, in either of which, in truth, one might roam for days through endless rooms and corridors without encountering other life. Tristano for his part, for reasons of this profound but unaccountable dislike, was more than content to provide her ladyship the wide berth she demanded, and would most gratefully have forsaken Lord W—'s hospitality altogether had not his lordship, much to his lady's vexation, remained adamant on the issue of the singer's residency. Young Lord Burlington kept Mr Handel in his mansion in Piccadilly; the composer was said to enjoy an entire apartment to himself in Burlington House.

—And no doubt the new Italian, Bononcini, will take up his residence there as well, his lordship had explained to her as the first of the twelve portmanteaus was opened in the grand atrium amid much excited commentary from the spaniels. I shall not therefore allow him the privilege of Tristano as well. No, I declare the fellow shall remain under *my* roof.

Her ladyship had cast a ribboned coif upon the floor and then wept fiercely into a blue mantua lately unpacked from the trunk.

—Pray do not pretend this contest is betwixt you and the Earl, she sobbed in a voice muffled by the silk, for it is one, surely, betwixt you and me!

—Then it is one in which I shall certainly triumph, he growled, his green eye glittering, since it is not one between equals! For your right to equality, my dearest lady, expired upon that fine day we were wedded together. Thus you shall now be governed by me in this as in all other things, and there an end to the matter!

Upon this pronouncement, which admitted of no appeal, her ladyship fled up the stairs and into her dressing-chamber, her spaniels in train, the last of the number receiving a blow upon its posteriors for valiantly rebuking his lordship with a series of yaps, apparently in defence of its disconsolate mistress.

Lady W— did not emerge from her luxurious chamber for three days. Her meals, placed outside the door, remained untouched, and even the milliner from New Bond Street—a much closer companion, in truth, than her husband—was turned away.

What may be said of her ladyship's character? She was, as his lordship frequently declared during her period of self-imposed exile in the boudoir, 'a most confoundedly perplexing creature' and (if he was less charitably inclined) 'a phlegmatic hypochondriac'. Indeed, she was the sport of

318

constant illnesses—whether real or imaginary Tristano could not precisely determine—which caused her to faint as well as to consult with her doctor ('a knavish quacksalver', according to his lordship) at least as frequently as with her milliner. She spent several hours each day treating herself with his prescriptions, which were variously gargled, swallowed, inhaled, bathed in, infused in tea, mixed with mustard, milk, or spa water, rubbed into her breastbone, dropped on to her tongue or into her eyes, or perhaps even (for so a rumour among the downstairs servants had it) inserted by special tubes into the orifices of her nether regions. Her boudoir—whenever Tristano scurried past it— smelled like an apothecary's shop or a witch's den, and its music was that of chinking bottles, rattling pills and a pestle fiercely scraping a mortar.

To Tristano her ladyship was not so much a person as an assemblage of practised gestures, bright possessions, inscrutable whimsies. It was difficult to form an accurate impression of her person, for on mornings when her apparently fragile constitution permitted her to venture from her bed this was frustrated at her *toilette*—disguised, perhaps— by her mirrors and many cosmetic powers. It was also concealed by the milliner from New Bond Street, who, once she finally relented, resumed his visits each morning as she rose at eleven o'clock; and perhaps also by the young dandy who every second afternoon tutored her in elocution. For she was regarded as somewhat deficient in this last area on account of having been born a Caledonian; having been born, that is, as Lady Sidney Hannah, daughter of a wealthy Scottish earl.

Who precisely her ladyship's arts were intended to benefit was not immediately obvious. Even when relations with his lordship stood on better ground—rare enough occurrences—she seldom left her chambers. Despite these elaborate *toilettes*, that is, she passed most of her days at home, out of sight, venturing out-of-doors only upon her husband's suggestion or with his permission—and, even then, never did she depart alone. Her efforts were not, however, intended to please his lordship; even on those infrequent occasions when their associations in the parlour or at the dining-table were unaccompanied by shouts or scolds or vexed weeping, he paid her very little heed beyond uttering commands about what she might or might not do, or where she might or might not travel. It was almost as if she were a captive in the mansion, with his lordship for her gaoler, her stern governor.

Yet Tristano presently had occasion to notice that Lord W—'s behaviour towards his wife differed remarkably whenever the two of them entered the company of people of fashion. For when they appeared together in St James's Park or elsewhere—at a concert or other such assembly— his ambivalence disappeared and he became exceedingly solicitous of her appearance, anxious that everyone present should appreciate and comment favourably upon her worth. Strangely, he now appeared to esteem his wife as diligently as he had previously ignored her. This ambition to have his wife recognised set him, however, upon the horns of a peculiar and unfortunate dilemma: for if anyone dared appreciate her worth too industriously, looking with an excess of familiarity upon this charming item he had presented so proudly for general observation, his lordship would abruptly retract the view and challenge the baffled connoisseur to a duel. In the past year three or four young gallants had been run through in such reprisals, or so at least it was rumoured. And so, though he was negligent of her in private, he was jealous—madly so—in the more public domains; almost as jealous of her, that is, as he was of Tristano.

Thus when Lord W— proposed a visit to Smithfield, Tristano was not slow to accept, since upon that day her ladyship's behaviour had been alternating between a brooding silence and the occasional angry rebuke, during which the lessons of her simpering young thrice-a-week coxcomb were cast aside, rendering her quite incomprehensible to Tristano, whose grasp of the new tongue was yet feeble at best. Thus far today she had accused him—both in and out of earshot—of being a heathen, a superstitious peasant, of subscribing to the errors of Rome, of being ugly to look upon, of mangling the English tongue, of speaking secretively in Italian while in her presence, and of being a thief (for one of her lace handkerchiefs—later recovered in the laundry-maid's basket—had temporarily gone missing).

The 'English carnival', however, proved a disappointing diversion from these trials. An endless parade of tumblers, fencers, posture-masters, men in loincloths eating stones, others devouring the flames of torches. Such lunacy! Puppet-shows in which 'operas' were performed in a gibberish lan-

320

guage; a dancing bear, an Iroquois monarch, a gigantic hog, a white tiger roaring unhappily in a wooden cage, a dusty cassowary, a wrinkled elephant whose owner proclaimed it would discharge a pistol and strike a target in fifteen minutes' time. Freaks, too, of course: everywhere posters outside the striped booths of monster-mongers displayed two-headed goats, maidens with great black mustachios, giantesses, hermaphrodite monkeys, calves with five legs, and a hundred other pieces of nonsense, all on display to the sound of hurdy-gurdies, salt-boxes, kettledrums, timbrels, and the cries of mountebanks selling juleps, fever powders, cephalic draughts, somnivolences, balsamic styptics—the very kind of wares, in short, that each morning rattled and clinked in Lady W—'s bedchamber, tolling her latest illness. The most successful of these quacks was loudly recommending a remedy for the plague, sold at a price of one guinea per bottle. A large group of people had deserted the other shows and stalls to assemble round his platform, and soon all were emptying their purses into the hands of his two assistants, who could scarcely keep pace with the demand for this miraculous product.

Yes—the plague. For the past fortnight Tristano had almost forgotten this giant's shadow that had seemed to be stalking him as it crept across France, up towards Paris, following his own route along the Rhône, the Saône, the Loire. He had almost forgotten it because with the fair the streets, even as far west as St James's Square, were filled once again, albeit only with roistering mobs, gamesters, roaring drunkards. With them, however, all of the heedless sanguineness of the previous month had, it seemed, returned. On St Bartholomew's Day—the day after Mr Britton's concert—there had been a mob at South Sea House, Lord W— included among it, hoping to register stock transfers. Then, too, the aristocracy and wealthiest merchants were soon to return from their spas and homes in the country for the London season: for the new season of masquerades, assemblies, plays and, especially, operas. With their arrival in town, with this new flood of wealth into London, the price of stocks—both in the South Sea Company and the Royal Academy—would, his lordship predicted, only begin to rise.

And so upon the eve of the final day of St Bartholomew's Fair his lordship had been in splendid spirits, proposing after

321

an hour of the most dubious entertainment that the two of
them depart for a chocolate-house in St James's Street
where a party of like-minded young lords were waiting, 'full
of purse and empty of brains'. Their plans were interrupted,
however, when upon departing into Pye Corner they were
startled by the sharp report of a pistol behind them—as
advertised, it was the elephant's—and then, ahead of them,
the sound of a mob in common cry. After a short moment
a swarm of men, perhaps a hundred in number, grew visible,
rushing east along Newgate Street. Their shouts drowned
out those of the hectoring mountebanks and even the
leather-lunged hawkers declaring that the performances by
the puppets and fire-eaters were about to commence. Was
this spectacle, Tristano wondered, another Smithfield show?
For this many-headed beast pressing along the thoroughfare
and through the narrow City gate—its body had reached
Christ's Hospital by now—made a stranger sight indeed
than the freaks and animals.

Lord W— was likewise puzzled. These fellows had
escaped, he speculated, from Newgate Gaol. No, no—they
were rushing and stumbling in the opposite direction,
towards the gaol, towards the City. Well-dressed fellows,
most of them; no prisoners, surely, among them. So, then—
what was it? The plague? The first deaths, perhaps, discovered in St Giles or Holborn, the inhabitants fleeing their
noxious precincts . . . ?

Others, too, were baffled. Murmurs ran round the fair as
the front line of the mob—its vociferating head—thrust into
Cheapside. The mountebanks had fallen into silence, and
some of the fair-goers were rushing down Giltspur Street
and into Newgate.

—What happens? one of them cried in a stout voice at a
half-dozen fellows bringing up the rear; the crumbling tail
of the beast. Whither do you go, sirs? What the devil grieves
you? The plague?

—'Tis a plague, sure, responded one member of this
strange company; a fellow in a handsome paduasoy coat
and a pair of buckled shoes whose shine not even the dirt
of Snow Hill and Newgate Street could quite disguise.

—The plague! cried the chorus of a dozen voices behind
Tristano. The plague, the plague!

—An abominable plague, the gentleman continued, still
marching towards the gate that had swallowed his fellows.
322

'Tis known as the South Sea Plague! Thousands are caught of it, he said, and all shall suffer the most terrible death!

The screams behind Tristano grew even louder, more desperate. From beside him came those of Lord W—, who was roaring like the white tiger in its wooden cage, as if seeking to split open the seams of the warm September sky. Loudest and most desperate of all, however, was the sound of humming in Tristano's skull—as if the trees and buildings and swarms of people had been struck like a tuning-fork and now trembled and buzzed with their own terrible music.

Thirty-three

 'It was here they stood,' Lady Beauclair said, gesturing with a gloved hand, 'not so very far from this spot.'

I peered out the window, but as the day was grown late—the bells of St Bartholomew the Great had just announced six o'clock—there was very little to distinguish along the short length of Giltspur Street, and I leaned back upon my cushion.

Why, I was wondering, had we come here? As we departed the White-Conduit House a few minutes before she had instructed our coachman to turn south, into St John's Street; and so now, having passed Smithfield Market—empty and dark—we were trotting alongside St Bartholomew's Hospital. A longer journey, surely—to wherever it was we might be travelling—but as her ladyship was paying the fare, and as our bodies were pressed together in the hack, bouncing into one another with each bump in the road, I voiced no complaints. I wondered, though, whether this diversion into Smithfield was for my benefit, or whether she was merely avoiding those neighbourhoods—Battle Bridge and the Seven Dials—where she had been most anxious not to be recognised.

Before I could reflect further upon the question, however, her hands commenced pinching and stroking mine. This form of intercourse between us had prevailed for most of the day, indeed almost all the while that she communicated her story. Its performance, however, occasioned a good many unwelcome observations from among our fellow patrons at the White-Conduit House. Some of them seated in booths nearby had been so rude as to snigger at us behind their hands and point; others whispered to companions, nodding in our direction; still others frowned as if in grave disapproval, swiftly looking away as though anxious to convince themselves we did not exist.

Quickly growing vexed by these impertinent attentions, her ladyship had any number of times declared that we must depart; but, unwilling to capitulate to such impudence on the part of these other tea-drinkers, I had become fiercely resolved that we should not budge one inch from our station. I therefore remained deaf to her pleas and, as she continued her story upon my command, recommenced caressing the back of her neck ever more fondly and obviously, all the while hotly challenging these spectators with my eyes. The conspicuous attentions of this audience were, however, a great puzzle to me. Why it was we were such special subjects of these titters and lingering glances I could not fathom, for the tea-room was by no means short of other pairs of ladies and gentlemen similarly engaged in displays of mutual affection; other pairs, however, whose amorous pleasures over their cups of tea were unaccountably immune to such commentary and observation.

Once inside the hack, it seemed my lady's reserve had vanished, and I was hoping to gain further favours from her lips. Now, however, our vehicle had turned up Holborn Hill—where the sun could be seen setting behind Gray's Inn, the fat clouds above it having turned the colour of goldfish—and suddenly she unclasped my hands and recommenced her story.

324

Thirty-four

 The curtain did not rise upon Mr Handel's new opera, called *Philomela*, until somewhat later than anticipated; not, that is, until the first week in December.

The King had returned from Hanover a month previously, after a rough crossing during which violent tempests had forced the royal squadron back into Helvoetsluys. The fierce tempests then endured for the rest of the year, as the equinoctial gales—interpreted by some as a divine retribution in lieu of the plague, which had failed to make its vengeful appearance—declined to abate. The King discovered his city, and his subjects, to be much altered since he departed from them in the summer. After the mobs and outcries of September—when stocks fell from 830 to 750, then below 700, then to 550, dragging all else with them, including stock in the Academy—all had fallen silent as people withdrew to contemplate their ruin. If the dire prediction of the gentleman in Newgate Street did not prove strictly true, some victims did indeed perish of the distemper. The nephew of a director of the Company cut his throat with a razor and a few unhappy investors leapt into the Fleet or the Thames, the pockets of their handsome silk coats filled with stones; while others, seeking a more dilatory end, were borne to their graves upon a river of gin. Less seriously, skirmishes broke out in Exchange Alley, occasionally someone was stabbed, and before September was out two stock-jobbers were fired upon in the street.

By October the streets and shops had emptied. In the coachmen's yards, the shipyards, the squares—once such restless hives—one now saw only, in place of the earlier activities, the lath skeletons of half-finished chariots, barges, mansions; as if these were so many crumbling beasts whose flesh had been gnawed, their bones picked, by invisible predators; bones through which, by spring, the grass would begin to grow. Those chariots, barges or mansions that had been finished remained unclaimed, as did thousands upon

325

thousands of embroidered coats, gold watches and buckles, panelled snuff-boxes, beaver hats, silver swords, marble canes. Two thousand tradesmen—mostly milliners, tailors, drapers, lace-makers, haberdashers, perfumers, and the like—were broken without having wagered a single guinea on the fortunes of the South Sea Company. And of course the rough-masons, carpenters, joiners, tilers, plumbers—well . . . Not even His Majesty—who some claimed commenced this madness in the first place—had been immune to the disaster, for it was rumoured that his £66,000 stocks, pledged the previous April, had declined in value to no better than £10,000.

But the King appeared to suffer his losses more philosophically than most. In November Tristano was summoned to meet him at Kensington House, in one of the new State Rooms, which, half-finished, was as skeletal and littered with dried gobs of plaster as anything in London. He was required to kneel in his silk stockings and velvet breeches upon a carpet that was freckled with dust and only partly unrolled. Before him, in a high-backed mahogany chair, lolled a less than regal-looking character. The monarch of the land looked indeed like nothing so much as a vulgar country squire: his shirt-ruffles and waistcoat were bespattered with snuff, his stockinged foot was elevated and bandaged on account of the gout, and he was conversing in jovial tones, and in German, with a lady—introduced as Madame Kielmansegge—and scarcely with anyone else. A long tobacco-pipe sat at one elbow, a mug of ale at the other; pleasures likewise partaken of by Madame Kielmansegge, who had a pipe and a mug of her own. She, it was rumoured, was one of the few wise enough to sell her shares before the violent waters of the South Seas crashed upon her doorstep.

Tristano had seen both of them the previous evening in the Haymarket, for the opening of the new opera season. It had commenced, in lieu of *Philomela*—which Mr Handel was yet composing, working both day and night, refusing all forms of sustenance but tobacco—with Signor Bononcini's *Astarto*. The King had been perched in his stage-box, chattering and laughing and playing cards with Madame Kielmansegge and two other ladies, each a duchess. Evidently these activities had prevented His Majesty from paying close attention to the opera, for he now commanded Tristano—

whom, quite unaccountably, he persisted in calling 'Signor Senesino'—to sing one of its arias. Tristano started to explain that he had not in fact performed in *Astarto*—the real Signor Senesino had sung instead—but Lord W—, who was standing behind him, quickly whispered:

—Sing anything—you may be sure the old dolt will not know the difference!

Astarto, surprisingly, had been a great success: twenty-four performances. Not even *Radamisto* had been favoured with so many. A remarkable feat by Signor Bononcini, all things—that is, the disaster of the Bubble—considered. Perhaps too remarkable a feat for some. Mr Handel, shut away in his apartment in Lord Burlington's mansion in Piccadilly, was rumoured to be jealous of the generous reception given Signor Bononcini; to be raging at Lord Burlington for traitorously bringing this new composer to London; to be most anxious for the triumph of his newest work, *Philomela*. Tristano might have given some credence to these rumours—for Mr Handel was certainly an irascible fellow— had he not also heard rumours that he himself was supposedly intriguing against Senesino.

In truth, however, Tristano had other things to worry about, things more serious than Senesino (who was, it must be admitted, a most vain, coarse creature). No—he had deeper worries, rather, about his position in England, which since he returned from Smithfield had become dangerously tenuous. For the Royal Academy of Music and Lord W— both—and especially the latter—had seen their fortunes turn for the worse in September.

—We shall have to set to packing and betake ourselves away, Lady W— had said quite calmly a day after the mob had rushed along Newgate Street in the direction of South Sea House. She had received the news of her husband's losses with much equanimity, as if they marked some *felix culpa*. He, however, not so. Indeed, he had been strangely bereft of the forbearance that always served him so well whenever he was forced to acknowledge his frequent losses at the gaming-tables. I doubt, she said in her steady tone, that there is aught else we may do.

—Ho! And wouldn't you love that, my dearest lady!

His lordship's hand was resting upon a bust of his father, the first Lord W—, who wore a King William cravat and a disapproving expression. So disapproving was the latter that this marble effigy appeared to have been put out of countenance upon being apprised of how the fortune his original had piled up in the Turkey trade was now demolished by the son in, as it were, a single afternoon; in the time it took to black a pair of boots.

—To drag me away thus, roared his lordship, out of London and into the country! Well, the mistress shall not be master just yet, upon my honour. No, I will not allow my losses to unman me thus!

—We shall have to sell all, her ladyship replied simply, then added, somewhat more harshly: And your Italian capon will have to be sold, too. We cannot afford to keep him and his finery now.

His lordship snorted.

—I should think, he said, that the pot has called the kettle black-arse.

—I will not tolerate him within my house a day longer.

—Then he must return to Italy, replied his lordship in no particular manner, for the Academy cannot pay him now.

—Then do so. Ship him back to Italy upon the next packet.

Tristano, as will be imagined, did not overhear this debate with indifference. Listening to the exchange from behind the open door of the library, he felt a douche of fear run down his loins and legs as the terrible visage of Count Provenzale—who yet choked him in the occasional dream— rose before his eyes. Then, however, his lordship said something most peculiar, unaccountable:

—Even if he is the means through which we may redeem ourselves?

—Whatever it is, her ladyship quickly responded, I will not pay any such price for redemption. Then she paused. My father, she continued, may redeem us as easily . . .

—I will not hear of it for an instant, he replied in a grim voice. I tell you, I will not be unmanned thus!

With a surly roar, and kicking over an encrusted bucket left by the plasterer (who had been released from his services the day before), he stomped up the spiral steps, whose banisters were unfinished and fated to remain so— like so much else about the house—for a good many months to come.

For the past day, since the coach-and-six returned from Smithfield, roles in the mansion in St James's Square had been neatly exchanged. Lady W— now issued the cold commands, while her husband fell prey to violent transports of emotion and disappeared for hours on end into his chamber, leaving his meals untouched outside the door. Her health, it seemed, had miraculously improved, while from his chambers there now came the rattle of bottles whose contents were seldom looked upon with favour even by the most unschooled quacks. Their dispute endured throughout September and into October, at the end of which Lady W— made threats to remove herself, along with her dogs and serving-maids, to Richmond; at other times, when the disagreement grew particularly fierce, to her father's castle in the Highlands. The central issue in the disagreement— perhaps in place of those larger things that neither could suffer to face—had become Tristano's continued residence in St James's Square. By early December Lady W— was upon the verge of a victory, for Tristano had begun arranging lodgings in Burlington House, where, he reasoned, not even the peevish Mr Handel could possibly prove so disagreeable as her ladyship. Yet quite unexpectedly, she underwent a change of opinion and, upon the eventful morning after the curtain at last rose upon *Philomela*, tossed away this impending triumph.

His lordship, returning from the snow of Hyde Park a victorious warrior with blood staining his shirt-ruffles, supposed it had been his fearsome appearance that morning— his manly expression and his bloody sword—that had at last altered her resolution. Little did he guess the true reason; at least, not for a time.

But again I run too far ahead of my story, and we must now return to the night of the opening performance of *Philomela*.

The opera's libretto—I have, I believe, a copy of it somewhere—was cobbled together for Mr Handel's opera from an earlier libretto written for Signor Piozzi by Gaetano, the stuttering poet, who in turn cobbled it together for the maestro's greatest opera, likewise called *Philomela*, from a still earlier libretto. A simple enough story, that of Philomela; none of the avenging armies and usurping brothers and magic spirits of Mr Handel's other more spectacular operas. No, merely a tale of how art and beauty—how painting and music—may grow out of the most horrible acts of barbarism.

Perhaps you have heard the story of Philomela, beautiful daughter of Pandion, King of Athens? Perhaps you know this tragic tale, the opera's *argomento*? Ah, so you have read of it in Ovid's *Metamorphoses*? Yes, good: then you will remember how the tale begins how most happy ones end—with a wedding. How Philomela's sister, Procne, weds her father's ally, King Tereus of Thrace. Alas, this wedding is not a happy occasion; the signs are not auspicious; the gods do not smile upon the union. But in time the new couple is blessed with a son, little Itys; the very image of his father. Then—tragedy. The treacherous Tereus, after inviting the virgin Philomela to Thrace, cruelly violates her, and then, to prevent his terrible deed from being exposed, cuts out her tongue with his sword. She communicates his guilt upon a loom to her sister Procne—Philomela weaves the most beautiful tapestry ever seen—who, in taking revenge upon her evil husband, murders Itys and serves his flesh in a dish to his villainous father. The barbarous Tereus pursues Philomela, but the gods are moved to pity and transform her into a nightingale. No longer mute—no longer mutilated—she sings to the world of her sufferings in the most beautiful voice ever heard.

Well, that at least is the story in its barest bones. What I have told in these few words now stretches to well over three hours; over three acts with eleven scenes each, with two intermezzi in which there are performances by, first, ballet dancers and then a viola d'amore. Thirty-two arias, four duets, three long recitatives . . .

Hush now—the performance begins. Outside in the Haymarket the colonnade is crowded with sedan-chairs, the stable-yards are full. Inside, the candles in the galleries are snuffed as the heavy curtain rises with a rattle and creak, swishing like a lady's petticoats across the floor of a great ballroom. So raised, it reveals two white columns—like a pair of legs beneath these skirts—and, behind them, sliding flats, a painted backcloth, other shapes yet in shadow.

Above the stage, shutters slap open, hands of cards are folded, heads crane. The murmuring ceases, a dammed river of babble. Orange-girls pick their way gingerly through the fresh darkness, mindful of toppling into the orchestra pit. The gentlemen at the pit doors become statues of themselves, while above their black tricornes the boxes and galleries are filled with row upon row of powdered heads. Among them, those of Lord and Lady W— in their taffeta-draped box prominently situated beneath the painted proscenium arch: the better for her ladyship to be relished by the eyes of the assembly. Count Heidegger is in his manager's box, having a moment before descended the staircase leading from his magnificent apartment above the opera house. A short distance away the King may be seen in the royal box, Madame Kielmansegge beside him with a jealousy glass. Never has the King seen so many of his subjects at one time, in one place. Indeed, so many tickets have been sold tonight that people are sitting upon the edges of the stage itself, legs crossed like tailors' apprentices; some fine lords and ladies among them. Or, rather, His Majesty *would* have seen this unsurpassed multitude were he not playing backgammon so attentively with Madame Kielmansegge.

Now in the wax-lights of the stage you may see Mr Handel—*there*—at his conductor's harpsichord, his periwig a white glow. 'Il Signor Giorgio Federico Handel', according to the libretto. Arranged about him in two tiered crescents are thirty-seven musicians. Violins, violas, cellos, lutes, basses, flutes, oboes, bassoons, kettledrums, even a harp. The peg-boxes, the violin bows and the narrow bells of the woodwinds all rise up in shadows, like reeds from the floor of a marsh in which the musicians sit waist-deep; the two tenor lutes with their bent peg-boxes like fat wooden geese, the long-necked theorbo a swan straining at a branch.

Now, beyond them, the first set, designed by Signor Roberto Scarabelli, has come more clearly into view. A new trickle of murmurs. *Atto primo, scena prima*—as the libretto explains—presents the Temple of Juno: a squat, domed construction standing at a short remove from the two Corinthian columns entwined with vines and flanked on either side by two palm trees in large pots—where the deuce did Signor Scarabelli come by *those*?—and the same number of barefooted maidens in white robes. Painted flats show a mountain range—truly more Alpine-looking than Grecian—and the distant shore of a ruffled blue sea. As the attendants step away from the temple, the goddess—likewise barefoot and wearing a white robe—emerges from its interior. At this same instant Mr Handel energetically strikes his keys—there will be no broken strings tonight—

331

and the instruments before him, the bows and bells, stir as if a wind has rushed over them. An overture rises from the dark marsh. Then after a moment the goddess, a soprano— 'La Signora Anastasia Robinson'—begins a dignified *aria di portimento*, holding the notes exquisitely in her throat and upon her lips, and thereby so impressing the audience (most of whom have not actually understood one word of her lament), that almost before she has finished the aria they are loudly voicing requests for its repetition.

But the goddess has disappeared back into her temple, and now the front of the stage is crowded with a dozen Furies, their faces garishly masked, the backs of their ragged red-and-black garb affixed with papier-mâché wings. In their hands they bear smoking torches, which they proceed to flourish vigorously in the air. Half their number have entered from above, descending to the stage—one rather too heavily, spilling on to her rump—on the invisible wires of an aerial machine, the pulleys clacking and whining. Now they rush to and fro with their torches among the columns and round the temple, screeching and laughing as a four-posted bed is lowered to the stage—likewise from the sky— then set alight by their torches. Flames dance upwards and a black smoke billows across the front of the stage—fanned by smoke operators hidden in the wings—as the Furies, still cackling, disappear through these clouds to either side of the stage or, flying upwards on their invisible strings, into the sky.

The audience has enjoyed this little spectacle even more than Juno's aria, and a loud clapping and cheering spills down from the galleries.

—Heigh-ho! cries Lord W— from his box, lustily joining these encomiums. Damnably good! Damn me if it is not an excellent business!

Her ladyship is more reserved with her comments. She has been conducted here only under duress. She is unwell. Epsom salts for her stomach, a cephalic draught for her head, volatile salts should she suddenly feel faint, a flask of spa water if thirsty ('ferruginous chalybeate', from the gardens of Sadler's Wells Theatre), as well as various other potions and elixirs sold by her doctor—all are ranged before her in the box, next to his lordship's snuff-box and bottle of claret, and all will be called anxiously into service before the evening is out. For her nerves, delicate at the best of

332

times, are, in these worst of times, in an intolerable condition. She fans herself with the pages of her libretto and wonders how much longer she must suffer in this place.

Scena seconda: a State Room in the palace of King Pandion. The stage has cleared of smoke, the bed has disappeared, and amid much slapping and banging a series of flats have slid into view, presenting not mountains but, through a bank of windows, the tall needles of obelisks, the round cuticles of domes. Burning candelabra, torchères, urns, framed paintings, rich tapestries and a tall-backed throne have all appeared. Between the two columns left over from the Temple of Juno there now emerges a bridal party, moving slowly as the violins sigh and wheeze, as the basses mumble happily; the chorus in a crescent behind them, all in white. A *recitativo* begins as the bridal pair—Tereus and Procne (the latter being 'La Signora Robinson' again, differently attired)—stand together, their heads garlanded with flowers. This piece, sung by the choristers but with additions by King Pandion, a bass, goes on for some time; goes on and on and . . . on: the history of the two nations, the late wars, the two kings like brothers, pledges of friendship—and so forth. The music—furiously paced for the exploits of the Furies—has now slowed to a soft river of flutes and strings with a sluggish bass undertow. The audience swiftly grows bored; feet shuffle; some, led by Lord W—, begin demanding a return of the Furies.

—Quiet, commands her ladyship, frowning. How much more of this nonsense? Oh, why did she ever submit to attend! Her doctor—*he* advised her to come, spoke of how music had powers to calm the tempestuous sallies of the soul and bring it into a state of proper harmony—more efficaciously even than her draughts and spa waters, or so he had claimed. But thus far the effects of the music are all bad. It is much too loud; already her head begins to ache. Besides, she is too warm, perspiring lightly: the heat of so many candles and torches on the stage, of so many cramped bodies. For the evening is so unseasonably warm for December. Warm and windy. The fierce gale that accompanied their coach journey from St James's Square to the stable-yard in the Haymarket—for she had stubbornly refused to walk the short distance, even though it was plain the streets were so crowded with coaches and chariots that the voyage from door to door would take thirty minutes or more—has greatly disturbed her hair, which was set only two days before, whorled like the shell of a snail. Now this smoke: it all seems to have floated up towards the proscenium arch, to her box. She is weak of chest and can now feel her delicate lungs being restricted by the noxious fumes, can feel a cough building—or perhaps even something more concerning.

—A wretched valetudinarian, his lordship had been snarling at her two hours before, through the closed door of her boudoir, that is what you are, madam. Upon my veracity, worse than an ancient dowager griping about her corns!

—Then it is you, my lord, who has made me so, she replied through the door as one of her serving-maids squeezed her into the corset and another trickled into her mouth a brandy cordial flavoured with aniseed and liquorice.

Earlier she had been pleading her health in an attempt to escape the performance, but his lordship would have none of it: a gown ordered from a dressmaker on the Pont au Change had finally arrived, and he was damned, he said, if she would not be wearing it—all 50 louis d'or's worth— and sitting at his side when the curtain rose. Her spirits, sinking ever lower, were revived only when, upon descending the stairs at the summons of the coachman, she glimpsed Tristano's portmanteaus—a battered-looking trio—stacked in the atrium, packed for their departure to Piccadilly.

Now because of the smoke and the heat and the noise she requires another draught of the cordial, whose trembling administration draws his lordship's attention from the stage. He snorts violently—Bah!—before recommencing his appeals for the Furies.

This cross exclamation in turn draws the attention of two fellows in the adjacent box, who turn to peer at their quarrelling neighbours, then to smile kindly at her ladyship as she treats herself with another draught. Her distressed hair and rapid breathing have given her an amorous appearance, as if she has recently emerged from the exertions of the bedchamber. The gentlemen's smiles widen, becoming ever more solicitous: for a weak constitution and delicate nerves are not universally despised among his lordship's race, and indeed among a certain sort of gentlemen are regarded with no mean esteem as tokens of the greatest virtue and sensibility.

334

—Madam, says the nearest of the gentlemen, bowing his head while retaining his smile.

On the stage, the *recitativo* has at long last ended with a few piercing notes from the flautist, and King Tereus, the bridegroom, now steps forward in all his nuptial finery. A tall soprano—'Il Signor Francesco Bernardi,' reports the libretto, 'otherwise known as *Senesino*'—he begins singing an aside to his servant, Lysander (in fact 'La Signora Margherita Rolli', an alto). His eyes are travelling this way and that, and he strokes a black moustachio as he confides to Lysander how his eye had been caught by his new sister-in-law, Philomela; how perchance he has wedded the wrong sister. His lust at the sight of her, he confesses, burns like ripe grain, like dried-out leaves, like old hay-ricks. To win her, he declares, he will bribe her guardians, her faithful nurse; he will even lose his kingdom! Why, he must have her! Oh, he *shall* have her—or die!

The audience's few imprecations at this shameful admission of dishonourable intent are scarcely voiced in the galleries before the fair creature who has raised these unworthy desires steps forth from among the chorus: indeed, a fine-looking lady, dressed for the occasion in white, adorned with flowers, her arms bare. A brief rustle of libretti ensues as the singer's name is sought in the libretto's *personaggi*: 'Il Signor Tristano Pieretti'.

Hardly has the audience had time to digest this fact—which occasions in the footman's gallery a few titters and catcalls ('A eunuch dressed in petticoats!') and, from Lady W—, a sigh of disgust—when a duet between the two sopranos commences. Perhaps, sings Tereus, Philomela will one day visit Thrace? No, it is much too far; her father is growing old and requires her in Athens. But if she pleases he will send a ship. No, she would be frightened to journey across the waves. Not even, then, to see her beloved sister, Procne? Of course she loves Procne, yet ... Why then, he insists—and so on and on in this vein: Tereus pleading, Philomela demurring; their voices interweaving, rising and falling, rushing and retreating, *largo* and then *presto*, echoed by tremolos from the violas and cellos.

Titters and catcalls repented or forgotten, the audience is still applauding—some are even standing, others weeping—as the company sweeps from the stage. Then a rapid scene change—more sliding and banging of flats—as the choristers announce (over the continuing cheers) that five years have now passed; five years during which time a son, Itys, has been born in Thrace: the future king, a darling boy, the perfect picture of his father. Five years, too, during which Philomela, yet unmarried, has pined desperately for her sister, for a sight of young Itys: all of this she confesses to her nurse as the two of them stroll through a bower shaded by palm trees.

The audience sits, shuffles again, prepared once more to be bored, but now one of the sliding-flats is withdrawn to display a small waterfall spilling into a pool. The audience stirs and murmurs at the sight, then stirs and murmurs even more as two swans—live ones, surely?—are delivered into it through an attached conduit, their wings flapping in protest and, in doing so, extinguishing several of the candles. Then as the swans make their exit through another channel—to cries of acclaim from the galleries and demands for an encore—King Pandion appears in his great purple-and-ermine robe, several choristers in his train, now dressed smartly as courtiers. He is older now, stooped. Philomela rushes to him, wheedles, coaxes, pleads: O beloved father, I beg of you . . . No, Pandion sings in his strong bass, holding up his hand—she shall not go; he has already lost one daughter to the imperatives of geography, he is determined he shall not lose another.

—*T'amo, o bella Philomela*, this dignified old gentleman sings, *t'amo, il confesso*—and if she loves him in return, he says, she must stay, she must remain here, in Athens . . .

But the old king relents, of course—though only after ten more minutes of such exchanges—and Philomela now sings her farewell aria, a sorrowful *largo*: how she shall miss him, O her dearest father; how she shall hurry back into his arms once her eyes are satisfied with a tender glimpse of her beloved Procne . . . This is Tristano's first *aria cantabile*, a slow and pathetic piece, which, once completed—the last note hanging suspended in the still air of the theatre for, it seems, a full minute before gently disappearing—draws even louder endorsements than the swans, louder than for the duet with Senesino.

—Lawdy, declares Lord W—, they will be humming that ditty in the coffee-houses tomorrow, upon my word!

The audience is now chanting for the aria's repetition even as the lighting changes and the next scene begins.

Tristano is loudly pronounced by some in the upper galleries as the superior of the great Nicolini, by others as that even of the sublime Farinelli. No, protest a third faction, Senesino—*his* is surely the finest soprano voice of all. Why, his vibrato is that of a laughing angel tickled by swan's down! No, no, *no*, respond the others, it must be Tristano or no one!

—Senesino!

—Tristano!

—*Senesino*!

—*Tristano*! shouts Lady W— in the midst of this chorus, quite without premeditation, her voice the loudest of all. For there is no doubt in her mind: why, that voice—so sweet and impassioned—such a tone of pathos and sensibility! Yet her doctor was mistaken, for the sounds did not calm the wild transports of her soul; rather, they roused them to a more passionate pitch, to a height they had never before scaled. From this wondrous promontory with its rare and novel air she gazes down upon Tristano, seeing him as if for the first time: how different he now seems, this celestial creature upon the stage, from the ugly, murmuring little monster with the bent nose and black eyes who has been haunting her chambers for these past four months. During the exchange with Pandion she was dizzy and in need of a constant succession of draughts and powders (thus attracting the ever more interested attention of the fellows in the next box), yet now the apothecary shop scattered before her is quite forgotten and, with the others, she cries for an encore.

But now, drowning out these cries, there comes a rumble and screech of casters as a ship is rolled on to the stage, the palm trees off. An immense construction, this ship, with webby rigging and a slack foresail throwing the pit into shadow. The bowsprit seems to terminate a few scant feet short of the proscenium arch. Her ladyship grows dizzy again simply looking at it. A new backcloth drops, representing a blue sea with great pyramidal waves crested white; a pattern soon repeated by the sliding-flats. Alas, the impression of the vastness of this sea beyond the vessel—rocking on its casters now—is somewhat diminished, first by the sight of a fellow from the audience taking a pinch of snuff with an apparent unconcern for the murderous waves towering above his periwig, then by the sight of part of the painted grove formerly seen comprising the pleasant bower.

Only when the audience laughs with pleasure at the incongruous spectacle are the trees retracted and hastily replaced by rolling waves.

Philomela appears on the ship's deck, below the mizensail, attired in an aquamarine gown fitted with dozens of gold brocades, bows, froggings. A pose similar to that of the Lydian princess in Signor Piozzi's *Oeneus*. The choristers have become sailors, who are battening hatches, cinching knots, raising a papier-mâché anchor, rushing fore and aft. Evidently a tempest has blown up: the ship begins rocking, rocking, sliding this way and that. With the ostrich feathers on her behatted head bowing and rising she grasps one of the spars and begins another aria, this time with much accompaniment: the timpani are smitten violently, the cellists' hands shiver on the necks of their instruments as the bows parry and thrust like rapiers.

The tempest aria, a furious *presto*. Blow you winds, she sings. O you perilous zephyrs, blow me to Thrace, swiftly, swiftly. O you tempestuous breezes, blow, blow; then blow me back once more to Athens. And so forth. A coloratura piece, one as difficult as anything produced by the quill of Signor Piozzi; a true trial of strength, a challenge from Mr Handel's quill to Tristano's throat. His voice matches the C in the middle of the composer's harpsichord, then rises, miraculously, two notes above it; each note so clear and full, so exquisite . . .

Cheers rise up from among Tristano's noisy faction, hoots of derision from the supporters of Senesino. But Signor Scarabelli has tricks in store, which soon succeed in quieting all of them. As Philomela advances, slipping and sliding, towards the main-mast—whose sail, on account of the rocking, is now flapping like laundry in a breeze—a pasteboard dolphin suddenly appears on the starboard side, nodding and bobbing in the vat of water into which, earlier, the fountain has flowed. Scarcely does the audience have opportunity to appreciate the artfulness of the fish's design before a rocket concealed in its tail fin sizzles and pops. Projected with a splash from the vat, it crosses in a parabola before the ship's bow, then in a flash travels across the stage through the air. This voyage terminates only when the creature's body—slightly mangled on account of the charge, its wires and lead weights visible—comes to rest against the alarmed snuff-taker (now seated comfortably before the thundering waves), who promptly spills half the contents of his snuff-box on to the blunt head of this new arrival, the remainder into his own shirt-ruffles.

The audience roars its approval at the dolphin's progress—though many have recently seen a version of this stunt performed in Winstanley's Water Theatre behind St James's Park—but then exclaims even louder as, the aria finishing, the Furies reappear with their masks and torches, flapping their papier-mâché wings and in a chorus warning Philomela to turn back. The music from the pit grows ever more portentous, the bassoons and double-basses grumbling ominously, the violins shrieking above them. Turn back, O turn back . . .

Too late: the coast of Thrace has come into view with a hard slam. Then a few more slams and, as the waves disappear, Thrace proves to be a rocky desert filled with caves and precipices; a most unpromising land. The ship ceases its back-and-forth motions. The Furies have disappeared, as have the sailors, many of whom have been tumbling about on the deck like dice on a draught-board. With Philomela still perched beneath the now drooping mizen-sail Tereus—there he is, the villain, upon the shore, still stroking his moustachio—sings a song of welcome, accompanied only by Lysander. But where, Philomela inquires, interrupting, is Procne? Why, at home with Itys, he replies; awaiting her arrival. Come, O fair lady, he sings, and you shall greet her. Yes, she replies, such a journey have I had . . .

The timpani thump and pound, the double-basses rumble and thrum.

Then I beg of you, come here, sings Tereus, and I shall lead you to her, straight away. I bid you welcome. O come, your sister awaits us; my son awaits us . . .

She descends the gangplank, is embraced by Tereus, who leads her from the stage, leaning upon her, leering, fondling her. This way, he sings as the music thrashes; this is the way, O my dearest sister, why should you resist? Come with me, O come with me, dearest sister . . .

They disappear, slowly, into the dark coulisses, followed by Lysander. Then, silence. The figures in the orchestra pit grow still, like posed waxworks. Then after a long moment—after the timpani begin their rumble, after the tragic bleating of the cellos and the high-pitched shivering of the violins commence—Philomela stumblingly reappears: her blue

339

dress is torn, the bows and ribbons scattering before her feet like golden petals.

O agony! Such sorrow! Can tongue express, ears receive? Another *aria cantabile*, this one recounting in a plaintive vibrato how she has been betrayed, violated, destroyed. In the pit the strings weep, the wood-winds sing like the wind in a lonely grotto; silken sounds whose beauty is surpassed only by that of Tristano's voice. Such beauty that even Senesino's camp is being won over! But then even before she finishes—she has fallen to her knees now—the cruel Tereus has appeared behind her, has withdrawn a knife from his belt, has grasped a handful of her hair and tipped back her head . . .

—My salts, Lady W— is saying, fumbling about in the dimness of the stage-box, knocking over bottles: her own cordials and ferruginous chalybeate, then the half-finished claret. The latter event occasions a sharp bellow from his lordship, who applies a handkerchief to the groin of his velvet breeches and squirms about in his seat as if the bottle had contained not claret but hot coals.

—Damn you your eyes, he is cursing as he appraises the dark red stain. Lookee, my breeches! What the deuce—?

—My salts, she whimpers, this time spilling his snuff-box on to the floor with a loud clatter. Every nerve in her body vibrates, every membrane swells. She makes to stand and then, venting a loud shriek—a cry much louder than his lordship's, and much louder, even, than the loud lament of disconsolate Philomela—collapses to the floor of the box.

But before her brow has struck his lordship's boots two things—or, rather, a hundred things—have happened. For in the second of her scream a hundred heads have swung from the stage to his lordship's box, those of the gentlemen in the next box included. Both of these fellows rapidly spring to their feet, as if their end of an invisible see-saw has propelled them into the air whilst her ladyship's has bounced her to the ground.

And upon the stage, unseen now by everyone, Tereus is so startled by the sound as he wields the knife before Philomela's face—is it *she*, he wonders, who screams?—that his hand quavers and the gleaming blade slips quickly through his kneeling victim's astonished flesh.

Thirty-five

'Exactly a fortnight after this performance, Tristano departed in his lordship's coach for Bath.'

Lady Beauclair, her back to me, was riffling through the contents of a bureau. From without and below came the clopping sounds of our departing hack, and through the window-panes the lobster's tail of St Giles-in-the-Fields looked to be on fire, so brilliant was the sun—still not quite set—spread out behind it.

'Tell me, Mr Cautley, have you ever perchance visited this great Pool of Bethesda? It is, more than anywhere else upon our island,' she recommended before I had opportunity to respond to this inquiry, 'a place of hope, of promises, perhaps even of miracles. A place of many pilgrimages, though not ones undertaken for the sake of the soul—like Canterbury—but those suffered for the aid of the body and its many complaints. A place where the flesh and bones of the fragile and weak'—rummage, rummage—'are healed of their wounds and diseases. So many disfigured bodies seeking a cure. Wealthy gentlemen with intestinal hernias and venereal complaints, fashionable ladies with melancholy or scorbulic humours, noble children with catarrhs and chancres, old admirals with gout, gumboils and the scars of victorious sea battles—all becoming pilgrims to this spa, all making themselves supplicants'—rummage, rummage—'before its hot waters.'

Leaving off her efforts, she straightened with a dull sigh. She had been in search of the libretto, removing from the bureau great sheafs of paper: what looked to be dozens of letters, their wax seals still clinging in red splotches to the outer pages; also a pamphlet, whose title I could not quite read: *A True and Genuine Narrative of* ... Of what? Of something. Of someone.

'No,' she said as if to herself, 'I fancy it is not here ...'

I swiftly averted my eyes as she turned round, for while bringing the copper tea-kettle to the boil over a spirit-lamp and preparing an infusion of green tea—this task she assigned me upon our arrival at her lodgings a few moments before—I had been craftily studying her ankles, tantalisingly exposed as she leaned over the bureau's drawers. The nape of her neck was likewise disclosed to my hungry view as her ringlets of hair—an untinctured black again in the semidarkness of the chamber—slipped forward from her crown in the midst of her search.

'Perhaps I have packed it away in the portmanteau—yes, yes, I believe so. Please, if you will excuse me . . .'

Her skirts swirled as she disappeared into the bedchamber, which quickly became the source of a great number of grunts and clunks, as if something were being manufactured inside.

'First,' she was calling to me through the open door, 'first of all came the Ancient Britons—led by the leprous king, Bladud—then the Romans, then Queen Bess and later Queen Henrietta Maria and Queen Nan. Ugh!'

Something was dropped to the floor, then I heard the door of the wardrobe creak and sigh. The kettle gurgled, and I quickly poured its contents into the china teapot; a brief cavernous roar, the tea-leaves swimming and dancing.

'King Charles II,' she continued, 'brought his bride, Catherine of Braganza, in the hope that she might be cured of barrenness by the salubrious waters; and then Mary of Modena visited for similar reasons a short while later—alas, with much better success, for shortly thereafter the Pretender was born'—another thump—'and our nation's freedoms lay in the utmost peril. I believe the papists have erected a monument to this occasion in one of the baths . . .'

'I have never journeyed to this spa,' I called to her when this speech seemed to have run its length, replaced now by a series of rustles and flaps. 'My health being sound, I have been so fortunate as never to require such a recourse.'

'I pray it may always be so,' came her reply. 'But, "fortunate"? You would not say so had you but paid a visit during the season. During the time of balls and other entertainments, that is, when the card-room is full, the parades crowded with the finest ladies and gentlemen, the bells in the great Abbey ringing as the carriage of each new Person of Quality appears in the London Road . . .'

A long pause, filled with more rustles and flaps. I

342

wondered, should I offer my assistance? After a moment, though, she continued:

'I travelled there with Tristano. When? Not so very long ago. A matter of a few years. It was a place—perhaps the *sole* place—where, albeit for a very short time, he was truly happy. Bath then was greatly different from the place it is today. Fifty years ago it was much smaller, its narrow streets like dunghills, its roof spouts generously anointing the head of each passer-by. No squares, crescents, parades, terraces. Cramped lodgings, few water-closets. Then, too, he arrived in the winter season—Oh, I am getting so far ahead of myself here . . .'

By now the strange noises had ceased, and in an ensuing silence she appeared in the doorway.

'Here, sir,' she said in a quieter tone, extending her hand, which clutched what looked to be a loose sheaf of papers. 'I have discovered the libretto. It is Lady W—'s copy. The copy she had with her in the box upon that fateful evening.'

'Fateful . . .?'

My eyes were swiftly drawn away from this object of her search, however, as were my thoughts from her story: for in the bedchamber she had also found not only the libretto but also the Turkish costume, in which she was now attired, thus exposing—as she turned round for my appraisal—more of those regions I had been studying so secretively a few moments before. The light from behind the steeple fell across her shoulders—almost bare—setting the smooth skin alight.

And then, turning my eyes from this sight, I saw the opened drawer of the bureau, where the title of the pamphlet was now decipherable: *A True and Genuine Narrative of Signor Tristano Pieretti, Late of the King's Opera House.*

'The tea,' I whispered through my suddenly dry lips. 'Shall I now pour the tea, my lady?'

Thirty-six

A fortnight after the performance at the King's Theatre, Tristano departed for Bath in his lordship's coach. Strapped to the top of the vehicle were two of his three portmanteaus; inside, beside him, Lady W— and two of her serving-maids. Also her potions, salts, drops, chalybeates, medicinal herbs; enough of them for the two-day journey. The bottles rattled and chimed, making their sad music as the coach travelled westward: through Kensington, Hammersmith, Hounslow, then on to the Bath Road, past Cranford, Longford, Colnbrook, Windsor; all white and asleep under snow.

His face, bandaged, bled on to his ruffles, giving him the aspect of Lord W— upon that strangest of mornings a fortnight before. The morning, that is, when he awoke in his bedchamber—upon his bloodied linen—to hear his lordship's bellows echoing up through the banisterless staircase, as if from the bottom of a well. These were followed by her ladyship's cries—was she pleading?—which in turn were followed by more of his lordship's bellows, though of a more moderated variety. The outcome of this discussion, Tristano had no doubt, would prove most unfavourable to his position in the household.

He was therefore greatly perplexed when, upon encountering Lady W— as he crept down the stairs some thirty minutes later—just after the long-case clock outside his door chimed the hour of nine—he was greeted with a polite smile and a sympathetic inquiry regarding his health.

—Do not reply, she swiftly appended before he could respond. Doctor Lightholder says you must rest your voice.

His lordship, seated at the dining-table, had been less willing to observe such precautions.

—Are you quite well enough to journey? he demanded. His bloody shirt was still on his back and an enormous meal—potted venison, buttered turnips, plum pudding—sat half-consumed before him. He was refilling his cup with

344

Rhenish wine, the red stream wagging into his goblet and plashing a few drops on to the table.

Through his bandages Tristano replied in the affirmative, observing (with much pain to his lips involved in the effort) that Piccadilly was not in fact so far distant, a matter of a few short steps.

—Piccadilly? His lordship vigorously shook his head as he sucked at his fingers and then wiped them on his breeches, likewise stained with a blood evidently—judging from his enormous appetite—not that of his own veins. Piccadilly! he roared through a mouthful of turnips, which then sluiced noisily down his gullet, hurriedly pursued by three gulps of wine. You will not be going to Piccadilly! No, no—a change in plan, a change in plan. Prepare your trunks for Bath! Yes—Bath, I say!

For whatever reason—the prospect of travelling to this unknown town, the recent loss of so much of his own blood, the sight of someone else's profusely staining his lordship's clothing, the smell of such rich food at this hour of the morning, the onset of the dangerous fever that was to afflict him for the next eight days, or some profoundly dizzying combination of all—Tristano's sole response to this proclamation had been to collapse to the floor, where his brow struck his lordship's blood-spattered boots, to which a few fresh drops were added.

Now, as the coach travelled westward through Middlesex, his blood was steaming the cold air in thin tendrils that rose and lolled before his eyes. Afterwards, as the hours passed, it froze and stiffened the ruffles so that, as the coach bounced along, these scratched at his throat like finger-nails.

At an inn on the Buckinghamshire side of the River Colne the horses were exchanged and he replaced the plasters, which were made into a kind of poultice with the addition of extracts of periwinkle, Lady's mantle and pimpernel, all supplied upon Lady W—'s concerned initiative. He was also assisted in the operation by a parson who, seeking relief from rheumatism and a gouty toe, was likewise on his way to Bath and, owing to a broken wheel and a dislodged horseshoe, had been invited to share their carriage for the remainder of the journey.

Why did the wound not begin to heal? The stitchings, sewn a fortnight before, had yesterday been removed by the surgeon. He scarcely remembered either the fellow or

345

his house. After the accident—which was not interpreted as such by his supporters, much to the discredit of the unfortunate Senesino—he had been transported to the home of the renowned surgeon in Hanover Square. Dr Lightholder proved an ancient fellow whose infirm body—assisted in its slow journey to the door by both a cane and a more vigorous young manservant—inspired no great confidence in Tristano, who abruptly fainted beneath the Ionic porch. That he arrived upon the porch at all had been a miracle of sorts. He had fairly bled to death upon the stage before a few members of the audience could be persuaded that the spectacle they were beholding—the spreading pool of Philomela's blood—was not in fact one of Signor Scarabelli's latest clever tricks, and that as Senesino leapt about the stage, screeching incomprehensibly in Italian, he was completely sincere in his grief at having mutilated the figure lying prone before his feet.

Tristano had been revived—first upon the stage and then this short time later in Hanover Square—by Lady W—'s smelling bottle, opening his eyes each time to see through his panicked confusion her anxious but gentle expression, as well as something further that had not heretofore visited her features. After this second restoration of the senses Dr Lightholder lit a lamp and, blinking slowly (on account of being roused from a slumber made all the more restful by a strong potion of his own invention), daubed, stitched and then bandaged Tristano's right cheek and lips: for Tereus's startled and unwitting knife had laid these regions open in a long gash that stretched down from Tristano's right ear at a 45-degree angle to his crooked nose.

—As for your tongue, there is no need, the old man said, for 'tis not so badly cut and will heal itself in time.

—But I am a singer, Tristano had wanted to say. I shall require the offices of my tongue. I am nothing without my tongue—an ordinary man. A nothing. Senesino might as well have cut my throat as cut my tongue.

But of course on account of the wound—on account of his nicked tongue and sliced lips—he could utter not a word.

Her ladyship spoke for him.

—The good *signore* shall surely sing once more, she whispered with a gentle smile, though it seemed a note of urgency basted together this hopeful pronouncement.

Good *signore*?

His duties accomplished, Dr Lightholder—assisted again by the cane and the servant—had shuffled off to his bed. But then at first light he was roused by another pounding at his door and, summoning the manservant with the ring of a bell, shuffled back to the entrance.

—I fear we have arrived too late, a young gentleman shivering beneath the pediment had lamented, pointing to another of his kind who proceeded to topple through the door of his sedan-chair to the paving-stones as if diving into a clear blue lake.

Yet as fate would have it, this party had not in fact arrived too late, for after breaching the watered silk waistcoat, the sword—Lord W—'s—had missed the young fellow's liver by a clear inch.

—Then next time I shall slit the rascal's throat, his lordship proclaimed when this news was conducted to him in St James's Square by his second, a young marquess. He had consumed his turnips, venison and pudding by this point, and was now engaging both a gingerbread and a Scotch cake. Tristano, revived for a third time by her ladyship's smelling bottle, had been conducted upstairs, Dr Lightholder sent for.

—If the devil lays his paws on my wife again...! he growled to the marquess before the remainder of this threat was submerged beneath a mouthful of gingerbread.

—A doctor of physick, my arse, replied the marquess, reaching for a crumb of cake.

—He had been eyeballing her all evening—don't think I missed a bit of it!

—Not at all, my lord.

—His insinuating manner—his vile mischief—loosening her stays like that ... His voice was the very sound of sharp, tarry shingle turned by the winter waves.

The marquess cleared his throat delicately, while Lord W—'s visage resumed its murderous frown.

—Her ladyship looks very well this morning.

—That shall be unwelcome news to her, responded his lordship. Pray, Bob, do not say so to her face or she shall be much aggrieved.

—Then truly she is ill?

His lordship snorted. Why, undoubtedly!

—What ails her, then?

—Nothing but a disease called life. The cake dispatched,

347

he stood up, showering the floor with crumbs. She shall go to Bath.

—Then you will—?

He snorted again. Bath to him was—apart from its gaming—the most odious of places. Built upon a quagmire, impenetrable to the beams of the sun, so inaccessible that one risked breaking one's neck to reach it, only to find it filled, once one did arrive, with bony-haunched old men and their hypochondriac old dames . . .

—No, no, he replied, I shall remain in London and be devilish glad of it.

—Is that so very wise, my lord? It was the turn of the marquess to frown.

His lordship laughed grimly as the murderous frown threatened a reappearance.

—Yes, he said, there are many such 'doctors of physick' in Bath at this time of the season, are there not? Upon my word, many hands willing to assist her—*fondle* her—should she faint. No, you are perfectly right, Bob. Therefore she must needs be accompanied by a guardian. Someone I may trust utterly, as with a bag of gold. Ah—Dr Lightholder! Up the staircase—yes, just so—up, up—mind the banisters! Then muttering: Old fool!

The marquess, biting his lip, seemed perplexed. An ancient codger such as that . . .?

His lordship chuckled merrily: the sound of a rusted clapper striking the cracked fragments of a bell.

—No, Bob, he said, I must unpuzzle you—here, lookee—haw haw haw! Read it aloud, dear fellow, read it aloud.

He drew from his bloodied shirt and thrust into the marquess's hand a broadsheet purchased that morning from a ballad-monger in Brick Street, off Hyde Park Corner. Entitled 'An Epistle from Signor T——o P——i to a Young Lady', the poem—an anonymous composition rushed into print for the opening of *Philomela*—advanced the theory that the castrato made a perfectly virtuous companion for the ladies. The marquess, something balked by the blood stains, held the paper delicately by its corners.

—*An Eunuch's Song thine Ear shall take*, he commenced in a dignified tone, as if reciting the catechism. No, he broke off, surely this is silly stuff.

—No, Bob, read it, I beg you!

—*An Eunuch's Song thine Ear shall take*, the marquess

348

resumed after a few seconds, though in a voice now grown more hushed than in the initial essay,

> *Yet never shall its Membrane break.*
> *And never shall it shock thy Taste,*
> *For the Surgeon's Blade hath made it Chaste.*
> *Though robb'd not of the Means to Please,*
> *My Song of Love may only tease.*
> *Therefore seek ye virtuoso Joys*
> *Without the Curse of Girls and Boys.*
> *For when the Pope of Rome behoov'd,*
> *The Doctor had my Cods remov'd!—*

—Stay—there is yet another stanza, his lordship urged, laughing mightily, in which he is compared to Tantalus.

—Silly stuff indeed, murmured the marquess, folding the broadsheet and then hastily attempting to conceal it upon glimpsing Lady W—, who had unexpectedly appeared at the foot of the staircase.

—Tristano shall go with you to spa, his lordship was briskly announcing to her some hours later, after Dr Lightholder confirmed that the patient's life was in no immediate danger.

—Whatever you command, my lord, she replied, disguising something like a smile behind her folding-fan.

—He must recover so he may sing again. Hang it! How I shall lose my money in this business! That clumsy oaf, Senesino! His vaulting eyebrows that were like the feathers upon arrows descended, almost concealing his vividly antithetical eyes. Yes, yes—he must restore himself, and quickly!

—Whatever you command.

Tristano's face had at last stopped bleeding by the time the coach reached its destination. A day before, in the Marlborough Downs, the snow had disappeared, replaced by a foggy rain. The mist now briefly lifting, he caught a glimpse of the city from the steep crest of Kingsdown: a hexagon confined in a sharp bend in the river, surrounded by walls and, beyond those, a series of hills. A damp and miserable place, he thought before the mist descended again and they rode along Walcot Street to York House, the final stage. A place where a person was more likely to catch his death of fever, surely, than be cured of one.

349

—A place of scoundrels and villains, his lordship had explained to him two mornings before, upon his departure, huffing and puffing great funnels of steam into the dark winter air. You must keep a peeled eye upon her ladyship each step of the way. Mind she is a sly one! Harkee, you shall be my eyes and ears!

—A place of healing, his wife had said a day after the departure, as they rested for an hour at a public house. A place, she continued, where the disfigured body is rendered whole. Pray, good *signore*, do you know the legend of King Bladud?

He being unable to speak, rendered wellnigh mute by the erring knife, her ladyship showed a great enthusiasm for filling the silences of the journey herself: indicating flashes of red deer among the man-high bracken, the groves of peaches and apricots owned by great statesmen, the sandy and barren heaths frequented by equally famous highwaymen, and a score of other well-loved landmarks on the route past Windsor Forest and into the Berkshire Downs. For she had been to Bath, she explained, above a half-dozen times.

Bladud, the son of Lud Hudibras and the father of King Lear (she now expounded as twilight coloured the mullioned windows of the public house), had been infected in his youth with leprosy and was, according to the practice of those barbarous times, expelled from the royal court. His subsequent career as a humble swine-herd was likewise jeopardised when the grave affliction was unwittingly transmitted to the pigs in his charge. These creatures were miraculously cured of their ailments after wallowing (as is their wont) in the mud above some hot springs on the western side of the Kingdom. Shrewdly following the example of these proverbially canny beasts, young Bladud was himself instantly cured of the disease, his body renewed, unscathed by the tribulations of disease; and in time he succeeded to his father's throne and set up his court upon the site of these wondrous springs and their redeeming muck.

—Thus can we see that the ailing body may be cured, the parson, Mr Trumbull, had appended by way of a moral, only by abasing itself in the lowliest of substances.

He was peering at the two of them over his ale mug and rhythmically masticating the stem of his tobacco-pipe. He was a tall, pale gentleman of middle years with a chin that appeared to have crumbled away, like an outcrop from a

350

chalky cliff, and a pair of watery grey eyes animated with a mischievous spark that, like his fondness for both hop and grape, was not ordinarily identified with country clergymen.

—Our fine silk clothes, he continued with a grand gesture at his own fine waistcoat, our hats and gloves, our silks and linens, our comfortable homes and carriages purchased at the dearest cost to our purses—these things that divide us like pattens from the muck and grime of the world, in the end none can shape the body anew or inoculate it against the diseases and complaints to which the flesh is prone. No, the Almighty with his famously fine sense of humour has seen to it that we may only discover the solace we seek in vain through these glittering trinkets in, rather, a puddle of muck and a pool of stinking water!

After quacking voraciously at this piece of wisdom he called for a quart of eggnog and more tobacco. He was proving a most convivial companion, though one whose lack of restraint, especially where his tobacco-pipe was concerned, did not endear him to her ladyship. To her increasing chagrin, he was also proving an omnipresent companion. After confiding his ignorance of Bath and his worries about being duped because of this ignorance into paying an exorbitant rent for his chambers, he wondered if he might perchance lodge in the residence of their party. Lady W— was in the midst of explaining how from what she knew of them her lodgings would be quite confined as it was, when the fellow's countenance assumed so sorrowful an expression, and his eyes began observing his pocket-book with such a degree of anxiety, that she swiftly relented and the matter was closed.

Their lodgings did indeed prove confined; also damp, draughty and miserable. They stood in Green Street, one of the newer avenues, though it seemed the house, like his lordship's mansion, was in some state of incompletion. Tristano's chambers—two rooms for which he paid ten shillings per week—were scarcely more commodious than those of a butler. Unpainted wainscots, a whitewashed chimney-piece, a cane-bottomed chair, a fireplace with neither coal, tongs, poker nor shovel. A tiny mirror in whose flawed glass he inspected his face for damage immediately upon arrival.

Mr Trumbull's chambers, located farther along a narrow corridor, were apparently no more hospitable, for not ten minutes after ensconcing himself he knocked upon Tristano's door and asked if he might borrow any cups, saucers or buckets in order to capture the drips of rain making their entrance through his ceiling. Tristano found himself unable to oblige, having already employed a variety of such housewares in defence against the drips from his own ceiling; and so Mr Trumbull departed murmuring cheerfully about the 'muck of the world'.

Even her ladyship's chambers, one floor below, were no better despite their much less economical rate of £3 per week. Tristano was afforded many opportunities to inspect the surprisingly meagre conditions of these lodgings, being often invited, in those first few days, to consume tea in her withdrawing-room in the afternoon or to pass an hour or two at reversi, her favourite board game.

Yet these activities—which were often interrupted and then joined in by Mr Trumbull—were truly the least of their acquaintance. Yes, Tristano had been raised from the bloody stage, and then from his feverish sick-bed, to discover that the world, and most especially perhaps Lady W—, had altered quite immeasurably. A sea change had occurred over those eight days, as if the sharp scent of the smelling-bottle had powers to change the chemistry of his brain, to make the world look different. As if her bottle held not volatile salts but some magical witch's potion that resolved the world at an angle unfamiliar to itself.

Whether or not this new world was for the better, though, he could not at this point precisely say. During these first days in Bath he was scarcely absent from her side. Each morning at six o'clock the two of them were transported in sedan-chairs along Stall Street to either the King's Bath or the Cross Bath, in whose waters they sat for an hour before being wrapped in towels and borne home for breakfast, still swaddled thus, their hands tender and red and wrinkled like walnuts. Or sometimes they took their breakfast—buttered Bath buns, chocolate, dishes of coffee or tea—in the Assembly Rooms, to the accompaniment of French horns and clarinets, their table set with silver. Then after this to the Pump Room to drink a sulphurous and muddy liquid supplied hot from a marble-cased pump while a group of musicians—a poorly trained lot—sawed and whined in a gallery above their heads. Next, tea of a brew scarcely any more refreshing than the water, served, once again, in the Assembly Rooms; after which, if her ladyship's constitution

352

permitted, a promenade through the gardens of Harrison's Walk. In the afternoon, two hours in bed, 'preserving' themselves. Gaming-tables in the evening: faro, basset, hazard, even-and-odd, ace of hearts. Cards ruffling and snapping, dice rattling in a cup or skipping across taut green velvet: if he closed his eyes he might have been back in the Villa Provenzale. Then every second night it seemed there were dances in a ballroom, newly built, where upon a waxed floor that looked like a giant's draught-board her ladyship introduced him to the steps and arm movements of the minuet.

Mr Trumbull, as was his wont, often sought to encroach upon these activities, going so far as to insist upon dancing minuets with Lady W—, and proving remarkably adept for a clergyman who professed no previous acquaintance with the entertainments of Bath. He was also a determined gambler whose winnings could not be attributed solely to that pagan goddess whom he so modestly claimed favoured him each day with her attentions. It was not many days before Tristano noticed how her ladyship sought with a powerful determination to avoid the merry parson and appeared to be repenting the hospitality she had shown after discovering him stranded in the snow of the Bath Road.

Other effects of this sea change? *Philomela* had closed even before his delirium abated, not to be revived. On the evening following the disastrous début, never of course completed, Signora Rolli—the servant, Lysander—had assumed the roll of Philomela. The audience—the supporters of Tristano and Senesino alike—hooted and hissed without pity, until, in the middle of her duet with Tereus, she fled the stage in tears. Tristano's supporters visited their derision with equal abundance upon the head of Senesino, to which practice this virtuoso's defenders objected with the blows of a few librettos and then, when these projectiles were promptly returned, their fists. As Mr Handel led his orchestra through the final *presto* stages of the duet with no vocal accompaniment apart from the screams and insults of the best part of the audience, this debate spilled into the King's Stable-yard and Market Lane. Beneath the colonnade in the Haymarket, sedan-chairs were knocked on to their sides, fine ladies on to their side-hoops. The doors to the stable-yards were opened, great carriages pulled riderless into Charing Cross. Chair-men struck one another—and anyone else within their range—with their poles; some of the most violent of these gesticulations broke the window-panes in the shops of the wine merchant and royal perfumer. The crowd was not dispersed until twenty minutes later—by which point the performance had once more been abandoned, this time for ever.

A last change: Tristano's career upon the stage was ended. At first this event was neither apparent nor expected. A spa in Bath: this was certain to cure both the wounds in his singing parts as well as the feverish affliction of the throat that Dr Lightholder attributed to an adverse effect of the late equinoctial gales upon the ratio of his radical heat to his radical moisture. Yes—a spa in Bath, this place of healing, was just the thing. Who might have known that the end of his career lay within this hope for its resumption?

No—the end was neither apparent nor expected. Indeed, after little more than a fortnight in Bath, Tristano was—whether because of the waters or Lady W—'s medicinal herbs—sufficiently recovered to submit to Mr Trumbull's proposal that he sing in the Assembly Rooms upon the evening of 'a Masquerade Ball in the Venetian Manner' (as the engraved tickets named this diversion) to be held ten days hence. As this endeavour naturally required a great deal of practice, he gingerly performed a few roulades and trills in his chambers each afternoon as Lady W— preserved herself one floor below. After two days he was able to sing, however imperfectly and uncertainly, part of the tempest aria from *Philomela*. At which point—in the middle of one such session—there came a knock upon his door.

—If you wish, good *signore*, I will be your audience. Lady W—, wearing a flower-printed mantua and a cap with cherry-coloured ribbons, was a bewitching sight. Come, come—your voice sounds as perfect, as beautiful to me, as ever.

So as she sat upon the cane-bottomed chair, hands folded demurely in her lap, head inclined like that of a true *connoisseuse*, he once again executed the aria. *Mobil ondo che rupe circonda*, he trilled over the last remnants of pain, his voice echoing against the bare, water-stained walls,

Spuma e piange,
in se stessa si frange
e del vento la scuote il furore—

354

He ceased in the exertions after a moment in order to cough and sip from a flask of pump water. She had recommended eight pints of this liquid each day, besides her various other drops and potions.

—*The hurtling waves*, he translated for her as he wiped his brow with a handkerchief, *frothing and moaning round the rocks*—

—No, she said, her eyes regarding him from under the cap with a peculiar and unidentifiable significance. Sing! The words matter not. *Sing*, I beg of you.

At some point during their long journey along the Bath Road she had explained how listening to his singing voice was like sniffing the scent of sweet marjoram mixed with basil, both of which together, she vouched, took away sighing and sorrow and made the heart merry and glad. Yet it appeared that his voice had another effect upon her heart—and perhaps also upon some other organ—for scarcely had he resumed the aria, when she rose from her chair, almost as if pushed. She approached swiftly to where he was gripping an imaginary mizen-mast with one hand and repelling the spray and spume with the other.

—Beautiful, she murmured. So beautiful . . .

He broke off.

—My lady . . .?

The doctor, she decided, had been right: the flesh was forgotten—only the soul remained.

—*Sing*!

As he recommenced she approached even nearer, until he could smell her skin; the sulphur of the bath, the spiced scent of perfume rising above it, the more imprecise and bracing smell of her many potions. The unaccountable expression yet had possession of her features as she suddenly knelt before him and without hesitation, and with only a few practised flicks, unbuttoned his breeches and, before he could respond, jiggered them down his hips.

—Ah yes, she whispered, as if unfastening the ribbons of a gift-box. Then she pushed up his frock and imprinted his belly with a series of soft kisses, which descended ever lower, lower, lower . . . until the song—for, remarkably, he was still gamely warbling the tempest aria, gulping at the perfume-tinctured air—died in his throat and he released the invisible mizen-mast.

—Please continue, good *signore*, she urged, as politely as

if the two of them were sitting in her withdrawing-room, playing reversi. At the same time she began disencumbering herself of her mantua, petticoats and stays: a few shifts and twitches, like a strange and beautiful creature on the floor below him being born from a chrysalis.

Continue? With all his many injunctions the great Maestro Piozzi had neglected to instruct his pupils how to perform roulades under these special conditions. But with much confusion he resumed the aria, choking slightly as her shoulders were bared, then the small round breasts beneath, then her white belly with its splotch of navel.

—Sing no more, she said, moving to his small bed, scuttling backwards like a crab, tugging his hands. Come to me—come . . .

Thirty-seven

 'Come to me—come,' Lady Beauclair was saying, drawing me past the sideboard and into the bedchamber. The Turkish dress hung limply from her shoulders, as if in exhaustion, while in her other hand she held a candle, whose light, playing uncertainly across her face, rendered her features quite inscrutable. 'Inside, Mr Cautley. Come, I have something to show you . . .'

As Madam Chapuy and Esmeralda were absent for the evening, my lady had fixed our pretty dinner herself: stewed hare, anchovy toast, beetroot pancakes, boiled artichokes, as well as a claret, into which she swizzled a generous amount of chocolate. I ate from my dish and drank from my cup with a great enthusiasm, though the feast I most desired was all the while seated across the table from me, her foot touching mine. The preparation of this repast afforded me an opportunity to visit hitherto unknown regions of the house—viz., the downstairs kitchen with its boiler, hot plate, Dutch oven, and the many hanging copper pots and low joists upon which I bumped my head a half-dozen times as we frolicked and embraced, waiting for our

356

stew to bubble. Yet the region I most wished to visit—and, as it were, experience—was that unlighted one into which I was now being drawn.

Believing her ladyship was disposed at last to accommodate my hottest wishes, I did not therefore scruple to resist her commands and found myself a few seconds later in the bedchamber, which in the past few hours I had visited a hundred times in my wanton imagination. Yet I did not have long to appreciate the sight of this *sanctum sanctorum* of my desires, for upon our entrance the candle was extinguished—because of the haste with which I (having taken the lead) propelled us through the door—and we were cast into darkness.

As she released my hand I heard the quiet rustle of damask, as of the garment being drawn over her shoulders and head. 'O Tantalus,' I thought, 'at last you shall drink of those sweet waters!' Rejoicing in my fortune, I began fumbling after her with my left hand while with the right I just as frantically groped at the buttons on my breeches. So many of them—how I cursed their inventor! I had just released from its buttonhole the last of those that supported my trousers and, with my left hand, had just laid hold of her ladyship—who, strangely, yet seemed to be costumed—when nearby my ear a flint was struck.

In the sudden aureole of light I now could see my lady—still costumed indeed—pointing at, and stepping towards, an object hanging upon the wall. As her candle moved, so moved the shadows—so that for a second the chamber seemed to be shifting this way and the other, like the swaying cabin in a storm-tossed ship. Then all fell still and I found myself staring at the oil-portrait of a lady.

As I fumbled at my trousers, in as much desperate haste to raise them now as formerly I had been to drop them, her ladyship (whose back, mercifully, was turned to me) said in a voice barely more than a whisper: 'Here—see, it is her . . .'

'It is whom, my lady?' I had succeeded in drawing my breeches over my hips and posteriors and in fastening one button, albeit only half the distance into its hole.

'Lady W—,' she replied in the same whisper.

I relented in my struggles and squinted in the faltering light, which now revealed how the lady in the portrait—a most beautiful creature—was attired in a Turkish habit of

357

ultramarine damask; and thus, as Lady Beauclair now turned to face me, I was presented with the most remarkable double image: for so alike was this pair that it seemed my lady truly might have stepped from out of the gilt frame behind her head.

I drew in my breath at this sight, at which point my button escaped its incomplete confinement and my breeches once more descended.

'Come,' said her ladyship. She blew out the candle, reached for my hand and drew me towards an invisible bed, whose mattress was stuffed, she whispered, with the hair of stallions.

Thirty-eight

 Such, then, was Tristano's première in Bath: a short and somewhat clumsy, though impassioned, performance for which an encore was eagerly demanded and duly accomplished. Scarcely was this début ended, however, when there came another knock upon the—unlocked—door as they lay gasping together, breathing plumes of steam at the water-splotched ceiling.

—Signor Pieretti? It was Mr Trumbull's voice. Are you quite well? Your singing . . .

Only after a frantic moment was he permitted inside. Her ladyship had by this time ducked and thrust her way into her petticoats, Tristano into his breeches. The parson then sat upon the bed—rapidly smoothed before his entry—and, discreetly ignoring any immodest evidence that might have betrayed itself, began discussing the fashionable ladies with whom he hoped to dance a minuet that evening: Miss This and Lady That, Countess Something-or-other visiting from Paris or Poland . . .

Tristano barely heard a word of this chatter, for despite himself he could not remove his eyes from the blushing countenance of Lady W—. Only when Mr Trumbull bounced out of the room twenty minutes later did it occur to him that the waters must have done the parson a world of good indeed, as neither his gout nor his rheumatism could quite manage to incommode the vigour of his performances in the Assembly Rooms.

Two mornings later, after the previous day saw a repeat performance—including two encores—in the greater privacy of her ladyship's bedchamber, Tristano arrived with her at the King's Bath a little later than was their usual custom. After receiving their special garments from the attendants inside the King's Bath—her ladyship's consisted of sulphur-yellowed canvas petticoats, his of breeches and a smock of similar material and hue—they were assisted into the steaming cistern by the sergeant.

A place of diseased and withering flesh. Nearby, an old gentleman with scrofulous ulcers sat up to his neck. Beside him, another old fellow was complaining of cramps and windiness to a young lady, who in turn was describing the tribulations visited upon her by an asthma and a convulsive twitch. The sergeant was assisting into the waters yet another old fellow, this one bereft of his left leg. On the other side, however, could be seen groups and pairs of bathers of both sexes who—if their laughter and splashing frolics with one another were any measure of their health—possessed strong constitutions indeed. There appeared to be many such dubious invalids in Bath, Mr Trumbull foremost among them.

Oh, the waters were pleasant. At first. The heat—they were, truly, boiling hot—presently gave Tristano a headache, or else the headache was caused by the strong smell of sulphur. According to Lady W—, this smell was beneficial for the humours, but none the less it made him terribly dizzy.

—... might if we wish go to Scotland, she was now saying, apparently immune to the perils of the waters, which had swallowed all but her head.

—Scotland? Eyes closed, he had been paying her little heed.

—We might safely go there—to my father's estate.

—Go there, my lady? His eyes opened.

—Elope, if you like.

Her hands were making short sallies through the water like a pair of dorsal fins, the ripples so caused disturbing the floating dish into which her handkerchief and a nosegay had been placed. In lieu of the wood-chip bonnet worn by most of the bathers, she had elected, as usual, to wear a cap decorated with yellow ribbons. It was adequately maintaining its shape, but the mouse-skin patch applied to her cheekbone had slipped an inch or two in the heat and moisture and now was stuck alongside her nose. This accident went unremedied as—for the sake of privacy, it now was clear—she had for the morning dismissed the serving-maid, Susie, who usually attended her in the waters.

—My stars, she said somewhat maliciously, how I should like to see his face! She paused when he did not reply. Why, *signore*, are you ill? Shall I summon the sergeant?

The sergeant had just dropped the wheezily rotund spouse of the legless fellow into the pool, occasioning a loud splash followed by much cursing.

—It is . . . nothing.

But he was indeed ill. Bathers were instructed to water their wine the night before, though Tristano had done no such thing; in fact, for the past two evenings he had rather imprudently, though with great deliberation, consumed two entire bottles of wine before retiring to bed, to dreams in which the burgundy visage of the Count had translated itself into the handsomely frowning one of Lord W—.

—If you fancy, we may travel incognito, she said as if relishing the prospect. (During some thaw in their relations Lord W— had evidently described to her their flight across the Lombardy Plain.) In disguise, she continued, all the way to Edinburgh. We may purchase our costumes from the habit-maker in Westgate Street and invent new names for ourselves. Or, if you wish, to your own homeland. I fancy I might pass for a countess . . .

So—another flight. As she continued, inventing new lives for the two of them, he listened in silence and with as much detachment as if she truly described two different people who were wildly dedicating themselves to Fortune, braving this challenge, risking that adversity, imperilling both their purses and their necks. He was almost upon the brink of denying to himself that the hazards were worth the prize, when something—her bare foot, perhaps—touched his ankle and he felt a rush of warmth that could not entirely be attributed to the temperature of the waters. He was then almost upon the brink of submitting to her latest proposal—something about him adopting a Caledonian brogue and

360

fleeing with her into the Highlands—when the unexpected source of this persuasive touch suddenly broke the surface of the waters.

—Mr Trumbull, gasped her ladyship, propelling herself backwards with a splash. Sir! What on earth . . .? You will frighten me to death!

The parson quacked with mirth as he scrubbed the water from his skull, which without its wig was completely bald and, as a result of the hot waters in which it had been momentarily submerged, red as a crustacean.

—I failed to see you at first, he said, blinking his grey eyes and bobbing up and down in the water. The bath, he explained, is so confoundingly filled with steam.

—Neither did we see *you*, her ladyship replied in a tone strongly implying that she would have been more than content to keep the situation thus.

The parson did not seize upon this connotation and now, with much splashing, interposed himself between the two of them. After making inquiries after their health, with particular reference to Tristano's voice, he began describing costumes for the coming masquerade.

—For did I just now hear you make mention of the habit-maker in Westgate Street?

Despite the heat of the bath, Lady W—'s complexion seemed to bleed quite dramatically of its ruddy colour.

—I'm quite sure you are mistaken, sir, she muttered tensely, looking round in some ill-concealed distress, her beauty-patch in the process sliding closer to her lips as her bright colour returned in spades. Yet the parson did not linger long upon this question.

—As this fellow's prices are too dear for my modest purse I am contriving to fashion a costume with my own hands. Yes, I shall work like a seamstress! Oh, but it is nothing— a small matter—a simple costume. He smiled widely, displaying a set of teeth that had not happily weathered the debauches of his tobacco-pipe.

—What, Tristano inquired when her ladyship (now studiously ignoring this interloper) failed to rise to the bait that dangled upon this smile, what, sir, he asked, shall this costume represent?

Mr Trumbull's smile widened.

—Death, he replied, with more glee in his voice than was normal to afford this noun. The dark reaper of souls!

361

As he described his black cloak and the sickle he hoped to fashion from a broomstick and papier mâché, Lady W—'s complexion once again turned preternaturally white. Tristano felt her hand—her finger-nails—clutch at his submerged forearm. Scarcely had she undertaken this action, however, than the parson's disembodied head suddenly lurched towards her and, with no further ado, he rose half-way from the waters and kissed her with much passion upon the lips.

—Mr *Trumbull*!

The parson's quacking laughter again rose up over the steam, and over her ladyship's remonstrating voice, which demanded an account of this impudent behaviour. When his fit of merriment subsided he explained that, as her beauty-patch in slipping down the contours of her face had reached the corner of her lips, he was merely obeying the code.

—For is it not so that whereas a beauty spot placed near the eye signifies chastity, one nearer the lady's lips coyly exclaims 'Kiss me!' to the gentlemen, who are then obliged to, as it were, oblige?

He quacked once more as he bade them farewell, his bald head bobbing across the steaming waters before once more vanishing beneath the surface.

Upon this explanation her ladyship had swiftly torn the traitorous patch from her face altogether and flung it into the waters. Then, without waiting for the assistance of the sergeant, she scrambled out of the water, so weighed down by her water-gorged petticoats, however, that her motions were slow and heavy, like those of a sleep-walker. All the while she was wiping her lips so frantically with her handkerchief that it appeared she almost believed it was Death who had kissed them.

Three days later, during which time he had maintained an uncustomarily low profile, Mr Trumbull knocked tentatively upon the door of Tristano's chamber. It was three days before the masquerade. By this time Tristano and Lady W— had permitted themselves to forget the parson's impudence in the King's Bath. Indeed, they had allowed themselves to forget everything except that, on the morning after the masquerade, they would leave Bath—and England—for ever.

—I wonder, inquired Mr Trumbull, whose head intruded no more than three inches into the chamber, whether, *signore*, you might possess a copy of a newspaper?

Tristano answered in the negative, confessing how, alas, he read very little English and therefore had no particular need for a newspaper subscription.

—For you see, the parson continued as if he had not heard this response, I am fashioning my sickle (the object peeped through the aperture, a paste-slathered glob of newspaper scraps imperfectly concealing a wire bent into a crescent shape and attached to the tip of a broomstick), and I have unfortunately run short of newspaper.

—Perhaps Lady W—, Tristano began, regretting the words even before they left his lips.

Mr Trumbull shook his head, which was still hanging in the doorway, from which he now retracted the half-finished sickle.

—I fear the lady does not ... umm, umm ... Might I perchance enter? Thank you, *signore*. No, he said, seating himself in the cane-bottomed chair and revolving the broomstick in his palms as if desirous of drilling a hole through the floor with its end; in the process a few gobs of paste splattered about the chamber, to which he, in the midst of some reflection, remained oblivious. No, he said, the good lady does not fancy me, I am afraid, and that is that. No, it is so, it is so, I do assure thee. Well, and can I blame her? The tobacco-stained grin made its somewhat grisly appearance. No, I do not. A humble clergyman like myself? She is my better, I must respect that. A simple man of the cloth ..., his voice trailed away.

—A noble calling ..., Tristano began, before his own voice trailed away.

By now the parson's attentions had drifted to the sickle, to which he gave a critical study before asking:

—What, I pray, sir, will you be wearing to the masquerade? Come, come, he said when Tristano demurred, we are friends, I hope. No, I beg you, sir, tell me. Surely we have no need of subterfuge and tricks?

—I will be an easy one to spot, Tristano replied without further resistance, for I shall be Philomela. He gestured at the opera costume, which hung in the *armoire*. Its blood stains had been removed by Susie after many sulphurous soakings. The better, he said, for me to sing.

—Indeed! Mr Trumbull leaned forward. And ... Lady W—?

Now Tristano did scruple.

—I cannot ... that is, I do not ...

—Come, come, the fellow insisted, tapping his sickle sharply upon the floor. We shall all go together, the three of us! Tap-tap-*tap*.

—It will be a costume I have given her, he replied after a moment, a very precious one ... Oh, very well, sir, I shall show you, then.

As the tapping halted and Mr Trumbull observed with much alacrity, he walked to one of the two portmanteaus, hoisted open the lid and pointed to the costume folded on top.

—Very beautiful indeed, said the parson after giving a short whistle of approval. Turkish, is it? Why, the embroidery! And *ultramarine*—a most beautiful colour! She will make a ravishing appearance, upon my word!

Tristano closed the lid and these raptures abruptly ceased, as if they, too, had been shut away.

—A most appropriate costume, I should say, observed the parson in a casual tone as he struggled with the broomstick while lighting his tobacco-pipe.

—Sir?

—If I am not mistaken, his lordship gained his fortune through the Turkey trade?

This was so. Or, more precisely, the major part derived from his father, the first Lord W—, who (before being elevated to the peerage for courtesies of a financial nature extended to King William early in his reign) had harvested some of the commercial benefits accruing from the military expeditions led against the Ottomans in the Mediterranean regions by the Venetian admiral Francesco Morosini. His lordship—that is, the son—had undertaken a number of ambitious journeys into the Levant himself, though, it must be said, without effecting any marked improvement in the family's fortunes.

—Yes, Tristano said vaguely, I believe you are right.

Since this mention of Lord W— the parson's grey eyes had begun regarding Tristano with an expression of sympathy mingled with gravity. After a few seconds of such study he cleared his throat and inquired:

—May I speak to you—very frankly—about certain mat-

364

ters? I can see, he continued before Tristano could respond either way, that you think very much of Lady W—, and she, for aught I can see, of you. Mutual esteem, that is. The grisly smile reappeared, then swiftly vanished as the sympathetically grave expression reasserted itself over it. Lord W— is, I believe, a fine gentleman, he began in an uncertain manner, tapping the stem of his pipe against his teeth.

—His lordship is my patron.

—Indeed? This reply seemed to set Mr Trumbull to much reflection and several further murmurings: indeed, yes indeed. Then he sat forward and inquired in a confidential tone:

—This husband ... does her ladyship ...? That is, are they ...?

—She loves him no more than he loves her.

—Ah! Mr Trumbull furrowed his brow and looked sorrowful. He recommenced drilling through the floor, though at a moderated pace. I believe I have heard, he said at length, of his association with her ladyship, of his character. Nothing much, you must understand: tittle-tattle, that is all. Yet ... The drilling ceased; pipe-smoke crept through the air like a vine. I have been witness, he resumed, to many things in my career as a clergyman. Things that might make your wig curl. Now ... might you not consider, *signore*, might it not be *possible* that she is merely—how shall I phrase it?—*using you* in a revenge plot against her husband, whom you imply she dislikes? As I say, in my profession I have been witness to many things, privy to many scheming hearts ...

Inwardly, Tristano winced.

—I do not believe it, sir.

—Fly, said Mr Trumbull, who gave no indication of having hearkened to this response. His pipe had been removed from his teeth and his right cheek was twitching like the flank of a horse.

—Sir ...?

—*Fly, signore*—flee this place. She is a witch! Put as many miles between you and her ladyship as is possible! Do not for one instant look over your shoulder! Return, if you must, to Italy. He paused long enough for his twitching features to modify themselves and assume a more gentle expression. I am most concerned for your safety, he said in a voice that was now scarcely above a whisper. Danger awaits you here, for if all I know of his lordship is true ...!

365

Tristano's face, reflected back at him in the small, flawed looking-glass, appeared to have turned completely white. A grotesque white mask; a halfpenny engraving of Fear. Yet before long his alarm at this heated recommendation turned to anger, and now his warped face grew blotches of a bright red. For suddenly all was clear: what a fool he was not to have seen it before. Yes—the parson was envious! He wished to possess Lady W— for himself, to be rid of the impediments, to frighten him away! His constant inter-positions and interferences, his behaviour in the King's Bath—yes, now all so obvious!

—Oh, I shall fly, that much is certain, he told the parson, endeavouring to bank down this rage that he might pro-nounce his reply and so scuttle the fellow's ambitions once and for all. I shall go to Italy and I shall not look back, you may be sure of that. But I must own, sir, that Lady W— will be at my side.

The grey eyes widened beneath raised eyebrows.

—No!

—Yes, returned Tristano, whose image in the glass now revealed a triumphant smirk. Why, the silly parson was as easy to read as a book! We shall be departing for Italy—for Naples.

—Naples! repeated Mr Trumbull as if this place were a strange novelty, as incredible as the New Atlantis or the Seven Cities of Cibola. Then he stood, clutching the dripping broomstick before him like a mitre. One person here means you well, he said, another harm. You must discover for yourself, sir, which is which.

—I have done so, sir.

—If you are resigned to this course, the parson said in a grave voice, then I cannot alter your mind. But may God have mercy upon your souls!

So saying, he spun on his boot heels and exited the cham-ber, though not before Tristano, whose grasp of written English was, as he admitted, small, none the less was able to read the small print of a newspaper plastered on to the half-finished sickle of Death which proclaimed: 'IL PIOZZINO ARRIVES IN LONDON'.

Yet what mattered this news? he asked himself hours later as he lay in her ladyship's bedchamber, feeling the soft tendrils of her hair resting upon his bare chest and shoulder, smelling the lavender and rose-water of her bed-linen, the musk-scented powder on her skin. Of what possible concern was it? He was leaving England. In six days he would be in France, travelling south. Yes, it was in fact good news. *Good* news. What could go wrong?

Thirty-nine

Strong gales arrived upon the morning of the masquerade. Tristano had awakened in her ladyship's bedchamber to the sound of the leaded window-panes rattling in their frames, of the naked branches of a cherry tree in the back garden scraping the ashlar. Throughout the forenoon, slate was blown from mossy roof-tops, branches from old trees. Wheeled Bath chairs squirmed this way and that as their chair-men strained at the handles, their eyes reduced to slits against the rain. Old ladies on their way to the King's Bath were pinned by the wind's force to the walls in Westgate Street, their petticoats filling and flapping like staysails.

Braving these elements, Tristano went alone to Cold Bath House in Widcombe, crossing the river on the Old Bridge. After undressing he plunged into the cold water and then, to warm himself afterwards—and as the bath appeared to be empty—began singing the tempest aria he would perform this evening. His voice, once more in fine fettle, resounded against the plaster walls, against the stone of the bath. In accompaniment, the wind howled like a flute in the eaves and the rain beat its percussion against the sash-window above his head. A fine day indeed for a tempest aria.

Only when he was dressing a few moments later did he see the tall form of Mr Trumbull in the architraved doorway. The parson appeared determined to ignore him, as if his watery grey eyes had lost the power to see his successful rival; as if he were blind now as well as afflicted by gout or rheumatism—or whatever mysterious ailments had brought him to Bath.

—Oh, the frail frame of flesh, this singular fellow proclaimed to no one in particular a minute later, plunging with a short splash into the cool mineral waters dispensed by the lion-head fountain. God have mercy upon it!

And only after he crossed the bridge again, rain lashing against the windows of his coach, the wind curry-combing Widcombe Hill, did Tristano stop to wonder how Mr Trumbull, having abandoned his carriage in the snow of the Bath Road, now managed to transport himself to Widcombe on such a tempestuous morning as this.

By evening these gales had grown yet more fierce. Each time the door leading into the vestibule of the Assembly Rooms was opened a violent gust rushed through the ballroom, rippling the feathers and ribbons on the costumes of the guests and fluttering the scores of the musicians in the gallery. Lady W—, in her Turkish dress, confessed to being cold. Yes: the *villeggiatura* was one thing, Bath in the midst of winter quite another. She was required to don a shawl.

—Where do you look? she asked Tristano. Whom do you seek? For, ever since their arrival, his head had been swivelling this way and that, peering at the masks of the arriving guests. Perhaps, she said, you have in mind some intrigue?

—No one, my lady, he replied somewhat brusquely. It is nothing. I shall find us a cup. No, he thought as he walked away, *I* am not the intriguer.

He had made no mention of his confrontation with Mr Trumbull, either the one in his own chamber or that in the Cold Bath House. There was no need to alarm her about this adversary or rival—whatever he was—in their midst. Already she was speaking somewhat fearfully of the young gentlemen gored in the past year by his lordship's blade: it seemed there had in fact been a good dozen of them. Yet was there something more than fear in her voice? For the affections of one or two of the victims—strong fellows with reputations for swordsmanship—she confessed to having encouraged in the hope that the outcome in Hyde Park might have been the reverse.

—I shall not fight him, Tristano had been swift to reply upon learning of the frequency and extent of these bloody contests.

—Of course not, she replied, for he would kill you in a minute.

This much, he owned, was true. But as she spoke he had been wondering if she was having doubts. Or was she testing him? Testing his courage, his devotion? Yet she claimed to love him—yes, this word had passed her lips—because he was, as she said, the antipode of his lordship; not a man of the sword but, as she put it, a 'man of the heart', a 'man of sensibility and feelings' and, even, 'a female man'.

—In any case, she had continued, his lordship could not satisfy his honour in a place such as this, as our master of the revels, Mr Beau Nash, has forbidden gentlemen the privilege of wearing swords and fighting duels while in Bath. For this spa is a place where we lay aside the rougher passions of men and cultivate the softer ones—those for which you, good *signore*, are the most beautiful emblem.

But knowledge of this prohibition had been small comfort hours later as he fell into a dream in which Lord W—, paddling furiously and dressed in a brown linen smock, pursued him through the steaming waters of the King's Bath. Catching hold of him, his lordship had thrust him beneath the surface and held him down until the air was expelled from his lungs and rose above his head in scores of warping silver bubbles.

Now, after a minute's further searching, he laid eyes upon Mr Trumbull, who was seated at a card-table, playing whist. Despite his self-pity about his pocket-book and the immodest prices of the habit-maker, the parson had obviously succeeded in laying his hands upon a few shillings—perhaps through his good fortune at the card-tables—for his black cloak and hood proved to be of a fine satin, rippling and shining in the wax-lights. His white mask, likewise satin, was in the shape of a grotesque skull. As Tristano passed, it rose briefly from the hand of cards over which it had been hovering, then swiftly dipped. The rogue made a fearsome appearance, Tristano had to admit; one from which not even the makeshift sickle—clutched in his right hand, which was gloved in white—quite managed to detract. He appeared to have found comfort for his loss of Lady W—, being seated next to a pink domino with whom his intercourse—judging from the proximity of their masks and thighs—appeared to be of the intimate variety.

The punch, a viscous liquid, had been made from pump water, whose sulphurous taste unfortunately succeeded in overwhelming most of the more palatable ingredients—

claret, brandy, nutmeg, lemon. Those gathered round the silver punch-bowl were complaining rather bitterly about this unexpected recipe, many of them being reluctant even to sample it.

—A waste of good claret, lamented a Pierrot, pouring the contents of his cup back into the silver bowl.

—Terrible, was Lady W—'s verdict as she sipped from her cup a moment later. Please, let us depart.

Despite the shawl she was yet shivering, though not, Tristano suspected, because of the cold breeze from the vestibule but on account of the many other fiercer trials which both knew lay beyond the doors of the Assembly Rooms.

—I am to sing, he reminded her as she abandoned the punch in favour of cordial-water. Come—the minuets begin.

They seated themselves at one of the tables, amid a party comprised of a black domino, two shepherdesses, a plague doctor with his strange beak-nosed head-dress, and a fur-clad fellow who claimed to be attired as someone named 'Robinson Crusoe, the castaway'. Several of these guests being nothing loath to sup the punch despite its composition, presently they became very loud and free with their comments about the dancers who stepped on to the floor, one couple at a time, to execute the long minuet. This lady they found awkward and poorly shaped, like a broken elbow-chair; that one, they conjectured from her gait, was ill-disguising a limp; a third, from her side-hoops, the size of her posteriors. The gentlemen they denounced as oafs and rustics even as the steps of the zigzagging dance brought these poor fellows within range of hearing. And they applauded loudly with rude cries of 'Mercy at last!' and 'Upon my word, I thought it should never finish!' when the music ended and the couples scurried back to their tables, unabashed in their relief.

Thus when it was her turn to dance with Tristano, her ladyship was understandably reluctant to take the floor. Only after a good deal of tugging and persuasion—much of the latter deriving, none too reassuringly, from her table-mates—did she lay aside her shawl and totter on to the chequerboard tiles.

Now as the conductor tapped his harpsichord and the violins struck up their seething sound, the two of them faced one another like duellists, ten paces apart, then stepped slowly forward, shoes clicking, across the beeswaxed floor:

stately and measured advances, both moving to their left, away from the other; draughtsmen being manoeuvred on a patterned game-board. Right foot forward now, poised; then heels together, knees bent, back straight; right foot forward again, to toes, and down. Arms aloft at the same time, revolved, lowered. Another step, still in opposing directions—her ladyship stuttering only very slightly, then recovering—their arms now travelling *de bas en haut*; now doubling up; now extending. Both swept to their right, moons drawn by the pull of an invisible planet between them; then approached the other; turned their shoulders; sheered away in opposite directions like ships rapidly changing tack in the breeze.

Some of the guests were applauding faintly now, though not on account of the minuet—performed with passable grace—so much as because Lady W— made such a remarkable appearance in her Turkish habit. The gentlemen among the sitters-by—even the plague doctor and Robinson Crusoe—were willing to forgive any few infelicities in her steps for the sake of seeing the ultramarine damask swirl about her shoulders and hips.

—... which indeed are finely turned, the Crusoe was whispering to the plague doctor, as if from an expert's lathe ...

The two of them might have scored a small triumph upon that evening had Lady W—'s graceful steps not now brought her within reach of the card-tables: that is, within sight of Mr Trumbull, whose preoccupation with both his game of whist and the pink domino had formerly precluded him from taking particular note of the dances, even though his table was situated at the edge of the floor. Now, however, the skull-mask rose above the fan of cards and, as she passed, Lady W—, seeing it for the first time that evening, gave a kind of gasp—from ten paces away Tristano heard it over the violins—then promptly collapsed to the floor like a marionette whose strings were cut.

—The lady faints!

—A doctor!

—Hasten, bring my salts!

—Stand clear, stand clear, I say!

A dozen costumed figures quickly crowded round, each holding a smelling-bottle, each giving instructions to another. The attendance of so many volatile salts and flut-

371

tering fans may have revived her from the swoon, but the nature of her injury was soon judged more serious, for it was conjectured that in falling she had struck her brow upon the tiles.

—A doctor, a doctor!

Tristano was not one of those who immediately rushed to her prone body, and when at last he realised what had occurred the horseshoe-shaped throng about her prevented him from advancing. He was not one of those who rushed forward, that is, because in the second before she gasped and collapsed he had been seeing not Lady W— but rather Maddalena, whom he envisioned dancing in this same ultramarine habit on a warm summer evening at the Villa Provenzale barely six months before. And he had arrived at the conclusion that, throughout his life, but most especially since that particular night, he had been a passive creature, blown about as if by the trade winds: loaded on to, and unloaded from, ships and carriages, transported hither and yon like an exotic foreign ware purchased and consumed in order to satisfy restless and competitive yearnings for luxury. A commodity of adornment, like taffeta, muslin, cochineal, damasks, diamonds, spices—those disposable spoils from other lands for which upon his arrival in London there had been such a frenzy of purchasing; those things unloaded on lighters at the Port of London that the poet Mr Pope had called the emblems of vanity, corruption and the loss of masculine self-government. A loss that, in his case, extended as far back into his past as the sun-scorched and fly-buzzed afternoon when he sat alone in the vestry of his village church and listened to the soft jingle of coins knelling his fate . . .

And so, in the second that her ladyship dropped to the floor, he had come to the further conclusion that he would not be departing for Italy after all, at least not with Lady W—.

—Stand back, stand back, I say!

—Dr Collins, where is he? Dr Collins!

—Don't push, don't push!

Yet whatever the conviction Tristano reached in those few seconds, it was swiftly made doubtful, even irrelevant. For as he fought his way towards the prostrate marionette on the chequerboard tiles he was bumped roughly by one of the guests, and looking up was startled to see the mask of

372

Death, whose eyes as they took a fierce account of him were not watery grey but green and brown: those of his rough antipode.

Forty

One day later—the day, that is, after the one that commenced under the auspices of Mars in Hyde Park and concluded under those gentler ones of Venus in Lady Beauclair's bedchamber—I was to follow in Tristano's path; to follow him, as it were, along the Bath Road in a stage-coach. This was an unfamiliar and—at that time—an unexpected road, though perhaps not half so unfamiliar and unexpected as that path which in the preceding hours conducted me into it. Even now, after all these decades have passed, the events composing those days seem strange, a marvel, scarcely to be believed, less now even than then.

So you will have guessed that I now come to the conclusion of my story. What is that? What do you say? I have not yet finished Tristano's story? No, no—you are quite right. But, patience—all shall be told in good time. Why must the young, those blessed with so much time, forever be so impatient?

So, my Ganymede—am I to understand, then, that you wish to hear *his* story more than mine? That you are caught in *her* web, not in mine? No matter. I take no offence. For, you see, his story and mine are perhaps the same one.

Though I had returned from St Giles at a very late hour—as you might well conceive—I was awakened early upon the morrow by the sounds of Samson and Delilah, as well as by those of the carters urging their clopping nags along the Haymarket and a river of water ringing in my spouts and, only a little less abundantly, dripping on to my floorboards. I was awakened, that is, as I had been awakened a hundred times before.

That this new day should have commenced in so ordinary

a fashion seemed impossible to me: for upon this dreary London morning with its surly sounds of every day I felt as if during the previous hours—viz., in my lady's bed-chamber—the black stallions had come to life beneath us and borne us at a gallop across broad green meadows; as if I had been transported across the skies to touch the peaks of unscaled mountains, the rings and moons of undiscovered planets, the sharp new points of frozen stars. And, too, its bleak ordinariness seemed impossible in retrospect—a few days hence, that is, when I had time to think—for this day was fated to be even more eventful than that from which I had now awakened.

As my feet touched the floor (cold, as usual) and I lit a small fire from the chunks of coal so purposefully arranged (as always) in my grate, I wondered if when I peered into my looking-glass in a few minutes I might fail to recognise myself. The shape of the outer man, my father argued in *The Compleat Physiognomist*, changes with that of the inner, which is its mould, and which is in turn moulded by our experiences. My eyes, my lips, my nose—perhaps they would be different, moulded anew, reshaped by my novel experi-ence of last evening? Perhaps their familiar shapes and dimensions would have been altered so utterly that when I sat across from them, across from the teapot and halfpenny rolls on the breakfast table, the Sharps, too, would fail to know me, and would blink in uncomprehending wonder at this stranger in their midst.

Alas, this spotty and dishevelled stranger. When I did look into the glass a few minutes later I was indeed sur-prised—though somewhat unpleasantly—by the George Cautley who squinted back at me, since at some point during this night of transmogrifying wonders a pimple with the dimensions of a marrow pea had grown on the tip of his nose (perhaps on account of the chocolate swizzled into his wine) and a canker of some species at the corner of his mouth (its cause less readily identifiable); while his short brown hair, until it was hastily concealed by his ill-fitting periwig, stood up from his crown at a series of improbable angles, defiant of all powers either gravitational or tonsorial.

'Oh, I am unworthy of thy beauty,' I murmured to the subject of *A Lady by Candle-light* as I kissed her painted lips, which smelled of oil and turpentine. Tonight I fancied I would be kissing their original, for once again I was to meet with Lady Beauclair, this time at a masquerade in the King's Theatre. My elation at this prospect—her invitation—was only slightly qualified by her refusal once again to reveal her costume.

I dressed myself and stumbled down the stair to eat my dish of curds and whey among the Sharps. Whereupon I discovered that, far from finding me an incomprehensible stranger, the youngest and most obstreperous of these were dismayingly familiar in their attentions, for they clambered on to my lap, pinched my nose and endeavoured to feed me from their spoons or themselves with the curds in my dish.

Throughout this meal I was watched with a particularly wide-eyed solicitude by Jeremiah, who in turn was being watched with somewhat sterner expressions by Mr and Mrs Sharp. Occasionally the gazes of these latter rested upon my countenance as well, their severity scarcely mitigated for this variation in their object. I was greatly perplexed by these attentions. Only after I excused myself from the table and returned to my chamber was I informed by a quietly agitated Samuel (who had followed me up the stair and then knocked upon my door) that yesterday morning Jeremiah had been surprised by Mrs Sharp in the act of returning Mr Sharp's pistols. As a result of the distress and consternation occasioned by this discovery, he was now to be assigned extra duties in the shop, and as further punishment all of his recreations, liberties and privileges had been withdrawn for an indefinite period. Judging from their accusing glances at the breakfast table, Mr and Mrs Sharp suspected my part in the affair, whatever it had been; but as Jeremiah, my loyal servant, had, as Samuel explained, 'kept his gob clapped', no incriminating evidence could be presented against my charge.

Samuel was obviously hoping for my intercession in the matter; hoping for me to vouch to his parents that Jeremiah was not, as Mrs Sharp feared, a budding footpad, housebreaker or highwayman. And so—mainly to speed his departure from the chamber—I made vague promises to say something on the lad's behalf. Yet the truth was that as I left the house ten minutes later, stepping into the cold air of the Haymarket without having delivered on this promise, I was relieved not to have Jeremiah at my heels, not to have to fob him off or feel his presence weigh me down. For I was travelling forward, to the future, and the Sharps, I knew, were a part of my past.

'Goodbye, Jeremiah,' I had murmured to him in a voice acknowledging nothing other than, perhaps, a pitilessness, which hitherto was quite unlike me.

'Goodbye, Mr Cautley,' he replied as sorrowfully as if I were departing not for St Martin's Lane but, rather, for Frobisher Bay or Timbuktu, and leaving him behind to a fate of sweeping spilt powder and shorn side-whiskers from the floor.

And thus as the door sighed behind me and the shop exhaled its powdery warmth into my back, I reflected that perhaps this morning I *was* changed after all.

Yes: I was moving into the future, and my first stop on this journey was, as I have said, St Martin's Lane.

Mr Middleton's shop stood in this street, of course, but this establishment was not my destination; or, rather, it was not my destination until upon passing it I remembered I required spirits of turpentine and so stepped inside to purchase a pot. No, my destination was a quite different shop, one that upon other mornings I had often passed with a slyly knowing smirk directed at its scurrying clientele, though a smirk hollowed out by the strangest envy. For this establishment—above an apothecary's shop in a nondescript, cringing little building—catered both to those who sought love and those who, having found it, wished to protect themselves against, or even cure themselves from, its various unfortunate effects.

As I had paid a visit to the premises two months before in the company of Toppie (who, on account of having been imperfectly cured of his ailment in Lisbon, was bent upon purchasing a course of 'Van Sweeten's Corrosive Mercury'), I was not surprised by what I saw after slipping through the door. The objects of my visit sat near the clerk's desk—I knew exactly where to find them since on that previous occasion Toppie had made the further purchase of three of them in order to, as he said, 'close the door for good upon Signor Gonorrhoea'—yet I could not help lingering for a moment to browse the crowded shelves. Toppie's choice of corrosive mercury—beneficial, according to the bottle, 'for the Italian Pox'—sat alongside a number of other bottles and phials, whose labels proclaimed the contents most effi-

376

cacious in mending 'all of the loathsome Distempers of Venus', including, one such sample boasted, 'Gonorrhoeas more difficult to be cured than those contracted from Women'. Beside these were ranged various pills and powders advanced as cures for stranguaries and itches; excessive nocturnal emissions; enervations of the member and its rarer and even more inconvenient opposite, priapism; and a host of other strange complaints peculiar to the gentleman. Meanwhile the ladies—there were indeed several inside the shop—could choose from any number of remedies for barrenness, venereal indifference, green-sickness, Cupid's itch and, of course, 'Poxes of all Varieties', as well as curious imports from France named 'Bijoux Indiscrets', described as being contrived 'for the Amusement of Single Ladies'.

Many of the other wares I could scarcely bring myself to gawp upon, for they reminded me unhappily—especially the engraved prints from a recent edition of an obviously scurrilous work entitled *Memoirs of a Woman of Pleasure*— of my last evening with Sir Endymion in the Carv'd Balcony Tavern; while others simply set the mind to boggling: *A Treatise on the Use of Flogging in Venereal Affairs* by J. H. Meibom, *The Fifteen Plagues of a Maiden-head* by James Read, the scurrilous *Memoirs of a Woman of Pleasure* itself—to name merely a few of the titles in this vicious library. Finally, hanging upon the walls were bone-handled riding whips and what looked like some new species of cricket bat; this equipment for outdoor recreation naturally looking somewhat out of its element among these other less salubrious amusements.

After making my purchase I hurried into the street and back to my lodgings, where I unwrapped and then carefully inspected this novel item. No instructions were provided, but the little piece of armour—fashioned, so it appeared, from sheepskin—seemed to be fastened, once unrolled into place, by a red ribbon. Once convinced of its means of deployment I placed it in the fob-pocket of the waistcoat I was to wear that evening and, whistling, commenced powdering my periwig and then shining my shoe-buckles in preparation for the masquerade.

An explanation for my mission to St Martin's Lane is, I own, in order. I should report that though her ladyship and I had thrashed about upon her bed for what seemed like many hours, making the mattress shift and wriggle as much as a coach dragged bucketing and bouncing down a rutted carriageway by wild and rearing stallions, our progress in this rattling voyage had been impeded and then abruptly halted some distance short of our destination. Lady Beauclair, that is, had been reluctant despite our vigorous ardours (and despite my stiffest opposition) to allow me access to those most desirable precincts, that veritable South Sea of wanton pleasure behind the curved horizon. Only under my interrogations as I was seeking to remove the Turkish costume—which she, however, refused to shed completely— did she confess that it was for want of one of these small scraps of sheepskin and ribbon that, however temporarily, I must be denied this last precious passage.

Now, however, I possessed my passport: this evening as our journey recommenced my documents would be found in order and I motioned by the guards across a border and into those intemperate new regions.

At this hungry prospect I began to dance a happy little jig, in the middle of which my foot slipped on the puddle of water collecting in ever greater quantities on my floor. Oh, fateful puddle! I stumbled, first forwards, then backwards, before finally knocking my new pot of turpentine from the chair; whereupon its lid flew off and its contents splattered with a surprising profusion about the small chamber, including across my stockinged ankles and shin-bones and—more alarmingly—the glazed surface of *A Lady by Candle-light*.

Alternately praying and blaspheming, I rushed to the canvas and commenced daubing with a handkerchief at Lady Beauclair's visage. I reproached myself bitterly when I observed how the asphaltum, yellow lake and carmine were coming away on the lace: so much so, indeed, that the turpentine-soaked countenance over which I had spent so many cautious hours now appeared to be melting in a matter of a few brief seconds. Oh, addlepate! Clumsy lubber! Baffle-head!

My self-reproaches as well as my panicked ministrations with the handkerchief were halted, however, when a series of the most curious phenomena successively became apparent to my eyes. First of all, as if perhaps Art had come alive to mimic Life, the visage of Lady Beauclair as it dripped and melted away assumed the precise appearance of its fair original upon that evening of the débâcle with the tobacco-

378

pipe, when the tears sluicing down her cheeks had ploughed furrows through her *maquillage*. In my head now I heard her voice shouting in its tone of inexplicable distress as her face bled rouge and powdered lead: 'Do not gaze upon me!'

Yet I had little opportunity to reflect upon either the sight or the unpleasant memory, for the second event immediately following was still more curious and alarming. After another frantic swipe with my handkerchief at a rivulet of turpentine-impregnated yellow lake carving a course down the canvas and in the process attracting a number of tributaries, the portrait of my lady with her now discomposed features began to disappear altogether, to be replaced by the mysterious one—the painted revenant—that lay beneath but now appeared, in contrast, to be superimposing itself. Indeed, the image upon the canvas was now becoming a double one, each seemingly half-finished, each bleeding into the other. Then, as the rivulet of yellow lake swelled, my own efforts became less recognisable, those of the unknown artist more. Even the ultramarine ash of the Turkish habit—painted so carefully, in such detail, and at such expense to my purse— had begun fading and sliding, until her ladyship appeared to be shedding her bright costume in favour of a darker and less distinguishable garment.

For a long moment I contemplated this new garment, as well as the new nose, cheek and upper lip now partially supplanting the features I had painted. Then, as my sorrow and disappointment were overborne by my curiosity about this portrait that—for some mysterious reason—my lady had so detested, I squatted on my haunches and picked up the handkerchief.

Well . . . what else might I have done? The painting—*my* painting—was destroyed; its colours were now dripping on to the floor in an increasingly murky *mélange*. And so I dipped the handkerchief into the puddle of turpentine and applied it tentatively to the canvas. I rubbed slowly, in ever-growing circles; then, as the features began appearing, I continued more swiftly, almost too affrighted to keep my eyes open as the aperture dilated and the smudged nether image slowly resolved itself.

And it was with very good reason that I was affrighted. For it was not long at all—a matter of only a few short moments—before my exertions subsided and I found myself staring in great confusion at the familiar sight of a gold-edged tricorne, and, beneath this, a less familiar display: the mysteriously smiling countenance of Mr Robert Hannah.

Mightily confounded, my heart pounding and my brow as slick as if it, too, were melting, I rose to my feet and tossed the handkerchief aside. What on earth could this mean? Lady Beauclair had claimed—I was sure of this—that the hated portrait had been one of *her*. So she had lied to me—and not for the first time where Robert was concerned. But then I remembered her strange outburst against the varlet as we arrived at the White-Conduit House: about how she had finished with him, how she wished to see him no more. Now I had evidence of this determination (albeit an earlier, and perhaps a repented, one) to paint him out of her life, to rid herself of him for good. Well, she had slathered his smirking features with a thick coat of priming—surely this was an auspicious sign that she was done with the devil!

My heart briefly lifted, but then its fluttering tether dramatically slackened as I peered more closely at this visage that, in the flesh, had always denied me any glimpses of itself. And upon this more minute inspection I realised—how may I describe my shock?—that it was not truly so unfamiliar after all: for even in the absence of a folding-fan and a heavy *maquillage* it was identical in every feature to that most beautiful one now effaced by my handkerchief and spirits of turpentine.

Forty-one

Now, surely, no one recognised me. Now, surely, I was transformed utterly and for ever. The Inner Man had leapt up, twisting, pulling, peeling.

Upon the stair ten minutes later I encountered Samuel and Hetty, the former gasping at the sight of me, the latter suddenly breaking into tears. As I stumbled blindly towards the street door—where I was going I knew not—several more Sharps peered round corners and

380

through doorways at this inexplicable presence fleeing their midst, their gawps and half-finished questions only curtailed when the door banged behind me and I was blown into the street as if on the currents of a bellows.

Blown into the street to wander blindly through the rain. Into streets whose gritty physiognomies looked as altered as mine felt. All about me, as I stumbled forth, looked, strangely, to be reversed, to be a reflection of itself, as if formerly I had seen only sharp engravings on the bright copper plate, and now the print had been peeled from the rolling-press, black and smudged and mirror-imaged. This unreal furniture of the earth: swelling kennels, fish-stalls, dead yellow leaves, newspaper boys, carts loaded with hogs' heads, rubble, dung.

I pushed my way through, kicking and cursing, until I caught my own reflection—my own unreal double—in the window of a hosier's shop. My wig, I saw, was lopsided, my face slick with tears, rain, sweat, my cravat undone and flapping weakly at my throat like the wing of a snared fowl. I must have cut a fantastical appearance indeed, for in every street carters and pot-boys and dustmen—and whichever other spectres I might have bumped into and cursed—stopped to gaze in wonder upon me. But for once I gave a fig neither for my appearance nor for anyone's opinion of it. For with my handkerchief and turpentine I had scrubbed a hole—breached a great whistling cavity—through the false and flimsy canvas of appearance.

Some while later—how much time had passed I do not know—I found myself near Queen's Square; near to the house, that is, of my kinsman Sir Henry Pollixfen. I must have crossed through St James's Park—traversed the paths along which, impossibly, I had trodden only a day before, through the rising mists. And though I have no true memory of this passage, I do hold in my head an image of my blind and blundering progress through these stately precincts. For among the sedan-chairs and gentlefolk in promenade along the well-tended paths I must have looked as desperate and as lost as the mad dog that three winters before appeared out of the mists upon the pleasant green acres of Buckling Common, slavering and growling at the demons menacing it from within the fog, until its tortures were ended in the melancholy bark of my brother William's blunderbuss.

381

But as there was no one to relieve my misery, I arrived, as I have said, in Queen's Square. At the sight of the handsome buildings—and, in particular, that belonging to my kinsman—I briefly recovered something of my senses and paused for a moment in my mad perambulations. This street, I recollected, had been the first stop upon my arrival in London, and so it now seemed that—as I was resolved to leave the city this very day—I had travelled in a vast circuit throughout the metropolis, arriving at the end of my futile journey back at this forbidding—and forbidden—porch.

I peered up at the windows, two of which had been bricked up to avoid the window tax, thereby giving the upper storey of the building the appearance of being asleep. As the lower windows were dark, some of them draped with great blue-and-gold folds, I took it to be unoccupied and so stepped forward, only to be surprised in this action as suddenly the door was flung open and out stepped the elongated footman who had once threatened me with his cane. He was followed by a gentleman whose physiognomy, shrewd and austere, was of the sort often seen in courtiers and high-ranking ecclesiastics: that, I knew, of my esteemed kinsman.

I did not think either had taken account of me, standing as I was some yards distant. Yet as Sir Henry placed a buckled shoe upon the step of the waiting carriage, his tricorned head swivelled in my direction and in the stern and uncongenial tones of a watchman he commanded: 'Clear off, you young beggar!'

'You heard Sir Henry,' the footman added, advancing a step in my direction and raising his cane as if desirous of making good on the harsh promise tendered some months before.

Hardly had I begun to comply with these instructions than the carriage's polished doors—which, I noticed with a fish hook of pain catching at my heart, bore the Pollixfen coat of arms—clunked shut and the vehicle raced forward. Almost striking me with one of its wheels as it rushed past, it entered Park Street and then disappeared into the narrow court that conducted into Queen Street; into those premises, I suddenly and for no particular reason recollected, where fifty years before the great new South Sea House had been destined to stand.

As new freckles of rain had begun appearing on the drying cobbles, I took the risk of sitting for a moment beneath the porch of the neighbouring house, my head in my hands, reflecting how my journey now ended exactly as it had begun, and how my Bubble, too, had burst. I did not know, of course, that my journey—albeit one of a quite different sort—was about to recommence.

I walked south next, to Birdcage Walk, and thence east towards New Palace Yard, along the bank of the river. Once again I was wandering without purpose, letting each new street choose me, letting my scuffed shoes take the lead. Yet as I now approached Westminster Bridge—thick upon this Monday morning with wheel traffic from Southwark and Kent—I paused in Bridge Street, as I had in Queen's Square, then turned into Channel Row and walked down to the Manchester Stairs: down to where—how many days before?—I once sat with my sketch-book on my lap and my wig in my pocket.

I had been seated in the same spot for some moments, hugging my knees, when from behind me I heard a rustle, as of rubbish being blown against a wall. But, upon turning my head after another moment, I discovered the source of this sound to be—remarkably—my lost sketch-book with its drawings of Buckingham House, St George's Hospital, Mr Wren's churches and the most recent one of the bridge (in truth still looking more like a sea monster) stretching across the river. Some of the pages were torn, and all of them sodden, as if someone had looked upon my efforts and wept copious tears; but none the less I gathered up the book with its dripping physiognomical studies of the city and carefully smoothed the disintegrating pages with my palms.

By now the rain had recommenced in such great force that soon I was as sopping wet as my pictures. And I thought to myself, suddenly, how in all my days in London my grandest and most hopeful portrait had not been of one of Mr Sharp's bald-pated clients, nor of his frolicksome children, nor of Westminster Bridge, nor of Mr Wren's churches, nor even of Lady Beauclair. Rather, it had been one of myself: my own self-portrait, to which each day I had with great determination added new brush strokes, new tints and colours, only to have it, like all else, melt and disappear before my eyes.

It was as I was returning through Manchester Court a few minutes later I remembered that on the day my sketch-book was lost I had not been alone—rather, sharing the steps with Eleanora. The memory came as a gentle shock, for I had not so much as thought of Eleanora this past day, nor of that other portrait I had begun to paint. But now, I realised, the two of us shared a certain sad kinship, having both been so cruelly duped by Robert Hannah—if such was in fact the true name of this villain—and by Sir Endymion as well.

And so—perhaps for the first time since my arrival in London—I thought of someone other than myself, and as I did so I turned north, towards St Alban's Street. Taking the first steps, that is, upon my perilous new course.

Forty-two

 One morning later, at an hour so black and early it truly seemed to be in the middle of the night, I assisted Eleanora aboard the stage-coach—'the Flying Machine'—departing from the Old White Horse in Piccadilly. The vehicle was slow to commence, preceded by a great business of small boys polishing its flanks and doors, porters loading its roof with two high alps of luggage, and grooms curry-combing its three horses, all of whom looked as tired and unwilling at this hour of the day as the passengers they were to tow. The Flying Machine itself looked like a violoncello case—or perhaps, I thought grimly, like a coffin—set upon four great roulette wheels and pierced with oval windows, each with a leathern curtain. It was advertised as having been hung upon steel springs, a luxury for which we paid an extra pence per mile since, being in great haste—and, as we believed, in great danger—we dared not await one of the mail-coaches departing that evening at seven o'clock.

And believing ourselves in this great danger we boarded only at the last minute, only after carefully watching the faces of the other passengers—six of them—who climbed in ahead of us, and only after the last of the baggage had been strapped to the top or stowed in the basket behind. We

384

ourselves had no luggage other than a canvas bag, filled with little more than my paint-box and a single change of clothes each, placed between us.

'Five pence a mile,' the gentleman in the tiny booking-office had said, regarding the two of us with a squint. He was a tall fellow, thin and sharp like a wading bird. 'How far will you go?'

'Bath, sir,' I replied in a whisper, as if fearful of being overheard. 'When shall we arrive?'

'Day after the morrow. Baggage?'

I raised the canvas sack. It occurred to me, not for the first time this morning, that I was departing from London with even less than I had carried into it upon the back of the pack-horse. This lamentable absence of worldly possessions seemed to raise suspicion rather than pity in the heron behind the counter. His squint deepened at the sight of the solitary sack and then took a conspicuous view of a number of handbills fixed with pins to the pocked wall of his office. These recounted the names, general aspects and sometimes even the engraved likenesses of various highwaymen, gaol-breakers, absconded servants, refugees from debtors' prisons and other individuals who had escaped custody or otherwise run afoul of justice; and only after satisfying himself that neither of us was represented in this gallery of infamy did the surly fellow suffer to sell us our passage. No doubt his suspicions would have been greatly raised and his gaze taken further account of the handbills had he but known that the coins with which I paid our fares were stolen ones.

No doubt the fellow's suspicions would have been raised, as well, had he known I was in disguise. Yes: if my appearance had not been altered and unrecognisable yesterday morning when I peered into my glass, it certainly was upon this day. Indeed, so changed was it that when I glimpsed my head and trunk in the window of the booking-office a moment before I scarcely knew myself: for upon this desperate morning my face was heavily powdered and patched, I was attired in a long black topcoat and a pair of gloves of white leather, and my head was crested not by my late father's second-best hat but by a handsome black tricorne trimmed with gold *point d'Espagne*.

And no doubt, too—finally—the surly fellow would have hesitated over the two bills of passage had he known that

I, George Cautley, was a murderer, the lady shivering beside me my accomplice.

But fortunately he could have known none of these facts—and indeed I could scarcely believe them myself—and so our journey at last commenced. The Flying Machine crunched and jolted through the darkness on its way to the open fields of Kensington, its advertised springs screeching at each bump like a gelded pig. During this progress, like the clerk our fellow passengers seemed to regard us with ill-concealed suspicion, as if I were Dick Turpin and my companion Black Bess. Perhaps they, too, suspected something? Perhaps already our descriptions were circulating about the metropolis, posted upon the door of each tavern and coffee-house? Or perhaps these slouching citizens were merely jealous of my foppish attire. Most looked like humble tradesmen—stationers, hosiers, and the like—accompanied by their wives or maiden sisters; a glum little group in drab attire on their way to drink the waters and rub elbows with their betters. Certainly there were no Persons of Quality among them: Persons of Quality, I supposed, did not ride the Flying Machine. Whatever the case, we were the subject of their suspicious stares until, reaching Hammersmith Road, they one by one were claimed by sleep.

In another time I might have read their physiognomies for symptoms of amicability or malice, for clues as to their station or destiny but by now I had repudiated this practice, *The Compleat Physiognomist* not being among those few possessions stuffed into the canvas bag. I was, in any case, too alarmed and too exhausted by the events of the past day. And so as we approached Chiswick and I caught brief glimpses through my oval window of Mr Pope's old house in Mawson's Row, the ghostly shocks of reaped osiers slumped together outside a rushlit tavern, and then the thinly smoking chimney of Sir Endymion's house beside the river, it was fear alone that kept me awake as the others dozed.

Fear that grew as the haloed sun rose behind us. For only after we passed St Nicholas's Church—and the grave of Mr Hogarth—was the illumination through the oval windows sufficient for me to read the print on the newspaper in the lap of the gentleman dozing opposite: 'Body Discovered in St James's Square'.

Upon climbing its narrow stairs one morning earlier I had

found the house in St Alban's Street much as I left it two days previously. There were no new tokens of Sir Endymion's reappearance, and in the absence of aromatic herbs and jonquils—only a small shower of curled and shrunken yellow petals from the latter remained—the small chambers had resumed their unpleasant scent, that of a canvas tent pitched too long in the rain. Eleanora, too, I found much as I left her, though her customary melancholy was now edged with a certain resentment at my having been absent for so long.

'I was engaged in other matters,' I falteringly explained, not knowing whether I should feel guilty or flattered—or indeed anything at all.

'Neither have you finished my portrait,' she said somewhat reproachfully, gesturing at the work propped on the easel. It sat before *The Fair Garreteer*, likewise resting on an easel. They appeared as images of someone before and then after some dreadful catastrophe. One might have been an allegory of Hope, the other of Despair: those two dispositions between which I had these last weeks and months bounced like a shuttlecock.

'The portrait . . .' I replied vaguely, blinking at my half-finished effort. 'No—I am done with painting.'

'The light is still fine.' She did not seem to have heard me, and, having suddenly brightened, was busily arranging the brushes and paints. 'You will finish it today, I think. I am anxious to see it completed. Where shall I stand? Here by the window?'

'I am done with portraits,' I repeated more firmly. 'This day I am departing for Upper Buckling—for Shropshire. I came to bid you farewell.'

She set down the pigments and took a closer account of my dress and mien. I must have looked a madman some moments before, appearing unexpectedly upon the stair, wet and bedraggled, the sodden sketch-book under my arm dripping and shedding its churches and mansions. I had attempted—none too successfully—to compose myself before the Carv'd Balcony Tavern, though the tiny leaded windows had not served the purpose at all well. As my reflection was fragmented among the many panes, a dozen tiny dishevelled George Cautleys had been busily tying their floppy cravats and straightening their periwigs before my eyes, none in the end especially presentable.

387

'Done with painting, sir? Departing for Shropshire?' She seemed incredulous—as if her own dreams had not likewise been exploited and betrayed in this great metropolis. 'Why, whatever for?'

'It is my home.'

She was still appraising my wet and bedraggled appearance. 'You appear ill.'

'And I feel the worse.' She waited for me to elaborate. I had been determined as I tripped up the stairs to tell her nothing, to spare her my miserable knowledge. But upon seeing her sympathetic expression I had a strong and sudden wish to disburden myself, to share my sense of betrayal. 'I know where Robert lives,' I said simply, as if this fact alone adequately accounted for my distressed appearance and sudden wish to abandon my profession and flee back to my home in the Welsh Marches.

'Robert?' Her face was a study in contrasts, brightening and then darkening; a wintry heath over which the wind chases the fleeing shadows of clouds. '*My* Robert . . .?'

I was, I admit, greatly surprised by this response, which I had thought would be the sympathetic reflection of my own revulsion. Yet now the portrait was forgotten; even her mistreatment at this villain's hands was forgotten. For now she only wished to rush back to him, to embrace him, to forgive him. Why, the silly little fool fairly begged me! I believe she would have done most anything for me had I promised to divulge my secret.

All at once growing resentful, even angry, I sternly refused any such divulgation. Wishing to moderate her unreasonable response, I explained that there were things she did not know about him; that her love of him—if it still kindled and burned, as I could see it did—was as wasted and as hopeless as mine.

'But I do not understand.' Her brow was knit. '*Your* love? What has he to do with *your* love?'

'I shall tell you what,' I said in the grimmest tone, no longer wishing to spare her anything at all. My resentment— against her as well as against Robert—was (if this was possible in Robert's case) increasing. A few reeds of light had fallen slantwise across her countenance, sharply lighting her wan and sorrowful features. 'I shall tell you,' I repeated, picking up a paintbrush and moving to the easel, to her wan and sorrowful ghost.

388

'Where are we?' Eleanora, having come awake, was leaning across my chest to peer through the tiny window.

'Turnham Green.'

'Turnham Green?' There was a note of panic in her sleep-thickened voice. 'Why, isn't that very near—?'

'Yes,' I replied. Through the window I could see dawn lighting the trees on Chiswick Common. Eleanora peered through them very fearfully, as if expecting in each second to see Sir Endymion—or perhaps an officer of justice—emerge from the mists skirting their trunks.

'Why do we stop?'

'Breakfast. You are hungry?'

'No.' She rubbed her eyes. The rays of the sun were falling more confidently through the small oval window behind our heads. 'How long since . . . ?'

'Ten minutes. A little more.' Through the window of the inn—which had swelled our numbers by one—I could perceive the heads of our fellow passengers, bent as if praying over plates of gammon and eggs. 'Not long now.'

After a moment she said: 'He will follow us.'

'Not if he knows not where to follow.'

'He will pursue. He is most fond of me,' she continued as if not hearing me, and sounding, to my surprise, somewhat fond herself. Perhaps she was disappointed that he had not emerged from the trees? Perhaps she had been hoping he would pursue her, thereby affording proofs of his 'fondness'? Drained a day before of Robert, the empty cavity of her heart had now, it seemed, been filled with Sir Endymion.

'That I can see,' I replied somewhat gruffly. 'Indeed, very fond.'

'Do not judge so harshly.'

My laugh was short and bitter. 'You ask me not to judge a man who, if what you say is true, will slit my throat should he find me.'

'Yes,' she replied, the fondness in her voice seemingly undiluted by the prospect of Sir Endymion displaying his devotion in such a manner. 'He would slit your throat, that is true.'

Why, I wondered, was the creature so strangely devoted to those who mistreated her? Had she kissed his hands, dreamed of, and yearned for, the brutish fellow who had flogged her naked back in Bridewell? Had she mistaken those whippings before the alderman and the lasciviously roaring crowd for some testament of love? Perhaps she took the scars upon her shoulders to be proof of his esteem?

What opinion, then, might she hold of me, whose only crime against her person was one of protecting and comforting, of freeing?

When the time finally came to depart—almost twenty minutes later—the newest passenger entered first and sat down opposite Eleanora. He was a tall fellow with a black beard of scarcely plausible profusion that rose at its highest to a point just below his eyes, and at its lowest and densest to the middle button of his extravagantly brocaded waistcoat. After introducing himself as 'Mr Jonah Scroggins', a brewer from Chiswick, he appraised Eleanora and then afforded me a wink. What this gesture was meant to symbolise I did not know; but as the Flying Machine creaked and juddered past Strand on the Green, where the Thames rose to meet us, and then Brentford, where it dropped away again, I was not at all easy in my mind. At long last, though, I fell asleep, cushioned by the newspaper—filched as its owner consumed his breakfast—folded inside my topcoat.

As I spoke, there had come through the window of the garret, from without and below, a great commotion of carriages, travelling it seemed to Pall Mall or the Haymarket. Jingling harnesses, clopping hoofs, occasional laughter rising up like silver bubbles from the bottom of a vat. By the time I finished—what length of time had passed I do not know—all had fallen silent, and the window was as dark as the asphaltum I was rubbing from my fingers.

'Disguised thus?' Eleanora's brow had been so creased as she listened that I thought for the sake of verisimilitude I should perhaps be required to paint into her portrait some of those lines of deliberation. The conclusion of my story—the revelation of the result of my experiment with *A Lady by Candle-light*—had caused her to gasp and then begin her confused protestations. 'I do not understand. That Robert should attire himself as a lady!'

She wished me to give answers, but since I, too, had only questions I could only shrug my shoulders or shake my head, responding with jerks and twitches as if suddenly palsied either by my story or the events of the last fortnight. The strange performances at the Globe Tavern? she

390

wondered. His association with Mr Larkins, whose eccentric taste in dress she herself had known first-hand?

I little knew how to respond to any of these inquiries, so as she watched me with her searching gaze I merely jerked and twitched and then resumed replacing Sir Endymion's paints. I was thinking, however, that perhaps Mr Berkeley had spoken the truth in his debate with Count Heidegger: perhaps clothing did alter behaviour; perhaps it was the thin end of a wedge at whose thick end were vices of the vilest sort. Mr Larkins, for example: had not Eleanora described how this symbol for every vice and evil was wont to dress himself—and her—in the strangest and most unnatural garb? Yes—perhaps she now spoke truly: perhaps Robert had caught the infection from this treacherous impresario. Little wonder, then, that Lady Beauclair—that Robert, as I told myself I must now both say and think—had been unwilling to discuss the 'scandal' that forced him from the stage.

I had heard of other such cases, of course—of men who attired themselves as ladies, whether upon the stage or elsewhere, only to become strangely addicted to the unnatural custom and thereafter surrender themselves to every sort of iniquity. Indeed, at least once a year my father spoke a persuasive sermon upon this very topic, sternly and without qualification condemning the practice upon the precedent of the Book of Deuteronomy. For these particular Sundays he reserved a tremendous gravity that was otherwise (unless he was denouncing the evils of the theatre) quite rare in his performances. On these occasions he described to his congregation how Sporus, Sardanapalus and those two most debauched Roman emperors of all, Elagabalus and Caligula—as well as several other moral villains whose names, even now, are unknown to me, their deeds a mystery—commenced their pernicious careers by disguising themselves as ladies. For the distinction between the sexes marked by skirts and breeches (my father had argued, getting quite as lathered and out of breath in his exertions at the pulpit as a horse at Newmarket) was no less important to the structure of society as the distinction of rank, likewise observed in dress. For when the prescribed distinction between them was lost or no longer observed, men and women—as well as men and men, and women and women— might 'converse together', I could yet hear him storm, 'with the utmost licence and freedom, given a cover to commit those sins for which the Almighty destroyed Sodom'.

But I did not burden Eleanora with the wisdom of this sermon. Instead, at length I merely said: 'Whatever reasons may lie behind it, you at least know the truth, and you must be content with that much. You, like me, in searching for love and truth, discovered only perfidy and deceit. What can we say but that we now are wiser and shall not trust so easily again?'

I gathered up my sketch-book. Its pages had dried but were now so rippled by bubbles that their smudged-charcoal buildings seemed to occupy novel and distorting worlds, part of an unfathomed Atlantis or a vaporous planet. Part of a London as startling and as outlandish as that which this morning had presented itself to my eyes.

'And now, Miss Eleanora,' I said as I walked uphill to the door, 'I fear I must depart.'

'But the painting . . .'

'You may do with it what you will.'

As I looked upon the painting, which I had decided upon its completion to call *A Lady in a Garret*, I almost regretted these dismissive words. It was superior to—as true to life as—anything else I had ever attempted. I did not doubt, too, that it was superior to *The Fair Garreteer*.

'The beauty and grandeur of art,' Sir Endymion had said during one of our conversations upon this topic, 'consists in being able to rise above singular forms, accidents and petty details. It must be absolutely hollowed of everything particular to the individual, the truth in painting being approached only in this manner.'

This dictum had turned round and round in my head as I finished the portrait of Eleanora. The truth in painting? What truth was there, I wondered, in *The Fair Garreteer*? I now realised that, as she told me her story three days before, I had been determined that my own painting should present her as she truly appeared, all accidents and petty details included; as if through it her tragic story of misery and suffering might be told. *The Fair Garreteer* I now knew to be a lie and a mask, one that covered the infamy not of Eleanora but of her portraitist. I remembered what my master was forever claiming about clothing being a disguise, about nakedness being, as he once told Eleanora, an 'anti-costume'; and I thought that perhaps *A Lady in a Garret* was, by this same logic, an 'anti-painting'. For I had painted away a disguise, so to speak—as if in completing my work I had rubbed a turpentine-soaked cloth through the dissembling surface of *The Fair Garreteer*, thereby exposing to view all that lay beneath: the barbarism and suffering that, as he so often said, gave rise to the greatest works of art.

Perhaps it was the thought of her misery and suffering that caused me to relent when she begged me not to depart just yet, and then again when, a few minutes later, she requested the privilege of an escorted stroll into Piccadilly or Whitehall. Had I in that moment denied her and walked through the door alone, I am convinced I should certainly have returned to Shropshire, if not upon that evening's mail-coach for Shrewsbury—for perhaps I had already missed it—then upon the morrow's. And who knows what course my life may then have taken?

But I did not walk through the door alone. Instead I extended my arm.

'Very well,' I said. 'Where, then, shall we walk?'

I did not wake until we were on the edge of Hounslow Town. Fresh horses were being harnessed. We disembarked to stretch and tramp about in the pebbles and dirt—my neck was cramped, my legs tingling—and to breathe the morning air for a few moments. Then we climbed back inside at the behest of our coachman, a gentleman in a frock-coat of an almost military scarlet. He was joined in the box-seat by a thickset fellow clutching a golden bugle in one hand and a blunderbuss in the other, while the postilion, a young fellow in a cocked hat and riding-coat, was seated on the front horse.

As we set out, the guard—a very jovial fellow—put his lips to his bugle and played 'Death of the Stag' and 'The Lass of Richmond Hill', songs that had earlier embroidered their way into my sleep. His limited repertoire thereafter exhausted, the first number was repeated before, upon irritated complaints from the coachman, he set aside the instrument and sang merrily in his own voice, which rang across the empty heath:

> *'What memories these roads bequeath*
> *That traverse the dreaded Hounslow Heath.*

393

> Where ev'ry tree might hold beneath
> A masked and pistolled rider.
> Dick Turpin rode his gallant mare
> Along the moonlit roads, near where
> Gavotte was danced by ladye faire,
> With Claude Duval beside her.

'Bung it,' commanded the coachman. 'On your guard.'

I believe that upon the inspiration of this song each of us was anxiously on his guard, for no traveller fails to assume a paler hue as his coach sways toward the lonely wastes of Hounslow Heath. Indeed, all of us now were sitting forward, those facing to the front of the coach thereby frequently bumping noses and brows into those facing to the rear.

At length our guard pointed to the right of the coach with the bell end of his bugle. Heads and noses bumped again, until—far in the greyish distance, past the thin stand of wind-racked elms at the brink of the barren heath—two gibbets could be seen on the stark horizon. A still form was suspended from each, twisting and swaying in unison with the other, as if dreamily executing a *pas de deux* through the air.

'Highwaymen,' the guard declared, his cawing laughter drifting across the heath and seeming to stir up from the grasses a quartet of rooks, who responded in kind as they circled above us with ragged and sleepy flaps.

Before journeying another league through the furze bushes and grassy mounds of this infamous common and at last attaining the Colnbrook Turnpike, we were witness to four more such bodies hanging in their chains, their eyes pecked away, their flesh stinking. One corpse we encountered at the junction of the road to Staines and Exeter even displayed white lengths of skeleton through the remains of what had once been, it was clear, a handsome suit of clothing. For not even a fortnight of rain, sun and wind had entirely managed to fade the hyacinth blue of his silk frockcoat nor pick away its epaulettes, gold embroiderings or lace trimmings. His stockings, though slouching towards his ankles and thereby displaying his naked shin-bones, boasted a similar brocade terminating an inch above his shoes, whose gold buckles yet reflected the sunlight.

Before I averted my face from the window it appeared that, from beneath a delicate lace cuff, the rotten hand of this fellow—and, in particular, his fleshless index finger—

was gesturing westward, along the road we were to take. The skull, moreover, lolled backwards—the neck having been broken, I supposed, upon the scaffold at Tyburn—so that he looked to have tossed back his head as if to laugh at our folly in malicious though silent mirth.

Perhaps Mr Scroggins detected my shiverings, for he said into his great black holly bush: 'Perchance you recognise the gentleman?'

I shook my head vigorously. 'Sir, I hope not!'

His beard made a twitching motion, as if beneath its prodigious hairs he was smiling. ''Tis no other than Jack Potter,' he said.

'Jack Potter!' exclaimed two of the ladies, craning their necks, apparently desirous of a better view of the horrid spectacle.

'No other. Also known, I believe, as "The Ladies' Hero".' The holly bush twitched again, the eyes a fraction of an inch above it wrinkling into black cuticles. 'A perfect gentleman, Jack Potter was,' Mr Scroggins continued. 'Always conducted his business with the greatest good breeding, always dressed himself in the finest garb. Why, the rogue had the manners and bearing of a courtier! After prigging their purses he even kissed the ladies—'

The two sitting opposite me swiftly endorsed this claim with rapid nods and excited testimonies derived from recent personal experience: 'Yes, yes, yes—exactly so!'

'—and shook the hands of the gentlemen. Lived many a year in St James's, mixing with the Quality, who thought him one of them, a country squire. Great respect had they for him, old Jack. Alack, he was hanged at Tyburn this past se'ennight,' he concluded somewhat ruefully, 'dressed, as you see him, in his finest clothes, as always. I believe half of New Bond Street wept at the sight, and many a lady too.'

The two ladies in our party, upon hearing this conclusion to Mr Scroggins's story, did indeed look somewhat sorrowful of heart. Then above our heads the guard tootled a few notes of 'The Lass of Richmond Hill'.

'Bung it,' snarled the coachman.

We swayed and bounced for a mile in silence. When I closed my eyes I could yet see Jack Potter revolving slowly in his irons, only now his rotting countenance had transmogrified itself into my own. Who, I wondered, might gather and weep when my neck was cracked at Tyburn? Who would remember and recount my bloody deed? And what finery, I wondered as I fell asleep, might I wear to my own fatal appointment?

I did not awake until the coachman announced that we had reached Slough, twenty miles from Tyburn.

In the end we did not stroll far. Turning into Market Lane we discovered the narrow passage to be greatly impeded by carriages, chariots, phaetons and sedan-chairs, all of them empty. We picked our way among the wheels and poles to the west side of the King's Theatre, whose face rose darkly above us. The winged stallions surmounting the pediments on the opposite side in the Haymarket were visible from our station, though in the darkness they might have been gesticulating winged demons frozen into the sky.

'An Italian opera,' said Eleanora, her voice excited. 'Or perhaps a play. Look, it finishes.' She nodded her bonnet at one of the doors, through which several figures now emerged, unlighted.

'You are mistaken,' I said after a minute, suddenly remembering my forfeited assignation with Lady Beauclair. I was picking a North-west Passage for us through the vehicles and into Pall Mall, now thronged with people, all of them costumed, spilling through the doors. ''Tis a masquerade.'

'A masquerade?'

'I was to meet with Robert.' Taking her hand, I conducted us round a clutch of chair-men.

'Meet with Robert . . .?'

'Lady Beauclair, if you prefer.'

We were nearly swept into Cockspur Street by the growing crowd of maskers, by scores of Indian kings, Quakers, Jews, Arabians, Lucifers and dominoes, all muffled in capes and hoods. I would have relented peacefully to these pressures and been carried into Charing Cross or Whitehall had not Eleanora tugged fiercely at my hand, endeavouring to proceed into the Haymarket, now as crowded as upon market-days. I was puzzled by this insistence. Perhaps she wished to appreciate these fantastic habits in the greater light of the wider street? I tried to dissuade her, fearing that at any moment we may bump into a black domino topped by a certain gold-laced tricorne, but she succeeded in conducting us northwards. Only when we had with much effort

396

attained the theatre's marching colonnade did I realise with a squirm of fear that this encounter was precisely the one she sought.

'So he is here.' Her eyes were shining beneath the crystal globes of sputtering light, illuminated not by fondness, as I first suspected, but, rather, by the terrible rage I had seen upon those occasions when she gripped the iron salamander with such murderous intent. Yes—how the poor vixen's passions oscillated so easily and so frightfully between love and hate, which it appeared she sometimes had difficulties distinguishing one from the other. All plans of embracing him, of forgiving him, had suddenly burst, been thrust away. 'I will know him, disguise or no,' she was saying in a determined voice. 'Now may we eat our dish of revenge!'

I made some demur, but this Lady Macbeth thrust me forward into the crowd, fairly screeching 'Find him! Find him!' into my ear. The tide of maskers at this moment shifted, so we found ourselves pressed northwards, in some peril of being trampled beneath the hoofs of horses and the wheels of carriages. Indeed, I was knocked to the pavement by a horse's great swinging rump, but Eleanora merely grasped my collar and raised me to my feet, wellnigh strangling me in the process.

' . . . shall find him,' she was breathing through her clenched teeth. 'Come, let us now find him!'

Were it not for the brightness of the Turkish habit, this imperative would certainly have been impossible to fulfil; yet, as it was, by some impossible chance I soon glimpsed a flash of ultramarine before an inn standing on the north side of the theatre. I truly believe I would have said nothing then—I would almost certainly have allowed Robert to disappear again into the crowd and pass for ever from my life—had not Eleanora, following my gaze, suddenly exulted and cried: 'There! The dress!'

'No,' I said, 'I don't believe—'

'Yes, the very same! To him!' She was pushing her hands into the small of my back. 'Follow, follow!'

Another push and we were giving chase. Upon seeing us approach, the masked figure—there was now no doubt in my mind who it was—turned quickly into the inn's stable-yard: a flight that only seemed to confirm his identity.

'He flees! After, after!'

The stable-yard communicated with a narrow court, which

in turn communicated with Market Lane. After the noise and bustle of the Haymarket these precincts seemed eerie, their dark silence interrupted only by the snorts of stabled horses and now our pairs of running feet. With my greater pace I had caught the villain weeks earlier as he fled into Marybone Street. Now I was on the verge of laying hold of him again—laying hold of the damask flying behind his head like a pair of flimsy wings—when, turning south in Market Lane, I stumbled over a horseshoe and toppled headlong into straw and stones.

'Up, up, up!' Seconds later Eleanora, close behind me in this pursuit, was grasping at my collar. 'He flees into Charles Street! Quickly!'

Up, up—up. My palms were bleeding, my knees were sore, and somewhere I had lost a shoe. Kicking off the other, I ran more furiously now, cursing the receding shape ahead of me, as if my injuries and the loss of my footwear now spurred my wish for revenge more sharply than anything else that had passed between us.

He ran through Charles Street—somewhat more slowly now, seemingly exhausted and, rather than turning into St Alban's Street, he kept to a straight course, hastening directly, it appeared, into St James's Square. Yes—fleeing towards the mansion where first we met.

By the time I caught him a few short steps from the porch he was, as I suspected, quite exhausted. This perhaps accounts in some manner for his next action. As I grasped hold of his shoulder and spun him round, he produced a knife from the loose folds of the garment. I saw this instrument too late, however, and had already closed with him, our brief and furious struggle now being one of Mars rather than, as one short evening before, of Venus.

The briefest of struggles, as I say—which made its conclusion all the more curious. Indeed, we had concluded our rough engagement even before Eleanora arrived, though at least she had a final comfort—or perhaps it was a crueller satisfaction—in knowing that the last word gurgling from his lips after the knife pierced his heart was her name.

'Miss Eleanora . . .' he whispered through his satin mask before his words suddenly liquefied.

The shock at what I had done—quite by accident, I do assure you—caused me to fall backwards. It was then, as I watched in disbelief the dark stain spread outwards and cover the front of the habit, that I heard the terrible howl, coming, it seemed, from high above my head; a frozen wind whirling and screeching about a sharp alpine peak.

And it was then, upon raising my head as the first of the warm blood reached my cold toes, that in one of the mansion's many windows I glimpsed the face with the crooked nose and close-set eyes, its mouth in the darkness a perfect black circle of pain.

Forty-three

 Grizzled beeches and wych-elms, broken tracts of thornbreak and briar, buff-green hills, ancient barrows, soggy lowland marshes, heaths as featureless as the deserts of Arabia, everywhere great oaks, whose scaled trunks descending from the mists were the twisted forelegs of dragons ...

The scenery scrolled before us, as if at one end of the roller was London, at the other Bath, and our journey but an unwinding, a transfer of the scrolled leaves from one cylinder to the other, all glimpsed through one of the oval windows framed by leathern curtains. Or as if we had paid our fare and entered a tiny swaying theatre to watch optical effects cut from pasteboard, painted upon transparent paper, or projected by lights and reflectors on to cloud-cloths: here a country inn or blacksmith's, there a village of half-timbered cottages looking in the half-light of the chalk upland like a flock of nesting magpies; here a broken necklace of birds passing overhead, there a bounding hare or a young buck startled on the edge of a thick coppice.

The proprietors of these entertainments paid little attention, alas, to the elegant accommodations of the company, as the roads and hostelry were both of them abominable. The Bath Road was flooded in its lower parts, hard with frost in the high, and at times even seemed to turn entirely to muck or else disappear altogether from beneath our wheels. Some distance west of Reading we broke a gear and then, after its repair, became stuck fast in clay two miles short of Newbury, where we spent our first evening. During our exertions to liberate ourselves by pressing our shoulders to the muddy wheels we were watched by a flock of dirty sheep. In the end we walked the distance to the dark town, where neither the fleas nor the discomfort of our narrow beds could quite prevent our sleep.

Next morning, after the heads in the ordinary room bowed devotionally over more gammon and eggs, then cakes and ale, the last half of the scroll unwound itself: Hungerford, Marlborough, Overton, Calne, Black Dog Hill, Chippenham, Bath. At dusk the oval window showed scenes of a looping river, sharp spires, scaffolds crawling up the sides of half-finished buildings along the slopes of Walcot Parade, other slate-roofed terraces in the distance slinking up a hill into the sunset like the segments of giant buckling caterpillars. Finally Stall Street and the White Hart Inn, where the scroll, untethered, flapped and then blew away, borne rattlingly into the distance.

We had not dared to stop running before we lost ourselves in the dark capillaries spreading north of Piccadilly, somewhere in the vicinity of Golden Square. Twice in the course of this flight—once in the middle of Piccadilly and then again in Little Swallow Street—I had stopped to retch on to the paving-stones, watched with amusement each time by costumed revellers from the Haymarket, their wedge-shaped masks peering through the windows of phaetons and glass-chairs.

'Must ... find ... my shoes,' I was gasping as I leaned upon a butcher's cart and felt my stomach threaten to disgorge itself a third time.

'Your shoes, is that all you can worry about? Come—this way.'

'I cannot.' I was in great despair. 'No farther ...' Great heavens! I was now a murderer!

'*Come*.'

Earlier Eleanora had taken the lead, pulling me away from the blood-haloed body and hastening me out of the square and now into—where were we?—Soho. During our desperate flight she had retained a grim and seemingly unwholesome satisfaction, which could not have contrasted more sharply with my distress. Now as she caught at my hand I vomited a third time, into the cart, which in the midst of my groans and contortions I saw, too late, was occupied by a sleeping cur, who came to life as the first drops of my bitter libation anointed his matted brow. Snarling, he sank his teeth into my fingers.

'Come!' Eleanora's growl was fiercer, her pull stronger, than the dog's. 'This way!'

Where to? Left. Straight. Right. Left, left. Straight. Right and right again. Slinking and stumbling. Away from the light of Golden Square, the wider avenues of Pulteney or Broad Street, the clutches of figures crossing Soho Square or lingering in Milk Alley. Pursued only—so we hoped—by the matted cur, who began licking the blood from my stockings when, over Eleanora's protests, I wearily slumped down in Hog Lane.

Hog Lane. I raised my head. Over Eleanora's skewed bonnet I could see in black profile the lobster's-tail steeple in St Giles's.

'Not here,' she said. 'Someone comes.'

I cowered beneath a bow-window. An echoic *pop-pop-pop* of horseshoes grew louder, accompanied by the thin chime of a bridle. The cur bared his fangs and barked as the hack passed. The sharp noise brought a head to the window, at which point Eleanora, gripping my hand, allowed it to drop, crying suddenly: 'Robert, Robert, Robert, my love!'

The hack drew to an abrupt halt. A portrait—for so it appeared—rose in the window, framed by crimson curtains: white satin mask, black lace veil, silk hood collapsing to expose the gold-trimmed hat. Two white-gloved hands clutching the door as if to steady it.

We took lodgings in Green Street. The lease I signed in the names of 'Mr and Mrs Robert Hannah'—Eleanora's idea—paying our first week's rent from the coins she had sewn into her petticoats. In the first days I wondered if our chambers were those occupied by Tristano fifty years before. Certainly they were damp, miserable, meagre. Dead wet leaves the colour of egg yolk stuck like plasters to the window-panes. A mapwork of cracks crept across the ceiling, down the walls. On nights when it rained the clogged waterspout beneath the cornice choked and gurgled like the dying gasps of a hanged man. Like I would choke and gurgle

401

(I would think as I came awake, gasping, on my pallet) when I wriggled about like a worm on Tyburn's fatal tree. Or other times I would shout myself awake when the rain admitted through one of the cracks in the ceiling struck my forehead and, in my dreams, was translated into spraying droplets of blood.

'I beg you, mercy!' In the darkness Eleanora's voice, impatient, irritated, would seem only inches from my ear. 'Silence, please!'

Even when awake I could yet see the blood spreading across the blue habit, behind the death-drooped head, seeping uncontained towards my feet; as if this dark pool had been a living creature, something that grew flourishingly before my eyes, like the frond or blossom of some voracious plant.

Would the waters of Bath, I wondered, cure me of these dreams and memories? A place of hope, promises, miracles: so Lady Beauclair had described the city. A place where the sick and weary body is rendered whole. Alas, in my case its curative powers at first seemed curiously inverted, for we had not been two days in Bath before, perhaps because of my agitating dreams, I fell dangerously ill. For three days I lay sweating and shaking upon my pallet. Through my night-shirt I soon felt the undulations of my ribs and the sharp points of my hip-bones, as if I, like Jack Potter, were turning into a gnarled skeleton. And hearing distant hammers bark as the new Assembly Rooms were being constructed to the north, in the Upper Town, I imagined in my delirium that this commotion was my scaffold being built at Tyburn; each new nail bringing me closer and closer to a terrible and unavoidable fate.

Eleanora during this miserable period proved an indifferent nurse, but in spite of her many absences and her lacklustre administrations of spa water, drops and purgatives I awoke on the fourth day from dreams of my rising scaffold and, feeling stronger, walked alone into Green Street. The hour of dawn had only just arrived—the clouds behind Widcombe Hill held a dim butter-coloured smudge—but already people were returning from the baths, swaddled in Bath chairs, ghosts of steam rising from their necks and shoulders as they were borne up Milsom Street. In Queen Square others were taking a morning walk, dressed even at this hour in their frilled and laced finery. Yet so ill-looking and

402

emaciated were most of them—like I myself was—that I was reminded once again of Jack Potter foppishly rotting upon the gibbet. Then I remembered the ancient Briton's name for the city—Ackmanchester, 'City of Diseased People' (had Lady Beauclair told me this?)—and at the sight of these parading skeletons I once more felt a trembling in my limbs and a feverish sweat sprouting upon my brow.

Indeed, so unwholesome were the appearances of these inhabitants that immediately I felt I must abandon my initial plan, which had been to earn a living here as a portraitist. Bath, I knew, was the only city in England apart from London where one might survive in such a trade. Sir Endymion himself, as he once told me, had spent several profitable seasons here, and he often spoke with a mixture of envy and scorn of the many commissions earned by his Bath friend, Mr Gainsborough. Yet *now* . . .

'How, then, do you propose we shall eat?' Eleanora had wondered in an impatient tone when, later that morning, I unwisely informed her of my doubts. We were sitting neck-deep in the Cross Bath, the water lapping at our chins. A light rain was falling, stippling the surface, which in turn was sending up great columns of steam. So great and dense were these clouds that moments before, walking along Cheap Street and then into Westgate, I had feared some mighty conflagration.

''Tis merely the baths—there being the Cross Bath,' Eleanora had said, impatiently, as she pointed, 'there the King's.'

During my illness she had evidently become familiar with the baths, as well as with some of the other bathers: rough young fellows who first recognised, then hailed, her and finally splashed her sportively from the waters as we emerged from the dressing-rooms. This conviviality perhaps explained why her behaviour at my sick-bed had been so negligent.

'We shall eat, perhaps, when you make your first appearance upon the stage,' I now responded rather harshly to her inquiry. For this was the second reason why we had fled to Bath: Eleanora believed she might find work in the Orchard Street Theatre. In our more private moments in the Flying Machine she had been able to talk of little else. Yet despite her immersion in the many amusements of Bath during the course of my illness, she had thus far omitted this particular establishment from her itinerary.

'I will not listen to this,' she replied hotly, sweeping away to the other side of the bath, the sleeves and skirts of her canvas garments inflating like sails, so that, tacking through the waters, she had the appearance of a fearsome man-o'-war.

As I climbed splashingly from the waters a minute later, alone, I wondered, as I had upon the evening of the Vauxhall masquerade, if perhaps I had rashly forfeited my life for the sake and at the behest of a lady who cared nothing for me, who would side with my enemy as he sought to kill me.

'I am yet a passenger in the racing phaeton,' I said to myself, 'driven by the invisible coachman.'

And I thought, suddenly, of Tristano—perhaps it was on account of the baths—and of his fears of passivity and the loss of—what? Self-government?

Indeed, I thought very much upon Tristano in that first week in Bath. In my delirium I would cry out in memory of his fate beneath the sword of Lord W—, which, shuddering and gasping, I imagined was to be mine as well. I had despised Tristano earlier, in those first anguished hours after the turpentine had dissolved my illusions. Had he not been the means—this notoriously seductive creature—by which I myself had been tricked and seduced? I saw him then as a figure for our deceitful age: this usurper, transgressor, picaro, shape-shifter, border-crosser. This half-man, half-woman, this *both* and *neither*. This figure of art and luxury whose price was the mutilation of the flesh. But when I heard his voice from the window—his mutilated voice—it had not been inhuman, unearthly; rather, something else.

'Who was that?' Eleanora, breathing hard, looking over her shoulder, had asked as we fled north from the square into York Street, towards Piccadilly and St James's Church.

'That,' I gasped, struggling to keep pace in my cobble-bruised feet, 'that was Robert's father.'

'Robert, Robert . . .' I was echoing Eleanora, though my voice, resounding off the walls of Hog Lane, was rendered much less amorous and fervid than hers by the startling sight before us in the hack. 'Robert . . .?'

Eleanora now rushed forward, her arms spread wide, while I yet slumped on the stones, the cur snuffling noisily

404

as it licked the blood-steeped dirt from my stockings. Licked *whose* blood?

Yes, whose blood? You may imagine my consternation. I was a murderer, but whom had I murdered if not Robert? I couldn't think, reason. Who, or what, was bona fide in this living masquerade, this perpetual Vauxhall of the senses? My thoughts were in a mighty jumble, though in those first seconds as we appraised one another—the figure in the hack as surprised at our appearance as we were by his—I wondered with a terrible wrench of fear if I had misinterpreted the painting after all; I wondered if in fact there had been a different, an innocent, explanation for what I had seen, not shocking proof of the vilest treachery. Perhaps Lady Beauclair had not been a disguise at all, in which case—this was truly too horrible to contemplate—I had murdered *her* instead of Robert, who now appeared before me, terrifyingly resurrected. But—no—I could not think, I was losing my reason, my senses—I feared I might faint.

'Robert, Robert . . .!' Eleanora, reaching the phaeton, was grasping at the black-caped figure, whose gloved hands were endeavouring to keep these attentions firmly at bay.

'Drive!' I heard a voice commanding in the last blackening second before my brow bumped the stones. '*Drive!*'

Then a swimming and turning in the head. Lights drifting above me like vanishing comets. Voices reaching out of the darkness, retreating into it. Smells—of candles, flowers, perfume. The touch of hands, both rough and soft. Opening my eyes—how much later?—to watch the ebb and rise of a phosphorescent surf. To watch, as its bright rinse slowly and imperfectly drained, a pulsing countenance—was it truly Lady Beauclair?—leaning close enough for me to feel the warm down of breath upon my cheek.

'Drink,' the voice whispered. 'This shall recruit your strength in a trice.'

Surely I dreamed? Surely I was back once more in Lord W—'s mansion, lying on my back upon the cold tiles, Cupid, Time and Love orbiting in their fairy dance high above my swirling head. Yes—all since that strangest of evenings was merely a dream . . .

'No, no'—hands pressed my shoulders—'you must not move. Miss Eleanora goes to fetch a doctor. It will be no more than a minute.'

The voice seemed distant, submerged, unfamiliar. I sagged

405

on to the horsehair mattress. The red tide again boiled and washed. Its waves lapped through the bedchamber. Lapped across the framed image on the wall of the figure who now lay dead in St James's Square. Across the jawless white mask peering at me—peering blindly—from a bedside table, upon which there also sat, on its side, as if discarded in haste, the gold-trimmed tricorne.

Empty shells out of which, like a beautiful crustacean, the figure above me—yet a mystery—had crawled to plunge and swim and drift through this dizzy surf.

Eleanora's discontentment with me appeared to increase when, after five days had passed, Sir Endymion failed to arrive in Bath. He did not appear in Walcot Street astride a dusty, snorting steed, his cutlass singing as it sliced the air, his bloody voice roaring my name to the clouds. Such exploits were reserved for my nightmares—and perhaps also, I feared, for Eleanora's overly fond imagination. And so, thus abandoned, she sulked and each morning departed for the baths alone.

Occasionally, though, we took long walks, as in London. Past the half-built Assembly Rooms, round the Circus, along the bow-shaped skeleton of the half-built Royal Crescent. The latter, sweeping through its trenched meadow, looked as if it had been disinterred, the disintegrating bones of some mythic beast stretching into a distant prospect. Or we strolled beside the river, with its new bridge, likewise half-built, arising from the dark waters; its pillars a spiky spine, its piers four stout legs, its incomplete arches a pair of wings, its rearing toll-house a Cyclopean skull. Another primitive beast wrenched by pulleys and winches and cranes from its tomb of muck.

On these occasions we talked, if at all, about Tristano. Eleanora had become strangely obsessed. I had commenced the history—upon her request—during our journey, then almost completed it on our first day in Bath, before I fell ill. Now, like a Grand Tourist seeking the sites of Homer's battles, she wished to set both foot and eye upon the places described: the Pump Room, the Cold Bath House, the old Assembly Rooms with their attached ballroom; even Claverton Down, where—against the dictates of Mr Nash—the duel was to have been fought. She also wished me to finish the story.

406

'Lord W—, then, had suspected some affair between his wife and Tristano? For this reason Mr Trumbull—if such was his name—was dispatched as a spy?'

'I know not Mr Trumbull's true name,' I replied, 'if it was not in fact Mr Trumbull.' We were on our eighth revolution of Queen Square, it having taken the first seven for me to recount the evening of the masquerade and—more time-consuming—to answer Eleanora's many attendant questions. 'But no, in London Lord W— suspected nothing. Tristano, to him, was a Tantalus, someone surrounded by a beauty that he could in no way touch or enjoy. He only doubted the singer's ability to maintain a close watch on his wife, whom he understood—quite rightly, perhaps—as a guileful creature. He feared cuckoldry as he feared nothing else, and Bath was the place where, he believed, men were most habitually made cuckolds.'

'So Mr Trumbull, whoever he was, was engaged by—'

'Yes—and it was he who wrote to Lord W— in London, though not before, as I have told you, he tried to warn Tristano, for whom he had come to hold some respect or affection.'

'And her ladyship was, I believe, at this time with child—'

'Stay—I shall come to that.' I was in some state of exasperation at these interruptions. We stepped round an old skeleton sunning herself in a Bath chair and lace bonnet while her guardian—a forward-looking young lady with a novel—idled beside her on a bench. From the distance, from the Crescent, came the echoing iron heartbeat of hammers.

'A duel, then, was fought?'

'Not yet. But yes—one was arranged that evening, to be fought at sunrise upon Claverton Down.' I pointed vaguely to the east, above Quiet Street—which at this hour of the morning was just that—as I squinted into the autumn sunlight. 'With swords. But Tristano, at Lady W—'s behest, did not appear to give the lord his satisfaction.'

'For he had fled with her to France.' Her countenance had assumed the fond expression I had seen so rarely since our arrival in Bath, and her hands squeezed my forearm more tightly. In the sunlight, and with her new smile, she looked in some degree healthier, though in the past days she had grown even thinner, as had I: for, as the coins in her petticoats grew scarce, we were reduced to one meal a day, and that a most modest one. Instead of Jack Potter or my scaffold I now sometimes dreamed of Madam Chapuy's kitchen with its dead partridges and flayed rabbits hanging upon sticks.

'No, to London. And he was travelling without her ladyship. At the hour when Lord W— was cursing and waggling his cutlass through the misty air of Claverton Down, Tristano was on a stage-coach in the London Road, her ladyship under the care of a doctor.'

'Lord W— pursued Tristano, of course, with his faster horses. Tristano, surely, could never have escaped—'

I shook my head. 'No, no—he escaped. Though only for a day or two.'

'He arrived in London.'

'Yes—that is to say, very nearly. But a little beyond Knightsbridge his coach became stuck fast in the mud. By the time the wheels were prised free—almost twenty minutes later—Lord W—, who was riding post, had appeared in the road behind them.'

Her fingers gripped my arm. 'So Tristano was taken, forced to fight the duel.'

'He was dragged from the coach and taken—dragged—into Hyde Park; yes. But a duel? Who can say what Lord W— was planning?' I shrugged, half to free myself from her clutches—unsuccessfully. We had seated ourselves upon one of the benches having the advantage of sunlight and overlooking the balustraded garden with its sun-brindled parterres, its stone-piered gate. 'Who knows what forces, apart from alcohol, drove him as he thundered across the downs and uplands . . .'

Eleanora's fingers remained tight on my sleeve. 'And . . .?'

'Tristano was dragged from the coach, as I say. Through Hyde Park Gate.' The grip tightened. The distant hammers inexplicably fell silent. 'It was dark—late evening. The park was deserted, the ground stiff, frozen. His cape fluttering behind him like a pair of wings, Lord W— fairly carried Tristano, grasping him by the collar, the smaller man's boots scuffing and kicking at the hard dirt: a falcon bearing his twitching prey back to its blood-soaked nest of sticks. The lord had drawn his sword now and pressed its blade to Tristano's throat, asking if he was a man, if he was accountable to the laws of honour—such mockery as this. "Will you give me satisfaction," he growled, "or shall I pierce thy golden throat? Shall I give you a close shave, you beardless

408

girl? No—I will do better than that—much, much better than that!"

'They had reached the Ring—the bloody nest—and here his lordship released him, throwing him roughly to the ground. Tristano rolled away, but Lord W— pressed his boot to his chest. Then, after sheathing his sword, he knelt and slowly withdrew a knife from his belt. Seizing the singer by a hank of hair—his periwig had fallen to the ground—he tipped back his head.

' "A fine disguise, that of a eunuch!" he snarled into Tristano's ear. "A fine disguise, was it not, to earn your privileges and liberties! You might have fooled all the husbands in the world with it for aught they know of your ways! Well—will you beg forgiveness? Will you sing for your forgiveness? Will you try to charm me, Orpheus, like you charmed my wife from her senses?" So saying, he pressed the knife against Tristano's throat, hard enough that droplets of blood appeared, scurrying downwards into his lace collar like insects startled by sunlight. "No—I declare you will never sing more! I purchased you, now I will dispose of you! I will make a sacrifice of you—I will clip your wings—I will tear up by its roots the source of your infamous powers!" '

I paused. The tiger-stripe shadows of the balustrade were lunging at our feet. The young lady with the novel was arduously pushing her ancient charge into Gay Street, uphill towards the Circus.

'He loved her,' Eleanora was whispering. 'Lord W—. She did not know—could not see—but he did. Surely he *must* have loved her.'

'Love?' My eyes were watering from the sunlight. Love? 'Love took no part in what he did.'

'What he . . .?'

I stood and, stepping behind the bench, seized her unbonneted yellow neck locks in my left hand and drew back her head. 'He tipped back his head—thus—and then, like the barbarous Tereus—'

'Yes?' Her eyes were closed, her face, exposed so to the sun, radiant and serene.

'He cut . . . he cut his . . . his, his . . . cut *out* his . . .'

I released her neck locks and, as her head sagged forward, fell silent—fell mute—as if through some terrible act I, too, had been amputated, for ever deprived of powers of speech or song.

As it turned out, Eleanora's mission had taken considerably longer than the promised minute. When the doctor finally arrived—a surly fellow with crooked eyes and noxious breath—his prescription of feverfew dissolved in sweet wine failed to recall me to my senses. I was, indeed, more bewildered upon its administration, for this treatment was accompanied by the most curious behaviour on the part of Eleanora, who all the while gazed fondly upon me, stroked my hands and brow, and uttered the softest murmurs of concern. Curious behaviour, that is, from someone who moments—or however long—before had been howling like a Fury for her revenge; and curious behaviour, moreover, to show to someone who, however long before, had become a murderer.

Whom, then, had I murdered? The Turkish costume with its stained bodice, its dark angel wings spreading on the cobbles—this was what had scrolled back and forth before my eyes as I opened them a second time. Thus before Eleanora's return, and after the pulsing surf had drained away, I had pointed at the portrait of the costumed Lady W—, babbling rapidly and, I suppose, incoherently, as if a spell had been cast upon my tongue: 'Who—who is—but who, who, *who* is—was—?'

'But I told you,' the soft voice had interrupted these owlish articulations. 'Last evening. Do you not remember? Do you not believe me? As I explained to you, Lady W— was my mother.'

No—I remembered nothing. So, still babbling, I had stammered my crime.

'Murthered my mother . . .?' The face as it hovered above me displayed all of its perplexity. 'But, Mr Cautley, my mother has been dead these past twenty years . . .'

Or so Lady Beauclair had claimed the evening before, as I was to remember when my senses finally returned. Lady W— had apparently wasted away and expired in her middle years, her constitution fatally weakened by decades of purging, bleeding, bathing, doses of quinine, opium and the more mysterious concoctions fed to her by the herbalists. Killed, in other words, by those things meant to preserve her.

'I thought you may have surmised,' Lady Beauclair had

410

responded to my inquiry on that previous occasion as she gazed impassively upon the framed portrait, her own painted effigy. She had been reclining beside me in the Turkish costume, the two of us supine on the horsehair mattress. 'It was Lady W—, no other, who was my mother.'

The portrait had been executed in Bath, she had claimed, shortly after her own birth. Yet my surprise at this revelation about her mother had been somewhat mitigated on account of it having come after that much stranger—and, I believed, less credible—one, namely that Tristano was her father. At this earlier, more curious divulgation I had not been slow to voice the perplexities that were, I am sure, plainly inscribed across my face.

''Tis not possible, surely, such a thing as this . . .?'

She had shaken her head, releasing the perfume of her hair, several shoots and tendrils of which had been liberated by our exertions of a few moments before. 'Have you not heard, in these last few years, of Signor Giusto Tenducci, the celebrated castrato who married Miss Dora Maunsell of Limerick, very much against the advice of the girl's guardians?' It was my turn to shake my head. 'I am surprised,' she said in response, 'for many scandalous pamphlets have been composed upon the subject.'

'A castrato marry?' The very idea had ploughed a furrow of doubt across my brow. 'How very strange indeed.' But my lady merely nodded gravely.

'Yes—so it is often thought. More, the ceremony is forbidden, particularly in Romish countries, where eunuchs are strictly denied all nuptial privileges. Why? Because, supposedly being bereft of all powers of generation, they may gratify only the basest wishes of the flesh, turning the delights of the body to an end in themselves: not the fulfilment of public duties—to wit, reproducing our species—but the satisfaction of private desires. Thus do the delights of the individual, in usurping this precedence, injure the well-being of civil society as a whole.' She drew a heavy breath. 'Do you follow me?' I nodded, but she had already resumed: 'It is well known, of course, how a lady is neither to admit nor exhibit these wanton appetites of the flesh, which may only be indulged in the name—under the guise, if need be—of propagation, of the biblical injunction to go forth and multiply. An injunction which this congress with the castrato so flagrantly mocks: for though he may, so to speak, go forth,

411

it is believed that he may not multiply. In such cases the dark act itself thereby becomes the *be-all* and *end-all*, and for all its passions and dangerous delights is finally as barren and issueless as one between two gentlemen or two ladies— likewise, of course, proscribed upon the dictates of this same logic.' A brief pause. 'Barren and issueless—yes. Though there are cases . . .'

Recalling several of my father's sterner sermons about the ladies, I interrupted in order to observe how the climate of opinion against female passions was scarcely any different on our island. Again she nodded very gravely.

'Precisely so. Two years before Tristano arrived in London a publisher rushed into print a work entitled *Eunuchism Display'd*, whose sole purpose, it is said, was to dissuade a young lady from marrying the great Nicolini. This work, as it turned out, proved a more successful ambassador than the guardians of Miss Maunsell, for the young lady married Signor Tenducci and—to universal surprise—bore him two children before being confined to a madhouse in Dublin. Her husband, though vindicated by the squawling babes from the presumed sin of his union, was none the less consigned to prison for violating the wishes of Miss Maunsell's guardians. You may read about this famous case, if you should wish, in *A True and Genuine*—'

'Two *children*, you say?' The stubborn oxen of doubt had ploughed even deeper trenches across my brow. 'Marriage I may believe, as well as conjugal acts, but children? No— the fellow was a cuckold without knowing.'

Her tresses shook, releasing more of their gentle perfume, more of their soft black filaments. 'On account of the danger of discovery, the operations were often of a primitive and inexpert variety, being conducted by the most disreputable surgeons. Therefore, through error or perhaps even through normal practice the boys were not always entirely deprived of the parts proper to generation; for one of the seminal glands, you must understand, sometimes remained. Neither did the operation make the castrati, as broadsheet ballads sometimes claimed, impotent or otherwise enervated.' She paused for a tick. 'And thus I believe they were quite capable of sustaining—'

'Sustaining?'

'Sustaining an . . .'

Ah. Sustaining what I was—and had for better than the

412

past hour been—sustaining, albeit concealing by the careful disposition of my knees. Her ladyship had smiled and delicately cleared her throat, while I felt my whole body flush, though with pleasure or embarrassment I could not quite have said.

'If he is indeed your father,' I had said quickly, wondering if I had properly absorbed all she had said, 'who, then, is your mother?'

'Mr Larkins!'

Greatly agitated, the figure before me was now biting a lip and pacing the bedchamber: back and forth, back and forth; the length of the bed, the length of my body, which was yet prone and supported by cushions.

'Mr Larkins?' I was blinking rapidly, though not on account of the revelation of this name, which indeed I had barely heard, but because I was endeavouring to take a clearer view of this—what shall I call it?—hermaphrodite pacing before me. This half-man, half-woman. For before me there strode the strangest sight ever seen, akin to something from a traveller's tale: a lady's head—Lady Beauclair's, to be precise—surmounting a gentleman's body, attired, like any gentleman's, in a ruffled shirt, a waistcoat, breeches, stockings and buckled shoes. Attired, that is, in the garb of Robert Hannah. So . . . a lady or a gentleman? A gentleman or a lady? This strange hybrid was at once, to my blinking eyes, *both* and *neither*; a cipher or nought that both invited and then frustrated my boggled interpretation.

'Mr Larkins . . .' I repeated the name in barely more than a whisper, scarcely hearing myself as I did so.

'The very same. Mr Larkins.' This name had been thrice repeated before my addled brain finally seized upon it in any sort of recognition. 'Dear, dear, dear—now dead, now dead!' At the foot of the bed the pacing ceased. 'I believe he was known to you?'

'Yes—no. Only a very little.' My faculties were returning, albeit slowly. My companion at the whist table; my sympathetic rescuer in the phaeton. 'But . . .?'

'But why?' I nodded and the pacing resumed. 'He was an acquaintance of mine. Oftentimes he wore the costume and tonight had insisted—' At the sound of feet clumping upon the stair the pacing abruptly stopped again. 'Oh, dear, dear, *dear*—you must flee. Now. Tonight. Where can you go?

Here—I shall give you coins. Here—you shall wear these. Tonight—yes, you must depart tonight.'

I would not have fled but for the inexplicably tender and attentive Eleanora, who had appeared with the foul-smelling doctor, in fact merely an apothecary. Her wish to flee London—to flee Sir Endymion, she said—was suddenly so urgent and strong that, in the end, it bore me with it, a silent passenger, in its frothing wake.

'Farewell,' this mixed creature said a few minutes later with teary eyes—whether they were for me or Mr Larkins I did not know—as a hack waited outside in the street. I was returning, briefly, to the Haymarket, there to collect my few possessions and—to my great shame—to plunder a few of Mr Sharp's less well-concealed coins. Yet I was already a murderer, I reasoned, so becoming a thief was almost an improvement, though both I knew to be hanging offences.

'Farewell,' I had whispered in return, one foot already upon the stair. The materials for my final transmogrification—the tricorne, gloves and topcoat—I held in my hands, my bloodied clothes having been discarded in the bedchamber.

A moment later as the hack clopped past the church I looked up to the window to see—without the confusions of its body—the countenance that, despite all, was still, and would remain, my *beau idéal*. I wondered when, or even if, I would set eyes upon it again.

Forty-four

 Increasingly now I walked alone; creeping through the streets of Bath, up the hills, looking ever more, as my clothes frayed and faded, as my flesh paled and shrank, like the swaddled skeletons everywhere about me.

It was upon one such walk in the Great Common north of the Weston Road that I looked back upon the town and saw how earlier I had been mistaken: for the half-built Crescent and the new bridge across the Avon—to be called

Pulteney Bridge—were no dead monsters of prehistory being exhumed by the workers with their buckets and spades; rather, they were shoots of new growth rising from the mire into sunlight, rising up like the stone angels climbing their ladders on the west front of the Abbey. Not of the foggy past but of a future, a new day, heaving into prospect. Part of a living creature; circulating, breathing. And the time had arrived, I knew, when I, too, must rise up, draw my breath, press forward.

Thus it was that less than a fortnight after our arrival I commenced my new work. Not painting portraits, as I had at first envisaged—for I was only ever to paint one more (that which you now hold, here, in your hand)—but labouring in Widcombe quarry, a short distance to the south of the city, behind Prior Park. Ten shillings per week I was paid for the task of chiselling loose the Bath freestone that lay beneath the wind-groomed grasses and loading these honey-coloured blocks on to wooden carts. They were transported along rails to the stoneworks beside the Avon, where the blocks, dressed by stone-cutters, were stacked like plates of armour into the gaunt hulk of the Royal Crescent and into the terraces taking shape along Walcot Parade; into the skin and bone of the gleaming city that, each new day, expanded around about me.

All built, in part, by my hands. I prised the limestone blocks, freeing them like new-born babes, from their yawning trenches, from their darkish bed of marl. When first exposed to the air these were tender children: moist, soft and tractable beneath the fingers when chiselled free, loaded on to the carts, hewn into cubes by the masons. Yet once in place against a core of rubble and further exposed to the sun and rain—to all rough adversities of climate—they became hard and immovable like granite.

And each new evening as I lay upon my pallet, feeling my palms and the balls of my fingers grow calloused, the muscles in my arms and back harden, I told myself that I, too, was being reborn, being hardened, being shaped anew by the blows of strife and rough adversity, the hard lashes of experience. The Outer Man hewn in stone or dressed in armour by the Inner . . .

But this was, like all else I had believed, an illusion. I was not a stone, and in the end I could not withstand the adversities awaiting me.

The first of these occurred after I had toiled in the quarry for little more than a week. How Eleanora amused herself during these days when I departed from Green Street at dawn and returned at dusk I had no idea, nor did I especially wish to know. Yet on this afternoon a heavy rain storm and then a shower of hail-stones swept in upon us, respectively filling the quarry with muddy water and violently pummelling our heads and shoulders, and in either case making our labours impossible. Thus it was that I returned to Green Street earlier than was my usual custom and then, as I paused on the stair outside our door, heard those same violent sounds—gasping, thumping, urgent cryings-out—which had greeted my startled ears upon the morning of The Unveiling.

At once it seemed my fever had returned. I shook so violently that, like a dog emerging from a duck-pond, I scattered droplets through the corridor, against the walls. The rain-slick floor—indeed, the whole building—seemed to list beneath my feet, and swaying with these motions I was certain I was soon destined to disgorge what had been, and would have to remain, my lone meal of the day. For there could be no question: Sir Endymion had arrived, as I had feared he would—and as Eleanora, I now knew, had wished. She had written to him; of this I was certain. But what, I wondered, had she written? That I had abducted her? For I knew she had wanted a testament of his love; some violent action. A duel—was this her game? Some violent action, yes—committed against me or, failing that, her.

I lurched down the stair and into the rain. For the best part of an hour I stood shivering beneath the portico of St Michael's Church, across Broad Street, watching our unlighted casement. Once again I was in a desperate confusion. What should I do? Challenge him? Or might he then make a challenge, demand satisfaction? Would he bear Eleanora away? Had he conducted an officer of justice to me? My capture, surely, was imminent . . .

The window flickered to life. A few moments later the street door opened to reveal not Sir Endymion but one of the young ruffians from the Cross Bath. The fellow took account of the sky before pulling his hat down firmly upon his brow and then, after mincing away through the puddles

416

in the direction of Milsom Street, climbed into a sedan-chair.

My fever now left me as I rushed to the door and up the stair. In our tiny chamber, huffing and puffing, I discovered Éleanora in the process of combing her unbound locks with a pair of handsomely carved tortoiseshell brushes, which I did not recall having stowed in our canvas sack in that first desperate hour of flight.

Her voice was impassive, and her back turned to me, as she asked: 'And do you not work today?'

'The rain.' I paused awkwardly, hating myself for that pause and for that awkwardness, then continued somewhat harshly: 'I see, Miss Eleanora, how your trade continues unabated.'

'Oh, does it rain?' Her voice was yet impassive, unconcerned, her back yet turned. She continued to work the brushes rhythmically through her hair, which under the influence of these attentions had reclaimed something of its lustre; something of the brightish hue of yellow orpiment. Yet now she appeared like the subject of neither *The Fair Garreteer* nor *A Lady in a Garret*; rather, someone quite different—someone whom I had no wish to paint. 'The draught,' she said in the same imperturbable voice, as though ordering a servant, which I realised I had in some ways been to her. 'If you will close the door.'

She was watching me—and I her—through our reflections in the small looking-glass before her. In the glass her reflection—warped by the many flaws—appeared to be frowning. Yet when she finally turned her head I saw that the glass had lied, for in fact she was smiling—albeit a smile that was not at all a pretty sight. I now noticed, too, that a strand of pearls encircled her neck, and that she was attired in a blue négligé of watered silk, whose purchase would surely have required me to labour many months in Widcombe quarry; to excavate enough Bath freestone to build a great colossus that would frown stonily from its heights upon my even greater stupidity.

That is to say, in this moment I noticed many things about Eleanora that I had hitherto failed to notice or recognise; as if, before, I had seen her only like this, through the false image of some warping piece of glass.

Unable to face this reflection I turned and, to the sounds of her laughter—as unpleasant and mirthless as her smile—

plunged down the stair and into the rain. I walked downhill, through deserted streets, borne along like the dead leaves in the flushing kennels, rain pattering upon my brow and shoulders. The quarry's limestone, clinging to my sleeves, was now wet and dissolving; and I felt I, too, was dissolving; cracking and crumbling to a core of rubble.

After wandering at some length past half-lit buildings and jumbles of empty Bath chairs, I found myself in Stall Street. Ghostly clouds of vapour—looking even more wet than usual—hung densely over the baths, from which I could hear the echoic sounds of splashing and shouting. I could smell the sulphurous waters and, at the scent, felt shiveringly ill.

More for the sake of warmth than anything else I stepped inside the White Hart Inn and ordered a pot of beer and tobacco, seating myself beside the fire. As the tavern was empty I sat alone for the next hour, drying myself and, as I studied the limestone beneath my finger-nails or the sawdust on the floor, thinking of, among other things, my mother's 'dioptrical bee-hive'; of how, though we think we see through its transparent glass to the inner workings, in fact this glass is warped, providing us with only the most distorted and untruthful view of its interior. And because of these twists and flaws the internal architecture, like the sentiments and passions of the human heart, may never be clearly glimpsed . . .

After I had drunk two more pots of beer and smoked innumerable bowls of tobacco I had further cause, if only I had known it, to reflect upon questions of the grim opacity of the human bosom, as two gentlemen, also smoking tobacco-pipes, now divested themselves of their wet cloaks and drew up chairs behind mine. The Flying Machine from London, one said, was late in its arrival, though hourly expected.

''Tis most foul weather for the journey,' said this voice as its owner noisily stumped his wet boots upon the floor.

'Just so. Your hat, sir—if you will permit me.'

After a pause filled with the scuttling of chairs, the first said: 'I believe 'twas set upon this time yesterday.'

'Indeed, sir?'

'Aye—near Newbury.'

'Then the losses must be great, for I hear a number of Persons of Quality are aboard upon this occasion.'

418

'You hear true; but the only losses were to the lives of the highwaymen. That of one of them at least—'

'Verily, sir?'

'—and the other rogue taken.'

'Praise be. Why, sir, we shall drink cheer to that! 'Twas the guard, then,' he inquired a moment later, after their drinks were brought and then promptly gulped in celebration of this death, 'who fired upon the rogues? Why, we shall toast the fellow's health when he arrives.'

A dismissive snort. 'No, no—save your money there, Mr Hooper, save your money. 'Twas not the guard. One of those cowards?' The snort was repeated, though in a quieter tone, as if someone present—for the rooms of the inn had begun to fill—might be among that occupation and take offence. 'Nay, 'twas someone other—a fearsome fellow, by all accounts. A wicked temper and a deft hand with the sword. Hang it—what's the fellow's name? The deuce! You will know it in an instant, for he is very well known here, upon my word . . .'

But this name was not recollected and it seemed to become the more tenuous and receding under the influence of further bumpers of port, until at last the topic was forgotten. And I, too, should have forgotten the subject had I not upon stumbling back to Green Street, hours later and after a further two pots of beer, heard the bells chiming in the Abbey's darkened tower, announcing the arrival of the Flying Machine with a cargo that included this valiant but mysterious Person of Quality.

'I bid you welcome to Bath!' I cried out, lurching drunkenly at the fork in Broad Street before St Michael's Church as the long-awaited vehicle creaked and jingled down Walcot and vanished into the fog of the High Street. Then I threw my hat high into the air as if in greeting, though the only response was that of the black bats who, mistaking it for one of their number, dived and swooped about it in rapid circles.

'Jealous,' Eleanora was saying two minutes later. She was still seated before the glass, her warped face watching me through it, and she was still attired in her négligé and string of pearls. Minutes rather than hours might have passed since my departure for the White Hart. 'You are in drink,' she

419

added as one of the brushes whipped through her hair, cawing softly. 'I shall not listen to your vile jealousy.'

Jealous? She had misread my reproach. My snort was now the perfect echo of the gentleman's in the tavern. 'Jealous?' I demanded. 'Jealous of those who pay for your favours? Jealous of your pearls and brushes?' I was wavering in the doorway, one hand on either side; Samson about to bring down the pillars. 'Self-respect is all I may covet now,' I growled thickly, 'for I have none of it left—though, alas, I see none before me now.'

'You are jealous of Sir Endymion,' she said in a confident tone. 'You dare not deny it.'

'What . . .?' Of the many things I felt for my old master, this was not one of them.

'Of his love for me,' she continued, 'and of mine for him.'

'Nonsense.' Still clinging to this illusion! Why, she was so easily deceived! I remembered how she had described the heart as a willing accomplice in its own betrayal—wise words indeed. Yes: she was wholly blind—as blind as those poor bats!—to the sentiments of others; perhaps, even worse, she was blind to her own. 'His love for you? Yes, yes—I shall laugh.'

She made no reply, but a desperate, vicious faith burned in her eyes: a faith I was certain was only illusion.

'A strange definition of love!' I continued, hoping to expunge this expression. 'In what dictionary might we find it? What grammar allows you to speak of it thus?' I tried to laugh again, to stand militarily erect, and then to make my drink-thickened voice sonorously magisterial as I said: 'No, miss—you are as deceived as ever. The physiognomy of the human heart is as unknown to you as—'

I broke off as she waved one of the tortoiseshell brushes at me. 'A fine one to talk! I shall take no lessons in this from *you*, sir.'

'Ah—but is there not a difference between us? Yes—for everywhere I look, I search for *truth*, whereas you'—my finger stabbed the air accusingly—'*you* would willingly be deceived. Yes, you are happily deceived because you are in love with deception! Your own and anyone else's! Yet you may tell yourself what you wish,' I recommenced after a short pause, 'and *still* he will not arrive! He will not arrive, for he does not—not—*not* . . .!'

There was no need to continue, for she had fallen silent.

Having turned away in the middle of this last reproach she was now watching me through the glass, which in its gruesomely unhappy frown at last reflected her true expression. Defeat showed in the slump of her thin shoulders, in her drooping yellow head. Yes: defeat. Sir Endymion had spurned even her last, most self-abasing wishes. Now only the two of us remained.

At once my anger drained and I felt a strange kind of sympathy for her. I stepped forward, wondering if I might comfort her as I had done on our journey; perhaps take her in my arms and lay her head upon my breast. Sympathy. What had Mr Larkins said about sympathy being the fundamental human passion? The glass by which, in the face of another, we recognise our own.

But as I advanced towards the distorted reflection in the glass I stumbled slightly on account of the four pots of beer, and at this suddenly violent and overly rapid progress Eleanora's head was swiftly raised, as was her hand, clutching a brush. Her eyes, misinterpreting my drunken expression—mistaking the sympathy in my face for something else—were fierce and narrowed.

'Do not dare *touch* me!' I was in the midst of a short protest, but at the same time as she shouted she released the brush, which now struck me in the middle of the brow, precisely where I had made contact with the cobbles of Hog Lane. Then the second arrived, bouncing off my nose.

Can those sharp blows or the four pots of beer consumed beside the fire explain—for of course they will never excuse—what happened next? I remember it now—and, indeed, see it in my mind—as if it is someone else: some person other than George Cautley who now rushes across the floor, screaming like a Bedlamite; who engages with frail Eleanora, the two of them twisting this way and that as if dancing a violent cotillion; who, after a few of these steps and turns, strikes her upon the cheek with the back of a limestone-roughened hand when his face is spat upon; who repeats the blow for greater effect when this hand is bitten where the cur has left its scar; who plucks her from the floor, shaking her shoulders, shouting hoarsely, drunkenly.

Who raises her up to find, to his surprise, how she is smiling: yes—that fond, almost rapturous expression he has seen so rarely and, as now, so unexpectedly. For as she

421

has misinterpreted his reproach and his abortive act of sympathy, so she now misinterprets his rage.

'Jealous,' she whispers, her eyes radiant. 'I knew, I *knew*! Your proof, your *proof*!'

Then, beneath her mad laughter, the gasp of a seam and the whisper of silk as the négligé is raised.

I know now, as I did not then, how a costume is not required to render a person mysterious, unfathomable. Those disguises we put on—the masks, veils, capes—are but the outward expressions of our unknown selves; the Outer Man, my father would have said, dressed in kind by—or reflecting—the dissembling Inner. Perhaps I might even speak of our *unknowing* selves, for are not we as much as others ignorant of, and forever duped by, the wilful opacity of our own hearts, swaddled as they are in unwhispered secrets? Are not our own hearts as ambiguous and occult as the faces of strangers?

Poor Eleanora, I have said, was blind in both such ways. The unfortunate creature, ever mistaking the one planet for the other in that troubled conjunction of Mars and Venus, took my anger—my violent maltreatment—for love, which she sought to return in the only way that, after so many years, she recognised. Love? No—love had nothing to do with it.

Nor, despite what she may have wished or thought, with what followed: my second adversity. For—perhaps already you can see?—I as much as Eleanora was blind to the hearts of others; and this blindness, in the end, was to cost me more.

I see the two of us as we were then, moments later, curled together on the pallet, nudging the bosom of sleep. Yet even now, in the tragic conjunction of which I have spoken, Mars slides into the ascendancy: for who has arrived on the Flying Machine? Yes—outside in the street, alighting from a glass-chair, the rain funnelling from the three corners of his hat brim, the fog licking at his silk umbrella as it is raised for a moment before the portico, Sir Endymion Starker may now be seen. I see him pay the chair-men, take three steps to the door, apply the knocker, consult with the landlady, place his feet upon the stair, its banister yet bearing the wet constellations of my earlier progress, its narrow steps the more geometrical imprints of my heels. Then he climbs silently to our chamber, to its unlocked door, his slim sword already half drawn from its silver scabbard before he touches the brass knob.

Forty-five

The trial of Lord W— before the House of Lords in 1721 was the event of what was otherwise a most unpromising spring season. True, there was still the opera. In April the Royal Academy's third season opened at the King's Theatre with the new opera *Muzio Scevola*, composed in collaboration by Signors Handel, Bononcini and Amadei; and *Radamisto* was then revived with much of its previous success. The Academy itself was to survive for another eight years, and before its collapse was to bring the two great sopranos Cuzzoni and Faustina—not to mention Il Piozzino—to the Haymarket. Yet the opera's companions, Count Heidegger's masquerades, were not the riotous assemblies of previous years. Indeed, there was now talk of their suppression by a royal proclamation, which was in fact enacted a few season later, making public masquerades unlawful. And there was talk, too, of a strong new Gaming Act—likewise subsequently passed into law in order to prevent the ruin of noble families through the practices of their profligate sons.

Thus, as if foreseeing they were soon to be deprived of their amusements, that spring the people of London were anxious to take their pleasures where they found them. So great was the demand for this latest entertainment that the proceedings were moved north through the dank, narrow corridors of the Palace of Westminster, from the House of Lords to the more capacious Westminster Hall. The galleries on the afternoon of the trial were as full as any of those in the King's Theatre, and even fuller than when, a few years before, the Earl of Oxford had been tried here for treason. The performance had been advertised for month upon month by ballad-mongers and the book- and printsellers who sold their wares outside the walls of the ancient Hall. Many of these publications had described in various competing versions the outline and more alluring details of the scandalous story: the attempted elopement of the lovers to Bath, the brutal reprisal in Hyde Park, the rumoured lying-in of Lady W— in Bath (whence she had not returned). These tracts were often read aloud in taverns, or sometimes, if a troupe of strolling players possessed the initiative, acted out with cruel portrayals upon makeshift stages: Tristano the simpering lecher, squeaking love-verses in Italian; Lady W— as a wanton hussy shaking her petticoats at him; his lordship, crowned with a pair of cuckold's horns, a foolishly meek and long-suffering husband.

This latter portrayal was seen for its ridiculous inaccuracy when his lordship was finally conducted from the Press-Yard in Newgate Prison—where he had hospitably entertained a liberal succession of Persons of Quality—to face the charge, punishable by hanging, of 'maliciously maiming or disfiguring'. Those who normally answered such charges, cowering in their fetters in the dock at, say, the Old Bailey, were often convicted by their appearance alone, being filthy and ragged beggars in the first place who during their incarceration had become even more filthy and more ragged from gaol fever. So noxious would they become, in fact, that the spectators and judges were obliged to carry nosegays, lumps of camphor, sprigs of rue, and pomanders filled with aromatic herbs, to which their noses took frequent resort throughout the course of the trial. And so these poor beggars generally made such a foul sight that in the end neither the spectators nor the judges could conclude anything else but that the tattered and stinking forms these fellows wore must be the sorry emblems of the most hideous moral natures.

Lord W—'s appearance in Westminster Hall was entirely otherwise, of course, though ultimately subject to the same prejudices. Dressed in one of his fine silk suits and a snowy bag-wig, he looked as though he might have been seated not in a dock but in his taffeta-draped box at the King's Theatre; and far from exhaling the evil fumes of gaol fever, he had anointed himself with the fragrant splashes of one of the scents purchased during his stay in Paris the previous year. And because people are so willing to believe that appearances intimately coincide with something deeper,

424

with some internal form that is their model, it was perhaps nothing more than this majestic façade which led, after the brief trial, to his acquittal by the lords; so that, one evening later, he truly *was* sitting in his box at the opera, tapping his marble cane, smiling to himself as Il Piozzino sang one of the final arias from *Muzio Scevola*, and considering, as he listened to this golden voice stretching itself across the theatre, how he might yet recover his investment.

Which in time, of course, he did, both through Il Piozzino and otherwise. That summer the craftsmen from Italy re-appeared in the mansion in St James's Square. Month upon month they hammered and plastered; moulded acanthus leaves and honeysuckles; put sashes on the windows and lintels on the doors; painted the allegory of Cupid, Time and Love; installed the marble cascade of the processional staircase; and laid the terracotta floor-tiles, where, a lifetime later, I was to bump my brow.

Who precisely was to reap the benefits of this new gran-deur was not immediately clear, as his lordship, because of growing commercial interests in the Levant, was rarely to be seen in London, let alone in the square. On those rare occasions when he returned to England he preferred the villa in Richmond, at which times Lady W— surrendered her occupancy and moved her court—her serving-maids and spaniels—not to St James's Square but Bath, Epsom or Tunbridge Wells. Despite this domestic arrangement an heir was eventually produced, albeit the boy was rumoured to be the offspring not of her ladyship but, rather, an Italian alto soprano who sang at the Theatre Royal in Covent Garden for a season in the year 1730. Another rumour held that Lady W— had given birth to a child of her own in Bath in 1721—one never acknowledged by his lordship—though the more sceptical asserted that the boy (or perhaps a girl, for the stories varied) had died at birth. Others claimed that the child's existence was merely an invention of ballad-mongers hoping to sell more of their broadsheets; still others that, far from being non-existent or having per-ished, it had been christened in Bath and then smuggled into Italy, where, decades later, after being reared in one of the *ospedali* and tutored by the great Farinelli, it would fulfil its father's blighted promise. Many more fantastic stories arose, too, including ones put forth in scurrilous treatises such as *The Scandalous Memoirs of Lady W—* and *A True and Genuine Narrative of Signor Tristano Pieretti*. These anonymous works of dubious authenticity contradicted one another on many points but allowed for the production of heirs of every possible identity and from every possible permutation of this *ménage à trois*. Indeed, for a while as many stories and speculations about Lady W—'s supposed lying-in abounded as at that time almost forty years before when hot-headed Jesuits and fanatical Protestants competed to establish the true facts regarding the birth of the Old Pretender.

But to return to the mansion in St James's Square. Despite his lordship's many absences in the eastern Mediterranean, this house did not quite remain empty. In the ensuing years it possessed, besides a collection of rather purposeless foot-men and serving-maids, a single occupant. For those who passed through the square in the evening might, if they looked up, see at a circular window in the top floor a face that in its silence, and because of its enduring presence, had inspired a hundred stories. Some of these portrayed their subject as a prisoner, yet being punished by Lord W—; the most fictional and allusive envisioned him in the role of Philomela, weaving upon a loom his tapestry of sorrow and accusation and, like her, awaiting a final redeeming transmogrification. Others more plausibly asserted that, after an *éclaircissement* with the singer, his lordship, plagued by guilt, kept the Italian in the most obscene luxury and, his guilt yet unabated, made long eastward journeys of a religious, rather than a commercial, nature. Much later a ferryman who plied the waters of the Thames between the Manchester Stairs and Richmond published his memoirs, in the middle of which he provided an account of how during the 1720s he had often transported a well-dressed foreigner—a gentleman who never once spoke a word—back and forth between Westminster and a landing-stage near Eel Pie Island, where a chariot from Lord W—'s nearby villa awaited. Yet the ferryman drew no conclusions, and by the time his memoirs were published the scandalous story of Lady W— and her lover was almost forgotten.

Yes: in time almost all of these stories were forgotten, and most people passing through St James's Square ceased to glance upwards at the window. Those who did simply wondered to themselves, only for a second before passing on, who this peculiar figure was or what he had been. And

426

in time only a few could be found, here or there, who might have told them.

There was no one to assist me, of course, as, recuperating from my wound in a hospital in Bath, I sought my own version of those events of fifty years ago. But then one night after a particularly vivid dream in which Lady Beauclair metamorphosed into Robert and then back into herself again, I awoke in my vinegar-scented sheets, thinking: *a child christened in Bath in the year 1721 . . .*

How long had I pondered my vital question—on the road to Bath and now in the town itself—before realising in the middle of the night how the wind-blown scraps of history, the scattered fragments of this secretive life, might be sorted, ordered, identified? How a mere inscription upon a page—concealed, perhaps, in the baptismal register of a parish church—might become the mark of truth, the answer to a mystery? Might become the sharp mould-board overturning the thick furrow-slices of rumour and deception?

The walk the next morning from St John's Hospital across Stall Street to the Abbey on that raw day in October consumed less than ten minutes, even though on account of my terrible wound—in the obscurest of places—I was limping, leaning heavily upon the oaken stick that accompanies me still. Despite my fever for explanation—for what Eleanora would have called proof—I rested before the west front of the Abbey. For a moment I peered up through the watery sunlight at the stone angels: those creatures inhabiting their margin between God and man, between man and woman; not rising, not descending, but suspended, undecidably, as if for all time, on ladders stretching both ways.

Then I limped through the open doors, gritting my teeth against the pain I yet carry with me.

Epilogue: London, 1812

My Ganymede frowns, his gaze travelling from the miniature to me, then back to the miniature. Then, suddenly impatient, it returns to me.

'And . . .?' he prompts.

Wearied, I close my eyes. In truth I had almost forgotten him.

'Please'—I am drawing to the dirtied wall—'shall we rest for a short time?'

So we stand for a moment in St Martin's Lane, horses and wheel traffic moving past us, south into the Seven Dials, their cloppings and grindings muffled by straw. The lights before us, to the north, are those of St Giles High Street, or rather, I should, I believe, say Broad Street; for the names, like the appearances, are forever changing. Will the building yet stand? Will I even recognise it if it does?

'How much longer?' He is impatient for our journey—both our walk and my story—to end.

'Not long now, not long. So,' I say after a moment as, at his anxious behest, we resume our walk, I with one hand on my stick, the other upon his shoulder, 'you would know what that scrap of paper read? You would know the truth, would you, inscribed in the vellum pages of the register stored in one of the mustier chambers of the Abbey? Perhaps you think these words are more incontrovertible than those of the pamphlets and broadsheets? That they present a "true and genuine narrative".' I see his impatient expression and continue: 'Very well, very well. I once believed so, too—that something such as this might remove the mask that obscured her face. Well, then—you shall know what proof I found, if proof it was.'

'Yes?' Beneath the passing oil lamp—for there are none of the new gaslights here, that has not changed—his face, turned to me, has become avid, expectant.

'A female child, baptized Petronella Hannah—'

'Ahh . . .'

'—whose godfather was signed "Captain John Smith". Who that might have been I do not know. The register gave

428

no details of parentage. The mother, I learned, wore a mask during her lying-in. Quite common in such cases, so that the midwives, notorious gossips, could not—'

'So Robert Hannah,' he interrupts, 'was the invention.'

'At this point it mattered not to me *which* was the invention,' I tell him. 'What mattered was that the invention, as you call it, could be separated from the true identity. That an identity, whatever it was, might be proved, settled. Either the one or the other. For I did not wish to see again the disjunction I had glimpsed through the opened window of *A Lady by Candle-light.*' I pause, breathing heavily from our pace. 'And so perhaps I was seeking the truth no more than Eleanora was, and in the end I saw only what I wished to see.'

A perplexed frown. 'What do you mean?'

I halt again. At last I see the steeple—the stone lobster's tail—of St Giles-in-the-Fields.

'What do you mean?' he repeats, ever impatient for explanation.

After the punishment of a suitable pause I say: 'You have heard of those instruments known as Claude glasses? No? Of course not—you do not paint. I have one in my lodgings, I believe . . . if it was not thrown overboard with the rest of the jetsam—my paintbox and brushes—when I abandoned my old trade and took up my new one.' His look grows more cross and impatient. My breathing labours. 'Small optical instruments, like opera glasses. If one held it to the eye its curved lenses reshaped the scene to present a prospect like those found in the poetic landscapes of the painter Claude Lorrain. Turned an ordinary scene into a poetic spectacle; everything tamed, ordered, arranged, familiar.'

He is not listening to this. 'No. I mean—the female child.' He is pondering. 'Why, then, she must have been—why, almost *fifty years of age* by the time . . .!' He shakes his head, as if in disbelief at some youthful ignorance. 'Then— *this* was her secret, the one she was affrighted you would pierce?' His voice is almost triumphant. 'The reason for her many paints and masks and deceptions.'

'Stay—patience.' We are walking again. I am thinking: Why must the young, who have so much time . . .?

'You returned to London,' he prompts.

After another pause: 'London, yes. Some months later, yes.'

429

'You saw her again?'

For the first time since our walk commenced—some ninety minutes earlier in Peter Street, near the new penitentiary in Tothill Fields—I feel a soft jab of pain in my stomach, in those vital regions where I am wounded. Tonight on our way to St Giles we have walked through Pall Mall, Piccadilly, the Haymarket—all of them now gaslit, bright—yet none of these precincts into which I now so rarely enter, and never without a sense of loss, quite disturbs me like these thoughts of what I did not do, did not see.

'No,' I reply. 'Not even at the end. Not even at the last.'

'The end?' He holds the miniature aloft. The countenance is illuminated by a hissing lamp, then darkened by shadow as we move on. 'But . . .?'

'Painted through memory.' The steeple to our right has shifted closer. 'Through that most distorting glass of all.'

'But—the end, sir.' He is almost pleading. To walk so slowly seems painful to him. 'Still you have not told me why she was hanged. She *was* hanged, this Petronella Hannah?'

'Patience.' I shy my white-gloved hand in an arc. The jab of pain remains. And the memory, that warping glass, remains—even though I myself did not go to Tyburn upon that morning. And with good reason, for in that last hour I was in my cell in the New Prison in Clerkenwell, unaware of what was happening. Yes, the officers of justice had finally arrived at my door; or rather, tormented by dreams, I arrived at theirs, confessing my crime. But I did not know as I lay on the stinking pallet and dreamed of the hammering men with their leathern aprons and the nails in their mouths that the scaffold rising at Tyburn, its shadow stretching ever nearer, was not in the end fated to be mine. For I—raving wildly—was judged a lunatic and in time set free. It was deemed I had read of the murder in the broadsheets, which were filled with ballads recounting this notorious stabbing in St James's Square, the murder of Mr Horatio Larkins of Covent Garden. For the truth is mistaken for a lie as often as a lie is for the truth.

Thus my scaffold was raised for someone else. It was Jeremiah who told me. How he had found me a few days earlier I was not to learn. But find me he did, and that afternoon, admitted by the turnkey, he told me that the procession had left from Newgate Prison at eleven o'clock. That there had been three condemned in three carts led by the sheriff's carriage. That each sat facing backwards, a prayer-book in hand, the coffin sitting beside like a great wooden violoncello case . . .

'I ask you, was she hanged? Lady Beauclair—I mean, Miss Hannah—or whatever she called herself . . .?'

To his frown I say: 'And is our name, then, a more reliable mark of identity than our face?'

We have reached Broad Street and turn to our right, Hog Lane opening darkly behind us. I lead now. Into Mr Hogarth's *Gin Lane*, everything different. Past the building—is this the one?—where the ladies displayed their scarlet petticoats. I should know the premises; after all, I came to know them well, those ladies, or ones like them. On their account I was flogged and fined and pilloried on more than one occasion (as of course were they, poor souls), but from them, and from my place of resort in Covent Garden—as famous in its day as Tom and Moll King's Coffee-House or the bagnio of Betty Careless—I once earned my squalid luxuries, my infamous reputation. With them I dazzled and inveigled the young fellows from the country—young fellows very like this one—who were what I once had been. Yes—as many George Cautleys came through my door each evening as I had glimpsed that unforgettable morning in the leaded panes of the Carv'd Balcony Tavern. I wished to remove their masks, those firm expressions of faith; to strip them of their bright illusions. Because, far from finding my place in the world, I had become an outcast from it, the 'uncouth monster' unable, as Mr Hume had said, to mingle and unite in society, to partake in the happier and more ordinary transactions of human commerce.

Why? How? I realise now that in those brief days spent in the garret Sir Endymion never managed to finish the story of Plato's cave. The story that ends, I have since learned, with an outcast. For after seeing the wooden cutouts, the prisoner whose fetters were broken is dragged forcibly from his subterranean home—this place of illusions—to the sunlit surface, where he is blinded by sun. Then upon returning to his place beside his fellows he finds himself blinded by the darkness that once nourished his visions and illusions; and when he speaks to his friends of the forms he has seen, and when he tries to convince them of the falseness—the fakery—of the shadows passing before them, he provokes only their laughter, doubt and disdain.

431

'She preferred the former name,' I say as we advance. 'That is, Lady Beauclair. I was not privy to how, or why, she invented it. Just as I was not privy to so many of her inventions. And yes,' I tell him: 'hanged . . .'

The route had been lined with people and the bells of St Sepulchre's were tolling as the procession—for it was exactly that—started up Snow Hill and thence into Holborn. Before the church, nosegays were handed to the condemned through the bars of their carts. Then arms waving, a thousand faces—a wall of people without a chink for a full league; for thirty full minutes. Constables marched on either side of the carts; ballad-mongers at a less restrained pace, bumping into one another as they hawked their broadsheets. Much else for sale, too: stalls selling gin, nuts, apples, gingerbread. Very profitable for business, a hanging. The carts moved through St Giles and along Oxford Street; then past the Pantheon, where a masquerade had been held only the night before, concluding at midnight as the bell knelling the fate of the condemned chimed outside the door to the narrow cell . . .

'Inventions?' He looks at me shrewdly. 'What do you mean, inventions? Robert, for example?'

'Ah. Yes—no.' We have stopped again. My pain is very great; like the pain that Abélard bears for Héloïse. 'That is, I only know what she told me, which was never enough to clear those clouds of dark suspicion from the sky. But faith, my Ganymede, is erected upon the stones of doubt.'

'What do you mean, "what she told you"?'

'There are many reasons, are there not, why in our world a lady should wish to dress as a gentleman? Two of our most accomplished actresses during the last century—Charlotte Charke and Susannah Centlivre—spent much of their working lives dressed as gentlemen. Yes, Mrs Charke, who as a hog merchant, pastry-cook, and valet, for a time imbibed the privileges and liberties—in short, the *life*—not extended to her sex . . .' He for once is silent and I continue: 'More to the point, then: the story about Mr Larkins and the Globe Tavern I believe to be true—in a sense—though much of that history my lady provided as we walked along Constitution Hill was, of course, deceit and lies. But truth and lies are not opposites or enemies, are they? Rather, neighbours, closely touching—'

432

'What lies for example?' he interrupts, regarding me suspiciously.

'As I say, they are woven through the fabric of what we like to call truth... You ask for an example? After my discovery in Bath I believed that the "scandal" which drove Robert from the theatre—perhaps you have guessed it?—was merely that he was discovered to be a lady. Discovered to be Petronella rather than Robert—rather like the Violas and Rosalinds he, or she, played on stage. For in this reversible world I thought I might discover the truth merely by turning the lie on its head, by peering *through* it to see the true shape on the opposite side, as I had peered through the transparent paintings at Vauxhall. I did not remember, alas, how the one image was not easily separated from the other.'

'A lady dressing as a man—this is no hanging offence,' he says a trifle impatiently. 'No—the *truth* now. Why did she hang?'

I pause. 'Because of me,' I then reply.

The cart had been creaking and jerking as it approached the green expanses of Tyburn Lane. Stands about the scaffold—there it was against the trees of Hyde Park, its shadow stretching away—were raked thirty feet high, filled row upon row from top to bottom; four cascades of people. They held as many spectators as—and ones as unruly as those in—the King's Theatre, also filled last night with many of these same.

The other two were hanged first—a highwayman and a man convicted of coining money—one after the other. Standing on the coffin balanced on top of the cart, a cap over the face, the noose round the neck. Two friends at the ready to perform a last service, to hang from the twitching legs to ensure the swift cracking of the neck, the split-second separation of the vertebrae. Then the horse was slapped and the hooded shape dropped faster than one would have imagined...

The boy's jaw drops. 'She was hanged for the murther of Mr Larkins?'

I am coughing—the cold air. Only after a moment am I able to continue: 'Each had been at the masquerade in the Haymarket. I believe they were lovers—of one sort or another—though it was said they had quarrelled, even fought, upon that evening. Do I wish to believe or to deny that the dispute, whatever it was, had been occasioned by me?' I close my eyes. 'A number of maskers came forward as witnesses. And though I was not there I can see so clearly how it must have been, this confused pantomime: the figure in the black domino dressed as Robert struggling with the one in the Turkish costume disguised as Lady Beauclair. As if two halves of a single self have come to blows, each struggling for mastery of the other, each perhaps as great an impostor as the other . . .'

Leaning heavily against a building, itself leaning as if in sympathetic exhaustion, I open my eyes and wonder: Is this the one? Was it here? These steps, that door? That darkened window above our heads? Or rather that building there? Or this other? I do not know—cannot tell. And as we shall not—as I *cannot*—proceed any farther in our journey, either forwards or backwards, perhaps I shall never learn, never know. Afterwards I came here—equally lost—in search of Madam Chapuy; but she by that time had died in a cell in Newgate, to which she had been consigned for keeping a common bawdy-house.

'There was very little evidence,' I continue. 'The only witness to the act itself—to *my* act—was Tristano. And he, perhaps thinking his child was dead, or else—more likely—seeing overlapping this costumed figure on the cobbles two other figures both dead and disappeared, became a lunatic. If in fact he had not already been such for many years. He died shortly thereafter, before the trial.'

'But surely Eleanora would . . .?'

I shy my hand more weakly now. 'I was never to see her again. No,' I shake my head, 'no, no—not strictly true. For I saw her face many times, in many windows—as goddesses or mythological queens in copperplate prints engraved from the paintings of Sir Endymion Starker. Perhaps you have seen *The Goddess of Truth prompting the Muse of History*? That is Eleanora in the centre, robed in white. Yet she would not have spoken the truth. She may even have been happy to see her betrayer hang.'

Cut down, the first corpse had been transported to Hounslow Heath to hang from a gibbet, the second for a more scholarly demonstration in the School of Anatomy in Great Windmill Street. Here in this last place, divested of garments, with the naked flesh exposed to a hovering scalpel, the best-preserved disguises of life are sometimes discovered as the surgeon who raises his blade finds that the specimen he is to dissect before his pupils this morning is not what he had specified; that in the chrysalis of a few garments a strange metamorphosis has occurred . . .

'But that Lady Beauclair—!' Now he shakes his head, though less vigorously. 'But how—*why* . . .?'

'That first question I can answer; the second, never.' I lean forward so that my face—so that my purplish and carbuncular nose—is scant inches from his face. 'She confessed to the murther.'

His face is grown more perplexed, more amazed than ever, his breathing almost as audible as my own wheezing. Had I looked like this—been the mirror of his incredulous countenance—when Jeremiah spoke these same words to me in gaol?

'The doctor, the apothecary who treated me with feverfew, *he* was the one responsible, the one who conducted the officers of justice to St Giles. My bloody clothes were discovered in her lodgings, of course. By this time, however, I had already fled. No,' I say before he can inquire again, 'I do not know why she did it. Just as I do not know so many other things about her, even now. But I believe it was an act of love—though, as I have said, I only believe what I wish to believe, knowing that, because the heart is so impenetrable, such faith may be an illusion.'

' "Other things"? What other things?'

I pause. For the first time I realise how late it is grown, notice that the streets are emptying. I glance down at this barely decipherable face, which peers into my own, into what had once been its double; and I see that it, too, is a reflecting glass, for in the clear brow and smooth contours, in the frank eyes and confused smile, I glimpse the outline of my own lost image. Yes—the minds of men, as Mr Larkins had said, are the mirrors of one another . . .

And suddenly I have no wish to alter this image, to expunge this light. I have no wish to see him vibrate—as I do—in a state of perpetual uncertainty. No: I shall let him believe what he wishes, that appearances coincide with something deeper, more meaningful. That, as Mr Locke writes, one thing cannot have two beginnings, nor two things one. And so I shake my head and do not tell him. He protests, grows angry, threatens to walk away. But still I do not tell him.

I do not tell him that after the hanging, and after my discharge, I returned in great confusion to Bath. I do not tell him that I wondered by this time if either Robert or Lady Beauclair had ever truly existed, or if each had perhaps been a vision sent by an evil genius to plunge me into a doubt from which belief and truth might never arise. I do not tell him that in that musty chamber I read the baptismal register once more and then, no wiser, visited St Swithin's churchyard, where Lady W— was buried. Where I read another version of her story, inscribed upon a marble tablet erected above a tiny nettle-overgrown stone lozenge. I do not tell him I discovered upon the authority of these tombstones—these stones of doubt—that her ladyship had been buried beside her daughter, Petronella; and that this daughter had not been hanged but—as one of the long-ago broadsheets had declared—perished in her infancy from a fever.

The hangman had placed the cap of black velvet over the face. A disguise placed over another disguise, layer upon layer, like the skin of an onion. How to separate reality, the truth—call it what we will—from its appearance, the mask? Faith from illusion? They are stitched together, the one seamlessly brocading the other.

The horse, its haunches slapped, ran towards the trees, dragging its tiny bumping chariot, the sunlight dancing across its flanks as, behind, the body contorted at the end of the oscillating rope. And as there was no one to hang upon the legs—no one to grasp the stockinged calves above the gold-buckled shoes or below the soft velvet breeches— 'Robert Hannah', so the broadsheets claimed the next morning, took a very long time in dying. The final words, they said, were—like so much else—indecipherable.

When I open my eyes he is gone, his shadow beneath the oil lamps leaping before him and then orbiting behind as he disappears into St Martin's Lane. I regret only that I shall no longer have his shoulder to lean upon.

Then I, too, begin walking—slowly, slowly, the skewers of pain sharp as ever. After a few steps I am surprised by my reflection in a shop window and, as the after-image of that lost favour yet floats before my eyes, for a second I do not recognise myself.

Author's Note

At the end of a novel implying the mutual embroidery of fact and fiction it is potentially embarrassing to unravel a few strands of 'historical truth' and present them outside the context of the 'fiction' they brocade. But it should be said that although like all historical novelists I attempt to render the period(s) in question as accurately as possible—in terms of, for example, food and fashions, the topographies of London, Venice and Bath, and historical events such as the Act of Parliament mentioned in Chapter Four—as this is a work of fiction certain historical liberties have naturally been taken. Foremost among these liberties is Handel's opera *Philomela*. He did not, of course, write an opera of this name or description, much less was such a work performed at the King's Theatre in the Haymarket, in December 1720. And while the concerts presented by Thomas Britton, the 'musical small-coals man', took place much as described and frequently featured Handel's presence, since Britton died in 1714 I must confess to having kept him alive to create his amusements for six more years. These brazen-faced liberties aside, many of the details concerning Handel and the Royal Academy, such as the performance of *Radamisto* and the arrivals of Senesino and Bononcini, are based on historical fact. Someone *not* based in fact, however, is Sir Endymion Starker: some readers may notice how his aesthetic is very close to that of Sir Joshua Reynolds, but the similarities are intended to stop there.

A few words about the castrati. Many of them appeared on the English stage after 1707; Nicolini, Senesino and Farinelli were only the most famous. In 1708, Nicolini (born Nicolo Grimaldi) sang in Scarlatti's *Pirro e Demetrio* at the Queen's Theatre, Haymarket, a performance whose enthusiastic reception was largely responsible for the importation of Italian opera into London in the decades that followed. The performances of the castrati in Italy date back much further. In 1565 they were singing in the Sistine Choir and within a few decades had begun to replace the falsettists.

438

By the middle of the seventeenth century, they were employed in choirs throughout Italy, after the Church's demand for beautiful music and impoverished parents' for gold had together overcome qualms about and sanctions against the mutilations to be endured. Since Pope Sixtus V's prohibition against women on the stage in the Papal States the castrati had been performing secular music as well, and in opera outside these domains they appeared as early as Monteverdi's *La Favola d'Orfeo* (1607), thereafter remaining in vogue long enough for Mozart to write for castrato voices in *La Clemenza di Tito* (1791).

The roles sung by the castrati may strike a modern reader or opera-goer as peculiar, for throughout the eighteenth century they, rather than the basses or tenors, had the privilege of the heroic singing parts: Handel's Julius Caesar, Gluck's Orpheus, Cavalli's Pompey, and so forth. The incongruity of the great masculine rulers of history settling the destiny of nations in women's voices was not, naturally, overlooked by English satirists. Two of the most articulate and vehement of these were Alexander Pope and Henry Fielding, each of whom regarded opera in general and the castrati in particular as the products of a foreign and decadent culture, and as such inimical not only to the arts in England but an affront to masculinity as well. How the castrati mock or subvert sexual identity is a vexed topic in many of the period's pamphlets. Playing transvestite roles on the stage as well as (less frequently) in life, they represented extreme examples of disguise, subversion and gender confusion in an age deeply conscious of such disruptions. In the last decade scholarship on gender—Ellen Pollak's *Poetics of Sexual Myth* (1985), for example—has suggested that the eighteenth century is the period when modern conceptions of sexual identity came into currency. Another work, Terry Castle's *Masquerade and Civilization* (1986), paints a compelling picture of eighteenth-century London as a place of a self-conscious and highly prevalent gender-crossing. This occurs, she argues, primarily at its masquerades and in its theatres—in Covent Garden and the Haymarket—where the topsy-turvy world of carnival fosters transgressions of the wonted distinctions between the sexes and the classes. Regardless of the virtues of either thesis, the paradox that the two seem to present if taken together seems highly suggestive: that sexual identity is created at the same time as it is playfully mocked and even subverted, and that identity is therefore closely linked to disguise, perhaps dependent upon it.

The castrati feature prominently in this process of veiling and unveiling. Their sexual abilities and disabilities, as well as notions of their sexual identity itself, became the subjects of prolific speculation throughout the first half of the eighteenth century. In 1737, for example, a pamphlet alleged that Farinelli (born Carlo Broschi) was a woman in the guise of a man and, what's more, was pregnant. A generation later the castrato Giusto Ferdinando Tenducci was supposed to have assumed an apparently even more impossible role, that of a father. His alleged fatherhood was reported by, among others, Casanova, who in his *Mémoires* confesses to having occasionally mistaken transvestite castrati for women. This problem of the castrato's sexual identity became particularly acute in one of the eighteenth century's more tragic cases of disguise, that of the transvestite castrato La Zambinella and his pursuit by the French sculptor Sarrasine, who proves less discriminating in the end than the more experienced Casanova. Unacquainted with the practices of Italian opera, the young sculptor mistakes the castrato for a woman and because of his amorous attentions is murdered by La Zambinella's protector, Cardinal Cicognara. The story is told in Balzac's 'Sarrasine', in which we are informed that by the nineteenth century the operation is no longer practised. In fact the production of castrati did not end until 1870, when the temporal sovereignty of the pope was ended by the Italian armies occupying Rome. The last known castrato, Alessandro Moreschi, died in 1922.

Lastly, a matter of debts. I wish to record my gratitude to Neil Taylor for his editorial assistance and enthusiasm for the novel from its start; and to my wife, Lynn Avery, for faith and support reaching back even farther.